Juli

Caesar's Commentaries on the Gallic and Civil Wars

Anatiposi

Julius Caesar

Caesar's Commentaries on the Gallic and Civil Wars

Reprint of the original, first published in 1859.

1st Edition 2023 | ISBN: 978-3-38230-712-7

Anatiposi Verlag is an imprint of Outlook Verlagsgesellschaft mbH.

Verlag (Publisher): Outlook Verlag GmbH, Zeilweg 44, 60439 Frankfurt, Deutschland
Vertretungsberechtigt (Authorized to represent): E. Roepke, Zeilweg 44, 60439 Frankfurt, Deutschland
Druck (Print): Books on Demand GmbH, In de Tarpen 42, 22848 Norderstedt, Deutschland

HARPER'S CLASSICAL LIBRARY.

CÆSAR'S COMMENTARIES.

TRANSLATED LITERALLY.

CÆSAR'S COMMENTARIES

ON THE

GALLIC AND CIVIL WARS:

WITH THE

Supplementary Books attributed to Hirtius;

INCLUDING THE

ALEXANDRIAN, AFRICAN, AND SPANISH WARS.

LITERALLY TRANSLATED,

WITH NOTES AND A VERY ELABORATE INDEX.

NEW YORK:
HARPER & BROTHERS,
329 & 331 PEARL STREET.
1859.

CÆSAR.

PREFACE.

The present is the most complete translation of Cæsar yet presented to the English public. Besides the books deemed authentic, it includes those variously attributed to Hirtius and others, namely, the eighth book of the Gallic War, and the Alexandrian, African, and Spanish Wars. In addition to these, the Fragments, consisting of quotations from various ancient authors relating to Cæsar, are now for the first time given in English.

The utmost attention has been paid to render the translation as closely literal as is consistent with neatness of style. The text which has been followed is that of Oudendorp, collated, however, with the labors of subsequent critics. The notes are of but limited extent, as the classical student is presumed to possess either Oudendorp's, Oberlin's, Anthon's, Prenderville's, or some other of the numerous editions which supply what he is likely to require in this department.

Although Cæsar can not be regarded as a difficult author, the publisher has had no little trouble in procuring a translation to his mind, in consequence of which considerable delay has arisen. The work has at length been completed, it is hoped satisfactorily, by Mr. W. A. McDevitte, B.A., of Trinity College, Dublin, in conjunction with W. S. Bohn.

THE

COMMENTARIES OF C. JULIUS CÆSAR

ON HIS

WAR IN GAUL.

BOOK I.

THE ARGUMENT.

I. Description of Gaul and its divisions. II.-IV. The ambitious designs of the Helvetii under Orgetorix, and the suspicious death of the latter. V.-VI. The Helvetii still proceed to carry out their designs. VIII.-XI. Cæsar's opposition and measures. XII. The battle at the River Arar. XIII. The Helvetii send embassadors to sue for peace. XIV. Cæsar's politic answer. XV. Another engagement with the Helvetii. XVI. Cæsar's reproof of the Ædui for not sending him the promised supplies. XVII.-XIX. The disclosures of Liscus respecting Dumnorix. XX. Divitiacus, his brother, pleads for Dumnorix. XXI.-XXVI. Various events in the war between Cæsar and the Helvetii. XXVII. The Helvetii, being worsted, offer a surrender, but some clandestinely return home. XXVIII.-XXIX. The numbers of the several Helvetian forces before and after the war. XXX. Certain parts of Gaul congratulate Cæsar and request a council. XXXI. Complaints are there made against Ariovistus. XXXII.-XXXVI. Cæsar's message to Ariovistus and the bold answer of the latter. XXXVII.-XXXIX. A panic in the Roman camp. XL. Cæsar's speech on that occasion. XLI. Its effects. XLII.-XLVI. Conference between Cæsar and Ariovistus. XLVII.-LII. Which terminates in war. LIII. The overthrow of the Germans and their flight from Gaul. LIV. Cæsar, having sent his army into winter-quarters among the Sequani, proceeds to perform the civil duties of his pro-consular office.

CHAP. I.—All Gaul is divided into three parts, one of which the Belgæ inhabit, the Aquitani another, those who in their own language are called Celts, in our Gauls, the third. All these differ from each other in language, customs and laws. The river Garonne separates the Gauls from the Aquitani; the Marne and the Seine separate them from the Belgæ. Of all these, the Belgæ are the bravest, because they are furthest from the civilization and refinement of [our] Province, and merchants least frequently resort to them, and import those things which tend to effeminate the mind; and they are the nearest to the Germans, who dwell beyond the Rhine, with whom they are continually waging war; for which reason the Helvetii also surpass the rest of the Gauls in valor, as they contend with the Germans in almost daily battles, when they either repel them from their own territories, or themselves wage war on their frontiers. One part of these,[1] which it has been said that the Gauls occupy, takes its beginning at the river Rhone; it is bounded by the river Garonne, the ocean, and the territories of the Belgæ; it borders, too, on the side of the Sequăni and the Helvetii, upon the river Rhine, and stretches toward the north.[2] The Belgæ rises from the extreme frontier of Gaul, extend to the lower part of the river Rhine; and look toward the north and the rising sun.[3] Aquitania extends from the river Garonne to the Pyrenæan mountains and to that part of the ocean which is near Spain:[4] it looks between the setting of the sun, and the north star.[5]

CHAP. II.—Among the Helvetii, Orgetorix was by far the most distinguished and wealthy. He, when Marcus Messāla and Marcus Piso[6] were consuls, incited by lust of sovereignty, formed a conspiracy among the nobility, and persuaded the people to go forth from their territories with all their possessions,[7] [saying] that it would be very easy,

[1] *Of these, i. e.* of the three divisions of the Gauls, (1) Celts, (2) Belgians, and (3) Aquitanians, not yet reduced by conquest to the state of provincials of Rome, as the *Allobroges* in the S. E. had been by *Q. Fabius Maximus Allobrogicus*, who was consul in B. C. 121 (the year of the famous vintage), with *L. Opimius Nepos*, the murderer of C. Gracchus in that year. This Fabius, who thence derived his surname, defeated them and triumphed over their ally Bituitus, king of the Averni [*Auvergne*] who was led captive in the victor's procession at Rome. So that before Cæsar's birth this was the *Provincia* (or Gallia Narbonensis vel Braccata). The modern *Provence* is only part of the old Roman *Provincia*.

[2] "To the north:" literally, to *the northern stars.*

[3] *i. e.* It has a north-east aspect.

[4] *i. e.* It has a north-west aspect.

[5] This "part of the ocean" is the Bay of Biscay, where it washes the north coast of Spain.

[6] The consulship of M. Valerius Messāla Niger and M. Pupius Piso, was in B. C. 61, the year in which Clodius profaned the rites of the Bona Dea, and in which Pompey the Great triumphed at Rome for his victories over the *Pirates*, and the kings *Tigranes*, and *Mithridates.*

[7] Cum omnibus copiis, *i. e.* πανδημεὶ, *with all their goods and chattels,* [conf. "cultum et *copias* Gallorum." Book i. § 31.]

since they excelled all in valor, to acquire the supremacy of the whole of Gaul. To this he the more easily persuaded them, because the Helvetii, are confined on every side by the nature of their situation; on one side by the Rhine, a very broad and deep river, which separates the Helvetian territory from the Germans; on a second side by the Jura, a very high mountain, which is [situated] between the Sequăni and the Helvetii; on a third by the Lake of Geneva, and by the river Rhone, which separates our Province from the Helvetii. From these circumstances it resulted, that they could range less widely, and could less easily make war upon their neighbors; for which reason men fond of war [as they were] were affected with great regret. They thought, that considering the extent of their population, and their renown for warfare and bravery, they had but narrow limits, although they extended in length 240, and in breadth 180 [Roman][1] miles.

CHAP. III.—Induced by these considerations, and influenced by the authority of Orgetŏrix, they determined to provide such things as were necessary for their expedition—to buy up as great a number as possible of beasts of burden and wagons—to make their sowings as large as possible, so that on their march plenty of corn might be in store—and to establish peace and friendship with the neighboring states. They reckoned that a term of two years would be sufficient for them to execute their designs; they fix by decree their departure for the third year. Orgetŏrix is chosen to complete these arrangements. He took upon himself the office of embassador to the states: on this journey he persuades Castĭcus, the son of Catamantalēdes (one of the Sequăni, whose father had possessed the sovereignty among the people for many years, and had been styled "*friend*" by the senate of the Roman people), to seize upon the sovereignty in his own state, which his father had held before him, and he likewise persuades Dumnŏrix, an Æduan, the brother of Divitiăcus, who at that time possessed the chief authority in the state, and was exceedingly beloved by the people, to attempt the same, and gives him his

[1] The Roman mile, mille passus=4,854 English feet, exactly=9·193 of English miles. So that the length, as in the text, would be about 217 English miles, the breadth 163. The real length of Helvetia from the Leman lake to Lake of Constance is hardly more than 40 geographical miles.

daughter in marriage. He proves to them that to accomplish their attempts was a thing very easy to be done, because he himself would obtain the government of his own state; that there was no doubt that the Helvetii were the most powerful of the whole of Gaul; he assures them that he will, with his own forces and his own army, acquire the sovereignty for them. Incited by this speech, they give a pledge and oath to one another, and hope that, when they have seized the sovereignty, they will, by means of the three most powerful and valiant nations, be enabled to obtain possession of the whole of Gaul.

CHAP. IV.—When this scheme was disclosed to the Helvetii by informers, they, according to their custom, compelled Orgetŏrix to plead his cause in chains; it was the law that the penalty of being burned by fire should await him if condemned. On the day appointed for the pleading of his cause, Orgetŏrix drew together from all quarters to the court, all his vassals to the number of ten thousand persons; and led together to the same place all his dependents and debtor-bondsmen, of whom he had a great number; by means of those he rescued himself from [the necessity of] pleading his cause. While the state, incensed at this act, was endeavoring to assert its right by arms, and the magistrates were mustering a large body of men from the country, Orgetŏrix died; and there is not wanting a suspicion, as the Helvetii think, of his having committed suicide.[1]

CHAP. V.—After his death, the Helvetii nevertheless attempt to do that which they had resolved on, namely, to go forth from their territories. When they thought that they were at length prepared for this undertaking, they set fire to all their towns, in number about twelve—to their villages about four hundred—and to the private dwellings that remained; they burn up all the corn, except what they intend to carry with them; that after destroying the hope of a return home, they might be the more ready for undergoing all dangers. They order every one to carry forth from home for himself provisions for three months, ready ground. They persuade the Raurăci, and the Tulingi, and the Latobrĭgi, their neigh-

[1] Literally, "nor is there absent a suspicion that he resolved on death for himself."

bors, to adopt the same plan, and after burning down their towns and villages, to set out with them: and they admit to their party and unite to themselves as confederates the Boii, who had dwelt on the other side of the Rhine,[1] and had crossed over into the Norican territory, and assaulted Noreia.[2]

CHAP. VI.—There were in all two routes, by which they could go forth from their country—one through the Sequăni[3] narrow and difficult, between Mount Jura and the river Rhone (by which scarcely one wagon at a time could be led; there was, moreover, a very high mountain overhanging, so that a very few might easily intercept them); the other, through our Province, much easier and freer from obstacles, because the Rhone flows between the boundaries of the Helvetii and those of the Allobroges, who had lately been subdued,[4] and is in some places crossed by a ford. The furthest town of the Allobroges, and the nearest to the territories of the Helvetii, is Geneva. From this town a bridge extends to the Helvetii. They thought that they should either persuade the Allobroges, because they did not seem as yet well-affected toward the Roman people, or compel them by force to allow them to pass through their territories. Having provided every thing for the expedition, they appoint a day, on which they should all meet on the bank of the Rhone. This day was the fifth before the kalends of April [i. e. the 28th[5] of March], in the consulship of Lucius Piso and Aulus Gabinius [B. C. 58.]

CHAP. VII.—When it was reported to Cæsar that they were attempting to make their route through our Province, he hastens to set out from the city, and, by as great marches as he can, proceeds to Further Gaul, and arrives at Geneva. He orders the whole Province [to furnish] as great a number of soldiers as possible, as there was in all only one legion in Further Gaul: he orders the bridge at Geneva to be

1 In the modern Bohemia and Bavaria, which both derive their names from the *Boii*.

2 Noreia seems to have been the old capital of Noricum.

3 The country of the *Sequani* is the modern *Franche Comté*.

4 C. Pomptinus, when prætor, defeated (B. C. 61) the Allobroges, who had invaded his province of Gallia Narbonensis. (They were perhaps insurgents.)

5 According to the *inclusive* reckoning of the ancients, whereby the 31st (last) day of March would be the day before [rather the 2d day of] the kalends of April, the 30th the 3d day before, etc., etc.

broken down. When the Helvetii are apprized of his arrival, they send to him, as embassadors, the most illustrious men of their state (in which embassy Numeius and Verudoctius held the chief place), to say "that it was their intention to march through the Province without doing any harm, because they had" [according to their own representations,][1] "no other route:—that they requested, they might be allowed to do so with his consent." Cæsar, inasmuch as he kept in remembrance that Lucius Cassius, the consul, had been slain,[2] and his army routed and made to pass under the yoke by the Helvetii, did not think that [their request] ought to be granted: nor was he of opinion that men of hostile disposition, if an opportunity of marching through the Province were given them, would abstain from outrage and mischief. Yet, in order that a period might intervene, until the soldiers whom he had ordered [to be furnished] should assemble, he replied to the ambassadors, that he would take time to deliberate; if they wanted any thing, they might return on the day before the ides[3] of April [on April 12th].

CHAP. VIII.—Meanwhile, with the legion which he had with him and the soldiers which had assembled from the Province, he carries along for nineteen [Roman, not quite eighteen English] miles a wall, to the height of sixteen feet,[4] and a trench, from the Lake of Geneva, which flows into the river Rhone, to Mount Jura, which separates the territories of the Sequăni from those of the Helvetii. When that work was finished, he distributes garrisons, and closely fortifies redoubts, in order that he may the more easily intercept them, if they should attempt to cross over against his will. When the day which he had appointed with the embassadors came, and

[1] Vid. Madvig's Lat. Gramm. (Wood's Translation), § 382. *Obs.* 3, p. 333. These parentheses are inserted to explain more fully the *precise* form of the Latin subjunctives ("haberent" . . . . "reverterentur, etc.) in the *oratio obliqua*, indirect citation, where not the fact but the *assertion* of it by somebody, is meant to be declared.

[2] By the *Tigurini*, B. C. 107, when consul (with the famous *C. Marius*). Vid. chap. xii.

[3] The ides of April being April 13th, and the ides of *every* month the 13th, save March, May, July, and, October, during which four months the ides fell on the 15th of each, two days later than usual.

[4] The Roman foot, *pes*, was equal to 97 English feet. The height of the wall would, therefore, be about 11 feet 10 inches, according to our mensuration.

they returned to him; he says, that he can not, consistently with the custom and precedent of the Roman people, grant any one a passage through the Province; and he gives them to understand,[1] that, if they should attempt to use violence he would oppose them. The Helvetti, disappointed in this hope, tried if they could force a passage (some by means of a bridge of boats and numerous rafts constructed for the purpose;[2] others, by the fords of the Rhone, where the depth of the river was least, sometimes by day, but more frequently by night), but being kept at bay by the strength of our works, and by the concourse of the soldiers, and by the missiles, they desisted from this attempt.

CHAP. IX.—There was left one way, [namely] through the Sequăni, by which, on account of its narrowness, they could not pass without the consent of the Sequăni. As they could not of themselves prevail on them, they send embassadors to Dumnŏrix the Æduan, that through his intercession, they might obtain their request from the Sequăni. Dumnŏrix, by his popularity and liberality, had great influence among the Sequăni, and was friendly to the Helvetii, because out of that state he had married the daughter of Orgetŏrix; and, incited by lust of sovereignty, was anxious for a revolution, and wished to have as many states as possible attached to him by his kindness toward them. He, therefore, undertakes the affair, and prevails upon the Sequăni to allow the Helvetii to march through their territories, and arranges that they should give hostages to each other—the Sequăni not to obstruct the Helvetii in their march—the Helvetii, to pass without mischief and outrage.

CHAP. X.—It is again told Cæsar, that the Helvetii intended to march through the country of the Sequăni and the Ædui into the territories of the Santŏnes, which are not far distant from those boundaries of the Tolŏsātes, which [viz. Tolŏsa, Toulouse] is a state in the Province. If this took place, he saw that it would be attended with great danger to the Province to have warlike men, enemies of the Roman

[1] "*Ostendere*" and "*demonstrare*" are often used by Cæsar for explicit *oral declaration.*

[2] That is, as a pontoon.

people, bordering upon[1] an open and very fertile tract of country. For these reasons he appointed Titus Labienus, his lieutenant, to the command of the fortification which he had made. He himself proceeds to Italy by forced marches, and there levies two legions, and leads out from winter-quarters three which were wintering around Aquileia,[2] and with these five legions marches[3] rapidly by the nearest route across the Alps into Further Gaul. Here the Centrōnes and the Graiocēli and the Caturīges,[4] having taken possession of the higher parts, attempt to obstruct the army in their march. After having routed these in several battles, he arrives in the territories of the Vocontii in the Further Province on the seventh day from Ocēlum,[5] which is the most remote town of the Hither Province; thence he leads his army into the country of the Allobroges, and from the Allobroges to the Segusiani.[6] These people are the first beyond the Province on the opposite side of the Rhone.[7]

Chap. XI.—The Helvetii had by this time led their forces over through the narrow defile and the territories of the Sequăni, and had arrived at the territories of the Ædui, and were ravaging their lands. The Ædui, as they could not defend themselves and their possessions against them, send embassadors to Cæsar to ask assistance, [pleading] that they had at all times so well deserved of the Roman people, that their fields ought not to have been laid waste—their children carried off into slavery—their towns stormed, almost within sight of our army. At the same time the Ambarri, the friends and kinsmen of the Ædui, apprize Cæsar, that it was not easy for them, now that their fields had been devastated,

1 Making "*locias patentibus*" directly dependent on "*finitimos,*" which seems the true (though overlooked) construction, and is perhaps the simplest.

2 A district in *Venetia*, which not in ancient only, but in more modern times and the middle ages, held the key of Italy on the north-east side.

3 *Contendit ire.* Literally, "hastens to go."

4 The Centrones in the Graian Alps, Caturiges (south of them) in the Cottian Alps, Graiocēli between the two.

5 *Ocēlum,* the chief town of *Graiocēli,* just on the frontiers of Transalpine Gaul: the present *Usseau* in *Piedmont.*

6 Considered, of course, not so much as tribes, but as districts. This is common enough in Cæsar.

7 The first independent people north of the Roman Province (near Lugdūnum, *Lyons*).

to ward off the violence of the enemy from their towns: the Allobroges likewise, who had villages and possessions on the other side of the Rhone, betake themselves in flight to Cæsar, and assure him that they had nothing remaining, except the soil of their land. Cæsar, induced by these circumstances, decides, that he ought not to wait until the Helvetii, after destroying all the property of his allies, should arrive among the Santŏnes.

CHAP. XII.—There is a river [called] the Saône, which flows through the territories of the Ædui and Sequăni into the Rhone with such incredible slowness, that it can not be determined by the eye in which direction it flows. This the Helvetii were crossing by rafts and boats joined together. When Cæsar was informed by spies that the Helvetii had already conveyed three parts of their forces across that river, but that the fourth part was left behind on this side of the Saône, he set out from the camp with three legions during the third watch,[1] and came up with that divison which had not yet crossed the river. Attacking them, encumbered with baggage, and not expecting him, he cut to pieces a great part of them; the rest betook themselves to flight, and concealed themselves in the nearest woods. That canton [which was cut down] was called the Tigurine;[2] for the whole Helvetian state is divided into four cantons. This single canton having left their country, within the recollection of our fathers, had slain Lucius Cassius the consul, and had made his army pass under the yoke,[3] [B. C. 107]. Thus, whether by chance, or by the design of the immortal gods, that part of the Helvetian state which had brought a signal calamity upon the Roman people, was the first to pay the penalty. In this Cæsar avenged not only the public but also his own personal wrongs, because the Tigurini had slain Lucius Piso[4] the lieutenant [of Cassius], the

[1] The night was divided by the Romans into four "watches," of three hours each; the *third* beginning at midnight, and the whole four lasting from six o'clock P.M. to six A.M. "*De*" seems often to mean "*about the middle of;*" "ut jugulent homines, surgunt *de nocte* (*at midnight*) latrones."—Horat. 1 Epist. ii. 32.

[2] The Canton of Zurich.

[3] This has been already mentioned in chap. vii.

[4] Consul in B.C. 112.

grandfather of Lucius Calpurnius Piso,[1] his [Cæsar's] father-in law, in the same battle as Cassius himself.

CHAP. XIII.—This battle ended, that he might be able to come up with the remaining forces of the Helvetii, he procures a bridge to be made across the Saône, and thus leads his army over. The Helvetii, confused by his sudden arrival, when they found that he had effected in one day, what they, themselves had with the utmost difficulty accomplished in twenty, namely, the crossing of the river, send embassadors to him; at the head of which embassy was Divíco, who had been commander of the Helvetii, in the war against Cassius. He thus treats with Cæsar:—that, "if the Roman people would make peace with the Helvetii they would go to that part and there remain, where Cæsar might appoint and desire them to be; but if he should persist in persecuting[2] them with war, that he ought to remember both the ancient disgrace of the Roman people and the characteristic valor of the Helvetii. As to his having attacked one canton by surprise, [at a time] when those who had crossed the river could not bring assistance to their friends, that he ought not on that account to ascribe very much to his own valor, or despise them; that they had so learned from their sires and ancestors, as to rely more on valor than on artifice and stratagem. Wherefore let him not bring it to pass[3] that the place, where they were standing, should acquire a name, from the disaster of the Roman people and the destruction of their army or transmit the remembrance [of such an event to posterity]."

CHAP. XIV.—To these words Cæsar thus replied:—that "on that very account he felt less hesitation, because he kept in remembrance those circumstances which the Helvetian embassadors had mentioned, and that he felt the more indignant at them, in proportion as they had happened undeservedly to the Roman people: for if they had been conscious of having done any wrong, it would not have been difficult

[1] Consul in B.C. 58, through Cæsar's influence, who had been consul in B.C. 59, and had married Piso's daughter *Calpurnia*.

[2] Turning the Latin from the oratio *obliqua* to the oratio *recta*, it would be:—"sin bello persequi perseveras, reminiscitor . . . . pristinæ virtutis Helvetiorum," etc.; and lower down (3) "ne committeret" would be "*ne commiseris*." Vid. Wood's Translation of Madvig's Lat. Gramm. § 404, 5, p. 354.

to be on their guard, but for that very reason had they been deceived, because neither were they aware that any offense had been given by them, on account of which they should be afraid, nor did they think that they ought to be afraid without cause. But even if he were willing to forget their former outrage, could he also lay aside[1] the remembrance of the late wrongs, in that they had against his will attempted a route through the Province by force, in that they had molested the Ædui, the Ambarri, and the Allobroges? That as to their so insolently boasting of their victory, and as to their being astonished that they had so long committed their outrages with impunity, [both these things] tended to the same point; for the immortal gods are wont to allow those persons whom they wish to punish for their guilt sometimes a greater prosperity and longer impunity, in order that they may suffer the more severely from a reverse of circumstances. Although these things are so, yet, if hostages were to be given him by them in order that he may be assured they will do what they promise, and provided they will give satisfaction to the Ædui for the outrages which they had committed against them and their allies, and likewise to the Allobroges, he [Cæsar] will make peace with them." Divico replied, that "the Helvetii had been so trained by their ancestors, that they were accustomed to receive, not to give hostages; of that fact the Roman people were witness." Having given this reply, he withdrew.

CHAP. XV.—On the following day they move their camp from that place; Cæsar does the same, and sends forward all his cavalry, to the number of four thousand (which he had drawn together from all parts of the Province and from the Ædui and their allies), to observe toward what parts the enemy are directing their march. These, having too eagerly pursued the enemy's rear, come to a battle with the cavalry of the Helvetii in a disadvantageous place, and a few of our men fall. The Helvetii, elated with this battle, because they had with five hundred horse repulsed so large a body of horse, began to face us more boldly, sometimes too from their rear to

[1] Si veteris contumeliæ oblivisci vellet, num etiam recentium injuriarum memoriam deponere, posse," without "*se*," would be in *oratio recta*, "si . . . volo"—"num . . . . possum?" For a fuller explanation see Madvig's Lat. Gramm. (Wood's Translation), § 405, *a*, page 354.

provoke our men by an attack. Cæsar [however] restrained his men from battle, deeming it sufficient for the present to prevent the enemy from rapine, forage, and depredation. They marched for about fifteen days in such a manner that there was not more than five or six miles between the enemy's rear and our van.

Chap. XVI.—Meanwhile, Cæsar kept daily importuning the Ædui for the corn which they had promised in the name of their state; for, in consequence of the coldness (Gaul, being, as before said, situated toward the north), not only was the corn in the fields not ripe, but there was not in store a sufficiently large quantity even of fodder: besides he was unable to use the corn which he had conveyed in ships up the river Saône, because the Helvetii, from whom he was unwilling to retire had diverted their march from the Saône. The Ædui kept deferring from day to day, and saying that it was being "collected—brought in—on the road." When he saw that he was put off too long, and that the day was close at hand on which he ought to serve out the corn to his soldiers;—having called together their chiefs, of whom he had a great number in his camp, among them Divitiăcus, and Liscus who was invested with the chief magistracy (whom the Ædui style the Vergobretus, and who is elected annually, and has power of life or death over his countrymen), he severely reprimands them, because he is not assisted by them on so urgent an occasion, when the enemy were so close at hand, and when [corn] could neither be bought nor taken from the fields, particularly as, in a great measure urged by their prayers, he had undertaken the war; much more bitterly, therefore, does he complain of his being forsaken.

Chap. XVII.—Then at length Liscus, moved by Cæsar's speech, discloses what he had hitherto kept secret:—that "there are some whose influences with the people is very great, who, though private men, have more power than the magistrates themselves: that these by seditions and violent language are deterring the populace from contributing the corn which they ought to supply; [by telling them] that, if they can not any longer retain the supremacy of Gaul, it were better to submit to the government of Gauls than of Romans, nor ought they to doubt that, if the Romans should overpower the Helvetii, they would wrest their freedom from the Ædui together with the remainder of Gaul. By these very men, [said he], are our plans, and whatever is done in the camp, disclosed to the enemy; that they could not be restrained by *him:* nay more, he was well aware, that though compelled by necessity, he had disclosed the matter to Cæsar, at how great a risk he had done it; and for that reason, he had been silent as long as he could."

CHAP. XVIII.—Cæsar perceived that, by this speech of Liscus, Dumnŏrix, the brother of Divitiăcus, was indicated; but, as he was unwilling that these matters should be discussed while so many were present, he speedily dismisses the council, but detains Liscus: he inquires from him when alone, about those things which he had said in the meeting. He [Liscus] speaks more unreservedly and boldly. He [Cæsar] makes inquiries on the same points privately of others, and discovers that it is all true; that "Dumnŏrix is the person, a man of the highest daring, in great favor with the people on account of his liberality, a man eager for a revolution: that for a great many years he has been in the habit of contracting for the customs and all the other taxes of the Ædui at a small cost, because when *he* bids, no one dares to bid against him. By these means he has both increased his own private property, and amassed great means for giving largesses; that he maintains constantly at his own expense and keeps about his own person a great number of cavalry, and that not only at home, but even among the neighboring states, he has great influence, and for the sake of strengthening this influence has given his mother in marriage among the Bitŭriges to a man the most noble and most influential there; that he has himself taken a wife from among the Helvetii, and has given his sister by the mother's side and his female relations in marriage into other states; that he favors and wishes well to the Helvetii on account of this connection; and that he hates Cæsar and the Romans, on his own account, because by their arrival his power was weakened, and his brother, Divitiăcus, restored to his former position of influence and dignity: that, if any thing should happen to the Romans, he entertains the highest hope of gaining the sovereignty by means of the Helvetii, but that under the government of the Roman people he despairs not only of royalty, but even of that influence which he already has." Cæsar discovered too, on inquiring into the unsuccessful cavalry engagement which had taken place a few days before, that the commencement of that flight had been made by Dumnŏrix and his cavalry (for Dumnŏrix was in command of the cavalry which the Ædui had sent for aid to Cæsar); that by their flight the rest of the cavalry were dismayed.

Chap. XIX—After learning these circumstances, since to these suspicions the most unequivocal facts were added, viz., that he had led the Helvetii through the territories of the Sequăni; that he had provided that hostages should be mutually given; that he had done all these things, not only without any orders of his [Cæsar's] and of his own state's, but even without their [the Ædui] knowing any thing of it themselves; that he [Dumnŏrix] was reprimanded by the [chief] magistrate of the Ædui; he [Cæsar] considered that there was sufficient reason, why he should either punish him himself, or order the state to do so. One thing [however] stood in the way of all this—that he had learned by experience his brother Divitiăcus's very high regard for the Roman people, his great affection toward him, his distinguished faithfulness, justice, and moderation; for he was afraid lest by the punishment of this man, he should hurt the feelings of Divitiăcus. Therefore, before he attempted any thing, he orders Divitiăcus to be summoned to him, and, when the ordinary interpreters had been withdrawn, converses with him through Caius Valerius Procillus, chief of the province of Gaul, an intimate friend of his, in whom he reposed the highest confidence in every thing; at the same time he reminds him of what was said about Dumnŏrix in the council of the Gauls, when he himself was present, and shows what each had said of him privately in his [Cæsar's] own presence; he begs and exhorts him, that, without offense to his feelings, he may either himself pass judgment on him [Dumnŏrix] after trying the case, or else order the [Æduan] state to do so.

Chap. XX.—Divitiăcus, embracing Cæsar, begins to implore him, with many tears, that "he would not pass any very severe sentence upon his brother; saying, that he knows that those charges are true, and that nobody suffered more pain on that account than he himself did; for when he himself could effect a very great deal by his influence at home and in the rest of Gaul, and he [Dumnŏrix] very little on account of his youth, the latter had become powerful through his means, which power and strength he used not only to the lessening of his [Divitiăcus] popularity, but almost to his ruin; that he, however, was influenced both by fraternal affection and by public opinion. But if any thing very severe from Cæsar should befall him [Dumnŏrix], no one would think that it had been done without his consent, since he himself held such a place in Cæsar's friendship: from which circumstance it would arise, that the affections of the whole of Gaul would be estranged from him." As he was with tears begging these things of Cæsar in many words, Cæsar takes his right hand, and, comforting him, begs him to make an end of entreating, and assures him that his regard for him is so great, that he forgives both the injuries of the republic and his private wrongs, at his desire and prayers. He summons Dumnŏrix to him; he brings in his brother; he points out what he censures in him; he lays before him what he of himself perceives, and what the state complains of; he warns him for the future to avoid all grounds of suspicion; he says that he pardons the past, for the sake of his brother, Divitiăcus. He sets spies over Dumnŏrix that he may be able to know what he does, and with whom he communicates.

CHAP. XXI.—Being on the same day informed by his scouts, that the enemy had encamped at the foot of a mountain eight miles from his own camp; he sent persons to ascertain what the nature of the mountain was, and of what kind the ascent on every side. Word was brought back, that it was easy. During the third watch[1] he orders Titus Labienus, his lieutenant with prætorian powers,[2] to ascend to the highest ridge of the mountain with two legions, and with those as guides who had examined the road; he explains what his plan is. He himself during the fourth watch,[1]

[1] For the *vigiliæ*, or watches of the night vid. note on book i. chap. 12.—

With the Romans	1st vigilia was from	6. P.M. to 9 P.M.	There being thus four of three hours each. "Vigiliæ" was a term connected with military night-duty.
	2d "	9 P.M. to midnight	
	3d "	midnight to 3 A.M.	
	4th "	3 A.M. to 3 A.M.	

[2] *Legatum pro prætore.*" The legati accompanied the generals into the field, or the proconsul [or prætor] to the provinces. They were *nominated (legati)* by the Consu, Prætor, or Dictator, under whom they served, after such nomination had been sanctioned by a decree of senate

hastens to them by the same route by which the enemy had gone, and sends on all the cavalry before him. Publius Considius, who was reputed to be very experienced in military affairs, and had been in the army of Lucius Sulla, and afterward in that of Marcus Crassus, is sent forward with the scouts.

CHAP. XXII.—At day-break, when the summit of the mountain was in the possession of Titus Labienus, and he himself was not further off than a mile and half[1] from the enemy's camp, nor, as he afterward ascertained from the captives, had either his arrival or that of Labienus been discovered; Considius, with his horse at full gallop, comes up to him—says that the mountain which he [Cæsar] wished should be seized by Labienus, is in possession of the enemy; that he has discovered this by the Gallic arms and ensigns. Cæsar leads off his forces to the next hill: [and] draws them up in battle-order. Labienus, as he had been ordered by Cæsar not to come to an engagement unless [Cæsar's] own forces were seen near the enemy's camp, that the attack upon the enemy might be made on every side at the same time, was, after having taken possession of the mountain, waiting for our men, and refraining from battle. When, at length, the day was far advanced, Cæsar learned through spies, that the mountain was in possession of his own men, and that the Helvetii had moved their camp, and that Considius, struck with fear, had reported to him, as seen, that which he had not seen. On that day he follows the enemy at his usual[2] distance, and pitches his camp three miles from theirs.

CHAP. XXIII.—The next day (as there remained in all only two day's space [to the time] when he must serve out the corn to his army, and as he was not more than eighteen miles from Bibracte,[3] by far the largest and best-stored town

[senatus consultum.] If the consul was absent from the army, or a proconsul left his province, the *legati*, or one of them, held the absent magistrate's power and insignia, in which case he was styled Legatus pro Prætore (or Vicegerent).

1 Bibracte, afterward *Augustodunam*, (*hence*) the modern *Autun* (on the river Aroux, in *Burgundy*).

2 Lit. "1500 paces." The passus (*pace*)=2 gradus=5 pedes=4 English feet, 10·248 inches.

3 Literally, "At the interval *at which he had been used*" (to follow, etc.)

of the Ædui), he thought that he ought to provide for a supply of corn; and diverted his march from the Helvetii, and advanced rapidly to Bibracte. This circumstance is reported to the enemy by some deserters from Lucius Æmilius, a captain,[1] of the Gallic horse. The Helvetii, either because they thought that the Romans, struck with terror, were retreating from them, the more so, as the day before, though they had seized on the higher grounds, they had not joined battle; or because they flattered themselves that they might be cut off from the provisions, altering their plan and changing their route, began to pursue, and to annoy our men in the rear.

CHAP. XXIV.—Cæsar, when he observes this, draws off his forces to the next hill, and sent the cavalry to sustain the attack of the enemy. He himself, meanwhile, drew up on the middle of the hill a triple line of his four veteran legions in such a manner, that he placed above him on the very summit the two legions, which he had lately levied in Hither Gaul,[2] and all the auxiliaries;[3] and he ordered that the whole mountain should be covered with men, and that meanwhile the baggage[4] should be brought together into one place, and the position be protected by those who were posted in the upper line. The Helvetii having followed with all their wagons, collected their baggage into one place: they themselves, after having repulsed our cavalry and formed a phalanx, advanced up to our front line in very close order.

CHAP. XXV.—Cæsar, having removed out of sight first his

[1] The regular complement (justus equitatus) of cavalry in a legion in Cæsar's time (the legion then was 5000 foot) was 300, *i. e.* 10 *turms* of 30 horseman each. [There were for each turm 3 decuriones, ἰλάρχαι.] But in Cæsar's time the decurio seems to have been captain of the whole turm, according to Vegetius.

[2] As is stated in chap. x. of this book.

[3] All the foreign socii were obliged to send subsidies in troops when Rome demanded them; these did not, however, like those of the socii Italici, serve in the line, but were used as light-armed soldiers, and were called "*auxilia.*"

[4] Sarcinæ (lit. "packages") is used of each solder's own baggage, which he carries for himself; but impedimenta is the army's baggage, carried on wagons or beasts of burden. The Roman soldier carried a vast load, 60 pounds weight, besides his armor, which last was considered part and parcel of the man himself. (Cic. Tusc. Qu. ii. 16.)

own horse, then those of all, that he might make the danger of all equal, and do away with the hope of flight, after encouraging his men, joined battle. His soldiers hurling their javelins from the higher ground, easily broke the enemy's phalanx. That being dispersed, they made a charge on them with drawn swords. It was a great hinderance to the Gauls in fighting, that, when several of their bucklers[1] had been by one stroke of the (Roman) javelins[2] pierced through and pinned fast together, as the point of the iron had bent itself, they could neither pluck it out, nor, with their left hand entangled, fight with sufficient ease; so that many, after having long tossed their arm about, chose rather to cast away the buckler from their hand, and to fight with their person unprotected. At length, worn out with wounds, they began to give way, and, as there was in the neighborhood a mountain about a mile off, to betake themselves thither. When the mountain had been gained, and our men were advancing up, the Boii and Tulingi, who with about 15,000 men closed the enemy's line of march and served as a guard to their rear, having assailed our men on the exposed flank as they advanced [prepared] to surround[3] them; upon seeing which, the Helvetii who had betaken themselves to the mountain, began to press on again and renew the battle. The Romans having faced about, advanced to the attack in two divisions;[4] the first and second line, to withstand those who had been de-

[1] Scutum, θυρεος of Polybius, was the (oblong) wooden (or wicker-work) buckler (strengthened with an iron rim and an iron boss) of the Roman heavy-armed infantry. It covered the left shoulder, and was 4 ft. long by 2½ broad. It was distinct from the (Greek) *clypeus* (shield), which was round, and was by the Romans discontinued for the Sabine *scutum*, about B.C. 400 (after the soldiers began to receive pay).

[2] The pilum, or ponderous javelin, ὑσσὸς (of which the Roman soldier carried two), to throw or to thrust with, was about 6 feet 9 inches in length. The shaft was 4½ feet, long; and of the same length was the barbed (three-square) iron head, which extended half-way down the shaft. This thick javelin was peculiar to the Roman heavy-armed soldier (with his long lance), as the *gosum* was to the Gauls.

[3] Circumvenire seems preferable to venere.

[4] "Romani conversa signa bipartito intulerunt," are the words "Signa inferre," "to bear the standards on," means to *attack;* and "signa convertere," "to turn the standards round," means to *face about.* The Romans, having faced about, advanced to the attack"—bipartito "from two different quarters," or "in two divisions."

feated and driven off the field; the third to receive those who were just arriving.

CHAP. XXVI.—Thus, was the contest long and vigorously carried on with doubtful success.[1] When they could no longer withstand the attacks of our men, the one division, as they had begun to do, betook themselves to the mountain; the other repaired to their baggage and wagons. For during the whole of this battle, although the fight lasted from the seventh hour [i. e. 12 (noon)—1 P. M.] to eventide, no one could see an enemy with his back turned. The fight was carried on also at the baggage till late in the night, for they had set wagons in the way as a rampart, and from the higher ground kept throwing weapons upon our men, as they came on, and some from between the wagons and the wheels kept darting their lances and javelins from beneath, and wounding our men. After the fight had lasted some time, our men gained possession of their baggage and camp. There the daughter and one of the sons of Orgetŏrix was taken. After the battle about 130,000 men [of the enemy] remained alive, who marched incessantly during the whole of that night; and after a march discontinued for no part of the night, arrived in the territories of the Lingŏnes on the fourth day, while our men, having stopped for three days, both on account of the wounds of the soldiers and the burial of the slain, had not been able to follow them. Cæsar sent letters and messengers to the Lingŏnes [with orders] that they should not assist them with corn or with any thing else; for that if they should assist them, he would regard them in the same light as the Helvetii. After the three days' interval he began to follow them himself with all his forces.

CHAP. XXVII.—The Helvetii, compelled by the want of every thing, sent embassadors to him about a surrender. When these had met him on the way and had thrown themselves at his feet, and speaking in suppliant tone had with tears sued for peace, and [when] he had ordered them to await his arrival, in the place,[2] where they then were, they obeyed

[1] The sense of "ancipiti prælio," to which the best commentators incline.

[2] Loco quo tum *essent*, "where they" (the whole body of the fugitive Helvetii) "then *were*," *essent*, (according to the embassador's statements, "where*ever*" on the faith of their statement "they were," though *where* exactly Cæsar knew not). This is the force of the subjunctive in the "*oratio obliqua*."

his commands. When Cæsar arrived at that place, he demanded hostages, their arms, and the slaves who had deserted to them. While those things are being sought for and got together, after a night's interval, about 6000 men of that canton which is called the Verbigene, whether terrified by fear, lest, after delivering up their arms, they should suffer punishment, or else induced by the hope of safety, because they supposed that, amid so vast a multitude of those who had surrendered themselves, *their* flight might either be concealed or entirely overlooked, having at night-fall departed out of the camp of the Helvetii, hastened to the Rhine and the territories of the Germans.

CHAP. XXVIII.—But when Cæsar discovered this, he commanded those through whose territory they had gone, to seek them out and to bring them back again, if they meant to be acquitted before him; and considered them, when brought back, in the light of enemies; he admitted all the rest to a surrender, upon their delivering up the hostages, arms, and deserters. He ordered the Helvetii, the Tulingi, and the Latobrĭgi, to return to their territories from which they had come, and as there was at home nothing whereby they might support their hunger, all the productions of the earth having been destroyed, he commanded the Allobrŏges to let them have a plentiful supply of corn; and ordered them to rebuild the towns and villages which they had burned. This he did, chiefly, on this account, because he was unwilling that the country, from which the Helvetii had departed, should be untenanted, lest the Germans, who dwell on the other side of the Rhine, should, on account of the excellence of the lands, cross over from their own territories into those of the Helvetii, and become borderers upon the province of Gaul and the Allobrŏges. He granted the petition[1] of the Ædui, that they might settle the Boii, in their own (i. e. in the Æduan) territories, as these were known to be of distinguished valor, to whom they gave lands, and whom they afterward admitted to the same state of rights and freedom as themselves.

CHAP. XXIX.—In the camp of the Helvetii, lists were

[1] Lit. "he granted to the Ædui, requesting it, that they (the Ædui) shall settle the Boii," etc. (where the *ut—collocarent* is governed by *concessit*).

found, drawn up in Greek characters, and were brought to Cæsar, in which an estimate had been drawn up, name by name, of the number which had gone forth from their country of those who were able to bear arms; and likewise the boys, the old men, and the women, separately. Of all which items the total was:

Of the *Helvetii* [lit. of the heads of the Helvetii]	263,000
Of the *Tulingi*	36,000
Of the *Latobrĭgi*	14,000
Of the *Raurăci*	23,000
Of the *Boii*	32,000
The sum of all amounted to . . .	368,000

Out of these, such as could bear arms, [amounted] to about 92,000. When the *census*[1] of those who returned home was taken, as Cæsar had commanded, the number was found to be 110,000.

CHAP. XXX.—When the war with the Helvetii was concluded, embassadors from almost all parts of Gaul, the chiefs of states, assembled to congratulate Cæsar, [saying] that they were well aware, that, although he had taken vengeance on the Helvetii in war, for the old wrongs done by them to the Roman people,[2] yet that circumstance had happened no less to the benefit of the land of Gaul than of the Roman people, because the Helvetii, while their affairs were most flourishing, had quitted their country with the design of making war upon the whole of Gaul, and seizing the government of it, and selecting, out of a great abundance, that spot for an abode, which they should judge to be the most convenient and most productive of all

[1] Probably, only an ordinary review, for the sake of a pretty accurate estimate.

[2] Helvetiorum—injuriis—populi Romani (use of the *double* genitive, Wood's *Madvig's Lat. Gram.* § 288), the wrongs of the Helvetii—i. e. which they *did* (*act*) implies the wrongs of the Roman people—i. e. which they *suffered* (*pass.*) [So "superior umdierum Sabini cunctatio," in Book iii. 18.] "Tametsi ab iis pœnas bello repetisset," is lit. "although from them he had sought back (re-claimed) penal-satisfactions in war." Pœnas petere, or *ex*petere, or *re*petere, capere or sumere, habere or persequi, to "*take satisfaction*" by *dealing punishment* or *vengeance.* Pœna, *expiatory* punishment [or tortures].

Gaul, and hold the rest of the states as tributaries. They requested that they might be allowed to proclaim an assembly of the whole of Gaul for[1] a particular day, and to do that with Cæsar's permission, [stating] that they had some things which, with the general consent, they wished to ask of him. This request having been granted, they appointed a day for the assembly, and ordained by an oath with each other, that no one should disclose [their deliberations] except those to whom this [office] should be assigned by the general assembly.

CHAP. XXXI.—When that assembly was dismissed, the same chiefs of states, who had before been to Cæsar, returned, and asked that they might be allowed to treat with him privately (in secret)[2] concerning the safety of themselves and of all. That request having been obtained, they all threw themselves in tears at Cæsar's feet, [saying] that they no less begged and earnestly desired that what they might say should not be disclosed, than that they might obtain those things which they wished for; inasmuch as they saw, that, if a disclosure was made, they should be put to the greatest tortures. For these Divitiăcus the Æduan spoke and told him:—"That there were two parties in the whole of Gaul: that the Ædui stood at the head of one of these, the Arverni of the other. After these had been violently struggling with one another for the superiority for many years, it came to pass that the Germans were called in for hire by the Arverni and the Sequăni. That about 15,000, of them [i. e. of the Germans] had at first crossed the Rhine: but after that these wild and savage men had become enamored of the lands and the refinement and the abundance of the Gauls, more were brought over, that there were now as many as 120,000 of them in Gaul: that with these the Ædui and their dependents had repeatedly struggled in arms—that they had been routed, and had sustained a great calamity—had lost all their nobility, all their senate, all their cavalry. And that broken by such engagements and calamities, although they had formerly been very powerful in Gaul, both from their own valor and from

[1] *i. e.* to make a proclamation, that such an assembly was to be holden upon a fixed day.

[2] Oudendorp has *secreto in occulto*, but more recent texts, and among them Bentley, regard *in occulto* as a gloss.

the Roman people's hospitality[1] and friendship, they were now compelled to give the chief nobles of their state, as hostages to the Sequăni, and to bind their state by an oath, that they would neither demand hostages in return, nor supplicate aid from the Roman people, nor refuse to be forever under their sway and empire. That he was the only one out of all the state of the Ædui, who could not be prevailed upon to take the oath or to give his children as hostages. On that account he had fled from his state and had gone to the senate at Rome[2] to beseech aid, as he alone was bound neither by oath nor hostages. But a worse thing had befallen the victorious Sequăni than the vanquished Ædui, for Ariovistus, the king of the Germans, had settled in their territories, and had seized upon a third of their land, which was[3] the best in the whole of Gaul, and was now ordering them to depart from another third part, because a few months previously 24,000 men of the Harūdes[4] had come to him, for whom room and settlements must be provided. The consequence would be, that in a few years they would all be driven from the territories of Gaul, and all the Germans would cross the Rhine; for neither must the land[5] of Gaul be compared with the land of the Germans, nor must the habit of living of the latter be put on a level with that of the former. Moreover, [as for] Ariovistus, no sooner did he defeat the forces of the Gauls in a battle, which took place at Magetobria, than [he began] to lord it haughtily and cruelly, to demand as hostages the children of all the principal nobles, and wreak on them every kind of cruelty, if every thing was not done at his nod or pleasure; that he was a savage, passionate, and reckless man, and that his commands could no longer be borne. Unless there was some aid in Cæsar and the Roman people, the Gauls must all do the same thing that the Helvetii have done, [viz.] emigrate from their country, and seek another dwelling place, other settlements

[1] The Roman "*hospitium*," public hospitality, was much the same as the Grecian προξενία.

[2] Romam ad senatum, lit. "to Rome to the senate (there)."

[3] *Esset* optimus, "was" *according to the speaker's representation*, "the best."

[4] Lit. "twenty-four thousands of the men" [called] "the *Harūdes*."

[5] *Agrum, land, i. e.* in the *agricultural* sense (arable soil).

[6] *Lit.* "as soon as (when once) he defeated the Gauls, etc., he [began to] lord it," etc.

remote from the Germans, and try whatever fortune may fall to their lot. If these things were to be disclosed to Ariovistus, [Divitiăcus adds] that he doubts not that he would inflict the most severe punishment on all the hostages who are in his possession, [and says] that Cæsar could, either by his own influence and by that of his army, or by his late victory, or by name of the Roman people, intimidate him, so as to prevent a greater number of Germans being brought over the Rhine, and could protect all Gaul from the outrages of Ariovistus.

Chap. XXXII.—When this speech had been delivered by Divitiăcus, all who were present began with loud lamentation to entreat assistance of Cæsar. Cæsar noticed that the Sequăni were the only people of all who did none of those things which the others did, but, with their heads bowed down, gazed on the earth in sadness. Wondering what was the reason of this conduct, he inquired of themselves. No reply did the Sequăni make, but silently continued in the same sadness. When he had repeatedly inquired of them and could not elicit any answer at all, the same Divitiăcus the Æduan answered, that —"the lot of the Sequăni was more wretched and grievous than that of the rest, on this account, because they alone durst not even in secret complain or supplicate aid; and shuddered at the cruelty of Ariovistus [even when] absent, just as if he were present; for, to the rest, despite of every thing,[1] there was an opportunity of flight given; but all tortures must be endured by the Sequăni, who had admitted Ariovistus within their territories, and whose towns were all in his power."

Chap. XXXIII.—Cæsar, on being informed of these things, cheered the minds of the Gauls with his words, and promised that this affair should be an object of his concern, [saying] that he had great hopes that Ariovistus, induced both by his kindness and his power, would put an end to his oppression. After delivering this speech, he dismissed the assembly; and, besides those statements, many circumstances induced him to think that this affair ought to be considered and taken up by him; especially as he saw that the Æudi, styled [as they had

[1] This elliptical use of *tamen*, (1) "*nevertheless*," (2) "*yet at least*," (3) "*but after all*," may be compared with that of the Greek ὅμως.

been] repeatedly by the senate "brethren" and "kinsmen," were held in the thraldom and dominion of the Germans, and understood that their hostages were with Ariovistus and the Sequăni, which in so mighty an empire [as that] of the Roman people he considered very disgraceful to himself and the republic. That, moreover, the Germans should by degrees become accustomed to cross the Rhine, and that a great body of them should come into Gaul, he saw [would be] dangerous to the Roman people, and judged, that wild and savage men would not be likely to restrain themselves, after they had possessed themselves of all Gaul, from going forth into the province and thence marching into Italy (as the Cimbri and Teutŏnes[1] had done before

[1] The Cimbri, says Niebuhr, were not real Gauls but Cymri (Celts in fact) of the same stock to which belong the Welsh—Basbretons—early Cumbrians, and inhabitants of the western coast of England. [The Picts of Scotland and the Belgæ were Cymri.] They extended eastward as far as the river Dnieper, where they were called Galatians. And he is equally sure that the Teutŏnes or (Teutŏni) were Germans. It is thought that Jutland and the regions whence came the Anglo-Saxons were the original seats of these Cimbri, who were driven from them by the progress of the Sarmatians, and migrated southward. They appeared B. C. 115 in Noricum, and thence descended into Illyricum, where, near Noreia (in the modern Carinthia), they defeated the consul Cn. Papririus Carbo, B. C. 113, who had been sent with a large army to protect the Carnians. They, however, now moved westward into Helvetia, and on their desolating course seem to have been joined by the Teutŏni, Ambrŏnes, Tigurini, to the number of about 300,000 fighting men, besides a vast multitude of women and children. With this nomad horde they spread over South Gaul. South-west Gaul (i. e. Languedoc and Provence, Dauphiné and Savoy, the country of the Allobrŏges) was now a Roman province, "provincia nostra," and the consul, M. Junius Silānus, was sent to protect it. He was defeated in 109 B. C. by the Cimbri. We have seen in previous chapters [§ 7 and 12] of these Commentaries, that in 107 B. C. the Tigurini defeated the consul L. Cassius Longinus, whose army was nearly cut to pieces, and himself slain, near the Lake of Geneva. In 105 B. C. M. Aurelius Scaurus, then consular legate in Gaul, was taken prisoner by the Cimbri, and put to death on the spot by Borŏrix (one of their leaders), for having warned them not to cross the Alps. In the same year, B. C. 105, on Oct. 6th, the Roman forces under the proconsul, Q. Servilius Cæpio, and the consul, Cn. Manlius Maximus, sustained a dreadful defeat, owing to the discord of the two generals; of the two consular armies, consisting of 80,000 soldiers, only ten men survived. After this, the Cimbri turned to Spain, which for two or three years they ravaged as ruthlessly as they had ravaged Gaul. They then, long-expected, moved into Italy, and mingled again with the Teutŏnes. The invaders advanced in two columns. The Cimbri entered

them), particularly as the Rhone [was the sole barrier that] separated the Sequăni from our province. Against which events he thought he ought to provide as speedily as possible. Moreover, Ariovistus, for his part, had assumed to himself such pride and arrogance, that he was felt to be quite insufferable.

CHAP. XXXIV.—He therefore determined to send embassadors to Ariovistus to demand of him to name some intermediate spot for a conference between the two, [saying] that he wished to treat him on state-business and matters of the highest importance to both of them. To this embassy Ariovistus replied, that if he himself had had need of any thing from Cæsar, he would have gone to him;[1] and that if Cæsar wanted any thing from him[2] he ought to come to him.

Italy on the north-east, crossing the passes of the Tyrolese Alps near Tridentum (*Trent*), to the Plain of the Po; while the Teutŏni [and Ambrŏnes] penetrated into Italy by *Nice*, round the coast of the Sinus Ligusticus (or *Gulf of Genoa*). The famous C. Marius, in his fourth consulate, B. C. 102, opposed the *Teutŏnes*, and, by means of an ambush of 3000 men under Claudius Marcellus in the barbarians' rear, vanquished and annihilated their immense army with terrible slaughter in a battle, fought on the banks of the Rhone near Aquæ Sextiæ (*Aix* in *Provence*). Marius's colleague, Q. Lutatius Catulus, who with (the afterward celebrated) Sulla for his lieutenant, had gone against the Cimbri and had taken up a strong position near the sources of the Athĕsis (*Adige*), was much less successful, for he was dislodged by a sudden onset of the Cimbri—forced to retreat—fall back behind the Po—and leave the whole of Transpadane Gaul (the rich plain of *Lombardy*) to the mercy of the enemy. This was in the spring of 101 B. C. Catulus this year was pro-consul; and Marius, now consul for the fifth time, started from Rome (where he had declined a triumph for his victory while the Cimbri were yet in Italy), to join his late colleague. Their united forces, amounting to 50,000 men, came up with the Cimbri near Vercellæ (*Vercelli* westward of *Milan*), and in the Raudii Campi (on July 30th), completely routed and destroyed the barbarian host, as Marius had the Teutŏnes. The brunt of this fearful conflict, and therefore the honor of the decisive victory which crowned it, belonged to Catulus, who with 20,000 men had occupied the center; Marius with the remainder, being posted on the wings, had (on account of a prodigious blinding dust which arose) quite missed the enemy, yet at Rome the whole merit was given to him. [Juvenal Sat., viii. 253.] The Tigurīni, who had been stationed at the passes of the Tyrol, fled and dispersed, when they heard of the overthrow and destruction of their allies—the Teutŏnes and Cimbri.

[1] "Sese ad eum *venturum fuisse*;" on this see Wood's translation of *Madvig's* Lat. Gramm. § 409 (the *Obs.* particularly), p. 357.

[2] "Si quid ille" (Cæsar) "se" (Ariovistum) "velit," where *se* is the

That, besides, neither dare he go without an army into those parts of Gaul which Cæsar had possession of, nor could he, without great expense and trouble, draw his army together to one place; that to him, moreover, it appeared strange, what business either Cæsar or the Roman people at all had in his own Gaul, which he had conquered in war.[1]

CHAP. XXXV.—When these answers were reported to Cæsar, he sends embassadors to him a second time with this message. "Since, after having been treated with so much kindness by himself and the Roman people (as he had in his consulship [B. C. 57] been styled 'king and friend' by the senate), he makes[2] this recompense to [Cæsar] himself and the Roman people, [viz.] that when invited to a conference he demurs, and does not think that it concerns him to advise and inform himself about an object of mutual interest, these are the things which he requires of him; first, that he do not[2] any more bring over any body of men across the Rhine into Gaul; in the next place, that he restore the hostages, which he has from the Ædui, and grant the Sequăni permission[3] to restore to them with his consent those hostages which they have, and that he neither provoke the Ædui by outrage nor make war upon them or their allies; if he would accordingly do this,"[4] [Cæsar says] that "he himself and the Roman people will entertain a perpetual feeling of favor and friendship toward him; but that if he [Cæsar] does not obtain [his desires] that he (forasmuch as in the consulship of Marcus Messāla and Marcus Piso [B. C. 61] the senate had decreed that, whoever should have the administration of the province of Gaul should, as far as he could do so consistently with the interests of the republic, protect the Ædui and the

accusative case; for "velle *aliquem aliquid*" is "to want something *of* (or *with*) somebody."

1 Lit. "What (sort) of business there was either to Cæsar, or to the Roman people at all, (i. e. what sort of business they had) in his" (*Ariovistus's*) "own Gaul," etc.

2 The *imperfects* subj. of the Latin *oratio obliqua*, are here translated by *present* tenses in English, this seeming better suited to our idiom. The imperfect is used in Latin, because the principal tense, legatos *mittit*, as an historic present, is equivalent to a past tense, which would require the subj. imperf.

3 Lit.—"grant permission that they should be allowed to restore."

4 Lit.—"if he should have done that so," *i. e.* "if he should have acted so in that case."

other friends of the Roman people), will not overlook the wrongs of the Ædui."

CHAP. XXXVI.—To this Ariovistus replied, that "the right of war was, that they who had conquered should govern those whom they had conquered, in what manner they pleased; that in that way the Roman people were wont to govern the nations which they had conquered, not according to the dictation of any other, but according to their own discretion. If he for his part did not dictate to the Roman people as to the manner in which they were to exercise their right, he ought not to be obstructed by the Roman people in his right; that the Ædui, inasmuch as they had tried the fortune of war and had engaged in arms and been conquered, had become tributaries to him; that Cæsar was doing a great injustice, in that by his arrival he was making his revenues less valuable to him; that he should not restore their hostages to the Ædui, but should not make war wrongfully either upon them or their allies, if they abided by that which had been agreed on, and paid their tribute annually: if they did *not* continue to do that, the Roman people's name of 'brothers' would avail them naught.[1] As to Cæsar's threatening him, that he would not overlook the wrongs of the Ædui, [he said] that no one had ever entered into a contest with *him* [Ariovistus] without utter ruin to himself. That Cæsar might enter the lists when he chose; he would feel what the invincible Germans, well-trained [as they were] beyond all others to arms, who for fourteen years[2] had not been beneath a roof, could achieve by their valor."

CHAP. XXXVII.—At the same time that this message was delivered to Cæsar, embassadors came from the Ædui and the Trevĭri; from the Ædui to complain that the Harūdes, who had lately been brought over into Gaul, were ravaging their territories; that they had not been able to purchase peace from Ariovistus, even by giving hostages: and from the Trevĭri, [to state] that a hundred cantons of the Suevi

[1] Lit.—"if they should *not* have done that, the Roman people's title of "brothers" would be far from being of any avail to them. "*Longe—procul—multum abesse,*" often means "to be utterly impotent, or disinclined, to be of no service."

[2] *Inter* annos XIV. means this: *intra* annos XIV. would be "*within* [in less than] fourteen years."

had encamped on the banks of the Rhine, and were attempting to cross it; that the brothers, Nasuas and Cimberius, headed them. Being greatly alarmed at these things, Cæsar thought that he ought to use all dispatch, lest, if this new band of Suevi should unite with the old troops of Ariovistus, he [Ariovistus] might be less easily withstood. Having therefore, as quickly as he could, provided a supply of corn, he hastened to Ariovistus by forced marches.

CHAP. XXXVIII.—When he had proceeded three days' journey, word was brought to him that Ariovistus was hastening with all his forces to seize on Vesontio,[1] which is the largest town of the Sequăni, and had advanced three days' journey from its territories. Cæsar thought that he ought to take the greatest precautions lest this should happen, for there was in that town a most ample supply of every thing which was serviceable for war; and so fortified was it by the nature of the ground, as to afford a great facility for protracting the war, inasmuch as the river Doubs almost surrounds the whole town, as though it were traced round it with a pair of compasses. A mountain of great height shuts in the remaining space, which is not more than 600 feet,[2] where the river leaves a gap, in such a manner that the roots of that mountain extend to the river's bank on either side. A wall thrown around it makes a citadel of this [mountain], and connects it with the town. Hither Cæsar hastens by forced marches by night and day, and, after having seized the town, stations a garrison there.

CHAP. XXXIX.—While he is tarrying a few days at Vesontio, on account of corn and provisions; from the inquiries of our men and the reports of the Gauls and traders (who asserted that the Germans were men of huge stature, of incredible valor and practice in arms—that oftentimes they, on encountering them, could not bear even their countenance, and the fierceness of their eyes)—so great a panic on a sudden seized the whole army, as to discompose the minds and spirits of all in no slight degree. This first arose from the tribunes

[1] Modern *Besançon*.

[2] Cæsar seems to have meant here not the common foot, but the *gradus* or pes sestertius (= 2½ feet), as the base of the mountain actually measures 1500 feet.

of the soldiers, the prefects and the rest, who, having followed Cæsar from the city [Rome] from motives of friendship, had no great experience in military affairs. And alleging, some of them one reason, some another, which they said made it necessary for them to depart, they requested that by his consent they might be allowed to withdraw; some, influenced by shame, stayed behind in order that they might avoid the suspicion of cowardice. These could neither compose their countenance,[1] nor even sometimes check their tears: but hidden in their tents, either bewailed their fate, or deplored with their comrades the general danger. Wills were sealed universally throughout the whole camp. By the expressions and cowardice of these men, even those who possessed great experience in the camp, both soldiers and centurions, and those [the decurions] who were in command of the cavalry, were gradually disconcerted. Such of them as wished to be considered less alarmed, said that they did not dread the enemy, but feared the narrowness of the roads and the vastness of the forests which lay between them and Ariovistus, or else that the supplies could not be brought up readily enough. Some even declared to Cæsar, that when he gave orders for the camp to be moved and the troops to advance,[2] the soldiers would not be obedient to the command, nor advance[3] in consequence of their fear.

CHAP. XL.—When Cæsar observed these things, having called a council, and summoned to it the centurions of all the companies, he severely reprimanded them, "particularly, for supposing that it belonged to them to inquire or conjecture, either in what direction they were marching, or with what object. That Ariovistus, during his [Cæsar's] consulship, had most anxiously sought after the friendship of the Roman people; why should any one judge that he would so rashly depart from his duty? He for his part was persuaded, that, when his demands were known and the fairness of the terms considered, he would reject neither his nor the Roman people's favor. But even if, driven on by rage and madness, he should

[1] With Cæsar's "vultum fingere" conf. *πλασαμενος τῇ ὄψει*, Thuc. vi. § 58, & Dem. 1122 12, 20.

[2] *i. e.* that his men should decamp from that place and march forward.

[3] Lit. "would not bear the standards."

make war upon them, what after all were they afraid of?—or why should they despair either of their own valor or of his zeal? Of that enemy a trial had been made within our fathers' recollection, when, on the defeat of the Cimbri and Teutŏnes by Caius Marius, the army was regarded as having deserved no less praise than their commander himself. It had been made lately, too, in Italy, during the rebellion of the slaves, whom, however, the experience and training which they had received from us, assisted in some respect. From which a judgment might be formed of the advantages which resolution carries with it—inasmuch as those whom for some time they had groundlessly dreaded when unarmed, they had afterward vanquished, when well armed and flushed with success. In short, that these were the same men whom the Helvetii, in frequent encounters, not only in their own territories, but also in theirs [the German], have generally vanquished, and yet can not have been a match for our army. If the unsuccessful battle and flight of the Gauls disquieted any, these, if they made inquiries, might discover that, when the Gauls had been tired out by the long duration of the war, Ariovistus, after he had many months kept himself in his camp and in the marshes, and had given no opportunity for an engagement, fell suddenly upon them, by this time despairing of a battle and scattered in all directions, and was victorious more through stratagem and cunning than valor. But though there had been room for such stratagem against savage and unskilled men, not even [Ariovistus] himself expected that thereby our armies could be entrapped. That those who ascribed their fear to a pretense about the [deficiency of] supplies and the narrowness of the roads, acted presumptuously, as they seemed either to distrust their general's discharge of his duty, or to dictate to him. That these things were his concern; that the Sequăni, the Leuci, and the Lingŏnes were to furnish the corn; and that it was already ripe in the fields; that as to the road they would soon be able to judge for themselves. As to its being reported that the soldiers would not be obedient to command, or advance, he was not at all disturbed at that; for he knew, that in the case of all those whose army had not been obedient to command, either upon some mismanagement of an affair, fortune had deserted them, or, that upon some crime being discovered, covetousness had been clearly proved [against them]. His integrity had been seen throughout his whole life, his good fortune in the war with the Helvetii. That he would therefore instantly set about what he had intended to put off till a more distant day, and would break up his camp the next night, in the fourth watch, that he might ascertain, as soon as possible, whether a sense of honor and duty, or whether fear had more influence with them. But that, if no one else should follow, yet he would go with only the tenth legion, of which he had no misgivings, and it should be his prætorian cohort."—This legion Cæsar had both greatly favored, and in it, on account of its valor, placed the greatest confidence.

CHAP. XLI.—Upon the delivery of this speech, the minds of all were changed in a surprising manner, and the highest ardor and eagerness for prosecuting the war were engendered; and the tenth legion was the first to return thanks to him, through their military tribunes, for his having expressed this most favorable opinion of them; and assured him that they were quite ready to prosecute the war. Then, the other legions endeavored, through their military tribunes and the centurions of the principal companies, to excuse themselves to Cæsar, [saying] that they had never either doubted or feared, or supposed that the determination of the conduct of the war was theirs and not their general's. Having accepted their excuse, and having had the road carefully reconnoitered by Divitiăcus, because in him of all others he had the greatest faith, [he found] that by a circuitous route of more than fifty miles[1] he might lead his army through open parts; he then set out in the fourth watch, as he had said [he would]. On the seventh day, as he did not discontinue his march, he was informed by scouts that the forces of Ariovistus were only four and twenty miles distant from ours.[1]

CHAP. XLII.—Upon being apprized of Cæsar's arrival, Ariovistus sends embassadors to him, [saying] that what he had before requested as to a conference, might now, as far as his permission went, take place, since he [Cæsar] had approached nearer, and he considered that he might now do it without

[1] See the note on p. 3.

danger. Cæsar did not reject the proposal and began to think that he was now returning to a rational state of mind, as he spontaneously proffered that which he had previously refused to him when requesting it; and was in great hopes that, in consideration of his own and the Roman people's great favors toward him, the issue would be that he would desist from his obstinacy upon his demands being made known. The fifth day after that was appointed as the day of conference. Meanwhile, as ambassadors were being often sent to and fro between them, Ariovistus demanded that Cæsar should not bring any foot-soldier with him to the conference, [saying] that "he was afraid of being ensnared by him through treachery; that both should come accompanied by cavalry; that he would not come on any other condition." Cæsar, as he neither wished that the conference should, by an excuse thrown in the way, be set aside, nor durst trust his life to the cavalry of the Gauls, decided that it would be most expedient to take away from the Gallic cavalry all their horses, and thereon to mount the[1] legionary soldiers of the tenth legion, in which he placed the greatest confidence, in order that he might have a body-guard as trustworthy as possible, should there be any need for action. And when this was done, one of the soldiers of the tenth legion said, not without a touch of humor, "that Cæsar did more for them than he had promised; he had promised to have the tenth legion in place of his prætorian cohort; but he now converted them into horse."

CHAP. XLIII.—There was a large plain, and in it a mound of earth of considerable size. This spot was at nearly an equal distance from both camps. Thither, as had been appointed, they came for the conference. Cæsar stationed the legion, which he had brought [with him] on horseback, 200 paces from this mound. The cavalry of Ariovistus also took their stand at an equal distance. Ariovistus then demanded that they should confer on horseback, and that, besides themselves, they should bring with them ten men each to the conference. When they were come to the place, Cæsar, in the opening of his speech, detailed his own and the senate's favors toward him [Ariovistus], in that he had been styled king, in that [he

[1] The regular troops of the legion are here called "legionary soldiers," to distinguish them from the Velites, or light-armed infantry.

had been styled] friend, by the senate—in that very considerable presents had been sent him; which circumstance he informed him had both fallen to the lot of few, and had usually been bestowed in consideration of important personal services; that he, although he had neither an introduction, nor a just ground for the request, had obtained these honors through the kindness and munificence of himself [Cæsar] and the senate. He informed him too, how old and how just were the grounds of connection that existed between themselves [the Romans] and the Ædui, what decrees of the senate had been passed in their favor, and how frequent and how honorable; how from time immemorial the Ædui had held the supremacy of the whole of Gaul; even [said Cæsar] before they had sought *our* friendship; that it was the custom of the Roman people to desire not only that its allies and friends should lose none of their property, but be advanced in influence, dignity, and honor: who then could endure that what they had brought with them to the friendship of the Roman people, should be torn from them?" He then made the same demands which he had commissioned the embassadors to make, that [Ariovistus] should not make war either upon the Ædui or their allies, that he should restore the hostages; that, if he could not send back to their country any part of the Germans, he should at all events suffer none of them any more to cross the Rhine.

Chap. XLIV.—Ariovistus briefly replied to the demands of Cæsar; but expatiated largely on his own virtues, "that he had crossed the Rhine not of his own accord, but on being invited and sent for by the Gauls; that he had not left home and kindred without great expectations and great rewards; that he had settlements in Gaul, granted by the Gauls themselves; that the hostages had been given by their own good-will; that he took by right of war the tribute which conquerors are accustomed to impose on the conquered; that he had not made war upon the Gauls, but the Gauls upon him; that all the states of Gaul came to attack him, and had encamped against him; that all their forces had been routed and beaten by him in a single battle; that if they chose to make a second trial, he was ready to encounter them again; but if they chose to enjoy peace, it was unfair to refuse the tribute, which of their own free-will they had paid up to that time. That the friendship of the Roman people ought to prove to him an ornament and a safeguard, not a detriment; and that he sought it with that expectation. But if through the Roman people the tribute was to be discontinued, and those who surrendered to be seduced from him, he would renounce the friendship of the Roman people no less heartily than he had sought it. As to his leading over a host of Germans into Gaul, that he was doing this with a view of securing himself, not of assaulting Gaul: that there was evidence of this, in that he did not come without being invited, and in that he did not make war, but merely warded it off. That he had come into Gaul before the Roman people. That never before this time did a Roman army go beyond the frontiers of the province of Gaul. What [said he] does [Cæsar] desire?—why come into his [Ariovistus] domains?—that this was his province of Gaul, just as that is ours. As it ought not to be pardoned in him, if he were to make an attack upon our territories; so, likewise, that we were unjust, to obstruct him in his prerogative. As for Cæsar's saying that the Ædui had been styled 'brethren' by the senate, he was not so uncivilized nor so ignorant of affairs, as not to know that the Ædui in the very last war with the Allobrŏges had neither rendered assistance to the Romans, nor received any from the Roman people in the struggles which the Ædui had been maintaining with him and with the Sequăni. He must feel suspicious, that Cæsar, though feigning friendship as the reason for his keeping an army in Gaul, was keeping it with the view of crushing him. And that unless he depart and withdraw his army from these parts, he shall regard him not as a friend, but as a foe; and that, even if he should put him to death, he should do what would please many of the nobles and leading men of the Roman people; he had assurance of that from themselves through their messengers, and could purchase the favor and the friendship of them all by his [Cæsar's] death. But if he would depart and resign to him the free possession of Gaul, he would recompense him with a great reward, and would bring to a close whatever wars he wished to be carried on, without any trouble or risk to him."

CHAP. XLV.—Many things were stated by Cæsar to the effect [to show]; "why he could not waive the business, and that neither his nor the Roman people's practice would suffer him to abandon most meritorious allies, nor did he deem that Gaul belonged to Ariovistus rather than to the Roman people; that the Arverni[1] and the Rutēni[2] had been subdued in war by Quintus Fabius Maximus,[3] and that the Roman people had pardoned them and had not reduced them into a province or imposed a tribute upon them. And if the most ancient period was to be regarded—then was the sovereignty of the Roman people in Gaul most just: if the decree of the Senate was to be observed, then ought Gaul to be free, which they [the Romans] had conquered in war, and had permitted to enjoy its own laws."

Chap. XLVI.—While these things are being transacted in the conference it was announced to Cæsar that the cavalry of Ariovistus were approaching nearer the mound, and were riding up to our men, and casting stones and weapons at them. Cæsar made an end of his speech and betook himself to his men; and commanded them that they should by no means return a weapon upon the enemy. For though he saw that an engagement with the cavalry would be without any danger to his chosen legion, yet he did not think proper to engage, lest, after the enemy were routed, it might be said that they had been insnared by him under the sanction of a conference. When it was spread abroad among the common soldiery with what haughtiness Ariovistus had behaved at the conference, and how he had ordered the Romans to quit Gaul, and how his cavalry had made an attack upon our men, and how this had broken off the conference, a much greater alacrity and eagerness for battle was infused into our army.

Chap. XLVII.—Two days after, Ariovistus sends embassadors to Cæsar, to state "that he wished to treat with him about those things which had been begun to be treated of between them, but had not been concluded;" [and to beg] that "he would either again appoint a day for a conference; or, if he were not willing to do that, that he would send one of his [officers] as an embassador to him." There did not appear to Cæsar any good reason for holding a conference; and the more so as the day before the Germans could not be

[1] Modern *Auvergne*.

[2] Modern *Le Roüergue*.

[3] We find mention made of this victory in the Epitomes of Livy, lib. lxi., and in Strabo, lib. iv.

restrained from casting weapons at our men. He thought he should not without great danger send to him as embassador one of his [Roman] officers, and should expose him to savage men. It seemed [therefore] most proper to send to him C. Valerius Procillus, the son of C. Valerius Caburus, a young man of the highest courage and accomplishments (whose father had been presented with the freedom of the city by C. Valerius Flaccus), both on account of his fidelity and on account of his knowledge of the Gallic language, which Ariovistus, by long practice, now spoke fluently; and because in his case the Germans would have no motive for committing violence;[1] and [as his colleague] M. Mettius, who had shared the hospitality of Ariovistus.[2] He commissioned them to learn what Ariovistus had to say, and to report to him. But when Ariovistus saw them before him in his camp, he cried out in the presence of his army, "Why were they come to him? was it for the purpose of acting as spies?" He stopped them when attempting to speak, and cast them into chains.

CHAP. XLVIII.—The same day he moved his camp forward and pitched under a hill six miles from Cæsar's camp. The day following he led his forces past Cæsar's camp, and encamped two miles beyond him; with this design—that he might cut off Cæsar from the corn and provisions, which might be conveyed to him from the Sequăni and the Ædui. For five successive days from that day, Cæsar drew out his forces before the camp, and put them in battle order, that, if Ariovistus should be willing to engage in battle, an opportunity might not be wanting to him. Ariovistus all this time kept his army in camp: but engaged daily in cavalry skirmishes. The method of battle in which the Germans had practiced themselves was this. There were 6,000 horse, and as many very active and courageous foot, one of whom each of the horse selected out of the whole army for his own protection. By these [foot] they

[1] Inasmuch as he was not a Roman, but a Gaul.

[2] Classical writers bear continual testimony to the sanctity of this relation. It appears from Aul. Gellius (1–13) to have ranked next to that of parents and clients. A league of the same nature, and bearing the same name, was sometimes entered into by persons at a distance from each other. The Roman people, at large, formed such a league with foreign States. The 31st section of the present book of Cæsar's Commentaries furnishes an allusion to this.

were constantly accompanied in their engagements; to these the horse retired; these on any emergency rushed forward; if any one, upon receiving a very severe wound, had fallen from his horse, they stood around him: if it was necessary to advance further than usual, or to retreat more rapidly, so great, from practice, was their swiftness, that, supported by the manes of the horses, they could keep pace with their speed.[1]

CHAP. XLIX.—Perceiving that Ariovistus kept himself in camp, Cæsar, that he might not any longer be cut off from provisions, chose a convenient position for a camp beyond that place in which the Germans had encamped, at about 600 paces from them, and having drawn up his army in three lines, marched to that place. He ordered the first and second lines to be under arms; the third to fortify the camp.[2] This place was distant from the enemy about 600 paces, as has been stated. Thither Ariovistus sent light troops, about 16,000 men in number, with all his cavalry; which forces were to intimidate our men, and hinder them in their fortification. Cæsar nevertheless, as he had before arranged, ordered two lines to drive off the enemy: the third to execute the work. The camp being fortified, he left there two legions and a por-

[1] Strange as this account may appear to us moderns, into whose military tactics nothing similar enters, it does not need the explanation which some have given of it—that the foot-soldiers here spoken of threw themselves into a body when an engagement began, and supported the cavalry in that form. They were, Cæsar expressly says, chosen *individually* to assist some *particular* cavalry soldier; and their duty was rather to perform that part, as occasion required, than to render any *direct* service against the enemy. The Romans had, before this time, practiced in a more scientific form, this piece of warfare. Livy relates, lib. xxvi. 41, that at the siege of Capua, upon the discovery that from all their engagements the legions returned victorious, while the cavalry were worsted, they adopted the plan of mounting behind each horse-soldier a man armed with a small shield and seven darts, who, upon a given signal, alighted and charged the enemy. This was attended with great success, and led, says Livy, to the origin of the *Velites*. Sallust, too, in his *Bell. Jugurth.*, tells us that Marius intermingled the *Velites* with the cavalry. Cæsar appears to have resorted to this plan in the encounter with Pompey at the river Genusus, after his defeat at Dyrrachium.

[2] The care with which the Romans fortified their camp in a remarkable feature in their military discipline. They never encamped even for a single night, without fortifying themselves with a rampart and a ditch. The encampment of a few hours presented the systematic and complete order of a station.

tion of the auxiliaries; and led back the other four legions into the larger camp.

CHAP. L.—The next day, according to his custom, Cæsar led out his forces from both camps, and having advanced a little from the larger one, drew up his line of battle, and gave the enemy an opportunity of fighting. When he found that they did not even then come out [from their intrenchments,] he led back his army into camp about noon. Then at last Ariovistus sent part of his forces to attack the lesser camp. The battle was vigorously maintained on both sides till the evening. At sunset, after many wounds had been inflicted and received, Ariovistus led back his forces into camp. When Cæsar inquired of his prisoners, wherefore Ariovistus did not come to an engagement, he discovered this to be the reason—that among the Germans it was the custom for their matrons to pronounce from lots and divination, whether it were expedient that the battle should be engaged in or not; that they had said, "that it was not the will of heaven that the Germans should conquer, if they engaged in battle before the new moon."[1]

CHAP. LI.—The day following, Cæsar left what seemed sufficient as a guard for both camps; [and then] drew up all the auxiliaries in sight of the enemy, before the lesser camp, because he was not very powerful in the number of legionary soldiers, considering the number of the enemy; that [thereby]

[1] Some suppose the women here referred to were Druidesses; but we know that the ancient Germans believed there was something sacred and prophetic (*quid sacrum*) in the female character. See Tacitus, Germania, cap. viii. Among the Romans, divination by "sortes" was usually performed by means of counters (*tesseræ*), mostly made of wood, thrown into an urn (*sitella*). To this, among other instances, Plautus alludes in his Casina, act iii. sc. v. The presage was drawn from the order in which the counters were taken out of the urn. There are many interesting records of the use of "sortes" in later times. The "sortes Virgilianæ," which are among these, derive their name from the custom of placing verses of the poet Virgil in an urn, or of opening his writings at chance, and discerning the events inquired into by the order in which the verses appeared in the former, or the passage on which the eye first rested in the latter method. To this St. Augustine alludes in the 4th book of his Confessions. The Mohammedans used the Koran, and the Christians the Bible, for the same purpose. The latter was forbidden by some of the early Ecclesiastical Councils. Tacitus says that the Germans were much given to divination (auspicia sortesque, ut qui maximè observant, Ger. 10). Plutarch relates that these German *fatidicæ* drew their observations from the motion of the water in rivers.

he might make use of his auxiliaries for appearance. He himself, having drawn up his army in three lines, advanced to the camp of the enemy. Then at last of necessity the Germans drew their forces out of camp, and disposed them canton by canton, at equal distances, the Harudes, Marcomanni, Triboci, Vangiones, Nemetes, Sedusii, Suevi; and surrounded their whole army with their chariots and wagons, that no hope might be left in flight. On these they placed their women, who, with disheveled hair and in tears, entreated the soldiers, as they went forward to battle, not to deliver them into slavery to the Romans.

CHAP. LII.—Cæsar appointed over each legion a lieutenant and a questor, that every one might have them as witnesses of his valor. He himself began the battle at the head of the right wing, because he had observed that part of the enemy to be the least strong. Accordingly our men, upon the signal being given, vigorously made an attack upon the enemy, and the enemy so suddenly and rapidly rushed forward, that there was no time for casting the javelins at them. Throwing aside [therefore] their javelins, they fought with swords hand to hand. But the Germans, according to their custom, rapidly forming a phalanx, sustained the attack of our swords. There were found very many of our soldiers who leaped upon the phalanx, and with their hands tore away the shields, and wounded the enemy from above. Although the army of the enemy was routed on the left wing and put to flight, they [still] pressed heavily on our men from the right wing, by the great number of their troops. On observing which, P. Crassus, a young man, who commanded the cavalry—as he was more disengaged than those who were employed in the fight—sent the third line as a relief to our men who were in distress.

CHAP. LIII.—Thereupon the engagement was renewed, and all the enemy turned their backs, nor did they cease to flee until they arrived at the river Rhine, about fifty miles from that place.[1] There some few, either relying on their strength, endeavored to swim over, or, finding boats, procured their safety. Among the latter was Ariovistus, who meeting with a small vessel tied to the bank, escaped in it; our horse pursued and slew all the rest of them. Ariovistus had two wives, one a Sue-

[1] Dion. Cassius, 38–48, narrates this war between Cæsar and Ariovistus.

van by nation, whom he brought with him from home; the other a Norican, the sister of king Vocion, whom he had married in Gaul, she having been sent [thither for that purpose] by her brother. Both perished in that flight. Of their two daughters, one was slain, the other captured. C. Valerius Procillus, as he was being dragged by his guards in the fight, bound with a triple chain, fell into the hands of Cæsar himself, as he was pursuing the enemy with his cavalry. This circumstance indeed afforded Cæsar no less pleasure than the victory itself; because he saw a man of the first rank in the province of Gaul, his intimate acquaintance and friend, rescued from the hand of the enemy, and restored to him, and that fortune had not diminished aught of the joy and exultation [of that day] by his destruction. He [Procillus] said that, in his own presence, the lots had been thrice consulted[1] respecting him, whether he should immediately be put to death by fire, or be reserved for another time: that by the favor of the lots he was uninjured. M. Mettius, also, was found and brought back to him [Cæsar.]

CHAP. LIV.—This battle having been reported beyond the Rhine, the Suevi, who had come to the banks of that river, began to return home, when the Ubii,[2] who dwelt nearest to the Rhine, pursuing them, while much alarmed, slew a great number of them. Cæsar having concluded two very important wars in one campaign, conducted his army into winter-quarters[3] among the Sequăni, a little earlier than the sea-

[1] Perhaps *three* was with the Germans, as with some other nations of antiquity, a sacred or mystical number.

[2] The Ubii were situated on the west side of the Rhine. Cologne is supposed to occupy the site of their capital.

[3] The winter-quarters (*hiberna*) of the Romans present one of the most striking characteristics of the warfare of antiquity. They were fortified with astonishing strength, and, besides being constructed with due regard to the relative dignity of the several ranks of the Roman army, were furnished, no less than the civilized towns of the period, with every accommodation. They covered a great space of ground. To Roman encampments many towns owe their origin. In our country (where this portion of military discipline was by no means remissly observed), those places in the names of which *cester* or *chester* appear, bespeak their having existed there. Nor is it on the authority of the name alone (where *cester* or *chester* is certainly from Castra, and not from a Saxon word) that this assertion is made. In those places, particularly, have Roman implements of war and other vestiges of the Roman sojourn in this island been discovered.

son of the year required. He appointed Labienus over the winter-quarters, and set out in person for Hither Gaul to hold the assizes.[1]

[1] The word "*conventus*" in the original, refers to those courts which the policy of the Romans established in countries which they had conquered. These may be represented by the expression, *provincial assizes*. Their business was to administer justice, to hear petitions, prescribe regulations as to taxes and levies, and affix seals to documents which required that process to render them legal. Over these it was the office of the proconsul to preside, assisted, usually, by twenty persons, selected, for the most part, from the Romans resident in that particular portion of the province, as his "*assessores*" or "*concilium*," or body of advisers. The proceedings of these courts, like all those of the governors of provinces, were conducted in Latin. (Val. Maximus, ii. 2.) Hence the proconsul was on these occasions attended by an interpreter. To this allusion is made, among other places, in Cicero's Third Oration against Verres, sect. 37

It will prove interesting to compare the Commentaries of Cæsar, as regards the Gauls, with the history of their wars with the Romans, given in the second Book of Polybius, and to read the account of their participation in the Punic war, given in his third Book.

BOOK II.

THE ARGUMENT.

I. The Belgæ, from various motives, enter into a confederacy against the Roman people. II. Cæsar, having received intelligence of it, proceeds against them. III. IV. The Remi submit to Cæsar, and give him information respecting the other Belgæ. V. He crosses the river Aisne and encamps beyond it. VI. VII. The attack on Bibrax by the Belgæ, and its relief by the Romans. VIII.-X. State of affairs between the Romans and the Belgæ. XI. The Bellovaci, withdrawing from the warfare to return home, are pursued by the Romans, and suffer severely. XII. Cæsar proceeds against the Suessiones. XIII. Then against the Bellovaci, and receives the surrender of both. XIV. Divitiacus pleads in behalf of the Bellovaci. XV. Cæsar's reply; the character of the Nervii. XVI.-XXIII. Engagements with them; a peculiarity in their mode of warfare; their extraordinary courage; they are finally subdued. XXIX. The Aduatuci. XXX. Their ridicule of the Roman engineering. XXXI. Their pretended submission to the Romans. XXXII. Cæsar's reply to their embassy. XXXIII. Their treachery and overthrow. XXXIV. P. Crassus announces that several nations had submitted to the Roman power. XXXV. Cæsar returns to Italy; a solemn thanksgiving is decreed by the senate.

CHAP. I.—While Cæsar was in winter quarters in Hither Gaul, as we have shown above, frequent reports were brought to him, and he was also informed by letters from Labienus, that all the Belgæ, who we have said are a third part of Gaul, were entering into a confederacy against the Roman people, and giving hostages to one another; that the reasons of the confederacy were these—first, because they feared that, after all [Celtic] Gaul was subdued, our army would be led against them; secondly, because they were instigated by several of the Gauls; some of whom as [on the one hand] they had been unwilling that the Germans should remain any longer in Gaul,[1] so

[1] The circumstances which led to the Germans going into Gaul, and the result of their introduction, are briefly given, book i. 31.

[on the other] they were dissatisfied that the army of the Roman people should pass the winter in it, and settle there; and others of them, from a natural instability and fickleness of disposition,[1] were anxious for a revolution; [the Belgæ were instigated] by several, also, because the government in Gaul was generally seized upon by the more powerful persons and by those who had the means of hiring troops, and they could less easily effect this object under our dominion.

CHAP. II.—Alarmed by these tidings and letters, Cæsar levied two new legions in Hither Gaul, and, at the beginning of summer, sent Q. Pedius, his lieutenant, to conduct them further into Gaul. He himself, as soon as there began to be plenty of forage, came to the army. He gives a commission to the Senŏnes and the other Gauls who were neighbors of the Belgæ, to learn what is going on among them [*i. e.* the Belgæ], and inform him of these matters. These all uniformly reported that troops were being raised, and that an army was being collected in one place. Then, indeed, he thought that he ought not to hesitate about proceeding toward them, and having provided supplies, moves his camp, and in about fifteen days arrives at the territories of the Belgæ.

CHAP. III.—As he arrived there unexpectedly and sooner than any one anticipated, the Remi, who are the nearest of the Belgæ to [Celtic] Gaul, sent to him Iccius and Antebrogius, [two of] the principal persons of the state, as their embassadors: to tell him that they surrendered themselves and all their possessions to the protection and disposal of the Roman people: and that they had neither combined with the rest of the Belgæ, nor entered into any confederacy against the Roman people: and were prepared to give hostages, to obey his commands, to receive him into their towns, and to aid him with corn and other things; that all the rest of the Belgæ were in arms; and that the Germans, who dwell on this side of the Rhine, had joined themselves to them; and that so great was the infatuation of them all, that they could not restrain even the Suessiones, their own brethren and kinsmen, who enjoy the same rights, and the same laws, and who have one government and one magistracy [in common] with themselves, from uniting with them.

[1] Polybius represents the Gauls, in general, as characterized by fickleness of mind and impetuosity of action. Hist. lib. ii. 35.

CHAP. IV.—When Cæsar inquired of them what states were in arms, how powerful they were, and what they could do in war, he received the following information: that the greater part of the Belgæ were sprung from the Germans, and that having crossed the Rhine at an early period, they had settled there, on account of the fertility of the country, and had driven out the Gauls who inhabited those regions; and that they were the only people who, in the memory of our fathers, when all Gaul was overrun, had prevented the Teutŏnes and the Cimbri from entering their territories; the effect of which was, that, from the recollection of those events, they assumed to themselves great authority and haughtiness in military matters. The Remi said, that they had known accurately every thing respecting their number, because being united to them by neighborhood and by alliances, they had learned what number each state had in the general council of the Belgæ promised for that war. That the Bellovăci were the most powerful among them in valor, influence, and the number of men; that these could muster 100,000 armed men, [and had] promised 60,000 picked men out of that number, and demanded for themselves the command of the whole war. That the Suessiónes[1] were their nearest neighbors and possessed a very extensive and fertile country; that among them, even in our own memory, Divitiacus, the most powerful man of all Gaul, had been king; who had held the government of a great part of these regions, as well as of Britain; that their king at present was Galba; that the direction of the whole war was conferred by the consent of all, upon him, on account of his integrity and prudence; that they had twelve towns; that they had promised 50,000 armed men; and that the Nervii, who are reckoned the most warlike among them, and are situated at a very great distance, [had promised] as many; the Atrébâtes 15,000; the Ambiani,[2] 10,000; the Morĭni,[3] 25,000; the Menapii,[4] 9,000; the Calēti,[5]

[1] A people of Gallia Belgica. *Suessiones,* their capital, is the modern *Soissons.*

[2] Ambiani. The territory of these people lay along the British Channel. Atrĕbātes (*Arras*), their capital, is by the Flemings called *Atrecht.*

[3] Morĭni. Their country lay along the coast opposite Kent.

[4] Menapii. They lay near the Mosa (the *Meuse*).

[5] Calĕti or Calĕtes. They lay to the north of the mouth of the Seine.

10,000; the Velocasses[1] and the Veromandui[2] as many; the Aduatŭci 19,000; that the Condrŭsi, the Eburŏnes, the Cæræsi, the Pæmāni, who are called by the common name of Germans [had promised], they thought, to the number of 40,000.

CHAP. V.—Cæsar, having encouraged the Remi, and addressed them courteously, ordered the whole senate to assemble before him, and the children of their chief men to be brought to him as hostages; all which commands they punctually performed by the day [appointed]. He, addressing himself to Divitiacus, the Æduan, with great earnestness, points out how much it concernes the republic and their common security, that the forces of the enemy should be divided, so that it might not be necessary to engage with so large a number at one time. [He asserts] that this might be effected if the Ædui would lead their forces into the territories of the Bellovăci, and begin to lay waste their country. With these instructions he dismissed him from his presence. After he perceived that all the forces of the Belgæ, which had been collected in one place, were approaching toward him, and learned from the scouts whom he had sent out, and [also] from the Remi, that they were then not far distant, he hastened to lead his army over the Aisne, which is on the borders of the Remi, and there pitched his camp. This position fortified one side of his camp by the banks of the river, rendered the country which lay in his rear secure from the enemy, and furthermore insured that provisions might without danger be brought to him by the Remi and the rest of the states. Over that river was a bridge: there he places a guard; and on the other side of the river he leaves Q. Titurius Sabinus, his lieutenant, with six cohorts. He orders him to

[1] Velocasses, or Bellocassi. Their territories were of considerable extent, and were bounded on the east by the Isere; on the south, by the Seine; on the west, by the regions of the Calĕti, and on the north by those of the Bellovăci.

[2] Vęromandui, etc. The Veromandui lay between the Nervii and the Suessiones. Their capital, Augusta Veromanduorum, is the modern *St. Quentin.* The Aduatuci lay on the west bank of the Meuse. The Condrŭsi lay on the Meuse; modern *Condrotz* derives its name from their territories. Eburŏnes (in some Greek authors, Euburŏnes), the greater part of whose territories lay on the west of the Meuse. The Cæræsi and the Pæmāni also lay on the Meuse.

fortify a camp with a rampart twelve feet in height, and a trench eighteen feet in breadth.

CHAP. VI.—There was a town of the Remi, by name Bibrax,[1] eight miles distant from this camp. This the Belgæ on their march began to attack with great vigor. [The assault] was with difficulty sustained for that day. The Gauls' mode of besieging is the same as that of the Belgæ: when after having drawn a large number of men around the whole of the fortifications, stones have begun to be cast against the wall on all sides, and the wall has been stripped of its defenders, [then], forming a testudo,[2] they advance to the gates and undermine the wall: which was easily effected on this occasion; for while so large a number were casting stones and darts, no one[3] was able to maintain his position upon the wall. When night had put an end to the assault, Iccius, who was then in command of the town, one of the Remi, a man of the highest rank and influence among his people, and one of those who had come to Cæsar as embassador [to sue] for peace, sends messengers to him, [to report] "That, unless assistance were sent to him he could not hold out any longer."

CHAP. VII.—Thither, immediately after midnight, Cæsar, using as guides the same persons who had come to him as messengers from Iccius, sends some Numidian and Cretan archers, and some Baleārian slingers[4] as a relief to the

[1] Bibrax. *Bièvre,* a town of the Remi, on the Aisne, must not be confounded with Bibracte, one of the largest and richest towns of the Ædui.

[2] A body of soldiers, in forming a testudo, held their shields firmly together over their heads, and were thus protected from such missiles as might be thrown from above, while those of the outer files held their shields sloping in such a manner as to protect the flanks of the entire body. They thus presented an appearance not unlike the back of a tortoise, "testudo;" from which circumstance the name was derived. By the testudo was also meant a penthouse moving on wheels, under cover of which the besiegers worked the battering-ram. The name in this case was readily suggested by the resemblance which the ram presented to a tortoise thrusting its head forward from its shell and drawing it back again.

[3] Literally, "No one had the power of standing his ground."

[4] Frequent mention is made by ancient writers of the Numidians and Cretans as archers, and of the Baleārians as slingers. These last took their name from three islands in the Mediterranean; two of which, from their distinctive titles of Major and Minor, are called *Majorca* and *Minorca;* the third *Yvica.* Pliny ascribes the invention of the sling to these people. Diodorus Siculus tells us that they could break a target or helmet, or, indeed, any piece of armor, with their national weapon. Nor

towns-people, by whose arrival both a desire to resist together with the hope of [making good their] defense, was infused into the Remi, and, for the same reason, the hope of gaining the town, abandoned the enemy. Therefore, after staying a short time before the town, and laying waste the country of the Remi, when all the villages and buildings which they could approach had been burned, they hastened with all their forces to the camp of Cæsar, and encamped within less than two miles [of it]; and their camp, as was indicated by the smoke and fires, extended more than eight miles in breadth.

CHAP. VIII.—Cæsar at first determined to decline a battle, as well on account of the great number of the enemy as their distinguished reputation for valor: daily, however, in cavalry actions, he strove to ascertain by frequent trials, what the enemy could effect by their prowess and what our men would dare. When he perceived that our men were not inferior, as the place before the camp was naturally convenient and suitable for marshaling an army (since the hill where the camp was pitched, rising gradually from the plain, extended forward in breadth as far as the space which the marshaled army could occupy, and had steep declines of its side in either direction, and gently sloping in front gradually sank to the plain); on either side of that hill he drew a cross trench of about four hundred paces, and at the extremities of that trench built forts, and placed there his military engines, lest, after he had marshaled his army, the enemy, since they were so powerful in point of number, should be able to surround his men in the flank, while fighting. After doing this, and leaving in the camp the two legions which he had last raised, that, if there should be any occasion, they might be brought as a reserve, he formed the other six legions in order of battle before the camp. The enemy, likewise, had drawn up their forces which they had brought out of the camp.

CHAP. IX.—There was a marsh of no great extent between our army and that of the enemy. The latter were waiting to see if our men would pass this; our men, also, were ready in

will that appear wonderful if we receive the assertion of Suidas, that they would cast a stone of a pound weight. Their usual missiles, however, were small stones and leaden bullets. The inhabitants of those islands are reported to excel in the use of the sling at the present day.

arms to attack them while disordered, if the first attempt to pass should be made by them. In the mean time battle was commenced between the two armies by a cavalry action. When neither army began to pass the marsh, Cæsar, upon the skirmishes of the horse [proving] favorable to our men, led back his forces into the camp. The enemy immediately hastened from that place to the river Aisne, which it has been stated was behind our camp. Finding a ford there, they endeavored to lead a part of their forces over it; with the design, that, if they could, they might carry by storm the fort which Q. Titurius, Cæsar's lieutenant, commanded, and might cut off the bridge; but, if they could not do that, they should lay waste the lands of the Remi, which were of great use to us in carrying on the war, and might hinder our men from foraging.

CHAP. X.—Cæsar, being apprized of this by Titurius, leads all his cavalry and light-armed Numidians, slingers and archers, over the bridge, and hastens toward them. There was a severe struggle in that place. Our men, attacking in the river the disordered enemy, slew a great part of them. By the immense number of their missiles they drove back the rest, who, in a most courageous manner were attempting to pass over their bodies, and surrounded with their cavalry, and cut to pieces those who had first crossed the river. The enemy, when they perceived that their hopes had deceived them both with regard to their taking the town by storm and also their passing the river, and did not see our men advance to a more disadvantageous place for the purpose of fighting, and when provisions began to fail them, having called a council, determined that it was best for each to return to his country, and resolved to assemble from all quarters to defend those into whose territories the Romans should first march an army; that they might contend in their own rather than in a foreign country, and might enjoy the stores of provision which they possessed at home. Together with other causes, this consideration also led them to that resolution, viz.: that they had learned that Divitiacus and the Ædui were approaching the territories of the Bellovaci. And it was impossible to persuade the latter to stay any longer, or to deter them from conveying succor to their own people.

CHAP. XI.—That matter being determined on, marching

out of their camp at the second watch, with great noise and confusion, in no fixed order, nor under any command, since each sought for himself the foremost place in the journey, and hastened to reach home, they made their departure appear very like a flight. Cæsar, immediately learning this through his scouts, [but] fearing an ambuscade, because he had not yet discovered for what reason they were departing, kept his army and cavalry within the camp. At day-break, the intelligence having been confirmed by the scouts, he sent forward his cavalry to harass their rear; and gave the command of it to two of his lieutenants, Q. Pedius, and L. Aurunculeius Cotta. He ordered T. Labienus, another of his lieutenants, to follow them closely with three legions. These, attacking their rear, and pursuing them for many miles, slew a great number of them as they were fleeing; while those in the rear with whom they had come up, halted, and bravely sustained the attack of our soldiers; the van, because they appeared to be removed from danger, and were not restrained by any necessity or command, as soon as the noise was heard, broke their ranks, and, to a man, rested their safety in flight. Thus without any risk [to themselves] our men killed as great a number of them as the length of the day allowed; and at sunset desisted from the pursuit, and betook themselves into the camp, as they had been commanded.

Chap. XII.—On the day following, before the enemy could recover from their terror and flight, Cæsar led his army into the territories of the Suessiones, which are next to the Remi, and having accomplished a long march, hastens to the town named Noviodunum.[1] Having attempted to take it by storm on his march, because he heard that it was destitute of [sufficient] defenders, he was not able to carry it by assault, on account of the breadth of the ditch and the height of the wall, though few were defending it. Therefore, having fortified the camp, he began to bring up the vineæ, and to provide whatever things were necessary for the storm. In the mean time the whole body of the Suessiones, after their flight,

[1] There were three cities of this name in Gaul:—1. Noviodunum Suessinum, called also simply Suessiones and Augusta, the modern Soissons, which is meant here. 2. Noviodunum Æduoum or Nevirnum, a city of the Ædui on the Loire, the modern Nevers. 3. Noviodunum Biturigum, the modern Neuvy or Neufry, about twenty miles west from Nevers.

came the next night into the town. The vineæ having been quickly brought up against the town, a mound thrown up, and towers built, the Gauls, amazed by the greatness of the works, such as they had neither seen nor heard of before, and struck also by the dispatch of the Romans, send embassadors to Cæsar respecting a surrender, and succeed in consequence of the Remi requesting that they [the Suessiones] might be spared.

CHAP. XIII.—Cæsar, having received as hostages the first men of the state, and even the two sons of king Galba himself; and all the arms in the town having been delivered up, admitted the Suessiones to a surrender, and led his army against the Bellovaci. Who, when they had conveyed themselves and all their possessions into the town called Bratuspantium,[1] and Cæsar with his army was about five miles distant from that town, all the old men, going out of the town, began to stretch out their hands to Cæsar, and to intimate by their voice that they would throw themselves on his protection and power, nor would contend in arms against the Roman people. In like manner, when he had come up to the town, and there pitched his camp, the boys and the women from the wall, with outstretched hands, after their custom, begged peace from the Romans.

CHAP. XIV.—For these Divitiacus pleads (for after the departure of the Belgæ, having dismissed the troops of the Ædui, he had returned to Cæsar). "The Bellovaci had at all times been in the alliance and friendship of the Æduan state; that they had revolted from the Ædui and made war upon the Roman people, being urged thereto by their nobles, who said that the Ædui, reduced to slavery by Cæsar, were suffering every indignity and insult. That they who had been the leaders of that plot, because they perceived how great a calamity they had brought upon the state, had fled into Britain. That not only the Bellovaci, but also the Ædui, entreated him to use his [accustomed] clemency and lenity toward them [the Bellovaci]: which if he did, he would increase the influence of the Ædui among all the Belgæ, by whose succor and resources they had been accustomed to support themselves whenever any wars occurred."[2]

[1] This town is supposed to have stood between Cæsaromagus, afterward Belvacus, Beauvais, and Samarobriva, Amiens.

[2] For the grammatical construction of the original of this passage ("Qui

CHAP. XV.—Cæsar said that on account of his respect for Divitiacus and the Æduans, he would receive them into his protection, and would spare them; but, because the state was of great influence among the Belgæ, and pre-eminent in the number of its population, he demanded 600 hostages. When these were delivered, and all the arms in the town collected, he went from that place into the territories of the Ambiăni, who, without delay, surrendered themselves and all their possessions. Upon their territories bordered the Nervii, concerning whose character and customs when Cæsar inquired he received the following information:—That there was no access for merchants to them; that they suffered no wine and other things tending to luxury to be imported; because they thought that by their use the mind is enervated and the courage impaired: that they were a savage people and of great bravery: that they upbraided and condemned the rest of the Belgæ who had surrendered themselves to the Roman people and thrown aside their national courage: that they openly declared they would neither send embassadors, nor accept any condition of peace."

CHAP. XVI.—After he had made three days' march through their territories, he discovered from some prisoners, that the river Sambre was not more than ten miles from his camp; that all the Nervii had stationed themselves on the other side of that river, and together with the Atrĕbătes and the Veromandui, their neighbors, were there awaiting the arrival of the Romans; for they had persuaded both these nations to try the same fortune of war [as themselves]: that the forces of the Aduatŭci were also expected by them, and were on their march; that they had put their women, and those who through age appeared useless for war, in a place to which there was no approach for an army, on account of the marshes.

CHAP. XVII.—Having learned these things, he sends forward scouts and centurions to choose a convenient place for the camp. And as a great many of the surrounding Belgæ and other Gauls, following Cæsar, marched with him; some of these, as was afterwards learned from the prisoners, having accurately observed, during those days, the army's method of marching, went by night to the Nervii, and informed them that a great number of baggage-trains passed between

hujus," etc.—"fuissent"—"intulissent"—"consuērint,") see the notes on the "oratio obliqua" and "oratio recta," book i., pp. 6, 10, 20.

the several legions, and that there would be no difficulty, when the first legion had come into the camp, and the other legions were at a great distance, to attack that legion while under baggage, which being routed, and the baggage-train seized, it would come to pass that the other legions would not dare to stand their ground. It added weight also to the advice of those who reported that circumstance, that the Nervii, from early times, because they were weak in cavalry, (for not even at this time do they attend to it, but accomplish by their infantry whatever they can,) in order that they might the more easily obstruct the cavalry of their neighbors if they came upon them for the purpose of plundering, having cut young trees, and bent them, by means of their numerous branches [extending] on to the sides, and the quick-briars and thorns springing up between them, had made these hedges present a fortification like a wall, through which it was not only impossible to enter, but even to penetrate with the eye.[1] Since [therefore] the march of our army would be obstructed by these things, the Nervii thought that the advice ought not to be neglected by them.

CHAP XVIII.—The nature of the ground which our men had chosen for the camp was this: A hill, declining evenly from the top, extending to the river Sambre, which we have mentioned above: from this river there arose a [second] hill of like ascent, on the other side and opposite to the former, and open for about 200 paces at the lower part; but in the upper part, woody, (so much so) that it was not easy to see through it into the interior. Within these woods the enemy kept themselves in concealment; a few troops of horse-soldiers appeared on the open ground, along the river. The depth of the river was about three feet.

CHAP. XIX.—Cæsar, having sent his cavalry on before, followed close after them with all his forces; but the plan and order of the march was different from that which the Belgæ had reported to the Nervii. For as he was approaching the enemy, Cæsar, according to his custom, led on [as the van]

[1] I have here adopted Anthon's reading and interpretation. Prendeville retains *enatis* in the text, punctuates differently, and translates as follows: "Having half cut young trees and twisted their thick branches in a lateral direction, and briars and thorns growing up and being dispersed between them (the trees), caused that these hedges could form a barrier like a wall."

six legions unencumbered by baggage; behind them he had placed the baggage-trains of the whole army; then the two legions which had been last raised closed the rear, and were a guard for the baggage-train. Our horse, with the slingers and archers, having passed the river, commenced action with the cavalry of the enemy. While they from time to time betook themselves into the woods to their companions, and again made an assault out of the wood upon our men, who did not dare to follow them in their retreat further than the limit to which the plain and open parts extended, in the mean time the six legions which had arrived first, having measured out the work, began to fortify the camp. When the first part of the baggage train of our army was seen by those who lay hid in the woods, which had been agreed on among them as the time for commencing action, as soon as they had arranged their line of battle and formed their ranks within the woods, and had encouraged one another, they rushed out suddenly with all their forces and made an attack upon our horse. The latter being easily routed and thrown into confusion, the Nervii ran down to the river with such incredible speed that they seemed to be in the woods, the river, and close upon us almost at the same time. And with the same speed they hastened up the hill to our camp, and to those who were employed in the works.

CHAP. XX.—Cæsar had every thing to do at one time:[1] the standard to be displayed, which was the sign when it was necessary to run to arms; the signal to be given by the trumpet; the soldiers to be called off from the works; those who had proceeded some distance for the purpose of seeking materials for the rampart, to be summoned; the order of battle to be formed; the soldiers to be encouraged;[2]

[1] Literally, "all things were to be done by Cæsar at one time."

[2] "When a general, after having consulted the auspices, had determined to lead forth his troops against the enemy, a red flag was displayed (*vexillum* vel *signum pugnæ proponebatur*), on a spear from the top of the Prætorium, Cæs. de Bell. Gall. ii. 20. Liv. xxii. 45, which was the signal to prepare for battle. Then having called an assembly by the sound of a trumpet (*classico, i. e.* tuba, *concione advocatâ*, Liv. iii. 62), he harangued the soldiers, who usually showed their approbation by shouts, by raising their right hands (Lucan i. 386), or by beating on their shields with their spears. This address was sometimes made in the open field from a tribunal raised of turf (*e tribunali cespititio, aut viride cespite exstructo*). Tacit. Ann. i. 18. Plin. Paneg. 50. Stat. Silv. v. 2—144."—Adam's Rom. Antiquities.

the watchword to be given. A great part of these arrangements was prevented by the shortness of time and the sudden approach and charge of the enemy. Under these difficulties two things proved of advantage; [first] the skill and experience of the soldiers, because, having been trained by former engagements, they could suggest to themselves what ought to be done, as conveniently as receive information from others; and [secondly] that Cæsar had forbidden his several lieutenants to depart from the works and their respective legions, before the camp was fortified. These, on account of the near approach and the speed of the enemy, did not then wait for any command from Cæsar, but of themselves executed whatever appeared proper.

CHAP. XXI.—Cæsar, having given the necessary orders, hastened to and fro into whatever quarter fortune carried him, to animate the troops, and came to the tenth legion. Having encouraged the soldiers with no further speech than that "they should keep up the remembrance of their wonted valor, and not be confused in mind, but valiantly sustain the assault of the enemy;" as the latter were not further from them than the distance to which a dart could be cast, he gave the signal for commencing battle. And having gone to another quarter for the purpose of encouraging [the soldiers], he finds them fighting. Such was the shortness of the time, and so determined was the mind of the enemy on fighting, that time was wanting not only for affixing the military insignia,[1] but even for putting on the helmets[2] and drawing off the covers from the shields.[3] To whatever part any one by chance came from the works (in which he had been employed), and whatever standards he saw first, at these he stood, lest in seeking his own company he should lose the time for fighting.

[1] "*Insignia*" here means those ornaments and badges of distinction worn by the Roman soldiers: probably it here refers especially to the devices upon the helmets. "The fictitious employment" of *insignia* "to deceive and mislead an enemy was among the stratagems of war. (Paus. iv. 28; Virg. Æn. ii. 389–392)." Smith's Diction. of Greek and Roman Antiq.

[2] It was the practice of the Roman soldiers when on the march, not to wear their helmets, but to carry them slung over their backs, or chests.

[3] As the shields of the soldiers, even at that period, were embellished with curious and expensive ornaments, they kept them, when either in camp or on the march, covered with leather, as a defense against the dust or rain.

Chap. XXII.—The army having been marshaled, rather as the nature of the ground and the declivity of the hill and the exigency of the time, than as the method and order of military matters required; while the legions in the different places were withstanding the enemy, some in one quarter, some in another, and the view was obstructed by the very thick hedges intervening, as we have before remarked, neither could proper reserves be posted, nor could the necessary measures be taken in each part, nor could all the commands be issued by one person. Therefore, in such an unfavorable state of affairs, various events of fortune followed.

Chap. XXIII.—The soldiers of the ninth and tenth legions, as they had been stationed on the left part of the army, casting their weapons, speedily drove the Atrĕbătes (for that division had been opposed to them,) who were breathless with running and fatigue, and worn out with wounds, from the higher ground into the river; and following them as they were endeavoring to pass it, slew with their swords a great part of them while impeded (therein). They themselves did not hesitate to pass the river; and having advanced to a disadvantageous place, when the battle was renewed, they [nevertheless] again put to flight the enemy, who had returned and were opposing them. In like manner, in another quarter two different legions, the eleventh and the eighth, having routed the Veromandui, with whom they had engaged, were fighting from the higher ground upon the very banks of the river. But, almost the whole camp on the front and on the left side being then exposed, since the twelfth legion was posted in the right wing, and the seventh at no great distance from it, all the Nervii, in a very close body, with Boduognatus, who held the chief command, as their leader, hastened toward that place; and part of them began to surround the legions on their unprotected flank, part to make for the highest point of the encampment.[1]

Chap. XXIV.—At the same time our horsemen, and light-armed infantry, who had been with those, who, as I have related, were routed by the first assault of the enemy, as they were betaking themselves into the camp, met the enemy face to face, and again sought flight into another quarter; and

[1] The highest point, perhaps, of the hill on which the camp was. The Greek paraphrast has πὸρς τὰ ἄκρα τείνουσι.

the camp-followers[1] who from the Decuman Gate,[2] and from the highest ridge of the hill had seen our men pass the river as victors, when, after going out for the purposes of plundering, they looked back and saw the enemy parading in our camp, committed themselves precipitately to flight; at the same time there arose the cry and shout of those who came with the baggage-train: and they (affrighted), were carried some one way, some another. By all these circumstances the cavalry of the Treviri were much alarmed, (whose reputation for courage is extraordinary among the Gauls, and who had come to Cæsar, being sent by their state as auxiliaries), and, when they saw our camp filled with a large number of the enemy, the legions hard pressed and almost held surrounded, the camp-retainers, horsemen, slingers, and Numidians fleeing on all sides divided and scattered, they, despairing of our affairs, hastened home, and related to their state that the Romans were routed and conquered, [and] that the enemy were in possession of their camp and baggage-train.

CHAP. XXV.—Cæsar proceeded, after encouraging the tenth legion, to the right wing; where he perceived that his men were hard pressed, and that in consequence of the standards of the twelfth legion being collected together in one place, the crowded soldiers were a hinderance to themselves in the fight; that all the centurions of the fourth cohort were slain, and the standard-bearer killed, the standard[3] itself lost, almost all the centurions of the other cohorts either wounded or slain, and among them the chief centurion of the legion[4] P. Sextius Baculus, a very valiant man, who was so exhausted by many and severe wounds,

[1] These *calones*, it is generally supposed, were slaves. From continual attendance upon the army they arrived at a considerable degree of skill in military matters. Cæsar, for the most part, uses the word *calones* by itself; whereas Tacitus uses it in conjunction with *lixæ*, as if the two words implied the same class of persons. The *lixæ*, however, were quite distinct from the *calones*. They were freemen, and followed the army for the purpose of trade; "lixæ, qui exercitum sequebantur, quæstus causâ." Festus. Thus Hirtius, de Bello Afric. 75, classes them with "*mercatores*:" "lixarum mercatorumque qui plaustris merces portabant."

[2] The Roman camp had four gates: "*porte prætoria*," nearest to the enemy; "*porta Decumana*," opposite to that, and thus furthest from them; "*porta principalis dectra*," and "*porta principalis sinistra*."

[3] Besides the *aquila* or standard of the legion, there were the subordinate standards of the *cohorts* and the *manipuli*.

[4] The *primopilus* was the first centurion of the first maniple of the

that he was already unable to support himself; he likewise perceived that the rest were slackening their efforts, and that some, deserted by those in the rear, were retiring from the battle and avoiding the weapons; that the enemy [on the other hand] though advancing from the lower ground, were not relaxing in front, and were [at the same time] pressing hard on both flanks; he also perceived that the affair was at a crisis, and that there was not any reserve which could be brought up; having therefore snatched a shield from one of the soldiers in the rear (for he himself had come without a shield), he advanced to the front of the line, and addressing the centurions by name, and encouraging the rest of the soldiers, he ordered them to carry forward the standards, and extend the companies, that they might the more easily use their swords. On his arrival, as hope was brought to the soldiers and their courage restored, while every one for his own part, in the sight of his general, desired to exert his utmost energy, the impetuosity of the enemy was a little checked.

CHAP. XXVI.—Cæsar, when he perceived that the seventh legion, which stood close by him, was also hard pressed by the enemy, directed the tribunes of the soldiers[1] to effect

Triarii (*centurio primi pili*), also called *primus centurio*, a person of great distinction in a legion. He had authority over the other centurions; ranked next to the *tribuni militum*, and had a place in the council of war. To him was committed the charge of the principal standard of the legion, whence he is, among other instances, referred to by Tacitus, Ann. i. 39, Hist. i. 56, by the title of *aquilifer*. To the lucrative nature of his office, at least under the empire, Juvenal alludes, when, Sat. xvi. 197, he says, "locupletem aquilam."

[1] *The tribunes of the soldiers.* In each legion there were in the time of Polybius, six *tribuni militum*, who commanded under the consul, usually in turns of a month each. During that period the tribune's authority extended over the whole legion. Up to the year B. C. 361, these officers were chosen, during the monarchy, by the kings; upon the institution of the consulate, by the consuls; and under the dictatorship, by the dictator. That year the people claimed the right of electing either the whole, or the greater part of them. From that period down to B. C. 207, they continued to elect them in this manner. Subsequently, several changes took place in the appointment of these officers. In battle, a military tribune had command of 1,000 men; whence their name in Greek is *χιλίαρχος* or *χιλιάρχης*. The office was for many years the reward of merit and long service. This rule was afterward fatally violated. The late emperors, in order to oblige as many of their friends as possible, frequently conferred the office for the period of six months only. Hence, Pliny, Epist. iv. 4, has "*semestri* tribunatu;" and Juvenal, Sat. vii. 8,

a junction of the legions gradually, and make their charge upon the enemy with a double front; which having been done, since they brought assistance the one to the other, nor feared lest their rear should be surrounded by the enemy, they began to stand their ground more boldly, and to fight more courageously. In the mean time, the soldiers of the two legions which had been in the rear of the army, as a guard for the baggage-train, upon the battle being reported to them, quickened their pace, and were seen by the enemy on the top of the hill; and Titus Labienus, having gained possession of the camp of the enemy, and observed from the higher ground what was going on in our camp, sent the tenth legion as a relief to our men, who, when they had learned from the flight of the horse and the sutlers in what position the affair was, and in how great danger the camp and the legion and the commander were involved, left undone nothing [which tended] to dispatch.

CHAP. XXVII.—By their arrival, so great a change of matters was made, that our men, even those who had fallen down exhausted with wounds, leaned on their shields, and renewed the fight: then the camp-retainers, though unarmed, seeing the enemy completely dismayed, attacked [them though] armed; the horsemen too, that they might by their valor blot the disgrace of their flight, thrust themselves before the legionary soldiers in all parts of the battle. But the enemy, even in the last hope of safety, displayed such great courage, that when the foremost of them had fallen, the next stood upon them prostrate, and fought from their bodies; when these were overthrown, and their corpses heaped up together, those who survived cast their weapons against our men [thence], as from a mound, and returned our darts which had fallen short between [the armies]; so that it ought not to be concluded, that men of such great courage had injudiciously dared to pass a very broad river, ascend very high banks, and come up to a very disadvantageous place; since their greatness of spirit had rendered these actions easy, although in themselves very difficult.

CHAP. XXVIII.—This battle being ended, and the na-

alluding at once to that practice and the gold ring which was one of the insignia of the tribune, has "*semestri auro*." The sixth book of Polybius may be here consulted.

tion and name of the Nervii being almost reduced to annihilation, their old men, whom together with the boys and women we have stated to have been collected together in the fenny places and marshes, on this battle having been reported to them, since they were convinced that nothing was an obstacle to the conquerors, and nothing safe to the conquered, sent embassadors to Cæsar by the consent of all who remained, and surrendered themselves to him; and in recounting the calamity of their state, said that their senators were reduced from 600 to three; that from 60,000 men they [were reduced] to scarcely 500 who could bear arms; whom Cæsar, that he might appear to use compassion toward the wretched and the suppliant, most carefully spared; and ordered them to enjoy their own territories and towns, and commanded their neighbors that they should restrain themselves and their dependents from offering injury or outrage [to them].

CHAP. XXIX.—When the Aduatuci, of whom we have written above, were coming up with all their forces to the assistance of the Nervii, upon this battle being reported to them, they returned home after they were on the march; deserting all their towns and forts, they conveyed together all their possessions into one town, eminently fortified by nature. While this town had on all sides around it very high rocks and precipices, there was left on one side a gently ascending approach, of not more than 200 feet in width; which place they had fortified with a very lofty double wall: besides, they had placed stones of great weight and sharpened stakes upon the walls. They were descended from the Cimbri and Teutones, who, when they were marching into our province and Italy, having deposited on this side the river Rhine such of their baggage-trains as they could not drive or convey with them, left 6,000 of their men as a guard and defense for them. These having, after the destruction of their countrymen, been harassed for many years by their neighbors, while one time they waged war offensively, and at another resisted it when waged against them, concluded a peace with the consent of all, and chose this place as their settlement.

CHAP. XXX.—And on the first arrival of our army they made frequent sallies from the town, and contended with our men in trifling skirmishes; afterward, when hemmed in by a rampart of twelve feet [in height], and fifteen miles in circuit, they kept themselves within the town. When, vineæ[1] having been brought up and a mound raised, they observed that a tower also was being built at a distance, they at first began to mock the Romans from their wall, and to taunt them with the following speeches. "For what purpose was so vast a machine constructed at so great a distance? With what hands," or "with what strength did they, especially [as they were] men of such very small stature" (for our shortness of stature, in comparison to the great size of their bodies, is generally a subject of much contempt to the men of Gaul) "trust to place against their walls a tower of such great weight."

CHAP. XXXI.—But when they saw that it was being moved, and was approaching their walls, startled by the new and unaccustomed sight, they sent embassadors to Cæsar [to treat] about peace; who spoke in the following manner: "That they did not believe the Romans waged war without divine aid, since they were able to move forward machines of such a height with so great speed, and thus fight from close quarters; that they resigned themselves and all their possessions to [Cæsar's] disposal: that they begged and earnestly entreated one thing, viz., that if perchance, agreeable to his clemency and humanity, which they had heard of from others, he should resolve that the Aduatuci were to be spared, he would not deprive them of their arms; that all their neighbors were enemies to them and envied their courage, from whom they could not defend themselves if their arms were delivered up: that it was better for them, if they should be reduced to that state, to suffer any fate from the Roman people, than to be tortured to death by those among whom they had been accustomed to rule."

CHAP. XXXII.—To these things Cæsar replied, "That he,

[1] The *vineæ* was a machine under the protection of which the besieging soldiery advanced to the walls of a town. It consisted of a roof, (formed of planks and wickerwork, covered over with raw hides or wet cloth), about sixteen feet long and seven broad, and resting upon posts eight feet in height. The sides of this were guarded also by a wickerwork. Though usually so light that the men might carry it, the *vineæ* was, in extraordinary cases, made so strong as to be too heavy for that mode of advancing it, and was then moved by wheels attached to the posts. Frequently, as perhaps in the above case, several of these were joined together; the besiegers being defended against the darts, stones, and fire of the town by the *vineæ*, conducted their operations of undermining or of attack by the battering-ram.

in accordance with his custom, rather than owing to their desert, should spare the state, if they should surrender themselves before the battering-ram[1] should touch the wall; but that there was no condition of surrender, except upon their arms being delivered up; that he should do to them that which he had done in the case of the Nervii, and would command their neighbors not to offer any injury to those who had surrendered to the Roman people." The matter being reported to their countrymen, they said that they would execute his commands. Having cast a very large quantity of their arms from the wall into the trench that was before the town, so that the heaps of arms almost equalled the top of the wall and the rampart, and nevertheless having retained and concealed, as we afterward discovered, about a third part in the town, the gates were opened, and they enjoyed peace for that day.

CHAP. XXXIII.—Toward evening Cæsar ordered the gates to be shut, and the soldiers to go out of the town, lest the towns-people should receive any injury from them by night. They [the Aduatuci], by a design before entered into, as we afterwards understood, because they believed that, as a surrender had been made, our men would dismiss their guards, or at least would keep watch less carefully, partly with those arms which they had retained and concealed, partly with shields made of bark or interwoven wickers, which they had hastily covered over with skins, (as the shortness of time required) in the third watch, suddenly made a sally from the town with all their forces [in that direction] in which the ascent to our fortifi-

[1] The battering-ram (*aries*) was, perhaps, the most effective instrument of ancient warfare. It may be called the artillery of olden times. The bas-reliefs on the column of Trajan at Rome present a portraiture of this war engine in its simple form; borne and impelled that is, by human force alone. In its more efficient form, iron rings were placed around the beam of the ram, by which it was suspended by means of ropes, or chains, to another beam fitted transversely over it. Velocity, and consequently power, were thus greatly increased. The head was made of iron or some hard metal, and formed to represent the head of a goat. Hence, as well as from its application, it was called by the Romans *aries*. The Romans borrowed it from the Greeks. They do not, however, appear to have made very much use of it before the siege of Syracuse, in the second Punic war. The beam to which the head was attached varied from eighty to a hundred and twenty feet in length, and the united strength of more than a hundred men was sometimes engaged in its operation.

cations seemed the least difficult. The signal having been immediately given by fires, as Cæsar had previously commanded, a rush was made thither [i. e. by the Roman soldiers] from the nearest fort; and the battle was fought by the enemy as vigorously as it ought to be fought by brave men, in the last hope of safety, in a disadvantageous place, and against those who were throwing their weapons from a rampart and from towers; since all hope of safety depended on their courage alone. About 4,000 of the men having been slain, the rest were forced back into the town. The day after, Cæsar, after breaking open the gates, which there was no one then to defend, and sending in our soldiers, sold the whole spoil of that town. The number of 53,000 persons was reported to him by those who had bought them.

CHAP. XXXIV.—At the same time he was informed by P. Crassus, whom he had sent with one legion against the Venĕti,[1] the Unelli, the Osismii, the Curiosolitæ, the Sesuvii, the Aulerci, and the Rhedŏnes, which are maritime states, and touch upon the [Atlantic] ocean, that all these nations were brought under the dominion and power of the Roman people.

CHAP. XXXV.—These things being achieved, [and] all Gaul being subdued, so high an opinion of this war was spread among the barbarians, that embassadors were sent to Cæsar by those nations who dwelt beyond the Rhine, to promise that they would give hostages and execute his commands. Which embassies Cæsar, because he was hastening into Italy and Illyricum, ordered to return to him at the beginning of the following summer. He himself, having led his legions into winter quarters among the Carnutes, the Andes, and the Turŏnes, which states were close to those regions in which he had waged war, set out for Italy; and a thanksgiving[2] of fifteen days was decreed for those achieve-

[1] *Veneti*, etc. These were nations of Gallia Celtica. The Veneti were situated in the west. The Unelli possessed a territory lying on the northwest of what is now called Normandy. Off their coast lay the islands Cæsarea, *Jersey;* Sarnia, *Guernsey;* and Reduna, *Alderney*. The Osismii occupied a territory afterward forming a part of the province of *Bretagne*, and now called *Finisterre*. The Curiosolitæ also occupied a part of the same province. The Sesuvii are supposed to have been situated on the coast near the Bay of Biscay.

[2] This (*supplicatio* or *supplicium*) was a great religious solemnity decreed by the senate, upon an extraordinary victory. It was designed as

ments, upon receiving Cæsar's letter; [an honor] which before that time[1] had been conferred on none.

an act of thanksgiving to the gods. The temples were then thrown open and the statues of the deities placed in public upon couches. Before these the people gave expression to their thankfulness. This part of the solemnity was called *lectisternium.* The value of the victory was supposed to determine the period of the duration of this sacred festival. Though sometimes decreed for one day, its usual period was three or five days. Pompey had a *supplicatio* of ten days decreed upon the conclusion of the war with Mithridates. Cæsar, as we read in the text, obtained one of fifteen days. This, he tells us, was the first occasion on which a Roman general had enjoyed that honor. Upon his victory over Vercingetorix, that illustrious enemy of the Roman power in Gaul, a *supplicatio* of twenty days was decreed him, as we read, De Bell. Gall. vii. 90. Dion Cassius mentions instances in which a forty, fifty, and even sixty days' *supplicatio* was decreed. Cicero obtained a *supplicatio* upon the suppression of the Catiline conspiracy—an honor which he took frequent opportunity of observing had never before been granted to manful achievements.

There was another solemnity bearing this name. The occasion of it, however, was very different from that already spoken of. In times of public distress or danger, and at the appearance of uncommon prodigies, the senate decreed a *supplicatio* to appease the deities and remove the present, or avert the anticipated evil.

[1] Literally, "happened to none."

BOOK III.

THE ARGUMENT.

I. Cæsar, at the close of the late campaign, sent Servius Galba into the territories of the Nantuates, Veragri, and Seduni, with permission to winter there, if expedient; his reason for this. Galba resolved to winter at Octodurus. II. The Seduni and Veragri combine against him. III. And attack his camp. IV.-VI. A fierce battle ensues; in which, as well as in several other engagements, Galba is successful. VII., VIII. An unexpected war in Gaul; the occasion of it. Veneti are the principal instigators. IX. Cæsar gives orders for the equipment of a fleet. The Veneti and other states augment their navy, and extend their alliances. X.-XII. Cæsar's difficulties; arising chiefly from the position of the Venetic towns. XIII. The structure of the Venetic ships accommodated to that position. XIV., XV. Cæsar surmounts these disadvantages; and in a naval engagement obtains a victory. XVI. Which terminated the war with the Veneti. XVII.-XIX. Titurius Sabinus is sent into the territories of the Unelli. Conduct of their king, Viridorix. Sabinus is compelled to resort to stratagems; he defeats the Unelli. XX., XXI. P. Crassus enters Aquitania, and is attacked by the Sotiates, who are signally worsted. XXII. The "Soldurii." XXIII. Crassus proceeds into the territories of the Vocates and Tarusates; who engage in measures of opposition. XXIV. He draws up his forces for a battle; which the enemy decline. XXV., XXVI. He then attacks their encampment, and is victorious. XXVIII. Cæsar advances against the Morini and Menapii; his motives for this: the enemy make a sudden assault on the Roman forces, and are repelled with great loss. XXIX. Cæsar's provision against such attacks: his operations interrupted by the inclemency of the season: the army is led into winter quarters.

CHAP. I.—When Cæsar was setting out for Italy, he sent Servius Galba with the twelfth legion and part of the cavalry, against the Nantuātes,[1] the Veragri, and Sedūni, who ex-

[1] The Nantuātes were an Alpine race, on the south of the Lake of Geneva; the Veragri, a tribe of the Roman province, also south of that lake, whose chief town, Octodurus, is the modern *Martigni*, and the Sedūni, a people lying between the east coast of it and the Rhone, whose capital, Seduni, is the modern *Sion*.

tend from the territories of the Allobroges, and the lake of Geneva, and the River Rhone to the top of the Alps. The reason for sending him was, that he desired that the pass along the Alps, through which [the Roman] merchants had been accustomed to travel with great danger, and under great imposts, should be opened. He permitted him, if he thought it necessary, to station the legion in these places, for the purpose of wintering. Galba having fought some successful battless and stormed several of their forts; upon embassadors being sent to him from all parts and hostages given and a peace concluded, determined to station two cohorts among the Nantuātes, and to winter in person with the other cohorts of that legion in a village of the Veragri, which is called Octodūrus; and this village being situated in a valley, with a small plain annexed to it, is bounded on all sides by very high mountains. As this village was divided into two parts by a river, he granted one part of it to the Gauls, and assigned the other, which had been left by them unoccupied, to the cohorts to winter in. He fortified this [latter] part with a rampart and a ditch.

CHAP. II.—When several days had elapsed in winter quarters, and he had ordered corn to be brought in he was suddenly informed by his scouts that all the people had gone off in the night from that part of the town which he had given up to the Gauls, and that the mountains which hung over it were occupied by a very large force of the Sedūni and Veragri. It had happened for several reasons that the Gauls suddenly formed the design of renewing the war and cutting off that legion. First, because they despised a single legion, on account of its small number, and that not quite full (two cohorts having been detached, and several individuals being absent, who had been dispatched for the purpose of seeking provision); then, likewise, because they thought that on account of the disadvantageous character of the situation, even their first attack could not be sustained [by us] when they would rush from the mountains into the valley, and discharge their weapons upon us. To this was added, that they were indignant that their children were torn from them under the title of hostages, and they were persuaded that the Romans designed to seize upon the summits of the Alps, and unite those parts to the neighboring province [of Gaul], not only to secure the passes,[1] but also a constant possession.

CHAP. III.—Having received these tidings, Galba, since the works of the winter-quarters and the fortifications were not fully completed, nor was sufficient preparation made with regard to corn and other provisions (since, as a surrender had been made, and hostages received, he had thought he need entertain no apprehension of war), speedily summoning a council, began to anxiously inquire their opinions. In which council, since so much sudden danger had happened contrary to the general expectation, and almost all the higher places were seen already covered with a multitude of armed men, nor could [either] troops come to their relief, or provisions be brought in, as the passes were blocked up [by the enemy]; safety being now nearly despaired of, some opinions of this sort were delivered: that, "leaving their baggage, and making a sally, they should hasten away for safety by the same routes by which they had come thither." To the greater part, however, it seemed best, reserving that measure to the last, to await the issue of the matter, and to defend the camp.

CHAP. IV.—A short time only having elapsed, so that time was scarcely given for arranging and executing those things which they had determined on, the enemy, upon the signal being given, rushed down [upon our men] from all parts, and discharged stones and darts[2] upon our rampart. Our men at first, while their strength was fresh, resisted bravely, nor did they cast any weapon ineffectually from their higher station. As soon as any part of the camp, being destitute of defenders, seemed to be hard pressed, thither they ran, and brought assistance. But they were over-matched in this, that the enemy when wearied by the long continuance of the battle, went out of the action, and others with fresh strength came in their place; none of which things could be done by our men, owing to the smallness of their number; and not only was permission not given to the wearied [Roman] to retire from the fight, but not even to the wounded [was liberty granted] to quit the post where he had been stationed, and recover.

CHAP. V.—When they had now been fighting for more than six hours, without cessation, and not only strength, but even

[1] Literally, "for the possession of the passes."

[2] The *gæsum*, a Celtic weapon, was adopted by the Romans.

weapons were failing our men, and the enemy were pressing on more rigorously, and had begun to demolish the rampart and to fill up the trench, while our men were becoming exhausted, and the matter was now brought to the last extremity, P. Sextius Baculus, a centurion of the first rank, whom we have related to have been disabled by severe wounds in the engagement with the Nervii, and also C. Volusenus, a tribune of the soldiers, a man of great skill and valor, hasten to Galba, and assure him that the only hope of safety[1] lay in making a sally, and trying the last resource. Whereupon assembling the centurions, he quickly gives orders to the soldiers to discontinue the fight a short time, and only collect the weapons flung [at them], and recruit themselves after their fatigue, and afterward, upon the signal being given, sally forth from the camp, and place in their valor all their hope of safety.

CHAP. VI.—They do what they were ordered; and, making a sudden sally from all the gates [of the camp], leave the enemy the means neither of knowing what was taking place, nor of collecting themselves. Fortune thus taking a turn, [our men] surround on every side, and slay those who had entertained the hope of gaining the camp and having killed more than the third part of an army of more than 30,000 men (which number of the barbarians it appeared certain had come up to our camp], put to flight the rest when panic-stricken, and do not suffer them to halt even upon the higher grounds. All the forces of the enemy being thus routed, and stripped of their arms, [our men] betake themselves to their camp and fortifications. Which battle being finished, inasmuch as Galba was unwilling to tempt fortune again, and remembered that he had come into winter quarters with one design, and saw that he had met with a different state of affairs; chiefly however urged by the want of corn and provision, having the next day burned all the buildings of that village, he hastens to return into the province; and as no enemy opposed or hindered his march, he brought the legion safe into the [country of the] Nantuates, thence into [that of] the Allobroges, and there wintered.

CHAP. VII.—These things being achieved, while Cæsar had every reason to suppose that Gaul was reduced to a state of tran-

[1] Literally, "the only hope of safety was, if a sally being made, they tried the last resource."

quillity, the Belgæ being overcome, the Germans expelled, the Sedūni among the Alps defeated, and when he had, therefore, in the beginning of winter, set out for Illyricum, as he wished to visit those nations, and acquire a knowledge of their countries, a sudden war sprang up in Gaul. The occasion of that war was this: P. Crassus, a young man, had taken up his winter quarters with the seventh legion among the Andes, who border upon the [Atlantic] ocean. He, as there was a scarcity of corn in those parts, sent out some officers of cavalry, and several military tribunes among the neighbouring states, for the purpose of procuring corn and provision; in which number T. Terrasidius was sent among the Esubii; M. Trebius Gallus among the Curiosolītæ; Q. Velanius, T. Silius, amongst the Veněti.

CHAP. VIII.—The influence of this state is by far the most considerable of any of the countries on the whole sea coast, because the Veněti both have a very great number of ships, with which they have been accustomed to sail to Britain, and [thus] excel the rest in their knowledge and experience of nautical affairs; and as only a few ports lie scattered along that stormy and open sea, of which they are in possession, they hold as tributaries almost all those who are accustomed to traffic in that sea. With them arose the beginning [of the revolt] by their detaining Silius and Velanius; for they thought that they should recover by their means the hostages which they had given to Crassus. The neighboring people led on by their influence (as the measures of the Gauls are sudden and hasty), detain Trebius and Terrasidius for the same motive; and quickly sending embassadors, by means of their leading men, they enter into a mutual compact to do nothing except by general consent, and abide the same issue of fortune; and they solicit the other states to choose rather to continue in that liberty which they had received from their ancestors, than endure slavery under the Romans. All the sea coast being quickly brought over to their sentiments, they send a common embassy to P. Crassus [to say], "If he wished to receive back his officers, let him send back to them their hostages."

CHAP. IX.—Cæsar, being informed of these things by Crassus, since he was so far distant himself, orders ships of war to be built in the mean time on the river Loire, which flows into the ocean; rowers to be raised from the province; sailors and pilots to be provided. These matters being quickly executed, he himself, as soon as the season of the year permits, hastens to the army. The Veneti, and the other states also, being informed of Cæsar's arrival, when they reflected how great a crime they had committed, in that, the embassadors (a character which had among all nations ever been sacred and inviolable)[1] had by them been detained and thrown into prison, resolve to prepare for a war in proportion to the greatness of their danger, and especially to provide those things which appertain to the service of a navy, with the greater confidence, inasmuch as they greatly relied on the nature of their situation. They knew that the passes by land were cut off by estuaries, that the approach by sea was most difficult, by reason of our ignorance of the localities, [and] the small number of the harbors, and they trusted that our army would not be able to stay very long among them, on account of the insufficiency of corn; and again, even if all these things should turn out contrary to their expectation, yet they were very powerful in their navy. They well understood that the Romans neither had any number of ships, nor were acquainted with the shallows, the harbors, or the islands of those parts where they would have to carry on the war; and the navigation was very different in a narrow sea[2] from what it was in the vast and open ocean. Having come to this resolution, they fortify their towns, convey corn into them from the country parts, bring together as many ships as possible to Venetia, where it appeared Cæsar would at first carry on the war. They unite to themselves as allies for that war, the Osismii, the Lexovii, the Nannĕtes,[3] the Ambiliati, the Morĭni, the Diablintes,[4] and the Menapii; and send for auxiliaries from Britain, which is situated over against those regions.

1 Frequent mention is made of the sacred and holy characters of embassadors by Roman writers.

2 Literally, "far different in a narrow sea and in the vast and open ocean."

3 The Nannĕtes, or Namnĕtes, were a Celtic tribe, whose capital, Condivicnum, afterward Nannĕtes, is the modern *Nantes*, which preserves the ancient name with a slight modification.

4 The Diablintes were a division of the Aulerci. Their capital, the name of which was changed from Neodūnum to Diablintes, is the modern *Gabliens*.

CHAP. X.—There were these difficulties which we have mentioned above, in carrying on the war, but many things, nevertheless, urged Cæsar to that war;—the open insult offered to the state in the detention of the Roman knights, the rebellion raised after surrendering, the revolt after hostages were given, the confederacy of so many states, but principally, lest if, [the conduct of] this part was overlooked, the other nations should think that the same thing was permitted them. Wherefore, since he reflected that almost all the Gauls were fond of revolution, and easily and quickly excited to war; that all men likewise, by nature, love liberty and hate the condition of slavery, he thought he ought to divide and more widely distribute his army, before more states should join the confederation.

CHAP. XI.—He therefore sends T. Labienus, his lieutenant, with the cavalry to the Treviri, who are nearest to the river Rhine. He charges him to visit the Remi and the other Belgians, and to keep them in their allegiance and repel the Germans (who where said to have been summoned by the Belgæ to their aid,) if they attempted to cross the river by force in their ships. He orders P. Crassus to proceed into Aquitania with twelve legionary cohorts and a great number of the cavalry, lest auxiliaries should be sent into Gaul by these states, and such great nations be united. He sends Q. Titurius Sabinus his lieutenant, with three legions, among the Unelli, the Curiosolītæ, and the Lexovii, to take care that their forces should be kept separate from the rest. He appoints D. Brutus, a young man, over the fleet and those Gallic vessels which he had ordered to be furnished[1] by the Pictŏnes and the Santŏni, and the other provinces which remained at peace; and commands him to proceed toward the Venĕti, as soon as he could. He himself hastens thither with the land forces.

CHAP. XII.—The sites of their towns were generally such that, being placed on extreme points[2] [of land] and on promontories, they neither had an approach by land when the tide had rushed in from the main ocean, which always happens twice in the space of twelve hours; nor by ships, because, upon the tide ebbing again, the ships were likely to be dashed upon the shoals. Thus, by either circumstance, was the storming of their towns rendered difficult; and if at any time

[1] Lit. "to assemble from among," etc.
[2] Lit. "small tongues."

perchance the Veneti overpowered by the greatness of our works, (the sea having been excluded by a mound and large dams, and the latter being made almost equal in height to the walls of the town) had begun to despair of their fortunes; bringing up a large number of ships, of which they had a very great quantity, they carried off all their property and betook themselves to the nearest towns; there they again defended themselves by the same advantages of situation. They did this the more easily during a great part of the summer, because our ships were kept back by storms, and the difficulty of sailing was very great in that vast and open sea, with its strong tides and its harbors far apart and exceedingly few in number.

Chap. XIII.—For their ships were built and equipped after this manner. The keels were somewhat flatter than those of our ships, whereby they could more easily encounter the shallows and the ebbing of the tide: the prows were raised very high, and, in like manner the sterns were adapted to the force of the waves and storms [which they were formed to sustain]. The ships were built wholly of oak, and designed to endure any force and violence whatever; the benches which were made of planks a foot in breadth, were fastened by iron spikes of the thickness of a man's thumb; the anchors were secured fast by iron chains instead of cables, and for sails they used skins and thin dressed leather. These [were used] either through their want of canvas and their ignorance of its application, or for this reason, which is more probable, that they thought that such storms of the ocean, and such violent gales of wind could not be resisted by sails, nor ships of such great burden be conveniently enough managed by them. The encounter of our fleet with these ships[1] was of such a nature that our fleet excelled in speed alone, and the plying of the oars; other things, considering the nature of the place [and] the violence of the storms, were more suitable and better adapted on their side; for neither could our ships injure theirs with their beaks[2] (so great was their strength), nor on account of

[1] *i. e.* the relative character of the two was, etc.

[2] "For neither could," etc. A similar remark is made in the next chapter. And yet the *rostrum* (more commonly *rostra*, Greek ἔμβολος, or ἔμβολον) supplied a very formidable instrument of ancient naval warfare. It was a beam springing from a part just below the prow, and topped

their height was a weapon easily cast up to them; and for the same reason they were less readily locked in by rocks. To this was added, that whenever a storm began to rage and they ran before the wind, they both could weather the storm more easily and heave to securely in the shallows, and when left by the tide feared nothing from rocks and shelves: the risk of all which things was much to be dreaded by our ships.

CHAP. XIV.—Cæsar, after taking many of their towns, perceiving that so much labor was spent in vain and that the flight of the enemy could not be prevented on the capture of their towns, and that injury could not be done them, he determined to wait for his fleet. As soon as it came up and was first seen by the enemy, about 220 of their ships, fully equipped and appointed with every kind of [naval] implement, sailed forth from the harbor, and drew up opposite to ours; nor did it appear clear to Brutus, who commanded the fleet, or to the tribunes of the soldiers and the centurions, to whom the several ships were assigned, what to do, or what system of tactics to adopt; for they knew that damage could not be done by their beaks; and that, although turrets were built [on their decks], yet the height of the stems of the barbarian ships exceeded these; so that weapons could not be cast up from [our] lower position with sufficient effect, and those cast by the Gauls fell the more forcibly upon us. One thing provided by our men was of great service, [viz.] sharp hooks[1] inserted into and fastened upon poles, of a form not unlike the hooks used in attacking town walls. When the ropes which fastened the sail-yards to the masts were caught by them and pulled, and our vessel vigorously impelled with the oars, they[2] [the ropes] were severed; and when they were cut away, the

with sharp iron points or an iron figure of a ram's head. Though formerly always above the water they were in latter times placed below it, and thus rendered more dangerous.

1 "Sharp hooks," (*falces præacutæ*). The *falces* here spoken of were, probably, those arms which were much used under that name. The *falx* was a large dagger with a coulter, or bill, projecting from one side. Such implements, when fixed upon poles, were employed at the siege of towns. One service of them was to loosen the stones of the walls. To this practice Cæsar refers, De Bell. Gall. vii. 22. But Vegetius, iv. 14, tells us that a large *falx* was sometimes employed, instead of the more common ram's head, for the purpose of attacking towns.

2 Literally, "gave themselves to the wind."

4

yards necessarily fell down; so that as all the hope of the Gallic vessels depended on their sails and rigging, upon these being cut away, the entire management of the ships was taken from them at the same time. The rest of the contest depended on[1] courage; in which our men decidedly had the advantage; and the more so, because the whole action was carried on in the sight of Cæsar and the entire army; so that no act, a little more valiant than ordinary, could pass unobserved, for all the hills and higher grounds, from which there was a near prospect of the sea were occupied by our army.

CHAP. XV.—The sail-yards [of the enemy], as we have said, being brought down, although two and [in some cases] three ships [of theirs] surrounded each one [of ours], the soldiers strove with the greatest energy to board the ships of the enemy; and, after the barbarians observed this taking place, as a great many of their ships were beaten, and as no relief for that evil could be discovered, they hastened to seek safety in flight. And, having now turned their vessels to that quarter in which the wind blew, so great a calm and lull suddenly arose, that they could not move out of their place, which circumstance, truly, was exceedingly opportune for finishing the business; for our men gave chase and took them one by one, so that very few out of all the number, [and those] by the intervention of night, arrived at the land, after the battle had lasted almost from the fourth hour[2] till sun-set.

CHAP. XVI.—By this battle the war with the Venĕti and the whole of the sea coast was finished; for both all the youth, and all, too, of more advanced age, in whom there was any discretion or rank, had assembled in that battle; and they had collected in that one place whatever naval forces they had any where; and when these were lost, the survivors had no place to retreat to, nor means of defending their towns. They accordingly surrendered themselves and all their possessions to Cæsar, on whom Cæsar thought that punishment should be inflicted the more severely, in order that for the future the rights of embassadors might be more carefully respected by barbarians; having, therefore, put to death all their senate, he sold the rest for slaves.

CHAP. XVII.—While these things are going on among the Venĕti, Q. Titurius Sabinus with those troops which he

[1] Lit. "was placed in." [2] Lit. "about ten in the morning."

had received from Cæsar, arrives in the territories of the Unelli. Over these people Viridovix ruled, and held the chief command of all those states which had revolted; from which he had collected a large and powerful army.[1] And in those few days, the Aulerci and the Sexovii, having slain their senate because they would not consent to be promoters of the war, shut their gates [against us] and united themselves to Viridovix; a great multitude besides of desperate men and robbers assembled out of Gaul from all quarters, whom the hope of plundering and the love of fighting had called away from husbandry and their daily labor. Sabinus kept himself within his camp, which was in a position convenient for everything; while Viridovix encamped over against him at a distance of two miles, and daily bringing out his forces, gave him an opportunity of fighting; so that Sabinus had now not only come into contempt with the enemy, but also was somewhat taunted by the speeches of our soldiers; and furnished so great a suspicion of his cowardice that the enemy presumed to approach even to the very rampart of our camp. He adopted this conduct for the following reason: because he did not think that a lieutenant ought to engage in battle with so great a force, especially while he who held the chief command was absent, except on advantageous ground or some favorable circumstance presented itself.

CHAP. XVIII.—After having established this suspicion of his cowardice, he selected a certain suitable and crafty Gaul, who was one of those whom he had with him as auxiliaries. He induces him by great gifts and promises to go over to the enemy; and informs [him] of what he wished to be done. Who, when he arrives among them as a deserter, lays before them the fears of the Romans; and informs them by what difficulties Cæsar himself was harassed, and that the matter was not far removed from this—that Sabinus would the next night privately draw off his army out of the camp and set forth to Cæsar for the purpose of carrying [him] assistance, which, when they heard, they all cry out together that an opportunity of successfully conducting their enterprise, ought not to be thrown away: that they ought to go to the [Roman] camp. Many things persuaded the Gauls to this measure; the delay of Sabinus during the previous days; the

[1] Lit. "an army and large forces."

positive assertion of the [pretended] deserter; want of provisions, for a supply of which they had not taken the requisite precautions; the hope springing from the Venetic war; and [also] because in most cases men willingly believe what they wish. Influenced by these things they do not discharge Viridovix and the other leaders from the council, before they gained permission from them to take up arms and hasten to [our] camp; which being granted, rejoicing as if victory were fully certain, they collected faggots and brushwood, with which to fill up the Roman trenches, and hasten to the camp.

CHAP. XIX.—The situation of the camp was a rising ground, gently sloping from the bottom for about a mile. Thither they proceeded with great speed (in order that as little time as possible might be given to the Romans to collect and arm themselves), and arrived quite out of breath. Sabinus having encouraged his men, gives them the signal, which they earnestly desired. While the enemy were encumbered by reason of the burdens which they were carrying, he orders a sally to be made suddenly from two gates [of the camp]. It happened, by the advantage of situation, by the unskilfulness and the fatigue of the enemy, by the valor of our soldiers, and their experience in former battles, that they could not stand one attack of our men, and immediately turned their backs; and our men with full vigor followed them while disordered, and slew a great number of them; the horse pursuing the rest, left but few, who escaped by flight. Thus at the same time, Sabinus was informed of the naval battle and Cæsar of victory gained by Sabinus; and all the states immediately surrendered themselves to Titurius: for as the temper of the Gauls is impetuous and ready to undertake wars, so their mind is weak, and by no means resolute in enduring calamities.[1]

CHAP. XX.—About the same time, P. Crassus, when he had arrived in Aquitania (which, as has been before said, both from its extent of territory and the great number of its people, is to be reckoned a third part of Gaul,[2]) understanding that he was to wage war in these parts, where a few years before, L. Valerius Præconinus, the lieu-

[1] Polybius's character of the Gauls perfectly agrees with that of Cæsar's in both the points spoken of in the passage above.

[2] Book i. 1.

tenant had been killed, and his army routed, and from which L. Manilius, the proconsul, had fled with the loss of his baggage, he perceived that no ordinary care must be used by him. Wherefore, having provided corn, procured auxiliaries and cavalry, [and] having summoned by name many valiant men from Tolosa, Carcaso, and Narbo, which are the states of the province of Gaul, that border on these regions [Aquitania], he led his army into the territories of the Sotiātes. On his arrival being known, the Sotiātes having brought together great forces and [much] cavalry, in which their strength principally lay,[1] and assailing our army on the march, engaged first in a cavalry action, then when their cavalry was routed, and our men pursuing, they suddenly display their infantry forces, which they had placed in ambuscade in a valley. These attacked our men [while] disordered, and renewed the fight.

CHAP. XXI.—The battle was long and vigorously contested, since the Sotiātes, relying on their former victories, imagined that the safety of the whole of Aquitania rested on their valor; [and] our men, on the other hand, desired it might be seen what they could accomplish without their general and without the other legions, under a very young commander; at length the enemy, worn out with wounds, began to turn their backs, and a great number of them being slain, Crassus began to besiege the [principal] town of the Sotiātes on his march. Upon their valiantly resisting, he raised vineæ and turrets. They at one time attempting a sally, at another forming mines[2] to our rampart and vineæ (at which the Aquitani are eminently skilled, because in many places among them there are copper mines); when they perceived that nothing could be gained by these operations through

[1] It need scarcely be observed that the infantry were then regarded as the main part of an army.

[2] When a town could not be approached by *vineæ*, the operations of the siege were often carried on by the means of mines. These were sometimes carried into the very heart of the place. When the object was principally to sap the foundations of the walls, the part to be destroyed was supported by upright wooden beams, which being fired, left the wall to come down. This piece of warfare, we find, then, was also applied to the fortifications of a camp. Another instance of this is found, De Bell. Gall., vii. 22; where Cæsar speaks also of skill derived from the civil workings of mines applied to military purposes.

the perseverance of our men, they send embassadors to Crassus, and entreat him to admit them to a surrender. Having obtained it, they, being ordered to deliver up their arms, comply.

CHAP. XXII.—And while the attention of our men is engaged in that matter, in another part Adcantuannus, who held the chief command, with 600 devoted followers whom they call soldurii[1] (the conditions of whose association are these,—that they enjoy all the conveniences of life with those to whose friendship they have devoted themselves: if any thing calamitous happen to them, either they endure the same destiny together with them, or commit suicide: nor hitherto, in the memory of men, has there been found any one who, upon his being slain to whose friendship he had devoted himself, refused to die); Adcantuannus, [I say] endeavoring to make a sally with these, when our soldiers had rushed together to arms, upon a shout being raised at that part of the fortification, and a fierce battle had been fought there, was driven back into the town, yet he obtained from Crassus [the indulgence] that he should enjoy the same terms of surrender [as the other inhabitants].

CHAP. XXIII.—Crassus, having received their arms and hostages, marched into the territories of the Vocātes and the Tarusātes. But then, the barbarians being alarmed, because they had heard that a town fortified by the nature of the place and by art,[2] had been taken by us in a few days after our arrival there, began to send embassadors into all quarters, to combine, to give hostages one to another, to raise troops. Embassadors also are sent to those states of Hither Spain which are nearest to Aquitania, and auxiliaries and leaders are summoned from them; on whose arrival they proceed to carry on the war with great confidence, and with a great host of men. They who had been with Q. Sertorius the whole period [of his war in

[1] *Soldurii.* This seems a Celtic word. That the soldurii were persons lying under feudal obligations to the persons whom they attended in battle, and are to be regarded in the same light as the persons (ambacti clientesque) spoken of in book vi. 15, is at least doubtful. Plutarch speaks of persons among the Egyptians devoting themselves to the service of others for life and death (*συναποθνήσκοντες*). It is probable that the soldurii acted only on *sacred* principles in this self-devotion, and were thus an *ἱερος λόχος*.

[2] Lit. "by hand."

Spain] and were supposed to have very great skill in military matters, are chosen leaders. These, adopting the practice of the Roman people, begin to select [advantageous] places, to fortify their camp, to cut off our men from provisions, which, when Crassus observes, [and likewise] that his forces, on account of their small number could not safely be separated; that the enemy both made excursions and beset the passes, and [yet] left sufficient guard for their camp; that on that account, corn and provision could not very conveniently be brought up to him, and that the number of the enemy was daily increased, he thought that he ought not to delay in giving battle. This matter being brought to a council, when he discovered that all thought the same thing, he appointed the next day for the fight.

CHAP. XXIV.—Having drawn out all his forces at the break of day, and marshaled them in a double line, he posted the auxiliaries in the center, and waited to see what measures the enemy would take. They, although on account of their great number and their ancient renown in war, and the small number of our men, they supposed they might safely fight, nevertheless considered it safer to gain the victory without any wound, by besetting the passes [and] cutting off the provisions: and if the Romans, on account of the want of corn, should begin to retreat they intended to attack them while encumbered in their march and depressed in spirit [as being assailed while] under baggage. This measure being approved of by the leaders and the forces of the Romans drawn out, the enemy [still] kept themselves in their camp. Crassus having remarked this circumstance, since the enemy, intimidated by their own delay, and by the reputation [*i. e.* for cowardice arising thence] had rendered our soldiers more eager for fighting, and the remarks of all were heard [declaring] that no longer ought delay to be made in going to the camp, after encouraging his men, he marches to the camp of the enemy, to the great gratification of his own troops.[1]

CHAP. XXV.—There, while some were filling up the ditch, and others, by throwing a large number of darts, were driving the defenders from the rampart and fortifications, and the auxiliaries, on whom Crassus did not much rely in the battle, by supplying stones and weapons [to the soldiers], and by conveying

[1] Lit. "all earnestly wishing it"

turf to the mound, presented the appearance and character of men engaged in fighting; while also the enemy were fighting resolutely and boldly, and their weapons, discharged from their higher position, fell[1] with great effect; the horse, having gone round the camp of the enemy, reported to Crassus that the camp was not fortified with equal care on the side of the Decuman gate, and had an easy approach.

CHAP. XXVI.—Crassus, having exhorted the commanders of the horse to animate their men by great rewards and promises, points out to them what he wished to have done. They, a they had been commanded, having brought out the four cohorts, which, as they had been left as a guard for the camp, were not fatigued by exertion, and having led them round by a somewhat longer way, lest they could be seen from the camp of the enemy, when the eyes and minds of all were intent upon the battle, quickly arrived at those fortifications which we have spoken of, and, having demolished these, stood in the camp of the enemy before they were seen by them, or it was known what was going on. And then, a shout being heard in that quarter, our men, their strength having been recruited, (which[2] usually occurs on the hope of victory), began to fight more vigorously. The enemy surrounded on all sides, [and] all their affairs being despaired of, made great attempts to cast themselves down over the ramparts and to seek safety in flight. These the cavalry pursued over the very open plains, and after leaving scarcely a fourth part out of the number of 50,000, which it was certain had assembled out of Aquitania and from the Cantabri, returned late at night to the camp.

CHAP. XXVII.—Having heard of this battle, the greatest part of Aquitania surrendered itself to Crassus, and of its own accord sent hostages, in which number were the Tarbelli,[3] the Bigerriones, the Preciani, the Vocasātes, the Tarusātes, the Elurates, the Garites, the Ausci, the Garumni, the Sibuzates, the Cocosates. A few [and those] most remote nations, relying on the time of the year, because winter was at hand, neglected to do this.

CHAP. XXVIII.—About the same time Cæsar, although the summer was nearly past, yet, since, all Gaul being re-

1 Literally, "not ineffectively."
2 Literally, "which generally is accustomed to happen."
3 For the situations of these several people, see the map.

duced, the Morini and the Menapii alone remained in arms, and had never sent embassadors to him [to make a treaty] of peace, speedily led his army thither, thinking that that war might soon be terminated. They resolved to conduct the war on a very different method from the rest of the Gauls; for as they perceived that the greatest nations [of Gaul] who had engaged in war, had been routed and overcome, and as they possessed continuous ranges of forests and morasses, they removed themselves and all their property thither. When Cæsar had arrived at the opening of these forests, and had began to fortify his camp, and no enemy was in the mean time seen, while our men were dispersed on their respective duties, they suddenly rushed out from all parts of the forest, and made an attack on our men. The latter quickly took up arms and drove them back again to their forests; and having killed a great many, lost a few of their own men while pursuing them too far through those intricate places.

CHAP. XXIX.—During the remaining days after this, Cæsar began to cut down the forests; and that no attack might be made on the flank of the soldiers, while unarmed and not foreseeing it, he placed together (opposite to the enemy) all that timber which was cut down, and piled it up as a rampart on either flank. When a great space had been, with incredible speed, cleared in a few days, when the cattle [of the enemy] and the rear of their baggage train were already seized by our men, and they themselves were seeking for the thickest parts of the forests, storms of such a kind came on that the work was necessarily suspended, and, through the continuance of the rains, the soldiers could not any longer remain in their tents. Therefore, having laid waste all their country, [and] having burned their villages and houses, Cæsar led back his army and stationed them in winter quarters among the Aulerci and Lexovii, and the other states which had made war upon him last.

BOOK IV.

THE ARGUMENT.

I.-III. The Usipĕtes and Tenchtheri, oppressed by the Suevi, migrate from Germany into Gaul; the national character of the Suevi. IV. The Usipĕtes and Tenchtheri possess themselves of the estates of the Menapii. V., VI. Cæsar resolves to make war upon the Germans. VII.-IX. Receives an overture of peace from them; their treacherous designs. X. Description of the Meuse and the Rhine. XI.-XV. The perfidy of the Germans; their overthrow and retreat. XVI.-XVII. Cæsar's bridge over the Rhine. XVIII., XIX. Cæsar leads his army into Germany; punishes the Sigambri; frees the Ubii from the tyranny of the Suevi, and returns into Gaul. XX.-XXII. His design upon Britain; preparations for the expedition. XXIII.-XXVII. Carries it into effect; the defeat and surrender of the Britons. XXVIII., XXIX. The Roman vessels overtaken by a storm. XXX. The Britons think to take advantage of this. XXXI. Cæsar defeats their designs. XXXII. A stratagem of the Britons for attacking a Roman legion. XXXIII. Their mode of fighting with chariots. XXXIV. They advance to the Roman camp. XXXV. Are defeated. XXXVI. Sue for peace. XXXVII., XXXVIII. The Morini attack two legions which had just returned from Britain and suffer a severe loss; Cæsar goes into winter quarters among the Belgæ; a thanksgiving of twenty days decreed by the senate for the success of this campaign.

Chap. I.—The following winter (this was the year in which Cn. Pompey and M. Crassus were consuls),[1] those Germans [called] the Usipĕtes, and likewise the Tenchtheri, with a great number of men, crossed the Rhine, not far from the place at which that river discharges itself into the sea.[2] The motive for crossing [that river] was, that having been for several years harassed by the Suevi, they were constantly engaged in war, and hindered from the pursuits of agriculture. The nation of the Suevi is by far the largest and the most warlike nation of all

[1] This was the year 699, after the building of Rome: 55 before Christ. It was the fourth year of the Gallic war.

[2] Lit. "not far from the sea, where the Rhine flows into it."

the Germans. They are said to possess a hundred cantons,[1] from each of which they yearly send from their territories for the purpose of war a thousand armed men: the others who remain at home, maintain [both] themselves and those engaged in the expedition. The latter again, in their turn, are in arms the year after: the former remain at home. Thus neither husbandry, nor the art and practice of war are neglected. But among them there exists no private and separate land; nor are they permitted to remain more than one year in one place for the purpose of residence. They do not live much on corn, but subsist for the most part on milk and flesh, and are much [engaged] in hunting; which circumstance must, by the nature of their food, and by their daily exercise and the freedom of their life (for having from boyhood been accustomed to no employment, or discipline, they do nothing at all contrary to their inclination), both promote their strength and render them men of vast stature of body.[2] And to such a habit have they brought themselves, that even in the coldest parts they wear no clothing whatever except skins,[3] by reason of the scantiness of which, a great portion of their body is bare, and besides they bathe in open rivers.[4]

CHAP. II.—Merchants have access to them rather that they may have persons to whom they may sell those things which they have taken in war, than because they need any commodity to be imported to them. Moreover, even as to laboring cattle, in which the Gauls take the greatest pleasure, and which they procure at a great price, the Germans do not employ such as are imported, but those poor[5] and ill-shaped animals, which belong to their country; these, however, they render capable of the greatest labor by daily exercise. In cavalry actions they

1 The correctness of this statement of Cæsar's has been doubted. But Tacitus, in his Germania, ch. xxxix. has "centum pagis habitantur," in speaking of a German nation.

2 Tacitus, Germania, ch. iv., describing the personal appearance of the Germans, speaks of them in a similar manner: "magna corpora."

3 See book vi., ch. 21.

4 In the above mentioned work, ch. iv., Tacitus further says of the Germans: "*frigora* atque inediam cœlo solove assueverint." Their bathings in the open rivers, in their cold climate, and perhaps without much respect to seasons, would to the Romans be an evidence of their hardihood,

5 Some editions have *parva*. Davis and Clark have the better reading *prava*. The Greek paraphrast has *μικρὰς*. The classical Greek writers use πονηρὸς, as the Latin do *pravus*, to denote what is *inferior*. Xeno-

frequently leap from their horses and fight on foot; and train their horses to stand still in the very spot on which they leave them, to which they retreat with great activity when there is occasion; nor, according to their practice, is any thing regarded as more unseemly, or more unmanly, than to use housings.[1] Accordingly, they have the courage, though they be themselves but few, to advance against any number whatever of horse mounted with housings. They on no account permit wine to be imported to them, because they consider that men degenerate in their powers of enduring fatigue, and are rendered effeminate by that commodity.

Chap. III.—They esteem it their greatest praise as a nation, that the lands about their territories lie unoccupied to a very great extent, inasmuch as [they think] that by this circumstance is indicated, that a great number of nations can not withstand their power; and thus on one side of the Suevi the lands are said to lie desolate for about six hundred miles. On the other side they border on the Ubii, whose state was large and flourishing, considering the condition of the Germans, and who are somewhat more refined than those of the same race and the rest [of the Germans], and that because they border on the Rhine, and are much resorted to by merchants, and are accustomed to the manners of the Gauls, by reason of their approximity to them. Though the Suevi, after making the attempt frequently and in several wars, could not expel this nation from their territories, on account of the extent and population of their state, yet they made them tributaries, and rendered them less distinguished and powerful [than they had ever been].[2]

Chap. IV.—In the same condition were the Usipĕtes and the Tenchtheri (whom we have mentioned above), who, for many years, resisted the power of the Suevi, but being at last driven from their possessions, and having wandered through many parts of Germany, came to the Rhine, to districts which

phon, Cyropæd. book i. The account of the cattle of the Germans given by Tacitus, Germania, ch. v., agrees with that given here by Cæsar. He describes their country as "pecorum fœcunda, sed plerumque improcera;" adding, "ne armentis quidem suus honor aut gloria frontis."

[1] Livy, lib. xxxv. ch. xi., says, that the Numidian horse did not use bridles.

[2] So we have thought fit to translate "*humiliores*," the literal meaning of which is *more lowly*.

the Menapii inhabited, and where they had lands, houses, and villages on either side of the river. The latter people, alarmed by the arrival of so great a multitude, removed from those houses which they had on the other side of the river, and having placed guards on this side the Rhine, proceeded to hinder the Germans from crossing. They, finding themselves, after they had tried all means, unable either to force a passage on account of their deficiency in shipping, or cross by stealth on account of the guards of the Menapii, pretended to return to their own settlements and districts; and, after having proceeded three days' march, returned; and their cavalry having performed the whole of this journey in one night, cut off the Menapii, who were ignorant of, and did not expect [their approach, and] who, having moreover been informed of the departure of the Germans by their scouts, had, without apprehension, returned to their villages beyond the Rhine. Having slain these, and seized their ships, they crossed the river before that part of the Menapii, who were at peace in their settlements over the Rhine, were apprized of [their intention]; and seizing all their houses, maintained themselves upon their provisions during the rest of the winter.

CHAP. V.—Cæsar, when informed of these matters, fearing the fickle disposition of the Gauls, who are easily prompted to take up resolutions, and much addicted to change, considered that nothing was to be intrusted to them; for it is the custom of that people to compel travelers to stop, even against their inclination, and inquire what they may have heard, or may know, respecting any matter; and in towns the common people throng around merchants and force them to state from what countries they come, and what affairs they know of there. They often engage in resolutions concerning the most important matters, induced by these reports and stories alone; of which they must necessarily instantly repent, since they yield to mere unauthorized reports;[1] and since most people give to their questions answers framed agreeably to their wishes.

CHAP. VI.—Cæsar, being aware of their custom, in order that he might not encounter a more formidable war,[2] sets forward to

[1] "Quum incertis rumoribus *serviant.*" Oudendorp cites a collateral passage from Plautus, "Nec tuis depellor dictis, quin *rumore serviam.*"

[2] Than by delay he would.

the army earlier in the year than he was accustomed to do. When he had arrived there, he discovered that those things, which he had suspected would occur, had taken place; that embassies had been sent to the Germans by some of the states, and that they had been entreated to leave the Rhine, and had been promised that all things which they desired should be provided by the Gauls. Allured by this hope, the Germans were then making excursions to greater distances, and had advanced to the territories of the Eburŏnes and the Condrusi, who are under the protection[1] of the Treviri. After summoning the chiefs of Gaul, Cæsar thought proper to pretend ignorance of the things which he had discovered; and having conciliated and confirmed their minds,[2] and ordered some cavalry to be raised, resolved to make war against the Germans.

CHAP. VII.—Having provided corn and selected his cavalry, he began to direct his march toward those parts in which he heard the Germans were. When he was distant from them only a few days' march, embassadors came to him from their state, whose speech was as follows: "That the Germans neither make war upon the Roman people first, nor do they decline, if they are provoked, to engage with them in arms; for that this was the custom of the Germans handed down to them from their forefathers,—to resist whatsoever people make war upon them and not to avert it by entreaty;[3] this, however, they confessed,—that they had come hither reluctantly,[4] having been expelled from their country. If the Romans were disposed[5] to accept their friendship, they might be serviceable allies to them; and let them either assign them lands, or permit them to retain those which they had acquired by their arms; that they are inferior to the Suevi alone, to whom not even the immortal gods can show themselves equal; that there was none at all besides on earth whom they could not conquer."

CHAP. VIII.—To these remarks Cæsar replied in such terms as he thought proper; but the conclusion[6] of his

1 "Qui sunt Trevirorum *clientes*."
2 *i. e.* in their allegiance to the Roman people.
3 "*Deprecari.*"
4 "*Invitos*," *i. e.* not by design, but by necessity.
5 *Velint.* The Greek θέλω has a like sense.
6 "*Exitus.*" Conclusion, *i. e.* substance.

speech was, "That he could make no alliance with them, if they continued in Gaul; that it was not probable that they who were not able to defend their own territories, should get possession of those of others, nor were there any lands lying waste in Gaul, which could be given away, especially to so great a number of men, without doing wrong [to others]; but they might, if they were desirous, settle in the territories of the Ubii; whose embassadors were then with him, and were complaining of the aggressions of the Suevi, and requesting assistance from him; and that he would obtain this request from them."

CHAP. IX.—The embassadors said that they would report these things to their country men; and, after having deliberated on the matter, would return to Cæsar after the third day, they begged that he would not in the mean time advance his camp nearer to them. Cæsar said that he could not grant them even that; for he had learned that they had sent a great part of their cavalry over the Meuse to the Ambivarīti,[1] some days before, for the purpose of plundering and procuring forage. He supposed that they were then waiting for these horse, and that the delay was caused on this account.

CHAP. X.[2]—The Meuse rises from mount Le Vosge,[3] which is in the territories of the Lingones; and, having received a branch of the Rhine, which is called the Waal, forms the island of the Batavi, and not more than eighty miles from it it falls into the ocean. But the Rhine takes its source among the Lepontii, who inhabit the Alps, and is carried with a rapid current for a long distance through the territories of the Sarunates, Helvetii, Sequani, Mediomatrici,[4] Tribuci, and Treviri, and when it approaches the ocean, divides into several branches; and, having formed many and extensive islands, a great part of which are inhabited by savage and barbarous

[1] The Ambivarīti lay between the Meuse and the Rhine.

[2] This tenth chapter has, though without any reason, been supposed to be a gloss.

[3] Vosegus (sometimes written Vogesus and Vosaga), the present *Vosge*, is a branch of mount Jura.

[4] The Mediomatrici, or -rices, were a people of Gallia Belgica. Till crippled by the Roman conquests in Gaul, they were a powerful people, and possessed of an extensive country. The modern *Metz* derives its name from their chief town, Mediomatrici. The Tribuci lay in the east of Gallia Belgica. They were of German origin.

nations (of whom there are some who are supposed to live on fish and the eggs of sea-fowl), flows into the ocean by several mouths.[1]

CHAP. XI—When Cæsar was not more than twelve miles distant from the enemy, the embassadors return to him, as had been arranged; who meeting him on the march, earnestly entreated him not to advance any further. When they could not obtain this, they begged him to send on a dispatch to those who had marched in advance of the main army, and forbid them to engage; and grant them permission to send embassadors to the Ubii, and if the princes and senate of the latter would give them security by oath, they assured Cæsar that they would accept such conditions as might be proposed by him; and requested that he would give them the space of three days for negociating these affairs. Cæsar thought that these things tended to the self-same point [as their other proposal]; [namely] that, in consequence of a delay of three days intervening, their horse, which were at a distance, might return; however, he said, that he would not that day advance further than four miles for the purpose of procuring water; he ordered that they should assemble at that place in as large a number as possible, the following day, that he might inquire into their demands. In the mean time he sends messengers to the officers who had marched in advance with all the cavalry, to order them not to provoke the enemy to an engagement, and if they themselves were assailed, to sustain the attack until he came up with the army.

CHAP. XII.—But the enemy, as soon as they saw our horse, the number of which was 5000, whereas they themselves had not more than 800 horse, because those which had gone over the Meuse for the purpose of foraging had not returned, while our men had no apprehensions, because their embassadors had gone away from Cæsar a little before, and that day had been requested by them as a period of truce, made an onset on our men, and soon threw them into disorder. When our men, in their turn, made a stand, they, according to their practice, leaped from their horses to their feet, and stabbing our horses in the belly and overthrowing a great many of our men, put the

[1] "Multisque capitibus," etc. Contrary to the use of the Latin writers, Cæsar here employs *caput* to signify, not the source of the river, but the part at which it flows into the sea.

rest to flight, and drove them forward so much alarmed that they did not desist from their retreat till they had come in sight of our army. In that encounter seventy-four of our horse were slain; among them, Piso, an Aquitanian, a most valiant man, and descended from a very illustrious family; whose grandfather had held the sovereignty of his state, and had been styled friend by our senate. He, while he was endeavoring to render assistance to his brother who was surrounded by the enemy, and whom he rescued from danger, was himself thrown from his horse, which was wounded under him, but still opposed [his antagonists] with the greatest intrepidity, as long as he was able to maintain the conflict. When at length he fell, surrounded on all sides and after receiving many wounds, and his brother, who had then retired from the fight, observed it from a distance, he spurred on his horse, threw himself upon the enemy, and was killed.

CHAP. XIII.—After this engagement, Cæsar considered that neither ought embassadors to be received to audience, nor conditions be accepted by him from those who, after having sued for peace by way of stratagem and treachery, had made war without provocation. And to wait until the enemy's forces were augmented and their cavalry had returned, he concluded, would be the greatest madness; and knowing the fickleness of the Gauls, he felt how much influence the enemy had already acquired among them by this one skirmish. He [therefore] deemed that no time for concerting measures ought to be afforded them. After having resolved on those things and communicated his plans to his lieutenants and quæstor[1] in order that he might not suffer any opportunity for engaging to escape him, a very seasonable event occurred, namely, that on the morning of the next day, a large body of

[1] From the city quæstors (*quæstores urbani*), whose office was nearly coeval with the building of Rome, other functionaries of the state, from the corresponding character of their duties, derived their name, with the distinctive title of Militares, or Provinciales. The duties of the former were, principally, to take charge of the treasury, which was kept in the temple of Saturn; to receive and expend the public money (of which they were required to render an account); exact the fines imposed by the state and provide for the accomodation of foreign embassadors. Those of the military, or provincial, quæstors, were to attend the consuls or prætors, into their provinces; see that provisions and pay were there furnished to the army; take charge of the money deposited by the soldiers; raise the taxes and tributes of the state; have charge of the money and sell the

Germans, consisting of their princes and old men, came to the camp to him to practice the same treachery and dissimulation; but, as they asserted, for the purpose of acquitting themselves for having engaged in a skirmish the day before, contrary to what had been agreed and to what indeed, they themselves had requested; and also if they could by any means obtain a truce by deceiving him. Cæsar, rejoicing that they had fallen into his power, ordered them to be detained.[1] He then drew all his forces out of the camp, and commanded the cavalry, because he thought they were intimidated by the late skirmish, to follow in the rear.

Chap. XIV.—Having marshalled his army in three lines, and in a short time performed a march of eight miles, he arrived at the camp of the enemy before the Germans could perceive what was going on; who being suddenly alarmed by all the circumstances, both by the speediness of our arrival and the absence of their own officers, as time was afforded neither for concerting measures nor for seizing their arms, are perplexed as to whether it would be better to lead out their forces against the enemy, or to defend their camp, or seek their safety by flight. Their consternation being made apparent by their noise and tumult, our soldiers, excited by the treachery of the preceding day, rushed into the camp: such of them as could readily get their arms, for a short time withstood our men, and gave battle among their carts and baggage wagons; but the rest of the people,[2] [consisting] of boys and women (for they had left their country and crossed the Rhine with all their families) began to fly in all directions; in pursuit of whom Cæsar sent the cavalry.

Chap. XV.—The Germans when, upon hearing a noise behind them, [they looked and] saw that their families were being slain,

spoils taken in war; and, like the city quæstors, render an account of their receipts and disbursements.

[1] Plutarch, in his life of Cæsar, records, on the authority of this passage, this act of perfidy on the part of the Germans; but further intimates that, when a public thanksgiving for this victory was proposed in the senate, Cato (not altogether a friend of Cæsar's) was so displeased with the Roman general's conduct in attacking the Germans while their embassadors were in his camp, as to declare that he ought to have been delivered up to the enemy as one who had violated a treaty.

[2] "Reliqua multitudo;" the rest of that large body of people; *i. e.* the Germans.

throwing away their arms and abandoning their standards, fled out of the camp, and when they had arrived at the confluence of the Meuse and the Rhine, the survivors despairing of further escape, as a great number of their countrymen had been killed, threw themselves into the river and there perished, overcome by fear, fatigue, and the violence of the stream. Our soldiers, after the alarm of so great a war, for the number of the enemy amounted to 430,000,[1] returned to their camp, all safe to a man, very few being even wounded. Cæsar granted those whom he had detained in the camp liberty of departing. They however, dreading revenge and torture from the Gauls, whose lands they had harassed, said that they desired to remain with him. Cæsar granted them permission.

CHAP. XVI.—The German war being finished, Cæsar thought it expedient for him to cross the Rhine, for many reasons; of which this was the most weighty, that, since he saw the Germans were so easily urged to go into Gaul, he desired they should have their fears for their own territories, when they discovered that the army of the Roman people both could and dared pass the Rhine. There was added also, that portion of the cavalry of the Usipĕtes and the Tenchtheri, which I have above related to have crossed the Meuse for the purpose of plundering and procuring forage, and was not present at the engagement, had betaken themselves, after the retreat of their countrymen, across the Rhine into the territories of the Sigambri, and united themselves to them. When Cæsar sent embassadors to them, to demand that they should give up to him those who had made war against him and against Gaul, they replied, "That the Rhine bounded the empire of the Roman people; if he did not think it just for the Germans to pass over into Gaul against his consent, why did he claim that any thing beyond the Rhine should be subject to his dominion or power?" The Ubii, also, who alone, out of all the nations lying beyond the Rhine, had sent embassadors to Cæsar, and formed an alliance and given hostages, earnestly entreated "that he would bring them assistance, because they were grievously oppressed by the Suevi; or, if he was prevented from doing so by the business of the commonwealth, he would at least transport his army over the Rhine; that that would

[1] Including women and children.

be sufficient for their present assistance and their hope for the future; that so great was the name and the reputation of his army, even among the most remote nations of the Germans, arising from the defeat of Ariovistus and this last battle which was fought, that they might be safe under the fame and friendship of the Roman people." They promised a large number of ships for transporting the army.

CHAP. XVII.—Cæsar, for those reasons which I[1] have mentioned, had resolved to cross the Rhine; but to cross by ships he neither deemed to be sufficiently safe, nor considered consistent with his own dignity or that of the Roman people. Therefore, although the greatest difficulty in forming a bridge was presented to him, on account of the breadth, rapidity, and depth of the river, he nevertheless considered that it ought to be attempted by him, or that his army ought not otherwise to be led over. He devised this plan of a bridge. He joined together at the distance of two feet, two piles, each a foot and a half thick, sharpened a little at the lower end, and proportioned in length, to the depth of the river. After he had, by means of engines, sunk these into the river, and fixed them at the bottom, and then driven them in with rammers, not quite perpendicularly, like a stake, but bending forward and sloping, so as to incline in the direction of the current of the river; he also placed two [other piles] opposite to these, at the distance of forty feet lower down, fastened together in the same manner, but directed against the force and current of the river. Both these, moreover, were kept firmly apart by beams two feet thick (the space which the binding of the piles occupied), laid in at their extremities between two braces on each side, and in consequence of these being in different directions and fastened on sides the one opposite to the other, so great was the strength of the work, and such the arrangement of the materials, that in proportion as the greater body of water dashed against the bridge, so much the closer were its parts held fastened together. These beams were bound together by timber laid over them,[2] in the direction of the length of the bridge, and were [then] covered over with laths and hurdles; and in addi-

[1] "Commemoravi." Here, as in ch. 27, Cæsar, contrary to his practice, uses the first person *singular*.

[2] I have here adopted Clarke's explanation, which is supported by the authority of Lipsius.

tion to this, piles were driven into the water obliquely, at the lower side of the bridge, and these, serving as buttresses, and being connected with every portion of the work, sustained the force of the stream: and there were others also above the bridge, at a moderate distance; that if trunks of trees or vessels were floated down the river by the barbarians for the purpose of destroying the work, the violence of such things might be diminished by these defenses, and might not injure the bridge.

CHAP. XVIII. Within ten days after the timber began to be collected, the whole work was completed, and the whole army led over. Cæsar, leaving a strong guard at each end of the bridge, hastens into the territories of the Sigambri. In the mean time, embassadors from several nations come to him, whom, on their suing for peace and alliance, he answers in a courteous manner, and orders hostages to be brought to him. But the Sigambri, at the very time the bridge was begun to be built, made preparations for a flight (by the advice of such of the Tenchtheri and Usipětes as they had among them), and quitted their territories, and conveyed away all their possessions, and concealed themselves in deserts and woods.

CHAP. XIX.—Cæsar, having remained in their territories a few days, and burned all their villages and houses, and cut down their corn, proceeded into the territories of the Ubii; and having promised them his assistance, if they were ever harassed by the Suevi, he learned from them these particulars: that the Suevi, after they had by means of their scouts found that the bridge was being built, had called a council, according to their custom, and sent orders to all parts of their state to remove from the towns and convey their children, wives, and all their possessions into the woods, and that all who could bear arms should assemble in one place; that the place thus chosen was nearly the centre of those regions which the Suevi possessed; that in this spot they had resolved to await the arrival of the Romans, and give them battle there. When Cæsar discovered this, having already accomplished all these things on account of which he had resolved to lead his army over, namely, to strike fear into the Germans, take vengeance on the Sigambri, and free the Ubii from the invasion of the Suevi, having spent altogether eighteen days beyond the Rhine, and thinking he had advanced far enough to serve both honor and interest, he returned into Gaul, and cut down the bridge.

CHAP. XX. During the short part of summer which remained, Cæsar, although in these countries, as all Gaul lies toward the north, the winters are early, nevertheless resolved to proceed into Britain,[1] because he discovered that in almost all the wars with the Gauls succors had been furnished to our enemy from that country; and even if the time of year should be insufficient for carrying on the war, yet he thought it would be of great service to him if he only entered the island, and saw into the character of the people, and got knowledge of their localities, harbors, and landing-places, all which were for the most part unknown to the Gauls. For neither does any one except merchants generally go thither, nor even to them was any portion of it known, except the sea-coast and those parts which are opposite to Gaul. Therefore, after having called up to him the merchants from all parts, he could learn neither what was the size of the island, nor what or how numerous were the nations which inhabited it, nor what system of war they followed, nor what customs they used, nor what harbors were convenient for a great number of large ships.[2]

CHAP. XXI.—He sends before him Caius Volusenus with a ship of war, to acquire a knowledge of these particulars before he in person should make a descent[3] into the island, as he was convinced that this was a judicious measure. He commissioned him to thoroughly examine into all matters, and then return to him as soon as possible. He himself proceeds to the Morini with all his forces. He orders ships from all parts of the neighboring countries, and the fleet which the

1 Ouberlin remarks in his note on this passage, that Dion Cassius asserts that Cæsar's expedition against Britain tended to the advantage neither of the general nor of Rome, beyond the mere extension of the empire; and adds, that Plutarch assented to that opinion. He further reminds us that Suetonius assigns as Cæsar's motive for the expedition, the very strange one of his wishing to obtain pearls, in which he had heard the island abounded. He, lastly, cites the passage from Pliny (lib. ix., c. 517), in which that writer relates that Cæsar dedicated to Venus, from whom he boasted his descent, a breast-plate formed, as he wished it to be believed, of British pearls.

2 The earliest accredited account of the ancient Britons is that given in these Commentaries. Tacitus, in his Agricola, c. 10, in entering on his description of that people, represents them as "multis scriptoribus memoratos." After Cæsar (in this and the fifth book of the Gallic War), Livy, Strabo, Fabius Rusticus, Pomponius Mela, Pliny, and Tacitus himself, in his Agricola, left records of them.

preceding summer he had built for the war with the Venĕti, to assemble in this place. In the mean time, his purpose having been discovered, and reported to the Britons by merchants, embassadors come to him from several states of the island, to promise that they will give hostages, and submit to the government of the Roman people. Having given them an audience, he after promising liberally, and exhorting them to continue in that purpose, sends them back to their own country, and [dispatches] with them Commius, whom, upon subduing the Atrebătes, he had created king there, a man whose courage and conduct he esteemed, and who he thought would be faithful to him, and whose influence ranked highly[1] in those countries. He orders him to visit as many states as he could, and persuade them to embrace the protection of the Roman people, and apprize them that he would shortly come thither. Volusenus, having viewed the localities as far as means could be afforded one who dared not leave his ship and trust himself to barbarians, returns to Cæsar on the fifth day, and reports what he had there observed.

CHAP. XXII. While Cæsar remains in these parts for the purpose of procuring ships, embassadors come to him from a great portion of the Morini, to plead their excuse respecting their conduct on the late occasion; alleging that it was as men uncivilized, and as those who were unacquainted with our custom, that they had made war upon the Roman people, and promising to perform what he should command. Cæsar, thinking that this had happened fortunately enough for him, because he neither wished to leave an enemy behind him, nor had an opportunity for carrying on a war, by reason of the time of year, nor considered that employment in such trifling matters was to be preferred to his enterprise on Britain, imposes a large number of hostages; and when these were brought, he received them to his protection. Having collected together, and provided[2] about eighty transport ships, as many as he thought necessary for conveying over two legions, he assigned such

[1] Or, "whose character was highly prized;" "whose reputation for integrity and ability stood high."

[2] "Navibus circiter LXXX. onerariis coactis contractisque." The Greek paraphrast distinguishes *coactis* and *contractis* in this passage, by *συναλίς ειν, to assemble*, and *ἐκλεγεσθαι, to select; i. e.* some from the whole number *assembled.*

[ships] of war as he had besides to the quæstor, his lieutenants, and officers of cavalry. There were in addition to these eighteen ships of burden which were prevented, eight miles from that place, by winds, from being able to reach the same port. These he distributed among the horse; the rest of the army, he delivered to Q. Titurius Sabinus and L. Aurunculeius Cotta, his lieutenants, to lead into the territories of the Menapii and those cantons of the Morini from which embassadors had not come to him. He ordered P. Sulpicius Rufus, his lieutenant, to hold possession of the harbor, with such a garrison as he thought sufficient.

CHAP. XXIII.—These matters being arranged, finding the weather favorable for his voyage, he set sail about the third watch, and ordered the horse to march forward to the further port, and there embark and follow him. As this was performed rather tardily by them, he himself reached Britain with the first squadron of ships, about the fourth hour of the day, and there saw the forces of the enemy drawn up in arms on all the hills. The nature of the place was this: the sea was confined by mountains so close to it that a dart could be thrown from their summit upon the shore. Considering this by no means a fit place for disembarking, he remained at anchor till the ninth hour, for the other ships to arrive there. Having in the mean time assembled the lieutenants and military tribunes, he told them both what he had learned from Volusenus, and what he wished to be done; and enjoined them (as the principle of military matters, and especially as maritime affairs, which have a precipitate and uncertain action, required) that all things should be performed by them at a nod and at the instant. Having dismissed them, meeting both with wind and tide favorable at the same time, the signal being given and the anchor weighed, he advanced about seven miles from that place, and stationed his fleet over against an open and level shore.

CHAP. XXIV. But the barbarians, upon perceiving the design of the Romans, sent forward their cavalry and charioteers, a class of warriors of whom it is their practice to make great use in their battles,[1] and following with the rest

[1] Lit. "which class" or "kind, they are accustomed for the most part to use in battles." The clause applies to the charioteers (*essedarii*). See note on page 100.

of their forces, endeavored to prevent our men landing. In this was the greatest difficulty, for the following reasons, namely, because our ships, on account of their great size, could be stationed only in deep water; and our soldiers, in places unknown to them, with their hands embarrassed, oppressed with a large and heavy weight of armor, had at the same time to leap from the ships, stand amid the waves, and encounter the enemy; whereas they, either on dry ground, or advancing a little way into the water, free in all their limbs, in places thoroughly known to them, could confidently throw their weapons and spur on their horses, which were accustomed to this kind of service. Dismayed by these circumstances and altogether untrained in this mode of battle, our men did not all exert the same vigor and eagerness which they had been wont to exert in engagements on dry ground.

CHAP. XXV.—When Cæsar observed this, he ordered the ships of war, the appearance of which was somewhat strange to the barbarians and the motion more ready for service, to be withdrawn a little from the transport vessels, and to be propelled by their oars, and be stationed toward the open flank of the enemy, and the enemy to be beaten off and driven away, with slings, arrows, and engines: which plan was of great service to our men; for the barbarians being startled by the form of our ships and the motions of our oars and the nature of our engines, which was strange to them, stopped, and shortly after retreated a little. And while our men were hesitating [whether they should advance to the shore], chiefly on account of the depth of the sea, he who carried the eagle of the tenth legion, after supplicating the gods that the matter might turn out favorably to the legion, exclaimed, "Leap, fellow soldiers, unless you wish to betray your eagle to the enemy. I, for my part, will perform my duty to the commonwealth and my general." When he had said this with a loud voice, he leaped from the ship and proceeded to bear the eagle toward the enemy. Then our men, exhorting one another that so great a disgrace should not be incurred, all leaped from the ship. When those in the nearest vessels saw them, they speedily followed and approached the enemy.

CHAP XXVI.—The battle was maintained vigorously on both sides. Our men, however, as they could neither keep their ranks, nor get firm footing, nor follow their standards, and as one from one ship and another from another assembled around whatever standards they met, were thrown into great confusion. But the enemy, who were acquainted with all the shallows, when from the shore they saw any coming from a ship one by one, spurred on their horses, and attacked them while embarrassed; many surrounded a few, others threw their weapons upon our collected forces on their exposed flank. When Cæsar observed this, he ordered the boats of the ships of war and the spy sloops to be filled with soldiers, and sent them up to the succor of those whom he had observed in distress. Our men, as soon as they made good their footing on dry ground, and all their comrades had joined them, made an attack upon the enemy, and put them to flight, but could not pursue them very far, because the horse had not been able to maintain their course at sea and reach the island. This alone was wanting to Cæsar's accustomed success.[1]

CHAP. XXVII.—The enemy being thus vanquished in battle, as soon as they recovered after their flight, instantly sent embassadors to Cæsar to negotiate about peace. They promised to give hostages and perform what he should command. Together with these embassadors came Commius the Altrebatian, who, as I have above said, had been sent by Cæsar into Britain. Him they had seized upon when leaving his ship, although in the character of embassador he bore the general's commission to them, and thrown into chains: then after the battle was fought, they sent him back, and in suing for peace cast the blame of that act upon the common people, and entreated that it might be pardoned on account of their indiscretion. Cæsar, complaining, that after they had sued for peace, and had voluntarily sent embassadors into the continent for that purpose, they had made war without a reason, said that he would pardon their indiscretion, and imposed hostages, a part of whom they gave immediately; the rest they said they would give in a few days, since they were sent for from remote places. In the mean time they ordered their people to return to the country parts, and the chiefs assembled from all quarters, and proceeded to surrender themselves and their states to Cæsar.

1 "Hoc unum ad pristinam fortunam Cæsari defuit;" where "ad pris. fort." has the idea of *coming up to the mark, or standard,* of his olden, or former, *i. e.* his completely good fortune in war.

CHAP. XXVIII.—A peace being established by these proceedings four days after we had come into Britain, the eighteen ships, to which reference has been made above, and which conveyed the cavalry, set sail from the upper port with a gentle gale, when, however, they were approaching Britain and were seen from the camp, so great a storm suddenly arose that none of them could maintain their course at sea; and some were taken back to the same port from which they had started;—others, to their great danger, were driven to the lower part of the island, nearer to the west; which, however, after having cast anchor, as they were getting filled with water, put out to sea through necessity in a stormy night, and made for the continent.

CHAP. XXIX.—It happened that night to be full moon, which usually occasions very high tides in that ocean; and that circumstance was unknown to our men. Thus, at the same time, the tide began to fill the ships of war which Cæsar had provided to convey over his army, and which he had drawn up on the strand; and the storm began to dash the ships of burden which were riding at anchor against each other; nor was any means afforded our men of either managing them or of rendering any service. A great many ships having been wrecked, inasmuch as the rest, having lost their cables, anchors, and other tackling, were unfit for sailing, a great confusion, as would necessarily happen, arose throughout the army; for there were no other ships in which they could be conveyed back, and all things which are of service in repairing vessels were wanting, and, corn for the winter had not been provided in those places, because it was understood by all that they would certainly winter in Gaul.

CHAP. XXX.—On discovering these things the chiefs of Britain, who had come up after the battle was fought to perform those conditions which Cæsar had imposed, held a conference, when they perceived that cavalry, and ships, and corn were wanting to the Romans, and discovered the small number of our soldiers from the small extent of the camp (which, too, was on this account more limited than ordinary, because Cæsar had conveyed over his legions without baggage), and thought that the best plan was to renew the war, and cut off our men from corn and provisions and protract the affair till winter; because they felt confident, that, if they were vanquished or cut off from a return, no one would afterward pass over into Britain for the purpose of making war. Therefore, again entering into a conspiracy, they began to depart from the camp by degrees and secretly bring up their people from the country parts.

CHAP. XXXI.—But Cæsar, although he had not as yet discovered their measures, yet, both from what had occurred to his ships, and from the circumstance that they had neglected to give the promised hostages, suspected that the thing would come to pass which really did happen. He therefore provided remedies against all contingencies; for he daily conveyed corn from the country parts into the camp, used the timber and brass of such ships as were most seriously damaged for repairing the rest, and ordered whatever things besides were necessary for this object to be brought to him from the continent. And thus, since that business was executed by the soldiers with the greatest energy, he effected that, after the loss of twelve ships, a voyage could be made well enough in the rest.

CHAP. XXXII.—While these things are being transacted, one legion had been sent to forage, according to custom, and no suspicion of war had arisen as yet, and some of the people[1] remained in the country parts, others went backward and forward to the camp, they who were on duty at the gates of the camp reported to Cæsar that a greater dust than was usual[2] was seen in that direction in which the legion had marched. Cæsar, suspecting that which was [really the case],—that some new enterprise was undertaken by the barbarians, ordered the two cohorts which were on duty, to march into that quarter with him, and two other cohorts to relieve them on duty; the rest to be armed and follow him immediately. When he had advanced some little way from the camp, he saw that his men were overpowered by the enemy and scarcely able to stand their ground, and that, the legion being crowded together, weapons were being cast on them from all sides. For as all the corn was reaped in every part with the exception of one, the enemy, suspecting that our men would repair to that, had concealed themselves in the woods during the night.

[1] *Hominum.* This refers, not to the Romans, but the Britons; contrary to the probable meaning of the text and the testimony of commentators; some translators, however, and among them Duncan, have referred it to the former.

[2] Lit. than custom produced.

Then attacking them suddenly, scattered as they were, and when they had laid aside their arms, and were engaged in reaping, they killed a small number, threw the rest into confusion, and surrounded them with their cavalry and chariots.

CHAP. XXXIII.—Their mode of fighting with their chariots is this: firstly, they drive about in all directions and throw their weapons and generally break the ranks of the enemy with the very dread of their horses and the noise of their wheels; and when they have worked themselves in between the troops of horse, leap from their chariots and engage on foot. The charioteers in the mean time withdraw some little distance from the battle, and so place themselves with the chariots that, if their masters are overpowered by the number of the enemy, they may have a ready retreat to their own troops. Thus they display in battle the speed of horse, [together with] the firmness of infantry; and by daily practice and exercise attain to such expertness that they are accustomed, even on a declining and steep place, to check their horses at full speed, and manage and turn them in an instant and run along the pole, and stand on the yoke, and thence betake themselves with the greatest celerity to their chariots again.[1]

CHAP. XXXIV.—Under these circumstances, our men being dismayed by the novelty of this mode of battle, Cæsar most seasonably brought assistance; for upon his arrival the enemy paused, and our men recovered from their fear; upon which thinking the time unfavorable for provoking the enemy and coming to an action, he kept himself in his own quarter, and, a short time having intervened, drew back the legions into the camp. While these things are going on, and all our men engaged, the rest of the Britons, who were in the fields, departed. Storms then set in for several successive days, which both confined our men to the camp and hindered the enemy from attacking us. In the mean time the barbarians despatched messengers to all parts, and reported to their people the small number of our soldiers, and how good an opportunity was given for obtaining spoil and for liberating themselves forever, if they should only drive the Romans from their camp. Having by these means

[1] Though common among the ancient nations of the east, the mode of fighting with chariots seems to have been confined to the Britons in Europe. This serves the early historian, Geoffry of Monmouth, as an argument in his attempt to prove that the Britons were of Trojan origin.

speedily got together a large force of infantry and of cavalry, they came up to the camp.

CHAP. XXXV.—Although Cæsar anticipated that the same thing which had happened on former occasions would then occur—that, if the enemy were routed, they would escape from danger by their speed; still, having got about thirty horse, which Commius the Atrebatian, of whom mention has been made, had brought over with him [from Gaul], he drew up the legions in order of battle before the camp. When the action commenced, the enemy were unable to sustain the attack of our men long, and turned their backs; our men pursued them as far as their speed and strength permitted, and slew a great number of them; then, having destroyed and burned every thing far and wide, they retreated to their camp.

CHAP. XXXVI.—The same day, embassadors sent by the enemy came to Cæsar to negotiate a peace. Cæsar doubled the number of hostages which he had before demanded; and ordered that they should be brought over to the continent, because, since the time of the equinox was near, he did not consider that, with his ships out of repair, the voyage ought to be deferred till winter. Having met with favorable weather, he set sail a little after midnight, and all his fleet arrived safe at the continent, except two of the ships of burden which could not make the same port which the other ships did, and were carried a little lower down.

CHAP. XXXVII.—When our soldiers, about 300 in number, had been drawn out of these two ships, and were marching to the camp, the Morini, whom Cæsar, when setting forth for Britain, had left in a state of peace, excited by the hope of spoil, at first surrounded them with a small number of men, and ordered them to lay down their arms, if they did not wish to be slain; afterward however, when they, forming a circle, stood on their defense, a shout was raised and about 6000 of the enemy soon assembled; which being reported, Cæsar sent all the cavalry in the camp as a relief to his men. In the mean time our soldiers sustained the attack of the enemy, and fought most valiantly for more than four hours, and, receiving but few wounds themselves, slew several of them. But after our cavalry came in sight, the enemy, throwing away their arms, turned their backs, and a great number of them were killed.

CHAP. XXXVIII.—The day following Cæsar sent Labienus, his lieutenant, with those legions which he had brought back from Britain, against the Morini, who had revolted; who, as they had no place to which they might retreat, on account of the drying up of their marshes (which they had availed themselves of as a place of refuge the preceding year), almost all fell into the power of Labienus. In the mean time Cæsar's lieutenants, Q. Titurius and L. Cotta, who had led the legions into the territories of the Menapii, having laid waste all their lands, cut down their corn and burned their houses, returned to Cæsar because the Menapii had all concealed themselves in their thickest woods. Cæsar fixed the winter quarters of all the legions among the Belgæ. Thither only two British states sent hostages; the rest omitted to do so. For these successes, a thanksgiving[1] of twenty days was decreed by the senate upon receiving Cæsar's letter.

[1] In addition to the note at the end of the 2d Book of these Commentaries, it may be here remarked, that Livy, lib. iii., c. lxiii., gives an instance in which two victories over the Sabines having been included in one day's "supplicatio," by the senate, the people, indignant at it, of their own accord, celebrated the following day with still greater solemnity than they had that appointed by the state.

BOOK V.

THE ARGUMENT.

I. Cæsar orders a large fleet of peculiarly constructed ships to be built; proceeds against the Pirustæ; they submit. II. Returns into Hither Gaul; marches against the Treviri. III. Indutiomarus and Cingetorix. V. Cæsar goes to port Itius; his policy in taking certain Gallic chieftains with him to Britain. VI. Dumnorix, who was to have been in that number, by craft and violence, escapes attending Cæsar, but is slain. VII. Cæsar proceeds on his second expedition against Britain. IX. The bold resistance of the Britons; they are defeated. X. The Roman fleet suffers severely in a storm. XI. Cæsar gives orders to Labienus to build more ships; Cassivellaunus. XII.-XIV. Description of Britain and its inhabitants. XVII. The Britons again prepare for war, and receive a signal defeat. XVIII. Cæsar advances into the territories of Cassivellaunus as far as the Thames; an engagement with that prince. XIX. The stratagem of Cassivellaunus. XX. The Trinobantes send embassadors to Cæsar respecting the conduct of Cassivellaunus toward Mandubratius. XXII. The latter induces four princes of Cantium to attack the Romans, by whom they are defeated. XXIII. Cæsar receives hostages, and leads back his army into Gaul. XXIV. He quarters his forces, contrary to his custom, in several divisions. XXV. Tasgetius. XXVI The revolt of Ambiorix and Cativolcus. XXVII. Ambiorix defends himself in reference to his share in the Gallic combination. XXVIII.-XXXI. Dispute between Titurius and Cotta. XXXII. The valor and conduct of Cotta. XXXVIII.-XLII. The quarters of Cicero attacked by the Eburones; he sends intelligence to Cæsar. XLIV. The noble conduct of Pulfio and Varenus. XLVIII.-LII. Cæsar marches to the relief of Cicero; defeats the Enbrones: LIII. Indutiomarus is thereby deterred from attacking the camp of Labienus. LVI.-LVIII. Reinforced, Indutiomarus attacks Labienus; his forces are routed, and he is slain; Gaul becomes more tranquil.

CHAP. I.—Lucius Domitius and Appius Claudius being consuls,[1] Cæsar, when departing from his winter quarters into Italy, as he had been accustomed to do yearly, commands the lieutenants whom he appointed over the legions to take care that during the winter as many ships as possible should be built, and the old repaired. He plans the size and shape

[1] This was 700 years after the building of Rome.

of them. For dispatch of lading, and for drawing them on shore,[1] he makes them a little lower than those which we have been accustomed to use in our sea; and that so much the more, because he knew that, on account of the frequent changes of the tide, less swells occurred there; for the purpose of transporting burdens and a great number of horses,[2] [he makes them] a little broader than those which we use in other seas. All these he orders to be constructed for lightness and expedition,[3] to which object their lowness contributes greatly. He orders those things which are necessary for equipping ships to be brought thither from Spain. He himself, on the assizes of Hither Gaul being concluded, proceeds into Illyricum, because he heard that the part of the province nearest them was being laid waste by the incursions of the Pirustæ. When he had arrived there, he levies soldiers upon the states, and orders them to assemble at an appointed place. Which circumstance having been reported [to them], the Pirustæ send embassadors to him to inform him that no part of those proceedings was done by public deliberation, and assert that they were ready to make compensation by all means for the injuries [inflicted]. Cæsar, accepting their defense, demands hostages, and orders them to be brought to him on a specified day, and assures them that unless they did so he would visit their state with war. These being brought to him on the day which he had ordered, he appoints arbitrators between the states, who should estimate the damages and determine the reparation.

CHAP. II.—These things being finished, and the assizes being concluded, he returns into Hither Gaul, and proceeds thence to the army. When he had arrived there, having made a survey of the winter quarter, he finds that, by the extraordinary ardor of the soldiers, amid the utmost scarcity of all materials, about six hundred ships of that kind which we have described above, and twenty-eight ships of war, had been built,[4]

[1] This refers to the ancient practice of drawing ships on to the shore for the winter, or on other occasions.

[2] "Jumentorum." Horses seem here to be *especially* meant. "Equi et alia jumenta."—Livy.

[3] "Constructed for lightness," etc. The original, *actuarias*, is a distinctive term for a class of ships, the character of which the above translation conveys, but for which we have no established corresponding expression.

[4] "Built and were," etc. Though *in*built, *structas*, they were not

and were not far from that state, that they might be launched in a few days. Having commended the soldiers and those who had presided over the work, he informs them what he wishes to be done, and orders all the ships to assemble at port Itius,[1] from which port he had learned that the passage into Britain was shortest, [being only] about thirty miles from the continent. He left what seemed a sufficient number of soldiers for that design; he himself proceeds into the territories of the Treviri with four legions without baggage, and 800 horse, because they neither came to the general diets [of Gaul], nor obeyed his commands, and were moreover, said to be tampering with the Germans beyond the Rhine.

CHAP. III.—This state is by far the most powerful of all Gaul in cavalry, and has great forces of infantry, and as we have remarked above, borders on the Rhine. In that state, two persons, Indutiomărus[2] and Cingetorix, were then contending with each other[3] for the supreme power; one of whom, as soon as the arrival of Cæsar and his legions was known, came to him; assures him that he and all his party would continue in their allegiance, and not revolt from the alliance of the Roman people, and informs him of the things which were going on among the Treviri. But Indutiomărus began to collect cavalry and infantry, and make preparations for war, having concealed those who by reason of their age could not be under arms, in the forest Arduenna, which is of immense size, [and] extends from the Rhine across the country of the Treviri to the frontiers of the Remi. But after that, some of the chief persons of the state, both influenced by their friendship for Cingetorix, and alarmed at the arrival of our army, came to Cæsar and began to solicit him privately about their own interests, since they could not provide for the safety of the state; Indutiomărus, dreading lest he should be abandoned by all, sends embassadors to Cæsar, to declare that he absented himself from his countrymen, and refrained from coming to him[4] on this account, that he might the more easily

completely equipped with all necessary naval appointments, their *arma* or *armamenta*.

1 "Port Itius," some take this to be *Wissant;* others, *Boulogne.*

2 This is the person so named in Cicero's Oration for Fonteius.

3 Lit. "between themselves."

4 That is, he did not join those Gauls who attended on Cæsar at the provincial diets, for the reason following.

keep the state in its allegiance, lest on the departure of all the nobility the commonalty should, in their indiscretion, revolt. And thus the whole state was at his control; and that he, if Cæsar would permit, would come to the camp to him, and would commit his own fortunes and those of the state to his good faith.

CHAP. IV.—Cæsar, though he discerned from what motive these things were said, and what circumstances deterred him from his meditated plan, still, in order that he might not be compelled to waste the summer among the Treviri, while all things were prepared for the war with Britain, ordered Indutiomărus to come to him with 200 hostages. When these were brought, [and] among them his son and near relations, whom he had demanded by name, he consoled Indutiomărus, and enjoined him to continue in his allegiance; yet, nevertheless, summoning to him the chief men of the Treviri, he reconciled them individually to Cingetorix: this he both thought should be done by him in justice to the merits of the latter, and also judged that it was of great importance that the influence of one whose singular attachment toward him he had fully seen, should prevail as much as possible among his people. Indutiomărus was very much offended at this act, [seeing that] his influence was diminished among his countrymen; and he, who already before had borne a hostile mind toward us, was much more violently inflamed against us through resentment at this.

CHAP. V.—These matters being settled, Cæsar went to port Itius with the legions. There he discovers that forty ships, which had been built in the country of the Meldi,[1] having been driven back by a storm, had been unable to maintain their course, and had returned to the same port from which they had set out; he finds the rest ready for sailing, and furnished with every thing. In the same place, the cavalry of the whole of Gaul, in number 4,000, assembles, and [also] the chief persons of all the states; he had determined to leave in Gaul a very few of them, whose fidelity toward him he had clearly discerned, and take the rest with him as hostages; because he feared a commotion in Gaul when he should be absent.

[1] "In Meldis." Some copies have "*in Belgis;*" a reading not so probable as the former

Chap. VI.—There was together with the others, Dumnorix, the Æduan, of whom we have made previous mention. Him, in particular, he had resolved to have with him, because he had discovered him to be fond of change, fond of power, possessing great resolution, and great influence among the Gauls. To this was added, that Dumnorix had before said in an assembly of Æduans, that the sovereignty of the state had been made over to him by Cæsar; which speech the Ædui bore with impatience and yet dared not send embassadors to Cæsar for the purpose of either rejecting or deprecating [that appointment]. That fact Cæsar had learned from his own personal friends.[1] He at first strove to obtain by every entreaty that he should be left in Gaul; partly, because, being unaccustomed to sailing, he feared the sea; partly, because he said he was prevented by divine admonitions.[2] After he saw that this request was firmly refused him, all hope of success being lost, he began to tamper with the chief persons of the Gauls, to call them apart singly and exhort them to remain on the continent; to agitate them with the fear that it was not without reason that Gaul should be stripped of all her nobility; that it was Cæsar's design, to bring over to Britain and put to death all those whom he feared to slay in the sight of Gaul, to pledge his honor to the rest, to ask for their oath that they would by common deliberation execute what they should perceive to be necessary for Gaul. These things were reported to Cæsar by several persons.

Chap. VII.—Having learned this fact, Cæsar, because he had conferred so much honor upon the Æduan state, determined that Dumnorix should be restrained and deterred by whatever means he could; and that, because he perceived his insane designs to be proceeding further and further, care should be taken lest he might be able to injure him and the commonwealth. Therefore, having stayed about twenty-five days in that place, because the north wind, which usually blows a great part of every season, prevented the voyage, he exerted himself to keep Dumnorix in his allegiance [and] nevertheless learn all

1 "Ex suis hospitibus:" Those between whom and Cæsar there existed the much-reverenced bond of *hospitium*, already spoken of in these notes.

2 "Religionibus:" not, probably, in reference to engagement in any religious solemnities then celebrating, or to be celebrated; but to presentiments, omens, or auguries.

his measures: having at length met with favorable weather, he orders the foot soldiers[1] and the horse to embark in the ships. But, while the minds of all were occupied, Dumnorix began to take his departure from the camp homeward with the cavalry of the Ædui, Cæsar being ignorant of it. Cæsar, on this matter being reported to him, ceasing from his expedition and deferring all other affairs, sends a great part of the cavalry to pursue him, and commands that he be brought back; he orders that if he use violence and do not submit, that he be slain; considering that Dumnorix would do nothing as a rational man while he himself was absent, since he had disregarded his command even when present. He, however, when recalled, began to resist and defend himself with his hand,[2] and implore the support of his people, often exclaiming that "he was free and the subject of a free state."[3] They surround and kill the man as they had been commanded; but the Æduan horsemen all return to Cæsar.

CHAP. VIII.—When these things were done [and] Labienus, left on the continent with three legions and 2,000 horse, to defend the harbors and provide corn, and discover what was going on in Gaul, and take measures according to the occasion and according to the circumstance; he himself, with five legions and a number of horse, equal to that which he was leaving on the continent, set sail at sun-set, and [though for a time] borne forward by a gentle south-west wind, he did not maintain his course, in consequence of the wind dying away about midnight, and being carried on too far by the tide, when the sun rose, espied Britain passed on his left. Then, again, following the change of tide, he urged on with the oars that he might make that part of the island in which he had discovered the preceding summer, that there was the best landing-place, and in this affair the spirit of our soldiers was very much to be extolled; for they with the transports and heavy ships, the labor of rowing not being [for a moment] discontinued, equaled the speed of the ships of war. All the ships reached Britain

[1] "Milites." A Roman army was composed principally of infantry. Hence, *milites* was used to denote, by way of eminence, that larger and more important division of their service.

[2] "Manu;" with active and determined resistance.

[3] The Æduan state had not been reduced into the form of province.

nearly at mid-day; nor was there seen a [single] enemy in that place, but, as Cæsar afterward found from some prisoners, though large bodies of troops had assembled there, yet being alarmed by the great number of our ships, more than eight hundred of which, including the ships of the preceding year,[1] and those private vessels which each had built for his own convenience, had appeared at one time, they had quitted the coast and concealed themselves among the higher points.

Chap. IX.—Cæsar, having disembarked his army and chosen a convenient place for the camp, when he discovered from the prisoners in what part the forces of the enemy had lodged themselves, having left ten cohorts and 300 horse at the sea, to be a guard to the ships, hastens to the enemy, at the third watch,[2] fearing the less for the ships, for this reason because he was leaving them fastened at anchor upon an even and open shore; and he placed Q. Atrius over the guard of the ships. He himself, having advanced by night about twelve miles, espied the forces of the enemy. They, advancing to the river with their cavalry and chariots from the higher ground, began to annoy our men and give battle. Being repulsed by our cavalry, they concealed themselves in woods, as they had secured a place admirably fortified by nature and by art, which, as it seemed, they had before prepared on account of a civil war; for all entrances to it were shut up by a great number of felled trees. They themselves rushed out of the woods to fight here and there,[3] and prevented our men from entering their fortifications. But the soldiers of the seventh legion, having formed a testudo and thrown up a rampart against the fortification, took the place and drove them out of the woods, receiving only a few wounds. But Cæsar forbade his men to pursue them in ther flight any great distance;[4] both because he was ignorant of the nature of the ground, and because, as a great part of the day was spent, he wished time to be left for the fortification of the camp.

1 "Cum annotinis." Some copies have *annonariis*, *provision-ships*, from *annona*. The correct reading seems to be that of Oudendorp and others, as quoted and translated above. The Greek paraphrast has σὺν ταῖς τοῦ πρόσθεν ἔτους.

2 See the note, book i., ch. xxi.

3 "Here and there:" rari, in small detached parties.

4 "Longius." The comparative degree has often this sense.

CHAP. X.—The next day, early in the morning, he sent both foot-soldiers and horse in three divisions on an expedition to pursue those who had fled. These having advanced a little way, when already the rear [of the enemy] was in sight, some horse came to Cæsar from Quintus Atrius, to report that the preceding night, a very great storm having arisen, almost all the ships were dashed to pieces and cast upon the shore, because neither the anchors and cables could resist, nor could the sailors and pilots sustain the violence of the storm; and thus great damage was received by that collision of the ships.

CHAP. XI.—These things being known [to him], Cæsar orders the legions and cavalry to be recalled and to cease from their march; he himself returns to the ships: he sees clearly before him almost the same things which he had heard of from the messengers and by letter, so that, about forty ships being lost, the remainder seemed capable of being repaired with much labor. Therefore he selects workmen from the legions, and orders others to be sent for from the continent; he writes to Labienus to build as many ships as he could with those legions which were with him. He himself, though the matter was one of great difficulty and labor, yet thought it to be most expedient for all the ships to be brought up on shore and joined with the camp by one fortification. In these matters he employed about ten days, the labor of the soldiers being unremitting even during the hours of night. The ships having been brought up on shore and the camp strongly[1] fortified, he left the same forces as he did before as a guard for the ships; he sets out in person for the same place that he had returned from. When he had come thither, greater forces of the Britons had already assembled at that place, the chief command and management of the war having been intrusted to Cassivellaunus, whose territories a river, which is called the Thames, separates, from the maritime states at about eighty miles from the sea. At an earlier period perpetual wars had taken place between him and the other states; but, greatly alarmed by our arrival, the Britons had placed him over the whole war and the conduct of it.

CHAP. XII.—The interior portion of Britain is inhabited by those of whom they say that it is handed down by tradition

[1] "Egregiè," here does not mean *eminently*, or *peculiarly*; but simply, *with* great *attention, admirably*.

that they were born in the island itself:[1] the maritime portion by those who had passed over from the country of the Belgæ for the purpose of plunder and making war; almost all of whom are called by the names of those states from which being sprung they went thither, and having waged war, continued there and began to cultivate the lands. The number of the people is countless, and their buildings exceedingly numerous, for the most part very like those of the Gauls: the number of cattle is great. They use either brass[2] or iron rings, determined at a certain weight, as their money. Tin is produced in the midland regions; in the maritime, iron; but the quantity of it is small: they employ brass, which is imported. There, as in Gaul, is timber of every description, except beech and fir. They do not regard it lawful[3] to eat the hare, and the cock, and the goose; they, however, breed them for amusement and pleasure. The climate is more temperate than in Gaul, the colds being less severe.

CHAP. XIII.—The island is triangular in its form, and one of its sides is opposite to Gaul. One angle of this side, which is in Kent, whither almost all ships from Gaul are directed, [looks] to the east; the lower looks to the south. This side extends about 500 miles. Another side lies toward Spain[4] and the west, on which part is Ireland, less, as is reckoned, than Britain, by one half: but the passage [from it] into Britain is of equal distance with that from Gaul. In the middle of this voyage, is an island, which is called Mona:[5] many smaller islands besides are supposed to lie [there], of which islands some have written that at the time of the winter solstice it is night there for thirty consecutive days. We, in our inquiries about that matter, ascertained nothing, except that, by accurate measurements with water,[6] we per-

[1] "Quos natos in insula ipsa memoria proditum dicunt:" *i. e.* that they were those whom the Greek writers call αὐτοχθόνες; aborigines; descendants from the first inhabitants. *Memoria* denotes either *written record*, or *traditionary report*. Here it denotes the latter.

[2] Tacitus, in his life of Agricola, mentions silver and gold as the productions of Britain.

[3] The *nefas*, or impiety of eating those animals does not appear, however, to arise from their having been victims offered in sacrifice.

[4] This statement of Cæsar's is incorrect, as Spain lies to the south, not to the west of Britain.

[5] "Mona," the isle of Man. Tacitus applies this name to Anglesey. Annal. xiv. 29.

[6] The instrument used for this purpose was called *clepsydra*. Vegetius

ceived the nights to be shorter there than on the continent. The length of this side, as their account states, is 700 miles. The third side is toward the north, to which portion of the island no land is opposite; but an angle of that side looks principally toward Germany. This side is considered to be 800 miles in length. Thus the whole island is [about] 2,000 miles in circumference.

CHAP. XIV.—The most civilized of all these nations are they who inhabit Kent, which is entirely a maritime district, nor do they differ much from the Gallic customs. Most of the inland inhabitants do not sow corn, but live on milk and flesh, and are clad with skins. All the Britains, indeed, dye themselves[1] with wood, which occasions a bluish color, and thereby have a more terrible appearance in fight. They wear their hair long, and have every part of their body shaved except their head and upper lip. Ten and even twelve have wives common to them, and particularly brothers among brothers, and parents among their children; but if there be any issue by these wives, they are reputed to be the children of those by whom respectively each was first espoused when a virgin.

CHAP. XV.—The horse and charioteers of the enemy contended vigorously in a skirmish with our cavalry on the march; yet so that our men were conquerors in all parts, and drove them to their woods and hills; but, having slain a great many, they pursued too eagerly, and lost some of their men. But the enemy, after some time had elapsed, when our men were off their guard, and occupied in the fortification of the camp, rushed out of the woods, and making an attack upon those who were placed on duty before the camp, fought in a determined manner; and two cohorts being sent by Cæsar to their relief, and these severally the first of two legions, when these had taken up their position at a very small distance from each other, as our men were disconcerted by the unusual mode of battle, the enemy broke through the middle of them most

tells us that they were commonly used in the army. They were also used at the bar to measure the time allowed to the several advocates for speaking. Sand-glasses (which resemble them in form), were once used in England to limit the time which public speakers designed to allow themselves.

[1] Pomponius Mela and Pliny have related the same thing.

courageously, and retreated thence in safety. That day, Q. Laberius Durus, a tribune of the soldiers, was slain. The enemy, since more cohorts were sent against them, were repulsed.

CHAP. XVI.—In the whole of this method of fighting since the engagement took place under the eyes of all and before the camp, it was perceived that our men, on account of the weight of their arms, inasmuch as they could neither pursue [the enemy when] retreating, nor dare quit their standards, were little suited to this kind of enemy; that the horse also fought with great danger, because they [the Britons] generally retreated even designedly, and, when they had drawn off our men a short distance from the legions, leaped from their chariots aad fought on foot in unequal [and to them advantageous] battle. But the system of cavalry engagement is wont to produce equal danger, and indeed the same, both to those who retreat and to those who pursue. To this was added, that they never fought in close order, but in small parties and at great distances, and had detachments placed [in different parts], and then the one relieved the other, and the vigorous and fresh succeeded the wearied.

CHAP. XVII.—The following day the enemy halted on the hills, a distance from our camp, and presented themselves in small parties, and began to challenge our horse to battle with less spirit than the day before. But at noon, when Cæsar had sent three legions, and all the cavalry, with C. Trebonius, the lieutenant, for the purpose of foraging, they flew upon the foragers suddenly from all quarters, so that they did not keep off [even] from the standards and the legions. Our men making an attack on them vigorously, repulsed them; nor did they cease to pursue them until the horse, relying on relief, as they saw the legions behind them, drove the enemy precipitately before them, and slaying a great number of them, did not give them the opportunity either of rallying, or halting, or leaping from their chariots. Immediately after this retreat, the auxiliaries who had assembled from all sides, departed; nor after that time did the enemy ever engage with us in very large numbers.

CHAP. XVIII.—Cæsar, discovering their design, leads his army into the territories of Cassivellaunus to the river Thames; which river can be forded in one place only, and that with difficulty. When he had arrived there, he perceives that numerous forces of the enemy were marshaled on the other bank of the river; the bank also was defended by sharp stakes[1] fixed in front, and stakes of the same kind fixed under the water were covered by the river. These things being discovered from [some] prisoners and deserters, Cæsar, sending forward the cavalry, ordered the legions to follow them immediately. But the soldiers advanced with such speed and such ardor, though they stood above the water by their heads only, that the enemy could not sustain the attack of the legions and of the horse, and quitted the banks, and committed themselves to flight.

CHAP. XIX.—Cassivellaunus, as we have stated above, all hope [rising out] of battle being laid aside, the greater part of his forces being dismissed, and about 4,000 charioteers only being left, used to observe our marches and retire a little from the road, and conceal himself in intricate and woody places, and in those neighborhoods in which he had discovered we were about to march, he used to drive the cattle and the inhabitants from the fields into the woods; and, when our cavalry, for the sake of plundering and ravaging the more freely, scattered themselves among the fields, he used to send out charioteers from the woods by all the well-known roads and paths, and to the great danger of our horse, engage with them; and this source of fear hindered them from straggling very extensively. The result was[2] that Cæsar did not allow excursions to be made to a great distance from the main body of the legions, and ordered that damage should be done to the enemy in ravaging their lands, and kindling fires only so far as the legionary soldiers could, by their own exertion and marching, accomplish it.

CHAP. XX.—In the mean time, the Trinobantes,[3] almost the most powerful state of those parts, from which the young man, Mandubratius embracing the protection of Cæsar had come to the continent of Gaul to [meet] him (whose father, Imanuentius, had possessed the sovereignty in that state, and

[1] Bede, the learned and devout monk of the noble Benedictine monastery of Yarrow (8th century), so deservedly called "the venerable Bede," states that the remains of these stakes existed in his time.

[2] "Relinquebatur." Literally, "it remained."

[3] The territories of the Trinobantes comprehended Essex and Middlesex.

had been killed by Cassivellaunus; he himself had escaped death by flight), send embassadors to Cæsar, and promise that they will surrender themselves to him and perform his commands; they entreat him to protect Mandubratius from the violence of Cassivellaunus, and send to their state some one to preside over it, and possess the government. Cæsar demands forty hostages from them, and corn for his army, and sends Mandubratius to them. They speedily performed the things demanded, and sent hostages to the number appointed, and the corn.

CHAP. XXI.—The Trinobantes being protected and secured from any violence of the soldiers, the Cenimagni, the Segontiăci, the Ancalites, the Bibrŏci, and the Cassi, sending embassies, surrendered themselves to Cæsar.[1] From them he

[1] Tacitus says that Britain was rather surveyed than reduced, by Cæsar; claiming for his father-in-law, Agricola, the honor of the conquest. The Roman arms, it need scarcely be remarked, owe much to the military virtues of Agricola, as displayed here; but Cæsar did what no one had done before him, he levied a tribute upon the Britons, and effectually paved the way for all that Rome subsequently accomplished in this island.

The following may be given as a very brief and general account of the condition of Britain in relation to the Romans during the period of the twelve Cæsars. Augustus and Tiberius, from motives of policy, rested satisfied with the achievements of their predecessor, Julius, there. Nor did it suffer any thing at the hands of Caligula, who merely proposed, but did not attempt to execute, a design upon it. Legions and auxiliaries were introduced by Claudius, who, after absurdly arrogating to himself the honors of victory, sent thither, first Aulius Plautus, and afterward Ostorius, as proprætor or governor. This latter overthrew Caractacus, and led him in triumph at Rome—a spectacle, says Tacitus, Annal. book xii. 38, which the senators pronounced to be no less glorious than when P. Scipio exhibited Syphax, or L. Paulus paraded the Macedonian Perseus in the streets of that city. Britain was next under the governorship of Didius Gallus, who, infirm by age and contented with his present glory, left matters as he received them from his predecessors in the command. It was next governed by Veranus, a man of a stern and, it would seem, boastful temper. He died after holding his office about one year. Under the proprætorship of Suetonius Paulinus, who succeeded Veranus, Anglesey was invaded, and the Iceni, under the conduct of their renowned queen, Boadicea, were signally defeated. His discipline in Britain gave offense, and Petronius Turpilianus was appointed to succeed him. His sway was very mild. Many, also, were the indulgences of the Britons under his successor, Trebellius Maximus. Nor had they any reason to complain of the severity of their next governor, Vectius Bolanus. Petilius Cærealis, who succeeded him, sought to remedy the evils which the

learns that the capital town of Cassivellaunus was not far from that place, and was defended by woods and morasses, and a very large number of men and of cattle had been collected in it. (Now the Britons, when they have fortified the intricate woods, in which they are wont to assemble for the purpose of avoiding the incursion of an enemy, with an intrenchment and a rampart, call them a town.) Thither he proceeds with his legions: he finds the place admirably fortified by nature and art; he, however, undertakes to attack it in two directions. The enemy, having remained only a short time, did not sustain the attack of our soldiers, and hurried away on the other side of the town. A great amount of cattle was found there, and many of the enemy were taken and slain in their flight.

CHAP. XXII.—While these things are going forward in those places, Cassivellaunus sends messengers into Kent, which, we have observed above, is on the sea, over which districts four several kings reigned, Cingetorix, Carvilius, Taximagŭlus and Segŏnax, and commands them to collect all their forces, and unexpectedly assail and storm the naval camp. When they had come to the camp, our men, after making a sally, slaying many of their men, and also capturing a distinguished leader named Lugotorix, brought back their own men in safety. Cassivellaunus, when this battle was reported to him as so many losses had been sustained, and his territories laid waste, being alarmed most of all by the desertion of the states, sends embassadors to Cæsar [to treat] about a surrender through the mediation of Commius the Atrebatian. Cæsar, since he had determined to pass the winter on the continent, on account of the sudden revolts of Gaul, and as much of the summer did not remain, and he perceived that even that could be easily protracted, demands hostages, and prescribes what tribute Britain should pay each year to the Roman people; he forbids and commands Cassivellaunus that he wage not war against Mandubratius or the Trinobantes.

laxity of the last three had induced; and under him the Brigantes were subdued. Britain was next governed by Julius Frontinus, who conquered the Silures. Then came Agricola of whom it has been said that "he was as fortunate in many battles against the Britons as he was unhappy in his reward;" for Domitian, having become envious of his fame, recalled him from his propraetorship, and, as is reported, afterward procured his death by poison.

CHAP. XXIII.—When he had received the hostages, he leads back the army to the sea, and finds the ships repaired. After launching these, because he had a large number of prisoners, and some of the ships had been lost in the storm, he determines to convey back his army at two embarkations. And it so happened, that out of so large a number of ships, in so many voyages, neither in this nor in the previous year was any ship missing which conveyed soldiers; but very few out of those which were sent back to him from the continent empty, as the soldiers of the former convoy had been disembarked, and out of those (sixty in number) which Labienus had taken care to have built, reached their destination; almost all the rest were driven back, and when Cæsar had waited for them for some time in vain, lest he should be debarred from a voyage by the season of the year, inasmuch as the equinox was at hand, he of necessity stowed his soldiers the more closely, and, a very great calm coming on, after he had weighed anchor at the beginning of the second watch, he reached land at break of day and brought in all the ships in safety.

CHAP. XXIV.—The ships having been drawn up and a general assembly of the Gauls held at Samarobriva, because the corn that year had not prospered in Gaul by reason of the droughts, he was compelled to station his army in its winter-quarters differently from the former years, and to distribute the legions among several states: one of them he gave to C. Fabius, his lieutenant, to be marched into the territories of the Morini; a second to Q. Cicero, into those of the Nervii; a third to L. Roscius, into those of the Essui; a fourth he ordered to winter with T. Labienus among the Remi in the confines of the Treviri; he stationed three in Belgium; over these he appointed M. Crassus, his questor, and L. Munatius Plancus and C. Trebonius, his lieutenants. One legion which he had raised last on the other side of the Po, and five cohorts, he sent among the Eburones, the greatest portion of whom lie between the Meuse and the Rhine, [and] who were under the government of Ambiorix and Cativolcus. He ordered Q. Titurius Sabinus and L. Aurunculeius Cotta, his lieutenants, to take command of these soldiers. The legions being distributed in this manner, he thought he could most easily remedy the scarcity of corn; and yet the winter-quarters of all these legions (except that which he had given to L. Roscius, to be led into the most peaceful and tranquil neighborhood) were comprehended within [about] 100 miles.[1] He himself in the mean while, until he had stationed the legions and knew that the several winter-quarters were fortified, determined to stay in Gaul.

CHAP. XXV.—There was among the Carnutes a man named Tasgetius, born of very high rank, whose ancestors had held the sovereignty in his state. To him Cæsar had restored the position of his ancestors, in consideration of his prowess and attachment toward him, because in all his wars he had availed himself of his valuable services. His personal enemies had killed him when in the third year of his reign, many even of his own state being openly promoters [of that act]. This event is related to Cæsar. He fearing, because several were involved in the act, that the state might revolt at their instigation, orders Lucius Plancus, with a legion, to proceed quickly from Belgium to the Carnutes, and winter there, and arrest and send to him the persons by whose instrumentality he should discover that Tasgetius was slain. In the mean time, he was apprised by all the lieutenants and questors to whom he had assigned the legions, that they had arrived in winter-quarters, and that the place for the quarters was fortified.

CHAP. XXVI.—About fifteen days after they had come into winter-quarters, the beginning of a sudden insurrection and revolt arose from Ambiorix and Cativolcus, who, though they had met with Sabinus and Cotta at the borders of their kingdom, and had conveyed corn into our winter-quarters, induced by the messages of Indutiomărus, one of the Treviri, excited their people, and after having suddenly assailed the soldiers engaged in procuring wood, came with a large body to attack the camp. When our men had speedily taken up arms and had ascended the rampart, and sending out some Spanish horse on one side, had proved conquerors in a cavalry action, the enemy, despairing of success, drew off their troops from the assault. Then they shouted, according to their custom,

[1] There must be an error (whatever be the occasion of it), in this statement of the space intervening between the two *extreme* encampments. The distance from that among the Eburones to that spoken of as being in *Belgium*, would be about 180 miles.

that some of our men should go forward to a conference, [alleging] that they had some things which they desired to say respecting the common interest, by which they trusted their disputes could be removed.

CHAP. XXVII.—C. Arpineius, a Roman knight, the intimate friend of Q. Titurius, and with him, Q. Junius, a certain person from Spain, who already on previous occasions, had been accustomed to go to Ambiorix, at Cæsar's mission, is sent to them for the purpose of a conference: before them Ambiorix spoke to this effect: "That he confessed, that for Cæsar's kindness toward him, he was very much indebted to him, inasmuch as by his aid he had been freed from a tribute which he had been accustomed to pay to the Aduatuci, his neighbors; and because his own son and the son of his brother had been sent back to him, whom, when sent in the number of hostages, the Aduatuci had detained among them in slavery and in chains; and that he had not done that which he had done in regard to the attacking of the camp, either by his own judgment or desire, but by the compulsion of his state; and that his government was of that nature, that the people had as much authority over him as he over the people. To the state moreover the occasion of the war was this—that it could not withstand the sudden combination of the Gauls; that he could easily prove this from his own weakness, since he was not so little versed in affairs as to presume that with his forces he could conquer the Roman people; but that it was the common resolution of Gaul; that that day was appointed for the storming of all Cæsar's winter-quarters, in order that no legion should be able to come to the relief of another legion, that Gauls could not easily deny Gauls, especially when a measure seemed entered into for recovering their common freedom. Since he had performed his duty to them on the score of patriotism [he said], he has now regard to gratitude for the kindness of Cæsar; that he warned, that he prayed Titurius by the claims of hospitality, to consult for his and his soldiers' safety; that a large force of the Germans had been hired and had passed the Rhine; that it would arrive in two days: that it was for them to consider whether they thought fit, before the nearest people perceived it, to lead off their soldiers when drawn out of winter-quarters, either to Cicero or to Labienus; one of whom was about fifty miles distant from them, the other rather more;

that this he promised and confirmed by oath, that he would give them a safe passage through his territories; and when he did that, he was both consulting for his own state, because it would be relieved from the winter-quarters, and also making a requital to Cæsar for his obligations."

CHAP. XXVIII.—Arpineius and Junius relate to the lieutenants what they had heard. They, greatly alarmed by the unexpected affair, though those things were spoken by an enemy, still thought they were not to be disregarded; and they were especially influenced by this consideration, that it was scarcely credible that the obscure and humble state of the Eburones had dared to make war upon the Roman people of their own accord. Accordingly, they refer the matter to a council, and a great controversy arises among them. L. Aurunculeius, and several tribunes of the soldiers and the centurions of the first rank, were of opinion "that nothing should be done hastily, and that they should not depart from the camp without Cæsar's orders;" they declared, "that any forces of the Germans, however great, might be encountered by fortified winter-quarters; that this fact was a proof [of it]; that they had sustained the first assault of the Germans most valiantly, inflicting many wounds upon them; that they were not distressed for corn; that in the mean time relief would come both from the nearest winter-quarters and from Cæsar; lastly, they put the query, "what could be more undetermined, more undignified, than to adopt measures respecting the most important affairs on the authority of an enemy?"

CHAP. XXIX.—In opposition to these things, Titurius exclaimed, "That they would do this too late, when greater forces of the enemy, after a junction with the Germans, should have assembled; or when some disaster had been received in the neighboring winter-quarters; that the opportunity for deliberating was short; that he believed that Cæsar had set forth into Italy, as the Carnutes would not otherwise have taken the measure of slaying Tasgetius, nor would the Eburones, if he had been present, have come to the camp with so great defiance of us; that he did not regard the enemy, but the fact, as the authority; that the Rhine was near; that the death of Ariovistus and our previous victories were subjects of great indignation to the Germans; that Gaul was inflamed, that after having received so many defeats she was reduced under the sway of the Roman people, her pristine glory in military matters being extinguished." Lastly, "who would persuade himself of this, that Ambiorix had resorted to a design of that nature without sure grounds? That his own opinion was safe on either side; if there be nothing very formidable, they would go without danger to the nearest legion; if all Gaul conspired with the Germans, their only safety lay in dispatch. What issue would the advice of Cotta and of those who differed from him, have? from which, if immediate danger was not to be dreaded, yet certainly famine, by a protracted siege, was."

CHAP. XXX.—This discussion having been held on the two sides, when opposition was offered strenuously by Cotta and the principal officers, "Prevail," said Sabinus, "if so you wish it;" and he said it with a louder voice, that a great portion of the soldiers might hear him; "nor am I the person among you," he said, "who is most powerfully alarmed by the danger of death; these will be aware of it, and then, if any thing disastrous shall have occurred, they will demand a reckoning at your hands; these, who, if it were permitted by you, united three days hence with the nearest winter-quarters, may encounter the common condition of war with the rest, and not, as if forced away and separated far from the rest, perish either by the sword or by famine."

CHAP. XXXI.—They rise from the council, detain both, and entreat, that "they do not bring the matter into the greatest jeopardy by their dissension and obstinacy; the affair was an easy one, if only they all thought and approved of the same thing, whether they remain or depart; on the other hand, they saw no security in dissension." The matter is prolonged by debate till midnight. At last Cotta, being overruled, yields his assent;[1] the opinion of Sabinus prevails. It is proclaimed that they will march at day-break; the remainder of the night is spent without sleep, since every soldier was inspecting his property, [to see] what he could carry with him, and what, out of the appurtenances of the winter-quarters, he

[1] "Dat manus," lit. *gives his hands;* an expression derived from the attitude of the vanquished when holding out their hands in the form of supplication (more generally, however, *tendens* than *dans manus*), or to receive their chains, which, at once, sealed their submission and preserved their lives.

would be compelled to leave; every reason is suggested to show why they could not stay without danger, and how that danger would be increased by the fatigue of the soldiers and their want of sleep. At break of day they quit the camp, in a very extended line and with a very large amount of baggage, in such a maner as men who were convinced that the advice was given by Ambiorix, not as an enemy, but as most friendly [toward them].

CHAP. XXXII.—But the enemy, after they had made the discovery of their intended departure by the noise during the night and their not retiring to rest, having placed an ambuscade in two divisions in the woods, in a suitable and concealed place, two miles from the camp, waited for the arrival of the Romans: and when the greater part of the line of march had descended into a considerable valley, they suddenly presented themselves on either side of that valley, and began both to harass the rear and hinder the van from ascending, and to give battle in a place exceedingly disadvantageous to our men.

CHAP. XXXIII.—Then at length Titurius, as one who had provided nothing beforehand, was confused, ran to and fro, and set about arranging his troops; these very things, however, he did timidly and in such a manner that all resources seemed to fail him: which generally happens to those who are compelled to take council in the action itself. But Cotta, who had reflected that these things might occur on the march, and on that account had not been an adviser of the departure, was wanting to the common safety in no respect; both in addressing and encouraging the soldiers, he performed the duties of a general, and in the battle those of a soldier. And since they [Titurius and Cotta] could less easily perform every thing by themselves, and provide what was to be done in each place, by reason of the length of the line of march, they ordered [the officers] to give the command that they should leave the baggage and form themselves into an orb,[1] which measure, though in a contingency of that nature it was not to be condemned, still turned out unfortunately; for it both diminished the hope of our soldiers and

[1] When surrounded by an enemy, they threw themselves in an order called *orbis*, or *globus*, from its form. This is further referred to in ch. xxxvii. of book iv. of the Gallic peace, and the fifteenth chapter of the African War. The phrases are, *orbem facere*, or, *volvere; in orbem se tutari*, or, *conglobare; in orbem pugnant;* and, upon halting, *in orbem consistunt.*

rendered the enemy more eager for the fight, because it appeared that this was not done without the greatest fear and despair. Besides that happened, which would necessarily be the case, that the soldiers for the most part quitted their ensigns and hurried to seek and carry off from the baggage whatever each thought valuable, and all parts were filled with uproar and lamentation.

CHAP. XXXIV.—But judgment was not wanting to the barbarians; for their leaders ordered [the officers] to proclaim through the ranks "that no man should quit his place; that the booty was theirs, and for them was reserved whatever the Romans should leave; therefore let them consider that all things depended on their victory.[1] Our men were equal to them in fighting, both in courage and in number, and though they were deserted by their leader and by fortune, yet they still placed all hope of safety in their valor, and as often as any cohort sallied forth on that side, a great number of the enemy usually fell. Ambiorix, when he observed this, orders the command to be issued that they throw their weapons from a distance and do not approach too near, and in whatever direction the Romans should make an attack, there give way (from the lightness of their appointments and from their daily practice no damage could be done them); [but] pursue them when betaking themselves to their standards again.

CHAP. XXXV.—Which command having been most carefully obeyed, when any cohort had quitted the circle and made a charge, the enemy fled very precipitately. In the mean time, that part of the Roman army, of necessity, was left unprotected, and the weapons received on their open flank. Again, when they had begun to return to that place from which they had advanced, they were surrounded both by those who had retreated and by those who stood next them; but if, on the other hand, they wish to keep their place, neither was an opportunity left for valor, nor could they, being crowded together, escape the weapons cast by so large a body of men. Yet, though assailed by so many disadvantages, [and] having received many wounds, they withstood the enemy, and, a great portion of the day being spent, though they fought from day-break till the eighth hour, they did nothing which was unworthy of them. At length, each thigh of T. Balventius, who the year before had

[1] "Posita," etc., lit. *lay in*, etc.

been chief centurion,[1] a brave man and one of great authority, is pierced with a javelin; Q. Lucanius, of the same rank, fighting most valiantly, is slain while he assists his son when surrounded by the enemy; L. Cotta, the lieutenant, when encouraging all the cohorts and companies, is wounded full in the mouth by a sling.

CHAP. XXXVI.—Much troubled by these events, Q. Titurius, when he had perceived Ambiorix in the distance encouraging his men, sends to him his interpreter, Cn. Pompey, to beg that he would spare him and his soldiers. He, when addressed, replied, "If he wishes to confer with him, it was permitted; that he hoped what pertained to the safety of the soldiers could be obtained from the people; that to him however certainly no injury would be done, and that he pledged his faith to that effect." He consults with Cotta, who had been wounded, whether it would appear right to retire from battle, and confer with Ambiorix; [saying] that he hoped to be able to succeed respecting his own and the soldiers' safety. Cotta says he will not go to an armed enemy, and in that perseveres.

CHAP. XXXVII.—Sabinus orders those tribunes of the soldiers whom he had at the time around him, and the centurions of the first ranks, to follow him, and when he had approached near to Ambiorix, being ordered to throw down his arms, he obeys the order and commands his men to do the same. In the mean time, while they treat upon the terms, and a longer debate than necessary is designedly entered into by Ambiorix, being surrounded by degrees, he is slain. Then they, according to their custom, shout out "Victory," and raise their war-cry, and, making an attack on our men, break their ranks. There L. Cotta, while figting, is slain, together with the greater part of the soldiers; the rest betake themselves to the camp, from which they had marched forth, and one of them, L. Petrosidius, the standard bearer, when he was operpowered by the great number of the enemy, threw the eagle within the intrenchments and is himself slain while figting with the greatest courage before the camp. They with difficulty sustain the attack till night; despairing of safety, they all to a man destroy themselves in the night. A few escaping from

[1] "Qui primum pilum duxerat." See the note, book ii., ch. xxv.; or book iii., ch. v.

the battle, made their way to Labienus at winter-quarters, after wandering at random through the woods, and inform him of these events.

CHAP. XXXVIII.—Elated by this victory, Ambiorix marches immediately with his cavalry to the Aduatuci, who bordered on his kingdom; he halts neither day nor night, and orders the infantry to follow him closely. Having related the exploit and roused the Aduatuci, the next day he arrived among the Nervii, and entreats "that they should not throw away the opportunity of liberating themselves forever and of punishing the Romans for those wrongs which they had received from them;"[1] [he tells them] "that two lieutenants have been slain, and that a large portion of the army has perished; that it was not a matter of difficulty for the legion which was wintering with Cicero to be cut off, when suddenly assaulted; he declares himself ready to co-operate in that design. He easily gains over the Nervii by this speech.

CHAP. XXXIX.—Accordingly, messengers having been forthwith dispatched to the Centrones, the Grudii, the Levaci, the Pleumoxii, and the Geiduni, all of whom are under their government, they assemble as large bodies as they can, and rush unexpectedly to the winter-quarters of Cicero, the report of the death of Titurius not having as yet been conveyed to him. That also occurred to him, which was the consequence of a necessary work—that some soldiers who had gone off into the woods for the purpose of procuring timber and therewith constructing fortifications, were intercepted by the sudden arrival of [the enemy's] horse. These having been entrapped, the Eburones, the Nervii, and the Aduatici and all their allies and dependants, begin to attack the legion: our men quickly run together to arms and mount the rampart; they sustained the attack that day with great difficulty, since the enemy placed all their hope in dispatch, and felt assured that, if they obtained this victory, they would be conquerors forever.

CHAP. XL.—Letters are immediately sent to Cæsar by Cicero, great rewards being offered [to the messengers] if they carried them through. All these passes having been beset, those who were sent are intercepted. During the night as many as

[1] See a statement of the calamity of the Nervii, made by themselves, book ii. ch. xxviii. For a signal defeat of the Aduatuci, see ch. xxxiii. of the same book.

120 towers are raised with incredible dispatch out of the timber which they had collected for the purpose of fortification: the things which seemed necessary to the work are completed. The following day the enemy, having collected far greater forces, attack the camp [and] fill up the ditch. Resistance is made by our men in the same manner as the day before; this same thing is done afterward during the remaining days. The work is carried on incessantly in the night:[1] not even to the sick, or wounded, is opportunity given for rest: whatever things are required for resisting the assault of the next day are provided during the night: many stakes burned at the end, and a large number of mural pikes are procured: towers are built up, battlements and parapets are formed of interwoven hurdles. Cicero himself, though he was in very weak health, did not leave himself the night-time for repose, so that he was forced to spare himself by the spontaneous movement and entreaties of the soldiers.

CHAP. XLI.—Then these leaders and chiefs of the Nervii, who had any intimacy and grounds of friendship with Cicero, say they desire to confer with him. When permission was granted, they recount the same things which Ambiorix had related to Titurius, namely, "that all Gaul was in arms, that the Germans had passed the Rhine, that the winter-quarters of Cæsar and of the others were attacked." They report in addition also, about the death of Sabinus. They point to Ambiorix for the purpose of obtaining credence; "they are mistaken," say they, "if they hoped for any relief from those who distrust their own affairs; that they bear such feelings toward Cicero and the Roman people that they deny them nothing but winter-quarters, and are unwilling that the practice[2] should become constant; that through their [the Nervii's] means it is possible for them [the Romans] to depart from their winter-quarters safely and to proceed without fear into whatever parts they desire." To these Cicero made only one reply: "that it is not the custom of the Roman people to accept any condition from an armed enemy: if they are willing to lay down their arms, they may employ him as their advocate and send embassadors to Cæsar: that he believed, from his [Cæsar's] justice, they would obtain the things which they might request."

[1] Literally, "No portion of the night-time is intermitted to the work.

[2] The practice of occupying winter-quarters in Gaul.

CHAP. XLII.—Disappointed in this hope, the Nervii surround the winter-quarters with a rampart eleven feet high, and a ditch thirteen feet in depth. These military works they had learned from our men in the intercourse of former years, and, having taken some of our army prisoners, were instructed by them: but, as they had no supply of iron tools which are requisite for this service, they were forced to cut the turf with their swords, and to empty out the earth with their hands and cloaks, from which circumstance, the vast number of the men could be inferred; for in less than three hours they completed a fortification of ten miles in circumference; and during the rest of the days they began to prepare and construct towers of the height of the ramparts, and grappling irons, and mantelets, which the same prisoners had taught them.

CHAP. XLIII.—On the seventh day of the attack, a very high wind having sprung up, they began to discharge by their slings hot balls made of burned or hardened clay, and heated javelins, upon the huts, which, after the Gallic custom, were thatched with straw. These quickly took fire, and by the violence of the wind, scattered their flames in every part of the camp. The enemy following up their success with a very loud shout, as if victory were already obtained and secured, began to advance their towers and mantelets, and climb the rampart with ladders. But so great was the courage of our soldiers, and such their presence of mind, that though they were scorched on all sides, and harassed by a vast number of weapons, and were aware that their baggage and their possessions were burning, not only did no one quit the rampart for the purpose of withdrawing from the scene, but scarcely did any one even then look behind; and they all fought most vigorously and most valiantly. This day was by far the most calamitous to our men; it had this result, however, that on that day the largest number of the enemy was wounded and slain, since they had crowded beneath the very rampart, and the hindmost did not afford the foremost a retreat. The flame having abated a little, and a tower having been brought up in a particular place and touching the rampart, the centurions of the third cohort retired from the place in which they were standing, and drew off all their men: they began to call on the enemy by gestures and by words, to enter if they wished; but none of them dared to advance. Then stones having been cast from every quarter, the enemy were dislodged, and their tower set on fire.

CHAP. XLIV.—In that legion there were two very brave men, centurions, who were now approaching the first ranks, T. Pulfio,[1] and L. Varenus. These used to have continual disputes between them which of them should be preferred, and every year used to contend for promotion with the utmost animosity. When the fight was going on most vigorously before the fortifications, Pulfio, one of them, says, "Why do you hesitate, Varenus? or what [better] opportunity of signalizing your valor do you seek? This very day shall decide our disputes." When he had uttered these words, he proceeds beyond the fortifications, and rushes on that part of the enemy which appeared the thickest. Nor does Varenus remain within the rampart, but respecting the high opinion of all, follows close after. Then, when an inconsiderable space intervened, Pulfio throws his javelin at the enemy, and pierces one of the multitude who was running up, and while the latter was wounded and slain, the enemy cover him with their shields, and all throw their weapons at the other and afford him no opportunity of retreating. The shield of Pulfio is pierced and a javelin is fastened in his belt. This circumstance turns aside his scabbard and obstructs his right hand when attempting to draw his sword: the enemy crowd around him when [thus] embarrassed. His rival runs up to him and succors him in this emergency. Immediately the whole host turn from Pulfio to him, supposing the other to be pierced through by the javelin. Varenus rushes on briskly with his sword and carries on the combat hand to hand, and having slain one man, for a short time drove back the rest: while he urges on too eagerly, slipping into a hollow,[2] he fell. To him, in his turn, when surrounded, Pulfio brings relief; and both having slain

[1] The Delphin annotator here remarks, that, from the circumstances of this Pulfio's having been a strenuous partisan of Pompey, in the civil war, either Cæsar had not leisure to read over his Commentaries and blot out this incident, so favorable to Pulfio; or that having published them before that person's espousal of Pompey's cause, he could not retract it; or, that he was too noble-minded to withhold such a well deserved tribute of praise, even from one who had become his opponent. The annotator, however, does not favor this third supposition.

[2] "In locum dejectus inferiorem concidit."

a great number, retreat into the fortifications amid the highest applause. Fortune so dealt with both in this rivalry and conflict, that the one competitor was a succor and a safeguard to the other, nor could it be determined which of the two appeared worthy of being preferred to the other.

CHAP. XLV.—In proportion as the attack became daily more formidable and violent, and particularly, because, as a great number of the soldiers were exhausted with wounds, the matter had come to a small number of defenders, more frequent letters and messages were sent to Cæsar; a part of which messengers were taken and tortured to death in the sight of our soldiers. There was within our camp a certain Nervian, by name Vertico, born in a distinguished position, who in the beginning of the blockade had deserted to Cicero, and had exhibited his fidelity to him. He persuades his slave, by the hope of freedom, and by great rewards, to convey a letter to Cæsar. This he carries out bound about his javelin; and mixing among the Gauls without any suspicion by being a Gaul, he reaches Cæsar. From him they received information of the imminent danger of Cicero and the legion.

CHAP. XLVI.—Cæsar having received the letter about the eleventh hour of the day, immediately sends a messenger to the Bellovaci, to M. Crassus, questor there, whose winter-quarters were twenty-five miles distant from him. He orders the legion to set forward in the middle of the night, and come to him with dispatch. Crassus sets out with the messenger. He sends another to C. Fabius, the lieutenant, ordering him to lead forth his legion into the territories of the Atrebates, to which he knew his march must be made. He writes to Labienus to come with his legion to the frontiers of the Nervii, if he could do so to the advantage of the commonwealth: he does not consider that the remaining portion of the army, because it was somewhat further distant, should be waited for; but assembles about 400 horse from the nearest winter-quarters.

CHAP. XLVII.—Having been apprised of the arrival of Crassus by the scouts at about the third hour, he advances twenty miles that day. He appoints Crassus over Samarobriva and assigns him a legion, because he was leaving there the baggage of the army, the hostages of the states, the public documents, and all the corn, which he had conveyed thither for passing the winter. Fabius, without delaying a moment, meets him on the march with his legion, as he had been commanded. Labienus, having learned the death of Sabinus and the destruction of the cohorts, as all the forces of the Treviri had come against him, beginning to fear lest, if he made a departure from his winter-quarters, resembling a flight, he should not be able to support the attack of the enemy, particularly since he knew them to be elated by their recent victory, sends back a letter to Cæsar, informing him with what great hazard he would lead out his legion from winter-quarters; he relates at large the affairs which had taken place among the Eburones; he informs him that all the infantry and cavalry of the Treviri had encamped at a distance of only three miles from his own camp.

CHAP. XLVIII.—Cæsar, approving of his motives, although he was disappointed in his expectation of three legions, and reduced to two, yet placed his only hopes of the common safety in dispatch. He goes into the territories of the Nervii by long marches. There he learns from some prisoners what things are going on in the camp of Cicero, and in how great jeopardy the affair is. Then with great rewards he induces a certain man of the Gallic horse to convey a letter to Cicero. This he sends written in Greek characters,[1] lest the letter being intercepted, our measures should be discovered by the enemy. He directs him, if he should be unable to enter, to throw his spear with the letter fastened to the thong, inside the fortifica-

[1] In the twenty-fifth chapter of the first book of these Commentaries, Cæsar is said to have found in the camp of the Helvetii (left there upon their departure), an account of their forces, written in Greek characters. In the fourteenth chapter of the sixth book, we are told that the Gauls used those characters both in their public and their private matters. Here we have it assigned as a reason for Cæsar's using them in this letter, that if it were intercepted by the Gauls, it might be unintelligible to them. Some have attempted to reconcile these apparent discrepancies, by supposing that, though the Gauls used the letters of the Greek alphabet, they only applied them to their own language. But Cæsar is not here said to have written this letter in Greek; he is only said to have done so in Greek characters, which leaves this passage still seemingly opposed to the other two. It has, therefore, been conjectured that he wrote not only, as the original would imply in the Greek characters, with which he seems twice to represent that the Gauls were acquainted, but also in the Greek language, of which they were ignorant.

tions of the camp. He writes in the letter, that he having set out with his legions, will quickly be there: he entreats him to maintain his ancient valor. The Gaul apprehending danger, throws his spear as he has been directed. Is by chance stuck in a tower, and, not being observed by our men for two days, was seen by a certain soldier on the third day: when taken down, it was carried to Cicero. He, after perusing it, reads it out in an assembly of the soldiers, and fills all with the greatest joy. Then the smoke of the fires was seen in the distance, a circumstance which banished all doubt of the arrival of the legions.

CHAP. XLIX.—The Gauls, having discovered the matter through their scouts, abandon the blockade, and march toward Cæsar with all their forces; these were about 60,000 armed men. Cicero, an opportunity being now afforded, again begs of that Vertico, the Gaul, whom we mentioned above, to convey back a letter to Cæsar; he advises him to perform his journey warily; he writes in the letter that the enemy had departed and had turned their entire force against him. When this letter was brought to him about the middle of the night, Cæsar apprises his soldiers of its contents, and inspires them with courage for fighting: the following day, at the dawn, he moves his camp, and, having proceeded four miles, he espies the forces of the enemy on the other side of a considerable valley and rivulet. It was an affair of great danger to fight with such large forces in a disadvantageous situation. For the present, therefore, inasmuch as he knew that Cicero was released from the blockade, and thought that he might, on that account, relax his speed, he halted there and fortifies a camp in the most favorable position he can. And this, though it was small in itself, [there being] scarcely 7,000 men, and these too without baggage, still by the narrowness of the passages,[1] he contracts as much as he can, with this object, that he may come into the greatest contempt with the enemy. In the mean while scouts having been sent in all directions, he examines by what most convenient path he might cross the valley.

[1] "Augustiis viarum." The spaces between the different divisions of the Roman camp were called *viæ*. Of these, besides several subordinate ones, there were eight of considerable width; five of which ran from the *Decuman* to the *Prætorian* side of the camp, and three from the one to the other of the two remaining sides. These Cæsar on this occasion very much contracted, with the design stated in the text.

CHAP. L.—That day, slight skirmishes of cavalry having taken place near the river, both armies kept in their own positions: the Gauls, because they were awaiting larger forces which had not then arrived; Cæsar, [to see] if perchance by pretense of fear he could allure the enemy toward his position, so that he might engage in battle, in front of his camp, on this side of the valley; if he could not accomplish this, that, having inquired about the passes, he might cross the valley and the river with the less hazard. At daybreak the cavalry of the enemy approaches to the camp and joins battle with our horse. Cæsar orders the horse to give way purposely, and retreat to the camp: at the same time he orders the camp to be fortified with a higher rampart in all directions, the gates to be barricaded, and in executing these things as much confusion to be shown as possible, and to perform them under the pretense of fear.

CHAP. LI.—Induced by all these things, the enemy lead over their forces and draw up their line in a disadvantageous position; and as our men also had been led down from the ramparts, they approach nearer, and throw their weapons into the fortification from all sides, and sending heralds round, order it to be proclaimed that, if "any, either Gaul or Roman, was willing to go over to them before the third hour, it was permitted; after that time there would not be permission;"[1] and so much did they disregard our men, that the gates having been blocked up with single rows of turf as a mere appearance, because they did not seem able to burst in that way, some began to pull down the rampart with their hands, others to fill up the trenches. Then Cæsar, making a sally from all the gates, and sending out the cavalry, soon puts the enemy to flight, so that no one at all stood his ground with the intention of fighting; and he slew a great number of them, and deprived all of their arms.

CHAP. LII.—Cæsar, fearing to pursue them very far, because woods and morasses intervened, and also [because] he saw that they suffered no small loss in abandoning their position, reaches Cicero the same day with all his forces safe. He witnesses with surprise the towers, mantelets, and [other] fortifications belonging to the enemy: the legion having been drawn out, he finds that even every tenth soldier had not escaped without wounds. From all these things he judges with what danger and with

[1] "Non fore potestatem," lit. *there would not be the power.*

what great courage matters had been conducted; he commends Cicero according to his desert, and likewise the legion; he addresses individually the centurions and the tribunes of the soldiers, whose valor he had discovered to have been signal. He receives information of the death of Sabinus and Cotta from the prisoners. An assembly being held the following day, he states the occurrence; he consoles and encourages the soldiers; he suggests, that the disaster, which had been occasioned by the misconduct and rashness of his lieutenant, should be borne with a patient mind, because by the favor of the immortal gods and their own valor, neither was lasting joy left to the enemy, nor very lasting grief to them.

Chap. LIII.—In the mean while the report respecting the victory of Cæsar is conveyed to Labienus through the country of the Remi with incredible speed, so that, though he was about sixty miles distant from the winter-quarter of Cicero, and Cæsar had arrived there after the ninth hour, before midnight a shout arose at the gates of the camp, by which shout an indication of the victory and a congratulation on the part of the Remi were given to Labienus. This report having been carried to the Treviri, Indutiomărus, who had resolved to attack the camp of Labienus the following day, flies by night and leads back all his forces into the country of the Treviri. Cæsar sends back Fabius with his legion to his winter-quarters; he himself determines to winter with three legions near Samarobriva in three different quarters, and, because such great commotions had arisen in Gaul, he resolved to remain during the whole winter with the army himself. For the disaster respecting the death of Sabinus having been circulated among them, almost all the states of Gaul were deliberating about war, sending messengers and embassies into all quarters, inquiring what further measure they should take, and holding councils by night in secluded places. Nor did any period of the whole winter pass over without fresh anxiety to Cæsar, or,[1] without his receiving some intelligence respecting the meetings and commotions of the Gauls. Among these, he is informed by L. Roscius, the lieutenant whom he had placed over the thirteenth legion, that large forces of those states of the Gauls, which are called the Armoricæ, had assembled for the purpose of attacking him and were not more than eight

[1] Literally, "but that he received."

miles distant; but intelligence respecting the victory of Cæsar being carried [to them], had retreated in such a manner that their departure appeared like a flight.

CHAP. LIV.—But Cæsar, having summoned to him the principal persons of each state, in one case by alarming them, since he declared that he knew what was going on, and in another case by encouraging them, retained a great part of Gaul in its allegiance. The Senŏnes, however, which is a state eminently powerful and one of great influence among the Gauls, attempting by general design to slay Cavarinus, whom Cæsar had created king among them (whose brother, Moritasgus, had held the sovereignty at the period of the arrival of Cæsar in Gaul, and whose ancestors had also previously held it), when he discovered their plot and fled, pursued him even to the frontiers [of the state], and drove him from his kingdom and his home; and, after having sent embassadors to Cæsar for the purpose of concluding a peace, when he ordered all their senate to come to him, did not obey that command. So far did it operate among those barbarian people, that there were found some to be the first to wage war; and so great a change of inclinations did it produce in all, that, except the Ædui and the Remi, whom Cæsar had always held in especial honor, the one people for their long standing and uniform fidelity toward the Roman people, the other for their late service in the Gallic war, there was scarcely a state which was not suspected by us. And I do not know whether that ought much to be wondered at, as well for several other reasons, as particularly because they who ranked above all nations for prowess in war,[1] most keenly regretted that they had lost so much of that reputation as to submit to commands from the Roman people.

CHAP. LV.—But the Triviri and Indutiomărus let no part of the entire winter pass without sending embassadors across the Rhine, importuning the states, promising money, and asserting that, as a large portion of our army had been cut off, a much smaller portion remained. However, none of the German States could be induced to cross the Rhine, since "they had twice essayed it," they said, "in the war with Ariovistus and in the passage of the Tenchtheri there; that fortune was

[1] When they thought of their national glory in deeds of arms, doubtless they did not pass over their exploits in Italy and their sacking of Rome.

not to be tempted any more." Indutiomărus disappointed in this expectation, nevertheless began to raise troops, and discipline them, and procure horses from the neighboring people, and allure to him by great rewards the outlaws and convicts throughout Gaul. And such great influence had he already acquired for himself in Gaul by these means, that embassies were flocking to him in all directions, and seeking, publicly and privately, his favor and friendship.

CHAP. LVI.—When he perceived that they were coming to him voluntarily; that on the one side the Senones and the Carnutes were stimulated by their consciousness of guilt, on the other side the Nervii and the Aduatuci were preparing war against the Romans, and that forces of volunteers would not be wanting to him if he began to advance from his own territories, he proclaims an armed council (this according to the custom of the Gauls in the commencement of war) at which, by a common law, all the youth were wont to asssemble in arms, whoever of them comes last is killed in the sight of the whole assembly after being racked with every torture.[1] In that council he declares Cingetorix, the leader of the other faction, his own son-in-law (whom we have above mentioned, as having embraced the protection of Cæsar, and never having deserted him) an enemy and confiscates his property. When these things were finished, he asserts in the council that he, invited by the Senones and the Carnutes, and several other states of Gaul, was about to march thither through the territories of the Remi, devastate their lands, and attack the camp of Labienus: before he does that, he informs them of what he desires to be done.

CHAP. LVII.—Labienus, since he was confining himself within a camp strongly fortified by the nature of the ground and by art, had no apprehensions as to his own and the legion's danger, but was devising that he might throw away no opportunity of conducting the war successfully. Accordingly, the speech of Indutiomărus, which he had delivered in the council, having been made known [to him] by Cingetorix and his allies, he sends messengers to the neighboring states and summons horse from all quarters: he appoints to them a fixed day for

[1] Tacitus, then, when he tells us, in his Germania, that "even three days out of the space appointed for their assemblies were wasted by the delay of those who were to meet," must refer to councils of minor importance.

assembling. In the mean time, Indutiomărus, with all his cavalry, nearly every day used to parade close to his [Labienus'] camp; at one time, that he might inform himself of the situation of the camp; at another time, for the purpose of conferring with or of intimidating him. Labienus confined his men within the fortifications, and promoted the enemy's belief of his fear by whatever methods he could.

CHAP. LVIII.—Since Indutiomărus was daily advancing up to the camp with greater defiance, all the cavalry of the neighboring states which he [Labienus] had taken care to have sent for, having been admitted in one night, he confined all his men within the camp by guards with such great strictness, that that fact could by no means be reported or carried to the Treviri. In the mean while, Indutiomărus, according to his daily practice, advances up to the camp and spends a great part of the day there: his horse cast their weapons, and with very insulting language call out our men to battle. No reply being given by our men, the enemy, when they thought proper, depart toward evening in a disorderly and scattered manner, Labienus unexpectedly sends out all the cavalry by two gates; he gives this command and prohibition, that, when the enemy should be terrified and put to flight (which he foresaw would happen, as it did), they should all make for Indutiomărus, and no one wound any man before he should have seen him slain, because he was unwilling that he should escape, in consequence of gaining time by the delay [occasioned by the pursuit] of the rest. He offers great rewards for those who should kill him: he sends up the cohorts as a relief to the horse. The issue justifies[1] the policy of the man, and since all aimed at one, Indutiomărus is slain, having been overtaken at the very ford of the river, and his head is carried to the camp, the horse, when returning, pursue and slay all whom they can. This affair having been known, all the forces of the Eburōnes and the Nervii which had assembled, depart; and for a short time after this action, Cæsar[2] was less harassed in the government of Gaul.

[1] "Comprobat fortuna." One sense of comprobo, is, *to make good.*

[2] Literally, "Cæsar held Gaul more tranquil."

BOOK VI.

THE ARGUMENT.

Cæsar, apprehending commotions in Gaul, levies additional forces. II.-VI. Defeats the Nervii, Senones, Carnutes, and Menapii. VII., VIII. Labienus defeats the Treviri. IX. Cæsar again crosses the Rhine; the Ubii send embassadors to plead the defense of their state. XI.-XX. The political factions of the Gallic states. The Druids, the second order or knights, the third order or commonalty, and the mythology of the Gauls. XXI.-XXVIII. The Germans; their customs; account of some remarkable animals found in the Hercinian forest. XXIX.-XXXI. Cæsar returns to Gaul; Ambiorix is worsted; death of Cativoleus. XXXII.-XXXIV. The territories of the Eburones are plundered. XXXV.-XLII. The Sigambri attack the Roman camp; some extraordinary incidents connected therewith. Cæsar arrives and restores confidence. XLIII., XLIV. Cæsar holds an investigation respecting the conspiracy of the Senones; Acco suffers capital punishment; the appointment of winter-quarters; Cæsar departs for Italy.

CHAP. I.—Cæsar, expecting for many reasons[1] a greater commotion in Gaul, resolves to hold a levy by the means of M. Silanus C. Antistius Reginus, and T. Sextius, his lieutenants: at the same time he requested Cn. Pompey, the proconsul, that since he was remaining near the city invested with military command for the interests of the commonwealth,[2] he

[1] "For many reasons:" one of these may be inferred from the close of chap. 54, of book v.

[2] When Pompey was consul (which was the year 699 A.U.C.), Spain was decreed him, as his proconsular province, for a period of five years; and permission was given him to raise what forces, and in what parts, he chose. He consequently raised one legion in Cisalpine Gaul. While, however, upon the expiration of his consulate, he was preparing to proceed into the province which the senate had decreed him, an opposition was successfully made to the realization of his hopes by some of the tribunes of the commons, and Petreius and Afranius were sent to Spain in his stead. Pompey remained at Rome, and sought to diminish the unpleasant nature of his position by giving out that he remained in the city for the purpose of procuring corn. Cæsar requested that he would send him that legion which he had raised in Gaul. With this request Pompey

would command those men whom when consul he had levied by the military oath in Cisalpine Gaul, to join their respective corps,[1] and to proceed to him; thinking it of great importance, as far as regarded the opinion which the Gauls would entertain for the future, that that the resources of Italy should appear so great that if any loss should be sustained in war, not only could it be repaired in a short time, but likewise be further supplied by still larger forces. And when Pompey had granted this to the interests of the commonwealth and the claims of friendship, Cæsar having quickly completed the levy by means of his lieutenants, after three regiments had been both formed and brought to him before the winter [had] expired, and the number of those cohorts which he had lost under Q. Titurius had been doubled, taught the Gauls, both by his dispatch and by his forces what the discipline and the power of the Roman people could accomplish.

CHAP. II.—Indutiomărus having been slain, as we have stated, the government was conferred upon his relatives by the Treviri. They cease not to importune the neighboring Germans and to promise them money: when they could not obtain [their object] from those nearest them, they try those more remote. Having found some states willing to accede to their wishes, they enter into a compact with them by a mutual oath, and give hostages as a security for the money: they attach Ambiorix to them by an alliance and confederacy. Cæsar, on being informed of their acts, since he saw that war was being prepared on all sides, that the Nervii, Aduatuci, and Menapii, with the addition of all the Germans on this side of the Rhine were under arms, that the Senŏnes did not assemble according to his command, and were concerting measures with the Car-

complied, as an act of duty to the state and a tribute of friendship toward Cæsar. Pompey, however, afterward demanded his legion again. The circumstances which attended its return to him performed, as Plutarch relates, their part in the civil war.

With regard to the original of the rest of this sentence, it may be remarked, first, that some copies have "quos . . . consul is," etc., and others "quos . . . . consulis." Davis and Clark defend the latter reading as, agreeably with the genius and usage of the Latin language, denoting, after his consulate, an act performed during it. Secondly, that Livy, iii. 20, gives the substance of the military oath in his time; and, thirdly, that Vegetius, has left it as it was used under the Christian emperors, including these words, "per Deum et per Christum et per Spiritum Sanctum."

[1] Literally, "to assemble at their standards."

nutes and the neighboring states, that the Germans were importuned by the Treviri in frequent embassies, thought that he ought to take measures for the war earlier [than usual].

CHAP. III.—Accordingly, while the winter was not yet ended, having concentrated the four nearest legions, he marched unexpectedly into the territories of the Nervii, and before they could either assemble or retreat, after capturing a large number of cattle and of men, and wasting their lands and giving up that booty to the soldiers, compelled them to enter into a surrender and give him hostages. That business having been speedily executed, he again led his legions back into winter-quarters. Having proclaimed a council of Gaul in the beginning of the spring, as he had been accustomed [to do], when the deputies from the rest, except the Senŏnes, the Carnutes, and the Treviri, had come, judging this[1] to be the commencement of war and revolt, that he might appear to consider all things of less consequence [than that war], he transfers the council to Lutetia of the Parisii. These were adjacent to the Senŏnes, and had united their state to them during the memory of their fathers, but were thought to have no part in the present plot. Having proclaimed this from the tribunal, he advances the same day toward the Senŏnes with his legions, and arrives among them by long marches.

CHAP. IV.—Acco, who had been the author of that enterprise, on being informed of his arrival, orders the people to assemble in the towns; to them, while attempting this, and before it could be accomplished, news is brought that the Romans are close at hand: through necessity they give over their design and send embassadors to Cæsar for the purpose of imploring pardon; they make advances to him through the Ædui, whose state was from ancient times under the protection of Rome. Cæsar readily grants them pardon, and receives their excuse, at the request of the Ædui, because he thought that the summer season[2] was one for an impending war, not for an investigation. Having imposed one hundred hostages, he delivers these to the Ædui to be held in charge by them.

[1] Namely, the absence of the representatives of three fore-mentioned states.

[2] "The summer season, investigation;" *i. e.* it was to be employed in the war with the Treviri and Ambiorix, and not in an examination as to the merits of the defense set up in behalf of the Sonones.

To the same place the Carnutes send embassadors and hostages, employing as their mediators the Remi, under whose protection they were: they receive the same answers. Cæsar concludes the council and imposes a levy of cavalry on the states.

CHAP. V.—This part of Gaul having been tranquilized, he applies himself entirely both in mind and soul to the war with the Treviri and Ambiŏrix. He orders Cavarīnus to march with him with the cavalry of the Senŏnes, lest any commotion should arise either out of his hot temper, or out of the hatred of the state which he had incurred.[1] After arranging these things, as he considered it certain that Ambiorix would not contend in battle, he watched his other plans attentively. The Menapii bordered on the territories of the Eburones, and were protected by one continued extent of morasses and woods; and they alone out of Gaul had never sent embassadors to Cæsar on the subject of peace. Cæsar knew that a tie of hospitality subsisted between them and Ambiorix: he also discovered that the latter had entered into an alliance with the Germans by means of the Treviri. He thought that these auxiliaries ought to be detached from him before he provoked him to war; lest he, despairing of safety, should either proceed to conceal himself in the territories of the Menapii,[2] or should be driven to coalesce[3] with the Germans beyond the Rhine. Having entered upon this resolution, he sends the baggage of the whole army to Labienus, in the territories of the Treviri and orders two legions to proceed to him: he himself proceeds against the Menapii with five lightly-equipped legions. They, having assembled no troops, as they relied on the defense of their position, retreat into the woods and morasses, and convey thither all their property.

CHAP. VI.—Cæsar, having divided his forces with C. Fabius, his lieutenant, and M. Crassus his questor, and having hastily constructed some bridges, enters their country in three divisions, burns their houses and villages, and gets possession of a large

[1] In the original, "ex eo, quod meruerat, odio;" mereo referring as well to the *unfavorable*, as to the favorable effects of conduct, and results of fortune. Some copies have *metuerat*, a reading obviously erroneous.

[2] The "territories," etc., "*in Menapios abderet,*" the proposition here including the idea of his *going* to do so.

[3] In the original, "congredi." The Greek paraphrast has συμμαχιαν ποιεισθαι.

number of cattle and men. Constrained by these circumstances the Menapii send embassadors to him for the purpose of suing for peace. He, after receiving hostages, assures them that he will consider them in the number of his enemies if they shall receive within their territories either Ambiorix or his embassadors. Having determinately settled these things, he left among the Menapii, Commius the Atrĕbatian, with some cavalry as a guard;[1] he himself proceeds toward the Treviri.

CHAP. VII.—While these things are being performed by Cæsar, the Treviri, having drawn together large forces of infantry and cavalry, were preparing to attack Labienus and the legion which was wintering in their territories, and were already not further distant from him than a journey of two days, when they learn that two legions had arrived by the order of Cæsar. Having pitched their camp fifteen miles off, they resolve to await the support of the Germans. Labienus, having learned the design of the enemy, hoping that through their rashness there would be some opportunity of engaging, after leaving a guard of five cohorts for the baggage, advances against the enemy with twenty-five cohorts and a large body of cavalry, and, leaving the space of a mile between them, fortifies his camp. There was between Labienus and the enemy a river difficult to cross, and with steep banks: this neither did he himself design to cross, nor did he suppose the enemy would cross it. Their hope of auxiliaries was daily increasing. He [Labienus] openly says in a council that "since the Germans are said to be approaching, he would not bring into uncertainty his own and the army's fortunes, and the next day would move his camp at early dawn." These words are quickly carried to the enemy, since out of so large a number of cavalry composed of Gauls, nature compelled some to favor the Gallic interests. Labienus, having assembled the tribunes of the soldiers and principal centurions by night, states what his design is, and, that he may the more easily give the enemy a belief of his fears, he orders the camp to be moved with greater noise and confusion than was usual with the Roman people.[2] By these means he makes his departure

[1] "Custodis loco." "Id est, observatoris, speculatoris." Holomam. One appointed to observe and report proceedings.

[2] "Quam populi Romani fert consuetudo:" not *than the discipline of the Roman army allowed*, but, *than was customary with, or usually at-*

[appear] like a retreat. These things, also, since the camps were so near, are reported to the enemy by scouts before daylight.

CHAP. VIII.—Scarcely had the rear advanced beyond the fortifications when the Gauls, encouraging one another "not to cast from their hands the anticipated booty, that it was a tedious thing, while the Romans were panic-stricken, to be waiting for the aid of the Germans, and that their dignity did not suffer them to fear to attack with such great forces so small a band, particularly when retreating and encumbered," do not hesitate to cross the river and give battle in a disadvantageous position. Labienus suspecting that these things would happen, was proceeding quietly, and using the same pretense of a march, in order that he might entice them across the river. Then, having sent forward the baggage some short distance and placed it on a certain eminence, he says, "Soldiers, you have the opportunity you have sought: you hold the enemy in an encumbered and disadvantageous position: display to us, your leaders, the same valor you have ofttimes displayed to your general: imagine that he is present and actually sees these exploits." At the same time he orders the troops to face about toward the enemy and form in line of battle, and, dispatching a few troops of cavalry as a guard for the baggage, he places the rest of the horse on the wings. Our men, raising a shout, quickly throw their javelins at the enemy. They, when, contrary to their expectation, they saw those whom they believed to be retreating, advance toward them with threatening banners, were not able to sustain even the charge, and, being put to flight at the first onslaught sought the nearest woods; Labienus pursuing them with the cavalry, upon a large number being slain, and several taken prisoners, got possession of the state a few days after; for the Germans, who were coming to the aid of the Treviri, having been informed of their flight, retreated to their homes. The relations of Indutiomărus, who had been the promoters of the revolt, accompanying them, quitted their own state with them. The supreme power and government were delivered to Cingetorix, whom we have stated to have remained firm in his allegiance from the commencement.

tended it. *Fert consuetudo* is an expression employed in this way. Thus, book iv. ch. xxxii. we read that it was reported to Cæsar "pulverem majorem, quam *consuetudo ferret*—videri."

CHAP. IX.—Cæsar, after he came from the territories of the Menapii into those of the Treviri, resolved for two reasons to cross the Rhine; one of which was, because they[1] had sent assistance to the Treviri against him; the other, that Ambiorix might not have a retreat among them. Having determined on these matters, he began to build a bridge a little above that place where he had before conveyed over his army. The plan having been known and laid down, the work is accomplished in a few days by the great exertion of the soldiers. Having left a strong guard at the bridge on the side of the Treviri, lest any commotion should suddenly arise among them, he leads over the rest of the forces and the cavalry. The Ubii, who before had sent hostages and come to a capitulation, send embassadors to him, for the purpose of vindicating themselves, to assure him that "neither had auxiliaries been sent to the Treviri from their state, nor had they violated their allegiance;" they entreat and beseech him "to spare them, lest, in his common hatred of the Germans, the innocent should suffer the penalty of the guilty: they promise to give more hostages, if he desire them." Having investigated the case, Cæsar finds that the auxiliaries had been sent by the Suevi; he accepts the apology of the Ubii, and makes the minute inquiries concerning the approaches and the routes to the territories of the Suevi.

CHAP. X.—In the mean time he is informed by the Ubii, a few days after, that the Suevi are drawing all their forces into one place, and are giving orders to those nations which are under their government to send auxiliaries of infantry and of cavalry. Having learned these things, he provides a supply of corn, selects a proper place for his camp, and commands the Ubii to drive off their cattle and carry away all their possessions from the country parts into the towns, hoping that they, being a barbarous and ignorant people, when harassed by the want of provisions, might be brought to an engagement on disadvantageous terms: he orders them to send numerous scouts among the Suevi, and learn what things are going on among them. They execute the orders, and, a few days having intervened, report that all the Suevi, after certain intelligence concerning the army of the Romans had come, retreated with all their

[1] The Germans.

own forces and those of their allies, which they had assembled, to the utmost extremities of their territories: that there is a wood there of very great extent, which is called Bacĕnis; that this stretches a great way into the interior, and, being opposed as a natural barrier, defends from injuries and incursions the Cherusci against the Suevi, and the Suevi against the Cherusci: that at the entrance of that forest the Suevi had determined to await the coming up of the Romans.

CHAP. XI.—Since we have come to the place, it does not appear to be foreign to our subject to lay before the reader an account of the manners of Gaul and Germany, and wherein these nations differ from each other. In Gaul there are factions not only in all the states, and in all the cantons and their divisions, but almost in each family, and of these factions those are the leaders who are considered according to their judgment to possess the greatest influence, upon whose will and determination the management of all affairs and measures depends. And that seems to have been instituted in ancient times with this view, that no one of the common people should be in want of support against one more powerful; for, none [of those leaders] suffers his party to be oppressed and defrauded, and if he do otherwise, he has no influence among his party. This same policy exists throughout the whole of Gaul; for all the states are divided into two factions.

CHAP. XII.—When Cæsar arrived in Gaul, the Ædui were the leaders of one faction, the Sequăni of the other. Since the latter were less powerful by themselves, inasmuch as the chief influence was from of old among the Ædui, and their dependencies were great, they had united to themselves the Germans and Ariovistus, and had brought them over to their party by great sacrifices and promises. And having fought several successful battles and slain all the nobility of the Ædui, they had so far surpassed them in power, that they brought over, from the Ædui to themselves, a large portion of their dependents and received from them the sons of their leading men as hostages, and compelled them to swear in their public character that they would enter into no design against them; and held a portion of the neighboring land, seized on by force, and possessed the sovereignty of the whole of Gaul. Divitiacus urged by this necessity, had proceeded to Rome to the senate, for the purpose of entreating assistance, and had returned without accomplishing his object. A change of affairs ensued on the arrival of Cæsar, the hostages were returned to the Ædui, their old dependencies restored, and new acquired through Cæsar (because those who had attached themselves to their alliance saw that they enjoyed a better state and a milder government), their other interests, their influence, their reputation were likewise increased, and in consequence, the Sequăni lost the sovereignty. The Remi succeeded to their place, and, as it was perceived that they equaled the Ædui in favor with Cæsar,[1] those, who on account of their old animosities could by no means coalesce with the Ædui, consigned themselves in clientship to the Remi. The latter carefully protected them. Thus they possessed both a new and suddenly acquired influence. Affairs were then in that position that the Ædui were considered by far the leading people, and the Remi held the second post of honor.

CHAP. XIII.—Throughout all Gaul there are two orders of those men who are of any rank and dignity: for the commonality is held almost in the condition of slaves, and dares to undertake nothing of itself, and is admitted to no deliberation. The greater part, when they are pressed either by debt, or the large amount of their tributes, or the oppression of the more powerful, give themselves up in vassalage to the nobles, who possess over them the same rights without exception as masters over their slaves.[2] But of these two orders, one is that of the Druids, the other that of the knights. The former are engaged in things sacred, conduct the public and the private sacrifices, and interpret all matters of religion. To these a large number of the young men resort for the purpose of instruction, and they [the Druids] are in great honor among them. For they determine respecting almost all controversies, public and private; and if any crime has been perpetrated, if murder has been committed, if there be any dispute about an inheritance, if any about boundaries, these same persons decide it; they decree rewards and punishments; if any one, either in a private or public capacity, has not submitted to their decision,

[1] *i. e.*, that the *Remi* stood as high in Cæsar's favor as did the *Ædui*.

[2] As far as we can discover from remaining testimonies, the condition of vassalage, or the state of the feudal retainer, among the ancient Gauls was not so hard as that of a corresponding relation among some more polished people.

they interdict him from the sacrifices.[1] This among them is the most heavy punishment. Those who have been thus interdicted are esteemed in the number of the impious and the criminal: all shun them, and avoid their society and conversation, lest they receive some evil from their contact; nor is justice administered to them when seeking it, nor is any dignity bestowed on them. Over all these Druids one presides, who possesses supreme authority among them. Upon his death, if any individual among the rest is pre-eminent in dignity, he succeeds; but, if there are many equal, the election is made by the suffrages of the Druids; sometimes they even contend for the presidency with arms. These assemble at a fixed period of the year in a consecrated place in the territories of the Carnutes, which is reckoned the central region of the whole of Gaul. Hither all, who have disputes, assemble from every part, and submit to their decrees and determinations. This institution is supposed to have been devised in Britain, and to have been brought over from it into Gaul; and now those who desire to gain a more accurate knowledge of that system generally proceed thither for the purpose of studying it.[2]

CHAP. XIV.—The Druids do not go to war, nor pay tribute together with the rest; they have an exemption from military service and a dispensation in all matters. Induced by such great advantages, many embrace this profession of their own accord, and [many] are sent to it by their parents and relations. They are said there to learn by

[1] As judges not only in the most important civil causes, but, further, invested with the administration of capital justice; as priests among a people given, as all allow the Gauls were in a remarkable degree, to religious rites and ceremonies; as those who had the instructions of the sons of the great not only in the mysteries of religion, but also in the theories of government and the physical sciences, the Druids possessed unbounded influence. "They," says Chrysostom, "in truth, reigned; for kings, though sitting on thrones of gold, and dwelling in gorgeous palaces, and partaking of sumptuous banquets, were subservient to them."

[2] The Delphin commentator thinks this improbable. He supposes it more likely that this institution passed into Britain from Gaul. When it declined in Gaul it flourished in Britain. He illustrates his position by saying, that, though Judea was the fountain of Christianity, the faith is nearly extinct there while it shines in those regions which derived it thence; and asks who would go to Jerusalem rather than to Rome or Paris to study Christian divinity. He also observes that Cæsar does not assert it on his own authority.

heart a great number of verses; accordingly some remain in the course of training twenty years. Nor do they regard it lawful to commit these to writing, though in almost all other matters, in their public and private transactions, they use Greek characters. That practice they seem to me to have adopted for two reasons; because they neither desire their doctrines to be divulged among the mass of the people, nor those who learn, to devote themselves the less to the efforts of memory, relying on writing; since it generally occurs to most men, that, in their dependence on writing, they relax their diligence in learning thoroughly, and their employment of the memory. They wish to inculcate this as one of their leading tenets, that souls do not become extinct,[1] but pass after death from one body to another, and they think that men by this tenet are in a great degree excited to valor, the fear of death being disregarded. They likewise discuss and impart to the youth many things respecting the stars and their motion, respecting the extent of the world and of our earth, respecting the nature of things, respecting the power and the majesty of the immortal gods.[2]

CHAP. XV.—The other order is that of the knights.[3] These, when there is occasion and any war occurs (which before Cæsar's arrival was for the most part wont to happen every year, as either they on their part were inflicting injuries or repelling those which others inflicted on them), are all engaged in war. And those of them most distinguished by birth and resources, have the greatest number of vassals and dependents about them. They acknowledge this sort of influence and power only.

[1] Because Pythagoras is said by Diogenes Laertius to have visited not only the Greek, but likewise the *Barbarian* schools in pursuing his study of *Sacred Mysteries*, it has been thought that he derived his *Metempsychosis* from the Druids. But, though there is in another writer the additional record that Pythagoras had heard the Druids, the conjecture above stated will not be readily received.

Between the Druidical and the Pythagorean Metempsychosis there was this difference, that the latter maintained the migration of the soul into irrational animals, while the former restricted the dogma to the passage of the soul from man to man.

[2] Other ancient writers have referred to the sciences of the Druids.

[3] As Cæsar at the time of writing probably had in his mind the three Roman orders, "*patricii*," "*equites*," and "*plebs*," and "equites" there is commonly rendered "knights," we have thought fit (though that translation is not free from objections) to call this second order among the Gauls by that name.

CHAP. XVI.—The nation of all the Gauls is extremely devoted to superstitious rites; and on that account they who are troubled with unusually severe diseases, and they who are engaged in battles and dangers, either sacrifice men as victims,[1] or vow that they will sacrifice them, and employ the Druids as the performers of those sacrifices; because they think that unless the life of a man be offered for the life of a man, the mind of the immortal gods can not be rendered propitious, and they have sacrifices of that kind ordained for national purposes. Others have figures of vast size, the limbs of which formed of osiers they fill with living men, which being set on fire, the men perish enveloped in the flames. They consider that the oblation of such as have been taken in theft, or in robbery, or any other offense, is more acceptable to the immortal gods; but when a supply of that class is wanting, they have recourse to the oblation of even the innocent.

CHAP. XVII.—They worship as their divinity, Mercury[2] in particular, and have many images of him, and regard him as the inventor of all arts, they consider him the guide of their journeys and marches, and believe him to have great influence over the acquisition of gain and mercantile transactions. Next to him they worship Apollo, and Mars, and Jupiter, and Minerva; respecting these deities they have for the most part the same belief as other nations: that Apollo averts diseases, that Minerva imparts the invention of manufactures, that Jupiter possesses the sovereignty of the heavenly powers; that Mars presides over wars. To him, when they have determined to engage in battle, they commonly vow those things which they shall take[3] in war. When they have conquered, they sacrifice whatever captured animals may have survived the conflict,[4] and col-

1 To this Cicero refers in his Oration for Fonteius as to a well-known fact.

2 The student must not imagine that Cæsar found the names *Mercurius*, *Apollo*, etc., existing among the Gauls, as those of their *deities* here spoken of. Whether the names assigned by commentators (as *Woda*, *Mercury*, *Balenus*, *Apollo*, etc.), were, or were not, the Gallic, must remain a question; but it is to be understood that Cæsar applied to the *divinities* of the Gauls the names of those in the Roman mythology, whose attributes generally corresponded with them severally.

3 "*Ceperint*," not, as some copies, *ceperunt*, as the *vow* necessarily requires the former reading. The Greek paraphrast accordingly has *τὰ ληφθησόμενα*.

4 Athenæus remarks "that the Gauls sacrifice their captives to the gods."

lect the other things into one place. In many states you may see piles of these things heaped up in their consecrated spots; nor does it often happen that any one, disregarding the sanctity of the case,[1] dares either to secrete in his house things captured, or take away those deposited; and the most severe punishment, with torture, has been established for such a deed.

CHAP. XVIII.—All the Gauls assert that they are descended from the god Dis, and say that this tradition has been handed down by the Druids. For that reason they compute the divisions of every season, not by the number of days, but of nights; they keep birth-days and the beginnings of months and years in such an order that the day follows the night. Among the other usages of their life, they differ in this from almost all other nations, that they do not permit their children to approach them openly until they are grown up so as to be able to bear the service of war; and they regard it as indecorous for a son of boyish age to stand in public in the presence of his father.

CHAP. XIX.—Whatever sums of money the husbands have received in the name of dowry from their wives, making an estimate of it, they add the same amount out of their own estates. An account is kept of all this money conjointly, and the profits are laid by: whichever of them shall have survived [the other], to that one the portion of both reverts together with the profits of the previous time. Husbands have power of life and death over their wives as well as over their children: and when the father of a family, born in a more than commonly distinguished rank, has died, his relations assemble, and, if the circumstances of his death are suspicious, hold an investigation upon the wives in the manner adopted toward slaves; and, if proof be obtained, put them to severe torture, and kill them. Their funerals, considering the state of civilization among the Gauls, are magnificent and costly; and they cast into the fire all things, including living creatures, which they suppose to have been dear to them when alive; and, a little before this period, slaves and dependents, who[2] were ascer-

[1] "Neglectâ religione:" there are four *general* senses of the word *religio*. 1. Religion, devotion. 2. (in the plural) Religious ceremonies and mysteries. 3. Superstition. And, 4. The sanctity of any particular matter, or reverential feelings entertained with regard to a certain case. This last, not religion in its general acceptation, is the sense of the word in this passage.

[2] Literally "who, it was ascertained, was beloved by them."

tained to have been beloved by them, were,[1] after the regular funeral rites were completed, burnt together with them.

CHAP. XX.—Those states which are considered to conduct their commonwealth more judiciously, have it ordained by their laws, that, if any person shall have heard by rumor and report from his neighbors any thing concerning the commonwealth, he shall convey it to the magistrate, and not impart it to any other; because it has been discovered that inconsiderate and inexperienced men were often alarmed by false reports, and driven to some rash act, or else took hasty measures in affairs of the highest importance. The magistrates conceal those things which require to be kept unknown; and they disclose to the people whatever they determine to be expedient. It is not lawful to speak of the commonwealth, except in council.

CHAP. XXI.—The Germans differ much from these usages, for they have neither Druids to preside over sacred offices, nor do they pay great regard to sacrifices. They rank in the number of the gods those alone whom they behold, and by whose instrumentality they are obviously benefited, namely, the sun, fire, and the moon; they have not heard of the other deities even by report. Their whole life is occupied in hunting and in the pursuits of the military art; from childhood they devote themselves to fatigue and hardships. Those who have remained chaste for the longest time, receive the greatest commendation among their people; they think that by this the growth is promoted, by this the physical powers are increased and the sinews are strengthened. And to have had knowledge of a woman before the twentieth year they reckon among the most disgraceful acts; of which matter there is no concealment, because they bathe promiscuously in the rivers and [only] use skins or small cloaks of deers' hides, a large portion of the body being in consequence naked.

CHAP. XXII.—They do not pay much attention to agriculture, and a large portion of their food consists in milk, cheese, and flesh; nor has any one a fixed quantity of land or his own individual limits; but the magistrates and the leading men each year apportion to the tribes and families, who have united together, as much land as, and in the place in which, they think

[1] Otherwise thus, "when the funeral rites were rendered complete."

proper, and the year after compel them to remove elsewhere. For this enactment[1] they advance many reasons—lest seduced by long-continued custom, they may exchange their ardor in the waging of war for agriculture; lest they may be anxious to acquire extensive estates, and the more powerful drive the weaker from their possessions; lest they construct their houses with too great a desire to avoid cold and heat; lest the desire of wealth spring up, from which cause divisions and discords arise; and that they may keep the common people in a contented state of mind, when each sees his own means placed on an equality with [those of] the most powerful.

CHAP. XXIII. It is the greatest glory to the several states to have as wide deserts as possible around them, their frontiers having been laid waste. They consider this the real evidence of their prowess, that their neighbors shall be driven out of their lands and abandon them, and that no one dare settle near them; at the same time they think that they shall be on that account the more secure, because they have removed the apprehension of a sudden incursion. When a state either repels war waged against it, or wages it against another, magistrates are chosen to preside over that war with such authority, that they have power of life and death. In peace there is no common magistrate, but the chiefs of provinces and cantons administer justice and determine controversies among their own people. Robberies which are committed beyond the boundaries of each state bear no infamy, and they avow that these are committed for the purpose of disciplining their youth and of preventing sloth. And when any of their chiefs has said in an assembly "that he will be their leader, let those who are willing to follow, give in their names;" they who approve of both the enterprise and the man arise and promise their assistance and are applauded by the people; such of them as have not followed him are accounted in the number of deserters and traitors, and confidence in all matters is afterward refused them. To injure guests they regard as impious; they defend from wrong those who have come to them for any purpose whatever, and esteem them inviolable; to them the houses of all are open and maintenance is freely supplied.[2]

1 "Ejus rei."

2 "No nation," says Tacitus, speaking of them in his Germania, "more freely exercises entertainment and hospitality. To drive any one whomsoever from their houses, they consider a crime."

CHAP. XXIV.—And there was formerly a time when the Gauls excelled the Germans in prowess, and waged war on them offensively, and, on account of the great number of their people and the insufficiency of their land, sent colonies over the Rhine. Accordingly, the Volcæ Tectosăges,[1] seized on those parts of Germany which are the most fruitful [and lie] around the Hercynian forest[2] (which, I perceive, was known by report to Eratosthenes[3] and some other Greeks, and which they call Orcynia), and settled there. Which nation to this time retains its position in those settlements, and has a very high character for justice and military merit; now also they continue in the same scarcity, indigence, hardihood, as the Germans, and use the same food and dress; but their proximity to the Province and knowledge of commodities from countries beyond the sea supplies to the Gauls[4] many things tending to luxury as well as civilization. Accustomed by degrees to be overmatched and worsted in many engagements, they do not even compare themselves to the Germans in prowess.

CHAP. XXV.—The breadth of this Hercynian forest, which has been referred to above, is[5] to a quick traveler, a journey of nine days. For it can not be otherwise computed, nor are they acquainted with the measures of roads. It begins at the frontiers of the Helvetii, Nemetes, and Rauraci, and extends in a right line along the river Danube to the territories of the Daci and the Anartes; it bends thence to the left in a different direction from the river, and owing to its

1 The Volcæ were a large and powerful nation in the south-west of Gaul, and were divided into two great tribes. First, the Volcæ Arecomici, who inhabited the eastern part of the Province, whose chief city was Nimausus, Nismes. Second, the Volcæ Tectosages, who inhabited the western part of the Province, whose chief city was Narbo, Narbonne. It is highly probable that the migration to which Cæsar alludes here, is the same recorded by Livy, in the 34th chapter of the 5th book, and that the Volcæ Tectosages were the Gauls that followed Sigovesus into the wilds of the Hercynian forest.

2 The Hercynian forest is supposed to have derived its name from the German word, hartz "resin." Traces of the name are still preserved in the Harz and Erz mountains.

3 A famous mathematician and astronomer born in Africa. He was intrusted by the Egyptians with the care of the famous Alexandrian library, and was the second person who discharged that honorable office. He died 194 B.C.

4 Gallis meaning such of the Volcæ Tectosages as had not migrated into Germany.

5 Literally, "extends."

extent touches the confines of many nations; nor is there any person belonging to this part of Germany who says that he either has gone to the extremity of that forest, though he had advanced a journey of sixty days, or has heard in what place it begins. It is certain that many kinds of wild beast are produced in it which have not been seen in other parts; of which the following are such as differ principally from other animals, and appear worthy of being committed to record.

CHAP. XXVI.—There is an ox of the shape of a stag, between whose ears a horn rises from the middle of the forehead, higher and straighter than those horns which are known to us. From the top of this, branches, like palms, stretch out a considerable distance. The shape of the female and of the male is the same; the appearance and the size of the horns is the same.

CHAP. XXVII.—There are also [animals] which are called elks. The shape of these, and the varied color of their skins, is much like roes, but in size they surpass them a little and are destitute of horns, and have legs without joints and ligatures; nor do they lie down for the purpose of rest, nor, if they have been thrown down by any accident, can they raise or lift themselves up. Trees serve as beds to them; they lean themselves against them, and thus reclining only slightly, they take their rest; when the huntsmen have discovered from the footsteps of these animals whither they are accustomed to betake themselves, they either undermine all the trees at the roots, or cut into them so far that the upper part of the trees may appear to be left standing.[1] When they have leant upon them, according to their habit, they knock down by their weight the unsupported trees, and fall down themselves along with them.

CHAP. XXVIII.—There is a third kind, consisting of those animals which are called uri. These are a little below the elephant in size, and of the appearance, color, and shape of a bull. Their strength and speed are extraordinary; they spare neither man nor wild beast which they have espied. These the Germans take with much pains in pits and kill them. The young men harden themselves with this exercise, and practice themselves in this kind of hunting, and those who have slain the greatest number of them, having produced the horns in public, to serve as evidence, receive great praise. But not even when taken very young can they be rendered familiar to men and

[1] Literally, "that the appearance alone of them standing may be left."

tamed. The size, shape, and appearance of their horns differ much from the horns of our oxen. These they anxiously seek after, and bind at the tips with silver, and use as cups at their most sumptuous entertainments.

CHAP. XXIX.—Cæsar, after he discovered through the Ubian scouts that the Suevi had retired into their woods, apprehending a scarcity of corn, because, as we have observed above, all the Germans pay very little attention to agriculture, resolved not to proceed any further; but, that he might not altogether relieve the barbarians from the fear of his return, and that he might delay their succours, having led back his army, he breaks down, to the length of 200 feet, the further end of the bridge, which joined the banks of the Ubii, and at the extremity of the bridge raises towers of four stories, and stations a guard of twelve cohorts for the purpose of defending the bridge, and strengthens the place with considerable fortifications. Over that fort and guard he appointed C. Volcatius Tullus, a young man; he himself, when the corn began to ripen, having set forth for the war with Ambiorix (through the forest Arduenna,[1] which is the largest of all Gaul, and reaches from the banks of the Rhine and the frontiers of the Treviri to those of the Nervii, and extends over more than 500 miles), he sends forward L. Minucius Basilus with all the cavalry, to try if he might gain any advantage by rapid marches and the advantage of time, he warns him to forbid fires being made in the camp, lest any indication of his approach be given at a distance: he tells him that he will follow immediately.

CHAP. XXX.—Basilus does as he was commanded; having performed his march rapidly, and even surpassed[2] the expectations of all, he surprises in the fields many not expecting him; through their information he advances toward Ambiorix himself, to the place in which he was said to be with a few horse.

[1] Arduenna, the largest forest in ancient Gaul. The name is supposed to be derived from *ar denn*, "the deep" [forest]. *Ar* is the article, while *denn* in the Kymric, *don* in the Bas-Breton, and *domhainn* in Gaelic, denote respectively, "deep," "thick."—*Thiery Histoire de Gaulois*, vol. ii. p. 41. The name is still preserved in the 'forest of Ardennes," on the frontiers of France and Belgium, which is, however, but a small portion of the noble forest that extended from the bank of the Rhine, and the frontiers of the Treviri to those of the Nervii.

[2] Literally, "contrary to."

Fortune accomplishes much, not only in other matters, but also in the art of war. For as it happened by a remarkable chance, that he fell upon [Ambiorix] himself unguarded and unprepared, and that his arrival was seen by the people before the report or information of his arrival was carried thither; so it was an incident of extraordinary fortune that, although every implement of war which he was accustomed to have about him was seized, and his chariots and horses surprised, yet he himself escaped death. But it was effected owing to this circumstance, that his house being surrounded by a wood (as are generally the dwellings of the Gauls, who, for the purpose of avoiding heat, mostly seek the neighborhood of woods and rivers), his attendants and friends in a narrow spot sustained for a short time the attack of our horse. While they were fighting, one of his followers mounted him on a horse; the woods sheltered him as he fled. Thus fortune tended much[1] both toward his encountering and his escaping danger.

Chap. XXXI.—Whether Ambiorix did not collect his forces from cool deliberation, because he considered he ought not to engage in a battle, or [whether] he was debarred by time and prevented by the sudden arrival of our horse, when he supposed the rest of the army was closely following, is doubtful: but certainly, dispatching messengers through the country, he ordered every one to provide for himself; and a part of them fled into the forest Arduenna, a part into the extensive morasses; those who were nearest the ocean concealed themselves in the islands which the tides usually form; many, departing from their territories, committed themselves and all their possessions to perfect strangers. Cativolcus, king of one half of the Eburones, who had entered into the design together with Ambiorix, since, being now worn out by age, he was unable to endure the fatigue either of war or flight, having cursed Ambiorix with every imprecation, as the person who had been the contriver of that measure, destroyed himself with the juice of the yew-tree, of which there is a great abundance in Gaul and Germany.

Chap. XXXII.—The Segui and Condrusi, of the nation and number of the Germans, and who are between the Eburones and the Treviri, sent embassadors to Cæsar to entreat that he would not regard them in the number of his enemies, nor consider that the cause of all the Germans on

[1] "Multum valuit:" had much avail.

this side the Rhine was one and the same; that they had formed no plans of war, and had sent no auxiliaries to Ambiorix. Cæsar, having ascertained this fact by an examination of his prisoners, commanded that if any of the Eburones in their flight had repaired to them, they should be sent back to him; he assures them that if they did that, he will not injure their territories. Then, having divided his forces into three parts, he sent the baggage of all the legions to Aduatuca. That is the name of a fort. This is nearly in the middle of the Eburones, where Titurius and Aurunculeius had been quartered for the purpose of wintering. This place he selected as well on other accounts as because the fortifications of the previous year remained, in order that he might relieve the labor of the soldiers. He left the fourteenth legion as a guard for the baggage, one of those three which he had lately raised in Italy and brought over. Over that legion and camp he places Q. Tullius Cicero and gives him 200 horse.

CHAP. XXXIII.—Having divided the army, he orders T. Labienus to proceed with three legions toward the ocean into those parts which border on the Menapii; he sends C. Trebonius with a like number of legions to lay waste that district which lies contiguous to the Aduatuci; he himself determines to go with the remaining three to the river Sambre,[1] which flows into the Meuse, and to the most remote parts of Arduenna, whither he heard that Ambiorix had gone with a few horse. When departing, he promises that he will return before the end of the seventh day, on which day he was aware corn was due to that legion which was being left in garrison. He directs Labienus and Trebonius to return by the same day, if they can do so agreeably to the interests of the republic; so that their measures having been mutually imparted, and the plans of the enemy having been discovered, they might be able to commence a different line of operations.

CHAP. XXXIV.—There was, as we have above observed,[2] no regular army, nor a town, nor a garrison which could defend itself by arms; but the people were scattered in all

[1] I have here, without the least hesitation, adopted Anthon's reading, which is supported by the authority of the Greek paraphrase. The common reading is *Scaldis*, "the Scheldt;" but the Scheldt and Meuse do not form a junction, nor have we any reason to suppose that they did, either in Cæsar's time, or at any other time.

[2] Chapter xxxi.

directions. Where either a hidden valley, or a woody spot, or a difficult morass furnished any hope of protection or of security to any one, there he had fixed himself. These places were known to those who dwelt in the neighborhood, and the matter demanded great attention, not so much in protecting the main body of the army (for no peril could occur to them altogether from those alarmed and scattered troops), as in preserving individual soldiers; which in some measure tended to the safety of the army. For both the desire of booty was leading many too far, and the woods with their unknown and hidden routes would not allow them to go in large bodies. If he desired the business to be completed and the race of those infamous people to be cut off, more bodies of men must be sent in several directions and the soldiers must be detached on all sides; if he were disposed to keep the companies at their standards, as the established discipline and practice of the Roman army required, the situation itself was a safeguard to the barbarians, nor was there wanting to individuals the daring to lay secret ambuscades and beset scattered soldiers. But amid difficulties of this nature as far as precautions could be taken by vigilance, such precautions were taken; so that some opportunities of injuring the enemy were neglected, though the minds of all were burning to take revenge, rather than that injury should be effected with any loss to our soldiers. Cæsar dispatches messengers to the neighboring states; by the hope of booty he invites all to him, for the purpose of plundering the Eburones, in order that the life of the Gauls might be hazarded in the woods rather than the legionary soldiers; at the same time, in order that a large force being drawn around them, the race and name of that state may be annihilated for such a crime. A large number from all quarters speedily assembles.

CHAP. XXXV.—These things were going on in all parts of the territories of the Eburones, and the seventh day was drawing near, by which day Cæsar had purposed to return to the baggage and the legion. Here it might be learned how much fortune achieves in war, and how great casualties she produces. The enemy having been scattered and alarmed, as we related above, there was no force which might produce even a slight occasion of fear. The report extends beyond the Rhine to the Germans that the Eburones are being pillaged, and that all were without distinction[1] invited to the plunder. The Sigambri, who are nearest to the Rhine, by whom, we have mentioned above, the Tenchtheri and Usipetes were received after their retreat, collect 2,000 horse; they cross the Rhine in ships and barks thirty miles below that place where the bridge was entire and the garrison left by Cæsar; they arrive at the frontiers of the Eburones, surprise many who were scattered in flight, and get possession of a large amount of cattle, of which barbarians are extremely covetous. Allured by booty, they advance further; neither morass nor forest obstructs these men, born amid war and depredations; they inquire of their prisoners in what part Cæsar is; they find that he has advanced further, and learn that all the army has removed. Thereon one of the prisoners says, "Why do you pursue such wretched and trifling spoil; you, to whom it is granted to become even now most richly endowed by fortune? In three hours you can reach Aduatuca; there the Roman army has deposited all its fortunes; there is so little of a garrison that not even the wall can be manned, nor dare any one go beyond the fortifications." A hope having been presented them, the Germans leave in concealment the plunder they had acquired; they themselves hasten to Aduatuca, employing as their guide the same man by whose information they had become informed of these things.

CHAP. XXXVI.—Cicero, who during all the foregoing days had kept his soldiers in camp with the greatest exactness, and agreeable to the injunctions of Cæsar, had not permitted even any of the camp-followers to go beyond the fortification, distrusting on the seventh day that Cæsar would keep his promise as to the number of days, because he heard that he had proceeded further, and no report as to his return was brought to him, and being urged at the same time by the expressions of those who called his tolerance almost a siege, if, forsooth, it was not permitted them to go out of the camp, since he might expect no disaster, whereby he could be injured, within three miles of the camp, while nine legions and all the cavalry were under arms, and the enemy scattered and almost annihilated, sent five cohorts into the neighboring cornlands, between which and the camp only one hill intervened,

[1] "Ultro," or, *such as chose; freely.*

for the purpose of foraging. Many soldiers of the legions had been left invalided in the camp, of whom those who had recovered in this space of time, being about 300, are sent together under one standard; a large number of soldiers' attendants besides, with a great number of beasts of burden, which had remained in the camp, permission being granted, follow them.

CHAP. XXXVII.—At this very time, the German horse by chance came up, and immediately, with the same speed with which they had advanced, attempt to force the camp at the Decuman gate, nor were they seen, in consequence of woods lying in the way on that side, before they were just reaching the camp: so much so, that the sutlers who had their booths under the rampart had not an opportunity of retreating within the camp. Our men, not anticipating it, are perplexed by the sudden affair, and the cohort on the outpost scarcely sustains the first attack. The enemy spread themselves on the other sides to ascertain if they could find any access. Our men with difficulty defend the gates; the very position of itself and the fortification secures the other accesses. There is a panic in the entire camp, and one inquires of another the cause of the confusion, nor do they readily determine whither the standards should be borne, nor into what quarter each should betake himself. One avows that the camp is already taken, another maintains that, the enemy having destroyed the army and commander-in-chief, are come hither as conquerors; most form strange superstitious fancies from the spot, and place before their eyes the catastrophe of Cotta and Titurius, who had fallen in the same fort. All being greatly disconcerted by this alarm, the belief of the barbarians is strengthened that there is no garrison within, as they had heard from their prisoner. They endeavor to force an entrance and encourage one another not to cast from their hands so valuable a prize.

CHAP. XXXVIII.—P. Sextius Baculus, who had led a principal century under Cæsar (of whom we have made mention in previous engagements), had been left an invalid in the garrison, and had now been five days without food. He, distrusting his own safety and that of all, goes forth from his tent unarmed; he sees that the enemy are close at hand and that the matter is in the utmost danger; he snatches arms from those nearest, and stations himself at the gate. The centurions of that cohort which was on guard follow him; for a short time they sustain the fight together. Sextius faints, after receiving many wounds; he is with difficulty saved, drawn away by the hands of the soldiers. This space having intervened, the others resume courage so far as to venture to take their place on the fortifications and present the aspect of defenders.

CHAP. XXXIX.—The foraging having in the mean time been completed, our soldiers distinctly hear the shout; the horse hasten on before and discover in what danger the affair is. But here there is no fortification to receive them, in their alarm: those last enlisted, and unskilled in military discipline turn their faces to the military tribune and the centurions; they wait to find what orders may be given by them. No one is so courageous as not to be disconcerted by the suddenness of the affair. The barbarians, espying our standard in the distance, desist from the attack; at first they suppose that the legions, which they had learned from their prisoners had removed further off, had returned; afterward, despising their small number, they make an attack on them at all sides.

CHAP. XL.—The camp-followers run forward to the nearest rising ground; being speedily driven from this they throw themselves among the standards and companies: they thus so much the more alarm the soldiers already affrighted. Some propose that, forming a wedge,[1] they suddenly break through, since the camp was so near; and if any part should be surrounded and slain, they fully trust that at least the rest may be saved; others, that they take their stand on an eminence, and all undergo the same destiny. The veteran soldiers, whom we stated to have set out together [with the others] under a standard, do not approve of this. Therefore encouraging each other, under the conduct of Caius Trebonius, a Roman knight,

[1] "Cuneo facto." The *cuneus*, in its strict and proper sense, was a triangular figure. It was not peculiar to the Romans. Tacitus seems to speak of it as the ordinary battle array of the Germans. The Romans adopted it only under particular circumstances. They sometimes received the *cuneus* of their enemy by forming a figure called "forceps," from its resemblance to a pair of (opened) scissors or shears.

who had been appointed over them, they break through the midst of the enemy, and arrive in the camp safe to a man. The camp attendants and the horse following close upon them with the same impetuosity, are saved by the courage of the soldiers. But those who had taken their stand upon the eminence, having even now acquired no experience of military matters, neither could persevere in that resolution which they approved of, namely, to defend themselves from their higher position, nor imitate that vigor and speed which they had observed to have availed others; but, attempting to reach the camp, had descended into an unfavorable situation. The centurions, some of whom had been promoted for their valor from the lower ranks of other legions to higher ranks in this legion, in order that they might not forfeit their glory for military exploits previously acquired, fell together fighting most valiantly. The enemy having been dislodged by their valor, a part of the soldiers arrived safe in camp contrary to their expectations; a part perished, surrounded by the barbarians.

CHAP. XLI.—The Germans, despairing of taking the camp by storm, because they saw that our men had taken up their position on the fortifications, retreated beyond the Rhine with that plunder which they had deposited in the woods. And so great was the alarm, even after the departure of the enemy, that when C. Volusenus, who had been sent with the cavalry, arrived that night, he could not gain credence that Cæsar was close at hand with his army safe. Fear had so pre-occupied the minds of all, that their reason being almost estranged, they said that all the other forces having been cut off, the cavalry alone had arrived there by flight, and asserted that, if the army were safe, the Germans would not have attacked the camp; which fear the arrival of Cæsar removed.

CHAP. XLII.—He, on his return, being well aware of the casualties of war, complained of one thing [only], namely, that the cohorts had been sent away from the outposts and garrison [duty], and pointed out that room ought not to have been left for even the most trivial casualty; that fortune had exercised great influence in the sudden arrival of their enemy; much greater, in that she had turned the barbarians away from the very rampart and gates of the camp. Of all which events, it seemed the most surprising, that the Germans, who had crossed the Rhine with this object, that they might plunder the territories of Ambiorix, being led to the camp of the Romans, rendered Ambiorix a most acceptable service.

CHAP. XLIII.—Cæsar, having again marched to harass the enemy, after collecting a large number [of auxiliaries] from the neighboring states, dispatches them in all directions. All the villages and all the buildings, which each beheld, were on fire: spoil was being driven off from all parts; the corn not only was being consumed by so great numbers of cattle and men, but also had fallen to the earth, owing to the time of the year and the storms; so that if any had concealed themselves for the present, still, it appeared likely that they must perish through want of all things, when the army should be drawn off. And frequently it came to that point, as so large a body of cavalry had been sent abroad in all directions, that the prisoners declared Ambiorix had just then been seen by them in flight, and had not even passed out of sight, so that the hope of overtaking him being raised, and unbounded exertions having been resorted to, those who thought they should acquire the highest favor with Cæsar, nearly overcame nature by their ardor, and continually, a little only seemed wanting to complete success; but he rescued himself by [means of] lurking-places and forests, and, concealed by the night made for other districts and quarters, with no greater guard than that of four horsemen, to whom alone he ventured to confide his life.

CHAP. XLIV.—Having devastated the country in such a manner, Cæsar leads back his army with the loss of two cohorts to Durocortorum[1] of the Remi, and, having summoned a council of Gaul to assemble at that place, he resolved to hold an investigation respecting the conspiracy of the Senŏnes and Carnūtes, and having pronounced a most severe sentence upon Acco, who had been the contriver of that plot, he punished him after the custom of our ancestors.[2] Some fearing a trial,

1 "Durocortorum:" *Rheims.*

2 "The custom of our ancestors:" *more majorum.* What that was may be shown by a quotation from Suetonius's Life of Nero. "In the mean time he snatched some letters from the hands of a servant of Phaoñ, and, upon reading them discovers that he has been declared by the senate an enemy of the state, and was sought for, that he might be punished *more*

fled; when he had forbidden these fire and water,[1] he stationed in winter quarters two legions at the frontiers of the Treviri, two among the Lingŏnes, the remaining six at Agendīcum,[2] in the territories of the Senŏnes; and, having provided corn for the army, he set out for Italy, as he had determined, to hold the asssizes.

majorum. Upon which he inquired what kind of punishment that was, and was told it consisted in the criminal being stripped naked and lashed to death, with his neck fastened within a cross-bar (*furca*)." The question, however, may arise, how could Nero require such information?

[1] "Ignis et aquæ interdictio," the penalty here spoken of, as it applied to a Roman citizen, involved the necessity of seeking an abode beyond Italy. We may suppose the sentence was severely felt by these revolutionary Senones; at least for a time.

[2] "Agendīcum:" *Sens.*

BOOK VII.

THE ARGUMENT.

I.-III. Many of the Gallic nations conspire to assert their freedom, IV.-VII. And select Vercingetorix the Arvernian as Commander-in-chief. VIII., IX. Cæsar suddenly invades the country of the Arverni. X. Succors the Boii, XI. Takes Vellaunodunum and Genabum, XII.-XIV. And Noviodunum. XV.-XIX. The Gauls burn all the towns of the Bituriges, except Avaricum, into which they throw a strong garrison, as Cæsar was then besieging it. XX., XXI. In the mean time Vercingetorix, being accused of treachery by his countrymen, completely vindicates himself. XXII.-XXVII. Avaricum is for some time ably defended, XXVIII.-XXXI. But it is at length taken by storm. XXXII., XXXIII. Commotions among the Ædui divert Cæsar from the war. XXXIV.-XXXVI. After quelling them, he marches at the head of his army to Gergovia. XXXVII.-XLV. While he is carrying on the war there, disturbances break out a second time among the Ædui. XLVI. The Romans take possession of three different camps belonging to the enemy, XLVII.-LII. But attacking the town too impetuously, are repulsed with great loss. LIII.-LVII. Cæsar, despairing of being able to take the town, removes his camp into the country of the Ædui. LVIII.-LXI. Labienus, after carrying on the war successfully against the Parisii, LXII. Joins him. LXIII.-LXV. All the Gauls, with very few exceptions, follow the example of the Ædui, and revolt. LXVI., LXVII. Under the command of Vercingetorix, they attack Cæsar while marching into the country of the Sequani, and are completely defeated. LXVIII.-LXXIV. He pursues them as far as Alesia, and surrounds both the town and themselves, with a line of circumvallation. LXXV.-LXXXVI. The Gauls select the bravest men in their respective states, and endeavor to relieve their besieged countrymen. LXXXVII. They sustain a total defeat. LXXXIX. Alesia and Vercingetorix surrender, likewise the Ædui and several other states.

CHAP. I.—Gaul being tranquil, Cæsar, as he had determined, sets out for Italy to hold the provincial assizes. There he receives intelligence of the death of Clodius;[1] and, being

[1] Clodius, a noble but licentious Roman, who acted a prominent part in the scenes of anarchy and violence which disgraced, at this time, the Roman republic. He bore a bitter hatred to Cicero and became a ready tool in the hands of Pompey and others, who beheld, in the eloquence of Cicero, the greatest bulwark of the constitution. He succeeded in expelling the father of his country, who was, however, speedily recalled.

informed of the decree of the senate, [to the effect] that all the youth of Italy should take the military oath, he determined to hold a levy throughout the entire poovince. Report of these events is rapidly borne into Transalpine Gaul. The Gauls themselves add to the report, and invent, what the case seemed to require, [namely] that[1] Cæsar was detained by commotions in the city, and could not, amid so violent dissensions, come to his army. Animated by this opportunity, they who already, previously to this occurrence, were indignant that they were reduced beneath the dominion of Rome, begin to organize their plans for war more openly and daringly. The leading men of Gaul, having convened councils among themselves in the woods, and retired places, complain of the death of Acco: they point out that this fate may fall in turn on themselves: they bewail the unhappy fate of Gaul; and by every sort of promises and rewards, they earnestly solicit some to begin the war, and assert the freedom of Gaul at the hazard of their lives. They say that special care should be paid to this, that Cæsar should be cut off from his army before their secret plans should be divulged. That this was easy, because neither would the legions, in the absence of their general, dare to leave their winter quarters, nor could the general reach his army without a guard: finally, that it was better to be slain in battle, than not to recover their ancient glory in war, and that freedom which they had received from their forefathers.

CHAP. II.—While these things are in agitation, the Carnutes declare "that they would decline no danger for the sake of the general safety, 'and promise" that they would be the first of all to begin the war; and since they can not at present take precautions, by giving and receiving hostages, that the affair shall not be divulged, they require that a solemn assurance be given them by oath and plighted honor, their military

Clodius met a death worthy of his life, being slain by a gladiator in the service of Milo, one of his most hated political opponents. It was on the occasion of Milo's trial for the death of Clodius that Cicero pronounced his famous oration, "Pro Milone," which has attracted the admiration of all ages for the eloquence of the language and beauty of the diction.

[1] Plutarch well remarks, that had Vercingetorix waited a little longer until Cæsar had actually engaged in the civil war, the rising of the Gauls would have appeared as formidable to the Romans as the inroad of the Cimbri and Teutones.

standards being brought together (in which manner their most sacred obligations are made binding), that they should not be deserted by the rest of the Gauls on commencing the war.

CHAP. III.—When the appointed day came, the Carnutes, under the command of Cotuatus and Conetodunus, desperate men, meet together at Genabum, and slay the Roman citizens who had settled there for the purpose of trading (among the rest, Caius Fusius Cita, a distinguished Roman knight, who by Cæsar's orders had presided over the provision department), and plunder their property. The report is quickly spread among all the states of Gaul; for, whenever a more important and remarkable event takes place, they transmit the intelligence through their lands and districts by a shout;[1] the others take it up in succession, and pass it to their neighbors, as happened on this occasion; for the things which were done at Genabum at sunrise, were heard in the territories of the Arverni before the end of the first watch, which is an extent of more than a hundred and sixty miles.

CHAP. IV.—There in like manner, Vercingetorix[2] the son of Celtillus the Arvernian, a young man of the highest power (whose father had held the supremacy of entire Gaul, and had been put to death by his fellow-citizens, for this reason, because he aimed at sovereign power), summoned together his dependents, and easily excited them. On his design being made known, they rush to arms: he is expelled from the town of Gergovia,[3] by his uncle Gobanitio and the rest of the nobles, who were of opinion, that such an enterprise ought not to be hazarded: he did not however desist, but held in the country a

[1] Men were posted on heights to convey the intelligence from one to the other by shouts. This practice was adopted in Persia. The Spaniards, on their invasion of Peru, found that runners were stationed at short regular distances to convey any important intelligence to the government.

[2] Vercingetorix appears to have been by far the most talented of the Gallic chieftains that ever entered the lists against Cæsar; he certainly raised the most powerful combination against Rome which has been yet mentioned; and it was under him that the warrior Gauls made their last great effort to crush the overwhelming power of Rome, which is detailed in the present book. Celtic scholars derive the name Vercingetorix from Ver-cim-cedo-righ, which means, "chieftain of a hundred heads," or, in other words, "a great captain."

[3] Gergovia, a very strong town and fortress of the Arverni, built on a very high mountain, which was almost inaccessible: it lay to the west of the Albi, and is remarkable as being the only place in Gaul that foiled the arms of Cæsar. It is considered to be the modern *Mount Gergoie.*

levy of the needy and desperate. Having collected such a body of troops, he brings over to his sentiments such of his fellow-citizens as he has access to: he exhorts them to take up arms in behalf of the general freedom, and having assembled great forces he drives from the state his opponents, by whom he had been expelled a short time previously. He is saluted king by his partisans; he sends embassadors in every direction, he conjures them to adhere firmly to their promise. He quickly attaches to his interests the Senones, Parisii, Pictones, Cadurci, Turones, Aulerci, Lemovice, and all the others who border on the ocean; the supreme command is conferred on him by unanimous consent. On obtaining this authority, he demands hostages from all these states, he orders a fixed number of soldiers to be sent to him immediately; he determines what quantity of arms each state shall prepare at home, and before what time; he pays particular attention to the cavalry. To the utmost vigilance he adds the utmost rigor of authority; and by the severity of his punishments brings over the wavering: for on the commission of a greater crime[1] he puts the perpetrators to death by fire and every sort of tortures; for a slighter cause, he sends home the offenders with their ears cut off, or one of their eyes put out, that they may be an example to the rest, and frighten others by the severity of their punishment.

CHAP. V.—Having quickly collected an army by their punishments, he sends Lucterius, one of the Cadurci, a man of the utmost daring, with part of his forces, into the territory of the Ruteni; and marches in person into the country of the Bituriges. On his arrival, the Bituriges send embassadors to the Ædui, under whose protection they were, to solicit aid in order that they might more easily resist the forces of the enemy. The Ædui, by the advice of the lieutenants whom Cæsar had left with the army, send supplies of horse and foot to succor the Bituriges. When they came to the river Loire, which separates the Bituriges from the Ædui, they delayed a few days there, and, not daring to pass the river, return home, and send back word to the lieutenants that they had returned through fear of the treachery of the Bituriges, who, they ascertained, had formed this design, that if the Ædui should cross the river, the Bituriges on the one side, and the Arverni

[1] Than being lukewarm in the Gallic cause.

on the other, should surround them. Whether they did this for the reason which they alleged to the lieutenants, or influenced by treachery, we think that we ought not to state as certain, because we have no proof. On their departure, the Bituriges immediately unite themselves to the Arverni.

CHAP. VI.—These affairs being announced to Cæsar in Italy, at the time when he understood that matters in the city had been reduced to a more tranquil state by the energy of Cneius Pompey, he set out for Transalpine Gaul. After he had arrived there, he[1] was greatly at a loss to know by what means he could reach his army. For if he should summon the legions into the province, he was aware that on their march they would have to fight in his absence; he foresaw too, that if he himself should endeavor to reach the army, he would act injudiciously, in trusting his safety even to those who seemed to be tranquilized.

CHAP. VII.—In the mean time Lucterius the Cadurcan, having been sent into the country of the Ruteni, gains over that state to the Arverni. Having advanced into the country of the Nitiobriges, and Gabali, he receives hostages from both nations, and, assembling a numerous force, marches to make a descent on the province in the direction of Narbo. Cæsar, when this circumstance was announced to him, thought that the march to Narbo ought to take the precedence of all his other plans. When he arrived there, he encourages the timid, and stations garrisons among the Ruteni,[2] in the province of the Volcæ Arecomici, and the country around Narbo which was in the vicinity of the enemy; he orders a portion of the forces from the province, and the recruits which he had brought from Italy, to rendezvous among the Helvii who border on the territories of the Arverni.

CHAP. VIII.—These matters being arranged, and Lucterius now checked and forced to retreat, because he thought it dangerous to enter the line of Roman garrisons, Cæsar marches into the country of the Helvii; although mount Cevennes,[3] which separates the Arverni from the Helvii,

[1] Literally, "he was affected with great difficulty."

[2] Cæsar calls them the Ruteni of the province, to distinguish them from the Ruteni of Aquitania.

[3] Mount Cevenna, or Cebenna, the Cevennes, a lofty chain of mountains which separated Aquitania from Gallia Narbonensis, and joins Mount Jura.

blocked up the way with very deep snow, as it was the severest season of the year; yet having cleared away the snow to the depth of six feet, and having opened the roads, he reaches the territories of the Arverni, with infinite labor to his soldiers. This people being surprised, because they considered themselves defended by the Cevennes as by a wall, and the paths at this season of the year had never before been passable even to individuals, he orders the cavalry to extend themselves as far as they could, and strike as great a panic as possible into the enemy. These proceedings are speedily announced to Vercingetorix by rumor and his messengers. Around him all the Arverni crowd in alarm, and solemnly entreat him to protect their property, and not to suffer them to be plundered by the enemy, especially as he saw that all the war was transferred into their country. Being prevailed upon by their entreaties he moves his camp from the country of the Bituriges in the direction of the Arverni.

Chap. IX.—Cæsar, having delayed two days in that place, because he had anticipated that, in the natural course of events, such would be the conduct of Vercingetorix, leaves the army under pretense of raising recruits and cavalry: he places Brutus, a young man, in command of these forces; he gives him instructions that the cavalry should range as extensively as possible in all directions; that he would exert himself not to be absent from the camp longer than three days. Having arranged these matters, he marches to Vienna[1] by as long journeys as he can, when his own soldiers did not expect him. Finding there a fresh body of cavalry, which he had sent on to that place several days before, marching incessantly night and day, he advanced rapidly through the territory of the Ædui into that of the Lingones, in which two legions were wintering, that, if any plan affecting his own safety should have been organized by the Ædui, he might defeat it by the rapidity of his movements. When he arrived there, he sends information to the rest of the legions, and gathers all his army into one place before intelligence of his arrival could be announced to the Arverni.

Vercingetorix, on hearing this circumstance, leads back his

[1] Vienna, now *Vienne*, the chief town of the Allobroges, situated on the eastern bank of the Rhone.

army into the country of the Bituriges; and after marching from it to Gergovia, a town of the Boii, whom Cæsar had settled there after defeating them in the Helvetian war, and had rendered tributary to the Ædui, he determined to attack it.

CHAP. X.—This action caused great perplexity to Cæsar in the selection of his plans; [he feared] lest, if he should confine his legions in one place for the remaining portion of the winter, all Gaul should revolt when the tributaries of the Ædui were subdued, because it would appear that there was in him no protection for his friends; but if he should draw them too soon out of their winter quarters, he might be distressed by the want of provisions, in consequence of the difficulty of conveyance. It seemed better, however, to endure every hardship than to alienate the affections of all his allies, by submitting to such an insult. Having, therefore, impressed on the Ædui the necessity of supplying him with provisions, he sends forward messengers to the Boii to inform them of his arrival, and encourage them to remain firm in their allegiance, and resist the attack of the enemy with great resolution. Having left two legions and the luggage of the entire army at Agendicum,[1] he marches to the Boii.

CHAP. XI.—On the second day, when he came to Vellaunodunum,[2] a town of the Senones, he determined to attack it, in order that he might not leave an enemy in his rear, and might the more easily procure supplies of provisions, and draw a line of circumvallation around it in two days: on the third day, embassadors being sent from the town to treat of a capitulation, he orders their arms to be brought together, their cattle to be brought forth, and six hundred hostages to be given. He leaves Caius Trebonius his lieutenant, to complete these arrangements; he himself sets out with the intention of marching as soon as possible, to Genabum, a town of the Carnutes, who having then for the first time received information of the siege of Vellaunodunum, as they thought that it would be protracted to a longer time, were preparing a garrison to send to Genabum

[1] Agendicum, now *Sens*, the chief city of the Senones. It stood below the confluence of the Vanne and the Yonne, a southern branch of the Seine.

[2] Vellaunodunum, now *Beauns*, a town of the Senones, about fifty-five miles south of Paris.

for the defense of that town. Cæsar arrived here in two days; after pitching his camp before the town, being prevented by the time of the day, he defers the attack to the next day, and orders his soldiers to prepare whatever was necessary for that enterprise; and as a bridge over the Loire connected the town of Genabum[1] with the opposite bank, fearing lest the inhabitants should escape by night from the town, he orders two legions to keep watch under arms. The people of Genabum came forth silently from the city before midnight, and began to cross the river. When this circumstance was announced by scouts, Cæsar, having set fire to the gates, sends in the legions which he had ordered to be ready, and obtains possession of the town so completely, that very few of the whole number of the enemy escaped being taken alive, because the narrowness of the bridge and the roads prevented the multitude from escaping. He pillages and burns the town, gives the booty to the soldiers, then leads his army over the Loire, and marches into the territories of the Bituriges.

Chap. XII.—Vercingetorix, when he ascertained the arrival of Cæsar, desisted from the siege [of Gergovia], and marched to meet Cæsar. The latter had commenced to besiege Noviodunum; and when embassadors came from this town to beg that he would pardon them and spare their lives, in order that he might execute the rest of his designs with the rapidity by which he had accomplished most of them, he orders their arms to be collected, their horses to be brought forth, and hostages to be given. A part of the hostages being now delivered up, when the rest of the terms were being performed, a few centurions and soldiers being sent into the town to collect the arms and horses, the enemy's cavaly which had outstripped the main body of Vercingetorix's army, was seen at a distance; as soon as the townsmen beheld them, and entertained hopes of assistance, raising a shout, they began to take up arms, shut the gates, and line the walls. When the centurions in the town understood from the signal-making of the Gauls that they were forming some new design, they drew their swords and seized the gates, and recovered all their men safe.

Chap. XIII.—Cæsar orders the horse to be drawn out of

[1] Genabum, a town of the Areliani, situated on the Loire, which ran through it. It was subsequently called by the inhabitants Aurelianum, which by a slight change became the modern Orleans.

the camp, and commences a cavalry action. His men being now distressed, Cæsar sends to their aid about four hundred German horse, which he had determined, at the beginning, to keep with himself. The Gauls could not withstand their attack, but were put to flight, and retreated to their main body, after losing a great number of men. When they were routed, the townsmen, again intimidated, arrested those persons by whose exertions they thought that the mob had been roused, and brought them to Cæsar, and surrendered themselves to him. When these affairs were accomplished, Cæsar marched to the Avaricum,[1] which was the largest and best fortified town in the territories of the Bituriges, and situated in a most fertile tract of country; because he confidently expected that on taking that town, he would reduce beneath his dominion the state of the Bituriges.

CHAP. XIV.—Vercingetorix, after sustaining such a series of losses at Vellaunodunum, Genabum, and Noviodunum, summons his men to a council. He impresses on them "that the war must be prosecuted on a very different system from that which had been previously adopted; but they should by all means aim at this object, that the Romans should be prevented from foraging and procuring provisions; that this was easy, because they themselves were well supplied with cavalry, and were likewise assisted by the season of the year; that forage could not be cut; that the enemy must necessarily disperse, and look for it in the houses, that all these might be daily destroyed by the horse. Besides that the interests of private property must be neglected for the sake of the general safety; that the villages and houses ought to be fired, over such an extent of country in every direction from Boia, as the Romans appeared capable of scouring in their search for forage. That an abundance of these necessaries could be supplied to them, because they would be assisted by the resources of those in whose territories the war would be waged: that the Romans either would not bear the privation, or else would advance to any distance from the camp with considerable danger; and that it made no difference whether they slew them or stripped them of their baggage, since, if it was

[1] Avaricum, the modern *Bourges*, the largest and best fortified town of the Bituriges, whose name it subsequently bore. It derived its ancient appellation from the river Avara, the Euse, one of the southern branches of the Loire.

lost, they could not carry on the war. Besides that, the towns ought to be burned which were not secured against every danger by their fortifications or natural advantages; that there should not be places of retreat for their own countrymen for declining military service, nor be exposed to the Romans as inducements to carry off abundance of provisions and plunder. If these sacrifices should appear heavy or galling, that they ought to consider it much more distressing that their wives and children should be dragged off to slavery, and themselves slain; the evils which must necessarily befall the conquered.

Chap. XV.—This opinion having been approved of by unanimous consent, more than twenty towns of the Bituriges are burned in one day. Conflagrations are beheld in every quarter; and although all bore this with great regret, yet they laid before themselves this consolation, that, as the victory was certain, they could quickly recover their losses. There is a debate concerning Avaricum in the general council, whether they should decide, that it should be burned or defended. The Bituriges threw themselves at the feet of all the Gauls, and entreat that they should not be compelled to set fire with their own hands to the fairest city of almost the whole of Gaul, which was both a protection and ornament to the state; they say that "they could easily defend it, owing to the nature of the ground, for, being inclosed almost on every side by a river and a marsh, it had only one entrance, and that very narrow." Permission being granted to them at their earnest request, Vercingetorix at first dissuades them from it, but afterward concedes the point, owing to their entreaties and the compassion of the soldiers. A proper garrison is selected for the town.

Chap. XVI.—Vercingetorix follows closely upon Cæsar by shorter marches, and selects for his camp a place defended by woods and marshes, at the distance of fifteen miles from Avaricum. There he received intelligence by trusty scouts, every hour in the day, of what was going on at Avaricum, and ordered whatever he wished to be done; he closely watched all our expeditions for corn and forage, and whenever they were compelled to go to a greater distance, he attacked them when dispersed, and inflicted severe loss upon them; although the evil was remedied by our men, as far as precautions could be taken, by going forth at irregular times, and by different ways.

CHAP. XVII.—Cæsar pitching his camp at that side of the town which was not defended by the river and marsh, and had a very narrow approach, as we have mentioned, began to raise the vineæ and erect two towers: for the nature of the place prevented him from drawing a line of circumvallation. He never ceased to importune the Boii and Ædui for supplies of corn; of whom the one [the Ædui], because they were acting with no zeal, did not aid him much; the others [the Boii], as their resources were not great, quickly consumed what they had. Although the army was distressed by the greatest want of corn, through the poverty of the Boii, the apathy of the Ædui, and the burning of the houses, to such a degree, that for several days the soldiers were without corn, and satisfied their extreme hunger with cattle driven from the remote villages; yet no language was heard from them unworthy of the majesty of the Roman people and their former victories. Moreover, when Cæsar addressed the legions, one by one, when at work, and said that he would raise the siege, if they felt the scarcity too severely, they unanimously begged him "not to do so; that they had served for several years under his command in such a manner that they never submitted to insult, and never abandoned an enterprise without accomplishing it; that they should consider it a disgrace if they abandoned the siege after commencing it; that it was better to endure every hardship than to not avenge[1] the manes of the Roman citizens who perished at Genabum by the perfidy of the Gauls." They intrusted the same declarations to the centurions and military tribunes, that through them they might be communicated to Cæsar.

CHAP. XVIII.—When the towers had now approached the walls, Cæsar ascertained from the captives that Vercingetorix, after destroying the forage, had pitched his camp nearer Avaricum, and that he himself with the cavalry and light-armed infantry, who generally fought among the horse, had gone to lay an ambuscade in that quarter, to which he thought that our troops would come the next day to forage. On learning these facts, he set out from the camp secretly at midnight, and reached the camp of the enemy early in the morning.

[1] *Parento* means, properly, to celebrate the funeral obsequies of a parent or friend; hence, by an easy transition, it came to signify "to avenge the death of any one."

They having quickly learned the arrival of Cæsar by scouts, hid their cars and baggage in the thickest parts of the woods, and drew up all their forces in a lofty and open space: which circumstance being announced, Cæsar immediately ordered the baggage to be piled, and the arms to be got ready.

CHAP. XIX.—There was a hill of a gentle ascent from the bottom; a dangerous and impassable marsh, not more than fifty feet broad, begirt it on almost every side. The Gauls, having broken down the bridges, posted themselves on this hill, in confidence of their position, and being drawn up in tribes according to their respective states, held all the fords and passages of that marsh with trusty guards, thus determined that if the Romans should attempt to force the marsh, they would overpower them from the higher ground while sticking in it, so that whoever saw the nearness of the position, would imagine that the two armies were prepared to fight on almost equal terms; but whoever should view accurately the disadvantage of position, would discover that they were showing off an empty affectation of courage. Cæsar clearly points out to his soldiers, who were indignant that the enemy could bear the sight of them at the distance of so short a space, and were earnestly demanding the signal for action, "with how great loss and the death of how many gallant men the victory would necessarily be purchased: and when he saw them so determined to decline no danger for his renown, that he ought to be considered guilty of the utmost injustice if he did not hold their life dearer than his personal safety." Having thus consoled his soldiers, he leads them back on the same day to the camp, and determined to prepare the other things which were necessary for the siege of the town.

CHAP. XX.—Vercingetorix, when he had returned to his men, was accused of treason, in that he had moved his camp nearer the Romans, in that he had gone away with all the cavalry, in that he had left so great forces without a commander, in that, on his departure, the Romans had come at such a favorable season, and with such dispatch; that all these circumstances could not have happened accidentally or without design; that he preferred holding the sovereignty of Gaul by the grant of Cæsar to acquiring it by their favor. Being accused in such a manner, he made the following reply to these charges:—"That his moving his camp had been caused by want of forage, and had been done even by their advice; that his approaching near the Romans had been a measure dictated by the favorable nature of the ground, which would defend him by its natural strength; that the service of the cavalry could not have been requisite in marshy ground, and was useful in that place to which they had gone; that he, on his departure, had given the supreme command to no one intentionally, lest he should be induced by the eagerness of the multitude to hazard an engagement, to which he perceived that all were inclined, owing to their want of energy, because they were unable to endure fatigue any longer. That, if the Romans in the mean time came up by chance, they [the Gauls] should feel grateful to fortune; if invited by the information of some one they should feel grateful to him, because they were enabled to see distinctly from the higher ground the smallness of the number of their enemy, and despise the courage of those who, not daring to fight, retreated disgracefully into their camp. That he desired no power from Cæsar by treachery, since he could have it by victory, which was now assured to himself and to all the Gauls; nay, that he would even give them back the command, if they thought that they conferred honor on him, rather than received safety from him. That you may be assured," said he, "that I speak these words with truth;—listen to these Roman soldiers!" He produces some camp-followers whom he had surprised on a foraging expedition some days before, and had tortured by famine and confinement. They being previously instructed in what answers they should make when examined, say, "That they were legionary soldiers, that, urged by famine and want, they had recently gone forth from the camp, [to see] if they could find any corn or cattle in the fields; that the whole army was distressed by a similar scarcity, nor had any one now sufficient strength, nor could bear the labor of the work; and therefore that the general was determined, if he made no progress in the siege, to draw off his army in three days." "These benefits," says Vercingetorix, "you receive from me, whom you accuse of treason—me, by whose exertions you see so powerful and victorious an army almost destroyed by famine, without shedding one drop of your blood; and I have taken precautions that no state shall admit within its territories this army in its ignominious flight from this place."

Chap. XXI.—The whole multitude raise a shout and clash their arms, according to their custom, as they usually do in the case of him of whose speech they approve; [they exclaim] that Vercingetorix was a consummate general, and that they had no doubt of his honor; that the war could not be conducted with greater prudence. They determine that ten thousand men should be picked out of the entire army and sent into the town, and decide that the general safety should not be intrusted to the Bituriges alone, because they were aware that the glory of the victory must rest with the Bituriges, if they made good the defense of the town.

Chap. XXII.—To the extraordinary valor of our soldiers, devices of every sort were opposed by the Gauls; since they are a nation of consummate ingenuity, and most skillful in imitating and making those things which are imparted by any one; for they turned aside the hooks[1] with nooses, and when they had caught hold of them firmly, drew them on by means of engines, and undermined the mound the more skillfully on this account, because there are in their territories extensive iron mines, and consequently every description of mining operations is known and practiced by them. They had furnished, moreover, the whole wall on every side with turrets, and had covered them with skins. Besides, in their frequent sallies by day and night, they attempted either to set fire to the mound, or attack our soldiers when engaged in the works; and, moreover, by splicing the upright timbers of their own towers, they equaled the height of ours, as fast as the mound had daily raised them, and countermined our mines, and impeded the working of them by stakes bent and sharpened at the ends, and boiling pitch, and stones of very great weight, and prevented them from approaching the walls.

Chap. XXIII.—But this is usually the form of all the Gallic walls. Straight beams, connected lengthwise and two feet distant from each other at equal intervals, are placed together on the ground; these are mortised on the inside, and covered with plenty of earth. But the intervals which we have mentioned,

[1] These are the *falces murales.* When they were struck against the walls to tear out the stones, the Gauls standing on the top caught them by a sort of snares and prevented their blows, and drew them over the walls into the town. They also undermined the embankments of the Romans and rendered them useless.

are closed up in front by large stones. These being thus laid and cemented together, another row is added above, in such a manner, that the same interval may be observed, and that the beams may not touch one another, but equal spaces intervening, each row of beams is kept firmly in its place by a row of stones. In this manner the whole wall is consolidated, until the regular height of the wall be completed. This work, with respect to appearance and variety, is not unsightly, owing to the alternate rows of beams and stones, which preserve their order in right lines; and, besides, it possesses great advantages as regards utility and the defense of cities; for the stone protects it from fire, and the wood from the battering ram, since it [the wood] being mortised in the inside with rows of beams, generally forty feet each in length, can neither be broken through nor torn asunder.

CHAP. XXIV.—The siege having been impeded by so many disadvantages, the soldiers, although they were retarded during the whole time by the mud, cold, and constant showers, yet by their incessant labor overcame all these obstacles, and in twenty-five days raised a mound three hundred and thirty feet broad and eighty feet high. When it almost touched the enemy's walls, and Cæsar, according to his usual custom, kept watch at the work, and encouraged the soldiers not to discontinue the work for a moment: a little before the third watch they discovered that the mound was sinking, since the enemy had set it on fire by a mine; and at the same time a shout was raised along the entire wall, and a sally was made from two gates on each side of the turrets. Some at a distance were casting torches and dry wood from the wall on the mound, others were pouring on it pitch, and other materials, by which the flame might be excited, so that a plan could hardly be formed, as to where they should first run to the defense, or to what part aid should be brought. However, as two legions always kept guard before the camp by Cæsar's orders, and several of them were at stated times at the work, measures were promptly taken, that some should oppose the sallying party, others draw back the towers and make a cut in the rampart; and moreover, that the whole army should hasten from the camp to extinguish the flames.

CHAP. XXV.—When the battle was going on in every direction, the rest of the night being now spent, and fresh hopes of victory always arose before the enemy: the more so on this account because they saw the coverings of our towers burnt away, and perceived, that we, being exposed, could not easily go to give assistance, and they themselves were always relieving the weary with fresh men, and considered that all the safety of Gaul rested on this crisis; there happened in my own view a circumstance which, having appeared to be worthy of record, we thought it ought not to be omitted. A certain Gaul before the gate of the town, who was casting into the fire opposite the turret balls of tallow and fire which were passed along to him, was pierced with a dart on the right side and fell dead.[1] One of those next him stepped over him as he lay, and discharged the same office: when the second man was slain in the same manner by a wound from a cross-bow, a third succeeded him, and a fourth succeeded the third: nor was this post left vacant by the besieged, until, the fire of the mound having been extinguished, and the enemy repulsed in every direction, an end was put to the fighting.

Chap. XXVI.—The Gauls having tried every expedient, as nothing had succeeded, adopted the design of fleeing from the town the next day, by the advice and order of Vercingetorix. They hoped that, by attempting it at the dead of night, they would effect it without any great loss of men, because the camp of Vercingetorix was not far distant from the town, and the extensive marsh which intervened, was likely to retard the Romans in the pursuit. And they were now preparing to execute this by night, when the matrons suddenly ran out into the streets, and weeping cast themselves at the feet of their husbands, and requested of them, with every entreaty, that they should not abandon themselves and their common children to the enemy for punishment, because the weakness of their nature and physical powers prevented them from taking to flight. When they saw that they (as fear does not generally admit of mercy in extreme danger) persisted in their resolution, they began to shout aloud, and give intelligence of their flight to the Romans. The Gauls being intimidated by fear of this, lest the passes should be pre-occupid by the Roman cavalry, desisted from their design.

[1] These balls were passed from hand to hand until they came to him, and he was in the act of throwing them into the fire when he was struck by the arrow from the cross-bow.

CHAP. XXVII.—The next day Cæsar, the tower being advanced, and the works which he had determined to raise being arranged, a violent storm arising, thought this no bad time for executing his designs, because he observed the guards arranged on the walls a little too negligently, and therefore ordered his own men to engage in their work more remissly, and pointed out what he wished to be done. He drew up his soldiers in a secret position within the vineæ, and exhorts them to reap, at least, the harvest of victory proportionate to their exertions. He proposed a reward for those who should first scale the walls, and gave the signal to the soldiers. They suddenly flew out from all quarters and quickly filled the walls.

CHAP. XXVIII.—The enemy being alarmed by the suddenness of the attack, were dislodged from the wall and towers, and drew up, in form of a wedge, in the market place and the open streets, with this intention that, if an attack should be made on any side, they should fight with their line drawn up to receive it. When they saw no one descending to the level ground, and the enemy extending themselves along the entire wall in every direction, fearing lest every hope of flight should be cut off, they cast away their arms, and sought, without stopping, the most remote parts of the town. A part was then slain by the infantry when they were crowding upon one another in the narrow passage of the gates; and a part having got without the gates, were cut to pieces by the cavalry: nor was there one who was anxious for the plunder. Thus, being excited by the massacre at Genabum and the fatigue of the siege, they spared neither those worn out with years, women, or children. Finally, out of all that number, which amounted to about forty thousand, scarcely eight hundred, who fled from the town when they heard the first alarm, reached Vercingetorix in safety: and he, the night being now far spent, received them in silence after their flight (fearing that any sedition should arise in the camp from their entrance in a body and the compassion of the soldiers), so that, having arranged his friends and the chiefs of the states at a distance on the road, he took precautions that they should be separated and conducted to their fellow countrymen, to whatever part of the camp had been assigned to each state from the beginning.

CHAP. XXIX.—Vercingetorix having convened an assembly on the following day, consoled and encouraged his soldiers in the following words:—"That they should not be too much depressed in spirit, nor alarmed at their loss; that the Romans did not conquer by valor nor in the field, but by a kind of art and skill in assault, with which they themselves were unacquainted; that whoever expected every event in the war to be favorable, erred; that it never was his opinion that Avaricum should be defended, of the truth of which statement he had themselves as witnesses, but that it was owing to the imprudence of the Bituriges, and the too ready compliance of the rest, that this loss was sustained; that, however, he would soon compensate it by superior advantages; for that he would, by his exertions, bring over those states which severed themselves from the rest of the Gauls, and would create a general unanimity throughout the whole of Gaul, the union of which not even the whole earth could withstand, and that he had it already almost effected; that in the mean time it was reasonable that he should prevail on them, for the sake of the general safety, to begin to fortify their camp, in order that they might the more easily sustain the sudden attacks of the enemy."

CHAP. XXX.—This speech was not disagreeable to the Gauls, principally, because he himself was not disheartened by receiving so severe a loss, and had not concealed himself, nor shunned the eyes of the people: and he was believed to possess greater foresight and sounder judgment than the rest, because, when the affair was undecided, he had at first been of opinion that Avaricum should be burnt, and afterward that it should be abandoned. Accordingly, as ill success weakens the authority of other generals, so, on the contrary, his dignity increased daily, although a loss was sustained: at the same time they began to entertain hopes, on his assertion, of uniting the rest of the states to themselves, and on this occasion, for the first time, the Gauls[1] began to fortify their camps, and were so alarmed that although they were men unaccustomed to toil, yet they were of opinion that they ought to endure and suffer every thing which should be imposed upon them.

CHAP. XXXI.—Nor did Vercingetorix use less efforts than he had promised, to gain over the other states, and [in consequence] endeavored to entice their leaders by gifts and promises. For this object he selected fitting emissaries, by whose subtle

[1] The Nervii did so in the war with Cicero, but it now became a general custom.

pleading or private friendship, each of the nobles could be most easily influenced. He takes care that those who fled to him on the storming of Avaricum should be provided with arms and clothes. At the same time that his diminished forces should be recruited, he levies a fixed quota of soldiers from each state, and defines the number and day before which he should wish them brought to the camp, and orders all the archers, of whom there was a very great number in Gaul, to be collected and sent to him. By these means, the troops which were lost at Avaricum are speedily replaced. In the mean time, Teutomarus, the son of Ollovicon, the king of the Nitiobriges,[1] whose father had received the appellation of friend from our senate, came to him with a great number of his own horse and those whom he had hired from Aquitania.

CHAP. XXXII.—Cæsar, after delaying several days at Avaricum, and, finding there the greatest plenty of corn and other provisions, refreshed his army after their fatigue and privation. The winter being almost ended, when he was invited by the favorable season of the year to prosecute the war and march against the enemy, [and try] whether he could draw them from the marshes and woods, or else press them by a blockade; some noblemen of the Ædui came to him as embassadors to entreat "that in an extreme emergency he should succor their state; that their affairs were in the utmost danger, because, whereas single magistrates had been usually appointed in ancient times and held the power of king for a single year, two persons now exercised this office, and each asserted that he was appointed according to their laws. That one of them was Convictolitanis, a powerful and illustrious youth; the other Cotus, sprung from a most ancient family, and personally a man of very great influence and extensive connections. His brother Valetiacus had borne the same office during the last year: that the whole state was up in arms; the senate divided, the people divided; that each of them had his own adherents; and that if the animosity would be fomented any longer, the result would be that one part of the state would come to a collision with the other; that it rested with his activity and influence to prevent it."

CHAP. XXXIII.—Although Cæsar considered it ruinous to leave the war and the enemy, yet, being well aware what great

[1] The Nitiobriges were a people of Gallia, whose country was situated on both sides of the Garrone, where it receives the Olt.

evils generally arise from internal dissensions, lest a state so powerful and so closely connected with the Roman people, which he himself had always fostered and honored in every respect, should have recourse to violence and arms, and that the party which had less confidence in its own power should summon aid from Vercingetorix, he determined to anticipate this movement; and because, by the laws of the Ædui, it was not permitted those who held the supreme authority to leave the country, he determined to go in person to the Ædui, lest he should appear to infringe upon their government and laws, and summoned all the senate, and those between whom the dispute was, to meet him at Decetia.[1] When almost all the state had assembled there, and he was informed that one brother had been declared magistrate by the other, when only a few persons were privately summoned for the purpose, at a different time and place from what he ought, whereas the laws not only forbade two belonging to one family to be elected magistrates while each was alive, but even deterred them from being in the senate, he compelled Cotus to resign his office; he ordered Convictolitanis, who had been elected by the priests, according to the usage of the state,[2] in the presence of the magistrates, to hold the supreme authority.

Chap. XXXIV.—Having pronounced this decree between [the contending parties], he exhorted the Ædui to bury in oblivion their disputes and dissensions, and, laying aside all these things, devote themselves to the war, and expect from him, on the conquest of Gaul, those rewards which they should have earned, and send speedily to him all their cavalry and ten thousand infantry, which he might place in different garrisons to protect his convoys of provisions, and then divided his army into two parts: he gave Labienus four legions to lead into the country of the Senones and Parisii; and led in person six into the country of the Arverni, in the direction of the town of Gergovia, along the banks of the Allier.[3] He gave part of

[1] Decetia, now *Decize*, a town of the Ædui, situated in a rocky island in the Loire, about 153 miles south-east from Paris.

[2] I have here adopted the reading, "intromissis magistratibus," which is supported by the authority of the Greek paraphrases. Oberlins reads, "intermissis magistratibus," which may be rendered, "when the magistracy was vacant."

[3] Elaver, the Allier, a river of Gaul, which rises at the foot of Mount Lozere, runs nearly north, and, after a course of seventy-two leagues, falls into the Loire about three miles above Nevers.

the cavalry to Labienus and kept part to himself. Vercingetorix, on learning this circumstance, broke down all the bridges over the river and began to march on the other bank of the Allier.

CHAP. XXXV.—When each army was in sight of the other, and was pitching their camp almost opposite that of the enemy, scouts being distributed in every quarter, lest the Romans should build a bridge and bring over their troops; it was to Cæsar a matter attended with great difficulties, lest he should be hindered from passing the river during the greater part of the summer, as the Allier can not generally be forded before the autumn. Therefore, that this might not happen, having pitched his camp in a woody place opposite to one of those bridges which Vercingetorix had taken care should be broken down, the next day he stopped behind with two legions in a secret place; he sent on the rest of the forces as usual, with all the baggage, after having selected some cohorts, that the number of the legions might appear to be complete. Having ordered these to advance as far as they could, when now, from the time of day, he conjectured they had come to an encampment, he began to rebuild the bridge on the same piles, the lower part of which remained entire. Having quickly finished the work and led his legions across, he selected a fit place for a camp, and recalled the rest of his troops. Vercingetorix, on ascertaining this fact, went before him by forced marches, in order that he might not be compelled to come to an action against his will.

CHAP. XXXVI.—Cæsar, in five days' march, went from that place to Gergovia, and after engaging in a slight cavalry skirmish that day, on viewing the situation of the city, which, being built on a very high mountain, was very difficult of access, he despaired of taking it by storm, and determined to take no measures with regard to besieging it before he should secure a supply of provisions. But Vercingetorix, having pitched his camp on the mountain near the town, placed the forces of each state separately and at small intervals around himself, and having occupied all the hills of that range as far as they commanded a view [of the Roman encampment], he presented a formidable appearance; he ordered the rulers of the states, whom he had selected as his council of war, to come to him daily at the dawn, whether any measure seemed to require deliberation or execution. Nor did he allow almost any day to pass without testing in a cavalry action, the archers being intermixed, what spirit and valor there was in each of his own men. There was a hill opposite the town, at the very foot of that mountain, strongly fortified and precipitous on every side (which if our men could gain, they seemed likely to exclude the enemy from a great share of their supply of water, and from free foraging; but this place was occupied by them with a weak garrison): however, Cæsar set out from the camp in the silence of night, and dislodging the garrison before succor could come from the town, he got possession of the place and posted two legions there, and drew from the greater camp to the less a double trench twelve feet broad, so that the soldiers could even singly pass secure from any sudden attack of the enemy.

CHAP. XXXVII.—While these affairs were going on at Gergovia, Convictolanis, the Æduan, to whom we have observed the magistracy was adjudged by Cæsar, being bribed by the Arverni, holds a conference with certain young men, the chief of whom were Litavicus and his brothers, who were born of a most noble family. He shares the bribe with them, and exhorts them to "remember that they were free and born for empire; that the state of the Ædui was the only one which retarded the most certain victory of the Gauls; that the rest were held in check by its authority; and, if it was brought over, the Romans would not have room to stand on in Gaul; that he had received some kindness from Cæsar, only so far, however, as gaining a most just cause by his decision; but that he assigned more weight to the general freedom; for, why should the Ædui go to Cæsar to decide concerning their rights and laws, rather than the Romans come to the Ædui?" The young men being easily won over by the speech of the magistrate and the bribe, when they declared that they would even be leaders in the plot, a plan for accomplishing it was considered, because they were confident their state could not be induced to undertake the war on slight grounds. It was resolved that Litavicus should have the command of the ten thousand, which were being sent to Cæsar for the war, and should have charge of them on their march, and that his brothers should go before him to Cæsar. They arrange the other measures, and the manner in which they should have them done.

CHAP. XXXVIII.—Litavicus, having received the command of the army, suddenly convened the soldiers, when he was about thirty miles distant from Gergovia, and, weeping, said, "Soldiers, whither are we going? All our knights and all our nobles have perished. Eporedirix and Viridomarus, the principal men of the state, being accused of treason, have been slain by the Romans without any permission to plead their cause. Learn this intelligence from those who have escaped from the massacre; for I, since my brothers and all my relations have been slain, am prevented by grief from declaring what has taken place. Persons are brought forward whom he had instructed in what he would have them say, and make the same statements to the soldiery as Litavicus had made: that all the knights of the Ædui were slain because they were said to have held conferences with the Arverni; that they had concealed themselves among the multitude of soldiers, and had escaped from the midst of the slaughter. The Ædui shout aloud and conjure Litavicus to provide for their safety. As if, said he, it were a matter of deliberation, and not of necessity, for us to go to Gergovia and unite ourselves to the Arverni. Or have we any reasons to doubt that the Romans, after perpetrating the atrocious crime, are now hastening to slay us? Therefore, if there be any spirit in us, let us avenge the death of those who have perished in a most unworthy manner, and let us slay these robbers." He points to the Roman citizens, who had accompanied them, in reliance on his protection. He immediately seizes a great quantity of corn and provisions, cruelly tortures them, and then puts them to death, sends messengers throughout the entire state of the Ædui, and rouses them completely by the same falsehood concerning the slaughter of their knights and nobles; he earnestly advises them to avenge, in the same manner as he did, the wrongs, which they had received.

CHAP. XXXIX.—Eporedirix, the Æduan, a young man born in the highest rank and possessing very great influence at home, and, along with Viridomarus, of equal age and influence, but of inferior birth, whom Cæsar had raised from a humble position to the highest rank, on being recommended to him by Divitiacus, had come in the number of horse, being summoned by Cæsar by name. These had a dispute with each other for precedence, and in the struggle between the magistrates they had contended with their utmost efforts, the one for Convictolitanis, the other for Cotus. Of these Eporedirix, on learning the design of Litavicus, lays the matter before Cæsar almost at midnight; he entreats that Cæsar should not suffer their state to swerve from the alliance with the Roman people, owing to the depraved counsels of a few young men, which he foresaw would be the consequence if so many thousand men should unite themselves to the enemy, as their relations could not neglect their safety, nor the state regard it as a matter of slight importance.

CHAP. XL.—Cæsar felt great anxiety on this intelligence, because he had always especially indulged the state of the Ædui, and, without any hesitation, draws out from the camp four light-armed legions and all the cavalry: nor had he time, at such a crisis, to contract the camp, because the affair seemed to depend upon dispatch. He leaves Caius Fabius, his lieutenant, with two legions to guard the camp. When he ordered the brothers of Litavicus to be arrested, he discovers that they had fled a short time before to the camp of the enemy. He encouraged his soldiers "not to be disheartened by the labor of the journey on such a necessary occasion," and, after advancing twenty-five miles, all being most eager, he came in sight of the army of the Ædui, and, by sending on his cavalry, retards and impedes their march; he then issues strict orders to all his soldiers to kill no one. He commands Eporedirix and Viridomarus, who they thought were killed, to move among the cavalry and address their friends. When they were recognized and the treachery of Litavicus discovered, the Ædui began to extend their hands to intimate submission, and, laying down their arms, to deprecate death. Litavicus, with his clansmen, who after the custom of the Gauls consider it a crime to desert their patrons, even in extreme misfortune, flees forth to Gergovia.

CHAP. XLI.—Cæsar, after sending messengers to the state of the Ædui, to inform them that they whom he could have put to death by the right of war were spared through his kindness, and after giving three hours of the night to his army for his repose, directed his march to Gergovia. Almost in the middle of the journey, a party of horse that were sent by Fabius stated in how great danger matters were; they inform him that the camp was attacked by a very powerful army, while fresh men were frequently relieving the wearied, and exhausting our soldiers by the incessant toil, since on account of the size of the camp, they had constantly to remain on the rampart; that many had been wounded by the immense number of arrows and all kinds of missiles; that the engines were of great service in withstanding them; that Fabius, at their departure, leaving only two gates open, was blocking up the rest, and was adding breast-works to the ramparts, and was preparing himself for a similar casualty on the following day. Cæsar, after receiving this information, reached the camp before sunrise owing to the very great zeal of his soldiers.

CHAP. XLII.—While these things are going on at Gergovia, the Ædui, on receiving the first announcements from Litavicus, leave themselves no time to ascertain the truth of those statements. Some are stimulated by avarice, others by revenge and credulity, which is an innate propensity in that race of men to such a degree that they consider a slight rumor as an ascertained fact. They plunder the property of the Roman citizens, and either massacre them or drag them away to slavery. Convictolitanis increases the evil state of affairs, and goads on the people to fury, that by the commission of some outrage they may be ashamed to return to propriety. They entice from the town of Cabillonus, by a promise of safety, Marcus Aristius, a military tribune, who was on his march to his legion; they compel those who had settled there for the purpose of trading to do the same. By constantly attacking them on their march they strip them of all their baggage; they besiege day and night those that resisted; when many were slain on both sides, they excite a great number to arms.

CHAP. XLIII.—In the mean time, when intelligence was brought that all their soldiers were in Cæsar's power, they run in a body to Aristius; they assure him that nothing had been done by public authority; they order an inquiry to be made about the plundered property; they confiscate the property of Litavicus and his brothers; they send embassaders to Cæsar for the purpose of clearing themselves. They do all this with a view to recover their soldiers; but being contaminated by guilt, and charmed by the gains arising from the plundered property, as that act was shared in by many, and being tempted by the fear of punishment, they began to form plans of war and stir up the other states by embassies. Although Cæsar was aware of this proceeding, yet he addresses the embassadors with as much mildness as he can: "That he did not think worse of the state on account of the ignorance and fickleness of the mob, nor would diminish his regard for the Ædui." He himself, fearing a greater commotion in Gaul, in order to prevent his being surrounded by all the states, began to form plans as to the manner in which he should return from Gergovia and again concentrate his forces, lest a departure arising from the fear of a revolt should seem like a flight.

CHAP. XLIV.—While he was considering these things an opportunity of acting successfully seemed to offer. For, when he had come into the smaller camp for the purpose of securing the works, he noticed that the hill in the possession of the enemy was stripped of men, although, on the former days, it could scarcely be seen on account of the numbers on it. Being astonished, he inquires the reason of it from the deserters, a great number of whom flocked to him daily. They all concurred in asserting, what Cæsar himself had already ascertained by his scouts, that the back of that hill was almost level; but likewise woody and narrow, by which there was a pass to the other side of the town; that they had serious apprehensions for this place, and had no other idea, on the occupation of one hill by the Romans, than that, if they should lose the other, they would be almost surrounded, and cut off from all egress and foraging; that they were all summoned by Vercingetorix to fortify this place.

CHAP. XLV.—Cæsar, on being informed of this circumstance, sends several troops of horse to the place immediately after midnight; he orders them to range in every quarter with more tumult than usual. At dawn he orders a large quantity of baggage to be drawn out of the camp, and the muleteers with helmets, in the appearance and guise of horsemen, to ride round the hills. To these he adds a few cavalry, with instructions to range more widely to make a show. He orders them all to seek the same quarter by a long circuit; these proceedings were seen at a distance from the town, as Gergovia commanded a view of the camp, nor could the Gauls ascertain at so great a distance, what certainty there was in the maneuver. He sends one legion to the same hill, and after it had marched a little, stations it in the lower ground, and conceals it in the woods. The suspicion of the Gauls are increased, and all their forces are marched to that place to defend it. Cæsar, having perceived the camp of the enemy deserted, covers the military insignia of his men, conceals the standards, and transfers his soldiers in small bodies from the greater to the less camp, and points out to the lieutenants whom he had placed in command over the respective legions, what he should wish to be done; he particularly advises them to restrain their men from advancing too far, through their desire of fighting, or their hope of plunder; he sets before them what disadvantages the unfavorable nature of the ground carries with it; that they could be assisted by dispatch alone: that success depended on a surprise, and not on a battle. After stating these particulars, he gives the signal for action, and detaches the Ædui at the same time by another ascent on the right.

CHAP. XLVI.—The town wall was 1200 paces distant from the plain and foot of the ascent, in a straight line, if no gap intervened; whatever circuit was added to this ascent, to make the hill easy, increased the length of the route. But almost in the middle of the hill, the Gauls had previously built a wall six feet high, made of large stones, and extending in length as far as the nature of the ground permitted, as a barrier to retard the advance of our men; and leaving all the lower space empty, they had filled the upper part of the hill, as far as the wall of the town, with their camps very close to one another. The soldiers, on the signal being given, quickly advance to this fortification, and passing over it, make themselves masters of the separate camps. And so great was their activity in taking the camps, that Teutomarus, the king of the Nitiobriges, being suddenly surprised in his tent, as he had gone to rest at noon, with difficulty escaped from the hands of the plunderers, with the upper part of his person naked, and his horse wounded.

CHAP. XLVII.—Cæsar, having accomplished the object which he had in view, ordered the signal to be sounded for a retreat; and the soldiers of the tenth legion, by which he was then accompanied, halted. But the soldiers of the other legions, not hearing the sound of the trumpet, because there was a very large valley between them, were however kept back by the tribunes of the soldiers and the lieutenants, according to Cæsar's orders; but being animated by the prospect of speedy victory, and the flight of the enemy, and the favorable battles of former periods, they thought nothing so difficult that their bravery could not accomplish it; nor did they put an end to the pursuit, until they drew nigh to the wall of the town and the gates. But then, when a shout arose in every quarter of the city, those who were at a distance being alarmed by the sudden tumult, fled hastily from the town, since they thought that the enemy were within the gates. The matrons begin to cast their clothes and silver over the wall, and bending over as far as the lower part of the bosom, with outstretched hands beseech the Romans to spare them, and not to sacrifice to their resentment even women and children, as they had done at Avaricum. Some of them let themselves down from the walls by their hands, and surrendered to our soldiers. Lucius Fabius, a centurion of the eighth legion, who, it was ascertained, had said that day among his fellow soldiers that he was excited by the plunder of Avaricum, and would not allow any one to mount the wall before him, finding three men of his own company, and being raised up by them, scaled the wall. He himself, in turn, taking hold of them one by one drew them up to the wall.

Chap. XLVIII.—In the mean time those who had gone to the other part of the town to defend it, as we have mentioned above, at first, aroused by hearing the shouts, and, afterward, by frequent accounts, that the town was in possession of the Romans, sent forward their cavalry, and hastened in larger numbers to that quarter. As each first came he stood beneath the wall, and increased the number of his countrymen engaged in action. When a great multitude of them had assembled, the matrons, who a little before were stretching their hands from the walls to the Romans, began to beseech their countrymen, and after the Gallic fashion to show their disheveled hair, and bring their children into public view. Neither in position nor in numbers was the contest an equal one to the Romans; at the same time, being exhausted by running and the long continuation of the fight, they could not easily withstand fresh and vigorous troops.

Chap. XLIX.—Cæsar, when he perceived that his soldiers were fighting on unfavorable ground, and that the enemy's forces were increasing, being alarmed for the safety of his troops, sent orders to Titus Sextius, one of his lieutenants, whom he had left to guard the smaller camp, to lead out his cohorts quickly from the camp, and post them at the foot of the hill, on the right wing of the enemy; that if he should see our men driven from the ground, he should deter the enemy from following too closely. He himself, advancing with the legion a little from that place where he had taken his post, awaited the issue of the battle.

CHAP. L.—While the fight was going on most vigorously, hand to hand, and the enemy depended on their position and numbers, our men on their bravery, the Ædui suddenly appeared on our exposed flank, as Cæsar had sent them by another ascent on the right, for the sake of creating a diversion. These, from the similarity of their arms, greatly terrified our men; and although they were discovered to have their right shoulders bare,[1] which was usually the sign of those reduced to peace, yet the soldiers suspected that this very thing was done by the enemy to deceive them. At the same time Lucius Fabius the centurion, and those who had scaled the wall with him, being surrounded and slain, were cast from the wall. Marcus Petreius, a centurion of the same legion, after attempting to hew down the gates, was overpowered by numbers, and, despairing of his safety, having already received many wounds, said to the soldiers of his own company who followed him: "Since I can not save you as well as myself, I shall at least provide for your safety, since I, allured by the love of glory, led you into this danger, do you save yourselves when an opportunity is given." At the same time he rushed into the midst of the enemy, and slaying two of them, drove back the rest a little from the gate. When his men attempted to aid him, "In vain," he says, "you endeavor to procure me safety, since blood and strength are now failing me, therefore leave this, while you have the opportunity, and retreat to the legion." Thus he fell fighting a few moments after, and saved his men by his own death.

CHAP. LI.—Our soldiers, being hard pressed on every side, were dislodged from their position, with the loss of forty-six centurions; but the tenth legion, which had been posted in reserve on ground a little more level, checked the

[1] It is more than probable that Cæsar had entered into a compact with such of the Gallic states as he had brought under the sway and alliance of Rome, that when engaging in battle against their countrymen they should leave their right shoulders bare, in order that the Roman soldiers might be able to distinguish between friend and foe.

Gauls in their eager pursuit. It was supported by the cohorts of the thirteenth legion, which, being led from the smaller camp, had, under the command of Titus Sextius, occupied the higher ground. The legions, as soon as they reached the plain, halted and faced the enemy. Vercingetorix led back his men from the part of the hill within the fortifications. On that day little less than seven hundred[1] of the soldiers were missing.

CHAP. LII.—On the next day, Cæsar, having called a meeting, censured the rashness and avarice of his soldiers, "In that they had judged for themselves how far they ought to proceed, or what they ought to do, and could not be kept back by the tribunes of the soldiers and the lieutenants;" and stated, "what the disadvantage of the ground could effect, what opinion he himself had entertained at Avaricum, when having surprised the enemy without either general or cavalry, he had given up a certain victory, lest even a trifling loss should occur in the contest owing to the disadvantage of position. That as much as he admired the greatness of their courage, since neither the fortifications of the camp, nor the height of the mountain, nor the wall of the town could retard them; in the same degree he censured their licentiousness and arrogance, because they thought that they knew more than their general concerning victory, and the issue of actions: and that he required in his soldiers forbearance and self-command, not less than valor and magnanimity."

CHAP. LIII.—Having held this assembly, and having encouraged the soldiers at the conclusion of his speech, "That they should not be dispirited on this account, nor attribute to the valor of the enemy, what the disadvantage of position had caused;" entertaining the same views of his departure that he had previously had, he led forth the legions from the camp, and drew up his army in order of battle in a suitable place. When Vercingetorix, nevertheless, would not descend to the level ground, a slight cavalry action, and that a successful one, having taken place, he led back his army into the camp. When he had done this, the next day, thinking

[1] Prendeville well remarks that we might naturally infer from the number of officers that perished a much greater loss among the soldiers; however, it is by no means improbable that, as the rashness of the centurions contributed largely to the defeat of the troops, so they endeavored, by the reckless exposure of their lives, to atone for their misconduct.

that he had done enough to lower the pride of the Gauls, and to encourage the minds of his soldiers, he moved his camp in the direction of the Ædui. The enemy not even then pursuing us, on the third day he repaired the bridge over the river Allier, and led over his whole army.

CHAP. LIV.—Having then held an interview with Viridomarus and Eporedorix the Æduans, he learns that Litavicus had set out with all the cavalry to raise the Ædui; that it was necessary that they too should go before him to confirm the state in their allegiance. Although he now saw distinctly the treachery of the Ædui in many things, and was of opinion that the revolt of the entire state would be hastened by their departure; yet he thought that they should not be detained, lest he should appear either to offer an insult, or betray some suspicion of fear. He briefly states to them when departing his services toward the Ædui: in what a state and how humbled he had found them, driven into their towns, deprived of their lands, stripped of all their forces, a tribute imposed on them, and hostages wrested from them with the utmost insult; and to what condition and to what greatness[1] he had raised them, [so much so] that they had not only recovered their former position, but seemed to surpass the dignity and influence of all the previous eras of their history. After giving these admonitions he dismissed them.

CHAP. LV.—Noviodunum was a town of the Ædui, advantageously situated on the banks of the Loire. Cæsar had conveyed hither all the hostages of Gaul, the corn, public money, a great part of his own baggage and that of his army; he had sent hither a great number of horses, which he had purchased in Italy and Spain on account of this war. When Eporedorix and Viridomarus came to this place, and received information of the disposition of the state, that Litavicus had been admitted by the Ædui into Bibracte, which is a town of the greatest importance among them, that Convictolitanis the chief magistrate and a great part of the senate had gone to meet him, that embassadors had been publicly sent to Vercingetorix to negotiate a peace and alliance; they thought that so great an opportunity ought not to be neglected. Therefore, having put to the sword the garrison of Noviodunum, and those

[1] The Ædui at this time numbered among their dependents the Segusiani, Ambirareti, Boii, and Aulerci Brannovices.

who had assembled there for the purpose of trading or were on their march, they divided the money and horses among themselves; they took care that the hostages of the [different] states should be brought to Bibracte, to the chief magistrate; they burned the town to prevent its being of any service to the Romans, as they were of opinion that they could not hold it; they carried away in their vessels whatever corn they could in the hurry, they destroyed the remainder, by [throwing it] into the river or setting it on fire, they themselves began to collect forces from the neighboring country, to place guards and garrisons in different positions along the banks of the Loire, and to display the cavalry on all sides to strike terror into the Romans, [to try] if they could cut them off from a supply of provisions. In which expectation they were much aided, from the circumstance that the Loire had swollen to such a degree from the melting of the snows, that it did not seem capable of being forded at all.

CHAP. LVI.—Cæsar on being informed of these movements was of opinion that he ought to make haste, even if he should run some risk in completing the bridges, in order that he might engage before greater forces of the enemy should be collected in that place. For no one even then considered it an absolutely necessary act, that changing his design he should direct his march into the Province, both because the infamy and disgrace of the thing, and the intervening mount Cevennes, and the difficulty of the roads prevented him; and especially because he had serious apprehensions for the safety of Labienus whom he had detached, and those legions whom he had sent with him. Therefore, having made very long marches by day and night, he came to the river Loire, contrary to the expectation of all; and having by means of the cavalry, found out a ford, suitable enough considering the emergency, of such depth that their arms and shoulders could be above water for supporting their accoutrements, he dispersed his cavalry in such a manner as to break the force of the current, and having confounded the enemy at the first sight, led his army across the river in safety; and finding corn and cattle in the fields, after refreshing his army with them, he determined to march into the country of the Senones.

CHAP. LVII.—While these things are being done by

Cæsar, Labienus, leaving at Agendicum the recruits who had lately arrived from Italy, to guard the baggage, marches with four legions to Lutetia (which is a town of the Parisii, situated on an island on the river Seine), whose arrival being discovered by the enemy, numerous forces arrived from the neighboring states. The supreme command is intrusted to Camalugenus one of the Aulerci, who, although almost worn out with age, was called to that honor on account of his extraordinary knowledge of military tactics. He, when he observed that there was a large marsh[1] which communicated[2] with the Seine, and rendered all that country impassable, encamped there, and determined to prevent our troops from passing it.

CHAP. LVIII.—Labienus at first attempted to raise Vineæ, fill up the marsh with hurdles and clay, and secure a road. After he perceived that this was too difficult to accomplish, he issued in silence from his camp at the third watch, and reached Melodunum by the same route by which he came. This is a town of the Senones, situated on an island in the Seine, as we have just before observed of Lutetia. Having seized upon about fifty ships and quickly joined them together, and having placed soldiers in them, he intimidated by his unexpected arrival the inhabitants, of whom a great number had been called out to the war, and obtains possession of the town without a contest. Having repaired the bridge, which the enemy had broken down during the preceding days, he led over his army, and began to march along the banks of the river to Lutetia. The enemy, on learning the circumstance from those who had escaped from Melodunum, set fire to Lutetia, and order the bridges of that town to be broken down: they themselves set out from the marsh, and take their position on the banks of the Seine, over against Lutetia and opposite the camp of Labienus.

CHAP. LIX.—Cæsar was now reported to have departed from Gergovia; intelligence was likewise brought to them concerning the revolt of the Ædui, and a successful rising in Gaul; and that Cæsar, having been prevented from prosecuting his journey and crossing the Loire, and having been compelled by the want of corn, had marched hastily to the province.

[1] This, according to Achaintre, is the part of Paris known by the name of Le Marais.—A.

[2] Literally, "flowed into."

But the Bellovaci, who had been previously disaffected of themselves, on learning the revolt of the Ædui, began to assemble forces and openly to prepare for war. Then Labienus, as the change in affairs was so great, thought that he must adopt a very different system from what he had previously intended, and he did not now think of making any new acquisitions, or of provoking the enemy to an action; but that he might bring back his army safe to Agendicum. For, on one side, the Bellovaci, a state which held the highest reputation for prowess in Gaul, were pressing on him; and Camulogenus, with a disciplined and well-equipped army, held the other side; moreover, a very great river separated and cut off the legions from[1] the garrison and baggage. He saw that, in consequence of such great difficulties being thrown in his way, he must seek aid from his own energy of disposition.

Chap. LX.—Having, therefore, called a council of war a little before evening, he exhorted his soldiers to execute with diligence and energy such commands as he should give; he assigns the ships which he had brought from Melodunum to Roman knights, one to each, and orders them to fall down the river silently for four miles, at the end of the fourth watch, and there wait for him. He leaves the five cohorts, which he considered to be the most steady in action, to guard the camp; he orders the five remaining cohorts of the same legion to proceed a little after midnight up the river with all their baggage, in a great tumult. He collects also some small boats; and sends them in the same direction, with orders to make a loud noise in rowing. He himself, a little after, marched out in silence, and, at the head of three legions, seeks that place to which he had ordered the ships to be brought.

Chap. LXI.—When he had arrived there, the enemy's scouts, as they were stationed along every part of the river, not expecting an attack, because a great storm had suddenly arisen, were surprised by our soldiers: the infantry and cavalry are quickly transported, under the superintendence of the Roman knights, whom he had appointed to that office. Almost at the same time, a little before daylight, intelligence was given to the enemy that there was an unusual tumult in the camp of the Romans, and that a strong force was

[1] He refers to the garrison which he left at Agendicum to guard the baggage.

marching up the river, and that the sound of oars was distinctly heard in the same quarter, and that soldiers were being conveyed across in ships a little below. On hearing these things, because they were of opinion that the legions were passing in three different places, and that the entire army, being terrified by the revolt of the Ædui, were preparing for flight, they divided their forces also into three divisions. For leaving a guard opposite to the camp and sending a small body in the direction of Metiosedum,[1] with orders to advance as far as the ships would proceed, they led the rest of their troops against Labienus.

CHAP. LXII.—By day-break all our soldiers were brought across, and the army of the enemy was in sight. Labienus, having encouraged his soldiers "to retain the memory of their ancient valor, and so many most successful actions, and imagine Cæsar himself, under whose command they had so often routed the enemy, to be present," gives the signal for action. At the first onset the enemy are beaten and put to flight in the right wing, where the seventh legion stood: on the left wing, which position the twelfth legion held, although the first ranks fell transfixed by the javelins of the Romans, yet the rest resisted most bravely; nor did any one of them show the slightest intention of flying. Camulogenus, the general of the enemy, was present and encouraged his troops. But when the issue of the victory was still uncertain, and the circumstances which were taking place on the left wing were announced to the tribunes of the seventh legion, they faced about their legion to the enemy's rear and attacked it: not even then did any one retreat, but all were surrounded and slain. Camulogenus met the same fate. But those who were left as a guard opposite the camp of Labienus, when they heard that the battle was commenced, marched to aid their countrymen and take possession of a hill, but were unable to withstand the attack of the victorious soldiers. In this manner, mixed with their own fugitives, such as the woods and mountains did not shelter were cut to pieces by our cavalry. When this battle was finished, Labienus returns to Agendicum, where the baggage of the whole army had been left: from it he marched with all his forces to Cæsar.

CHAP. LXIII.—The revolt of the Ædui being known, the war

[1] Metiosedum now *Meudon*, situated on the Seine, below Paris.

grows more dangerous. Embassies are sent by them in all directions: as far as they can prevail by influence, authority, or money, they strive to excite the state [to revolt]. Having got possession of the hostages whom Cæsar had deposited with them, they terrify the hesitating by putting them to death. The Ædui request Vercingetorix to come to them and communicate his plans of conducting the war. On obtaining this request they insist that the chief command should be assigned to them; and when the affair became a disputed question, a council of all Gual is summoned to Bibracte. They came together in great numbers and from every quarter to the same place. The decision is left to the votes of the mass; all to a man approve of Vercingetorix as their general. The Remi, Lingones, and Treviri were absent from this meeting; the two former because they attached themselves to the alliance of Rome; the Treviri because they were very remote and were hard pressed by the Germans; which was also the reason of their being absent during the whole war, and their sending auxiliaries to neither party. The Ædui are highly indignant at being deprived of the chief command; they lament the change of fortune, and miss Cæsar's indulgence toward them; however, after engaging in the war, they do not dare to pursue their own measures apart from the rest. Eporedorix and Viridomarus, youths of the greatest promise, submit reluctantly to Vercingetorix.

Chap. LXIV.—The latter demands hostages from the remaining states; nay, more, appointed a day for this proceeding; he orders all the cavalry, fifteen thousand in number, to quickly assemble here; he says that he will be content with the infantry which he had before, and would not tempt fortune nor come to a regular engagement; but since he had abundance of cavalry, it would be very easy for him to prevent the Romans from obtaining forage or corn, provided that they themselves should resolutely destroy their corn and set fire to their houses; by which sacrifice of private property they would evidently obtain perpetual dominion and freedom. After arranging these matters, he levies ten thousand infantry on the Ædui and Segusiani,[1] who border on our province: to these he adds eight hundred horse. He sets over them the

[1] Segusiani, a people of Gallia Celtica, to the west of the Rhine. Their country was traversed by the Loire, near the source of that river.

brother of Eporedirix, and orders him to wage war against the Allobroges. On the other side he sends the Gabali and the nearest cantons of the Arverni against the Helvii; he likewise sends the Ruteni and Cadurci to lay waste the territories of the Volcæ Arecomici. Besides, by secret messages and embassies, he tampers with the Allobroges, whose minds, he hopes, had not yet settled down after the excitement of the late war. To their nobles he promises money, and to their state the dominion of the whole province.

CHAP. LXV.—The only guards provided against all these contingencies were twenty-two cohorts, which were collected from the entire province by Lucius Cæsar, the lieutenant, and opposed to the enemy in every quarter. The Helvii, voluntarily engaging in battle with their neighbors, are defeated, and Caius Valerius Donotaurus, the son of Caburus, the principal man of the state, and several others, being slain, they are forced to retire within their towns and fortifications. The Allobroges, placing guards along the course of the Rhine, defend their frontiers with great vigilance and energy. Cæsar, as he perceived that the enemy were superior in cavalry, and he himself could receive no aid from the Province or Italy, while all communication was cut off, sends across the Rhine into Germany to those states which he had subdued in the preceding campaigns, and summons from them cavalry and the light-armed infantry, who were accustomed to engage among them. On their arrival, as they were mounted on unserviceable horses, he takes horses from the military tribunes and the rest, nay, even from the Roman knights and veterans, and distributes them among the Germans.

CHAP. LXVI.—In the mean time, whilst these things are going on, the forces of the enemy from the Arverni, and the cavalry which had been demanded from all Gaul, meet together. A great number of these having been collected, when Cæsar was marching into the country of the Sequani, through the confines of the Lingones, in order that he might the more easily render aid to the province, Vercingetorix encamped in three camps, about ten miles from the Romans: and having summoned the commanders of the cavalry to a council, he shows that the time of victory was come; that the Romans were fleeing into the Province and leaving Gaul; that this was sufficient for obtaining immediate freedom; but was of little moment in acquiring peace and tranquillity for the future; for the Romans would return after assembling greafer forces, and would not put an end to the war. Therefore they should attack them on their march, when encumbered. If the infantry should [be obliged to] relieve their cavalry, and be retarded by doing so, the march could not be accomplished: if, abandoning their baggage they should provide for their safety (a result which, he trusted, was more like to ensue), they would lose both property and character. For as to the enemy's horse, they ought not to entertain a doubt that none of them would dare to advance beyond the main body. In order that they [the Gauls] may do so with greater spirit, he would marshal all their forces before the camp, and intimidate the enemy. The cavalry unanimously shout out, "That they ought to bind themselves by a most sacred oath, that he should not be received under a roof, nor have access to his children, parents, or wife, who shall not twice have ridden through the enemy's army."

CHAP. LXVII.—This proposal receiving general approbation, and all being forced to take the oath, on the next day the cavalry were divided into three parts, and two of these divisions made a demonstration on our two flanks; while one in front began to obstruct our march. On this circumstance being announced, Cæsar orders his cavalry also to form three divisions and charge the enemy. Then the action commences simultaneously in every part: the main body halts; the baggage is received within the ranks of the legions. If our men seemed to be distressed, or hard pressed in any quarter, Cæsar usually ordered the troops to advance, and the army to wheel round in that quarter; which conduct retarded the enemy in the pursuit, and encouraged our men by the hope of support. At length the Germans, on the right wing, having gained the top of the hill, dislodge the enemy from their position and pursue them even as far as the river at which Vercingetorix with the infantry was stationed, and slay several of them. The rest, on observing this action, fearing lest they should be surrounded, betake themselves to flight. A slaughter ensues in every direction, and three of the noblest of the Ædui are taken and brought to Cæsar: Cotus, the commander of the cavalry, who had been engaged in the contest with Convictolitanis the last election, Cavarillus, who had held the command of the infantry after the revolt of Litavicus, and Eporedorix, under whose command the Ædui had engaged in war against the Sequani, before the arrival of Cæsar.

CHAP. LXVIII.—All his cavalry being routed, Vercingetorix led back his troops in the same order as he had arranged them before the camp, and immediately began to march to Alesia, which is a town of the Mandubii, and ordered the baggage to be speedily brought forth from the camp, and follow him closely. Cæsar, having conveyed his baggage to the nearest hill, and having left two legions to guard it, pursued as far as the time of day would permit, and after slaying about three thousand of the rear of the enemy, encamped at Alesia[1] on the next day. On reconnoitering the situation of the city, finding that the enemy were panic-stricken, because the cavalry in which they placed their chief reliance, were beaten, he encouraged his men to endure the toil, and began to draw a line of circumvallation round Alesia.

CHAP. LXIX.—The town itself was situated on the top of a hill, in a very lofty position, so that it did not appear likely to be taken, except by a regular siege. Two rivers, on two different sides, washed the foot of the hill. Before the town lay a plain of about three miles in length; on every other side hills at a moderate distance, and of an equal degree of height, surrounded the town. The army of the Gauls had filled all the space under the wall, comprising a part of the hill which looked to the rising sun, and had drawn in front a trench and a stone wall six feet high. The circuit of that fortification, which was commenced by the Romans, comprised eleven miles. The camp was pitched in a strong position, and twenty-three redoubts were raised in it, in which sentinels

[1] Alesia, a strongly fortified town of the Mandubii, near the sources of the Seine, and situated on the summit of a mountain now Mount Auxois. It was washed on two sides by the small rivers Lutosa and Osera, now Oze and Ozerain. Alesia is famous for the siege it stood against Cæsar. It was taken and destroyed by him, but was afterward rebuilt and became a place of considerable consequence under the Roman emperors. At the foot of Mount Auxois is a village still called Alise. According to tradition, Alesia was founded by Hercules, which would imply that the place had been originally a Phœnican stronghold for purposes of inland traffic. The Greek writers, however, say that it took its name from the wanderings of that hero on his expedition into Spain, ἀπὸ τῆς κατὰ τὴν στρατεῖαν ἄλης.—A.

were placed by day, lest any sally should be made suddenly; and by night the same were occupied by watches and strong guards.

CHAP. LXX.—The work having been begun, a cavalry action ensues in that plain, which we have already described as broken by hills, and extending three miles in length. The contest is maintained on both sides with the utmost vigor; Cæsar sends the Germans to aid our troops when distressed, and draws up the legions in front of the camp, lest any sally should be suddenly made by the enemy's infantry. The courage of our men is increased by the additional support of the legions; the enemy being put to flight, hinder one another by their numbers, and as only the narrower gates were left open, are crowded together in them; then the Germans pursue them with vigor even to the fortifications. A great slaughter ensues; some leave their horses, and endeavor to cross the ditch and climb the wall. Cæsar orders the legions which he had drawn up in front of the rampart to advance a little. The Gauls, who were within the fortifications, were no less panic-stricken, thinking that the enemy were coming that moment against them, and unanimously shout "to arms;" some in their alarm rush into the town; Vercingetorix orders the gates to be shut, lest the camp should be left undefended. The Germans retreat, after slaying many and taking several horses.

CHAP. LXXI.—Vercingetorix adopts the design of sending away all his cavalry by night, before the fortifications should be completed by the Romans. He charges them when departing "that each of them should go to his respective state, and press for the war all who were old enough to bear arms; he states his own merits, and conjures them to consider his safety, and not surrender him who had deserved so well of the general freedom, to the enemy for torture; he points out to them that, if they should be remiss, eighty thousand chosen men would perish with him; that upon making a calculation, he had barely corn for thirty days, but could hold out a little longer by economy." After giving these instructions he silently dismisses the cavalry in the second watch, [on that side] where our works were not completed; he orders all the corn to be brought to himself; he ordains capital punishment to such as should not obey; he distributes among them, man by man, the cattle, great quantities of which had been driven there by the Mandubii; he began to measure out the corn sparingly, and by little and little; he receives into the town all the forces which he had posted in front of it. In this manner he prepares to await the succors from Gaul, and carry on the war.

CHAP. LXXII.—Cæsar, on learning these proceedings from the deserters and captives, adopted the following system of fortification; he dug a trench twenty feet deep, with perpendicular sides, in such a manner that the base of this trench should extend so far as the edges were apart at the top. He raised all his other works at a distance of four hundred feet from that ditch; [he did] that with this intention, lest (since he necessarily embraced so extensive an area, and the whole works could not be easily surrounded by a line of soldiers) a large number of the enemy should suddenly, or by night, sally against the fortifications; or lest they should by day cast weapons against our men while occupied with the works. Having left this interval, he drew two trenches fifteen feet broad, and of the same depth; the innermost of them, being in low and level ground, he filled with water conveyed from the river. Behind these he raised a rampart and wall twelve feet high; to this he added a parapet and battlements, with large stakes cut like stags' horns, projecting from the junction of the parapet and battlements, to prevent the enemy from scaling it, and surrounded the entire work with turrets, which were eighty feet distant from one another.

CHAP. LXXIII.—It was necessary, at one and the same time, to procure timber [for the rampart], lay in supplies of corn, and raise also extensive fortifications, and the available troops were in consequence of this reduced in number, since they used to advance to some distance from the camp, and sometimes the Gauls endeavored to attack our works, and to make a sally from the town by several gates and in great force. On which Cæsar thought that further additions should be made to these works, in order that the fortifications might be defensible by a small number of soldiers. Having, therefore, cut down the trunks of trees or very thick branches, and having stripped their tops of the bark, and sharpened them into a point, he drew a continued trench every where five feet deep. These stakes being sunk into this trench, and fastened firmly at the bottom, to prevent the possibility of their being torn up, had their branches only projecting from the ground. There were five rows in connection with, and intersecting each other; and whoever entered within them were likely to impale themselves on very sharp stakes. The soldiers called these "cippi." Before these, which were arranged in oblique rows in the form of a quincunx, pits three feet deep were dug, which gradually diminished in depth to the bottom. In these pits tapering stakes, of the thickness of a man's thigh, sharpened at the top and hardened in the fire, were sunk in such a manner as to project from the ground not more than four inches; at the same time for the purpose of giving them strength and stability, they were each filled with trampled clay to the height of one foot from the bottom: the rest of the pit was covered over with osiers and twigs, to conceal the deceit. Eight rows of this kind were dug, and were three feet distant from each other. They called this a lily from its resemblance to that flower. Stakes a foot long, with iron hooks attached to them, were entirely sunk in the ground before these, and were planted in every place at small intervals; these they called spurs.

CHAP. LXXIV.—After completing these works, having selected as level ground as he could, considering the nature of the country, and having inclosed an area of fourteen miles, he constructed, against an external enemy, fortifications of the same kind in every respect, and separate from these, so that the guards of the fortifications could not be surrounded even by immense numbers, if such a circumstance should take place owing to the departure of the enemy's cavalry; and in order that the Roman soldiers might not be compelled to go out of the camp with great risk, he orders all to provide forage and corn for thirty days.

CHAP. LXXV.—While those things are carried on at Alesia, the Gauls, having convened a council of their chief nobility, determine that all who could bear arms should not be called out, which was the opinion of Vercingetorix, but that a fixed number should be levied from each state; lest, when so great a multitude assembled together, they could neither govern nor distinguish their men, nor have the means of supplying them with corn. They demand thirty-five thousand men from the Ædui and their dependents, the Segusiani, Ambivareti, and Aulerci Brannovices; an equal number from the Arverni in conjunction with the Eleuteti Cadurci, Gabali, and Velauni, who were accustomed to be under the command of the Arverni; twelve thousand each from the Senones, Sequani, Bituriges, Sentones, Ruteni, and Carnutes; ten thousand from the Bellovaci; the same number from the Lemovici; eight thousand each from the Pictones, and Turoni, and Parisii, and Helvii; five thousand each from the Suessiones, Ambiani, Mediomatrici, Petrocorii, Nervii, Morini, and Nitiobriges; the same number from the Aulerci Cenomani; four thousand from the Atrebates; three thousand each from the Bellocassi, Lexovii, and Aulerci Eburovices; thirty thousand from the Rauraci, and Boii; six thousand from all the states together, which border on the Atlantic, and which in their dialect are called Armoricæ[1] (in which number are comprehended the Curisolites, Rhedones, Ambibari, Caltes, Osismii, Lemovices, Veneti, and Unelli). Of these the Bellovaci did not contribute their number, as they said that they would wage war against the Romans on their own account, and at their own discretion, and would not obey the order of any one: however, at the request of Commius, they sent two thousand, in consideration of a tie of hospitality which subsisted between him and them.

CHAP. LXXVI.—Cæsar had, as we have previously narrated, availed himself of the faithful and valuable services of this Commius, in Britain, in former years: in consideration of which merits he had exempted from taxes his [Commius's] state, and had conferred on Commius himself the country of the Morini. Yet such was the unanimity of the Gauls in asserting their freedom, and recovering their ancient renown in war, that they were influenced neither by favors, nor by the recollection of private friendship; and all earnestly directed their energies and resources to that war, and collected eight thousand cavalry, and about two hundred and forty thousand infantry. These were reviewed in the country of the Ædui, and a calculation was made of their numbers: commanders were appointed: the supreme command is intrusted to Commius the Atrebatian, Viridomarus and Eporedorix the Æduans, and Vergasillaunus the Arvernan, the cousin-german

[1] Armorica, or Aremorica, a Celtic term applied in strictness to all parts of Gaul lying along the ocean. Cæsar, however, confines the appellation merely to the tract of country which corresponds to Normandy and Brittany. The name is derived from the Celtic Ar Moer, that is, Am Mur, "on the sea."—A.

of Vercingetorix. To them are assigned men selected from each state, by whose advice the war should be conducted. All march to Alesia, sanguine and full of confidence: nor was there a single individual who imagined that the Romans could withstand the sight of such an immense host: especially in an action carried on both in front and rear, when [on the inside] the besieged would sally from the town and attack the enemy, and on the outside so great forces of cavalry and infantry would be seen.

CHAP. LXXVII.—But those who were blockaded at Alesia, the day being past, on which they had expected auxiliaries from their countrymen, and all their corn being consumed ignorant of what was going on among the Ædui, convened an assembly and deliberated on the exigency of their situation. After various opinions had been expressed among them, some of which proposed a surrender, others a sally, while their strength would support it, the speech of Critognatus ought not to be omitted for its singular and detestable cruelty. He sprung from the noblest family among the Arverni, and possessing great influence, says, "I shall pay no attention to the opinion of those who call a most disgraceful surrender by the name of a capitulation; nor do I think that they ought to be considered as citizens, or summoned to the council. My business is with those who approve of a sally: in whose advice the memory of our ancient prowess seems to dwell in the opinion of you all. To be unable to bear privation for a short time is disgraceful cowardice, not true valor. Those who voluntarily offer themselves to death are more easily found than those who would calmly endure distress. And I would approve of this opinion (for honor is a powerful motive with me), could I foresee no other loss, save that of life; but let us, in adopting our design, look back on all Gaul, which we have stirred up to our aid. What courage do you think would our relatives and friends have, if eighty thousand men were butchered in one spot, supposing that they should be forced to come to an action almost over our corpses? Do not utterly deprive them of your aid, for they have spurned all thoughts of personal danger on account of your safety; nor by your folly, rashness, and cowardice, crush all Gaul and doom it to an eternal slavery. Do you doubt their fidelity and firmness because they have not come at the appointed day? What then? Do you suppose that the Romans are employed every day in the outer fortifications for mere amusement? If you can not be assured by their dispatches, since every avenue is blocked up, take the Romans as evidence that there approach is drawing near; since they, intimidated by alarm at this, labor night and day at their works. What, therefore, is my design? To do as our ancestors did in the war against the Cimbri and Teutones, which was by no means equally momentous who, when driven into their towns, and oppressed by similar privations, supported life by the corpses of those who appeared useless for war on account of their age, and did not surrender to the enemy: and even if we had not a precedent for such cruel conduct, still I should consider it most glorious that one should be established, and delivered to posterity. For in what was that war like this? The Cimbri, after laying Gaul waste, and inflicting great calamities, at length departed from our country, and sought other lands; they left us our rights, laws, lands, and liberty. But what other motive or wish have the Romans, than, induced by envy, to settle in the lands and states of those whom they have learned by fame to be noble and powerful in war, and impose on them perpetual slavery? For they never have carried on wars on any other terms. But if you know not these things which are going on in distant countries, look to the neighboring Gaul, which being reduced to the form of a province, stripped of its rights and laws, and subjected to Roman despotism,[1] is oppressed by perpetual slavery."

CHAP. LXXVIII.—When different opinions were expressed, they determined that those who, owing to age or ill health, were unserviceable for war, should depart from the town, and that themselves should try every expedient before they had recourse to the advice of Critognatus: however, that they would rather adopt that design, if circumstances should compel them and their allies should delay, than accept any terms of a surrender or peace. The Mandubii, who had admitted them into the town, are compelled to go forth with their wives and children. When these came to the Roman fortifications, weeping, they begged of the soldiers by every entreaty to receive them as slaves and relieve them with

[1] Literally, "axes," alluding to the *secures* carried by the Roman lictors.

food. But Cæsar, placing guards on the rampart, forbade them to be admitted.

CHAP. LXXIX.—In the mean time, Commius and the rest of the leaders, to whom the supreme command had been intrusted, came with all their forces to Alesia, and having occupied the entire hill, encamped not more than a mile from our fortifications. The following day, having led forth their cavalry from the camp, they fill all that plain, which, we have related, extended three miles in length, and drew out their infantry a little from that place, and post them on the higher ground. The town Alesia commanded a view of the whole plain. The besieged run together when these auxiliaries were seen; mutual congratulations ensue, and the minds of all are elated with joy. Accordingly, drawing out their troops, they encamp before the town, and cover the nearest trench with hurdles and fill it up with earth, and make ready for a sally and every casualty.

CHAP. LXXX.—Cæsar, having stationed his army on both sides of the fortifications, in order that, if occasion should arise, each should hold and know his own post, orders the cavalry to issue forth from the camp and commence action. There was a commanding view from the entire camp, which occupied a ridge of hills; and the minds of all the soldiers anxiously awaited the issue of the battle. The Gauls had scattered archers and light-armed infantry here and there, among their cavalry, to give relief to their retreating troops, and sustain the impetuosity of our cavalry. Several of our soldiers were unexpectedly wounded by these, and left the battle. When the Gauls were confident that their countrymen were the conquerors in the action, and beheld our men hard pressed by numbers, both those who were hemmed in by the line of circumvallation and those who had come to aid them, supported the spirits of their men by shouts and yells from every quarter. As the action was carried on in sight of all, neither a brave nor cowardly act could be concealed; both the desire of praise and the fear of ignominy, urged on each party to valor. After fighting from noon almost to sunset, without victory inclining in favor of either, the Germans, on one side, made a charge against the enemy in a compact body, and drove them back; and, when they were put to flight, the archers were surrounded and cut to pieces. In other parts, likewise, our men pursued to the camp the retreating enemy, and did not give them an opportunity of rallying. But those who had come forth from Alesia returned into the town dejected and almost despairing of success.

CHAP. LXXXI.—The Gauls, after the interval of a day, and after making, during that time, an immense number of hurdles, scaling-ladders, and iron hooks, silently went forth from the camp at midnight and approached the fortifications in the plain. Raising a shout suddenly, that by this intimation those who were beseiged in the town might learn their arrival, they began to cast down hurdles and dislodge our men from the rampart by slings, arrows, and stones, and executed the other movements which are requisite in storming. At the same time, Vercingetorix, having heard the shout, gives the signal to his troops by a trumpet, and leads them forth from the town. Our troops, as each man's post had been assigned him some days before, man the fortifications; they intimidate the Gauls by slings, large stones, stakes which they had placed along the works, and bullets. All view being prevented by the darkness, many wounds are received on both sides; several missiles, are thrown from the engines. But Marcus Antonius, and Caius Trebonius, the lieutenants, to whom the defense of these parts had been allotted, draughted troops from the redoubts which were more remote, and sent them to aid our troops, in whatever direction they understood that they were hard pressed.

CHAP. LXXXII.—While the Gauls were at a distance from the fortification, they did more execution, owing to the immense number of their weapons: after they came nearer, they either unawares empaled themselves on the spurs,[1] or were pierced by the mural darts from the ramparts and towers, and thus perished. After receiving many wounds on all sides, and having forced no part of the works, when day drew nigh, fearing lest they should be surrounded by a sally made from the higher camp on the exposed flank, they retreated to their countrymen. But those within, while they bring forward those things which had been prepared by Vercingetorix for a sally, fill up the nearest trenches; having delayed a long time in executing these movements, they learned the retreat

[1] Cæsar, at the end of the seventy-third chapter, explains what these were.

of their countrymen before they drew nigh to the fortifications. Thus they returned to the town without accomplishing their object.

CHAP. LXXXIII.—The Gauls, having been twice repulsed with great loss, consult what they should do; they avail themselves of the information of those who were well acquainted with the country; from them they ascertain the position and fortification of the upper camp. There was, on the north side, a hill, which our men could not include in their works, on account of the extent of the circuit, and had necessarily made their camp in ground almost disadvantageous, and pretty steep. Caius Antistius Reginus, and Caius Caninius Rebilus, two of the lieutenants, with two legions, were in possession of this camp. The leaders of the enemy, having reconnoitered the country by their scouts, select from the entire army sixty thousand men, belonging to those states, which bear the highest character for courage; they privately arrange among themselves what they wished to be done, and in what manner; they decide that the attack should take place when it should seem to be noon. They appoint over their forces Vergasillaunus, the Arvernian, one of the four generals, and a near relative of Vercingetorix. He, having issued from the camp at the first watch, and having almost completed his march a little before the dawn, hid himself behind the mountain, and ordered his soldiers to refresh themselves after their labor during the night. When noon now seemed to draw nigh, he marched hastily against that camp which we have mentioned before; and, at the same time, the cavalry began to approach the fortifications in the plain, and the rest of the forces to make a demonstration in front of the camp.

CHAP. LXXXIV.—Vercingetorix, having beheld his countrymen from the citadel of Alesia, issues forth from the town; he brings forth from the camp long hooks, movable pent-houses, mural hooks, and other things, which he had prepared for the purpose of making a sally. They engage on all sides at once and every expedient is adopted. They flocked to whatever part of the works seemed weakest. The army of the Romans is distributed along their extensive lines, and with difficulty meets the enemy in every quarter. The shouts which were raised by the combatants in their rear, had a great tendency to intimidate our men, because they perceived that their danger rested on the valor of others: for generally all evils which are distant most powerfully alarm men's minds.

CHAP. LXXXV.—Cæsar, having selected a commanding situation, sees distinctly whatever is going on in every quarter, and sends assistance to his troops when hard pressed. The idea uppermost in the minds of both parties is, that the present is the time in which they would have the fairest opportunity of making a struggle; the Gauls despairing of all safety, unless they should succeed in forcing the lines: the Romans expecting an end to all their labors if they should gain the day. The principal struggle is at the upper lines, to which as we have said Vergasillaunus was sent. The least elevation of ground, added to a declivity, exercises a momentous influence. Some are casting missiles, others, forming a testudo, advance to the attack; fresh men by turns relieve the wearied. The earth, heaped up by all against the fortifications, gives the means of ascent to the Gauls, and covers those works which the Romans had concealed in the ground. Our men have no longer arms or strength.

CHAP. LXXXVI.—Cæsar, on observing these movements, sends Labienus with six cohorts to relieve his distressed soldiers: he orders him, if he should be unable to withstand them, to draw off the cohorts and make a sally; but not to do this except through necessity. He himself goes to the rest, and exhorts them not to succumb to the toil; he shows them that the fruits of all former engagements depend on that day and hour. The Gauls within, despairing of forcing the fortifications in the plains on account of the greatness of the works, attempt the places precipitous in ascent: hither they bring the engines which they had prepared; by the immense number of their missiles they dislodge the defenders from the turrets: they fill the ditches with clay and hurdles, then clear the way; they tear down the rampart and breast-work with hooks.

CHAP. LXXXVII.—Cæsar sends at first young Brutus, with six cohorts, and afterward Caius Fabius, his lieutenant, with seven others: finally, as they fought more obstinately, he leads up fresh men to the assistance of his soldiers. After renewing the action, and repulsing the enemy, he marches in the direction in which he had sent Labienus, drafts four cohorts from the nearest redoubt, and orders part of the cavalry to follow him, and part to make the circuit of the external fortifications and attack the enemy in the rear. Labienus, when neither the ramparts or ditches could check the onset of the enemy, informs Cæsar by messengers of what he intended to do. Cæsar hastens to share in the action.

CHAP. LXXXVIII.—His arrival being known from the color of his robe,[1] and the troops of cavalry, and the cohorts which he had ordered to follow him being seen, as these low and sloping grounds were plainly visible from the eminences, the enemy join battle. A shout being raised by both sides, it was succeeded by a general shout along the ramparts and whole line of fortifications. Our troops, laying aside their javelins, carry on the engagement with their swords. The cavalry is suddenly seen in the rear of the Gauls; the other cohorts advance rapidly; the enemy turn their backs; the cavalry intercept them in their flight, and a great slaughter ensues. Sedulius the general and chief of the Lemovices is slain; Vergasillaunus, the Arvernian, is taken alive in the flight, seventy-four military standards are brought to Cæsar, and few out of so great a number return safe to their camp. The besieged, beholding from the town the slaughter and flight of their countrymen, despairing of safety, lead back their troops from the fortifications. A flight of the Gauls from their camp immediately ensues on hearing of this disaster, and had not the soldiers been wearied by sending frequent reinforcements, and the labor of the entire day, all the enemy's forces could have been destroyed. Immediately after midnight, the cavalry are sent out and overtake the rear, a great number are taken or cut to pieces, the rest by flight escape in different directions to their respective states. Vercingetorix, having convened a council the following day, declares, "That he had undertaken that war, not on account of his own exigences, but on account of the general freedom; and since he must yield to fortune, he offered himself to them for either purpose, whether they should wish to atone to the Romans by his death, or surrender him alive. Embassadors are sent to Cæsar

[1] The Roman generals usually wore a white or purple robe (*paludamentum*) over their armor. We find in Valerius Maximus the following allusion to the color of the robe:—"Crassus was about to lead his army from Carræ against the Parthians. A dark-colored military robe was given him, although a white or purple robe was usually given to the generals going forth to the field of battle."

on this subject. He orders their arms to be surrendered, and their chieftains delivered up. He seated himself at the head of the lines in front of the camp, the Gallic chieftains are brought before him. They surrender Vercingetorix,[1] and lay down their arms. Reserving the Ædui and Arverni, [to try] if he could gain over, through their influence, their respective states, he distributes one of the remaining captives to each soldier, throughout the entire army, as plunder.

CHAP. XC.—After making these arrangements, he marches into the [country of the] Ædui, and recovers that state. To this place embassadors are sent by the Arveni, who promise that they will execute his commands. He demands a great number of hostages. He sends the legions to winter-quarters; he restores about twenty thousand captives to the Ædui and Arverni; he orders Titus Labienus to march into the [country of the] Sequani with two legions and the cavalry, and to him he attaches Marcus Sempronius Rutilus; he places Caius Fabius, and Lucius Minucius Basilus, with two legions in the country of the Remi, lest they should sustain any loss from the Bellovaci in their neighborhood. He sends Caius Antistius Reginus into the [country of the] Ambivareti, Titus Sextius into the territories of the Bituriges, and Caius Caninius Rebilus into those of the Ruteni, with one legion each. He stations Quintus Tullius Cicero, and Publius Sulpicius among the Ædui at Cabillo and Matisco on the Saône, to procure supplies of corn. He himself determines to winter at Bibracte. A supplication of twenty days is decreed by the senate at Rome, on learning these successes from Cæsar's dispatches.

[1] According to Plutarch the Gallic chief arrayed himself in his most splendid armor, and having caparisoned his horse, sallied out from the gates of the town. After he had taken some circuits around Cæsar, as the latter was sitting in his tribunal, he dismounted, put off his armor, and seated himself at the feet of the Roman general. There he remained in silence until Cæsar ordered him to be taken away and reserved for his triumph. Dion Cassius states that he relied on Cæsar's former friendship for forgiveness. This reliance, however, proved unavailing; since, after having been led in triumph at Rome, he was put to death in prison.

BOOK VIII.

WRITTEN BY AULUS HIRTIUS.[1]

THE ARGUMENT.

I. Disturbances in Gaul. III. The Bituriges compelled to give hostages. IV. The Carnutes obliged to disperse. VII. Cæsar marches against the Bellovaci, XV. And compels them to retreat. XVIII. They lie in ambush for the Romans; but are defeated with great loss. XXIII. And give hostages. XXVI. Dumnacus besieges Limonum, XXIX. But is obliged to raise the siege, and loses his baggage. XXXI. The Carnutes and states called Armoricæ submit to Fabius. XXXVI. Drapes is taken prisoner by Caninius. XL. Cæsar and Caninius invest Uxellodunum. XLIV. The town is taken, and the inhabitants treated with extraordinary severity. XLV. Labienus's success against the Treviri. XLVIII. Comius surrenders to Antony. L. Cæsar goes to Italy, and is most honorably received. LII. He discovers the designs of his enemies. LV. And sets out again for Italy.

AULUS HIRTIUS'S PREFACE.

PREVAILED on by your continued solicitations, Balbus, I have engaged in a most difficult task, as my daily refusals appear to plead not my inability, but indolence, as an excuse. I have compiled a continuation of the Commentaries of our Cæsar's Wars in Gaul, not indeed to be compared to his writings, which either precede or follow them; and recently, I have completed what he left imperfect after the transactions in Alexandria, to the end, not indeed of the civil broils, to which

[1] We learn from Suetonius, in the life of Cæsar, that there was even in his time a doubt about the writer of this book: his words are, "For the author of the Alexandrian, African, and Spanish wars, has not been ascertained, since some think it was Oppius, others Hirtius, who also wrote a supplement to the last and unfinished book of the Gallic war." Many editors have attributed it to a certain Hirtius Pansa: but there can be no doubt that Hirtius and Pansa were quite different individuals. The mistake appears to have originated in the error of some of the librarians (a class of men whose services to Belles Lettres have been repaid by charging them with the corruption of the different texts which they transcribed), who from the circumstance of Aulus Hirtius and Caius Vibius Pansa being associated in the consulate, A.U.C. 710, fell into the error of supposing them the same individual.

we see no issue, but of Cæsar's life. I wish that those who may read them could know how unwillingly I undertook to write them, as then I might the more readily escape the imputation of folly and arrogance, in presuming to intrude among Cæsar's writings. For it is agreed on all hands, that no composition was ever executed with so great care, that it is not exceeded in elegance by these Commentaries, which were published for the use of historians, that they might not want memoirs of such achievements; and they stand so high in the esteem of all men, that historians seem rather deprived of, than furnished with material. At which we have more reason to be surprised than other men; for they can only appreciate the elegance and correctness with which he finished them, while we know with what ease and expediton. Cæsar possessed not only an uncommon flow of language and elegance of style, but also a thorough knowledge of the method of conveying his ideas. But I had not even the good fortune to share in the Alexandrian or African war; and though these were partly communicated to me by Cæsar himself, in conversation, yet we listen with a different degree of attention to those things which strike us with admiration by their novelty, and those which we design to attest to posterity. But, in truth, while I urge every apology, that I may not be compared to Cæsar, I incur the charge of vanity, by thinking it possible that I can in the judgment of any one be put in competition with him. Farewell.

CHAP. I.—Gaul being entirely reduced, when Cæsar having waged war incessantly during the former summer, wished to recruit his soldiers after so much fatigue, by repose in winter quarters, news was brought him that several states were simultaneously renewing their hostile intention, and forming combinations. For which a probable reason was assigned: namely, that the Gauls were convinced that they were not able to resist the Romans, with any force they could collect in one place; and hoped that if several states made war in different places at the same time, the Roman army would neither have aid, nor time, nor forces, to prosecute them all: nor ought any single state to decline any inconveniences that might befall them, provided that by such delay, the rest should be enabled to assert their liberty.

CHAP. II.—That this notion might not be confirmed among the Gauls, Cæsar left Marcus Antonius,[1] his quæstor, in charge of his quarters, and set out himself with a guard of horse,[2] the day before the kalends of January, from the town Bibracte, to the thirteenth legion, which he had stationed in the country of the Bituriges, not far from the territories of the Ædui, and joined to it the eleventh legion which was next it. Leaving two cohorts to guard the baggage, he leads the rest of his army into the most plentiful part of the country of the Bituriges; who, possessing an extensive territory and several towns, were not to be deterred, by a single legion quartered among them, from making warlike preparation, and forming combinations.

CHAP. III.—By Cæsar's sudden arrival, it happened, as it necessarily must, to an unprovided and dispersed people, that they were surprised by our horse, while cultivating the fields without any apprehensions, before they had time to fly to their towns. For the usual sign of an enemy's invasion, which is generally intimated by the burning of their towns, was forbidden by Cæsar's orders; lest if he advanced far, forage and corn should become scarce, or the enemy be warned by the fires to make their escape. Many thousands being taken, as many of the Bituriges as were able to escape the first coming of the Romans, fled to the neighboring states, relying either on private friendship, or public alliance. In vain; for Cæsar, by hasty marches, anticipated them in every place, nor did he allow any state leisure to consider the safety of others, in preference to their own. By this activity, he both retained his friends in their loyalty, and by fear, obliged the wavering to accept offers of peace. Such offers being made to the Bituriges, when they perceived that through Cæsar's clemency, an avenue was open to his friendship, and that the neighboring states had given hostages, without incurring any punishment, and had been received under his protection, they did the same.

CHAP. IV.—Cæsar promises his soldiers, as a reward for their labor and patience, in cheerfully submitting to hardships from the severity of the winter, the difficulty of the roads, and the intolerable cold, two hundred sestertii each, and to every centurian two thousand, to be given instead of plunder; and send

[1] So familiar to the reader of Shakespeare as Mark Antony.
[2] The 30th of December.

ing his legions back to quarters, he himself returned on the fortieth day to Bibracte. While he was dispensing justice there, the Biturgies send embassadors to him, to entreat his aid against the Carnutes, who they complained had made war against them. Upon this intelligence, though he had not remained more than eighteen days in winter quarters, he draws the fourteenth and sixth legion out of quarters on the Saône, where he had posted them as mentioned in a former Commentary, to procure supplies of corn. With these two legions he marches in pursuit of the Carnutes.

CHAP. V.—When the news of the approach of our army reached the enemy, the Carnutes, terrified by the suffering of other states, deserted their villages and towns (which were small buildings, raised in a hurry, to meet the immediate necessity, in which they lived to shelter themselves against the winter, for, being lately conquered, they had lost several towns), and dispersed and fled. Cæsar, unwilling to expose his soldiers to the violent storms that break out, especially at that season, took up his quarters at Genabum, a town of the Carnutes; and lodged his men in houses, partly belonging to the Gauls, and partly built to shelter the tents, and hastily covered with thatch. But the horse and auxiliaries he sends to all parts to which he was told the enemy had marched; and not without effect, as our men generally returned loaded with booty. The Carnutes, overpowered by the severity of the winter, and the fear of danger, and not daring to continue long in any place, as they were driven from their houses, and not finding sufficient protection in the woods, from the violence of the storms, after losing a considerable number of their men, disperse, and take refuge among the neighboring states.

CHAP. VI.—Cæsar, being contented, at so severe a season, to disperse the gathering foes, and prevent any new war from breaking out, and being convinced, as far as reason could foresee, that no war of consequence could be set on foot in the summer campaign, stationed Caius Trebonius, with the two legions which he had with him, in quarters at Genabum: and being informed by frequent embassies from the Remi, that the Bellovaci (who exceed all the Gauls and Belgæ in military prowess), and the neighboring states, headed by Correus, one of the Bellovaci, and Comius, the Atrebatian, were raising an army, and assembling at a general rendezvous, designing with their united forces to invade the territories of the Suessiones, who were put under the patronage of the Remi: and moreover, considering that not only his honor, but his interest was concerned, that such of his allies, as deserved well of the republic, should suffer no calamity; he again draws the eleventh legion out of quarters, and writes besides to Caius Fabius, to march with his two legions to the country of the Suessiones; and he sends to Trebonius for one of his two legions. Thus, as far as the convenience of the quarters, and the management of the war admitted, he laid the burden of the expedition on the legions by turns, without any intermission to his own toils.

CHAP. VII.—As soon as his troops were collected, he marched against the Bellovaci: and pitching his camp in their territories, detached troops of horse all round the country, to take prisoners, from whom he might learn the enemy's plan. The horse, having executed his orders, bring him back word, that but few were found in the houses: and that even these had not stayed at home to cultivate their lands (for the emigration was general from all parts) but had been sent back to watch our motions. Upon Cæsar's inquiring from them, where the main body of the Bellovaci were posted, and what was their design: they made answer, "that all the Bellovaci, fit for carrying arms, had assembled in one place, and along with them the Ambiani, Aulerci, Caletes, Velocasses, and Atrebates, and that they had chosen for their camp, an elevated position, surrounded by a dangerous morass: that they had conveyed all their baggage into the most remote woods: that several noblemen were united in the management of the war; but that the people were most inclined to be governed by Correus, because they knew that he had the strongest aversion to the name of the Roman people: that a few days before Comius had left the camp to engage the Germans to their aid whose nation bordered on theirs, and whose numbers were countless: that the Bellovaci had come to a resolution, with the consent of all the generals and the earnest desire of the people, if Cæsar should come with only three legions, as was reported, to give him battle, that they might not be obliged to encounter his whole army on a future occasion, when they should be in a more wretched and distressed condition; but if he brought a stronger force, they intended to remain in the position they had chosen, and by ambuscade to prevent the Romans from getting forage (which at that season was both scarce and much scattered), corn, and other necessaries."

CHAP. VIII.—When Cæsar was convinced of the truth of this account from the concurring testimony of several persons, and perceived that the plans which were proposed were full of prudence, and very unlike the rash resolves of a barbarous people, he considered it incumbent on him to use every exertion, in order that the enemy might despise his small force and come to an action. For he had three veteran legions of distinguished valor, the seventh, eighth and ninth. The eleventh consisted of chosen youth of great hopes, who had served eight campaigns, but who, compared with the others, had not yet acquired any great reputation for experience and valor. Calling therefore a council, and laying before it the intelligence which he had received, he encouraged his soldiers. In order if possible to entice the enemy to an engagement by the appearance of only three legions, he ranged his army in the following manner, that the seventh, eighth, and ninth legions should march before all the baggage; that then the eleventh should bring up the rear of the whole train of baggage (which however was but small, as is usual on such expeditions), so that the enemy could not get a sight of a greater number than they themselves were willing to encounter. By this disposition he formed his army almost into a square, and brought them within sight of the enemy sooner than was anticipated.

CHAP. IX.—When the Gauls, whose bold resolutions had been reported to Cæsar, saw the legions advance with a regular motion, drawn up in battle array; either from the danger of an engagement, or our sudden approach, or with the design of watching our movements, they drew up their forces before the camp, and did not quit the rising ground. Though Cæsar wished to bring them to battle, yet being surprised to see so vast a host of the enemy, he encamped opposite to them, with a valley between them, deep rather than extensive. He ordered his camp to be fortified with a rampart twelve feet high, with breastworks built on it proportioned to its height; and two trenches, each fifteen feet broad, with perpendicular sides to be sunk: likewise several turrets, three stories high, to be raised, with a communication to each other by galleries laid across and covered over; which should be guarded in front by small parapets of osiers; that the enemy might be repulsed by two rows of soldiers. The one of whom, being more secure from danger by their height might throw their darts with more daring and to a greater distance; the other which was nearer the enemy, being stationed on the rampart, would be protected by their galleries from darts falling on their heads. At the entrance he erected gates and turrets of a considerable height.

Chap. X.—Cæsar had a double design in this fortification; for he both hoped that the strength of his works, and his [apparent] fears would raise confidence in the barbarians; and when there should be occasion to make a distant excursion to get forage or corn, he saw that his camp would be secured by the works with a very small force. In the mean time there were frequent skirmishes across the marsh, a few on both sides sallying out between the two camps. Sometimes, however, our Gallic or German auxiliaries crossed the marsh, and furiously pursued the enemy; or on the other hand the enemy passed it and beat back our men. Moreover there happened in the course of our daily foraging, what must of necessity happen, when corn is to be collected by a few scattered men out of private houses, that our foragers dispersing in an intricate country were surrounded by the enemy; by which, though we suffered but an inconsiderable loss of cattle and servants, yet it raised foolish hopes in the barbarians; but more especially, because Comius, who I said had gone to get aid from the Germans, returned with some cavalry, and though the Germans were only 500, yet the barbarians were elated by their arrival.

Chap. XI.—Cæsar, observing that the enemy kept for several days within their camp, which was well secured by a morass and its natural situation, and that it could not be assaulted without a dangerous engagement, nor the place inclosed with lines without an addition to his army, wrote to Trebonius to send with all dispatch for the thirteenth legion which was in winter quarters among the Bituriges under Titus Sextius, one of his lieutenants; and then to come to him by forced marches with the three legions. He himself sent the cavalry of the Remi, and Lingones, and other states, from whom he had required a vast number, to guard his foraging parties, and to support them in case of any sudden attack of the enemy.

Chap. XII.—As this continued for several days, and their

vigilance was relaxed by custom (an effect which is generally produced by time), the Bellovaci, having made themselves acquainted with the daily stations of our horse, lie in ambush with a select body of foot in a place covered with woods; to it they sent their horse the next day, who were first to decoy our men into the ambuscade, and then when they were surrounded, to attack them. It was the lot of the Remi to fall into this snare, to whom that day had been allotted to perform this duty; for, having suddenly got sight of the enemy's cavalry, and despising their weakness, in consequence of their superior numbers, they pursued them too eagerly, and were surrounded on every side by the foot. Being by this means thrown into disorder they returned with more precipitation than is usual in cavalry actions, with the loss of Vertiscus the governor of their state, and the general of their horse who, though scarcely able to sit on horseback through years, neither, in accordance with the custom of the Gauls, pleaded his age in excuse for not accepting the command, nor would he suffer them to fight without him. The spirits of the barbarians were puffed up, and inflated at the success of this battle, in killing the prince, and general of the Remi; and our men were taught by this loss, to examine the country, and post their guards with more caution, and to be more moderate in pursuing a retreating enemy.

CHAP. XIII.—In the mean time daily skirmishes take place continually in view of both camps; these were fought at the ford and pass of the morass. In one of these contests the Germans, whom Cæsar had brought over the Rhine, to fight, intermixed with the horse, having resolutely crossed the marsh, and slain the few who made resistance, and boldly pursued the rest, so terrified them, that not only those who were attacked hand to hand, or wounded at a distance, but even those who were stationed at a greater distance to support them, fled disgracefully; and being often beaten from the rising grounds, did not stop till they had retired into their camp, or some, impelled by fear had fled further. Their danger threw their whole army into such confusion, that it was difficult to judge whether they were more insolent after a slight advantage, or more dejected by a trifling calamity.

CHAP. XIV.—After spending several days in the same camp, the guards of the Bellovaci, learning that Caius Trebonius was advancing nearer with his legions and fearing a siege like that of Alesia, send off by night all who were disabled by age or infirmity, or unarmed, and along with them their whole baggage. While they are preparing their disorderly and confused troop for march (for the Gauls are always attended by a vast multitude of wagons, even when they have very light baggage), being overtaken by day-light, they drew their forces out before their camp, to prevent the Romans attempting a pursuit before the line of their baggage had advanced to a considerable distance. But Cæsar did not think it prudent to attack them when standing on their defense, with such a steep hill in their favor, nor keep his legions at such a distance that they could quit their post without danger: but, perceiving that his camp was divided from the enemy's by a deep morass, so difficult to cross that he could not pursue with expedition, and that the hill beyond the morass, which extended almost to the enemy's camp, was separated from it only by a small valley, he laid a bridge over the morass and led his army across, and soon reached the plain on the top of the hill, which was fortified on either side by a steep ascent. Having there drawn up his army in order of battle, he marched to the furthest hill, from which he could, with his engines, shower darts upon the thickest of the enemy.

CHAP. XV.—The Gauls, confiding in the natural strength of their position, though they would not decline an engagement if the Romans attempted to ascend the hill, yet dared not divide their forces into small parties, lest they should be thrown into disorder by being dispersed, and therefore remained in order of battle. Cæsar, perceiving that they persisted in their resolution, kept twenty cohorts in battle array, and, measuring out ground there for a camp, ordered it to be fortified. Having completed his works, he drew up his legions before the rampart and stationed the cavalry in certain positions, with their horses bridled. When the Bellovaci saw the Romans prepared to pursue them, and that they could not wait the whole night, or continue longer in the same place without provisions, they formed the following plan to secure a retreat. They handed to one another the bundles of straw and sticks on which they sat (for it is the custom of the Gauls to sit when drawn up in order of battle, as has been asserted in former commentaries), of which they had great plenty in their camp, and piled them in the front of their line; and at the close of the day, on a certain signal, set them all on fire at one and the same time. The continued blaze soon screened all their forces from the sight of the Romans, which no sooner happened than the barbarians fled with the greatest precipitation.

CHAP. XVI.—Though Cæsar could not perceive the retreat of the enemy for the intervention of the fire, yet, suspecting that they had adopted that method to favor their escape, he made his legions advance, and sent a party of horse to pursue them; but, apprehensive of an ambuscade, and that the enemy might remain in the same place and endeavor to draw our men into a disadvantageous situation, he advances himself but slowly. The horse, being afraid to venture into the smoke and dense line of flame, and those who were bold enough to attempt it being scarcely able to see their horse's heads, gave the enemy free liberty to retreat, through fear of an ambuscade. Thus by a flight, full at once of cowardice and address, they advanced without any loss about ten miles, and encamped in a very strong position. From which, laying numerous ambuscades, both of horse and foot, they did considerable damage to the Roman foragers.

CHAP. XVII.—After this had happened several times, Cæsar discovered from a certain prisoner, that Correus, the general of the Bellovaci, had selected six thousand of his bravest foot and a thousand horse, with which he designed to lie in ambush in a place to which he suspected the Romans would send to look for forage, on account of the abundance of corn and grass. Upon receiving information of their design Cæsar drew out more legions than he usually did, and sent forward his cavalry as usual, to protect the foragers. With these he intermixed a guard of light infantry, and himself advanced with the legions as fast as he could.

CHAP. XVIII.—The Gauls, placed in ambush, had chosen for the seat of action a level piece of ground, not more than a mile in extent, inclosed on every side by a thick wood or a very deep river, as by a toil, and this they surrounded. Our men, apprised of the enemy's design, marched in good order to the ground, ready both in heart and hand to give battle, and willing to hazard any engagement when the legions were at their back. On their approach, as Correus supposed that he had got an opportunity of effecting his purpose, he at first shows himself with a small party and attacks the foremost troops. Our men resolutely stood the charge, and did not crowd together in one place, as commonly happens from surprise in engagements between the horse, whose numbers prove injurious to themselves.

CHAP. XIX.—When by the judicious arrangement of our forces only a few of our men fought by turns, and did not suffer themselves to be surrounded, the rest of the enemy broke out from the woods while Correus was engaged. The battle was maintained in different parts with great vigor, and continued for a long time undecided, till at length a body of foot gradually advanced from the woods in order of battle and forced our horse to give ground: the light infantry, which were sent before the legions to the assistance of the cavalry, soon came up, and, mixing with the horse, fought with great courage. The battle was for some time doubtful, but, as usually happens, our men, who stood the enemy's first charge, became superior from this very circumstance that, though suddenly attacked from an ambuscade, they had sustained no loss. In the mean time the legions were approaching, and several messengers arrived with notice to our men and the enemy that the [Roman] general was near at hand, with his forces in battle array. Upon this intelligence, our men, confiding in the support of the cohorts, fought most resolutely, fearing, lest if they should be slow in their operations they should let the legions participate in the glory of the conquest. The enemy lose courage and attempt to escape by different ways. In vain; for they were themselves entangled in that labyrinth in which they thought to entrap the Romans. Being defeated and put to the rout, and having lost the greater part of their men, they fled in consternation whithersoever chance carried them; some sought the woods, others the river, but were vigorously pursued by our men and put to the sword. Yet, in the mean time, Correus, unconquered by calamity, could not be prevailed on to quit the field and take refuge in the woods, or accept our offers of quarter, but, fighting courageously and wounding several, provoked our men, elated with victory, to discharge their weapons against him.

CHAP. XX.—After this transaction, Cæsar, having come up immediately after the battle, and imagining that the enemy, upon receiving the news of so great a defeat, would be so depressed that they would abandon their camp, which was not above eight miles distant from the scene of action, though he saw his passage obstructed by the river, yet he marched his army over and advanced. But the Bellovaci and the other states, being informed of the loss they had sustained by a few wounded men who having escaped by the shelter of the woods, had returned to them after the defeat, and learning that every thing had turned out unfavorable, that Correus was slain, and the horse and most valiant of their foot cut off, imagined that the Romans were marching against them, and calling a council in haste by sound of trumpet, unanimously cry out to send embassadors and hostages to Cæsar.

CHAP. XXI.—This proposal having met with general approbation, Comius the Atrebatian fled to those Germans from whom he had borrowed auxiliaries for that war. The rest instantly send embassadors to Cæsar; and requested that he would be contented with that punishment of his enemy, which if he had possessed the power to inflict on them before the engagement, when they were yet uninjured, they were persuaded from his usual clemency and mercy, he never would have inflicted; that the power of the Bellovaci was crushed by the cavalry action; that many thousand of their choicest foot had fallen, that scarce a man had escaped to bring the fatal news. That, however, the Bellovaci had derived from the battle one advantage, of some importance, considering their loss; that Correus, the author of the rebellion, and agitator of the people, was slain: for that while he lived the senate had never equal influence in the state with the giddy populace.

CHAP. XXII.—Cæsar reminded the embassadors who made these supplications, that the Bellovaci had at the same season the year before, in conjunction with other states of Gaul, undertaken a war, and that they had persevered the most obstinately of all in their purpose, and were not brought to a proper way of thinking by the submission of the rest: that he knew and was aware that the guilt of a crime was easily transferred to the dead; but that no one person could have such influence, as to be able by the feeble support of the multitude to raise a war and carry it on without the consent of the nobles, in opposition to the senate, and in despite of every virtuous man; however he was satisfied with the punishment, which they had drawn upon themselves.

CHAP. XXIII.—The night following the embassadors bring back his answer to their countrymen, and prepare the hostages.

Embassadors flock in from the other states, which were waiting for the issue of the [war with the] Bellovaci: they give hostages, and receive his orders; all except Comius, whose fears restrained him from intrusting his safety to any person's honor. For the year before, while Cæsar was holding the assizes in Hither Gaul, Titus Labienus, having discovered that Comius was tampering with the state, and raising a conspiracy against Cæsar, thought he might punish his infidelity without perfidy; but judging that he would not come to his camp at his invitation, and unwilling to put him on his guard by the attempt, he sent Caius Volusenus Quadratus, with orders to have him put to death under pretense of conference. To effect his purpose, he sent with him some chosen centurions. When they came to the conference, and Volusenus, as had been agreed on, had taken hold of Comius by the hand, and one of the centurions, as if surprised at so uncommon an incident, attempted to kill him, he was prevented by the friends of Comius, but wounded him severely in the head by the first blow. Swords were drawn on both sides, not so much with a design to fight as to effect an escape, our men believing that Comius had received a mortal stroke; and the Gauls, from the treachery which they had seen, dreading that a deeper design lay concealed. Upon this transaction, it was said that Comius made a resolution never to come within sight of any Roman.

Chap. XXIV.—When Cæsar, having completely conquered the most warlike nations, perceived that there was now no state which could make preparations for war to oppose him, but that some were removing and fleeing from their country to avoid present subjection, he resolved to detach his army into different parts of the country. He kept with himself Marcus Antonius the quæstor, with the eleventh legion; Caius Fabius was detached with twenty-five cohorts into the remotest part of Gaul, because it was rumored that some states had risen in arms, and he did not think that Caius Caninius Rebilus, who had the charge of that country, was strong enough to protect it with two legions. He ordered Titus Labienus to attend himself, and sent the twelfth legion which had been under him in winter quarters, to Hither Gaul, to protect the Roman colonies, and prevent any loss by the inroads of barbarians similar to that which had happened the year before to the

Tergestines,[1] who were cut off by a sudden depredation and attack. He himself marched to depopulate the country of Ambiorix, whom he had terrified and forced to fly, but despaired of being able to reduce under his power; but he thought it most consistent with his honor to waste his country both of inhabitants, cattle, and buildings, so that from the abhorrence of his countrymen, if fortune suffered any to survive, he might be excluded from a return to his state for the calamities which he had brought on it.

CHAP. XXV.—After he had sent either his legions or auxiliaries through every part of Ambiorix's dominions, and wasted the whole country by sword, fire, and rapine, and had killed or taken prodigious numbers, he sent Labienus with two legions against the Treviri, whose state, from its vicinity to Germany, being engaged in constant war, differed but little from the Germans, in civilization and savage barbarity; and never continued in its allegiance, except when awed by the presence of his army.

CHAP. XXVI.—In the mean time Caius Caninius, a lieutenant, having received information by letters and messages from Duracius, who had always continued in friendship to the Roman people, though a part of his state had revolted, that a great multitude of the enemy were in arms in the country of the Pictones, marched to the town Limonum.[2] When he was approaching it, he was informed by some prisoners, that Duracius was shut up by several thousand men, under the command of Dumnacus, general of the Andes, and that Limonum was besieged, but not daring to face the enemy with his weak legions, he encamped in a strong position: Dumnacus, having notice of Caninius's approach, turned his whole force against the legions, and prepared to assault the Roman camp. But after spending several days in the attempt, and losing a considerable number of men, without being able to make a breach in any part of the works, he returned again to the siege of Limonum.

[1] The inhabitants of Tergeste, *Trieste*, a Roman colony on the confines of Istria and the Carni.

[2] Limonum, called also Pictavi, modern *Poictiers*, the chief city of the Pictones, or Pictavi, a peaceful and extensive tribe, in the north of Aquitania Secunda, lying close to the mouth and along the south bank of the Loire.

CHAP. XXVII.—At the same time, Caius Fabius, a lieutenant, brings back many states to their allegiance, and confirms their submission by taking hostages; he was then informed by letters from Caninius, of the proceedings among the Pictones. Upon which he set off to bring assistance to Duracius. But Dumnacus, hearing of the approch of Fabius, and despairing of safety, if at the same time he should be forced to withstand the Roman army without, and observe, and be under apprehension from the town's people, made a precipitate retreat from that place with all his forces. Nor did he think that he should be sufficiently secure from danger, unless he led his army across the Loire, which was too deep a river to pass except by a bridge. Though Fabius had not yet come within sight of the enemy, nor joined Caninius; yet being informed of the nature of the country, by persons acquainted with it, he judged it most likely that the enemy would take that way, which he found they did take. He therefore marched to that bridge with his army, and ordered his cavalry to advance no farther before the legions than that they could return to the same camp at night, without fatiguing their horses. Our horse pursued according to orders, and fell upon Dumnacus's rear and attacking them on their march, while fleeing, dismayed, and laden with baggage, they slew a great number, and took a rich booty. Having executed the affair so successfully, they retired to the camp.

CHAP. XXVIII.—The night following, Fabius sent his horse before him, with orders to engage the enemy, and delay their march till he himself should come up. That his orders might be faithfully performed, Quintus Atius Varus, general of the horse, a man of uncommon spirit and skill, encouraged his men, and pursuing the enemy, disposed some of his troops in convenient places, and with the rest gave battle to the enemy. The enemy's cavalry made a bold stand, the foot relieving each other, and making a general halt, to assist their horse against ours. The battle was warmly contested. For our men, despising the enemy whom they had conquered the day before, and knowing that the legions were following them, animated both by the disgrace of retreating, and a desire of concluding the battle expeditiously by their own courage, fought most valiantly against the foot: and the enemy, imagining that no more forces would come against them, as they had experienced the day before, thought they had got a favorable opportunity of destroying our whole cavalry.

CHAP. XXIX.—After the conflict had continued for some time with great violence, Dumnacus drew out his army in such a manner, that the foot should by turns assist the horse. Then the legions, marching in close order, came suddenly in sight of the enemy. At this sight, the barbarian horse were so astonished, and the foot so terrified, that breaking through the line of baggage, they betook themselves to flight with a loud shout, and in great disorder. But our horse, who a little before had vigorously engaged them, while they made resistance, being elated with joy at their victory, raising a shout on every side, poured round them as they ran, and as long as their horses had strength to pursue, or their arms to give a blow, so long did they continue the slaughter of the enemy in that battle, and having killed above twelve thousand men in arms, or such as threw away their arms through fear, they took their whole train of baggage.

CHAP. XXX.—After this defeat when it was ascertained that Drapes, a Senonian (who in the beginning of the revolt of Gaul had collected from all quarters men of desperate fortunes, invited the slaves to liberty, called in the exiles of the whole kingdom, given an asylum to robbers, and intercepted the Roman baggage and provisions), was marching to the province with five thousand men, being all he could collect after the defeat, and that Luterius a Cadurcian who, as it has been observed in a former commentary, had designed to make an attack on the Province in the first revolt of Gaul, had formed a junction with him, Caius Caninius went in pursuit of them with two legions, lest great disgrace might be incurred from the fears or injuries done to the Province by the depredations of a band of desperate men.

CHAP. XXXI.—Caius Fabius set off with the rest of the army to the Carnutes and those other states, whose force he was informed, had served as auxiliaries in that battle, which he fought against Dumnacus. For he had no doubt that they would be more submissive after their recent sufferings, but if respite and time were given them, they might be easily excited by the earnest solicitations of the same Dumnacus. On this occasion Fabius was extremely fortunate and expeditious in recovering the states. For the Carnutes, who, though often harassed had never mentioned peace, submitted and gave hostages: and the other states, which lie in the remotest parts of Gaul, adjoining the ocean, and which are called Armoricæ, influenced by the example of the Carnutes, as soon as Fabius arrived with his legions, without delay comply with his command. Dumnacus, expelled from his own territories, wandering and skulking about, was forced to seek refuge by himself in the most remote parts of Gaul.

CHAP. XXXII.—But Drapes in conjunction with Luterius, knowing that Caninius was at hand with the legions, and that they themselves could not without certain destruction enter the boundaries of the province, while an army was in pursuit of them, and being no longer at liberty to roam up and down and pillage, halt in the country of the Cadurci, as Luterius had once in his prosperity possessed a powerful influence over the inhabitants, who were his countrymen, and being always the author of new projects, had considerable authority among the barbarians; with his own and Drapes' troops he seized Uxellodunum,[1] a town formerly in vassalage to him, and strongly fortified by its natural situation; and prevailed on the inhabitants to join him.

CHAP. XXXIII.—After Caninius had rapidly marched to this place, and perceived that all parts of the town were secured by very craggy rocks, which it would be difficult for men in arms to climb even if they met with no resistance; and moreover, observing that the town's people were possessed of effects, to a considerable amount, and that if they attempted to convey them away in a clandestine manner, they could not escape our horse, or even our legions; he divided his forces into three parts, and pitched three camps on very high ground, with the intention of drawing lines round the town by degrees, as his forces could bear the fatigue.

CHAP. XXXIV.—When the townsmen perceived his design, being terrified by the recollection of the distress at Alesia, they began to dread similar consequences from a siege; and above all Luterius, who had experienced that fatal event, cautioned

[1] Uxellodunum, *Le Puyd' Issolu*, one of the principal towns of the Cadurci: it was situated on the river Duranius, *Dordogne*, which enters the Garonne below Bourdeaux, and was remarkable for the siege which it sustained against Cæsar, being the last place in Gaul, which held out against him.—Arrowsmith's Ancient Geography.

them to make provisions of corn; they therefore resolve by general consent to leave part of their troops behind, and set out with their light troops to bring in corn. The scheme having met with approbation, the following night Drapes and Luterius leaving two thousand men in the garrison, marched out of the town with the rest. After a few days' stay in the country of the Cadurci (some of whom were disposed to assist them with corn, and others were unable to prevent their taking it) they collected a great store. Sometimes also attacks were made on our little forts by sallies at night. For this reason Caninius deferred drawing his works round the whole town, lest he should be unable to protect them when completed, or by disposing his garrisons in several places, should make them too weak.

CHAP. XXXV.—Drapes and Luterius, having laid in a large supply of corn, occupying a position at about ten miles distance from the town, intending from it to convey the corn into the town by degrees. They chose each his respective department. Drapes stayed behind in the camp with part of the army to protect it; Luterius conveys the train with provisions into the town. Accordingly, having disposed guards here and there along the road, about the tenth hour of the night, he set out by narrow paths through the woods, to fetch the corn into the town. But their noise being heard by the sentinels of our camp, and the scouts which we had sent out, having brought an account of what was going on, Caninius instantly with the ready-armed cohorts from the nearest turrets made an attack on the convoy at the break of day. They, alarmed at so unexpected an evil, fled by different ways to their guard: which as soon as our men perceived, they fell with great fury on the escort, and did not allow a single man to be taken alive. Luterius escaped thence with a few followers, but did not return to the camp.

CHAP. XXXVI.—After this success, Caninius learned from some prisoners, that a part of the forces was encamped with Drapes, not more than ten miles off: which being confirmed by several, supposing that after the defeat of one general, the rest would be terrified, and might be easily conquered, he thought it a most fortunate event that none of the enemy had fled back from the slaughter to the camp, to give Drapes notice of the calamity which had befallen him. And as he could see no danger in making the attempt, he sent forward all his cavalry and the German foot, men of great activity, to the enemy's camp. He divides one legion among the three camps, and takes the other without baggage along with him. When he had advanced near the enemy, he was informed by scouts, which he had sent before him, that the enemy's camp, as is the custom of barbarians, was pitched low, near the banks of a river, and that the higher grounds were unoccupied: but that the German horse had made a sudden attack on them, and had begun the battle. Upon this intelligence, he marched up with his legion, armed and in order of battle. Then, on a signal being suddenly given on every side, our men took possession of the higher grounds. Upon this the German horse observing the Roman colors, fought with great vigor. Immediately all the cohorts attack them on every side; and having either killed or made prisoners of them all, gained great booty. In that battle, Drapes himself was taken prisoner.

Chap. XXXVII.—Caninius, having accomplished the business so successfully, without having scarcely a man wounded, returned to besiege the town; and, having destroyed the enemy without, for fear of whom he had been prevented from strengthening his redoubts, and surrounding the enemy with his lines, he orders the work to be completed on every side. The next day, Caius Fabius came to join him with his forces, and took upon him the siege of one side.

Chap. XXXVIII.—In the mean time, Cæsar left Caius Antonius in the country of the Bellovaci, with fifteen cohorts, that the Belgæ might have no opportunity of forming new plans in future. He himself visits the other states, demands a great number of hostages, and by his encouraging language allays the apprehensions of all. When he came to the Carnutes, in whose state he has in a former commentary mentioned that the war first broke out; observing, that from a consciousness of their guilt, they seemed to be in the greatest terror: to relieve the state the sooner from its fear, he demanded that Guturvatus, the promoter of that treason, and the instigator of that rebellion, should be delivered up to punishment. And though the latter did not dare to trust his life even to his own countrymen, yet such diligent search was made by them all, that he was soon brought to our camp. Cæsar was forced to punish him, by the clamors of the soldiers, contrary to his natural humanity, for they alleged that all the dangers and losses incurred in that war, ought to be imputed to Guturvatus. Accordingly, he was whipped to death, and his head cut off.

CHAP. XXXIX.—Here Cæsar was informed by numerous letters from Caninius of what had happened to Drapes and Luterius, and in what conduct the town's people persisted: and though he despised the smallness of their numbers, yet he thought their obstinacy deserving a severe punishment, lest Gaul in general should adopt an idea that she did not want strength but perseverance to oppose the Romans; and lest the other states, relying on the advantage of situation, should follow their example and assert their liberty; especially as he knew that all the Gauls understood that his command was to continue but one summer longer, and if they could hold out for that time, that they would have no further danger to apprehend. He therefore left Quintus Calenus, one of his lieutenants, behind him, with two legions, and instructions to follow him by regular marches. He hastened as much at he could with all the cavalry to Caninius.

CHAP. XL.—Having arrived at Uxellodunum, contrary to the general expectation, and perceiving that the town was surrounded by the works, and that the enemy had no possible means of retiring from the assault, and being likewise informed by the deserters that the townsmen had abundance of corn, he endeavoured to prevent their getting water. A river divided the valley below, which almost surrounded the steep craggy mountain on which Uxellodunum was built. The nature of the ground prevented his turning the current: for it ran so low down at the foot of the mountain, that no drains could be sunk deep enough to draw it off in any direction. But the descent to it was so difficult, that if we made opposition, the besieged could neither come to the river nor retire up the precipice without hazard of their lives. Cæsar perceiving the difficulty, disposed archers and slingers, and in some places, opposite to the easiest descents, placed engines, and attempted to hinder the townsmen from getting water at the river, which obliged them afterward to go all to one place to procure water.

CHAP. XLI.—Close under the walls of the town, a copious spring gushed out on that part, which for the space of nearly three hundred feet,[1] was not surrounded by the river. While every other person wished that the besieged could be debarred

[1] Literally "wanted the circuit of the river."

from this spring, Cæsar alone saw that it could be effected, though not without great danger. Opposite to it he began to advance the vineæ toward the mountain, and to throw up a mound, with great labor and continual skirmishing. For the townsmen ran down from the high ground, and fought without any risk, and wounded several of our men, yet they obstinately pushed on and were not deterred from moving forward the vineæ, and from surmounting by their assiduity the difficulties of situation. At the same time they work mines, and move the crates and vineæ to the source of the fountain. This was the only work which they could do without danger or suspicion. A mound sixty feet high was raised; on it was erected a turret of ten stories, not with the intention that it should be on a level with the wall (for that could not be effected by any works), but to rise above the top of the spring. When our engines began to play from it upon the paths that led to the fountain, and the townsmen could not go for water without danger, not only the cattle designed for food and the working cattle, but a great number of men also died of thirst.

CHAP. XLII.—Alarmed at this calamity, the townsmen fill barrels with tallow, pitch, and dried wood: these they set on fire, and roll down on our works. At the same time, they fight most furiously, to deter the Romans, by the engagement and danger, from extinguishing the flames. Instantly a great blaze arose in the works. For whatever they threw down the precipice, striking against the vineæ and agger, communicated the fire to whatever was in the way. Our soldiers on the other hand, though they were engaged in a perilous sort of encounter, and laboring under the disadvantages of position, yet supported all with very great presence of mind. For the action happened in an elevated situation, and in sight of our army; and a great shout was raised on both sides; therefore every man faced the weapons of the enemy and the flames in as conspicuous a manner as he could, that his valor might be the better known and attested.

CHAP. XLIII.—Cæsar, observing that several of his men were wounded, ordered the cohorts to ascend the mountain on all sides, and, under pretense of assailing the walls, to raise a shout: at which the besieged being frightened, and not knowing what was going on in other places, call off their armed troops from attacking our works, and dispose them on the walls. Thus our men without hazarding a battle, gained time partly to extinguish the works which had caught fire, and partly to cut off the communication. As the townsmen still continued to make an obstinate resistance, and even, after losing the greatest part of their forces by drought, persevered in their resolution: at last the veins of the spring were cut across by our mines, and turned from their course. By this their constant spring was suddenly dried up, which reduced them to such despair that they imagined that it was not done by the art of man, but the will of the gods; forced, therefore, by necessity, they at length submitted.

CHAP. XLIV.—Cæsar, being convinced that his lenity was known to all men, and being under no fears of being thought to act severely from a natural cruelty, and perceiving that there would be no end to his troubles if several states should attempt to rebel in like manner and in different places, resolved to deter others by inflicting an exemplary punishment on these. Accordingly he cut off the hands of those who had borne arms against him. Their lives he spared, that the punishment of their rebellion might be the more conspicuous. Drapes, who I have said was taken by Caninius, either through indignation and grief arising from his captivity, or through fear of severer punishments, abstained from food for several days, and thus perished. At the same time, Luterius, who, I have related, had escaped from the battle, having fallen into the hands of Epasnactus, an Arvernian (for he frequently changed his quarters, and threw himself on the honor of several persons, as he saw that he dare not remain long in one place, and was conscious how great an enemy he deserved to have in Cæsar), was by this Epasnactus, the Arvernian, a sincere friend of the Roman people, delivered without any hesitation, a prisoner to Cæsar.

CHAP. XLV.—In the mean time, Labienus engages in a successful cavalry action among the Treviri; and, having killed several of them and of the Germans, who never refused their aid to any person against the Romans, he got their chiefs alive into his power, and, among them, Surus, an Æduan, who was highly renowned both for his valor and birth, and was the only Æduan that had continued in arms till that time. Cæsar, being informed of this, and perceiving that he had met with good success in all parts of Gaul, and reflecting that, in former campaigns [Celtic] Gaul had been conquered and subdued; but that he had never gone in person to Aquitania, but had made a conquest of it, in some degree, by Marcus Crassus, set out for it with two legions, designing to spend the latter part of the summer there. This affair he executed with his usual dispatch and good fortune. For all the states of Aquitania sent embassadors to him and delivered hostages. These affairs being concluded, he marched with a guard of cavalry toward Narbo, and drew off his army into winter quarters by his lieutenants. He posted four legions in the country of the Belgæ, under Marcus Antonius, Caius Trebonius, Publius Vatinius, and Quintus Tullius, his lieutenants. Two he detached to the Ædui, knowing them to have a very powerful influence throughout all Gaul. Two he placed among the Turoni, near the confines of the Carnutes, to keep in awe the entire tract of country bordering on the ocean; the other two he placed in the territories of the Lemovices, at a small distance from the Arverni, that no part of Gaul might be without an army. Having spent a few days in the province, he quickly ran through all the business of the assizes, settled all public disputes, and distributed rewards to the most deserving; for he had a good opportunity of learning how every person was disposed toward the republic during the general revolt of Gaul, which he had withstood by the fidelity and assistance of the Province.

Chap. XLVII.—Having finished these affairs, he returned to his legions among the Belgæ and wintered at Nemetocenna: there he got intelligence that Comius, the Atrebatian had had an engagement with his cavalry. For when Antonius had gone into winter quarters, and the state of the Atrebates continued in their allegiance, Comius, who, after that wound which I before mentioned, was always ready to join his countrymen upon every commotion, that they might not want a person to advise and head them in the management of the war, when his state submitted to the Romans, supported himself and his adherents on plunder by means of his cavalry, infested the roads, and intercepted several convoys which were bringing provisions to the Roman quarters.

Chap. XLVIII.—Caius Volusenus Quadratus was appointed commander of the horse under Antonius, to winter with him: Antonius sent him in pursuit of the enemy's cavalry; now Volusenus added to that valor which was pre-eminent in him, a great aversion to Comius, on which account he executed the more willingly the orders which he received. Having, therefore, laid ambuscades, he had several encounters with his cavalry and came off successful. At last, when a violent contest ensued, and Volusenus, through eagerness to intercept Comius, had obstinately pursued him with a small party; and Comius had, by the rapidity of his flight, drawn Volusenus to a considerable distance from his troops, he, on a sudden, appealed to the honor of all about him for assistance not to suffer the wound, which he had perfidiously received, to go without vengeance; and, wheeling his horse about, rode unguardedly before the rest up to the commander. All his horse following his example, made a few of our men turn their backs and pursued them. Comius, clapping spurs to his horse, rode up to Volusenus, and, pointing his lance, pierced him in the thigh with great force. When their commander was wounded, our men no longer hesitated to make resistance, and, facing about, beat back the enemy. When this occurred, several of the enemy, repulsed by the great impetuosity of our men, were wounded, and some were trampled to death in striving to escape, and some were made prisoners. Their general escaped this misfortune by the swiftness of his horse. Our commander, being severely wounded, so much so that he appeared to run the risk of losing his life, was carried back to the camp. But Comius, having either gratified his resentment, or, because he had lost the greatest part of his followers, sent embassadors to Antonius, and assured him that he would give hostages as a security that he would go wherever Antonius should prescribe, and would comply with his orders, and only entreated that this concession should be made to his fears, that he should not be obliged to go into the presence of any Roman. As Antonius judged that his request originated in a just apprehension, he indulged him in it and accepted his hostages.

Cæsar, I know, has made a separate commentary of each year's transactions, which I have not thought it necessary for me to do, because the following year, in which Lucius Paulus and Caius Marcellus were consuls, produced no remarkable occurrences in Gaul. But that no person may be left in ignorance of the place where Cæsar and his army were at that time, I have thought proper to write a few words in addition to this commentary.

CHAP. XLIX.—Cæsar, while in winter quarters in the country of the Belgæ, made it his only business to keep the states in amity with him, and to give none either hopes of, or pretext for a revolt. For nothing was further from his wishes than to be under the necessity of engaging in another war at his departure; lest, when he was drawing his army out of the country, any war should be left unfinished, which the Gauls would cheerfully undertake, when there was no immediate danger. Therefore, by treating the states with respect, making rich presents to the leading men, imposing no new burdens, and making the terms of their subjection lighter, he easily kept Gaul (already exhausted by so many unsuccessful battles) in obedience.

CHAP. L.—When the winter quarters were broken up he himself, contrary to his usual practice, proceeded to Italy, by the longest possible stages, in order to visit the free towns and colonies, that he might recommend to them the petition of Marcus Antonius, his treasurer, for the priesthood. For he exerted his interest both cheerfully in favor of a man strongly attached to him, whom he had sent home before him to attend the election, and zealously to oppose the faction and power of a few men, who, by rejecting Marcus Antonius, wished to undermine Cæsar's influence when going out of office. Though Cæsar heard on the road, before he reached Italy that he was created augur, yet he thought himself in honor bound to visit the free towns and colonies, to return them thanks for rendering such service to Antonius by their presence in such great numbers [at the election], and at the same time to recommend to them himself, and his honor in his suit for the consulate the ensuing year For his adversaries arrogantly boasted that Lucius Lentulus and Caius Marcellus had been appointed consuls, who would strip Cæsar of all honor and dignity: and that the consulate had been injuriously taken from Sergius Galba, though he had been much superior in votes and interest, because he was united to Cæsar, both by friendship, and by serving as lieutenant under him.

CHAP. LI.—Cæsar, on his arrival, was received by the principal towns and colonies with incredible respect and affection; for this was the first time he came since the war against united Gaul. Nothing was omitted which could be thought of for the ornament of the gates, roads, and every place through which Cæsar was to pass. All the people with their children went out to meet him. Sacrifices were offered up in every quarter. The market places and temples were laid out with entertainments, as if anticipating the joy of a most splendid triumph. So great was the magnificence of the richer and zeal of the poorer ranks of the people.

CHAP. LII.—When Cæsar had gone through all the states of Cisalpine Gaul, he returned with the greatest haste to the army at Nemetocenna; and having ordered all his legions to march from winter quarters to the territories of the Treviri, he went thither and reviewed them. He made Titus Labienus governor of Cisalpine Gaul, that he might be the more inclined to support him in his suit for the consulate. He himself made such journeys as he thought would conduce to the health of his men by change of air; and though he was frequently told that Labienus was solicited by his enemies, and was assured that a scheme was in agitation by the contrivance of a few, that the senate should interpose their authority to deprive him of a part of his army; yet he neither gave credit to any story concerning Labienus, nor could be prevailed upon to do any thing in opposition to the authority of the senate; for he thought that his cause would be easily gained by the free voice of the senators. For Caius Curio, one of the tribunes of the people, having undertaken to defend Cæsar's cause and dignity, had often proposed to the senate, "that if the dread of Cæsar's arms rendered any apprehensive, as Pompey's authority and arms were no less formidable to the forum, both should resign their command, and disband their armies. That then the city would be free, and enjoy its due rights." And he not only proposed this, but of himself called upon the senate to divide on the question. But the consuls and Pompey's friends interposed to prevent it; and regulating matters as they desired, they broke up the meeting.

CHAP. LIII.—This testimony of the unanimous voice of the senate was very great, and consistent with their former conduct; for the preceding year, when Marcellus attacked Cæsar's dignity, he proposed to the senate, contrary to the law of Pompey and Crassus, to dispose of Cæsar's province, before the expiration of his command, and when the votes were called for, and Marcellus, who endeavored to advance his own dignity, by raising envy against Cæsar, wanted a division, the full senate went over to the opposite side. The spirit of

Cæsar's foes was not broken by this, but it taught them, that they ought to strengthen their interest by enlarging their connections, so as to force the senate to comply with whatever they had resolved on.

CHAP. LIV.—After this a decree was passed by the senate, that one legion should be sent by Pompey, and another by Cæsar, to the Parthian war. But these two legions were evidently drawn from Cæsar alone. For the first legion which Pompey sent to Cæsar, he gave Cæsar, as if it belonged to himself, though it was levied in Cæsar's province. Cæsar, however, though no one could doubt the design of his enemies, sent the legion back to Cneius Pompey, and in compliance with the decree of the senate, ordered the fifteenth, belonging to himself, and which was quartered in Cisalpine Gaul, to be delivered up. In its room he sent the thirteenth into Italy, to protect the garrisons from which he had drafted the fifteenth. He disposed his army in winter quarters, placed Caius Trebonius, with four legions among the Belgæ, and detached Caius Fabius, with four more, to the Ædui; for he thought that Gaul would be most secure, if the Belgæ, a people of the greatest valor, and the Ædui, who possessed the most powerful influence, were kept in awe by his armies.

CHAP. LV.—He himself set out for Italy; where he was informed on his arrival, that the two legions sent home by him, and which by the senate's decree, should have been sent to the Parthian war, had been delivered over to Pompey, by Caius Marcellus the consul, and were retained in Italy. Although from this transaction it was evident to every one that war was designed against Cæsar, yet he resolved to submit to any thing, as long as there were hopes left of deciding the dispute in an equitable manner, rather than to have recourse to arms.

THE

COMMENTARIES OF C. JULIUS CÆSAR

ON THE

CIVIL WAR.

BOOK I.

THE ARGUMENT.

I. The various causes and origin of the civil war. VIII. Cæsar makes himself master of Italy with great ease, owing to the municipal towns being devoted to his interests. XXV. He besieges Pompey at Brundusium. XXVIII. The latter effects his escape, and the town surrenders. XXX. Cæsar's partisans expel Cotta from Sardinia, And Cato from Sicily. XXXII. Cæsar sets out for Rome. XXXIII. But the plans, which he had in contemplation being immature, he proceeds into Transalpine Gaul, XXXVI. With the intention of besieging Massilia by land and sea. XXXVII. He previously sends Fabius, one of his lieutenants, into Spain. XXXIX. He follows in person, leaving Caius Trebonius, and Decimus Brutus, to besiege Massilia, XLI. And carries on war against Afranius and Petreius, Pompey's lieutenants, in the vicinity of Ilerda. XLVIII. Cæsar is hemmed in between the Segre and Cinca, in consequence of a violent storm, which sweeps away the bridges over these rivers. LIV. Nevertheless, he surmounts all his difficulties. LVI. In the meantime, the inhabitants of Massilia are conquered in a naval battle. LIX. Cæsar henceforth is successful in all his operations in Spain. LXIII. He follows the enemy closely in all their marches and countermarches, and by his cavalry, prevents them from foraging, LXXXI. And at length intercepts them, and compels them to surrender.

VOSSIUS'S SUPPLEMENT TO THE FIRST BOOK.

I WILL now say nothing concerning the absurd opinion of those who assert that the following Commentaries on the Civil War were not written by Cæsar himself. Even without the authority of Suetonius, the diction itself would be sufficient to convince the most skeptical that Cæsar and no other was the author. I am of the opinion of those who think that the beginning of these Commentaries is lost. For I can not be convinced that Cæsar commenced so abruptly; and History itself gives sufficient evidence that many circumstances required to be previously stated. For which reason we thought that it would be well worth our attention to compile from Plutarch, Appian, and Dion, a narrative of such facts as seemed necessary to fill up the chasm; these facts are as follows:

"When Cæsar, after reducing all Transalpine Gaul, had passed into Cisalpine Gaul, he determined for many reasons to send embassadors to Rome to request for him the consulate, and a proolongation of the command of his province. Pompey, who was estranged from Cæsar, although he was not as yet at open enmity with him, determined neither to aid him by his influence nor openly oppose him on this occasion. But the consuls Lentulus and Marcellus, who had previously been on unfriendly terms with Cæsar, resolved to use all means in their power to prevent him from gaining his object. Marcellus in particular did not hesitate to offer Cæsar other insults. Cæsar had lately planned the colony of Novumcomum in Gaul: Marcellus, not content with taking from it the right of citizenship, ordered the principal man of the colony to be arrested and scourged at Rome, and sent him to make his complaints to Cæsar: an insult of this description had never before been offered to a Roman citizen. While these transactions are taking place, Caius Curio, tribune of the commons, comes to Cæsar in his province. Curio had made many and energetic struggles, in behalf of the republic and Cæsar's cause: at length when he perceived that all his efforts were vain, he fled through fear of his adversaries, and informed Cæsar of all the transactions that had taken place, and of the efforts made by his enemies to crush him. Cæsar received Curio with great kindness, as he was a man of the highest rank, and had great claims on himself and the republic, and thanked him warmly for his numerous personal favors. But Curio, as war was being openly prepared against Cæsar, advised him to concentrate his troops, and rescue the republic now oppressed by a few daring men. Cæsar, although he was not ignorant of the real state of affairs, was however of opinion that particular regard should be paid to the tranquillity of the republic, lest any one should suppose that he was the originator of the war. Therefore, through his friends, he made this one request, that two legions, and the province of Cisalpine Gaul, and Illyricum, should be left him. All these acts were performed by Cæsar, with the hope that his enemies might be induced by the justice of his demands, to preserve the peace of the republic. Even Pompey himself did not dare to oppose them. But when Cæsar could not obtain his request from the consuls, he wrote to the senate a letter, in which he briefly stated his exploits and public services, and entreated that he should not be deprived of the favor of the people, who had ordered, that he, although absent, should be considered a candidate at the next elections; and he stated also that he would disband his army, if the senate and people of Rome would pass a resolution to that effect, provided that Pompey would do the same. That, as long as the latter should retain the command of his army, no just reason could exist that he [Cæsar] should disband his troops and expose himself to the insults of his enemies. He intrusts this letter to Curio to bear to its destination; the latter traveled one hundred and sixty miles with incredible dispatch, and reached the city in three days' time, before the beginning of January, and before the consuls could pass any decree concerning Cæsar's command. Curio, after accomplishing his journey, kept the letter, and did not give it up, until there was a crowded meeting of the senate, and the tribunes of the commons were present; for he was afraid, lest, if he gave it up previously, the consuls should suppress it."

CHAP. I.—When Cæsar's letter was delivered to the consuls, they were with great difficulty, and a hard struggle of the tribunes,[1] prevailed on to suffer it to be read in the senate; but the tribunes could not prevail, that any question should be put to the senate on the subject of the letter. The consuls put the question on the regulation of the state, Lucius Lentulus the consul promises that he will not fail the senate and republic, "if they declared their sentiments boldly and resolutely, but if they turned their regard to Cæsar, and courted his favor, as they did on former occasions, he would adopt a plan for himself, and not submit to the authority of the senate: that he too had a means of regaining Cæsar's favor and friendship." Scipio spoke to the same purport, "that it was Pompey's intention not to abandon the republic,

[1] Plutarch says that Mark Antony, who was then tribune, read the letter to the people, which, says Cicero, made them very reluctant to enlist, when Pompey ordered a levy.—P.

if the senate would support him; but if they should hesitate and act without energy, they would in vain implore his aid, if they should require it hereafter."

CHAP. II.—This speech of Scipio's, as the senate was convened in the city, and Pompey[1] was near at hand, seemed to have fallen from the lips of Pompey himself. Some delivered their sentiments with more moderation, as Marcellus first, who in the beginning of his speech, said, "that the question ought not to be put to the senate on this matter, till levies were made throughout all Italy, and armies raised under whose protection the senate might freely and safely pass such resolutions as they thought proper;" as Marcus Calidius afterward, who was of opinion, "that Pompey should set out for his province, that there might be no cause for arms; that Cæsar[2] was naturally apprehensive as two legions were forced from him, that Pompey was retaining those troops, and keeping them near the city to do him injury:" as Marcus Rufus, who followed Calidius almost word for word. They were all harshly rebuked by Lentulus, who peremptorily refused to propose Calidius's motion. Marcellus, overawed by his reproofs, retracted his opinion. Thus most of the senate, intimidated by the expressions of the consul, by the fears of a present army, and the threats of Pompey's friends, unwillingly and reluctantly adopted Scipio's opinion, that Cæsar should disband his army by a certain day, and should he not do so, he should be considered as acting against the state. Marcus Antonius, and Quintus Cassius, tribunes of the people, interposed.[3] The question was immediately put on their interposition. Violent opinions were expressed; whoever spoke with the greatest acrimony and cruelty, was most highly commended by Cæsar's enemies.

CHAP. III.—The senate having broken up in the evening,

[1] As Pompey was at the head of an army (being appointed proconsul of Spain and Africa) he could not come within the city while invested with power.—P.

[2] A decree of the senate had been passed some time before, that Cæsar and Pompey should each contribute, out of their forces, a legion to be sent against the Parthians. Pompey had previously lent Cæsar one legion, which he now returned, with the fifteenth legion belonging to himself. Pompey kept both.—P.

[3] The tribunes by their intercession, were able to paralyze the measures of the senate, and prevent any obnoxious measures from passing.

all who belonged to that order were summoned by Pompey. He applauded the forward, and secured their votes for the next day; the more moderate he reproved and excited against Cæsar. Many veterans, from all parts, who had served in Pompey's armies, were invited to his standard by the hopes of rewards and promotions. Several officers belonging to the two legions, which had been delivered up by Cæsar, were sent for. The city and the comitium were crowded with tribunes, centurions, and veterans. All the consul's friends, all Pompey's connections, all those who bore any ancient enmity to Cæsar, were forced into the senate house. By their concourse and declarations the timid were awed, the irresolute confirmed, and the greater part deprived of the power of speaking their sentiments with freedom. Lucius Piso, the censor, offered to go to Cæsar: as did likewise Lucius Roscius, the prætor, to inform him of these affairs, and require only six days' time to finish the business. Opinions were expressed by some to the effect that commissioners should be sent to Cæsar to acquaint him with the senate's pleasure.

CHAP. IV.—All these proposals were rejected, and opposition made to them all, in the speeches of the consul, Scipio, and Cato. An old grudge against Cæsar and chagrin at a defeat actuated Cato. Lentulus was wrought upon by the magnitude of his debts, and the hopes of having the government of an army and provinces, and by the presents[1] which he expected from such princes as should receive the title of friends of the Roman people, and boasted among his friends, that he would be a second Sylla[2] to whom the supreme authority should return. Similar hopes of a province and armies, which he expected to share with Pompey on account of his connection[3] with him, urged on Scipio; and moreover [he was influenced by] the fear of being called to trial, and the

[1] The Roman commander often gave foreign princes the title of king in the name of the Roman people; and as this honor seemed to imply a recognition of their authority, immense sums were occasionally given for it.

[2] Alluding to the well-known prophecy of the Sybil, that three of the Cornelii should have the supreme power at Rome. Lentulus, who played such a prominent part in Catiline's conspiracy, frequently quoted the same prophecy, which seems to have lured the Cornelii to their doom by the bright vision of supreme power.

[3] Pompey married Cornelia, Scipio's daughter, on the death of Julia, whom her father Cæsar had bestowed on Pompey, to attach him more firmly to his interests.

adulation and an ostentatious display of himself and his friends in power, who at that time had great influence in the republic, and courts of judicature. Pompey himself, incited by Cæsar's enemies, because he was unwilling that any person should bear an equal degree of dignity, had wholly alienated himself from Cæsar's friendship, and procured a reconciliation with their common enemies; the greatest part of whom he had himself brought upon Cæsar during his affinity with him. At the same time, chagrined at the disgrace which he had incurred by converting the two legions from their expedition through Asia and Syria, to [augment] his own power and authority, he was anxious to bring matters to a war.

CHAP. V.—For these reasons every thing was done in a hasty and disorderly manner, and neither was time given to Cæsar's relations to inform him [of the state of affairs] nor liberty to the tribunes of the people to deprecate their own danger, nor even to retain the last privilege, which Sylla had left them, the interposing their authority; but on the seventh day they were obliged to think of their own safety, which the most turbulent tribunes of the people were not accustomed to attend to, nor to fear being called to an account for their actions, till the eighth month. Recourse is had to that extreme and final decree of the senate (which was never resorted to even by daring proposers except when the city was in danger of being set on fire, or when the public safety was despaired of). "That the consuls, prætors, tribunes of the people, and proconsuls in the city, should take care that the state received no injury." These decrees are dated the eighth day before the ides of January;[1] therefore, in the first five days, on which the senate could meet, from the day on which Lentulus entered into his consulate, the two days of election excepted, the severest and most virulent decrees were passed against Cæsar's government, and against those most illustrious characters, the tribunes of the people. The latter immediately made their escape from the city, and withdrew to Cæsar, who was then at Ravenna, awaiting an answer to his moderate demands; [to see] if matters could be brought to a peaceful termination by any equitable act on the part of his enemies.

CHAP. VI.—During the succeeding days the senate is convened outside the city. Pompey repeated the same things

[1] The 8th of January.

which he had declared through Scipio. He applauded the courage and firmness of the senate, acquainted them with his force, and told them that he had ten legions ready; that he was moreover informed and assured that Cæsar's soldiers were disaffected, and that he could not persuade them to defend or even follow him. Motions were made in the senate concerning other matters; that levies should be made through all Italy; that Faustus Sylla should be sent as proprætor into Mauritania; that money should be granted to Pompey from the public treasury. It was also put to the vote that king Juba should be [honored with the title of] friend and ally. But Marcellus said that he would not allow this motion for the present. Philip, one of the tribunes, stopped [the appointment of] Sylla; the resolutions respecting the other matters passed. The provinces, two of which were consular, the remainder prætorian, were decreed to private persons; Scipio got Syria, Lucius Domitius Gaul: Philip and Marcellus were omitted, from a private motive, and their lots were not even admitted. To the other provinces prætors were sent, nor was time granted as in former years, to refer to the people on their appointment, nor to make them take the usual oath, and march out of the city in a public manner, robed in the military habit, after offering their vows: a circumstance which had never before happened. Both the consuls leave the city, and private men had lictors in the city and capital, contrary to all precedents of former times. Levies were made throughout Italy, arms demanded, and money exacted from the municipal towns, and violently taken from the temples. All distinctions between things human and divine, are confounded.

Chap. VII.—These things being made known to Cæsar, he harangued his soldiers; he reminded them "of the wrongs done to him at all times by his enemies, and complained that Pompey had been alienated from him and led astray by them through envy and a malicious opposition to his glory, though he had always favored and promoted Pompey's honor and dignity. He complained that an innovation had been introduced into the republic, that the intercession of the tribunes, which had been restored a few years before by Sylla, was branded as a crime, and suppressed by force of arms; that Sylla, who had stripped the tribunes of every other power, had, nevertheless, left the privilege of intercession unrestrained; that

Pompey, who pretended to restore what they had lost, had taken away the privileges which they formerly had; that whenever the senate decreed, 'that the magistrates should take care that the republic sustained no injury' (by which words and decree the Roman people were obliged to repair to arms), it was only when pernicious laws were proposed; when the tribunes attempted violent measures; when the people seceded,[1] and possessed themselves of the temples and eminences of the city; (and these instances of former times, he showed them were expiated by the fate of Saturninus and the Gracchi): that nothing of this kind was attempted now, nor even thought of: that no law was promulgated, no intrigue with the people going forward, no secession made; he exhorted them to defend from the malice of his enemies the reputation and honor of that general under whose command they had for nine years most successfully supported the state; fought many successful battles, and subdued all Gaul and Germany." The soldiers of the thirteenth legion, which was present (for in the beginning of the disturbances he had called it out, his other legions not having yet arrived), all cry out that they are ready to defend their general, and the tribunes of the commons, from all injuries.

Chap. VIII.—Having made himself acquainted with the disposition of his soldiers, Cæsar set off with that legion to Ariminum, and there met the tribunes, who had fled to him for protection; he called his other legions from winter quarters, and ordered them to follow him. Thither came Lucius Cæsar, a young man, whose father was a lieutenant-general under Cæsar. He, after concluding the rest of his speech, and stating for what purpose he had come, told Cæsar that he had commands of a private nature for him from Pompey; that Pompey wished to clear himself to Cæsar, lest he should impute those actions which he did for the republic, to a design of affronting

[1] Three secessions of the Commons are recorded in history. The first, which was occasioned by the tyranny of the Patricians, led to the creation of the tribunes of the Commons. The second, which was occasioned by the licentiousness of Appius Claudius, and the murder of Siccius Dentatus led to the expulsion of the decemvirs. The third and last, which, according to some writers, was occasioned by the pressure of debt, according to others, by the attempt of the Patricians to cancel the Ogulnian law (which admitted the Plebians to the priesthood), occurred B. C. 286, and led to the complete equalization of the orders, from which we may date the brightest period of Rome's history.

him; that he had ever preferred the interest of the state to his own private connections; that Cæsar, too, for his own honor, ought to sacrifice his desires and resentment to the public good, and not vent his anger so violently against his enemies, lest in his hopes of injuring them, he should injure the republic. He spoke a few words to the same purport from himself, in addition to Pompey's apology. Roscius, the prætor, conferred with Cæsar almost in the same words, and on the same subject, and declared that Pompey had empowered him to do so.

CHAP. IX.—Though these things seemed to have no tendency toward redressing his injuries, yet having got proper persons by whom he could communicate his wishes to Pompey; he required of them both, that, as they had conveyed Pompey's demands to him, they should not refuse to convey his demands to Pompey; if by so little trouble they could terminate a great dispute, and liberate all Italy from her fears. "That the honor of the republic had ever been his first object, and dearer to him than life; that he was chagrined, that the favor of the Roman people was wrested from him by the injurious reports of his enemies; that he was deprived of a half-year's command, and dragged back to the city, though the people had ordered that regard should be paid to his suit for the consulate at the next election, though he was not present; that, however, he had patiently submitted to this loss of honor, for the sake of the republic; that when he wrote letters to the senate, requiring that all persons should resign the command of their armies, he did not obtain even that request; that levies were made throughout Italy; that the two legions which had been taken from him, under the pretense of the Parthian war, were kept at home, and that the state was in arms. To what did all these things tend, unless to his ruin? But, nevertheless, he was ready to condescend to any terms, and to endure every thing for the sake of the republic. Let Pompey[1] go to his own province; let them both disband their armies; let all persons in

[1] When Cæsar and Pompey were reconciled, they and Crassus divided the provinces between them. Cæsar got Hither and Further Gaul; Crassus, Parthia; and Pompey, Spain and Africa. The others set out for their respective provinces. Pompey dispatched his lieutenants to manage his provinces, and remained himself in Italy with an army, which Cæsar thought a great stretch of power, that he should command both his own provinces and Italy at the same time.—P.

Italy lay down their arms; let all fears be removed from the city; let free elections, and the whole republic be resigned to the direction of the senate and Roman people. That these things might be the more easily performed, and conditions secured and confirmed by oath, either let Pompey come to Cæsar, or allow Cæsar to go to him; it might be that all their disputes would be settled by an interview."

CHAP. X.—Roscius and Lucius Cæsar, having received this message, went to Capua, where they met the consuls and Pompey, and declared to them Cæsar's terms. Having deliberated on the matter, they replied, and sent written proposals to him by the same persons, the purport of which was, that Cæsar should return into Gaul, leave Ariminum, and disband his army: if he complied with this, that Pompey would go to Spain. In the mean time, until security was given that Cæsar would perform his promises, that the consuls and Pompey would not give over their levies.

CHAP. XI.—It was not an equitable proposal, to require that Cæsar should quit Ariminum and return to his province; but that he [Pompey] should himself retain his province and the legions that belonged to another, and desire that Cæsar's army should be disbanded, while he himself was making new levies: and that he should merely promise to go to his province, without naming the day on which he would set out; so that if he should not set out till after Cæsar's consulate expired, yet he would not appear bound by any religious scruples about asserting a falsehood. But his not granting time for a conference, nor promising to set out to meet him, made the expectation of peace appear very hopeless. Cæsar, therefore, sent Marcus Antonius, with five cohorts from Ariminum to Arretium; he himself staid at Ariminum with two legions, with the intention of raising levies there. He secured Pisaurus, Fanum, and Ancona, with a cohort each.

CHAP. XII.—In the mean time, being informed that Thermus the prætor was in possession of Iguvium, with five cohorts, and was fortifying the town, but that the affections of all the inhabitants were very well inclined toward himself, he detached Curio with three cohorts, which he had at Ariminum and Pisaurus. Upon notice of his approach, Thermus, distrusting the affections of the townsmen, drew his cohorts out of it, and made his escape; his soldiers deserted him on the road, and returned home. Curio recovered Iguvium, with the cheerful concurrence of all the inhabitants. Cæsar, having received an account of this, and relying on the affections of the municipal towns, drafted all the cohorts of the thirteenth legion from the garrison, and set out for Auximum, a town into which Attius had brought his cohorts, and of which he had taken possession, and from which he had sent senators round about the country of Picenum, to raise new levies.

CHAP. XIII.—Upon news of Cæsar's approach, the senate of Auximum went in a body to Attius Varus; and told him that it was not a subject for them to determine upon: yet neither they, nor the rest of the freemen would suffer Caius Cæsar, a general, who had merited so well of the republic, after performing such great achievements, to be excluded from their town and walls; wherefore he ought to pay some regard to the opinion of posterity, and his own danger. Alarmed at this declaration, Attius Varus drew out of the town the garrison which he had introduced, and fled. A few of Cæsar's front rank having pursued him, obliged him to halt, and when the battle began, Varus is deserted by his troops: some of them disperse to their homes, the rest come over to Cæsar; and along with them, Lucius Pupius, the chief centurion, is taken prisoner and brought to Cæsar. He had held the same rank before in Cneius Pompey's army. But Cæsar applauded the soldiers of Attius, set Pupius at liberty, returned thanks to the people of Auximum, and promised to be grateful for their conduct.

CHAP. XIV.—Intelligence of this being brought to Rome, so great a panic spread on a sudden that when Lentulus, the consul, came to open the treasury, to deliver money to Pompey by the senate's decree, immediately on opening the hallowed door he fled from the city. For it was falsely rumored that Cæsar was approaching, and that his cavalry were already at the gates. Marcellus, his colleague, followed him, and so did most of the magistrates. Cneius Pompey had left the city the day before, and was on his march to those legions which he had received from Cæsar, and had disposed in winter quarters in Apulia. The levies were stopped within the city. No place on this side of Capua was thought secure. At Capua they first began to take courage and to rally, and determined to raise levies in the colonies, which had been sent thither by the Julian law: and Lentulus brought into the public market place the gladiators which Cæsar maintained there for the entertainment of the people, and confirmed them in their liberty, and gave them horses and ordered them to attend him; but afterward, being warned by his friends that this action was censured by the judgment of all, he distributed them among the slaves of the district of Campania, to keep guard there.

CHAP. XV.—Cæsar, having moved forward from Auximum, traversed the whole country of Picenum. All the governors in these countries most cheerfully received him, and aided his army with every necessary. Embassadors came to him even from Cingulum, a town which Labienus had laid out and built at his own expense, and offered most earnestly to comply with his orders. He demanded soldiers: they sent them. In the mean time, the twelfth legion came to join Cæsar; with these two he marched to Asculum, the chief town of Picenum. Lentulus Spinther occupied that town with ten cohorts; but, on being informed of Cæsar's approach, he fled from the town, and, in attempting to bring off his cohorts with him, was deserted by a great part of his men. Being left on the road with a small number, he fell in with Vibullius Rufus, who was sent by Pompey into Picenum to confirm the people [in their allegiance]. Vibullius, being informed by him of the transactions in Picenum, takes his soldiers from him and dismisses him. He collects, likewise, from the neighboring countries, as many cohorts as he can from Pompey's new levies. Among them he meets with Uleilles Hirrus fleeing from Camerinum, with six cohorts, which he had in the garrison there; by a junction with which he made up thirteen cohorts. With them he marched by hasty journeys to Corfinium, to Domitius Ænobarbus, and informed him that Cæsar was advancing with two legions. Domitius had collected about twenty cohorts from Alba, and the Marsians, Pelignians, and neighboring states.

CHAP. XVI.—Cæsar, having recovered Asculum and driven out Lentulus, ordered the soldiers that had deserted from him to be sought out and a muster to be made; and, having delayed for one day there to provide corn, he marched to Corfinium. On his approach, five cohorts, sent by Domitius from the town, were breaking down a bridge which was over the river, at three miles' distance from it. An engagement taking place there with Cæsar's advanced-guard, Domitius's men were quickly beaten off from the bridge and retreated precipitately into the town. Cæsar, having marched his legions over, halted before the town and encamped close by the walls.

CHAP. XVII.—Domitius, upon observing this, sent messengers well acquainted with the country, encouraged by a promise of being amply rewarded, with dispatches to Pompey to Apulia, to beg and entreat him to come to his assistance. That Cæsar could be easily inclosed by the two armies, through the narrowness of the country, and prevented from obtaining supplies: unless he did so, that he and upward of thirty cohorts, and a great number of senators and Roman knights, would be in extreme danger. In the mean time he encouraged his troops, disposed engines on the walls, and assigned to each man a particular part of the city to defend. In a speech to the soldiers he promised them lands out of his own estate; to every private soldier four acres, and a corresponding share to the centurions and veterans.

CHAP. XVIII.—In the mean time, word was brought to Cæsar that the people of Sulmo, a town about seven miles distant from Corfinium, were ready to obey his orders, but were prevented by Quintus Lucretius, a senator, and Attius, a Pelignian, who were in possession of the town with a garrison of seven cohorts. He sent Marcus Antonius thither, with five cohorts of the eighth legion. The inhabitants, as soon as they saw our standards, threw open their gates, and all the people, both citizens and soldiers, went out to meet and welcome Antonius. Lucretius and Attius leaped off the walls. Attius, being brought before Antonius, begged that he might be sent to Cæsar. Antonius returned the same day on which he had set out with the cohorts and Attius. Cæsar added these cohorts to his own army, and sent Attius away in safety. The three first days Cæsar employed in fortifying his camp with strong works, in bringing in corn from the neighboring free towns, and waiting for the rest of his forces. Within the three days the eighth legion came to him, and twenty-two cohorts of the new levies in Gaul, and about three hundred horse from the king of Noricum.[1] On their arrival he made a second camp on

[1] We learn from the fifty-third chapter of the first book of the Gallic war, that Vocio, brother-in-law of Ariovistus, was king of Noricum.

another part of the town, and gave the command of it to Curio. He determined to surround the town with a rampart and turrets during the remainder of the time. Nearly at the time when the greatest part of the work was completed, all the messengers sent to Pompey returned.

CHAP. XIX.—Having read Pompey's letter, Domitius, concealing the truth, gave out in council that Pompey would speedily come to their assistance; and encouraged them not to despond, but to provide every thing necessary for the defense of the town. He held private conferences with a few of his most intimate friends, and determined on the design of fleeing. As Domitius's countenance did not agree with his words, and he did every thing with more confusion and fear than he had shown on the preceding days, and as he had several private meetings with his friends, contrary to his usual practice, in order to take their advice, and as he avoided all public councils and assemblies of the people, the truth could be no longer hid nor dissembled; for Pompey had written back in answer, "That he would not put matters to the last hazard; that Domitius had retreated into the town of Corfinium without either his advice or consent. Therefore, if any opportunity should offer, he [Domitius] should come to him with the whole force." But the blockade and works round the town prevented his escape.

CHAP. XX.—Domitius's design being noised abroad, the soldiers in Corfinium early in the evening began to mutiny, and held a conference with each other by their tribunes and centurions, and the most respectable among themselves: "that they were besieged by Cæsar; that his works and fortifications were almost finished; that their general, Domitius, on whose hopes and expectations they had confided, had thrown them off, and was meditating his own escape; that they ought to provide for their own safety." At first the Marsians differed in opinion, and possessed themselves of that part of the town which they thought the strongest. And so violent a dispute arose between them, that they attempted to fight and decide it by arms. However, in a little time, by messengers sent from one side to the other, they were informed of Domitius's meditated flight, of which they were previously ignorant. Therefore they all, with one consent brought Domitius into public view, gathered round him, and guarded him; and sent deputies out of their number to Cæsar, to say that they were ready to throw open their gates, to do whatever he should order, and deliver up Domitius alive into his hands."

CHAP. XXI.—Upon intelligence of these matters, though Cæsar thought it of great consequence to become master of the town as soon as possible, and to transfer the cohorts to his own camp, lest any change should be wrought on their inclinations by bribes, encouragement, or ficticious messages, because in war great events are often brought about by trifling circumstances; yet, dreading lest the town should be plundered by the soldiers entering into it, and taking advantage of the darkness of the night, he commended the persons who came to him, and sent them back to the town, and ordered the gates and walls to be secured. He disposed his soldiers on the works which he had begun, not at certain intervals, as was his practice before, but in one continued range of sentinels and stations, so that they touched each other, and formed a circle round the whole fortification; he ordered the tribunes and general officers to ride round: and exhorted them not only to be on their guard against sallies from the town, but also to watch that no single person should get out privately. Nor was any man so negligent or drowsy as to sleep that night. To so great height was their expectation raised, that they were carried away, heart and soul, each to different objects, what would become of the Corfinians, what of Domitius, what of Lentulus, what of the rest; what event would be the consequence of another.

CHAP. XXII.—About the fourth watch, Lentulus Spinther said to our sentinels and guards from the walls, that he desired to have an interview with Cæsar, if permission were given him. Having obtained it, he was escorted out of town; nor did the soldiers of Domitius leave him till they brought him into Cæsar's presence. He pleaded with Cæsar for his life, and entreated him to spare him, and reminded him of their former friendship; and acknowledged that Cæsar's favors to him were very great; in that through his interest he had been admitted into the college of priests; in that after his prætorship he had been appointed to the government of Spain; in that he had been assisted by him in his suit for the consulate. Cæsar interrupted him in his speech, and told him, "that he had not left his province to do mischief [to any man], but to protect himself from the injuries of his enemies; to restore to their dignity the tribunes of the people who had been driven out of the city on his account, and to assert his own liberty, and that of the Roman people, who were oppressed by a few factious men. Encouraged by this address, Lentulus begged leave to return to the town, that the security which he had obtained for himself might be an encouragement to the rest to hope for theirs; saying that some were so terrified that they were induced to make desperate attempts on their own lives. Leave being granted him, he departed.

CHAP. XXIII.—When day appeared, Cæsar ordered all the senators and their children, the tribunes of the soldiers, and the Roman knights to be brought before him. Among the persons of senatorial rank were Lucius Domitius, Publius Lentulus Spinther, Lucius Vibullius Rufus, Sextus Quintilius Varus, the quæstor, and Lucius Rubrius, besides the son of Domitius, and several other young men, and a great number of Roman knights and burgesses, whom Domitius had summoned from the municipal towns. When they were brought before him he protected them from the insolence and taunts of the soldiers; told them in few words that they had not made him a grateful return, on their part, for his very extraordinary kindness to them, and dismissed them all in safety. Sixty sestertia, which Domitius had brought with him and lodged in the public treasury, being brought to Cæsar by the magistrates of Corfinium, he gave them back to Domitius, that he might not appear more moderate with respect to the life of men than in money matters, though he knew that it was public money, and had been given by Pompey to pay his army. He ordered Domitius's soldiers to take the oath to himself, and that day decamped and performed the regular march.[1] He staid only seven days before Corfinium, and marched into Apulia through the country of the Marrucinians, Frentanian's and Larinates.

CHAP. XXIV.—Pompey, being informed of what had passed at Corfinium, marches from Luceria to Canusium, and thence to Brundusium.[2] He orders all the forces raised every where by the new levies to repair to him. He gives arms to

[1] The regular march was about twenty Roman miles.

[2] Brundusium, modern Brindisi, a city of Calabria, in the south of Italy.

the slaves that attended the flocks, and appoints horses for them. Of these he made up about three hundred horse. Lucius, the prætor, fled from Alba, with six cohorts: Rutilus Lupus, the prætor, from Tarracina, with three. These having descried Cæsar's cavalry at a distance, which were commanded by Bivius Curius, and having deserted the prætor, carried their colors to Curius and went over to him. In like manner, during the rest of his march, several cohorts fell in with the main body of Cæsar's army, others with his horse. Cneius Magius, from Cremona, engineer-general to Pompey, was taken prisoner on the road and brought to Cæsar, but sent back by him to Pompey with this message: "As hitherto he had not been allowed an interview, and was now on his march to him at Brundusium, that it deeply concerned the commonwealth and general safety that he should have an interview with Pompey; and that the same advantage could not be gained at a great distance when the proposals were conveyed to them by others, as if terms were argued by them both in person."

CHAP. XXV.—Having delivered this message he marched to Brundusium with six legions, four of them veterans: the rest those which he had raised in the late levy and completed on his march, for he had sent all Domitius's cohorts immediately from Corfinium to Sicily. He discovered that the consuls were gone to Dyrrachium with a considerable part of the army, and that Pompey remained at Brundusium with twenty cohorts; but could not find out, for a certainty, whether Pompey staid behind to keep possession of Brundusium, that he might the more easily command the whole Adriatic sea, with the extremities of Italy and the coast of Greece, and be able to conduct the war on either side of it, or whether he remained there for want of shipping; and, being afraid that Pompey would come to the conclusion that he ought not to relinquish Italy, he determined to deprive him of the means of communication afforded by the harbor of Brundusium. The plan of his work was as follows:—Where the mouth of the port was narrowest he threw up a mole of earth on either side, because in these places the sea was shallow. Having gone out so far that the mole could not be continued in the deep water, he fixed double floats, thirty feet on either side, before the mole. These he fastened with four anchors at the four corners, that they might not be carried away by the waves. Having completed and secured them, he then joined to them other floats of equal size. These he covered over with earth and mold, that he might not be prevented from access to them to defend them, and in the front and on both sides he protected them with a parapet of wicker work; and on every fourth one raised a turret, two stories high, to secure them the better from being attacked by the shipping and set on fire.

CHAP. XXVI.—To counteract this, Pompey fitted out large merchant ships, which he found in the harbor of Brundusium: on them he erected turrets three stories high, and, having furnished them with several engines and all sorts of weapons, drove them among Cæsar's works, to break through the floats and interrupt the works; thus there happened skirmishes every day at a distance with slings, arrows, and other weapons. Cæsar conducted matters as if he thought that the hopes of peace were not yet to be given up. And though he was very much surprised that Magius, whom he had sent to Pompey with a message, was not sent back to him; and though his attempting a reconciliation often retarded the vigorous prosecution of his plans, yet he thought that he ought by all means to persevere in the same line of conduct. He therefore sent Caninius Rebilus to have an interview with Scribonius Libo, his intimate friend and relation. He charges him to exhort Libo to effect a peace, but, above all things, requires that he should be admitted to an interview with Pompey. He declared that he had great hopes, if that were allowed him, that the consequence would be that both parties would lay down their arms on equal terms; that a great share of the glory and reputation of that event would redound to Libo, if, through his advice and agency, hostilities should be ended. Libo, having parted from the conference with Caninius, went to Pompey, and, shortly after, returns with answer that, as the consuls were absent, no treaty of composition could be engaged in without them. Cæsar therefore thought it time at length to give over the attempt which he had often made in vain, and act with energy in the war.

CHAP. XXVII.—When Cæsar's works were nearly half finished, and after nine days were spent in them, the ships which had conveyed the first division of the army to Dyrrachium being sent back by the consuls, returned to Brundusium. Pompey, either frightened at Cæsar's works or determined from the beginning to quit Italy, began to prepare for his departure on the arrival of the ships; and the more effectually to retard Cæsar's attack, lest his soldiers should force their way into the town at the moment of his departure, he stopped up the gates, built walls across the streets and avenues, sunk trenches across the ways, and in them fixed palisadoes and sharp stakes, which he made level with the ground by means of hurdles and clay. But he barricaded with large beams fastened in the ground and sharpened at the ends two passages and roads without the walls, which led to the port. After making these arrangements, he ordered his soldiers to go on board without noise, and disposed here and there, on the wall and turrets, some light-armed veterans, archers and slingers. These he designed to call off by a certain signal, when all the soldiers were embarked, and left row-galleys for them in a secure place.

CHAP. XXVIII.—The people of Brundusium, irritated by the insolence of Pompey's soldiers, and the insults received from Pompey himself, were in favor of Cæsar's party. Therefore, as soon as they were aware of Pompey's departure, while his men were running up and down, and busied about their voyage, they made signs from the tops of the houses: Cæsar, being apprised of the design by them, ordered scaling-ladders to be got ready, and his men to take arms, that he might not lose any opportunity of coming to an action. Pompey weighed anchor at nightfall. The soldiers who had been posted on the wall to guard it, were called off by the signal which had been agreed on, and knowing the roads, ran down to the ships. Cæsar's soldiers fixed their ladders and scaled the walls: but being cautioned by the people to beware of the hidden stakes and covered trenches, they halted, and being conducted by the inhabitants by a long circuit, they reached the port, and captured with their long boats and small craft two of Pompey's ships, full of soldiers, which had struck against Cæsar's moles.

CHAP. XXIX.—Though Cæsar highly approved of collecting a fleet, and crossing the sea, and pursuing Pompey before he could strengthen himself with his transmarine auxiliaries, with the hope of bringing the war to a conclusion, yet he dreaded the delay and length of time necessary to effect it: because Pompey, by collecting all his ships, had deprived him of the means of pursuing him at present. The only resource left to Cæsar, was to wait for a fleet from the distant regions of Gaul, Picenum, and the straits of Gibraltar. But this, on account of the season of the year, appeared tedious and troublesome. He was unwilling that, in the mean time, the veteran army, and the two Spains, one of which was bound to Pompey by the strongest obligations, should be confirmed in his interest; that auxiliaries and cavalry should be provided, and Gaul and Italy reduced in his absence.

CHAP. XXX.—Therefore, for the present, he relinquished all intention of pursuing Pompey, and resolved to march to Spain, and commanded the magistrates of the free towns to procure him ships, and to have them conveyed to Brundusium. He detached Valerius, his lieutenant, with one legion to Sardinia; Curio, the proprætor, to Sicily with three legions; and ordered him, when he had recoverd Sicily, to immediately transport his army to Africa. Marcus Cotta was at this time governor of Sardinia: Marcus Cato,[1] of Sicily: and Tubero, by the lots, should have had the government of Africa. The Caralitani,[2] as soon as they heard that Valerius was sent against them, even before he left Italy, of their own accord drove Cotta out of the town; who, terrified because he understood that the whole province was combined [against him], fled from Sardinia to Africa. Cato was in Sicily, repairing the old ships of war, and demanding new ones from the states, and these things he performed with great zeal. He was raising levies of Roman citizens, among the Lucani and Brutii, by his lieutenants, and exacting a certain quota of horse and foot from the states of Sicily. When these things were nearly completed, being informed of Curio's approach, he made a complaint that he was abandoned and betrayed by Pompey, who had undertaken an unnecessary war, without making any preparation, and when questioned by him and other members in the senate,

[1] Marcus Cato, better known by the name of Cato of Utica, was one of the most determined enemies of Cæsar. He continued the struggle until affairs became desperate, and then committed suicide in Utica, a town of Africa. Cato the elder, surnamed the Censor, was the first distinguished man of the name. Livy remarked of him, that his talents were so great and so versatile, that he could have raised himself to the highest honors of any state in which he might have been born. He was a most deadly foe to Carthage, and concluded every debate in the senate with the well-known words, "delenda est Carthago."

[2] The inhabitants of Carales, now Cagliari, the modern capital of Sardinia, in the south of the island. It was built by the Carthaginians.

had assured them that every thing was ready and provided for the war. After having made these complaints in a public assembly, he fled from his province.

CHAP. XXXI.—Valerius found Sardinia, and Curio, Sicily, deserted by their governors when they arrived there with their armies. When Tubero arrived in Africa, he found Attius Varus in the government of the province, who, having lost his cohorts, as already related, at Auximum, had straightway fled to Africa, and finding it without a governor, had seized it of his own accord, and making levies, had raised two legions. From his acquaintance with the people and country, and his knowledge of that province, he found the means of effecting this; because a few years before, at the expiration of his prætorship, he had obtained that province. He, when Tubero came to Utica with his fleet, prevented his entering the port or town, and did not suffer his son, though laboring under sickness, to set foot on shore; but obliged him to weigh anchor and quit the place.

CHAP. XXXII.—When these affairs were dispatched, Cæsar, that there might be an intermission from labor for the rest of the season, drew off his soldiers to the nearest municipal towns, and set off in person for Rome. Having assembled the senate, he reminded them of the injustice of his enemies; and told them, "That he aimed at no extraordinary honor, but had waited for the time appointed by law,[1] for standing candidate for the consulate, being contented with what was allowed to every citizen. That a bill had been carried by the ten tribunes of the people (notwithstanding the resistance of his enemies, and a very violent opposition from Cato, who in his usual manner, consumed the day by a tedious harangue) that he should be allowed to stand candidate, though absent, even in the consulship of Pompey; and if the latter disapproved of the bill, why did he allow it to pass? if he approved of it, why should he debar him [Cæsar] from the people's favor? He made mention of his own patience, in that he had freely proposed that all armies should be disbanded, by which he himself would suffer the loss both of dignity and honor. He urged the virulence of his enemies, who refused to comply with what they required from others, and had rather that all things should be thrown

[1] Ten years had elapsed since his former consulate.

into confusion, than that they should lose their power and their armies. He expatiated on their injustice, in taking away his legions: their cruelty and insolence in abridging the privileges of the tribunes; the proposals he had made, and his entreaties of an interview which had been refused him. For which reasons, he begged and desired that they would undertake the management of the republic, and unite with him in the administration of it. But if through fear they declined it, he would not be a burden to them, but take the management of it on himself. That deputies ought to be sent to Pompey, to propose a reconciliation; as he did not regard what Pompey had lately asserted in the senate, that authority was acknowledged to be vested in those persons to whom embassadors were sent, and fear implied in those that sent them. That these were the sentiments of low, weak minds: that for his part, as he had made it his study to surpass others in glory, so he was desirous of excelling them in justice and equity."

CHAP. XXXIII.—The senate approved of sending deputies, but none could be found fit to execute the commission: for every person, from his own private fears, declined the office. For Pompey, on leaving the city, had declared in the open senate, that he would hold in the same degree of estimation, those who staid in Rome and those in Cæsar's camp. Thus three days were wasted in disputes and excuses. Besides, Lucius Metellus, one of the tribunes, was suborned by Cæsar's enemies, to prevent this, and to embarrass[1] every thing else which Cæsar should propose. Cæsar having discovered his intention, after spending several days to no purpose, left the city, in order that he might not lose any more time,[2] and went to Transalpine Gaul, without effecting what he had intended.

[1] Before Cæsar left the city, he took out of the treasury a large sum of money, deposited there as a fund to defray the expenses of any war that might arise from the Gauls, of whom the Romans had a peculiar horror, alleging that, as he conquered the Gauls, there was no use for it. Metellus attempted to prevent him, but he drew his sword in an attitude of menace, saying, "Young man, it is as easy to do this as to say it." The money was soon expended, as Cæsar, not long after, was obliged to borrow money from his officers to pay his soldiers.—P.

[2] Cæsar intrusted Rome, on his departure, to the care of Marcus Lepidus: he gave the command of Italy to Mark Antony, of Sicily to Curio, of Sardinia to Valerius, of Illyricum to Caius Antonius, and of Hither Gaul, to Lucius Crassus.

CHAP. XXXIV.—On his arrival there, he was informed that Vibullius Rufus, whom he had taken a few days before at Corfinium, and set at liberty, was sent by Pompey into Spain; and that Domitius also was gone to seize Massilia with seven row-galleys, which were fitted up by some private persons at Igilium and Cosa, and which he had manned with his own slaves, freedmen, and colonists: and that some young noblemen of Massilia had been sent before him; whom Pompey, when leaving Rome had exhorted, that the late services of Cæsar should not erase from their minds the memory of his former favors. On receiving this message, the Massilians had shut their gates against Cæsar, and invited over to them the Albici, who had formerly been in alliance with them, and who inhabited the mountains that overhung Massilia: they had likewise conveyed the corn from the surrounding country, and from all the forts into the city; had opened armories in the city; and were repairing the walls, the fleet, and the gates.

CHAP. XXXV.—Cæsar sent for fifteen of the principal persons of Massilia to attend him. To prevent the war commencing among them, he remonstrates [in the following language]; "that they ought to follow the precedent set by all Italy, rather than submit to the will of any one man." He made use of such arguments as he thought would tend to bring them to reason. The deputies reported his speech to their countrymen, and by the authority of the state bring him back this answer: "That they understood that the Roman people was divided into two factions: that they had neither judgment nor abilities to decide which had the juster cause; but that the heads of these factions were Cneius Pompey and Caius Cæsar, the two patrons of the state: the former of whom had granted to their state the lands of the Vocæ Arecomici, and Helvii; the latter had assigned them a part of his conquests in Gaul, and had augmented their revenue. Wherefore, having received equal favors from both, they ought to show equal affection to both, and assist neither against the other, nor admit either into their city or harbors."

CHAP. XXXVI.—While this treaty was going forward, Domitius arrived at Massilia with his fleet, and was received into the city, and made governor of it. The chief management of the war was intrusted to him. At his command they send the fleet to all parts; they seize all the merchantmen they could meet with, and carry them into the harbor; they apply the nails, timber, and rigging, with which they were furnished to rig and refit their other vessels.[1] They lay up in the public stores, all the corn that was found in the ships, and reserve the rest of their lading and convoy for the siege of the town, should such an event take place. Provoked at such ill treatment, Cæsar led three legions against Massilia, and resolved to provide turrets, and vineæ to assault the town, and to build twelve ships at Arelas, which being completed and rigged in thirty days (from the time the timber was cut down), and being brought to Massilia, he put under the command of Decimus Brutus; and left Caius Trebonius his lieutenant, to invest the city.

CHAP. XXXVII.—While he was preparing and getting these things in readiness, he sent Caius Fabius one of his lieutenants into Spain with three legions, which he had disposed to winter quarters in Narbo, and the neighboring country; and ordered him immediately to seize the passes of the Pyrenees, which were at that time occupied by detachments from Lucius Afranius, one of Pompey's lieutenants. He desired the other legions, which were passing the winter at a great distance, to follow close after him. Fabius, according to his orders, by using expedition, dislodged the party from the hills, and by hasty marches came up with the army of Afranius.

CHAP. XXXVIII.—On the arrival of Vibullius Rufus, whom, we have already mentioned, Pompey had sent into Spain, Afranius, Petreius, and Varro, his lieutenants (one of whom had the command of Hither Spain, with three legions; the second of the country from the forest of Castulo to the river[2] Guadiana with two legions; the third from the river Guadiana to the country of the Vettones and Lusitania, with the like number of legions) divided among themselves their respective departments. Petreius was to march from Lusitania through the Vettones, and join Afranius with all his forces;

[1] I have here adopted the reading "earum" the other reading is "parum:" which translate as follows: "they take those that are badly supplied with nails, timber and rigging, to equip and fit out their other vessels."

[2] The Guadiana, the ancient name of which was Anas, is one of the largest rivers in Spain. It has its source in some lakes or marshes in New Castile, flows through the provinces of Estremadura, and entering Lusitania, the modern Portugal, traverses part of Algarva, in which it changes its direction, and running south, falls, after a course of 470 miles into Mare Gaditanum, or Bæticum, the gulf of Cadiz.

Varro was to guard all Further Spain with what legions he had. These matters being settled, reinforcements of horse and foot were demanded from Lusitania, by Petreius; from the Celtiberi, Cantabri, and all the barbarous nations which border on the ocean, by Afranius. When they were raised, Petreius immediately marched through the Vettones to Afranius. They resolved by joint consent to carry on the war in the vicinity of Ilerba, on account of the advantages of its situation.

CHAP. XXXIX.—Afranius, as above mentioned, had three legions, Petreius two. There were besides about eighty cohorts raised in Hither and Further Spain (of which, the troops belonging to the former province had shields, those of the latter targets),[1] and about five thousand horse raised in both provinces. Cæsar had sent his legions into Spain, with about six thousand auxiliary foot, and three thousand horse, which had served under him in all his former wars, and the same number from Gaul, which he himself had provided, having expressly called out all the most noble and valiant men of each state. The bravest of these were from the Aquitani and the mountaineers, who border on the Province in Gaul. He had been informed that Pompey was marching through Mauritania with his legions to Spain, and would shortly arrive. He at the same time borrowed money from the tribunes and centurions, which he distributed among his soldiers. By this proceeding he gained two points; he secured the interest of the centurions by this pledge in his hands, and by his liberality he purchased the affections of his army.

CHAP. XL.—Fabius sounded the inclinations of the neighboring states by letters and messengers. He had made two bridges over the river Segre,[2] at the distance of four miles from each other. He sent foraging parties over these bridges, because he had already consumed all the forage that was on his side of the river. The generals of Pompey's army did almost the same thing, and for the same reason: and the horse had frequent skirmishes with each other. When two of Fabius's legions had, as was their constant practice, gone forth as the usual protection to the foragers, and had crossed the

[1] Cetratæ, armed with the Cetra, a light leather target, somewhat of a circular form, used by the Spaniards (hence often called cetrati), ancient Britons, and other barbarous nations.

[2] The Segre, called in ancient times Sicoris, a river of Spain, which rises in the Pyrenees, is joined by the Cinga modern Cinca, near Lerida, and empties itself into the Ebro.

river, and the baggage, and all the horse were following them, on a sudden, from the weight of the cattle, and the mass of water, the bridge fell, and all the horse were cut off from the main army, which being known to Petreius and Afranius, from the timber and hurdles that were carried down the river, Afranius immediately crossed his own bridge, which communicated between his camp and the town, with four legions and all the cavalry, and marched against Fabius's two legions. When his approach was announced, Lucius Plancus, who had the command of those legions, compelled by the emergency, took post on a rising ground; and drew up his army with two fronts, that it might not be surrounded by the cavalry. Thus, though engaged with superior numbers, he sustained the furious charge of the legions and the horse. When the battle was begun by the horse, there were observed at a distance by both sides the colors of two legions, which Caius Fabius had sent round by the further bridge to reinforce our men, suspecting, as the event verified, that the enemy's generals would take advantage of the opportunity which fortune had put in their way, to attack our men. Their approach put an end to the battle, and each general led back his legions to their respective camps.

CHAP. XLI.—In two days after Cæsar came to the camp with nine hundred horse, which he had retained for a body guard. The bridge which had been broken down by the storm was almost repaired, and he ordered it to be finished in the night. Being acquainted with the nature of the country, he left behind him six cohorts to guard the bridge, the camp, and all his baggage, and the next day set off in person for Ilerda,[1] with all his forces drawn up in three lines, and halted just before the camp of Afranius, and having remained there a short time under arms, he offered him battle on equal terms. When this affair was made, Afranius drew out his forces, and posted them on the middle of a hill, near his camp. When Cæsar perceived that Afranius declined coming to an engagement, he resolved to encamp at somewhat less than half a mile's distance from the very foot of the mountain; and that his soldiers while engaged in their works, might not be terrified by any sudden attack of the enemy, or disturbed in their work, he ordered them not to fortify it with a wall, which must

[1] Ilerda, now Lerida, a town of Hispania Tarraconensis, situated on the Segre, about four miles above its junction with the Cinca.

rise high, and be seen at a distance, but draw, on the front opposite the enemy, a trench fifteen feet broad. The first and second lines contiued under arms, as was from the first appointed. Behind them the third line was carrying on the work without being seen; so that the whole was completed before Afranius discovered that the camp was being fortified.

CHAP. XLII.—In the evening Cæsar drew his legions within this trench, and rested them under arms the next night. The day following he kept his whole army within it, and as it was necessary to bring materials from a considerable distance, he for the present pursued the same plan in his work; and to each legion, one after the other, he assigned one side of the camp to fortify, and ordered trenches of the same magnitude to be cut: he kept the rest of the legions under arms without baggage to oppose the enemy. Afranius and Petreius, to frighten us and obstruct the work, drew out their forces at the very foot of the mountain, and challenged us to battle. Cæsar, however, did not interrupt his work, relying on the protection of the three legions, and the strength of the fosse. After staying for a short time, and advancing no great distance from the bottom of the hill, they led back their forces to their camp. The third day Cæsar fortified his camp with a rampart, and ordered the other cohorts which he had left in the upper camp, and his baggage to be removed to it.

CHAP. XLIII.—Between the town of Ilerda and the next hill, on which Afranius and Petreius were encamped, there was a plain about three hundred paces broad, and near the middle of it an eminence somewhat raised above the level: Cæsar hoped that if he could get possession of this and fortify it, he should be able to cut off the enemy from the town, the bridge, and all the stores which they had laid up in the town. In expectation of this he led three legions out of the camp, and, drawing up his army in an advantageous position, he ordered the advanced men of one legion to hasten forward and seize the eminence. Upon intelligence of this the cohorts which were on guard before Afranius's camp were instantly sent a nearer way to occupy the same post. The two parties engage, and as Afranius's men had reached the eminence first, our men were repulsed, and, on a reinforcement being sent, they were obliged to turn their backs and retreat to the standards of legions.

CHAP. XLIV.—The manner of fighting of those soldiers was to run forward with great impetuosity and boldly take a post, and not to keep their ranks strictly, but to fight in small scattered parties: if hard pressed they thought it no disgrace to retire and give up the post, being accustomed to this manner of fighting among the Lusitanians and other barbarous nations; for it commonly happens that soldiers are strongly influenced by the customs of those countries in which they have spent much time. This method, however, alarmed our men, who were not used to such a description of warfare. For they imagined that they were about to be surrounded on their exposed flank by the single men who ran forward from their ranks; and they thought it their duty to keep their ranks, and not to quit their colors, nor, without good reason to give up the post which they had taken. Accordingly, when the advanced guard gave way, the legion which was stationed on that wing did not keep its ground, but retreated to the next hill.

CHAP. XLV.—Almost the whole army being daunted at this, because it had occurred contrary to their expectations and custom, Cæsar encouraged his men and led the ninth legion to their relief, and checked the insolent and eager pursuit of the enemy, and obliged them, in their turn, to show their backs, and retreat to Ilerda, and take post under the walls. But the soldiers of the ninth legion, being over zealous to repair the dishonor which had been sustained, having rashly pursued the fleeing enemy, advanced into disadvantageous ground and went up to the foot of the mountain on which the town Ilerda was built. And when they wished to retire they were again attacked by the enemy from the rising ground. The place was craggy in the front and steep on either side, and was so narrow that even three cohorts, drawn up in order of battle, would fill it; but no relief could be sent on the flanks, and the horse could be of no service to them when hard pressed. From the town, indeed, the precipice inclined with a gentle slope for near four hundred paces. Our men had to retreat this way, as they had, through their eagerness, advanced too inconsiderately. The greatest contest was in this place, which was much to the disadvantage of our troops, both on account of its narrowness, and because they were posted at the foot of the mountain, so that no weapon was thrown at them without effect; yet they exerted their valor and patience, and bore every wound. The enemy's forces were increasing, and cohorts were frequently sent to their aid from the camp through the town, that fresh men might relieve the weary. Cæsar was obliged to do the same, and relieve the fatigued by sending cohorts to that post.

CHAP. XLVI.—After the battle had in this manner continued incessantly for five hours, and our men had suffered much from superior numbers, having spent all their javelins, they drew their swords and charged the enemy up the hill, and, having killed a few, obliged the rest to fly. The cohorts being beaten back to the wall, and some being driven by their fears into the town, an easy retreat was afforded to our men. Our cavalry also, on either flank, though stationed on sloping or low ground, yet bravely struggled up to the top of the hill, and, riding between the two armies, made our retreat more easy and secure. Such were the various turns of fortune in the battle. In the first encounter about seventy of our men fell: among them Quintus Fulgenius, first centurion of the second line of the fourteenth legion, who, for his extraordinary valor, had been promoted from the lower ranks to that post. About six hundred were wounded. Of Afranius's party there were killed Titus Cæcilius, principal centurion, and four other centurions, and above two hundred men.

CHAP XLVII.—But this opinion is spread abroad concerning this day, that each party thought that they came off conquerors. Afranius's soldiers, because, though they were esteemed inferior in the opinion of all, yet they had stood our attack and sustained our charge, and, at first, had kept the post on the hill which had been the occasion of the dispute; and, in the first encounter, had obliged our men to fly: but ours, because, notwithstanding the disadvantage of the ground and the disparity of numbers, they had maintained the battle for five hours, had advanced up the hill sword in hand, and had forced the enemy to fly from the higher ground and driven them into the town. The enemy fortified the hill, about which the contest had been, with strong works and posted a garrison on it.

CHAP. XLVIII.—In two days after this transaction, there happened an unexpected misfortune. For so great a storm arose, that it was agreed that there were never seen higher floods in those countries; it swept down the snow from all the mountains, and broke over the banks of the river, and in one day carried away both the bridges which Fabius had built—a circumstance which caused great difficulties to Cæsar's army. For as our[1] camp, as already mentioned, was pitched between two rivers, the Segre and Cinca, and as neither of these could be forded for the space of thirty miles, they were all of necessity confined within these narrow limits. Neither could the states, which had espoused Cæsar's cause, furnish him with corn, nor the troops, which had gone far to forage, return, as they were stopped by the waters: nor could the convoys, coming from Italy and Gaul, make their way to the camp. Besides, it was the most distressing season of the year, when there was no corn in the blade, and it was nearly ripe: and the states were exhausted, because Afranius had conveyed almost all the corn, before Cæsar's arrival, into Ilerda, and whatever he had left, had been already consumed by Cæsar. The cattle, which might have served as a secondary resource against want, had been removed by the states to a great distance on account of the war. They who had gone out to get forage or corn, were chased by the light troops of the Lusitanians, and the targeteers of Hither Spain, who were well acquainted with the country, and could readily swim across the river, because it is the custom of all those people not to join their armies without bladders.

CHAP. XLIX.—But Afranius's army had abundance of every thing; a great stock of corn had been provided and laid in long before, a large quantity was coming in from the whole province: they had a good store of forage. The bridge of Ilerda afforded an opportunity of getting all these without any danger, and the places beyond the bridge, to which Cæsar had no access, were as yet untouched.

CHAP. L.—Those floods continued several days. Cæsar endeavored to repair the bridges, but the height of the water did not allow him: and the cohorts disposed along the banks did not suffer tham to be completed; and it was easy for them to prevent it, both from the nature of the river and the height of the water, but especially because their darts were thrown from the whole course of the bank on one confined spot; and it was no easy matter at one and the same time to execute a work in a very rapid flood, and to avoid the darts.

[1] Cæsar has not alluded to this circumstance previously, so we must conclude, either that he made an oversight, or that the Commentaries have not reached us entire.

CHAP. LI.—Intelligence was brought to Afranius that the great convoys, which were on their march to Cæsar, had halted at the river. Archers from the Rutheni, and horse from the Gauls, with a long train of baggage, according to the Gallic custom of traveling, had arrived there; there were besides about six thousand people of all descriptions, with slaves and freed men. But there was no order, or regular discipline, as every one followed his own humor, and all traveled without apprehension, taking the same liberty as on former marches. There were several young noblemen, sons of senators, and of equestrian rank; there were embassadors from several states; there were lieutenants of Cæsar's. The river stopped them all. To attack them by surprise, Afranius set out in the beginning of the night, with all his cavalry and three legions, and sent the horse on before, to fall on them unawares; but the Gallic horse soon got themselves in readiness, and attacked them. Though but few, they withstood the vast number of the enemy, as long as they fought on equal terms; but when the legions began to approach, having lost a few men, they retreated to the next mountains. The delay occasioned by this battle was of great importance to the security of our men; for having gained time, they retired to the higher grounds. There were missing that day about two hundred bow-men, a few horse, and an inconsiderable number of servants and baggage.

CHAP. LII.—However, by all these things, the price of provisions was raised, which is commonly a disaster attendant, not only on a time of present scarcity, but on the apprehension of future want. Provisions had now reached fifty denarii each bushel; and the want of corn had diminished the strength of the soldiers; and the inconveniences were increasing every day; and so great an alteration was wrought in a few days, and fortune had so changed sides, that our men had to struggle with the want of every necessary; while the enemy had an abundant supply of all things, and were considered to have the advantage. Cæsar demanded from those states which had acceded to his alliance, a supply of cattle, as they had but little corn. He sent away the camp followers to the more distant states, and endeavored to remedy the present scarcity by every resource in his power.

CHAP. LIII.—Afranius and Petreius, and their friends, sent fuller and more circumstantial accounts of these things to

Rome, to their acquaintances. Report exaggerated them so that the war appeared to be almost at an end. When these letters and dispatches were received at Rome, a great concourse of people resorted to the house of Afranius, and congratulations ran high; several went out of Italy to Cneius Pompey; some of them, to be the first to bring him the intelligence; others, that they might not be thought to have waited the issue of the war, and to have come last of all.

CHAP. LIV.—When Cæsar's affairs were in this unfavorable position, and all the passes were guarded by the soldiers and horse of Afranius, and the bridges could not be prepared, Cæsar ordered his soldiers to make ships of the kind that his knowledge of Britain a few years before had taught him. First, the keels and ribs were made of light timber, then, the rest of the hulk of the ships was wrought with wicker work, and covered over with hides. When these were finished, he drew them down to the river in wagons in one night, a distance of twenty-two miles from his camp, and transported in them some soldiers across the river, and on a sudden took possession of a hill adjoining the bank. This he immediately fortified, before he was perceived by the enemy. To this he afterward transported a legion: and having begun a bridge on both sides, he finished it in two days. By this means, he brought safe to his camp, the convoys, and those who had gone out to forage; and began to prepare a conveyance for the provisions.

CHAP. LV.—The same day he made a great part of his horse pass the river, who, falling on the foragers by surprise as they were dispersed without any suspicions, intercepted an incredible number of cattle and people; and when some Spanish light-armed cohorts were sent to reinforce the enemy, our men judiciously divided themselves into two parts, the one to protect the spoil, the other to resist the advancing foe, and to beat them back, and they cut off from the rest and surrounded one cohort, which had rashly ventured out of the line before the others, and after putting it to the sword, returned safe with considerable booty to the camp over the same bridge.

CHAP. LVI.—While these affairs are going forward at Ilerda, the Massilians, adopting the advice of Domitius, prepared seventeen ships of war, of which eleven were decked. To these they add several smaller vessels, that our fleet might be terrified by numbers; they man them with a great number of archers and of the Albici, of whom mention has been already made, and these they incited by rewards and promises. Domitius required certain ships for his own use, which he manned with colonists and shepherds, whom he had brought along with him. A fleet being thus furnished with every necessary, he advanced with great confidence against our ships, commanded by Decimus Brutus. It was stationed at an island opposite to Massilia.

CHAP. LVII.—Brutus was much inferior in number of ships; but Cæsar had appointed to that fleet the bravest men selected from all his legions, antesignani[1] and centurions, who had requested to be employed in that service. They had provided iron hooks and harpoons, and had furnished themselves with a vast number of javelins, darts, and missiles. Thus prepared, and being apprised of the enemy's approach, they put out from the harbor, and engaged the Massilians. Both sides fought with great courage and resolution; nor did the Albici, a hardy people, bred on the highlands and inured to arms, fall much short of our men in valor: and being lately come from the Massilians, they retained in their minds their recent promises: and the wild shepherds, encouraged by the hope of liberty, were eager to prove their zeal in the presence of their masters.

CHAP. LVIII.—The Massilians themselves, confiding in the quickness of their ships, and the skill of their pilots, eluded ours, and evaded the shock, and as long as they were permitted by clear space, lengthening their line they endeavored to surround us, or to attack single ships with several of theirs, or to run across our ships, and carry away our oars, if possible; but when necessity obliged them to come nearer, they had recourse, from the skill and art of the pilots, to the valor of the mountaineers. But our men, not having such expert seamen, or skillful pilots, for they had been hastily drafted from the merchant ships, and were not yet acquainted even with the names of the rigging, were moreover impeded by the heaviness and slowness of our vessels, which having been built in a hurry

[1] In the early ages of Rome the *Hastati* fought in front of the standards, and were thence denominated "Antesignani," to distinguish them from the Principes and Triarii, who fought behind the standards. In the time of Cæsar, as the military organization of Rome had undergone great changes, the Antesignani were the oldest and best soldiers, who at this time formed the front line.

and of green timber, were not so easily maneuvered. Therefore, when Cæsar's men had an opportunity of a close engagement, they cheerfully opposed two of the enemy's ships with one of theirs. And throwing in the grappling-irons, and holding both ships fast, they fought on both sides of the deck, and boarded the enemy's; and having killed numbers of the Albici and shepherds, they sank some of their ships, took others with the men on board, and drove the rest into the harbor. That day the Massilians lost nine ships, including those that were taken.

CHAP. LIX.—When news of this battle was brought to Cæsar at Ilerda, the bridge being completed at the same time, fortune soon took a turn. The enemy, daunted by the courage of our horse, did not scour the country as freely or as boldly as before: but sometimes advancing a small distance from the camp, that they might have a ready retreat, they foraged within narrower bounds: at other times, they took a longer circuit to avoid our outposts and parties of horse; or having sustained some loss, or descried our horse at a distance, they fled in the midst of their expedition, leaving their baggage behind them; at length they resolved to leave off foraging for several days, and, contrary to the practice of all nations, to go out at night.

CHAP. LX.—In the mean time the Oscenses and the Calagurritani, who were under the government of the Oscenses, send embassadors to Cæsar, and offer to submit to his orders. They are followed by the Tarraconenses, Jacetani, and Ausetani, and in a few days more by the Illurgavonenses, who dwell near the river Ebro. He requires of them all, to assist him with corn, to which they agreed, and having collected all the cattle in the country, they convey them into his camp. One entire cohort of the Illurgavonenses, knowing the design of their state, came over to Cæsar, from the place where they were stationed, and carried their colors with them. A great change is shortly made in the face of affairs. The bridge being finished, five powerful states being joined to Cæsar, a way opened for the receiving of corn, and the rumors of the assistance of legions which were said to be on their march, with Pompey at their head, through Mauritania, having died away, several of the more distant states revolt from Afranius, and enter into league with Cæsar.

CHAP. LI.—While the spirits of the enemy were dismayed at these things, Cæsar, that he might not be always obliged to send his horse a long circuit round by the bridge, having found a convenient place, began to sink several drains, thirty feet deep, by which he might draw off a part of the river Segre, and make a ford over it. When these were almost finished, Afranius and Petreius began to be greatly alarmed, lest they should be altogether cut off from corn and forage, because Cæsar was very strong in cavalry. They therefore resolved to quit their posts, and to transfer the war to Celtiberia. There was, moreover, a circumstance that confirmed them in this resolution: for of the two adverse parties, that, which had stood by Sertorius in the late war, being conquered by Pompey, still trembled at his name and sway, though absent: the other which had remained firm in Pompey's interest, loved him for the favors which they had received: but Cæsar's name was not known to the barbarians. From these they expected considerable aid, both of horse and foot, and hoped to protract the war till winter, in a friendly country. Having come to this resolution, they gave orders to collect all the ships in the river Ebro, and to bring them to Octogesa,[1] a town situated on the river Ebro, about twenty miles distant from their camp. At this part of the river, they ordered a bridge to be made of boats fastened together, and transported two legions over the river Segre, and fortified their camp with a rampart, twelve feet high.

Chap. LXII.—Notice of this being given by the scouts, Cæsar continued his work day and night, with very great fatigue to the soldiers, to drain the river, and so far effected his purpose, that the horse were both able and bold enough, though with some difficulty and danger, to pass the river; but the foot had only their shoulders and upper part of their breast above the water, so that their fording it was retarded, not only by the depth of the water, but also by the rapidity of the current. However, almost at the same instant, news was received of the bridge being nearly completed over the Ebro, and a ford was found in the Segre.

Chap. LXIII.—Now indeed the enemy began to think that they ought to hasten their march. Accordingly, leaving two auxiliary cohorts in the garrison at Ilerda, they crossed the Segre with their whole force, and formed one camp with the

[1] Octogesa, now *Mequinensa*, a town of Spain, situated on the northern bank of the Ebro, at its confluence with the Segre.

two legions which they had led across a few days before. Cæsar had no resource, but to annoy and cut down their rear; since with his cavalry to go by the bridge, required him to take a long circuit; so that they would arrive at the Ebro by a much shorter route. The horse, which he had detached, crossed the ford, and when Afranius and Petreius had broken up their camp about the third watch, they suddenly appeared on their rear, and spreading round them in great numbers, began to retard and impede their march.

CHAP. LXIV.—At break of day, it was perceived from the rising grounds which joined Cæsar's camp, that their rear was vigorously pressed by our horse; that the last line sometimes halted and was broken; at other times, that they joined battle and that our men were beaten back by a general charge of their cohorts, and, in their turn, pursued them when they wheeled about: but through the whole camp the soldiers gathered in parties, and declared their chagrin that the enemy had been suffered to escape from their hands and that the war had been unnecessarily protracted. They applied to their tribunes and centurions, and entreated them to inform Cæsar that he need not spare their labor or consider their danger; that they were ready and able, and would venture to ford the river where the horse had crossed. Cæsar, encouraged by their zeal and importunity, though he felt reluctant to expose his army to a river so exceedingly large, yet judged it prudent to attempt it and make a trial. Accordingly, he ordered all the weaker soldiers, whose spirit or strength seemed unequal to the fatigue, to be selected from each century, and left them, with one legion besides, to guard the camp: the rest of the legions he drew out without any baggage, and, having disposed a great number of horses in the river, above and below the ford, he led his army over. A few of his soldiers being carried away by the force of the current, were stopped by the horse and taken up, and not a man perished. His army being safe on the opposite bank, he drew out his forces and resolved to lead them forward in three battalions: and so great was the ardor of the soldiers that, notwithstanding the addition of a circuit of six miles and a considerable delay in fording the river, before the ninth hour of the day they came up with those who had set out at the third watch.

CHAP. LXV.—When Afranius, who was in company with Petreius, saw them at a distance, being affrighted at so unexpected a sight, he halted on a rising ground and drew up his army. Cæsar refreshed his army on the plain that he might not expose them to battle while fatigued; and when the enemy attempted to renew their march, he pursued and stopped them. They were obliged to pitch their camp sooner than they had intended, for there were mountains at a small distance; and difficult and narrow roads awaited them about five miles off. They retired behind these mountains that they might avoid Cæsar's cavalry, and, placing parties in the narrow roads, stop the progress of his army and lead their own forces across the Ebro without danger or apprehension. This it was their interest to attempt and to effect by any means possible; but, fatigued by the skirmishes all day, and by the labor of their march, they deferred it till the following day; Cæsar likewise encamped on the next hill.

CHAP. LXVI.—About midnight a few of their men who had gone some distance from the camp to fetch water, being taken by our horse, Cæsar is informed by them that the generals of the enemy were drawing their troops out of the camp without noise. Upon this information Cæsar ordered the signal to be given and the military shout to be raised for packing up the baggage. When they heard the shout, being afraid lest they should be stopped in the night and obliged to engage under their baggage, or lest they should be confined in the narrow roads by Cæsar's horse, they put a stop to their march and kept their forces in their camp. The next day Petreius went out privately with a few horse to reconnoitre the country. A similar movement was made from Cæsar's camp. Lucius Decidius Saxa, was detached with a small party to explore the nature of the country. Each returned with the same account to his camp, that there was a level road for the next five miles, that there then succeeded a rough and mountainous country. Whichever should first obtain possession of the defiles would have no trouble in preventing the other's progress.

CHAP. LXVII.—There was a debate in the council between Afranius and Petreius, and the time of marching was the subject. The majority were of opinion that they should begin their march at night, "for they might reach the defiles before they should be discovered." Others, because a shout had been raised the night before in Cæsar's camp, used this as an argument that they could not leave the camp unnoticed: "that Cæsar's cavalry were patrolling the whole night, and that all the ways and roads were beset; that battles at night ought to be avoided, because, in civil dissension, a soldier once daunted is more apt to consult his fears than his oath; that the daylight raised a strong sense of shame in the eyes of all, and that the presence of the tribunes and centurions had the same effect: by these things the soldiers would be restrained and awed to their duty. Wherefore they should, by all means, attempt to force their way by day; for, though a trifling loss might be sustained, yet the post which they desired might be secured with safety to the main body of the army." This opinion prevailed in the council, and the next day, at the dawn, they resolved to set forward.

CHAP. LXVIII.—Cæsar, having taken a view of the country, the moment the sky began to grow white, led his forces from the camp and marched at the head of his army by a long circuit, keeping to no regular road; for the road which led to the Ebro and Octogesa was occupied by the enemy's camp, which lay in Cæsar's way. His soldiers were obliged to cross extensive and difficult valleys. Craggy cliffs, in several places, interrupted their march, insomuch that their arms had to be handed to one another, and the soldiers were forced to perform a great part of their march unarmed, and were lifted up the rocks by each other. But not a man murmured at the fatigue, because they imagined that there would be a period to all their toils, if they could cut off the enemy from the Ebro and intercept their convoys.

CHAP. LXIX.—At first, Afranius's soldiers ran in high spirits from their camp to look at us, and in contumelious language upbraided us, "that we were forced, for want of necessary subsistence, to run away, and return to Ilerda." For our route was different fram what we proposed, and we appeared to be going a contrary way. But their generals applauded their own prudence in keeping within their camp, and it was a strong confirmation of their opinion, that they saw we marched without wagons or baggage, which made them confident that we could not long endure want. But when they saw our army gradually wheel to the right, and observed our van was already passing the line of their camp, there was nobody so stupid, or averse to fatigue, as not to think it necessary to march from the camp immediately, and oppose us. The cry to arms was raised, and all the army, except a few which were left to guard the camp, set out and marched the direct road to the Ebro.

CHAP. LXX.—The contest depended entirely on dispatch, which should first get possession of the defile and the mountains. The difficulty of the roads delayed Cæsar's army, but his cavalry pursuing Afranius's forces, retarded their march. However, the affair was necessarily reduced to this point, with respect to Afranius's men, that if they first gained the mountains, which they desired, they would themselves avoid all danger, but could not save the baggage of their whole army, nor the cohorts which they had left behind in the camps, to which, being intercepted by Cæsar's army, by no means could assistance be given. Cæsar first accomplished the march, and having found a plain behind large rocks, drew up his army there in order of battle and facing the enemy. Afranius, perceiving that his rear was galled by our cavalry, and seeing the enemy before him, having come to a hill, made a halt on it. Thence he detached four cohorts of Spanish light infantry to the highest mountain which was in view: to this he ordered them to hasten with all expedition, and to take possession of it, with the intention of going to the same place with all his forces, then altering his route, and crossing the hills to Octogesa. As the Spaniards were making toward it in an oblique direction, Cæsar's horse espied them and attacked them, nor were they able to withstand the charge of the cavalry even for a moment, but were all surrounded and cut to pieces in the sight of the two armies.

CHAP. LXXI.—There was now an opportunity for managing affairs successfully, nor did it escape Cæsar, that an army daunted at suffering such a loss before their eyes, could not stand, especially as they were surrounded by our horse, and the engagement would take place on even and open ground. To this he was importuned on all sides. The lieutenants, centurions, and tribunes, gathered round him, and begged "that he would not hesitate to begin the battle: that the hearts of all the soldiers were very anxious for it: that Afranius's men had by several circumstances betrayed signs of fear; in that they had not assisted their party; in that they had not quitted the hill; in that they did not sustain the charge of our cavalry, but crowding their standards into one place, did not observe either rank or order. But if he had any apprehensions from the disadvantage of the ground, that an opportunity would be given him of coming to battle in some other place: for that Afranius must certainly come down, and would not be able to remain there for want of water."

CHAP. LXXII.—Cæsar had conceived hopes of ending the affair without an engagement, or without striking a blow, because he had cut off the enemy's supplies. Why should he hazard the loss of any of his men, even in a successful battle? Why should he expose soldiers to be wounded, who had deserved so well of him? Why, in short, should he tempt fortune? especially when it was as much a general's duty to conquer by tactics as by the sword. Besides, he was moved with compassion for those citizens, who, he foresaw, must fall: and he had rather gain his object without any loss or injury to them. This resolution of Cæsar was not generally approved of; but the soldiers openly declared to each other that since such an opportunity of victory was let pass, they would not come to an engagement, even when Cæsar should wish it. He persevered however in his resolution, and retired a little from that place to abate the enemy's fears. Petreius and Afranius, having got this opportunity, retired to their camp. Cæsar, having disposed parties on the mountains, and cut off all access to the Ebro, fortified his camp as close to the enemy as he could.

CHAP. LXXIII.—The day following, the generals of his opponents, being alarmed that they had lost all prospect of supplies, and of access to the Ebro, consulted as to what other course they should take. There were two roads, one to Ilerda, if they chose to return, the other to Tarraco,[1] if they should march to it. While they were deliberating on these matters, intelligence was brought them that their watering parties were attacked by our horse: upon which information, they dispose several parties of horse and auxiliary foot along the road, and intermix some legionary cohorts, and begin to throw up a rampart from the camp to the water, that they might be able to procure water within their lines, both without fear, and without a guard. Petreius and Afranius divided this task between themselves,

[1] Tarraco, now *Tarragona*, a large city and sea-port of Spain, about eighty miles north of the Ebro. During the Roman occupation of Spain, it was a place of great strength, and gave name to the northern division of Spain. Hispania Tarraconensis

and went in person to some distance from their camp for the purpose of seeing it accomplished.

CHAP. LXXIV.—The soldiers having obtained by their absence a free opportunity of conversing with each other, came out in great numbers, and inquired each for whatever acquaintance or fellow-citizen he had in our camp, and invited him to him. First they returned them general thanks for sparing them the day before, when they were greatly terrified, and acknowledged that they were alive through their kindness; then they inquired about the honor of our general, and whether they could with safety intrust themselves to him; and declared their sorrow that they had not done so in the beginning, and that they had taken up arms against their relations and kinsmen. Encouraged by these conferences, they desired the general's parole for the lives of Petreius and Afranius, that they might not appear guilty of a crime, in having betrayed their generals. When they were assured of obtaining their demands, they promised that they would immediately remove their standards, and sent centurions of the first rank as deputies to treat with Cæsar about a peace. In the mean time some of them invite their acquaintances, and bring them to their camp, others are brought away by their friends, so that the two camps seemed to be united into one, and several of the tribunes and centurions came to Cæsar, and paid their respects to him. The same was done by some of the nobility of Spain, whom they summoned to their assistance, and kept in their camp as hostages. They inquired after their acquaintance and friends, by whom each might have the means of being recommended to Cæsar. Even Afranius's son, a young man, endeavored, by means of Sulpitius the lieutenant, to make terms for his own and his father's life. Every place was filled with mirth and congratulations; in the one army, because they thought they had escaped so impending danger; in the other, because they thought they had completed so important a matter without blows; and Cæsar, in every man's judgment, reaped the advantage of his former lenity, and his conduct was applauded by all.

CHAP. LXXV.—When these circumstances were announced to Afranius, he left the work which he had begun, and returned to his camp, determined as it appeared, whatever should be the event, to bear it with an even and steady mind. Petreius did not neglect himself; he armed his domestics; with them and the prætorian cohort of Spaniards, and a few foreign horse, his dependents, whom he commonly kept near him to guard his person, he suddenly flew to the rampart, interrupted the conferences of the soldiers, drove our men from the camp, and put to death as many as he caught. The rest formed into a body, and being alarmed by the unexpected danger, wrapped their left arms in their cloaks, and drew their swords, and in this manner, depending on the nearness of their camp, defended themselves against the Spaniards, and the horse, and made good their retreat to the camp, where they were protected by the cohorts which were on guard.

CHAP. LXXVI.—Petreius, after accomplishing this, went round every maniple, calling the soldiers by their names, and entreating with tears that they would not give up him and their absent general Pompey, as a sacrifice to the vengeance of their enemies. Immediately they ran in crowds to the general's pavilion, when he required them all to take an oath that they would not desert nor betray the army nor the generals, nor form any design distinct from the general interest. He himself swore first to the tenor of those words, and obliged Afranius to take the same oath. The tribunes and centurions followed their example; the soldiers were brought out by centuries, and took the same oath. They gave orders,[1] that whoever had any of Cæsar's soldiers should produce them; as soon as they were produced, they put them to death publicly in the prætorium, but most of them concealed those that they had entertained, and let them out at night over the rampart. Thus the terror raised by the generals, the cruelty of the punishments, the new obligation of an oath, removed all hopes of surrender for the present, changed the soldiers' minds, and reduced matters to the former state of war.

CHAP. LXXVII.—Cæsar ordered the enemy's soldiers, who had come into his camp to hold a conference, to be searched for with the strictest diligence, and sent back. But of the tribunes and centurions, several voluntarily remained with him, and he afterward treated them with great respect. The centurions he promoted to higher ranks, and conferred on the Roman knights the honor of tribunes.

[1] Literally, "that with whomsoever any of Cæsar's soldiers was, he should be brought forth."

CHAP. LXXVIII.—Afranius's men were distressed in foraging, and procured water with difficulty. The legionary soldiers had a tolerable supply of corn, because they had been ordered to bring from Ilerda sufficient to last twenty-two days; the Spanish and auxiliary forces had none, for they had but few opportunities of procuring any, and their bodies were not accustomed to bear burdens; and therefore a great number of them came over to Cæsar every day. Their affairs were under these difficulties; but of the two schemes proposed, the most expedient seemed to be to return to Ilerda, because they had left some corn there; and there they hoped to decide on a plan for their future conduct. Tarraco lay at a greater distance; and in such a space they knew affairs might admit of many changes. Their design having met with approbation, they set out from their camp. Cæsar having sent forward his cavalry, to annoy and retard their rear, followed close after with his legions. Not a moment passed in which their rear was not engaged with our horse.

CHAP. LXXIX.—Their manner of fighting was this: the light cohorts closed their rear, and frequently made a stand on the level grounds. If they had a mountain to ascend, the very nature of the place readily secured them from any danger; for the advanced guards, from the rising grounds, protected the rest in their ascent. When they approached a valley or declivity, and the advanced men could not impart assistance to the tardy, our horse threw their darts at them from the rising grounds with advantage; then their affairs were in a perilous situation; the only plan left was, that whenever they came near such places, they should give orders to the legions to halt, and by a violent effort repulse our horse; and these being forced to give way, they should suddenly, with the utmost speed, run all together down to the valley, and having passed it, should face about again on the next hill. For so far were they from deriving any assistance from their horse (of which they had a large number), that they were obliged to receive them into the center of their army, and themselves protect them, as they were daunted by former battles. And on their march no one could quit the line without being taken by Cæsar's horse.

CHAP. LXXX.—While skirmishes were fought in this manner, they advanced but slowly and gradually, and frequently halted to help their rear, as then happened. For having advanced four miles, and being very much harassed by our horse, they took post on a high mountain, and there intrenched themselves on the front only, facing the enemy; and did not take their baggage off their cattle. When they perceived that Cæsar's camp was pitched, and the tents fixed up, and his horse sent out to forage, they suddenly rushed out about twelve o'clock the same day, and, having hopes that we should be delayed by the absence of our horse, they began to march, which Cæsar perceiving, followed them with the legions that remained. He left a few cohorts to guard his baggage, and ordered the foragers to be called home at the tenth hour,[1] and the horse to follow him. The horse shortly returned to their daily duty on march, and charged the rear so vigorously, that they almost forced them to fly; and several privates and some centurions were killed. The main body of Cæsar's army was at hand, and universal ruin threatened them.

CHAP. LXXXI.—Then indeed, not having opportunity either to choose a convenient position for their camp, or to march forward, they were obliged to halt, and to encamp at a distance from water, and on ground naturally unfavorable. But for the reasons already given, Cæsar did not attack them, nor suffer a tent to be pitched that day, that his men might be the readier to pursue them whether they attempted to run off by night or by day. Observing the defect in their position, they spent the whole night in extending their work, and turning their camp to ours. The next day, at dawn, they do the same, and spend the whole day in that manner, but in proportion as they advanced their works, and extended their camp, they were further distant from the water; and one evil was remedied by another. The first night, no one went out for water. The next day, they left a guard in the camp, and led out all their forces to water: but not a person was sent to look for forage. Cæsar was more desirous that they should be humbled by these means, and forced to come to terms, than decide the contest by battle. Yet he endeavored to surround them with a wall and trench, that he might be able to check their most sudden sally, to which he imagined that they must have recourse. Hereupon, urged by want of fodder, that they might be the readier for a march, they killed all their baggage cattle.

[1] Four o'clock.

CHAP. LXXXII.—In this work, and the deliberations on it, two days were spent. By the third day a considerable part of Cæsar's work was finished. To interrupt his progress, they drew out their legions about the eighth hour,[1] by a certain signal, and placed them in order of battle before their camp. Cæsar calling his legions off from their work, and ordering the horse to hold themselves in readiness, marshaled his army: for to appear to decline an engagement contrary to the opinion of the soldiers and the general voice, would have been attended with great disadvantage. But for the reasons already known, he was dissuaded from wishing to engage, and the more especially, because the short space between the camps, even if the enemy were put to flight, would not contribute much to a decisive victory; for the two camps were not distant from each other above two thousand feet. Two parts of this were occupied by the armies, and one third left for the soldiers to charge and make their attack. If a battle should be begun, the nearness of the camps would afford a ready retreat to the conquered party in the flight. For this reason Cæsar had resolved to make resistance if they attacked him, but not to be the first to provoke the battle.

CHAP. LXXXIII.—Afranius's five legions were drawn up in two lines, the auxiliary cohorts formed the third line, and acted as reserves. Cæsar had three lines, four cohorts out of each of the five legions formed the first line. Three more from each legion followed them, as reserves: and three others were behind these. The slingers and archers were stationed in the center of the line; the cavalry closed the flanks. The hostile armies being arranged in this manner, each seemed determined to adhere to his first intention: Cæsar not to hazard a battle, unless forced to it; Afranius to interrupt Cæsar's works. However, the matter was deferred, and both armies kept under arms till sunset; when they both returned to their camp. The next day Cæsar prepared to finish the works which he had begun. The enemy attempted to pass the river Segre by a ford. Cæsar, having perceived this, sent some light armed Germans and a party of horse across the river, and disposed several parties along the banks to guard them.

CHAP. LXXXIV.—At length, beset on all sides, their cattle

[1] About 2 o'clock.

having been four days without fodder, and having no water, wood, or corn, they beg a conference; and that, if possible, in a place remote from the soldiers. When this was refused by Cæsar, but a public interview offered if they chose it, Afranius's son was given as a hostage to Cæsar. They met in the place appointed by Cæsar. In the hearing of both armies, Afranius spoke thus: "That Cæsar ought not to be displeased either with him or his soldiers, for wishing to preserve their attachment to their general, Cneius Pompey. That they had now sufficiently discharged their duty to him, and had suffered punishment enough, in having endured the want of every necessary: but now, pent up almost like wild beasts, they were prevented from procuring water, and prevented from walking abroad; and were not able to bear the bodily pain or the mental disgrace: but confessed themselves vanquished: and begged and entreated, if there was any room left for mercy, that they should not be necessitated to suffer the most severe penalties." These sentiments were delivered in the most submissive and humble language.

Chap. LXXXV.—Cæsar replied, "That either to complain or sue for mercy became no man less than him: for that every other person had done their duty: himself, in having declined to engage on favorable terms, in an advantageous situation and time, that all things tending to a peace might be totally unembarrassed: his army, in having preserved and protected the men whom they had in their power, notwithstanding the injuries which they had received, and the murder of their comrades; and even Afranius's soldiers, who of themselves treated about concluding a peace, by which they thought that they would secure the lives of all. Thus, that the parties on both sides inclined to mercy: that the generals only were averse to peace: that they paid no regard to the laws either of conference or truce; and had most inhumanly put to death ignorant persons, who were deceived by a conference: that therefore, they had met that fate which usually befalls men from excessive obstinacy and arrogance; and were obliged to have recourse, and most earnestly desire that which they had shortly before disdained. That for his part, he would not avail himself of their present humiliation, or his present advantage, to require terms by which his power might be increased, but only that those armies, which they had maintained for so many years to oppose him, should be disbanded: for six legions had been sent into Spain, and a seventh raised there, and many and powerful fleets provided, and generals of great military experience sent to command them, for no other purpose than to oppose him: that none of these measures were adopted to keep the Spains in peace, or for the use of the province, which, from the length of the peace, stood in need of no such aid; that all these things were long since designed against him; that against him a new sort of government was established, that the same person should be at the gates of Rome, to direct the affairs of the city; and though absent, have the government of two most warlike provinces for so many years: that against him the laws of the magistrates had been altered; that the late prætors and consuls should not be sent to govern the provinces as had been the constant custom, but persons approved of and chosen by a faction. That against him the excuse of age was not admitted; but persons of tried experience in former wars were called up to take the command of the armies: that with respect to him only, the routine was not observed which had been allowed to all generals, that, after a successful war, they should return home and disband their armies, if not with some mark of honor, at least without disgrace; that he had submitted to all these things patiently, and would still submit to them; nor did he now desire to take their army from them and keep it to himself (which, however, would not be a difficult matter), but only that they should not have it to employ against him: and therefore, as he said before, let them quit the provinces, and disband their army. If this was complied with, he would injure no person; that these were the last and only conditions of peace."

CHAP. LXXXVI.—It was very acceptable and agreeable to Afranius's soldiers, as might be easily known from their signs of joy, that they who expected some injury after this defeat, should obtain without solicitation the reward of a dismissal. For when a debate was introduced about the place and time of their dismissal, they all began to express, both by words and signs, from the rampart where they stood, that they should be discharged immediately; for although every security might be given, that they would be disbanded, still the matter would be uncertain, if it was deferred to a future day. After a short debate on either side, it was brought to this issue: that those who had any settlement or possession in Spain, should be immediately discharged: the rest at the river Var.[1] Cæsar gave security that they should receive no damage, and that no person should be obliged against his inclination to take the military oath under him.

CHAP. LXXXVII.—Cæsar promised to supply them with corn from the present time till they arrived at the river Var. He further adds, that whatever any of them lost in the war, which was in the possession of his soldiers, should be restored to those that lost them. To his soldiers he made a recompense in money for those things, a just valuation being made. Whatever disputes Afranius's soldiers had afterward among themselves, they voluntarily submitted to Cæsar's decision. Afranius and Petreius, when pay was demanded by the legions, a sedition almost breaking out, asserted that the time had not yet come, and required that Cæsar should take cognizance of it; and both parties were content with his decision. About a third part of their army being dismissed in two days, Cæsar ordered two of his legions, to go before, the rest to follow the vanquished enemy; that they should encamp at a small distance from each other. The execution of this business he gave in charge to Quintus Fufius Kalenus, one of his lieutenants. According to his directions, they marched from Spain to the river Var, and there the rest of the army was disbanded.

[1] The Varus, modern Var, a rapid river of Italy, which takes its rise in the Alps, runs in a southerly direction, and falls into the Mediterranean, a little to the west of Nice.

BOOK II.

THE ARGUMENT.

I. Massilia is closely besieged on every side. III. Lucius Nasidius brings a fleet to the relief of the town, and forms a junction with the fleet of the Massilians. VII. He engages unsuccessfully with Cæsar's fleet. VIII. Trebonius constructs engines of extraordinary size against the town. XII. The inhabitants grow terrified and seek a truce. XIV. They succeed in obtaining it, but subsequently break it and destroy Trebonius's works by a sudden sally. XV. The besiegers speedily restore them, and the townsmen propose a surrender. XVII. In the mean time, M. Varro prepares for war in Farther Spain. XX. But is deserted by his followers, and falls into the power of Cæsar. XXII. The Massilians surrender. XXIII. Curio is at first successful in Africa. XL. But afterward, rashly engaging in action against a superior force, is cut to pieces with his entire army.

CHAP. I.—While these things were going forward in Spain, Caius Trebonius, Cæsar's lieutenant, who had been left to conduct the assault of Massilia, began to raise a mound, vineæ, and turrets against the town, on two sides; one of which was next the harbor and docks, the other on that part where there is a passage from Gaul and Spain to that sea which forces itself up the mouth of the Rhone. For Massilia is washed almost on three sides by the sea, the remaining fourth part is the only side which has access by land. A part even of this space, which reaches to the fortress, being fortified by the nature of the country, and a very deep valley, required a long and difficult siege. To accomplish these works, Caius Trebonius sends for a great quantity of carriages and men from the whole Province, and orders hurdles and materials to be furnished. These things being provided, he raised a mound eighty feet in height.

CHAP. II.—But so great a store of every thing necessary for a war had been a long time before laid up in the town, and so great a number of engines, that no vineæ made of hurdles could withstand their force. For poles twelve feet in length, pointed with iron, and these too shot from very large engines, sank into the ground through four rows of hurdles. Therefore the arches of the vineæ were covered over with beams a foot thick, fastened together, and under this the materials of the agger were handed from one to another. Before this was carried a testudo sixty feet long, for leveling the ground, made also of very strong timber, and covered over with every thing that was capable of protecting it against the fire and stones thrown by the enemy. But the greatness of the works, the height of the wall and towers, and the multitude of engines retarded the progress of our works. Besides, frequent sallies were made from the town by the Albici, and fire was thrown on our mound and turrets. These our men easily repulsed, and, doing considerable damage to those who sallied, beat them back into the town.

CHAP. III.—In the mean time, Lucius Nasidius, being sent by Cneius Pompey with a fleet of sixteen sail, a few of which had beaks of brass, to the assistance of Lucius Domitius and the Massilians, passed the straits of Sicily without the knowledge or expectation of Curio, and, putting with his fleet into Messana, and making the nobles and senate take flight with the sudden terror, carried off one of their ships out of dock. Having joined this to his other ships, he made good his voyage to Massilia, and having sent in a galley privately, acquaints Domitius and the Massilians of his arrival, and earnestly encourages them to hazard another battle with Brutus's fleet with the addition of his aid.

CHAP. IV.—The Massilians, since their former loss, had brought the same number of old ships from the docks, and had repaired and fitted them out with great industry: they had a large supply of seamen and pilots. They had got several fishing-smacks, and covered them over, that the seamen might be secure against darts: these they filled with archers and engines. With a fleet thus appointed, encouraged by the entreaties and tears of all the old men, matrons, and virgins to succor the state in this hour of distress, they went on board with no less spirit and confidence than they had fought before. For it happens, from a common infirmity of human nature, that we are more flushed with confidence, or more vehemently alarmed at things unseen, concealed, and unkown, as was the case then. For the arrival of Lucius Nasidius had filled the state with the most sanguine hopes and wishes. Having got a fair wind, they sailed out of port and went to Nasidius to Taurois, which is a fort belonging to the Massilians, and there ranged their fleet and again encouraged each other to engage, and communicated their plan of operation. The command of the right division was given to the Massilians, that of the left to Nasidius.

CHAP. V.—Brutus sailed to the same place with an augmented fleet; for to those made by Cæsar at Arelas[1] were added six ships taken from the Massilians, which he had refitted since the last battle and had furnished with every necessary. Accordingly, having encouraged his men to despise a vanquished people whom they had conquered when yet unbroken, he advanced against them full of confidence and spirit. From Trebonius's camp and all the higher grounds it was easy to see into the town—how all the youth which remained in it, and all persons of more advanced years, with their wives and children, and the public guards, were either extending their hands from the wall to the heavens, or were repairing to the temples of the immortal gods, and prostrating themselves before their images, were entreating them to grant them victory. Nor was there a single person who did not imagine that his future fortune depended on the issue of that day; for the choice of their youth and the most respectable of every age, being expressly invited and solicited, had gone on board the fleet, that if any adverse fate should befall them they might see that nothing was left for them to attempt, and, if they proved victorious, they might have hopes of preserving the city, either by their internal resources or by foreign assistance.

CHAP. VI.—When the battle was begun, no effort of valor was wanting to the Massilians, but, mindful of the instructions which they had a little before received from their friends, they fought with such spirit as if they supposed that they would never have another opportunity to attempt a defense, and as if they believed that those whose lives should be endangered in the battle would not long precede the fate of the rest of the citizens, who, if the city was taken, must undergo the same fortune of war. Our ships being at some distance from each

[1] Arelas, now Arles, a town of the Salyes, on the east side of the Rhone, a short distance from its mouth.

other, room was allowed both for the skill of their pilots and the maneuvering of their ships; and if at any time ours, gaining an advantage by casting the iron hooks on board their ships, grappled with them, from all parts they assisted those who were distressed. Nor, after being joined by the Albici. did they decline coming to close engagement, nor were they much inferior to our men in valor. At the same time, showers of darts, thrown from a distance from the lesser ships, suddenly inflicted several wounds on our men when off their guard and otherwise engaged; and two of their three-decked galleys, having descried the ship of Decimus Brutus, which could be easily distinguished by its flag, rowed up against him with great violence from opposite sides: but Brutus, seeing into their designs, by the swiftness of his ship extricated himself with such address as to get clear, though only by a moment. From the velocity of their motion they struck against each other with such violence that they were both excessively injured by the shock; the beak, indeed, of one of them being broken off, the whole ship was ready to founder, which circumstance being observed, the ships of Brutus's fleet, which were nearest that station, attack them when in this disorder and sink them both.

Chap. VII.—But Nasidius's ships were of no use, and soon left the fight; for the sight of their country, or the entreaties of their relations, did not urge them to run a desperate risk of their lives. Therefore, of the number of the ships not one was lost: of the fleet of the Massilians five were sunk, four taken, and one ran off with Nasidius: all that escaped made the best of their way to Hither Spain, but one of the rest was sent forward to Massilia for the purpose of bearing this intelligence, and when it came near the city, the whole people crowded out to hear the tidings, and, on being informed of the event, were so oppressed with grief, that one would have imagined that the city had been taken by an enemy at the same moment. The Massilians, however, began to make the necessary preparations for the defense of their city with unwearied energy.

Chap. VIII.—The legionary soldiers who had the management of the works on the right side, observed, from the frequent sallies of the enemy, that it might prove a great protection to them to build a turret of brick under the wall for a fort and place of refuge, which they at first built low and small, [to guard them] against sudden attacks. To it they retreated, and from it they made defense if any superior force attacked them; and from it they sallied out either to repel or pursue the enemy. It extended thirty feet on every side, and the thickness of the walls was five feet. But afterward, as experience is the best master in every thing on which the wit of man is employed, it was found that it might be of considerable service if it was raised to the usual height of turrets, which was effected in the following manner.

CHAP. IX.—When the turret was raised to the height for flooring, they laid it on the walls in such a manner that the ends of the joists were covered by the outer face of the wall, that nothing should project to which the enemy's fire might adhere. They, moreover, built over the joists with small bricks as high as the protection of the plutei and vineæ permitted them; and on that place they laid two beams across, angle-ways, at a small distance from the outer walls, to support the rafters which were to cover the turret, and on the beams they laid joists across in a direct line, and on these they fastened down planks. These joists they made somewhat longer, to project beyond the outside of the wall, that they might serve to hang a curtain on them to defend and repel all blows while they were building the walls between that and the next floor, and the floor of this story they faced with bricks and mortar, that the enemy's fire might do them no damage; and on this they spread mattrasses, lest the weapons thrown from engines should break through the flooring, or stones from catapults should batter the brick work. They, moreover, made three mats of cable ropes, each of them the length of the turret walls, and four feet broad, and, hanging them round the turret on the three sides which faced the enemy, fastened them to the projecting joists. For this was the only sort of defense which, they had learned by experience in other places, could not be pierced by darts or engines. But when that part of the turret which was completed was protected and secured against every attempt of the enemy, they removed the plutei to other works. They began to suspend gradually, and raise by screws from the first-floor, the entire roof of the turret, and then they elevated it as high as the length of the mats allowed. Hid and secured within these coverings, they built up the walls with bricks, and again, by another turn of the screw, cleared a place for themselves to proceed with the building; and, when they thought it time to lay another floor, they laid the ends of the beams, covered in by the outer bricks in like manner as in the first story, and from that story they again raised the uppermost floor and the mat-work. In this manner, securely and without a blow or danger, they raised it six stories high, and in laying the materials left loop-holes in such places as they thought proper for working their engines.

CHAP. X.—When they were confident that they could protect the works which lay around from this turret, they resolved to build a musculus,[1] sixty feet long, of timber, two feet square, and to extend it from the brick tower to the enemy's tower and wall. This was the form of it: first, two beams of equal length were laid on the ground, at the distance of four feet from each other; and in them were fastened small pillars, five feet high, which were joined together by braces, with a gentle slope, on which the timber which they must place to support the roof of the musculus should be laid: upon this were laid beams, two feet square, bound with iron plates and nails. To the upper covering of the musculus and the upper beams, they fastened laths, four fingers square, to support the tiles which were to cover the musculus. The roof being thus sloped and laid over in rows in the same manner as the joists were laid on the braces, the musculus was covered with tiles and mortar, to secure it against fire, which might be thrown from the wall. Over the tiles hides are spread, to prevent the water let in on them by spouts from dissolving the cement of the bricks. Again, the hides were covered over with mattrasses, that they might not be destroyed by fire or stones. The soldiers under the protection of the vineæ, finish this whole work to the very tower; and suddenly, before the enemy were aware of it, moved it forward by naval machinery, by putting rollers under it, close

[1] The musculus was, according to the description of Vegetius, one of the smaller military machines, by which soldiers, besieging a town, were protected while engaged in filling up the ditches round the besieged places, so that the movable towers (turres ambulatoriæ) of the besiegers might be able to approach the walls without obstacle. A minute description of a musculus is given by Cæsar in the passage before us. The musculus described by Cæsar, was evidently designed for different purposes than the one mentioned by Vegetius, and the former appears to have been only a smaller, but a more indestructible kind of vinea than that commonly used.—Smyth's Dictionary of Greek and Roman Antiquities.

up to the enemy's turret, so that it even touched the building.

CHAP. XI.—The townsmen, affrighted at this unexpected stroke, bring forward with levers the largest stones they can procure, and pitching them from the wall, roll them down on the musculus. The strength of the timber withstood the shock; and whatever fell on it slid off, on account of the sloping roof. When they perceived this, they altered their plan, and set fire to barrels, filled with resin and tar, and rolled them down from the wall on the musculus. As soon as they fell on it, they slid off again, and were removed from its side by long poles and forks. In the mean time, the soldiers, under cover of the musculus, were rooting out with crow-bars the lowest stones of the enemy's turret, with which the foundation was laid. The musculus was defended by darts, thrown from engines by our men from the brick tower, and the enemy were beaten off from the wall and turrets; nor was a fair opportunity of defending the walls given them. At length several stones being picked away from the foundation of that turret next the musculus, part of it fell down suddenly, and the rest, as if following it, leaned forward.

CHAP. XII.—Hereupon, the enemy distressed at the sudden fall of the turret, surprised at the unforeseen calamity, awed by the wrath of the gods, and dreading the pillage of their city, rush all together out of the gate unarmed, with their temples bound with fillets, and suppliantly stretch out their hands to the officers and the army. At this uncommon occurrence, the whole progress of the war was stopped, and the soldiers, turning away from the battle, ran eagerly to hear and listen to them. When the enemy came up to the commanders and the army, they all fell down at their feet, and besought them "to wait till Cæsar's arrival; they saw that their city was taken, our works completed, and their tower undermined, therefore they desisted from a defense; that no obstacle could arise, to prevent their being instantly plundered at a beck, as soon as he arrived, if they refused to submit to his orders." They inform them that, "if the turret had entirely fallen down, the soldiers could not be withheld from forcing into the town and sacking it, in hopes of getting spoil." These and several other arguments to the same effect were delivered, as they were a people of great learning, with great pathos and lamentations.

CHAP. XIII.—The lieutenants moved with compassion,

draw off the soldiers from the work, desist from the assault, and leave sentinels on the works. A sort of truce having been made through compassion for the besieged, the arrival of Cæsar is anxiously awaited; not a dart was thrown from the walls or by our men, but all remit their care and diligence, as if the business was at an end. For Cæsar had given Trebonius strict charge not to suffer the town to be taken by storm, lest the soldiers, too much irritated both by abhorrence of their revolt, by the contempt shown to them, and by their long labor, should put to the sword all the grown up inhabitants, as they threatened to do. And it was with difficulty that they were then restrained from breaking into the town, and they were much displeased, because they imagined that they were prevented by Trebonius from taking possession of it.

CHAP. XIV.—But the enemy, destitute of all honor, only waited a time and opportunity for fraud and treachery. And after an interval of some days, when our men were careless and negligent, on a sudden, at noon, when some were dispersed, and others indulging themselves in rest on the very works, after the fatigue of the day, and their arms were all laid by and covered up, they sallied out from the gates, and, the wind being high and favorable to them, they set fire to our works; and the wind spread it in such a manner that, in the same instant, the agger, plutei, testudo, tower, and engines all caught the flames and were consumed before we could conceive how it had occurred. Our men, alarmed at such an unexpected turn of fortune, lay hold on such arms as they could find. Some rush from the camp; an attack is made on the enemy: but they were prevented, by arrows and engines from the walls, from pursuing them when they fled. They retired to their walls, and there, without fear, set the musculus and brick tower on fire. Thus, by the perfidy of the enemy and the violence of the storm, the labor of many months was destroyed in a moment. The Massilians made the same attempt the next day, having got such another storm. They sallied out against the other tower and agger, and fought with more confidence. But as our men had on the former occasion given up all thoughts of a contest, so, warned by the event of the preceding day, they had made every preparation for a defense. Accordingly, they slew several, and forced the rest to retreat into the town without effecting their design.

CHAP. XV.—Trebonius began to provide and repair what

had been destroyed, with much greater zeal on the part of the soldiers; for when they saw that their extraordinary pains and preparations had an unfortunate issue, they were fired with indignation that, in consequence of the impious violation of the truce, their valor should be held in derision. There was no place left them from which the materials for their mound could be fetched, in consequence of all the timber, far and wide, in the territories of the Massilians, having been cut down and carried away; they began therefore to make an agger of a new construction, never heard of before, of two walls of brick, each six feet thick, and to lay floors over them of almost the same breadth with the agger, made of timber. But wherever the space between the walls, or the weakness of the timber, seemed to require it, pillars were placed underneath and traversed beams laid on to strengthen the work, and the space which was floored was covered over with hurdles, and the hurdles plastered over with mortar. The soldiers, covered over head by the floor, on the right and left by the wall, and in the front by the mantlets, carried whatever materials were necessary for the building without danger: the business was soon finished—the loss of their laborious work was soon repaired by the dexterity and fortitude of the soldiers. Gates for making sallies were left in the wall in such places as they thought proper.

CHAP. XVI.—But when the enemy perceived that those works, which they had hoped could not be replaced without a great length of time, were put into so thorough repair by a few day's labor and diligence, that there was no room for perfidy or sallies, and that no means were left them by which they could either hurt the men by resistance or the works by fire, and when they found by former examples that their town could be surrounded with a wall and turrets on every part by which it was accessible by land, in such a manner that they could not have room to stand on their own fortifications, because our works were built almost on the top of their walls by our army, and darts could be thrown from our hands, and when they perceived that all advantage arising from their engines, on which they had built great hopes, was totally lost, and that though they had an opportunity of fighting with us on equal terms from walls and turrets, they could perceive that they were not equal to our men in bravery, they had recourse to the same proposals of surrender as before.

CHAP. XVII.—In Further Spain, Marcus Varro, in the beginning of the disturbances, when he heard of the circumstances which took place in Italy, being diffident of Pompey's success, used to speak in a very friendly manner of Cæsar. That though, being pre-engaged to Cneius Pompey in quality of lieutenant, he was bound in honor to him, that, nevertheless, there existed a very intimate tie between him and Cæsar; that he was not ignorant of what was the duty of a lieutenant, who bore an office of trust; nor of his own strength, nor of the disposition of the whole province to Cæsar. These sentiments he constantly expressed in his ordinary conversation, and did not attach himself to either party. But afterward, when he found that Cæsar was detained before Massilia, that the forces of Petreius had effected a junction with the army of Afranius, that considerable reinforcements had come to their assistance, that there were great hopes and expectations, and heard that the whole Hither province had entered into a confederacy, and of the difficulties to which Cæsar was reduced afterward at Ilerda for want of provisions, and Afranius wrote to him a fuller and more exaggerated account of these matters, he began to regulate his movements by those of fortune.

CHAP. XVIII.—He made levies throughout the province; and, having completed his two legions, he added to them about thirty auxiliary cohorts; he collected a large quantity of corn to send partly to the Masilians, partly to Afranius and Petreius. He commanded the inhabitants of Gades to build ten ships of war; besides, he took care that several others should be built in Spain. He removed all the money and ornaments from the temple[1] of Hercules to the town of Gades, and sent six cohorts thither from the province to guard them, and gave the command of the town of Gades to Caius Gallonius, a Roman knight, and friend of Domitius, who had come thither sent by Domitius to recover an estate for him; and he deposited all the arms, both public and private, in Gallonius's house. He himself [Varro] made severe harangues against Cæsar. He often pronounced from his tribunal that Cæsar had fought several unsuccessful battles, and that a great number of his

[1] It was thought that the bones of Hercules were buried here; hence great offerings were made at his shrine. It is recorded that Lucullus offered the tenth of his property there, and that Hannibal, before he set out for Italy, went there to make vows and offerings.

men had deserted to Afranius. That he had these accounts from undoubted messengers, and authority on which he could rely. By these means he terrified the Roman citizens of that province, and obliged them to promise him for the service of the state one hundred and ninety thousand sesterces, twenty thousand pounds weight of silver, and a hundred and twenty thousand bushels of wheat. He laid heavier burdens on those states which he thought were friendly disposed to Cæsar, and billeted troops on them; he passed judgment against some private persons, and condemned to confiscation the properties of those who had spoken or made orations against the republic, and forced the whole province to take an oath of allegiance to him and Pompey. Being informed of all that happened in Hither Spain, he prepared for war. This was his plan of operations. He was to retire with his two legions to Gades, and to lay up all the shipping and provisions there. For he had been informed that the whole province was inclined to favor Cæsar's party. He thought that the war might be easily protracted in an island, if he was provided with corn and shipping. Cæsar, although called back to Italy by many and important matters, yet had determined to leave no dregs of war behind him in Spain, because he knew that Pompey had many dependents and clients in the hither province.

CHAP. XIX.—Having therefore sent two legions into Further Spain under the command of Quintus Cassius, tribune of the people; he himself advances with six hundred horse by forced marches, and issues a proclamation, appointing a day on which the magistrates and nobility of all the states should attend him at Corduba. This proclamation being published through the whole province, there was not a state that did not send a part of their senate to Corduba, at the appointed time; and not a Roman citizen of any note but appeared that day. At the same time the senate at Corduba shut the gates of their own accord against Varro, and posted guards and sentinels on the wall and in the turrets, and detained two cohorts (called Colonicæ, which had come there accidentally), for the defense of the town. About the same time the people of Carmona, which is by far the strongest state in the whole province, of themselves drove out of the town the cohorts, and shut the gates against them, although three cohorts had been detached by Varro to garrison the citadel.

CHAP. XX.—But Varro was in greater haste on this account to reach Gades with his legion as soon as possible, lest he should be stopped either on his march or on crossing over to the island. The affection of the province to Cæsar proved so great and so favorable, that he received a letter from Gades, before he was far advanced on his march: that as soon as the nobility of Gades heard of Cæsar's proclamation, they had combined with the tribune of the cohorts, which were in garrison there, to drive Gallonius out of the town, and to secure the city and island for Cæsar. That having agreed on the design they had sent notice to Gallonius, to quit Gades of his own accord while he could do it with safety; if he did not, they would take measures for themselves; that for fear of this Gallonius had been induced to quit the town. When this was known, one of Varro's two legions, which was called Vernacula, carried off the colors from Varro's camp, he himself standing by and looking on, and retired to Hispalis, and took post in the market and public places without doing any injury, and the Roman citizens residing there approved so highly of this act, that every one most earnestly offered to entertain them in their houses. When Varro, terrified at these things, having altered his route, proposed going to Italica, he was informed by his friends that the gates were shut against him. Then indeed, when intercepted from every road, he sends word to Cæsar, that he was ready to deliver up the legion which he commanded. He sends to him Sextus Cæsar, and orders him to deliver it up to him. Varro, having delivered up the legion, went to Cæsar to Corduba, and having laid before him the public accounts, handed over to him most faithfully whatever money he had, and told him what quantity of corn and shipping he had, and where.

CHAP. XXI.—Cæsar made a public oration at Corduba, in which he returned thanks to all severally: to the Roman citizens, because they had been zealous to keep the town in their own power; to the Spaniards, for having driven out the garrison; to the Gaditani, for having defeated the attempts of his enemies, and asserted their own liberty; to the Tribunes and Centurions who had gone there as a guard, for having by their valor confirmed them in their purpose. He remitted the tax which the Roman citizens had promised to Varro for the public use: he restored their goods to those who he was informed had incurred that penalty by speaking too freely, having given public and private rewards to some: he filled the rest with flattering hopes of his future intentions; and having staid two days at Corduba, he set out for Gades; he ordered the money and ornaments which had been carried away from the temple of Hercules, and lodged in the houses of private persons, to be replaced in the temple. He made Quintus Cassius governor of the province, and assigned him four legions. He himself, with those ships which Marcus Varro had built, and others which the Gaditani had built by Varro's orders, arrived in a few days at Tarraco, where embassadors from the greatest part of the nearer province waited his arrival. Having in the same manner conferred marks of honor both publicly and privately on some states, he left Tarraco, and went thence by and to Narbo, and thence to Massilia. There he was informed that a law was passed for creating a dictator, and that he had been nominated dictator by Marcus Lepidus[1] the prætor.

CHAP. XXII.—The Massilians, wearied out by misfortunes of every sort, reduced to the lowest ebb for want of corn, conquered in two engagements at sea, defeated in their frequent sallies, and struggling moreover with a fatal pestilence, from their long confinement and change of victuals (for they all subsisted on old millet and damaged barley, which they had formerly provided and laid up in the public stores against an emergency of this kind), their turret being demolished, a great part of their wall having given way, and despairing of any aid, either from the provinces or their armies, for these they had heard had fallen into Cæsar's power, resolved to surrender now without dissimulation. But a few days before, Lucius Domitius, having discovered the intention of the Massilians, and having procured three ships, two of which he gave up to his friends, went on board the third himself, having got a brisk wind, put out to sea. Some ships, which by Brutus's orders were constantly cruising near the port, having espied him, weighed anchor, and pursued him. But of these, the ship on board of which he was, persevered itself, and continuing its flight, and by the aid of the wind

[1] This was the Lepidus who subsequently, with Mark Antony and Octavius Cæsar, formed the second triumvirate.

got out of sight: the other two, affrighted by the approach of our galleys put back again into the harbor. The Massilians conveyed their arms and engines out of the town, as they were ordered: brought their ships out of the port and docks, and delivered up the money in their treasury. When these affairs were dispatched, Cæsar, sparing the town more out of regard to their renown and antiquity than to any claim they could lay to his favor, left two legions in garrison there, sent the rest to Italy, and set out himself for Rome.

CHAP. XXIII.—About the same time Caius Curio, having sailed from Sicily to Africa, and from the first despising the forces of Publius Attius Varus, transported only two of the four legions which he had received from Cæsar, and five hundred horse, and having spent two days and three nights on the voyage, arrived at a place called Aquilaria, which is about twenty-two miles distant from Clupea, and in the summer season has a convenient harbor, and is inclosed by two projecting promontories. Lucius Cæsar the son, who was waiting his arrival near Clupea with ten ships which had been taken near Utica in a war with the pirates, and which Publius Attius had had repaired for this war, frightened at the number of our ships, fled the sea, and running his three-decked covered galley on the nearest shore, left her there and made his escape by land to Adrumetum. Caius Considius Longus, with a garrison of one legion, guarded this town. The rest of Cæsar's fleet, after his flight, retired to Adrumetum. Marcus Rufus, the quæstor, pursued him with twelve ships, which Curio had brought from Sicily as convoy to the merchantmen, and seeing a ship left on the shore, he brought her off by a towing rope, and returned with his fleet to Curio.

CHAP. XXIV.—Curio detached Marcus before with the fleet to Utica, and marched thither with his army. Having advanced two days, he came to the river Bagrada, and there left Caius Caninius Rebilus, the lieutenant, with the legions; and went forward himself with the horse to view the Cornelian camp, because that was reckoned a very eligible position for encamping. It is a straight ridge, projecting into the sea, steep and rough on both sides, but the ascent is more gentle on that part which lies opposite Utica. It is not more than a mile distant from Utica in a direct line. But on this road there is a spring, to which the sea comes up, and overflows; an extensive morass is thereby formed; and if a person would avoid it, he must make a circuit of six miles to reach the town.

CHAP. XXV.—Having examined this place, Curio got a view of Varus's camp, joining the wall and town, at the gate called Bellica, well fortified by its natural situation, on one side by the town itself, on the other by a theater which is before the town, the approaches to the town being rendered difficult and narrow by the very extensive out-buildings of that structure. At the same time he observed the roads very full of carriages and cattle, which they were conveying from the country into the town on the sudden alarm. He sent his cavalry after them to plunder them and get the spoil. And at the same time Varus had detached as a guard for them six hundred Numidian horse, and four hundred foot, which king Juba had sent to Utica as auxiliaries a few days before. There was a friendship subsisting between his [Juba's] father and Pompey, and a feud between him and Curio, because he, when a tribune of the people, had proposed a law, in which he endeavored to make public property of the kingdom of Juba. The horse engaged; but the Numidians were not able to stand our first charge; but a hundred and twenty being killed, the rest retreated into their camp near the town. In the mean time, on the arrival of his men of war, Curio ordered proclamation to be made to the merchant ships, which lay at anchor before Utica, in number about two hundred, that he would treat as enemies all that did not set sail immediately for the Cornelian camp. As soon as the proclamation was made, in an instant they all weighed anchor and left Utica, and repaired to the place commanded them. This circumstance furnished the army with plenty of every thing.

CHAP. XXVI.—After these transactions, Curio returned to his camp to Bragada; and by a general shout of the whole army was saluted imperator.[1] The next day he led his army to Utica, and encamped near the town. Before the works of the camp were finished, the horse upon guard brought him word that a large supply of horse and foot sent by king Juba were on their march to Utica, and at the same time a cloud of

[1] This was merely an honorary title bestowed by the army on their victorious general.

dust was observed, and in a moment the front of the line was in sight. Curio, surprised at the suddenness of the affair, sent on the horse to receive their first charge, and detain them. He immediately called off his legions from the work, and put them in battle array. The horse began the battle: and before the legions could be completely marshaled and take their ground, the king's entire forces being thrown into disorder and confusion, because they had marched without any order, and were under no apprehensions, betake themselves to flight: almost all the enemy's horse being safe, because they made a speedy retreat into the town along the shore, Cæsar's soldiers slay a great number of their infantry.

CHAP. XXVII.—The next night two Marsian centurions, with twenty-two men belonging to the companies, deserted from Curio's camp to Attius Varus. They, whether they uttered the sentiments which they really entertained, or wished to gratify Varus (for what we wish we readily give credit to, and what we think ourselves, we hope is the opinion of other men), assured him, that the minds of the whole army were disaffected to Curio, that it was very expedient that the armies should be brought in view of each other, and an opportunity of a conference be given. Induced by their opinion, Varus the next day led his troops out of the camp: Curio did so in like manner, and with only one small valley between them, each drew up his forces.

CHAP. XXVIII.—In Varus's army there was one Sextus Quintilius Varus who, as we have mentioned before, was at Corfinium. When Cæsar gave him his liberty, he went over to Africa; now, Curio had transported to Africa those legions which Cæsar had received under his command a short time before at Corfinium; so that the officers and companies were still the same, excepting the change of a few centurions. Quintilius, making this a pretext for addressing them, began to go round Curio's lines, and to entreat the soldiers "not to lose all recollection of the oath which they took first to Domitius and to him their quæstor, nor bear arms against those who had shared the same fortune, and endured the same hardships in a siege, nor fight for those by whom they had been opprobriously called deserters." To this he added a few words by way of encouragement, what they might expect from his own liberality, if they should follow him and Attius. On the delivery of this speech, no intimation of their future conduct is given by Curio's army, and thus both generals led back their troops to their camp.

CHAP. XXIX.—However, a great and general fear spread through Curio's camp, for it is soon increased by the various discourses of men. For every one formed an opinion of his own; and to what he had heard from others, added his own apprehensions. When this had spread from a single author to several persons, and was handed from one another, there appeared to be many authors for such sentiments as these: ["That it was a civil war; that they were men; and therefore that it was lawful for them to act freely, and follow which party they pleased." These were the legions which a short time before had belonged to the enemy; for the custom of offering free towns to those who joined the opposite party had changed Cæsar's kindness. For the harshest expressions of the soldiers in general did not proceed from the Marsi and Peligni, as those which passed in the tents the night before; and some of their fellow soldiers heard them with displeasure. Some additions were also made to them by those who wished to be thought more zealous in their duty].[1]

CHAP. XXX.—For these reasons, having called a council, Curio began to deliberate on the general welfare. There were some opinions, which advised by all means an attempt to be made, and an attack on Varus's camp; for when such sentiments prevailed among the soldiers, they thought idleness was improper. In short, they said "that it was better bravely to try the hazard of war in a battle, than to be deserted and surrounded by their own troops, and forced to submit to the greatest cruelties." There were some who gave their opinion, that they ought to withdraw at the third watch to the Cornelian camp; that by a longer interval of time the soldiers might be brought to a proper way of thinking; and also, that if any misfortune should befall them, they might have a safer and readier retreat to Sicily, from the great number of their ships.

CHAP. XXXI.—Curio, censuring both measures, said, "that the one was as deficient in spirit, as the other exceeded in it: that the latter advised a shameful flight, and the former recommended us to engage at a great disadvantage.

[1] The text is here very corrupt, but I have given the probable meaning of the passage.

For on what, says he, can we rely that we can storm a camp, fortified both by nature and art? Or, indeed, what advantage do we gain if we give over the assault, after having suffered considerable loss; as if success did not acquire for a general the affection of his army, and misfortune their hatred? But what does a change of camp imply but a shameful flight, and universal despair, and the alienation of the army? For neither ought the obedient to suspect that they are distrusted, nor the insolent to know that we fear them; because our fears augment the licentiousness of the latter, and diminish the zeal of the former. But if, says he, we were convinced of the truth of the reports of the disaffection of the army (which I indeed am confident are either altogether groundless, or at least less than they are supposed to be), how much better to conceal and hide our suspicions of it, than by our conduct confirm it? Ought not the defects of an army to be as carefully concealed as the wounds in our bodies, lest we should increase the enemy's hopes? but they moreover advise us to set out at midnight, in order, I suppose, that those who attempt to do wrong may have a fairer opportunity; for conduct of this kind is restrained either by shame or fear, to the display of which the night is most averse. Wherefore, I am neither so rash as to give my opinion that we ought to attack their camp without hopes of succeeding; nor so influenced by fear as to despond: and I imagine that every expedient ought first to be tried; and I am in a great degree confident that I shall form the same opinions as yourselves on this matter."

CHAP. XXXII.—Having broken up the council, he called the soldiers together, and reminded them "what advantage Cæsar had derived from their zeal at Corfinium; how by their good offices and influence he had brought over a great part of Italy to his interest. For, says he, all the municipal towns afterward imitated you and your conduct; nor was it without reason that Cæsar judged so favorably, and the enemy so harshly of you. For Pompey, though beaten in no engagement, yet was obliged to shift his ground, and leave Italy, from the precedent established by your conduct. Cæsar commited me, whom he considered his dearest friend, and the provinces of Sicily and Africa, without which he was not able to protect Rome or Italy, to your protection. There are some here present who encourage you to revolt from us; for what can they wish for more, than at once to ruin us, and to involve you in a heinous crime? or what baser opinions could they in their resentment entertain of you, than that you would betray those who acknowledged themselves indebted to you for every thing, and put yourselves in the power of those who think they have been ruined by you? Have you not heard of Cæsar's exploits in Spain? that he routed two armies conquered two generals, recovered two provinces, and effected all this within forty days after he came in sight of the enemy? Can those who were not able to stand against him while they were uninjured, resist him when they are ruined? Will you, who took part with Cæsar while victory was uncertain, take part with the conquered enemy when the fortune of the war is decided, and when you ought to reap the reward of your services? For they say that they have been deserted and betrayed by you, and remind you of a former oath. But did you desert Lucius Domitius, or did Lucius Domitius desert you? Did he not, when you were ready to submit to the greatest difficulties, cast you off? Did he not, without your privacy, endeavor to effect his own escape? When you were betrayed by him, were you not preserved by Cæsar's generosity? And how could he think you bound by your oath to him, when, after having thrown up the ensigns of power, and abdicated his government, he became a private person, and a captive in another's power? A new obligation is left upon you, that you should disregard the oath, by which you are at present bound; and have respect only to that which was invalidated by the surrender of your general, and his diminution of rank. But I suppose, although you are pleased with Cæsar, you are offended with me; however, I shall not boast of my services to you, which still are inferior to my own wishes or your expectations. But, however, soldiers have ever looked for the rewards of labor at the conclusion of a war; and what the issue of it is likely to be, not even you can doubt. But why should I omit to mention my own diligence and good fortune, and to what a happy crisis affairs are now arrived? Are you sorry that I transported the army safe and entire, without the loss of a single ship? That on my arrival, in the very first attack, I routed the enemy's fleet? That twice in two days I defeated the enemy's horse? That I carried out of the very harbor and bay two hundred of the enemy's victualers, and reduced them to that situation that they can receive no supplies either by land or sea? Will you divorce yourselves from this fortune and these generals; and prefer the disgrace of Corfinium, the defeat of Italy, the surrender of both Spains, and the prestige of the African war? I, for my part, wished to be called a soldier of Cæsar's; you honored me with the title of Imperator. If you repent your bounty, I give it back to you; restore to me my former name that you may not appear to have conferred the honor on me as a reproach."

CHAP. XXXIII.—The soldiers, being affected by this oration, frequently attempted to interrupt him while he was speaking, so that they appeared to bear with excessive anguish the suspicion of treachery, and when he was leaving the assembly they unanimously besought him to be of good spirits, and not hesitate to engage the enemy and put their fidelity and courage to a trial. As the wishes and opinions of all were changed by this act, Curio, with the general consent, determined, whenever opportunity offered, to hazard a battle. The next day he led out his forces and ranged them in order of battle on the same ground where they had been posted the preceding day; nor did Attius Varus hesitate to draw out his men, that, if any occasion should offer, either to tamper with our men or to engage on equal terms, he might not miss the opportunity.

CHAP. XXXIV.—There lay between the two armies a valley, as already mentioned, not very deep, but of a difficult and steep ascent. Each was waiting till the enemy's forces should attempt to pass it, that they might engage with the advantage of the ground. At the same time on the left wing, the entire cavalry of Publius Attius, and several light-armed infantry intermixed with them, were perceived descending into the valley. Against them Curio detached his cavalry and two cohorts of the Marrucini, whose first charge the enemy's horse were unable to stand, but, setting spurs to their horses, fled back to their friends: the light-infantry being deserted by those who had come out along with them, were surrounded and cut to pieces by our men. Varus's whole army, facing that way, saw their men flee and cut down. Upon which Rebilus, one of Cæsar's lieutenants, whom Curio had brought with him from Sicily knowing that he had great experience in military matters, cried out, "You see the enemy are daunted, Curio! why do you hesitate to take advantage of the opportunity?" Curio, having merely "expressed this, that the soldiers should keep in mind the professions which they had made to him the day before,' then ordered them to follow him, and ran far before them all. The valley was so difficult of ascent that the foremost men could not struggle up it unless assisted by those behind. But the minds of Attius's soldiers being prepossessed with fear and the flight and slaughter of their men, never thought of opposing us; and they all imagined that they were already surrounded by our horse, and, therefore, before a dart could be thrown, or our men come near them, Varus's whole army turned their backs and retreated to their camp.

CHAP. XXXV.—In this flight one Fabius, a Pelignian and common soldier in Curio's army, pursuing the enemy's rear, with a loud voice shouted to Varus by his name, and often called him, so that he seemed to be one of his soldiers, who wished to speak to him and give him advice. When Varus, after been repeatedly called, stopped and looked at him, and inquired who he was and what he wanted, he made a blow with his sword at his naked shoulder and was very near killing Varus, but he escaped the danger by raising his shield to ward off the blow. Fabius was surrounded by the soldiers near him and cut to pieces; and by the multitude and crowds of those that fled, the gates of the camps were thronged and the passage stopped, and a greater number perished in that place without a stroke than in the battle and flight. Nor were we far from driving them from this camp; and some of them ran straightway to the town without halting. But both the nature of the ground and the strength of the fortifications prevented our access to the camp; for Curio's soldiers, marching out to battle, were without those things which were requisite for storming a camp. Curio, therefore, led his army back to the camp, with all his troops safe except Fabius. Of the enemy about six hundred were killed and a thousand wounded, all of whom, after Curio's return, and several more, under pretext of their wounds, but in fact through fear, withdrew from the camp into the town, which Varus perceiving and knowing the terror of his army, leaving a trumpeter in his camp and a few tents for show, at the third watch led back his army quietly into the town.

CHAP. XXXVI.—The next day Curio resolved to besiege Utica, and to draw lines about it. In the town there was a multitude of people, ignorant of war, owing to the length of the peace; some of them Uticans, very well inclined to Cæsar, for his favors to them; the Roman population was composed of persons differing widely in their sentiments. The terror occasioned by former battles was very great; and therefore, they openly talked of surrendering, and argued with Attius that he should not suffer the fortune of them all to be ruined by his obstinacy. While these things were in agitation, couriers, who had been sent forward, arrived from king Juba, with the intelligence that he was on his march, with considerable forces, and encouraged them to protect and defend their city, a circumstance which greatly comforted their desponding hearts.

CHAP. XXXVII.—The same intelligence was brought to Curio; but for some time he could not give credit to it, because he had so great confidence in his own good fortune. And at this time Cæsar's success in Spain was announced in Africa by messages and letters. Being elated by all these things, he imagined that the king would not dare to attempt any thing against him. But when he found out, from undoubted authority, that his forces were less than twenty miles distant from Utica, abandoning his works, he retired to the Cornelian camp. Here he began to lay in corn and wood, and to fortify his camp, and immediately dispatched orders to Sicily, that his two legions and the remainder of his cavalry should be sent to him. His camp was well adapted for protracting a war, from the nature and strength of the situation, from its proximity to the sea, and the abundance of water and salt, of which a great quantity had been stored up from the neighboring salt-pits. Timber could not fail him from the number of trees, nor corn, with which the lands abounded. Wherefore, with the general consent, Curio determined to wait for the rest of his forces, and protract the war.

CHAP. XXXVIII.—This plan being settled, and his conduct approved of, he is informed by some deserters from the town that Juba had staid behind in his own kingdom, being called home by a neighboring war, and a dispute with the people of Leptis; and that Sabura, his commander-in-chief, who had been sent with a small force, was drawing near to Utica. Curio rashly believing this information, altered his design, and resolved to hazard a battle. His youth, his spirits, his former good fortune and confidence of success, contributed much to confirm this resolution. Induced by these motives, early in the night he sent all his cavalry to the enemy's camp near the river Bagrada, of which Sabura, of whom we have already spoken, was the commander. But the king was coming after them with all his forces, and was posted at a distance of six miles behind Sabura. The horse that were sent perform their march that night, and attack the enemy unawares and unexpectedly; for the Numidians, after the usual barbarous custom, encamped here and there without any regularity The cavalry having attacked them, when sunk in sleep and dispersed, killed a great number of them; many were frightened and ran away. After which the horse returned to Curio, and brought some prisoners with them.

CHAP. XXXIX.—Curio had set out at the fourth watch with all his forces, except five cohorts which he left to guard the camp. Having advanced six miles, he met the horse, heard what had happened and inquired from the captives who commanded the camp at Bagrada. They replied Sabura. Through eagerness to perform his journey, he neglected to make further inquiries, but looking back to the company next him, "Don't you see, soldiers," says he, "that the answer of the prisoners corresponds with the account of the deserters, that the king is not with him, and that he sent only a small force which was not able to withstand a few horse? Hasten then to spoil, to glory; that we may now begin to think of rewarding you, and returning you thanks." The achievements of the horse were great in themselves, especially if their small number be compared with the vast host of Numidians. However, the account was enlarged by themselves, as men are naturally inclined to boast of their own merit. Besides, many spoils were produced; the men and horses that were taken were brought into their sight, that they might imagine that every moment of time which intervened was a delay to their conquest. By this means the hope of Curio were seconded by the ardor of the soldiers. He ordered the horse to follow him, and hastened his march, that he might attack them as soon as possible, while in consternation after their flight. But the horse, fatigued by the expedition of the preceding night, were not able to keep up with him, but fell behind in different places. Even this did not abate Curio's hopes.

CHAP. XL.—Juba, being informed by Sabura of the battle in the night, sent to his relief two thousand Spanish and Gallic horse, which he was accustomed to keep near him to guard his person, and that part of his infantry on which he had the greatest dependence, and he himself followed slowly after with the rest of his forces and forty elephants, suspecting that as Curio had sent his horse before, he himself would follow them. Sabura drew up his army, both horse and foot, and commanded them to give way gradually and retreat through the pretense of fear; that when it was necessary he would give them the signal for battle, and such orders as he found circumstances required. Curio, as his idea of their present behavior was calculated to confirm his former hopes, imagined that the enemy were running away, and led his army from the rising grounds down to the plain.

CHAP. XLI.—And when he had advanced from this place about sixteen miles, his army being exhausted with the fatigue, he halted. Sabura gave his men the signal, marshaled his army, and began to go around his ranks and encourage them. But he made use of the foot only for show; and sent the horse to the charge: Curio was not deficient in skill, and encouraged his men to rest all their hopes in their valor. Neither were the soldiers, though wearied, nor the horse, though few and exhausted with fatigue, deficient in ardor to engage, and courage: but the latter were in number but two hundred: the rest had dropped behind on the march. Wherever they charged they forced the enemy to give ground, but they were not able to pursue them far when they fled, or to press their horses too severely. Besides, the enemy's cavalry began to surround us on both wings and to trample down our rear. When any cohorts ran forward out of the line, the Numidians, being fresh, by their speed avoided our charge, and surrounded ours when they attempted to return to their post, and cut them off from the main body. So that it did not appear safe either to keep their ground and maintain their ranks, or to issue from the line, and run the risk. The enemy's troops were frequently reinforced by assistance sent from Juba; strength began to fail our men through fatigue;

and those who had been wounded could neither quit the field nor retire to a place of safety, because the whole field was surrounded by the enemy's cavalry. Therefore, despairing of their own safety, as men usually do in the last moment of their lives, they either lamented their unhappy deaths, or recommended their parents to the survivors, if fortune should save any from the impending danger. All were full of fear and grief.

CHAP. XLII.—When Curio perceived that in the general consternation neither his exhortations nor entreaties were attended to, imagining that the only hope of escaping in their deplorable situation was to gain the nearest hills, he ordered the colors to be borne that way. But a party of horse, that had been sent by Sabura, had already got possession of them. Now indeed our men were reduced to extreme despair: and some of them were killed by the cavalry in attempting to escape: some fell to the ground unhurt. Cneius Domitius, commander of the cavalry, standing round Curio with a small party of horse, urged Curio to endeavor to escape by flight, and to hasten to his camp; and assured him that he would not forsake him. But Curio declared that he would never more appear in Cæsar's sight, after losing the army which had been committed by Cæsar, to his charge, and accordingly fought till he was killed. Very few of the horse escaped from that battle, but those who had staid behind to refresh their horses having perceived at a distance the defeat of the whole army, retired in safety to their camp.

CHAP. XLIII.—The soldiers were all killed to a man. Marcus Rufus, the quæstor, who was left behind in the camp by Curio, having got intelligence of these things, encouraged his men not to be disheartened. They beg and entreat to be transported to Sicily. He consented, and ordered the masters of the ships to have all the boats brought close to the shore early in the evening. But so great was the terror in general, that some said that Juba's forces were marching up, others that Varus was hastening with his legions, and that they already saw the dust raised by their coming; of which not one circumstance had happened: others suspected that the enemy's fleet would immediately be upon them. Therefore in the general consternation, every man consulted his own safety. Those who were on board of the fleet, were in a hurry to set sail, and their flight hastened the masters of the ships of burden. A few small fishing boats attended their duty and his orders. But as the shores were crowded, so great was the struggle to determine who of such a vast number should first get on board, that some of the vessels sank with the weight of the multitude, and the fears of the rest delayed them from coming to the shore.

CHAP. XLIV.—From which circumstances it happened that a few foot and aged men, that could prevail either through interest or pity, or who were able to swim to the ships, were taken on board, and landed safe in Sicily. The rest of the troops sent their centurions as deputies to Varus at night, and surrendered themselves to him. But Juba the next day having spied their cohorts before the town, claimed them as his booty, and ordered great part of them to be put to the sword; a few he selected and sent home to his own realm. Although Varus complained that his honor was insulted by Juba, yet he dare not oppose him: Juba rode on horseback into the town, attended by several senators, among whom were Servius Sulpicius and Licinius Damasippus, and in a few days arranged and ordered what he would have done in Utica, and in a few days more returned to his own kingdom, with all his forces.

BOOK III.

THE ARGUMENT.

I. Cæsar arranges affairs in Rome, VI. Passes over to Epirus, VIII. Occupies Salonæ, XI. Oricum, XII. Apollonia, and other towns. XIII. Pompey falls back on Dyrrachium. XVIII. Bibulus dies. XIX. Cæsar's reiterated attempts to come to conference fail. XXII. Commotions arise in the city, but are quelled. XXIII. Libo blocks up the port of Brundusium, but in vain. XXVI. Antony and Calenus arrive from Italy, with fresh forces, and form a junction with Cæsar. XXXI. The tyrannical conduct of Scipio in Syria. XXXVI. The proceedings in Macedon and Thessaly. XL. Pompey hemmed in by Cæsar at Dyrrachium. XLIV. Frequent skirmishes without any decided advantages to either party. LXII. Cæsar suffers severely on two occasions, and abandons the blockade. LXXVIII. He induces Pompey to follow him into Thessaly, LXXXV. Gains an opportunity of coming to an action, XCIII. And completely defeats him. In the mean time, D. Lælius besieges the port of Brundusium; CI. And Cassius burns Cæsar's fleet in Sicily. CIV. Pompey is slain in Egypt by Achillas and Septimius. CVI. Cæsar pursues him to Alexandria, and there becomes involved in a new war.

CHAP. I.—Julius Cæsar, holding the election as dictator,[1] was himself appointed consul with Publius Servilius; for this was the year[2] in which it was permitted by the laws that he should be chosen consul. This business being ended, as credit was beginning to fail in Italy, and the debts could not be paid, he determined that arbitrators should be appointed: and that they should make an estimate of the possessions and properties [of the debtors], how much they were worth before the war, and that they should be handed over in payment to the creditors. This he thought the most likely method to remove and

[1] Cæsar thought that his continuing to hold the dictatorship was a stretch of power likely to alienate several of his own party, and therefore caused himself to be appointed consul.

[2] The tenth after his last consulship; however, this usage was not always observed; as, for instance, in the case of Scipio Africanus.

abate the apprehension of an abolition of debt,[1] the usual consequence of civil wars and dissensions, and to support the credit of the debtors. He likewise restored to their former condition (the prætors and tribunes,[2] first submitting the question to the people[3]) some persons condemned for bribery at the elections, by virtue of Pompey's law, at the time when Pompey kept his legions quartered in the city (these trials were finished in a single day, one judge hearing the merits, and another pronouncing the sentences), because they had offered their service to him in the beginning of the civil war, if he chose to accept them; setting the same value on them as if he had accepted them, because they had put themselves in his power. For he had determined that they ought to be restored rather by the judgment of the people than appear admitted to it by his bounty: that he might neither appear ungrateful in repaying an obligation, nor arrogant in depriving the people of their prerogative of exercising this bounty.

CHAP. II.—In accomplishing these things, and celebrating the Latin festival,[4] and holding all the elections, he spent eleven

[1] "Novæ tabulæ," an abolition of debt, called by the Greeks, *χρεῶν ἀποκοπὴ*. Plutarch calls it, "*σεισαχθεία*," *i. e.* a shaking off the burdens, because the debtors were relieved from their old debts.

[2] Cæsar acted on the appeals made to the people, in behalf of those who were condemned, by the prætors and the tribunes.

[3] Bribery, or undue influence, at elections. Pompey, when invested with the whole guardianship of the state on the death of Clodius, passed a severe law against such practices, in consequence of the violent competition between Hypsæus and Milo, for the consulship; by this law, the case was decided in one day, contrary to the usual practice.

[4] Feriæ Latinæ, or simply Latinæ (the original name was Latiar), had, according to the Roman legends, been instituted by the last Tarquin, in commemoration of the alliance between the Romans and Latins. But Niebuhr has shown that the festival, which was originally a panegyris of the Latins, is of much higher antiquity; for we find it stated that the town of the Priscans and Latins received their shows of the sacrifices on the Alban mount—which was the place of its celebration—along with the Albans, and the thirty towns of the Alban commonwealth. All that the last Tarquin did was, to convert the original Latin festival into a Roman one, and to make it the means of hallowing and cementing the alliance between the two nations. The object of this panegyris on the Alban mount was the worship of Jupiter Latiaris, and, at least as long as the Latin republic existed, to deliberate and decide on matters of the confederacy, and to settle any disputes which might have arisen between its members. Respecting the duration of the Feriæ Latinæ, the common opinion formerly was that at first they only lasted for one day, to

days; and having resigned the dictatorship, set out from the city, and went to Brundusium, where he had ordered twelve legions and all his cavalry to meet him. But he scarcely found as many ships as would be sufficient to transport fifteen thousand legionary soldiers and five hundred horse. This [the scarcity of shipping] was the only thing that prevented Cæsar from putting a speedy conclusion to the war. And even these troops embarked very short of their number, because several had fallen in so many wars in Gaul, and the long march from Spain had lessened their number very much, and a severe autumn in Apulia and the district about Brundusium, after the very wholesome countries of Spain and Gaul, had impaired the health of the whole army.

CHAP. III.—Pompey having got a year's respite to provide forces, during which he was not engaged in war, nor employed by an enemy, had collected a numerous fleet from Asia, and the Cyclades, from Corcyra, Athens, Pontus, Bithynia, Syria, Cilicia, Phœnicia, and Egypt, and had given directions that a great number should be built in every other place. He had exacted a large sum of money from Asia, Syria, and all the kings, dynasts, tetrarchs, and free states of Achaia; and had obliged the corporations of those provinces, of which he himself had the government, to count down to him a large sum.

CHAP. IV.—He had made up nine legions of Roman citizens; five from Italy, which he had brought with him; one veteran legion from Sicily, which being composed of two he called the Gemella; one from Crete and Macedonia, of veterans who had been discharged by their former generals and had settled in those provinces; two from Asia, which had been levied by the activity of Lentulus. Besides, he had distributed among his legions a considerable number, by way of recruits, from Thessaly, Bœotia, Achaia, and Epirus: with his legions he also intermixed the soldiers[1] taken from Caius Antonius. Besides these, he expected two legions from Syria, with Scipio; from Crete, Lacedæmon, Pontus, Syria, and other

which subsequently a second, a third, and a fourth were added; but it is clear that this supposition was founded on a confusion of the Feriæ Latinæ with the Ludi Maximi, and that they lasted for six days; one for each decury of the Alban and Latin town.—Abbreviated from the article in Smyth's Dictionary of Greek and Roman Antiquities.

[1] He refers to the soldiers of C. Antonius, who were betrayed by I. Pulcio, and subsequently compelled to surrender.

states, he got about three thousand archers, six cohorts of slingers, two thousand mercenary soldiers, and seven thousand horse; six hundred of which, Deiotarus had brought from Gaul; Ariobarzanes, five hundred from Cappadocia. Cotus had given him about the same number from Thrace, and had sent his son Sadalis with them. From Macedonia there were two hundred, of extraordinary valor, commanded by Rascipolis; five hundred Gauls and Germans; Gabinius's troops from Alexandria, whom Aulus Gabinius had left with king Ptolemy, to guard his person. Pompey, the son, had brought in his fleet eight hundred, whom he had raised among his own and his shepherds' slaves. Tarcundarius, Castor and Donilaus, had given three hundred from Gallogræcia: one of these came himself, the other sent his son. Two hundred were sent from Syria by Comagenus Antiochus, whom Pompey rewarded amply. The most of them were archers. To these were added Dardanians and Bessians, some of them mercenaries; others procured by power and influence: also, Macedonians, Thessalians, and troops from other nations and states, which completed the number which we mentioned before.

Chap. V.—He had laid in vast quantities of corn from Thessaly, Asia, Egypt, Crete, Cyrene, and other countries. He had resolved to fix his winter quarters at Dyrrachium, Apollonia, and the other seaports, to hinder Cæsar from passing the sea: and for this purpose had stationed his fleet along the sea-coast. The Egyptian fleet was commanded by Pompey, the son: the Asiatic, by Decimus Lælius, and Caius Triarius: the Syrian, by Caius Cassius: the Rhodian, by Caius Marcellus, in conjunction with Caius Coponius: and the Liburnian and Achaian, by Scribonius Libo, and Marcus Octavius. But Marcus Bibulus was appointed commander-in-chief of the whole maritime department, and regulated every matter. The chief direction rested upon him.

Chap. VI.—When Cæsar came to Brundusium, he made a speech to the soldiers: "That since they were now almost arrived at the termination of their toils and dangers, they should patiently submit to leave their slaves and baggage in Italy, and to embark without luggage, that a greater number of men might be put on board: that they might expect every thing from victory and his liberality." They cried out with one voice, "he might give what orders he pleased, that they would cheerfully fulfill them." He accordingly set sail the fourth day of January, with seven legions on board, as already remarked. The next day he reached land, between the Ceraunian rocks and other dangerous places; meeting with a safe road for his shipping to ride in, and dreading all other ports which he imagined were in possession of the enemy, he landed his men at a place called Pharsalus, without the loss of a single vessel.

CHAP. VII.—Lucretius Vespillo and Minutius Rufus were at Oricum, with eighteen Asiatic ships, which were given into their charge by the orders of Decimus Lælius: Marcus Bibulus at Corcyra, with a hundred and ten ships. But they had not the confidence to dare to move out of the harbor; though Cæsar had brought only twelve ships as a convoy, only four of which had decks; nor did Bibulus, his fleet being disordered and his seamen dispersed, come up in time: for Cæsar was seen at the continent, before any account whatsoever of his approach had reached those regions.

CHAP. VIII.—Cæsar, having landed his soldiers, sent back his ships the same night to Brundusium, to transport the rest of his legions and cavalry. The charge of this business was committed to lieutenant Fufius Kalenus, with orders to be expeditious in transporting the legions. But the ships having put to sea too late, and not having taken advantage of the night breeze, fell a sacrifice on their return. For Bibulus, at Corcyra, being informed of Cæsar's approach, hoped to fall in with some part of our ships, with their cargoes, but found them empty; and having taken about thirty, vented on them his rage at his own remissness, and set them all on fire: and, with the same flames, he destroyed the mariners and masters of the vessels, hoping by the severity of the punishment to deter the rest. Having accomplished this affair, he filled all the harbors and shores from Salona to Oricum with his fleets. Having disposed his guard with great care, he lay on board himself in the depth of winter, declining no fatigue or duty, and not waiting for reinforcements, in hopes that he might come within Cæsar's reach.

CHAP. IX.—But after the departure of the Liburnian fleet, Marcus Octavius sailed from Illyricum with what ships he had to Salona; and having spirited up the Dalmatians, and other barbarous nations, he drew Issa off from its connection with

Cæsar; but not being able to prevail with the council of Salona, either by promises or menaces, he resolved to storm the town. But it was well fortified by its natural situation, and a hill. The Roman citizens built wooden towers, the better to secure it; but when they were unable to resist, on account of the smallness of their numbers, being weakened by several wounds, they stooped to the last resource, and set at liberty all the slaves old enough to bear arms; and cutting the hair off the womens' heads,[1] made ropes for their engines. Octavius, being informed of their determination, surrounded the town with five encampments, and began to press them at once with a siege and storm. They were determined to endure every hardship, and their greatest distress was the want of corn. They, therefore, sent deputies to Cæsar, and begged a supply from him; all other inconveniences they bore by their own resources, as well as they could: and after a long interval, when the length of the siege had made Octavius's troops more remiss than usual, having got an opportunity at noon, when the enemy were dispersed, they disposed their wives and children on the walls, to keep up the appearance of their usual attention; and forming themselves into one body, with the slaves whom they had lately enfranchised, they made an attack on Octavius's nearest camp, and having forced that, attacked the second with the same fury; and then the third and the fourth, and then the other, and beat them from them all: and having killed a great number, obliged the rest and Octavius himself to fly for refuge to their ships. This put an end to the blockade. Winter was now approaching, and Octavius, despairing of capturing the town, after sustaining such considerable losses, withdrew to Pompey, to Dyrrachium.

CHAP. X.—We have mentioned, that Vibullius Rufus, an officer of Pompey's had fallen twice into Cæsar's power; first at Corfinium, and afterward in Spain. Cæsar. thought him a proper person, on account of his favors conferred on him, to send with proposals to Pompey: and he knew that he had an influence over Pompey. This was the substance of his proposals: "That it was the duty of both, to put an end to their obstinacy, and forbear hostilities, and not tempt fortune any further; that sufficient loss had been suffered on both

[1] We find similar devotion displayed in the siege of Carthage.

sides, to serve as a lesson and instruction to them, to render them apprehensive of future calamities, by Pompey, in having been driven out of Italy, and having lost Sicily, Cardinia, and the two Spains, and one hundred and thirty cohorts of Roman citizens, in Italy and Spain: by himself, in the death of Curio, and the loss of so great an army in Africa, and the surrender of his soldiers in Corcyra. Wherefore, they should have pity on themselves, and the republic: for, from their own misfortunes, they had sufficient experience of what fortune can effect in war. That this was the only time to treat for peace; when each had confidence in his own strength, and both seemed on an equal footing. Since, if fortune showed ever so little favor to either, he who thought himself superior, would not submit to terms of accommodation; nor would be content with an equal division, when he might expect to obtain the whole. That as they could not agree before, the terms of peace ought to be submitted to the senate and people in Rome. That in the mean time, it ought to content the republic and themselves, if they both immediately took oath in a public assembly that they would disband their forces within the three following days. That having divested themselves of the arms and auxiliaries, on which they placed their present confidence, they must both of necessity acquiesce in the decision of the people and senate. To give Pompey the fuller assurance of his intentions, he would dismiss all his forces on the land, even his garrisons.

CHAP. XI.—Vibullius, having received this commission from Cæsar, thought it no less necessary to give Pompey notice of Cæsar's sudden approach, that he might adopt such plans as the circumstance required, than to inform him of Cæsar's message; and therefore continuing his journey by night as well as by day, and taking fresh horses for dispatch, he posted away to Pompey, to inform him that Cæsar was marching toward him with all his forces. Pompey was at this time in Candavia,[1] and was on his march from Macedonia to his winter quarters in Apollonia and Dyrrachium; but surprised at the unexpected news, he determined to go to Apollonia by speedy marches, to prevent Cæsar from becoming master of all the maritime states. But as soon as Cæsar had landed his troops,

[1] Candavia is supposed to have been a district of Macedonia.

he set off the same day for Oricum: when he arrived there, Lucius Torquatus, who was governor of the town by Pompey's appointment, and had a garrison of Parthinians in it, endeavored to shut the gates and defend the town, and ordered the Greeks to man the walls, and to take arms. But as they refused to fight against the power of the Roman people, and as the citizens made a spontaneous attempt to admit Cæsar, despairing of any assistance, he threw open the gates, and surrendered himself and the town to Cæsar, and was preserved safe from injury by him.

CHAP. XII.—Having taken Oricum, Cæsar marched without making any delay to Apollonia. Staberius the governor, hearing of his approach, began to bring water into the citadel, and to fortify it, and to demand hostages of the town's people. But they refuse to give any, or to shut their gates against the consul, or to take upon them to judge contrary to what all Italy and the Roman people had judged. As soon as he knew their inclinations, he made his escape privately. The inhabitants of Apollonia sent embassadors to Cæsar, and gave him admission into their town. Their example was followed by the inhabitants of Bullis,[1] Amantia,[2] and the other neighboring states, and all Epirus: and they sent embassadors to Cæsar, and promised to obey his commands.

CHAP. XIII.—But Pompey having received information of the transactions at Oricum and Apollonia, began to be alarmed for Dyrrachium, and endeavored to reach it, marching day and night. As soon as it was said that Cæsar was approaching, such a panic fell upon Pompey's army, because in his haste he had made no distinction between night and day, and had marched without intermission, that they almost every man deserted their colors in Epirus and the neighboring countries; several threw down their arms, and their march had the appearance of a flight. But when Pompey had halted near Dyrrachium, and had given orders for measuring out the ground for his camp, his army even yet continuing in their fright, Labienus first stepped forward and swore that he would never desert him, and would share whatever fate fortune

[1] Bullis was a town of Macedonia, in the gulf of Venice, nearly opposite to Hydrus in Italy.

[2] Amantia, modern Porto Raguseo, called formerly Abantia, from its having been founded by the Abantes of Eubœa, on their return from Troy.

should assign to him. The other lieutenants took the same oath, and the tribunes and centurions followed their example: and the whole army swore in like manner. Cæsar, finding the road to Dyrrachium already in the possession of Pompey, was in no great haste, but encamped by the river Apsus, in the territory of Apollonia, that the states which had deserved his support might be certain of protection from his out-guards and forts; and there he resolved to wait the arrival of his other legions from Italy, and to winter in tents. Pompey did the same; and pitching his camp on the other side of the river Apsus, collected there all his troops and auxiliaries.

CHAP. XIV.—Kalenus, having put the legions and cavalry on board at Brundusium, as Cæsar had directed him, as far as the number of his ships allowed, weighed anchor: and having sailed a little distance from port, received a letter from Cæsar, in which he was informed, that all the ports and the whole shore was occupied by the enemy's fleet: on receiving this information he returned into the harbor, and recalled all the vessels. One of them, which continued the voyage and did not obey Kalenus's command, because it carried no troops, but was private property, bore away for Oricum, and was taken by Bibulus, who spared neither slaves nor free men, nor even children; but put all to the sword. Thus the safety of the whole army depended on a very short space of time and a great casualty.

CHAP. XV.—Bibulus, as has been observed before, lay with his fleet near Oricum, and as he debarred Cæsar of the liberty of the sea and harbors, so he was deprived of all intercourse with the country by land; for the whole shore was occupied by parties disposed in different places by Cæsar. And he was not allowed to get either wood or water, or even anchor near the land. He was reduced to great difficulties, and distressed with extreme scarcity of every necessary; insomuch that he was obliged to bring, in transports from Corcyra, not only provisions, but even wood and water; and it once happened that, meeting with violent storms, they were forced to catch the dew by night which fell on the hides that covered their decks; yet all these difficulties they bore patiently and without repining, and thought they ought not to leave the shores and harbors free from blockade. But when they were suffering under the distress which I have mentioned, and Libo had joined Bibulus, they both called from on ship-board, to Marcus Acilius and Statius Marcus, the lieutenants, one of whom commanded the town, the other the guards on the coast, that they wished to speak to Cæsar on affairs of importance, if permission should be granted them. They add something further to strengthen the impression that they intended to treat about an accommodation. In the mean time they requested a truce, and obtained it from them; for what they proposed seemed to be of importance, and it was well known that Cæsar desired it above all things, and it was imagined that some advantage would be derived from Bibulus's proposals.

CHAP. XVI.—Cæsar having set out with one legion to gain possession of the more remote states, and to provide corn, of which he had but a small quantity, was at this time at Buthrotum, opposite to Corcyra. There receiving Acilius and Marcus's letters, informing him of Libo's and Bibulus's demands, he left his legion behind him, and returned himself to Oricum. When he arrived, they were invited to a conference. Libo came and made an apology for Bibulus, "that he was a man of strong passion, and had a private quarrel against Cæsar, contracted when he was ædile and prætor; that for this reason he had avoided the conference, lest affairs of the utmost importance and advantage might be impeded by the warmth of his temper. That it now was and ever had been Pompey's most earnest wish, that they should be reconciled and lay down their arms, but they were not authorized to treat on that subject, because they resigned the whole management of the war, and all other matters to Pompey, by order of the council. But when they were acquainted with Cæsar's demands, they would transmit them to Pompey, who would conclude all of himself by their persuasions. In the mean time, let the truce be continued till the messengers could return from him; and let no injury be done on either side." To this he added a few words of the cause for which they fought, and of his own forces and resources.

CHAP. XVII.—To this, Cæsar did not then think proper to make any reply, nor do we now think it worth recording. But Cæsar required "that he should be allowed to send commissioners to Pompey, who should suffer no personal injury; and that either they should grant it, or should take his commissioners in charge, and convey them to Pompey. That as to the truce, the war in its present state was so divided, that they by their fleet deprived him of his shipping and auxiliaries; while he prevented them from the use of the land and fresh water; and if they wished that this restraint should be removed from them, they should relinquish their blockade of the seas, but if they retained the one, he in like manner would retain the other; that nevertheless, the treaty of accommodation might still be carried on, though these points were not conceded, and that they need not be an impediment to it." They would neither receive Cæsar's commissioners, nor guarantee their safety, but referred the whole to Pompey. They urged and struggled eagerly to gain the one point respecting a truce. But when Cæsar perceived that they had proposed the conference merely to avoid present danger and distress, but that they offered no hopes or terms of peace, he applied[1] his thoughts to the prosecution of the war.

CHAP. XVIII.—Bibulus, being prevented from landing for several days, and being seized with a violent distemper from the cold and fatigue, as he could neither be cured on board, nor was willing to desert the charge which he had taken upon him, was unable to bear up against the violence of the disease. On his death, the sole command devolved on no single individual, but each admiral managed his own division separately, and at his own discretion. Vibullius, as soon as the alarm, which Cæsar's unexpected arrival had raised, was over, began again to deliver Cæsar's message in the presence of Libo, Lucius Lucceius, and Theophanes, to whom Pompey used to communicate his most confidential secrets. He had scarcely entered on the subject when Pompey interrupted him, and forbade him to proceed. "What need," says he, "have I of life or Rome, if the world shall think I enjoy them by the bounty of Cæsar: an opinion which can never be removed while it shall be thought that I have been brought back by him to Italy, from which I set out." After the conclusion of the war, Cæsar was informed of these expressions by some persons who were present at the conversation. He attempted, however, by other means to bring about a negotiation of peace.

CHAP. XIX.—Between Pompey's and Cæsar's camp there was only the river Apsus, and the soldiers frequently conversed with each other; and by a private arrangement among them-

[1] Literally, "he betook himself to forming plans for the rest of the war."

selves, no weapons were thrown during their conferences. Cæsar sent Publius Vatinius, one of his lieutenants, to the bank of the river, to make such proposals as should appear most conducive to peace; and to cry out frequently with a loud voice [asking], "Are citizens permitted to send deputies to citizens to treat of peace? a concession which had been made even to fugitives on the Pyrenean mountains, and to robbers, especially when by so doing they would prevent citizens from fighting against citizens." Having spoken much in humble language, as became a man pleading for his own and the general safety and being listened to with silence by the soldiers of both armies, he received an answer from the enemy's party that Aulus Varro proposed coming the next day to a conference, and that deputies from both sides might come without danger, and explain their wishes, and accordingly a fixed time was appointed for the interview. When the deputies met the next day, a great multitude from both sides assembled, and the expectations of every person concerning this subject were raised very high, and their minds seemed to be eagerly disposed for peace. Titus Labienus walked forward from the crowd, and in submissive terms began to speak of peace, and to argue with Vatinius. But their conversation was suddenly interrupted by darts thrown from all sides, from which Vatinius escaped by being protected by the arms of the soldiers. However, several were wounded; and among them Cornelius Balbus, Marcus Plotius, and Lucius Tiburtius, centurions, and some privates; hereupon Labienus exclaimed, "Forbear, then, to speak any more about an accommodation, for we can have no peace unless we carry Cæsar's head back with us."

CHAP. XX.—At the same time in Rome, Marcus Cælius Rufus, one of the prætors, having undertaken the cause of the debtors, on entering into his office, fixed his tribunal near the bench of Caius Trebonius, the city prætor, and promised if any person appealed to him in regard to the valuation and payment of debts made by arbitration, as appointed by Cæsar when in Rome, that he would relieve them. But it happened, from the justice of Trebonius's decrees and his humanity (for he thought that in such dangerous times justice should be administered with moderation and compassion), that not one could be found who would offer himself the first to lodge an appeal. For to plead poverty, to complain of his own private calamities, or the general distresses of the times, or to assert the difficulty of setting the goods to sale, is the behavior of a man even of a moderate temper; but to retain their possessions entire, and at the same time acknowledge themselves in debt, what sort of spirit, and what impudence would it not have argued! Therefore nobody was found so unreasonable as to make such demands. But Cælius proved more severe to those very persons for whose advantage it had been designed; and starting from this beginning, in order that he might not appear to have engaged in so dishonorable an affair without effecting something, he promulgated a law that all debts should be discharged in six equal payments, of six months each, without interest.

CHAP. XXI.—When Servilius, the consul, and the other magistrates opposed him, and he himself effected less than he expected, in order to raise the passions of the people, he dropped it, and promulgated two others; one, by which he remitted the annual rents of the houses to the tenants, the other, an act of insolvency: upon which the mob made an assault on Caius Trebonius, and having wounded several persons, drove him from his tribunal. The consul Servilius informed the senate of his proceedings, who passed a decree that Cælius should be removed from the management of the republic. Upon this decree, the consul forbade him the senate; and when he was attempting to harangue the people, turned him out of the rostrum. Stung with the ignominy and with resentment, he pretended in public that he would go to Cæsar, but privately sent messengers to Milo, who had murdered Clodius, and had been condemned for it; and having invited him into Italy, because he had engaged the remains of the gladiators to his interest, by making them ample presents, he joined him, and sent him to Thurinum to tamper with the shepherds. When he himself was on his road to Casilinum, at the same time that his military standards and arms were seized at Capua, his slaves seen at Naples, and the design of betraying the town discovered: his plots being revealed, and Capua shut against him, being apprehensive of danger, because the Roman citizens residing there had armed themselves, and thought he ought to be treated as an enemy to the state, he abandoned his first design, and changed his route.

CHAP. XXII.—Milo in the mean time dispatched letters to the free towns, purporting that he acted as he did by the orders and commands of Pompey, conveyed to him by Bibulus: and he endeavored to engage in his interest all persons whom he imagined were under difficulties by reason of their debts. But not being able to prevail with them, he set at liberty some slaves from the work-houses, and begant to assault Cosa in the district of Thurinum. There having received a blow of a stone thrown from the wall of the town which was commanded by Quintus Pedius with one legion, he died of it; and Cælius having set out, as he pretended for Cæsar, went to Thurii, where he was put to death as he was tampering with some of the freemen of the town, and was offering money to Cæsar's Gallic and Spanish horse, which he had sent there to strengthen the garrison. And thus these mighty beginnings, which had embroiled Italy, and kept the magistrates employed, found a speedy and happy issue.

CHAP. XXIII.—Libo having sailed from Oricum,[1] with a fleet of fifty ships, which he commanded, came to Brundusium, and seized an island, which lies opposite to the harbor; judging it better to guard that place, which was our only pass to sea, than to keep all the shores and ports blocked up by a fleet. By his sudden arrival, he fell in with some of our transports, and set them on fire, and carried off one laden with corn; he struck great terror into our men, and having in the night landed a party of soldiers and archers, he beat our guard of horse from their station, and gained so much by the advantage of situation, that he dispatched letters to Pompey, and if he pleased he might order the rest of the ships to be hauled upon shore and repaired; for that with his own fleet he could prevent Cæsar from receiving his auxiliaries.

CHAP. XXIV.—Antonius was at this time at Brundusium, and relying on the valor of his troops, covered about sixty of the long-boats belonging to the men-of-war with penthouses and bulwarks of hurdles, and put on board them select soldiers; and disposed them separately along the shore: and under the pretext of keeping the seamen in exercise, he ordered two three-banked galleys, which he had built at Brundusium, to row to the mouth of the port. When Libo saw them advancing

[1] Oricum, modern Ericho, a town of Macedon, founded by the Abantes, and surnamed Dardania, because Helenus and Andromache reigned there for some time after the fall of Troy.

boldly toward him, he sent five four-banked galleys against them, in hopes of intercepting them. When these came near our ships, our veteran soldiers retreated within the harbor. The enemy, urged by their eagerness to capture them, pursued them unguardedly: for instantly the boats of Antonius, on a certain signal, rowed with great violence from all parts against the enemy; and at the first charge took one of the four-banked galleys, with the seamen and marines, and forced the rest to flee disgracefully. In addition to this loss, they were prevented from getting water by the horse which Antonius had disposed along the sea-coast. Libo, vexed at the distress and disgrace, departed from Brundusium, and abandoned the blockade.

CHAP. XXV.—Several months had now elapsed, and winter was almost gone, and Cæsar's legions and shipping were not coming to him from Brundusium, and he imagined that some opportunities had been neglected, for the winds had at least been often favorable, and he thought that he must trust to them at last. And the longer it was deferred, the more eager were those who commanded Pompey's fleet to guard the coast, and were more confident of preventing our getting assistance: they received frequent reproofs from Pompey by letter, that as they had not prevented Cæsar's arrival at the first, they should at least stop the remainder of his army: and they were expecting that the season for transporting troops, would become more unfavorable every day, as the winds grew calmer.[1] Cæsar, feeling some trouble on this account, wrote in severe terms to his officers at Brundusium, [and gave them orders] that as soon as they found the wind to answer, they should not let the opportunity of setting sail pass by, if they were even to steer their course to the shore of Apollonia: because there they might run their ships on ground. That these parts principally were left unguarded by the enemy's fleet, because they dare not venture too far from the harbor.

CHAP. XXVI.—They [his officers], exerting boldness and courage, aided by the instructions of Marcus Antonius, and Fusius Kalenus, and animated by the soldiers strongly encourag-

[1] Plutarch, Appian, Val. Maximus, and Suetonius, say that it was on this occasion that Cæsar in disguise went into a boat to cross over, and when the rowers, in consequence of a storm wished to return, said, "be bold, fear nothing, you carry Cæsar and his fortunes."

ing them, and declining no danger for Cæsar's safety, having got a southerly wind, weighed anchor, and the next day were carried past Apollonia and Dyrrachium, and being seen from the continent, Quintus Coponius, who commanded the Rhodian fleet at Dyrrachium, put out of the port with his ships; and when they had almost come up with us, in consequence of the breeze dying away, the south wind sprang up afresh, and rescued us. However, he did not desist from his attempt, but hoped by the labor and perseverance of his seamen to be able to bear up against the violence of the storm; and although we were carried beyond Dyrrachium, by the violence of the wind, he nevertheless continued to chase us. Our men, taking advantage of fortune's kindness, for they were still afraid of being attacked by the enemy's fleet, if the wind abated, having come near a port, called Nymphæum, about three miles beyond Lissus, put into it (this port is protected from a south-west wind, but is not secure against a south wind); and thought less danger was to be apprehended from the storm than from the enemy. But as soon as they were within the port, the south wind, which had blown for two days, by extraordinary good luck veered round to the south-west.

Chap. XXVII.—Here one might observe the sudden turns of fortune. We who, a moment before, were alarmed for ourselves, were safely lodged in a very secure harbor: and they who had threatened ruin to our fleet, were forced to be uneasy on their own account: and thus, by a change of circumstances, the storm protected our ships, and damaged the Rhodian fleet to such a degree that all their decked ships, sixteen in number, foundered, without exception, and were wrecked: and of the prodigious number of seamen and soldiers, some lost their lives by being dashed against the rocks, others were taken by our men: but Cæsar sent them all safe home.

Chap. XXVIII.—Two of our ships, that had not kept up with the rest, being overtaken by the night, and not knowing what port the rest had made to, came to an anchor opposite Lissus.[1] Otacilius Crassus, who commanded Pompey's fleet, detached after them several barges and small craft, and at-

[1] Lissus, modern Alessio, a city of Illyricum, situated near the mouth of the Drino. It was the most southern city of Illyricum, and was defended by strong fortifications, said to have been built by Dionysius, tyrant of Syracuse.

tempted to take them. At the same time, he treated with them about capitulating, and promised them their lives if they would surrender. One of them carried two hundred and twenty recruits, the other was manned with somewhat less than two hundred veterans. Here it might be seen what security men derive from a resolute spirit. For the recruits, frightened at the number of vessels, and fatigued with the rolling of the sea, and with sea-sickness, surrendered to Otacilius, after having first received his oath, that the enemy would not injure them; but as soon as they were brought before him, contrary to the obligation of his oath, they were inhumanly put to death in his presence. But the soldiers of the veteran legion, who had also struggled, not only with the inclemency of the weather, but by laboring at the pump, thought it their duty to remit nothing of their former valor: and having protracted the beginning of the night in settling the terms, under pretense of surrendering, they obliged the pilot to run the ship aground: and having got a convenient place on the shore, they spent the rest of the night there, and at day-break, when Otacilius had sent against them a party of the horse, who guarded that part of the coast, to the number of four hundred, beside some armed men, who had followed them from the garrison, they made a brave defense, and having killed some of them, retreated in safety to our army.

CHAP. XXIX.—After this action, the Roman citizens, who resided at Lissus, a town which Cæsar had before assigned them, and had carefully fortified, received Antony into their town, and gave him every assistance. Otacilius, apprehensive for his own safety, escaped out of the town, and went to Pompey. All his forces, whose number amounted to three veteran legions, and one of recruits, and about eight hundred horse being landed, Antony sent most of his ships back to Italy, to transport the remainder of the soldiers and horse. The pontons, which are a sort of Gallic ships, he left at Lissus with this object, that if Pompey, imagining Italy defenseless, should transport his army thither (and this notion was spread among the common people), Cæsar might have some means of pursuing him; and he sent messengers to him with great dispatch, to inform him in what part of the country he had landed his army, and what number of troops he had brought over with him.

CHAP. XXX.—Cæsar and Pompey received this intelligence

almost at the same time; for they had seen the ships sail past Apollonia and Dyrrachium. They directed their march after them by land; but at first they were ignorant to what part they had been carried; but when they were informed of it, they each adopted a different plan; Cæsar, to form a junction with Antonius as soon as possible; Pompey, to oppose Antonius's forces on their march to Cæsar, and, if possible, to fall upon them unexpectedly from ambush. And the same day they both led out their armies from their winter encampment along the river Apsus; Pompey, privately by night; Cæsar, openly by day. But Cæsar had to march a longer circuit up the river to find a ford. Pompey's route being easy, because he was not obliged to cross the river, he advanced rapidly and by forced marches against Antonius, and being informed of his approach, chose a convenient situation, where he posted his forces; and kept his men close within camp, and forbade fires to be kindled, that his arrival might be the more secret. An account of this was immediately carried to Antonius by the Greeks. He dispatched messengers to Cæsar, and confined himself in his camp for one day. The next day Cæsar, came up with him. On learning his arrival, Pompey, to prevent his being hemmed in between two armies, quitted his position, and went with all his forces to Asparagium,[1] in the territory of Dyrrachium, and there encamped in a convenient situation.

Chap. XXXI.—During these times, Scipio, though he had sustained some losses near mount Amanus,[2] had assumed to himself the title of imperator, after which he demanded large sums of money from the states and princes. He had also exacted from the tax-gatherers, two years' rents that they owed; and enjoined them to lend him the amount of the next

[1] Asparagium, a town of Greece, situated on the southern bank of the river Apsus, the modern Crevesta.

[2] Amanus Mons, *Lockham*, or *Alma Daghy*, is a spur of Mount Taurus, which quits the main ridge on the borders of Cilicia, and terminates on the coast of the Mediterranean, a little above the mouth of the Orontes. It forms the great passes leading into Asia Minor, one of which, between it and the sea, was called Syriæ Pylæ, *Saggal Doutan;* the other leading into the interior of the country, was known as the Amanidæ Pylæ, and has left its name in the neighboring town of *Bylan:* they are rendered very interesting from the maneuvers of Alexander and Darius, previous to the fatal battle of Issus.—Arrowsmith's Ancient Geography.

year, and demanded a supply of horse from the whole province. When they were collected, leaving behind him his neighboring enemies, the Parthians (who shortly before had killed Marcus Crassus, the imperator, and had kept Marcus Bibulus besieged), he drew his legions and cavalry out of Syria; and when he came into the province, which was under great anxiety and fear of the Parthian war,[1] and heard some declarations of the soldiers, "That they would march against an enemy, if he would lead them on; but would never bear arms against a countryman and consul;" he drew off his legions to winter quarters to Pergamus, and the most wealthy cities, and made them rich presents: and in order to attach them more firmly to his interest, permitted them to plunder the cities.

CHAP. XXXII.—In the mean time, the money which had been demanded from the province at large, was most vigorously exacted. Besides, many new imposts of different kinds were

[1] On the formation of the first triumvirate, Syria and the Parthian war were assigned to Crassus, Gaul and Germany to Cæsar, Hither and Further Spain to Pompey. (Livy, Epitome of the 105th book.) Crassus crossed the Euphrates, and after a series of unfortunate maneuvers, was betrayed by his allies, and completely defeated at the battle of Carrhæ (A. U. C. 701). Crassus, with such of his troops as escaped the slaughter, occupied a hill; the Parthians being apprehensive lest he should escape, enticed him to a conference. Crassus perceiving their treachery when it was too late, and spurning the idea of falling into the hands of the enemy, fought bravely, and at length, after an obstinate struggle, fell sword in hand. Livy mentions that the name of the Parthian general on this occasion was Surena, while other writers state it was Monæses; these apparent discrepnacies are reconciled by supposing that Surena was the honorary title given by the Parthians to their commander-in-chief. The Parthians, after the defeat of Crassus, invaded Syria, but were driven back with great loss by Caius Cassius, Crassus's quæstor. We learn, from the Epitome of the 127th book of Livy, that the Parthians took advantage of the disastrous wars that occurred after the assassination of Cæsar, and invaded Syria. They were commanded on this occasion by Labienus, the son of that Labienus of whom so frequent and so honorable mention has been made in the Gallic war, who, when the civil war broke out between Cæsar and Pompey, espoused the party of the latter, and survived the defeat of Pharsalia to fall on the plains of Munda. Young Labienus was an ardent supporter of Brutus and Cassius, and after the decisive battle of Philippi, fled to the Parthians. The invading army was at first successful, and after defeating Decidius Saxa, Mark Antony's lieutenant, occupied the whole of Syria. Their triumph, however, was of short duration; they were subsequently defeated in a most signal manner by Publius Ventidius, another of Antony's lieutenants (on which occasion Labienus was slain), and driven out of Syria.

devised to gratify his avarice. A tax of so much a head was laid on every slave and child. Columns, doors, corn, soldiers, sailors, arms, engines, and carriages, were made subject to a duty. Wherever a name could be found for any thing, it was deemed a sufficient reason for levying money on it. Officers were appointed to collect it, not only in the cities, but in almost every village and fort: and whosoever of them acted with the greatest rigor and inhumanity, was esteemed the best man, and best citizen. The province was overrun with bailiffs and officers, and crowded with overseers and tax-gatherers; who, besides the duties imposed, exacted a gratuity for themselves; for they asserted, that being expelled from their own homes and countries, they stood in need of every necessary; endeavoring by a plausible pretense, to color the most infamous conduct. To this was added the most exorbitant interest, as usually happens in times of war; the whole sums being called in, on which occasion, they alleged that the delay of a single day was a donation. Therefore, in those two years, the debt of the province was doubled: but notwithstanding, taxes were exacted, not only from the Roman citizens, but from every corporation and every state. And they said that these were loans, exacted by the senate's decree. The taxes of the ensuing year were demanded beforehand as a loan from the collectors, as on their first appointment.

Chap. XXXIII.—Moreover, Scipio ordered the money formerly lodged in the temple of Diana at Ephesus,[1] to be taken out with the statues of that goddess, which remained there. When Scipio came to the temple, letters were delivered to him from Pompey, in the presence of several senators, whom he had called upon to attend him; [informing him] that Cæsar had crossed the sea with his legions; that Scipio should hasten to him with his army, and postpone all other business. As soon as he received the letter, he dismissed his attendants, and began to prepare for his journey to Macedonia; and a few

[1] Ephesus, Aiosolue, a famous city of Ionia, in Asia Minor, situated near the mouth of the river Cayster, the *Little Mendere*. The temple of Diana at Ephesus, 425 feet long and 220 feet broad, was distinguished for its architectural beauties, as well as its vast size. The roof was supported by 127 marble pillars, sixty feet high. It was considered one of the seven wonders of the world, and 220 years are said to have elapsed between its foundation and completion. It was burned by Eratostratus to immortalize his memory on the night in which Alexander was born.

days after set out. This circumstance saved the money at Ephesus.

CHAP. XXXIV.—Cæsar, having effected a junction with Antonius's army, and having drawn his legion out of Oricum, which he had left there to guard the coast, thought he ought to sound the inclination of the provinces, and march further into the country; and when embassadors came to him from Thessaly and Ætolia, to engage that the states in those countries would obey his orders, if he sent a garrison to protect them, he dispatched Lucius Cassius Longinus, with the twenty-seventh, a legion composed of young soldiers, and two hundred horse, to Thessaly: and Caius Calvisius Sabinus, with five cohorts, and a small party of horse, into Ætolia. He recommended them to be especially careful to provide corn, because those regions were nearest to him. He ordered Cneius Domitius Calvinus to march into Macedonia with two legions, the eleventh and twelfth, and five hundred horse; from which province, Menedemus, the principal man of those regions, on that side which is called the Free, having come as embassador, assured him of the most devoted affection of all his subjects.

CHAP. XXXV. Of these Calvisius, on his first arrival in Ætolia, being very kindly received, dislodged the enemy's garrisons in Calydon and Naupactus, and made himself master of the whole country. Cassius went to Thessaly with his legion. As there were two factions there, he found the citizens divided in their inclinations. Hegasaretus, a man of established power, favored Pompey's interest. Petreius, a young man of a most noble family, warmly supported Cæsar with his own and his friends' influence.

CHAP. XXXVI.—At the same time, Domitius arrived in Macedonia: and when numerous embassies had begun to wait on him from many of the states, news was brought that Scipio was approaching with his legions, which occasioned various opinions and reports; for in strange events, rumor generally goes before. Without making any delay in any part of Macedonia, he marched with great haste against Domitius; and when he was come within about twenty miles of him, wheeled on a sudden toward Cassius Longinus in Thessaly. He effected this with such celerity, that news of his march and arrival came together; for to render his march expeditious, he left the baggage of his legions behind him at the river Haliacmon, which divides Macedonia from Thessaly, under the care of Marcus Favonius, with a guard of eight cohorts, and ordered him to build a strong fort there. At the same time, Cotus's cavalry, which used to infest the neighborhood of Macedonia, flew to attack Cassius's camp, at which Cassius being alarmed, and having received information of Scipio's approach, and seen the horse, which he imagined to be Scipio's, he betook himself to the mountains that environ Thessaly, and thence began to make his route toward Ambracia.[1] But when Scipio was hastening to pursue him, dispatches overtook him from Favonius, that Domitius was marching against him with his legions, and that he could not maintain the garrison over which he was appointed, without Scipio's assistance. On receipt of these dispatches, Scipio changed his designs and his route, desisted from his pursuit of Cassius, and hastened to relieve Favonius. Accordingly, continuing his march day and night, he came to him so opportunely, that the dust raised by Domitius's army, and Scipio's advanced guard, were observed at the same instant. Thus, the vigilance of Domitius saved Cassius, and the expedition of Scipio, Favonius.

CHAP. XXXVII.—Scipio, having staid for two days in his camp, along the river Haliacmon, which ran between him and Domitius's camp, on the third day, at dawn, led his army across a ford, and having made a regular encampment the day following, drew up his forces in front of his camp. Domitius thought he ought not to show any reluctance, but should draw out his forces and hazard a battle. But as there was a plain six miles in breadth between the two camps, he posted his army before Scipio's camp; while the latter persevered in not quitting his intrenchment. However, Domitius with difficulty restrained his men, and prevented their beginning a battle; the more so as a rivulet with steep banks, joining Scipio's camp, retarded the progress of our men. When Scipio perceived the eagerness and alacrity of our troops to engage, suspecting that he should be obliged the next day, either to fight, against his inclination, or to incur great disgrace by keeping within his camp, though he had come

[1] Ambracia, a town of Epirus, founded by a Corinthian colony; it gave a name to the Sinus Ambracius, *Gulf of Arta.*]

with high expectation, yet by advancing rashly, made a shameful end; and at night crossed the river, without even giving the signal for breaking up the camp, and returned to the ground from which he came, and there encamped near the river, on an elevated situation. After a few days, he placed a party of horse in ambush in the night, where our men had usually gone to forage for several days before. And when Quintus Varus, commander of Domitius's horse, came there as usual, they suddenly rushed from their ambush. But our men bravely supported their charge, and returned quickly every man to his own rank, and in their turn, made a general charge on the enemy; and having killed about eighty of them, and put the rest to flight, retreated to their camp with the loss of only two men.

CHAP. XXXVIII.—After these transactions, Domitius, hoping to allure Scipio to a battle, pretended to be obliged to change his position through want of corn, and having given the signal for decamping, advanced about three miles, and posted his army and cavalry in a convenient place, concealed from the enemy's view. Scipio being in readiness to pursue him, detached his cavalry and a considerable number of light infantry to explore Domitius's route. When they had marched a short way, and their foremost troops were within reach of our ambush, their suspicions being raised by the neighing of the horses, they began to retreat: and the rest who followed them, observing with what speed they retreated, made a halt. Our men, perceiving that the enemy had discovered their plot, and thinking it in vain to wait for any more, having got two troops in their power, intercepted them. Among them was Marcus Opimius, general of the horse, but he made his escape: they either killed or took prisoners all the rest of these two troops, and brought them to Domitius.

CHAP. XXXIX.—Cæsar, having drawn his garrisons out of the sea-ports, as before mentioned, left three cohorts at Oricum to protect the town, and committed to them the charge of his ships of war, which he had transported from Italy. Acilius, as lieutenant-general, had the charge of this duty and the command of the town; he drew the ships into the inner part of the harbor, behind the town, and fastened them to the shore, and sank a merchant-ship in the mouth of the harbor to block it up; and near it he fixed another at anchor, on which he raised a turret, and faced it to the entrance of the port, and filled it with soldiers, and ordered them to keep guard against any sudden attack.

CHAP. XL.—Cneius, Pompey's son, who commanded the Egyptian fleet, having got intelligence of these things, came to Oricum, and weighed up the ship, that had been sunk, with a windlass, and by straining at it with several ropes, and attacked the other which had been placed by Acilius to watch the port with several ships, on which he had raised very high turrets, so that fighting as it were from an eminence, and sending fresh men constantly to relieve the fatigued, and at the same time attempting the town on all sides by land, with ladders and his fleet, in order to divide the force of his enemies, he overpowered our men by fatigue, and the immense number of darts, and took the ship, having beat off the men that were put on board to defend it, who, however, made their escape in small boats; and at the same time he seized a natural mole on the opposite side, which almost formed an island over against the town. He carried over land, into the inner part of the harbor, four galleys, by putting rollers under them, and driving them on with levers. Then attacking on both sides the ships of war which were moored to the shore, and were not manned, he carried off four of them, and set the rest on fire. After dispatching this business, he left Decimus Lælius, whom he had taken away from the command of the Asiatic fleet, to hinder provisions from being brought into the town from Biblis and Amantia, and went himself to Lissus, where he attacked thirty merchantmen, left within the port by Antonius, and set them on fire. He attempted to storm Lissus, but being delayed three days by the vigorous defense of the Roman citizens who belonged to that district, and of the soldiers which Cæsar had sent to keep garrison there, and having lost a few men in the assault, he returned without effecting his object.

CHAP. XLI.—As soon as Cæsar heard that Pompey was at Asparagium, he set out for that place with his army, and having taken the capital of the Parthinians on his march, where there was a garrison of Pompey's, he reached Pompey in Macedonia, on the third day, and encamped beside him; and the day following, having drawn out all his forces before his camp, he offered Pompey battle. But perceiving that he kept within his trenches, he led his army back to his camp, and thought of pursuing some other plan. Accordingly, the day following, he set out with all his forces by a long circuit, through a difficult and narrow road to Dyrrachium; hoping, either that Pompey would be compelled to follow him to Dyrrachium, or that his communication with it might be cut off, because he had deposited there all his provisions and material of war. And so it happened; for Pompey, at first not knowing his design, because he imagined he had taken a route in a different direction from that country, thought that the scarcity of provisions had obliged him to shift his quarters; but having afterward got true intelligence from his scouts, he decamped the day following, hoping to prevent him by taking a shorter road; which Cæsar suspecting might happen, encouraged his troops to submit cheerfully to the fatigue, and having halted a very small part of the night, he arrived early in the morning at Dyrrachium, when the van of Pompey's army was visible at a distance, and there he encamped.

CHAP. XLII.—Pompey, being cut off from Dyrrachium, as he was unable to effect his purpose, took a new resolution, and intrenched himself strongly on a rising ground, which is called Petra, where ships of a small size can come in, and be sheltered from some winds. Here he ordered a part of his men of war to attend him, and corn and provisions to be brought from Asia, and from all the countries of which he kept possession. Cæsar, imagining that the war would be protracted to too great a length, and despairing of his convoys from Italy, because all the coasts were guarded with great diligence by Pompey's adherents; and because his own fleets, which he had built during the winter, in Sicily, Gaul, and Italy, were detained; sent Lucius Canuleius into Epirus to procure corn; and because these countries were too remote, he fixed granaries in certain places, and regulated the carriage of the corn for the neighboring states. He likewise gave directions that search should be made for whatever corn was in Lissus, the country of the Parthini, and all the places of strength. The quantity was very small, both from the nature of the land (for the country is rough and mountainous, and the people commonly import what grain they use); and because Pompey had foreseen what would happen, and some days before had plundered the Parthini, and having ravaged and dug up their houses, carried off all the corn, which he collected by means of his horse.

CHAP. XLIII.—Cæsar, on being informed of these transactions, pursued measures suggested by the nature of the country. For round Pompey's camps there were several high and rough hills. These he first of all occupied with guards, and raised strong forts on them. Then drawing a fortification from one fort to another, as the nature of each position allowed, he began to draw a line of circumvallation round Pompey, with these views; as he had but a small quantity of corn, and Pompey was strong in cavalry, that he might furnish his army with corn and other necessaries from all sides with less danger; secondly, to prevent Pompey from foraging, and thereby render his horse ineffectual in the operations of the war; and thirdly, to lessen his reputation, on which he saw he depended greatly, among foreign nations, when a report should have spread throughout the world that he was blockaded by Cæsar, and dare not hazard a battle.

CHAP. XLIV.—Neither was Pompey willing to leave the sea and Dyrrachium, because he had lodged his material there, his weapons, arms, and engines; and supplied his army with corn from it by his ships; nor was he able to put a stop to Cæsar's works without hazarding a battle, which at that time he had determined not to do. Nothing was left but to adopt the last resource, namely, to possess himself of as many hills as he could, and cover as great an extent of country as possible with his troops, and divide Cæsar's forces as much as possible; and so it happened: for having raised twenty-four forts, and taken in a compass of fifteen miles, he got forage in this space, and within this circuit there were several fields lately sown, in which the cattle might feed in the mean time. And as our men, who had completed their works by drawing lines of communication from one fort to another, were afraid that Pompey's men would sally out from some part, and attack us in the rear; so the enemy were making a continued fortification in a circuit within ours to prevent us from breaking in on any side, or surrounding them on the rear. But they completed their works first; both because they had a greater number of men, and because they had a smaller compass to inclose. When Cæsar attempted to gain any place, though Pompey had resolved not to oppose him with his whole force, or to come to a general engagement, yet he detached to particular places slingers and archers, with which his army abounded, and several of our men were wounded, and filled with great dread of the arrows; and almost all the soldiers made coats or coverings for themselves of hair cloths, tarpaulins, or raw hides to defend them against the weapons.

CHAP. XLV.—In seizing the posts, each exerted his utmost power. Cæsar, to confine Pompey within as narrow a compass as possible; Pompey, to occupy as many hills as he could in as large a circuit as possible, and several skirmishes were fought in consequence of it. In one of these, when Cæsar's ninth legion had gained a certain post, and had begun to fortify it, Pompey possessed himself of a hill near to and opposite the same place, and endeavored to annoy the men while at work; and as the approach on one side was almost level, he first surrounded it with archers and slingers, and afterward by detaching a strong party of light infantry, and using his engines, he stopped our works; and it was no easy matter for our men at once to defend themselves, and to proceed with their fortifications. When Cæsar perceived that his troops were wounded from all sides, he determined to retreat and give up the post; his retreat was down a precipice, on which account they pushed on with more spirit, and would not allow us to retire, because they imagined that we resigned the place through fear. It is reported that Pompey said that day in triumph to his friends about him, "That he would consent to be accounted a general of no experience, if Cæsar's legions effected a retreat without considerable loss from that ground into which they had rashly advanced."

CHAP. XLVI.—Cæsar, being uneasy about the retreat of his soldiers, ordered hurdles to be carried to the further side of the hill, and to be placed opposite to the enemy, and behind them a trench of a moderate breadth to be sunk by his soldiers under shelter of the hurdles; and the ground to be made as difficult as possible. He himself disposed slingers in convenient places to cover our men in their retreat. These things being completed, he ordered his legions to file off. Pompey's men insultingly and boldly pursued and chased us, leveling the hurdles that were thrown up in the front of our works, in order to pass over the trench. Which as soon as Cæsar perceived, being afraid that his men would appear not to retreat, but to be repulsed, and that greater loss might be sustained, when his men were almost half way down the hill, he encouraged them by Antonius, who commanded that legion, ordered the signal of battle to be sounded, and a charge to be made on the enemy. The soldiers of the ninth legion suddenly closing their files, threw their javelins, and advancing impetuously from the low ground up the steep, drove Pompey's men precipitately before them, and obliged them to turn their backs; but their retreat was greatly impeded by the hurdles that lay in a long line before them, and the palisadoes which were in their way, and the trenches that were sunk. But our men being contented to retreat without injury, having killed several of the enemy, and lost but five of their own, very quietly retired, and having seized some other hills somewhat on this side of that place, completed their fortifications.

CHAP. XLVII.—This method of conducting a war was new and unusual, as well on account of the number of forts, the extent and greatness of the works, and the manner of attack and defense, as on account of other circumstances. For all who have attempted to besiege any person, have attacked the enemy when they were frightened or weak, or after a defeat; or have been kept in fear of some attack, when they themselves have had a superior force both of foot and horse. Besides, the usual design of a siege is to cut off the enemy's supplies. On the contrary, Cæsar, with an inferior force, was inclosing troops sound and unhurt, and who had abundance of all things. For there arrived every day a prodigious number of ships, which brought them provisions: nor could the wind blow from any point, that would not be favorable to some of them. Whereas, Cæsar, having consumed all the corn far and near, was in very great distress, but his soldiers bore all with uncommon patience. For they remembered that they lay under the same difficulties last year[1] in Spain, and yet by labor and patience had concluded a dangerous war. They recollected too that they had suffered an alarming scarcity at Alesia, and a much greater at Avaricum, and yet had returned victorious over mighty nations. They refused neither barley nor pulse when offered them, and they held in great esteem cattle, of which they got great quantities from Epirus.

CHAP. XLVIII.—There was a sort of root, called chara,

[1] When encamped near Ilerda.

discovered by the troops which served under Valerius. This they mixed up with milk, and it greatly contributed to relieve their want. They made it into a sort of bread. They had great plenty of it; loaves made of this, when Pompey's men upbraided ours with want, they frequently threw among them to damp their hopes.

CHAP. XLIX.—The corn was now beginning to ripen, and their hope supported their want, as they were confident of having abundance in a short time. And there were frequently heard declarations of the soldiers on guard, in discourse with each other, that they would rather live on the bark of the trees, than let Pompey escape from their hands. For they were often told by deserters, that they could scarcely maintain their horses, and that their other cattle was dead: that they themselves were not in good health from their confinement within so narrow a compass, from the noisome smell, the number of carcasses, and the constant fatigue to them, being men unaccustomed to work, and laboring under a great want of water. For Cæsar had either turned the course of all the rivers and streams which ran to the sea, or had dammed them up with strong works. And as the country was mountainous, and the valleys narrow at the bottom, he inclosed them with piles sunk in the ground, and heaped up mold against them to keep in the water. They were therefore obliged to search for low and marshy grounds, and to sink wells, and they had this labor in addition to their daily works. And even these springs were at a considerable distance from some of their posts, and soon dried up with the heat. But Cæsar's army enjoyed perfect health and abundance of water, and had plenty of all sorts of provisions except corn; and they had a prospect of better times approaching, and saw greater hopes laid before them by the ripening of the grain.

CHAP. L.—In this new kind of war, new methods of managing it were invented by both generals. Pompey's men, perceiving by our fires at night, at what part of the works our cohorts were on guard, coming silently upon them discharged their arrows at random among the whole multitude, and instantly retired to their camp; as a remedy against which our men were taught by experience to light their fires in one place, and keep guard in another.[1]

[1] The last two words, "alio excubarent," are wanting in all the manu-

* * * * * * *

CHAP. LI.—In the mean time, Publius Sylla, whom Cæsar at his departure had left governor of his camp, came up with two legions to assist the cohort; upon whose arrival Pompey's forces were easily repulsed. Nor did they stand the sight and charge of our men, and the foremost falling, the rest turned their backs and quitted the field. But Sylla called our men in from the pursuit, lest their ardor should carry them too far, but most people imagine that if he had consented to a vigorous pursuit, the war might have been ended that day. His conduct however does not appear to deserve censure; for the duties of a lieutenant-general, and of a commander-in-chief, are very different; the one is bound to act entirely according to his instructions, the other to regulate his conduct without control, as occasion requires. Sylla, being deputed by Cæsar to take care of the camp, and having rescued his men, was satisfied with that, and did not desire to hazard a battle (although this circumstance might probably have had a successful issue), that he might not be thought to have assumed the part of the general. One circumstance laid the Pompeians under great difficulty in making good a retreat: for they had advanced from disadvantageous ground, and were posted on the top of a hill. If they attempted to retire down the steep, they dreaded the pursuit of our men from the rising ground, and there was but a short time till sunset: for in hopes of completing the business, they had protracted the battle almost till night. Taking therefore measures suited to their exigency, and to the shortness of the time, Pompey possessed himself of an eminence, at such a distance from our fort that no weapon discharged from an engine could reach him. Here he took up a position, and fortified it, and kept all his forces there.

CHAP. LII.—At the same time, there were engagements in two other places; for Pompey had attacked several forts at once, in order to divide our forces; that no relief might be sent from the neighboring posts. In one place, Volcatius Tullus sustained the charge of a legion with three cohorts, and beat them off the field. In another, the Germans, having

scripts, and appeared to have been added by Aldus. There can be no doubt that some of the original is here lost, as the cause of the unaccountable absence of Cæsar and the commencement of the sally made by Pompey's soldiers, are not recorded.

sallied over our fortifications, slew several of the enemy, and retreated safe to our camp.

CHAP. LIII.—Thus six engagements having happened in one day, three at Dyrrachium, and three at the fortifications, when a computation was made of the number of slain, we found that about two thousand fell on Pompey's side, several of them volunteer veterans and centurions. Among them was Valerius, the son of Lucius Flaccus, who as prætor had formerly had the government of Asia, and six military standards were taken. Of our men, not more than twenty were missing in all the action. But in the fort, not a single soldier escaped without a wound; and in one cohort, four centurions lost their eyes. And being desirous to produce testimony of the fatigue they underwent, and the danger they sustained, they counted to Cæsar about thirty thousand arrows which had been thrown into the fort; and in the shield of the centurion Scæva, which was brought to him, were found two hundred and thirty holes. In reward for this man's services, both to himself and the public, Cæsar presented to him two hundred thousand pieces of copper money,[1] and declared him promoted from the eighth to the first centurion. For it appeared that the fort had been in a great measure saved by his exertions; and he afterward very amply rewarded the cohorts with double pay, corn, clothing, and other military honors.

CHAP. LIV.—Pompey, having made great additions to his works in the night, the following days built turrets, and having carried his works fifteen feet high, faced that part of his camp with mantelets; and after an interval of five days, taking advantage of a second cloudy night, he barricaded all the gates of his camp to hinder a pursuit, and about midnight, quietly marched off his army, and retreated to his old fortifications.

CHAP. LV.—Ætolia, Acarnania, and Amphilochis, being reduced, as we have related, by Cassius Longinus, and Calvisius Sabinus, Cæsar thought he ought to attempt the conquest of Achaia, and to advance further into the country. Accordingly, he detached Fufius thither, and ordered Quintus Sabinus and Cassius to join him with their cohorts. Upon notice of their approach, Rutilius Lupus, who commanded in Achaia, under Pompey, began to fortify the Isthmus, to prevent Fufius from

[1] About £729 3*s.* 4*d.*

coming into Achaia. Kalenus recovered Delphi, Thebes, and Orchomenus, by a voluntary submission of those states. Some he subdued by force, the rest he endeavored to win over to Cæsar's interest, by sending deputies round to them. In these things, principally, Fusius was employed.

CHAP. LVI.—Every day afterward, Cæsar drew up his army on a level ground, and offered Pompey battle, and led his legions almost close to Pompey's camp; and his front line was at no greater distance from the rampart than that no weapon from their engines could reach it. But Pompey, to save his credit and reputation with the world, drew out his legions, but so close to his camp, that his rear line might touch the rampart, and that his whole army, when drawn up, might be protected by the darts discharged from it.

CHAP. LVII.—While these things were going forward in Achaia and at Dyrrachium, and when it was certainly known that Scipio was arrived in Macedonia, Cæsar, never losing sight of his first intention, sends Clodius to him, an intimate friend to both, whom Cæsar, on the introduction and recommendation of Pompey, had admitted into the number of his acquaintance. To this man he gave letters and instructions to Pompey, the substance of which was as follows: "That he had made every effort toward peace, and imputed the ill success of those efforts to the fault of those whom he had employed to conduct those negotiations; because they were afraid to carry his proposals to Pompey at an improper time. That Scipio had such authority, that he could not only freely explain what conduct met his approbation, but even in some degree enforce his advice, and govern him [Pompey] if he persisted in error; that he commanded an army independent of Pompey, so that besides his authority, he had strength to compel; and if he did so, all men would be indebted to him for the quiet of Italy, the peace of the provinces, and the preservation of the empire." These proposals Clodius made to him, and for some days at the first appeared to have met with a favorable reception, but afterward was not admitted to an audience; for Scipio being reprimanded by Favonius, as we found afterward when the war was ended, and the negotiation having miscarried, Clodius returned to Cæsar.

CHAP. LVIII.—Cæsar, that he might the more easily keep Pompey's horse inclosed within Dyrrachium, and prevent them from foraging, fortified the two narrow passes already mentioned with strong works, and erected forts at them. Pompey perceiving that he derived no advantage from his cavalry, after a few days had them conveyed back to his camp by sea. Fodder was so exceedingly scarce that he was obliged to feed his horses upon leaves stripped off the trees, or the tender roots of reeds pounded. For the corn which had been sown within the lines was already consumed, and they would be obliged to supply themselves with fodder from Corcyra and Acarnania, over a long tract of sea; and as the quantity of that fell short, to increase it by mixing barley with it, and by these methods support their cavalry. But when not only the barley and fodder in these parts were consumed, and the herbs cut away, when the leaves too were not to be found on the trees, the horses being almost starved, Pompey thought he ought to make some attempt by a sally.

CHAP. LIX.—In the number of Cæsar's cavalry were two Allobrogians, brothers, named Roscillus and Ægus, the sons of Abducillus, who for several years possessed the chief power in his own state; men of singular valor, whose gallant services Cæsar had found very useful in all his wars in Gaul. To them, for these reasons, he had committed the offices of greatest honor in their own country, and took care to have them chosen into the senate at an unusual age, and had bestowed on them lands taken from the enemy, and large pecuniary rewards, and from being needy had made them affluent. Their valor had not only procured them Cæsar's esteem, but they were beloved by the whole army. But presuming on Cæsar's friendship, and elated with the arrogance natural to a foolish and barbarous people, they despised their countrymen, defrauded their cavalry of their pay, and applied all the plunder to their own use. Displeased at this conduct, their soldiers went in a body to Cæsar, and openly complained of their ill usage; and to their other charges added, that false musters were given in to Cæsar, and the surcharged pay applied to their own use.

CHAP. LX.—Cæsar, not thinking it a proper time to call them to account, and willing to pardon many faults, on account of their valor, deferred the whole matter, and gave them a private rebuke, for having made a traffic of their troops, and advised them to expect every thing from his friendship, and by his past favors to measure their future hopes. This however, gave them great offense, and made them contemptible in the eyes of the whole army. Of this they became sensible, as well from the reproaches of others, as from the judgment of their own minds, and a consciousness of guilt. Prompted then by shame, and perhaps imagining that they were not liberated from trial, but reserved to a future day, they resolved to break off from us, to put their fortune to a new hazard, and to make trial of new connections. And having conferred with a few of their clients, to whom they could venture to intrust so base an action, they first attempted to assassinate Caius Volusenus, general of the horse (as was discovered at the end of the war), that they might appear to have fled to Pompey after conferring an important service on him. But when that appeared too difficult to put in execution, and no opportunity offered to accomplish it, they borrowed all the money they could, as if they designed to make satisfaction and restitution for what they had defrauded: and having purchased a great number of horses, they deserted to Pompey along with those whom they had engaged in their plot.

CHAP. LXI.—As they were persons nobly descended and of liberal education, and had come with a great retinue, and several cattle, and were reckoned men of courage, and had been in great esteem with Cæsar, and as it was a new and uncommon event, Pompey carried them round all his works, and made an ostentatious show of them, for till that day, not a soldier, either horse or foot had deserted from Cæsar to Pompey, though there were desertions almost every day from Pompey to Cæsar: but more commonly among the soldiers levied in Epirus and Ætolia, and in those countries, which were in Cæsar's possession. But the brothers, having been acquainted with all things, either what was incomplete in our works, or what appeared to the best judges of military matters to be deficient, the particular times, the distance of places, and the various[1] attention of the guards, according to the different temper and character of the officer who commanded the different posts, gave an exact account of all to Pompey.

CHAP. LXII.—Upon receiving this intelligence, Pompey, who had already formed the design of attempting a sally, as before mentioned, ordered the soldiers to make ozier coverings

[1] This is the reading of Morus, Oberlin prefers *viribus et diligentia*, "strength and attention."

for their helmets, and to provide fascines. These things being prepared, he embarked on board small boats and row galleys by night, a considerable number of light infantry and archers, with all their fascines, and immediately after midnight, he marched sixty cohorts drafted from the greater camp and the outposts, to that part of our works which extended toward the sea, and were at the furthest distance from Cæsar's greater camp. To the same place he sent the ships, which he had freighted with the fascines and light-armed troops; and all the ships of war that lay at Dyrrachium; and to each he gave particular instructions: at this part of the lines Cæsar had posted Lentulus Marcellinus, the quæstor, with the ninth legion, and as he was not in a good state of health, Fulvius Costhumus was sent to assist him in the command.

CHAP. LXIII.—At this place, fronting the enemy, there was a ditch fifteen feet wide, and a rampart ten feet high, and the top of the rampart was ten feet in breadth. At an interval of six hundred feet from that there was another rampart turned the contrary way, with the works lower. For some days before, Cæsar, apprehending that our men might be surrounded by sea, had made a double rampart there, that if he should be attacked on both sides, he might have the means of defending himself. But the extent of the lines, and the incessant labor for so many days, because he had inclosed a circuit of seventeen miles with his works, did not allow time to finish them. Therefore the transverse rampart which should make a communication between the other two, was not yet completed. This circumstance was known to Pompey, being told to him by the Allobrogian deserters, and proved of great disadvantage to us. For when our cohorts of the ninth legion were on guard by the sea-side, Pompey's army arrived suddenly by break of day, and their approach was a surprise to our men, and at the same time, the soldiers that came by sea, cast their darts on the front rampart; and the ditches were filled with fascines: and the legionary soldiers terrified those that defended the inner rampart, by applying the scaling ladders, and by engines and weapons of all sorts, and a vast multitude of archers poured round upon them from every side. Besides, the coverings of oziers, which they had laid over their helmets, were a great security to them against the blows of stones which were the only weapons that our soldiers had.

And therefore, when our men were oppressed in every manner, and were scarcely able to make resistance, the defect in our works was observed, and Pompey's soldiers, landing between the two ramparts, where the work was unfinished, attacked our men in the rear, and having beat them from both sides of the fortification, obliged them to flee.

CHAP. LXIV.—Marcellinus, being informed of this disorder, detached some cohorts to the relief of our men, who seeing them flee from the camp, were neither able to persuade them to rally at their approach, nor themselves to sustain the enemy's charge. And in like manner, whatever additional assistance was sent, was infected by the fears of the defeated, and increased the terror and danger. For retreat was prevented by the multitude of the fugitives. In that battle, when the eagle-bearer was dangerously wounded, and began to grow weak, having got sight of our horse, he said to them, "This eagle have I defended with the greatest care for many years, at the hazard of my life, and now in my last moments restore it to Cæsar with the same fidelity. Do not, I conjure you, suffer a dishonor to be sustained in the field, which never before happened to Cæsar's army, but deliver it safe into his hands." By this accident the eagle was preserved, but all the centurions of the first cohorts were killed, except the principal.

CHAP. LXV.—And now the Pompeians, after great havoc of our troops, were approaching Marcellinus's camp, and had struck no small terror into the rest of the cohorts, when Marcus Antonius, who commanded the nearest fort, being informed of what had happened, was observed descending from the rising ground with twelve cohorts. His arrival checked the Pompeians, and encouraged our men to recover from their extreme affright. And shortly after, Cæsar having got notice by the smoke of all the forts, which was the usual signal on such occasions, drafted off some cohorts from the outposts, and went to the scene of action. And having there learned the loss he had sustained, and perceiving that Pompey had forced our works, and had encamped along the coast, so that he was at liberty to forage, and had a communication with his shipping, he altered his plan for conducting the war, as his design had not succeeded, and ordered a strong encampment to be made near Pompey.

CHAP. LXVI.—When this work was finished, Cæsar's

scouts observed that some cohorts, which to them appeared like a legion, were retired behind the wood, and were on their march to the old camp. The situation of the two camps was as follows: a few days before, when Cæsar's ninth legion had opposed a party of Pompey's troops, and were endeavoring to inclose them, Cæsar's troops formed a camp in that place. This camp joined a certain wood, and was not above four hundred paces distant from the sea. Afterward, changing his design for certain reasons, Cæsar removed his camp to a small distance beyond that place; and after a few days, Pompey took possession of it, and added more extensive works, leaving the inner rampart standing, as he intended to keep several legions there. By this means, the lesser camp, included within the greater, answered the purpose of a fort and citadel. He had also carried an intrenchment from the left angle of the camp to the river, about four hundred paces, that his soldiers might have more liberty and less danger in fetching water. But he too, changing his design for reasons not necessary to be mentioned, abandoned the place. In this condition the camp remained for several days, the works being all entire.

CHAP. LXVII.—Cæsar's scouts brought him word that the standard of a legion was carried to this place. That the same thing was seen he was assured by those in the higher forts. This place was a half a mile distant from Pompey's new camp. Cæsar, hoping to surprise this legion, and anxious to repair the loss sustained that day, left two cohorts employed in the works to make an appearance of intrenching himself, and by a different route, as privately as he could, with his other cohorts amounting to thirty-three, among which was the ninth legion, which had lost so many centurions, and whose privates were greatly reduced in number, he marched in two lines against Pompey's legion and his lesser camp. Nor did this first opinion deceive him. For he reached the place before Pompey could have notice of it; and though the works were strong, yet having made the attack with the left wing which he commanded in person, he obliged the Pompeians to quit the rampart in disorder. A barricade[1] had been raised before the gates, at which a short contest was maintained, our men endeavoring to force their way in, and the enemy to defend the

[1] The *ericius* was a sort of military engine, full of sharp spikes, and placed before the gate of a camp, to prevent the approach of an enemy.

camp; Titus Pulcio,[1] by whose means we have related that Caius Antonius's army was betrayed, defending them with singular courage. But the valor of our men prevailed, and having cut down the barricade, they first forced the greater camp, and after that the fort which was inclosed within it; and as the legion on its repulse had retired to this, they slew several defending themselves there.

CHAP. LXVIII.—But Fortune who exerts a powerful influence as well in other matters, as especially in war, effects great changes from trifling causes, as happened at this time. For the cohorts on Cæsar's right wing, through ignorance of the place, followed the direction of that rampart which ran along from the camp to the river, while they were in search of a gate, and imagined that it belonged to the camp. But when they found that it led to the river, and that nobody opposed them, they immediately climbed over the rampart, and were followed by all our cavalry.

CHAP. LXIX.—In the mean time Pompey, by the great delay which this occasioned, being informed of what had happened, marched with the fifth legion, which he called away from their work to support his party; and at the same time his cavalry were advancing up to ours, and an army in order of battle, was seen at a distance by our men who had taken possession of the camp, and the face of affairs was suddenly changed. For Pompey's legion, encouraged by the hope of speedy support, attempted to make a stand at the Decuman gate, and made a bold charge on our men. Cæsar's cavalry, who had mounted the rampart by a narrow breach, being apprehensive of their retreat, were the first to flee. The right wing which had been separated from the left, observing the terror of the cavalry, to prevent their being overpowered within the lines, were endeavoring to retreat by the same way as they burst in; and most of them, lest they should be engaged in the narrow passes, threw themselves down a rampart ten feet high into the trenches; and the first being trodden to death, the rest procured their safety, and escaped over their bodies. The soldiers of the left wing, peceiving from the rampart that Pompey was

[1] As Cæsar has not mentioned elsewhere the circumstance alluded to here, we naturally infer that some of the Commentaries are wanting, a supposition which is strengthened by the abrupt commencement of the first book, and the chasm at the end of the fiftieth chapter of this one.

advancing, and their own friends fleeing, being afraid that they should be inclosed between the two ramparts, as they had an enemy both within and without, strove to secure their retreat the same way they came. All was disorder, consternation, and flight; insomuch that, when Cæsar laid hold of the colors of those who were running away, and desired them to stand, some left their horses behind, and continued to run in the same manner; others through fear even threw away their colors, nor did a single man face about.

CHAP. LXX.—In this calamity, the following favorable circumstance occurred to prevent the ruin of our whole army, viz., that Pompey suspecting an ambuscade (because, as I suppose, the success had far exceeded his hopes, as he had seen his men a moment before fleeing from the camp), durst not for some time approach the fortification; and that his horse were retarded from pursuing, because the passes and gates were in possession of Cæsar's soldiers. Thus a trifling circumstance proved of great importance to each party; for the rampart drawn from the camp to the river, interrupted the progress and certainty of Cæsar's victory, after he had forced Pompey's camp. The same thing, by retarding the rapidity of the enemy's pursuit, preserved our army.

CHAP. LXXI.—In the two actions of this day, Cæsar lost nine hundred and sixty rank and file, several Roman knights of distinction, Felginas Tuticanus Gallus, a senator's son; Caius Felginas from Placentia; Aulus Gravius from Puteoli; Marcus Sacrativir from Capua; and thirty-two military tribunes and centurions. But the greatest part of all these perished without a wound, being trodden to death in the trenches, on the ramparts and banks of the river by reason of the terror and flight of their own men. Pompey, after this battle, was saluted Imperator; this title he retained, and allowed himself to be addressed by it afterward. But neither in his letters to the senate, nor in the fasces, did he use the laurel as a mark of honor. But Labienus, having obtained his consent that the prisoners should be delivered up to him, had them all brought out, as it appeared, to make a show of them, and that Pompey might place a greater confidence in him who was a deserter; and calling them fellow soldiers, and asking them in the most insulting manner whether it was usual with veterans to flee, ordered them to be put to death in the sight of the whole army.

CHAP. LXXII.—Pompey's party were so elated with confidence and spirit at this success, that they thought no more of the method of conducting the war, but thought that they were already conquerors. They did not consider that the smallness of our numbers, and the disadvantage of the place and the confined nature of the ground occasioned by their having first possessed themselves of the camp, and the double danger both from within and without the fortifications, and the separation of the army into two parts, so that the one could not give relief to the other, were the causes of our defeat. They did not consider, in addition, that the contest was not decided by a vigorous attack, nor a regular battle; and that our men had suffered greater loss from their numbers and want of room, than they had sustained from the enemy. In fine, they did not reflect on the common casualties of war; how trifling causes, either frem groundless suspicions, sudden affright, or religious scruples, have oftentimes been productive of considerable losses; how often an army has been unsuccessful either by the misconduct of the general, or the oversight of a tribune; but as if they had proved victorious by their valor, and as if no change could ever take place, they published the success of the day throughout the world by reports and letters.

CHAP. LXXIII.—Cæsar, disappointed in his first intentions, resolved to change the whole plan of his operations. Accordingly, he at once called in all outposts, gave over the siege, and collecting his army into one place, addressed his soldiers and encouraged them "not to be troubled at what had happened, nor to be dismayed at it, but to weigh their many successful engagements against one disappointment, and that, too, a trifling one. That they ought to be grateful to Fortune, through whose favor they had recovered Italy without the effusion of blood; through whose favor they had subdued the two Spains, though protected by a most warlike people under the command of the most skillful and experienced generals; through whose favor they had reduced to submission the neighboring states that abounded with corn; in fine, that they ought to remember with what success they had been all transported safe through blockading fleets of the enemy, which possessed not only the ports, but even the coasts; that if all their attempts were not crowned with success, the defects of Fortune must be supplied by industry; and whatever loss had been sustained, ought to be attributed rather to her caprices than to any faults in him: that he had chosen a safe ground for the engagement, that he had possessed himself of the enemy's camp; that he had beaten them out, and overcome them when they offered resistance; but whether their own terror or some mistake, or whether Fortune herself had interrupted a victory almost secured and certain, they ought all now to use their utmost efforts to repair by their valor the loss which had been incurred; if they did so, their misfortunes would turn to their advantage, as it happened at Gergovia, and those who feared to face the enemy would be the first to offer themselves to battle.

CHAP. LXXIV.—Having concluded his speech, he disgraced some standard-bearers, and reduced them to the ranks; for the whole army was seized with such grief at their loss, and with such an ardent desire of repairing their disgrace, that not a man required the command of his tribune or centurion, but they imposed each on himself severer labors than usual as a punishment, and at the same time were so inflamed with eagerness to meet the enemy, that the officers of the first rank, sensibly affected at their entreaties, were of opinion that they ought to continue in their present posts, and commit their fate to the hazard of a battle. But, on the other hand, Cæsar could not place sufficient confidence in men so lately thrown into consternation, and thought he ought to allow them time to recover their dejected spirits; and having abandoned his works, he was apprehensive of being distressed for want of corn.

CHAP. LXXV.—Accordingly, suffering no time to intervene but what was necessary for a proper attention to be paid to the sick and wounded, he sent on all his baggage privately in the beginning of the night from his camp to Apollonia, and ordered them not to halt till they had performed their journey; and he detached one legion with them as a convoy. This affair being concluded, having retained only two legions in his camp, he marched the rest of his army out at three o'clock in the morning by several gates, and sent them forward by the same route; and in a short space after, that the military practice might be preserved, and his march known as late as possible, he ordered the signal for decamping to be given; and setting out immediately, and following the rear of his own army, he was soon out of sight of the camp. Nor did Pompey, as soon as he had notice of his design, make any delay to pursue him; but with a view to surprise them while encumbered with baggage on their march, and not yet recovered from their fright, he led his army out of his camp, and sent his cavalry on to retard our rear; but was not able to come up with them, because Cæsar had got far before him, and marched without baggage. But when we reached the river Genusus, the banks being steep, their horse overtook our rear, and detained them by bringing them to action. To oppose whom, Cæsar sent his horse, and intermixed with them about four hundred of his advanced light troops, who attacked their horse with such success, that having routed them all, and killed several, they returned without any loss to the main body.

Chap. LXXVI.—Having performed the exact march which he had proposed that day, and having led his army over the river Genusus, Cæsar posted himself in his old camp opposite Asparagium; and kept his soldiers close within the intrenchments; and ordered the horse, who had been sent out under pretense of foraging, to retire immediately into the camp, through the Decuman gate. Pompey, in like manner, having completed the same day's march, took post in his old camp at Asparagium; and his soldiers, as they had no work (the fortifications being entire), made long excursions, some to collect wood and forage; others, invited by the nearness of the former camp, laid up their arms in their tents, and quitted the intrenchments in order to bring what they had left behind them, because the design of marching being adopted in a hurry, they had left a considerable part of their wagons and luggage behind. Being thus incapable of pursuing, as Cæsar had foreseen, about noon he gave the signal for marching, led out his army, and doubling that day's march, he advanced eight miles beyond Pompey's camp; who could not pursue him, because his troops were dispersed.

Chap. LXXVII.—The next day Cæsar sent his baggage forward early in the night, and marched off himself immediately after the fourth watch:[1] that if he should be under the necessity of risking an engagement, he might meet a sudden attack with an army free from incumbrance. He did so for

[1] About 3 o'clock.

several days successively, by which means he was enabled to effect his march over the deepest rivers, and through the most intricate roads without any loss. For Pompey, after the first day's delay, and the fatigue which he endured for some days in vain, though he exerted himself by forced marches, and was anxious to overtake us, who had got the start of him, on the fourth day desisted from the pursuit, and determined to follow other measures.

CHAP. LXXVIII.—Cæsar was obliged to go to Apollonia, to lodge his wounded, pay his army, confirm his friends, and leave garrisons in the towns. But for these matters, he allowed no more time than was necessary for a person in haste. And being apprehensive for Domitius, lest he should be surprised by Pompey's arrival, he hastened with all speed and earnestness to join him; for he planned the operations of the whole campaign on these principles: that if Pompey should march after him, he would be drawn off from the sea, and from those forces which he had provided in Dyrrachium, and separated from his corn and magazines, and be obliged to carry on the war on equal terms; but if he crossed over into Italy, Cæsar, having effected a junction with Domitius, would march through Illyricum to the relief of Italy; but if he endeavored to storm Apollonia and Oricum, and exclude him from the whole coast, he hoped, by besieging Scipio, to oblige him, of necessity, to come to his assistance. Accordingly, Cæsar dispatching couriers, writes to Domitius, and acquaints him with his wishes on the subject: and having stationed a garrison of four cohorts at Apollonia, one at Lissus, and three at Oricum, besides those who were sick of their wounds, he set forward on his march through Epirus and Acarnania. Pompey, also, guessing at Cæsar's design, determined to hasten to Scipio, that if Cæsar should march in that direction, he might be ready to relieve him; but that if Cæsar should be unwilling to quit the sea-coast and Corcyra, because he expected legions and cavalry from Italy, he himself might fall on Domitius with all his forces.

CHAP. LXXIX.—For these reasons, each of them studied dispatch, that he might succor his friends, and not miss an opportunity of surprising his enemies. But Cæsar's engagements at Apolonia had carried him aside from the direct road. Pompey had taken the short road to Macedonia, through Candavia. To this was added another unexpected disadvantage, that Domitius, who for several days had been encamped opposite Scipio, had quitted that post for the sake of provisions, and had marched to Heraclea Sentica, a city subject to Candavia; so that fortune herself seemed to throw him in Pompey's way. Of this, Cæsar was ignorant up to this time. Letters likewise being sent by Pompey through all the provinces and states, with an account of the action at Dyrrachium, very much enlarged and exaggerated beyond the real facts, a rumor had been circulated, that Cæsar had been defeated and forced to flee, and had lost almost all his forces. These reports had made the roads dangerous, and drawn off some states from his alliance: whence it happened, that the messengers dispatched by Cæsar, by several different roads to Domitius, and by Domitius to Cæsar, were not able by any means to accomplish their journey. But the Allobroges, who were in the retinue of Ægus and Roscillus, and who had deserted to Pompey, having met on the road a scouting party of Domitius; either from old acquaintance, because they had served together in Gaul, or elated with vain glory, gave them an account of all that had happened, and informed them of Cæsar's departure, and Pompey's arrival. Domitius, who was scarce four hours' march distant, having got intelligence from these, by the courtesy of the enemy, avoided the danger, and met Cæsar coming to join him at Æginium, a town on the confines of and opposite to Thessaly.

Chap. LXXX. — The two armies being united, Cæsar marched to Gomphi, which is the first town of Thessaly on the road from Epirus. Now, the Thessalians, a few months before, had of themselves sent embassadors to Cæsar, offering him the free use of every thing in their power, and requesting a garrison for their protection. But the report, already spoken of, of the battle at Dyrrachium, which it had exaggerated in many particulars, had arrived before him. In consequence of which, Androsthenes, the prætor of Thessaly, as he preferred to be the companion of Pompey's victory, rather than Cæsar's associate in his misfortunes, collected all the people, both slaves and freemen from the country into the town and shut the gates, and dispatched messengers to Scipio and Pompey "to come to his relief, that he could depend on the strength of the town, if succor was speedily sent; but that it could not withstand a long siege." Scipio, as soon as he received advice of the departure of the armies from Dyrrachium, had marched with his legions to Larissa: Pompey was not yet arrived near Thessaly. Cæsar having fortified his camp, ordered scaling-ladders and pent-houses to be made for a sudden assault, and hurdles to be provided. As soon as they were ready, he exhorted his soldiers, and told them of what advantage it would be to assist them with all sorts of necessaries, if they made themselves masters of a rich and plentiful town: and, at the same time to strike terror into other states by the example of this, and to effect this with speed, before auxiliaries could arrive. Accordingly, taking advantage of the unusual ardor of the soldiers, he began his assault on the town at a little after three o'clock on the very day on which he arrived, and took it, though defended with very high walls, before sunset, and gave it up to his army to plunder, and immediately decamped from before it, and marched to Metropolis, with such rapidity as to outstrip any messenger or rumor of the taking of Gomphi.

CHAP. LXXXI.—The inhabitants of Metropolis, at first influenced by the same rumors, followed the same measures, shut the gates and manned their walls. But when they were made acquainted with the fate of the city of Gomphi by some prisoners, whom Cæsar had ordered to be brought up to the walls, they threw open their gates. As he preserved them with the greatest care, there was not a state in Thessaly (except Larissa, which was awed by a strong army of Scipio's), but on comparing the fate of the inhabitants of Metropolis with the severe treatment of Gomphi, gave admission to Cæsar, and obeyed his orders. Having chosen a position convenient for procuring corn, which was now almost ripe on the ground, he determined there to wait Pompey's arrival, and to make it the center of all his warlike operations.

CHAP. LXXXII.—Pompey arrived in Thessaly a few days after, and having harangued the combined army, returned thanks to his own men, and exhorted Scipio's soldiers, that as the victory was now secured, they should endeavor to merit a part of the rewards and booty. And receiving all the legions into one camp, he shared his honors with Scipio, ordered the trumpet to be sounded at his tent, and a pavilion to be erected for him. The forces of Pompey being thus augmented, and two such powerful armies united, their former expectations were confirmed, and their hopes of victory so much increased, that whatever time intervened was considered as so much delay to their return into Italy; and whenever Pompey acted with slowness and caution, they used to exclaim, that it was the business only of a single day, but that he had a passion for power, and was delighted in having persons of consular and prætorian rank in the number of his slaves. And they now began to dispute openly about rewards and priesthoods, and disposed of the consulate for several years to come. Others put in their claims for the houses and properties of all who were in Cæsar's camp, and in that council there was a warm debate, whether Lucius Hirtius, who had been sent by Pompey against the Parthians, should be admitted a candidate for the prætorship in his absence at the next election; his friends imploring Pompey's honor to fulfill the engagements which he had made to him at his departure, that he might not seem deceived through his authority: while others, embarked in equal labor and danger, pleaded that no individual ought to have a preference before all the rest.

CHAP. LXXXIII.—Already Domitius, Scipio, and Lentulus Spinther, in their daily quarrels about Cæsar's priesthood, openly abused each other in the most scurrilous language. Lentulus urging the respect due to his age, Domitius boasting his interest in the city and his dignity, and Scipio presuming on his alliance with Pompey. Attius Rufus charged Lucius Afranius before Pompey with betraying the army in the action that happened in Spain, and Lucius Domitius declared in the council that it was his wish that, when the war should be ended, three billets should be given to all the senators, who had taken part with them in the war, and that they should pass sentence[1] on every single person who had staid behind at Rome, or who had been within Pompey's garrisons and had not contributed their assistance in the military operations; that by the first billet they should have power to acquit, by the

[1] There is here an allusion to the Roman system of trial, according to which the Prætor gave to each judge three tablets: on one of which was written the letter C. for *condemno*, I condemn; on another the letter A. for *absolvo*, I acquit; and on a third N. L. *non liquet* sc. *mihi*, I am not clear. Each of the judges threw which of these tablets he thought proper into an urn, and the Prætor pronounced judgment according to the majority.

second to pass sentence of death, and by the third to impose a pecuniary fine. In short, Pompey's whole army talked of nothing but the honors or sums of money which were to be their rewards, or of vengeance on their enemies; and never considered how they were to defeat their enemies, but in what manner they should use their victory.

CHAP. LXXXIV.—Corn being provided, and his soldiers refreshed, and a sufficient time having elapsed since the engagement at Dyrrachium, when Cæsar thought he had sufficiently sounded the disposition of his troops, he thought that he ought to try whether Pompey had any intention or inclination to come to a battle. Accordingly he led his troops out of the camp, and ranged them in order of battle, at first on their own ground, and at a small distance from Pompey's camp: but afterward for several days in succession, he advanced from his own camp, and led them up to the hills on which Pompey's troops were posted, which conduct inspired his army every day with fresh courage. However he adhered to his former purpose respecting his cavalry, for as he was by many degrees inferior in number, he selected the youngest and most active of the advanced guard, and desired them to fight intermixed with the horse, and they by constant practice acquired experience in this kind of battle. By these means it was brought to pass that a thousand of his horse would dare even on open ground, to stand against seven thousand of Pompey's, if occasion required, and would not be much terrified by their number. For even on one of those days he was successful in a cavalry action, and killed one of the two Allobrogians, who had deserted to Pompey, as we before observed, and several others.

CHAP. LXXXV.—Pompey, because he was encamped on a hill, drew up his army at the very foot of it, ever in expectation, as may be conjectured, that Cæsar would expose himself to this disadvantageous situation. Cæsar, seeing no likelihood of being able to bring Pompey to an action, judged it the most expedient method of conducting the war, to decamp from that post and to be always in motion: with this hope, that by shifting his camp and removing from place to place, he might be more conveniently supplied with corn, and also, that by being in motion he might get some opportunity of forcing them to battle, and might by constant marches harass Pompey's army, which was not accustomed to fatigue. These matters being settled, when the signal for marching was given, and the tents struck, it was observed that shortly before, contrary to his daily practice, Pompey's army had advanced further than usual from his intrenchments, so that it appeared possible to come to an action on equal ground. Then Cæsar addressed himself to his soldiers, when they were at the gates of the camp, ready to march out. "We must defer," says he, "our march at present, and set our thoughts on battle, which has been our constant wish; let us then meet the foe with resolute souls. We shall not hereafter easily find such an opportunity." He immediately marched out at the head of his troops.

Chap. LXXXVI.—Pompey also, as was afterward known, at the unanimous solicitation of his friends, had determined to try the fate of a battle. For he had even declared in council a few days before that, before the battalions came to battle, Cæsar's army would be put to the rout. When most people expressed their surprise at it, "I know," says he, "that I promise a thing almost incredible; but hear the plan on which I proceed, that you may march to battle with more confidence and resolution. I have persuaded our cavalry, and they have engaged to execute it, as soon as the two armies have met, to attack Cæsar's right wing on the flank, and inclosing their army on the rear, throw them into disorder, and put them to the rout, before we shall throw a weapon against the enemy. By this means we shall put an end to the war, without endangering the legions, and almost without a blow. Nor is this a difficult matter, as we far outnumber them in cavalry." At the same time he gave them notice to be ready for battle on the day following, and since the opportunity which they had so often wished for was now arrived, not to disappoint the opinion generally entertained of their experience and valor.

Chap. LXXXVII.—After him Labienus spoke, as well to express his contempt of Cæsar's forces, as to extol Pompey's scheme with the highest encomiums. "Think not, Pompey," says he, "that this is the army which conquered Gaul and Germany; I was present at all those battles, and do not speak at random on a subject to which I am a stranger: a very small part of that army now remains, great numbers lost their lives, as must necessarily happen in so many battles, many fell victims to the autumnal pestilence in Italy, many returned home, and many were left behind on the continent. Have you not heard that the cohorts at Brundusium are composed of invalids? The forces which you now behold, have been recruited by levies lately made in Hither Spain, and the greater part from the colonies beyond the Po; moreover, the flower of the forces perished in the two engagements at Dyrrachium." Having so said, he took an oath, never to return to his camp unless victorious; and he encouraged the rest to do the like. Pompey applauded his proposal, and took the same oath; nor did any person present hesitate to take it. After this had passed in the council they broke up full of hopes and joy, and in imagination anticipated victory; because they thought that in a matter of such importance, no groundless assertion could be made by a general of such experience.

CHAP. LXXXVIII.—When Cæsar had approached near Pompey's camp, he observed that his army was drawn up in the following manner:—On the left wing were the two legions, delivered over by Cæsar at the beginning of the disputes in compliance with the senate's decree, one of which was called the first, the other the third. Here Pompey commanded in person. Scipio with the Syrian legions commanded the center. The Cilician legion in conjunction with the Spanish cohorts, which we said were brought over by Afranius, were disposed on the right wing. These Pompey considered his steadiest troops. The rest he had interspersed between the center and the wing, and he had a hundred and ten complete cohorts; these amounted to forty-five thousand men. He had besides two cohorts of volunteers, who having received favors from him in former wars, flocked to his standard: these were dispersed through his whole army. The seven remaining cohorts he had disposed to protect his camp, and the neighboring forts. His right wing was secured by a river with steep banks; for which reason he placed all his cavalry, archers, and slingers, on his left wing.

CHAP. LXXXIX.—Cæsar, observing his former custom, had placed the tenth legion on the right, the ninth on the left, although it was very much weakened by the battles at Dyrrachium. He placed the eighth legion so close to the ninth, as to almost make one of the two, and ordered them to support one another. He drew up on the field eighty cohorts, making a total of twenty-two thousand men. He left two cohorts to guard the camp. He gave the command of the left wing to Antonius, of the right to P. Sulla, and of the center to Cn. Domitius: he himself took his post opposite Pompey. At the same time, fearing, from the disposition of the enemy which we have previously mentioned, lest his right wing might be surrounded by their numerous cavalry, he rapidly drafted a single cohort from each of the legions composing the third line, formed of them a fourth line, and opposed them to Pompey's cavalry, and, acquainting them with his wishes, admonished them that the success of that day depended on their courage. At the same time he ordered the third line, and the entire army not to charge without his command: that he would give the signal whenever he wished them to do so.

CHAP. XC.—When he was exhorting his army to battle, according to the military custom, and spoke to them of the favors that they had constantly received from him, he took especial care to remind them "that he could call his soldiers to witness the earnestness with which he had sought peace, the efforts that he had made by Vatinius to gain a conference [with Labienus], and likewise by Claudius to treat with Scipio, in what manner he had exerted himself at Oricum, to gain permission from Libo to send embassadors; that he had been always reluctant to shed the blood of his soldiers, and did not wish to deprive the republic of one or other of her armies." After delivering this speech, he gave by a trumpet the signal to his soldiers, who were eagerly demanding it, and were very impatient for the onset.

CHAP. XCI.—There was in Cæsar's army, a volunteer of the name of Crastinus, who the year before had been first centurion of the tenth legion, a man of pre-eminent bravery. He, when the signal was given, says, "Follow me, my old comrades, and display such exertions in behalf of your general as you have determined to do: this is our last battle, and when it shall be won, he will recover his dignity, and we our liberty." At the same time he looked back to Cæsar, and said, "General, I will act in such a manner to-day, that you will feel grateful to me living or dead." After uttering these words he charged first on the right wing, and about one hundred and twenty chosen volunteers of the same century followed.

CHAP. XCII.—There was so much space left between the two lines, as sufficed for the onset of the hostile armies: but Pompey had ordered his soldiers to await Cæsar's attack, and not to advance from their position, or suffer their line to be put into disorder. And he is said to have done this by the advice of Caius Triarius, that the impetuosity of the charge of Cæsar's soldiers might be checked, and their line broken, and that Pompey's troops remaining in their ranks, might attack them while in disorder; and he thought that the javelins would fall with less force if the soldiers were kept in their ground, than if they met them in their course; at the same time he trusted that Cæsar's soldiers, after running over double the usual ground, would become weary and exhausted by the fatigue. But to me Pompey seems to have acted without sufficient reason: for there is a certain impetuosity of spirit and an alacrity implanted by nature in the hearts of all men, which is inflamed by a desire to meet the foe. This a general should endeavor not to repress, but to increase; nor was it a vain institution of our ancestors, that the trumpets should sound on all sides, and a general shout be raised; by which they imagined that the enemy were struck with terror, and their own army inspired with courage.

CHAP. XCIII.—But our men, when the signal was given, rushed forward with their javelins ready to be launched, but perceiving that Pompey's men did not run to meet their charge, having acquired experience by custom, and being practiced in former battles, they of their own accord repressed their speed, and halted almost midway, that they might not come up with the enemy when their strength was exhausted, and after a short respite they again renewed their course, and threw their javelins, and instantly drew their swords, as Cæsar had ordered them. Nor did Pompey's men fail in this crisis, for they received our javelins, stood our charge, and maintained their ranks; and having launched their javelins, had recourse to their swords. At the same time Pompey's horse, according to their orders, rushed out at once from his left wing, and his whole host of archers poured after them. Our cavalry did not withstand their charge: but gave ground a little, upon which Pompey's horse pressed them more vigorously, and began to file off in troops, and flank our army. When Cæsar perceived this, he gave the signal to his fourth line, which he had formed of the six cohorts. They instantly rushed forward and charged Pompey's horse with such fury, that not a man of them stood; but all wheeling about, not only quitted their post, but galloped forward to seek a refuge in the highest mountains. By their retreat the archers and slingers, being left destitute and defenseless, were all cut to pieces. The cohorts, pursuing their success, wheeled about upon Pompey's left wing, while his infantry still continued to make battle, and attacked them in the rear.

CHAP. XCIV.—At the same time Cæsar ordered his third line to advance, which till then had not been engaged, but had kept their post. Thus, new and fresh troops having come to the assistance of the fatigued, and others having made an attack on their rear, Pompey's men were not able to maintain their ground, but all fled,[1] nor was Cæsar deceived in his opinion, that the victory, as he had declared in his speech to his soldiers, must have its beginning from those six cohorts, which he had placed as a fourth line to oppose the horse. For by them the cavalry were routed; by them the archers and slingers were cut to pieces; by them the left wing of Pompey's army was surrounded, and obliged to be the first to flee. But when Pompey saw his cavalry routed, and that part of his army on which he reposed his greatest hopes thrown into confusion, despairing of the rest, he quitted the field, and retreated straightway on horseback to his camp, and calling to the centurions, whom he had placed to guard the prætorian gate, with a loud voice, that the soldiers might hear: "Secure the camp," says he, "defend it with diligence, if any danger should threaten it; I will visit the other gates, and encourage the guards of the camp." Having thus said, he retired into his tent in utter despair, yet anxiously waiting the issue.

CHAP. XCV.—Cæsar having forced the Pompeians to flee into their intrenchment, and thinking that he ought not to allow them any respite to recover from their fright, exhorted his soldiers to take advantage of fortune's kindness, and to attack the camp. Though they were fatigued by the intense heat, for the battle had continued till mid-day, yet, being prepared to

[1] Historians state that Cæsar on this occasion advised his soldiers to aim at the faces of Pompey's cavalry, who, being composed principally of the young noblemen of Rome, dreaded a scar in the face more than death itself.

undergo any labor, they cheerfully obeyed his command. The camp was bravely defended by the cohorts which had been left to guard it, but with much more spirit by the Thracians and foreign auxiliaries. For the soldiers who had fled for refuge to it from the field of battle, affrighted and exhausted by fatigue, having thrown away their arms and military standards, had their thoughts more engaged on their further escape than on the defense of the camp. Nor could the troops who were posted on the battlements, long withstand the immense number of our darts, but fainting under their wounds, quitted the place, and under the conduct of their centurions and tribunes, fled, without stopping, to the high mountains which joined the camp.

CHAP. XCVI.—In Pompey's camp you might see arbors in which tables were laid, a large quantity of plate set out, the floors of the tents covered with fresh sods, the tents of Lucius Lentulus and others shaded with ivy, and many other things which were proofs of excessive luxury, and a confidence of victory, so that it might readily be inferred that they had no apprehensions of the issue of the day, as they indulged themselves in unnecessary pleasures, and yet upbraided with luxury Cæsar's army, distressed and suffering troops, who had always been in want of common necessaries. Pompey, as soon as our men had forced the trenches, mounting his horse, and stripping off his general's habit, went hastily out of the back gate of the camp, and galloped with all speed to Larissa. Nor did he stop there, but with the same dispatch, collecting a few of his flying troops, and halting neither day nor night, he arrived at the seaside, attended by only thirty horse, and went on board a victualing barque, often complaining, as we have been told, that he had been so deceived in his expectation, that he was almost persuaded that he had been betrayed by those from whom he had expected victory, as they began the fight.

CHAP. XCVII.—Cæsar having possessed himself of Pompey's camp, urged his soldiers not to be too intent on plunder, and lose the opportunity of completing their conquest. Having obtained their consent, he began to draw lines round the mountain. The Pompeians distrusting the position, as there was no water on the mountain, abandoned it, and all began to retreat toward Larissa; which Cæsar perceiving, divided his troops, and ordering part of his legions to remain in Pompey's camp, sent back a part to his own camp, and taking four legions with him, went by a shorter road to intercept the enemy: and having marched six miles, drew up his army. But the Pompeians observing this, took post on a mountain, whose foot was washed by a river. Cæsar having encouraged his troops, though they were greatly exhausted by incessant labor the whole day, and night was now approaching, by throwing up works cut off the communication between the river and the mountain, that the enemy might not get water in the night. As soon as the work was finished, they sent embassadors to treat about a capitulation. A few senators who had espoused that party, made their escape by night.

CHAP. XCVIII.—At break of day, Cæsar ordered all those who had taken post on the mountain, to come down from the higher grounds into the plain, and pile their arms. When they did this without refusal, and with outstretched arms, prostrating themselves on the ground, with tears, implored his mercy: he comforted them and bade them rise, and having spoken a few words of his own clemency to alleviate their fears, he pardoned them all, and gave orders to his soldiers, that no injury should be done to them, and nothing taken from them. Having used this diligence, he ordered the legions in his camp to come and meet him, and those which were with him to take their turn of rest, and go back to the camp: and the same day went to Larissa.

CHAP. XCIX.—In that battle, no more than two hundred privates were missing, but Cæsar lost about thirty centurions, valiant officers. Crastinus, also, of whom mention was made before, fighting most courageously, lost his life by the wound of a sword in the mouth; nor was that false which he declared when marching to battle: for Cæsar entertained the highest opinion of his behavior in that battle, and thought him highly deserving of his approbation. Of Pompey's army, there fell about fifteen thousand; but upwards of twenty-four thousand were made prisoners: for even the cohorts which were stationed in the forts, surrendered to Sylla. Several others took shelter in the neighboring states. One hundred and eighty stands of colors, and nine eagles, were brought to Cæsar. Lucius Domitius, fleeing from the camp to the mountains, his strength being exhausted by fatigue, was killed by the horse.

CHAP. C.—About this time, Decimus Lælius arrived with his

fleet at Brundusium and in the same manner, as Libo had done before, possessed himself of an island opposite the harbor of Brundusium. In like manner, Valinius, who was then governor of Brundusium, with a few decked barks, endeavored to entice Lælius's fleet, and took one five-banked galley and two smaller vessels that had ventured further than the rest into a narrow part of the harbor: and likewise disposing the horse along the shore, strove to prevent the enemy from procuring fresh water. But Lælius having chosen a more convenient season of the year for his expedition, supplied himself with water brought in transports from Corcyra and Dyrrachium, and was not deterred from his purpose; and till he had received advice of the battle in Thessaly, he could not be forced either by the disgrace of losing his ships, or by the want of necessaries, to quit the port and islands.

CHAP. CI.—Much about the same time, Cassius arrived in Sicily with a fleet of Syrians, Phœnicians, and Cicilians: and as Cæsar's fleet was divided into two parts, Publius Sulpicius the prætor commanding one division at Vibo near the straits, Pomponius the other at Messana, Cassius got into Messana with his fleet, before Pomponius had notice of his arrival, and having found him in disorder, without guards or discipline, and the wind being high and favorable, he filled several transports with fir, pitch, and tow, and other combustiblès, and sent them against Pomponius's fleet, and set fire to all his ships, thirty-five in number, twenty of which were armed with beaks: and this action struck such terror that though there was a legion in garrison at Messana, the town with difficulty held out, and had not the news of Cæsar's victory been brought at that instant by the horse stationed along the coast, it was generally imagined that it would have been lost, but the town was maintained till the news arrived very opportunely: and Cassius set sail from thence to attack Sulpicius's fleet at Vibo, and our ships being moored to the land, to strike the same terror, he acted in the same manner as before. The wind being favorable, he sent into the port about forty ships provided with combustibles, and the flame catching on both sides, five ships were burned to ashes. And when the fire began to spread wider by the violence of the wind, the soldiers of the veteran legions, who had been left to guard the fleet, being considered as invalids, could not endure the disgrace, but of themselves went on board the ships and weighed anchor, and having attacked Cassius's fleet, captured two five-banked galleys, in one of which was Cassius himself; but he made his escape by taking to a boat. Two three-banked galleys were taken besides. Intelligence was shortly after received of the action in Thessaly, so well authenticated, that the Pompeians themselves gave credit to it; for they had hitherto believed it a fiction of Cæsar's lieutenants and friends. Upon which intelligence Cassius departed with his fleet from that coast.

CHAP. CII.—Cæsar thought he ought to postpone all business and pursue Pompey, whithersoever he should retreat; that he might not be able to provide fresh forces, and renew the war; he therefore marched on every day, as far as his cavalry were able to advance, and ordered one legion to follow him by shorter journeys. A proclamation was issued by Pompey at Amphipolis, that all the young men of that province, Grecians and Roman citizens, should take the military oath; but whether he issued it with an intention of preventing suspicion, and to conceal as long as possible his design of fleeing further, or to endeavor to keep possession of Macedonia by new levies, if nobody pursued him, it is impossible to judge. He lay at anchor one night, and calling together his friends in Amphipolis, and collecting a sum of money for his necessary expenses, upon advice of Cæsar's approach, set sail from that place, and arrived in a few days at Mitylene. Here he was detained two days, and having added a few galleys to his fleet he went to Cilicia, and thence to Cyprus. There he is informed that, by the consent of all the inhabitants of Antioch[1]

[1] Antiochia, or Antioch, now called *Antakia*, was founded by Seleucus Nicanor, who named it after his father. It was not only the capital of Syria, but of all Asia, and was once the third city in the world for beauty, size, and population; it was the royal seat of the Syrian kings, and after the Roman conquest became the ordinary residence of the prefect, or governor of the eastern provinces. It was here that the disciples of Christ first received the name of Christians, A.D. 39, having been before commonly called Nazarenes and Galilæans; it was the birth-place of St. Luke, the evangelist, and was called in the middle ages, Theopolis; it was surnamed Antioch ad Orontem, from the river on which it stood, and ad Daphnen, from the neighboring grove Daphne, *Doueir*. This grove, which was of bay-trees, intermixed with cypress, was said, in the mythology of the Greeks, to be the scene of Daphne's metamorphosis, when pursued by Apollo; it was a delightful place, and was surrounded with beautiful buildings, in the midst of which rose the famous temple of Apollo

and Roman citizens who traded there, the castle had been seized to shut him out of the town; and that messengers had been dispatched to all those who were reported to have taken refuge in the neighboring states, that they should not come to Antioch; that if they did, that it would be attended with imminent danger to their lives. The same thing had happened to Lucius Lentulus, who had been consul the year before, and to Publius Lentulus a consular senator, and to several others at Rhodes,[1] who having followed Pompey in his flight, and arrived at the island, were not admitted into the town or port; and having received a message to leave that neighborhood, set sail much against their will; for the rumor of Cæsar's approach had now reached those states.

CHAP. CIII.—Pompey, being informed of these proceedings, laid aside his design of going to Syria, and having taken the public money from the farmers of the revenue, and borrowed more from some private friends, and having put on board his ships a large quantity of brass for military purposes, and two thousand armed men, whom he partly selected from the slaves of the tax farmers, and partly collected from the merchants, and such persons as each of his friends thought fit on this occasion, he sailed for Pelusium.[2] It happened that king Ptolemy, a minor, was there

and Diana. Pompey, who visited the grove, was so struck with its beauty, that he gave it a piece of land for its enlargement, and many of the Roman emperors are said to have indulged in its enjoyments, and here for a time to have forgotten the cares of government; it became, however, at last devoted to voluptuousness and the most infamous dissipation; hence the proverb "Daphnici mores."—Arrowsmith's Ancient Geography.

[1] Off the southern coast of Caria lies Rhodus, Rhodes, the largest island in the Ægean Sea, after Crete and Eubœa, and containing 460 square miles; it anciently bore several other names, and is said to have derived that of Rhodes, either from the beautiful nymph Rhode, a favorite of Apollo—or from the word *ῥόδον*, *rosa*, owing to the profusion of roses with which it abounded; or, as others say, from *ῥόθος*, *undarum strepitus*, from its shores being lashed by violent seas. It is presumed, however, to have obtained its appellation from the Dodanim, otherwise called Rhodanim, an opinion which seems to have been entertained by the seventy interpreters, who render the Hebrew word by *Ῥόδιοι*. Its capital was Rhodus, Rhodes, near the northern point of the island, famous for its immense brazen statue of the Sun, called the Colossus, and reckoned one of the seven wonders of the world. Its three other principal cities were Lindus, Ialysus, and Camirus.

[2] Pelusium, an ancient city of Egypt, situated at the eastern extremity of the Delta. It was very strongly fortified, and was considered the key

with a considerable army, engaged in war with his sister Cleopatra, whom a few months before, by the assistance of his relations and friends, he had expelled from the kingdom; and her camp lay at a small distance from his. To him Pompey applied to be permitted to take refuge in Alexandria,[1] and to be protected in his calamity by his powerful assistance, in consideration of the friendship and amity which had subsisted between his father and him. But Pompey's deputies having executed their commission, began to converse with less restraint with the king's troops, and to advise them to act with friendship to Pompey, and not to think meanly of his bad fortune. In Ptolemy's army were several of Pompey's soldiers, of whom Gabinius had received the command in Syria, and had brought them over to Alexandria, and at the conclusion of the war had left with Ptolemy the father of the young king.

CHAP. CIV.—The king's friends, who were regents of the kingdom during the minority, being informed of these things, either induced by fear, as they afterward declared, lest Pompey should corrupt the king's army, and seize on Alexandria and Egypt; or despising his bad fortune, as in adversity friends commonly change to enemies, in public gave a favorable

of Egypt, on its eastern frontier. It derived its name from the Greek work πηλος, clay, as it lay in the midst of marshes and morasses, formed by the overflow of the Nile. We find it frequently mentioned in the Bible, under the name of Sin, which also expresses its marshy situation. It continued to preserve its importance in a military view, until the waters of the Nile found their way into the Damietta branch of that river.

[1] Alexandria, still called *Alexandria*, or *Iskenderieh*, a city of lower Egypt, situated on a narrow neck of land, washed on one side by the Mediterranean, and on the other by the Lake Mareotis. It was founded by Alexander the Great, 331 B.C., from whom it derived its name. The breadth of the city did not exceed one third of a league, but its length extended to one and a half. The principal street, 2000 feet broad, and adorned with some of the most costly edifices and structures of marble, which, perhaps, the world ever saw, was crossed in the middle by another of the same breadth. Many of these ornaments were subsequently transferred to adorn Rome and Constantinople. Alexander's object in building this city, was to reap the profit of the whole trade between Asia and Europe, which, from this city's natural advantages, he foresaw that it could not fail to engross after the fall of Tyre. In consequence of a communication with the Nile by a canal, and a junction of that river with the Red Sea by another, it soon became the center of commerce for all the merchandize passing between Europe and the East Indies. It was, likewise, distinguished as a seat of learning, and possessed an extensive library, which, at one period, consisted of 700,000 volumes.

answer to his deputies, and desired him to come to the king; but secretly laid a plot against him, and dispatched Achillas, captain of the king's guards, a man of singular boldness, and Lucius Septimius a military tribune to assassinate him. Being kindly addressed by them, and deluded by an acquaintance with Septimius, because in the war with the pirates the latter had commanded a company under him he embarked in a small boat with a few attendants, and was there murdered by Achillas and Septimius. In like manner, Lucius Lentulus was seized by the king's order, and put to death in prison.

CHAP. CV.—When Cæsar arrived in Asia, he found that Titus Ampius had attempted to remove the money from the temple of Diana at Ephesus; and for this purpose had convened all the senators in the province that he might have them to attest the sum, but was interrupted by Cæsar's arrival, and had made his escape. Thus, on two occasions, Cæsar saved the money of Ephesus. It was also remarked at Elis, in the temple of Minerva, upon calculating and enumerating the days, that on the very day on which Cæsar had gained his battle, the image of Victory which was placed before Minerva, and faced her statue, turned about toward the portal and entrance of the temple; and the same day, at Antioch in Syria, such a shout of an army and sound of trumpets was twice heard that the citizens ran in arms to the walls. The same thing happened at Ptolemais; a sound of drums too was heard at Pergamus, in the private and retired parts of the temple, into which none but the priests are allowed admission, and which the Greeks call Adyta (the inaccessible), and likewise at Tralles, in the temple of Victory, in which there stood a statue consecrated to Cæsar; a palm-tree at that time was shown that had sprouted up from the pavement, through the joints of the stones, and shot up above the roof.

CHAP. CVI.—After a few days' delay in Asia, Cæsar, having heard that Pompey had been seen in Cyprus, and conjecturing that he had directed his course into Egypt, on account of his connection with that kingdom,[1] set out for Alexandria with two legions (one of which he ordered to follow him from Thessaly, the other he called in from Achaia, from Fufius, the lieutenant general), and with eight hundred

[1] He had been appointed by the senate, guardian to the young king.

horse, ten ships of war from Rhodes, and a few from Asia. These legions amounted but to three thousand two hundred men; the rest, disabled by wounds received in various battles, by fatigue and the length of their march, could not follow him. But Cæsar, relying on the fame of his exploits, did not hesitate to set forward with a feeble force, and thought that he would be secure in any place. At Alexandria he was informed of the death of Pompey: and at his landing there, heard a cry among the soldiers whom the king had left to garrison the town, and saw a crowd gathering toward him, because the fasces were carried before him; for this the whole multitude thought an infringement of the king's dignity. Though this tumult was appeased, frequent disturbances were raised for several days successively, by crowds of the populace, and a great many of his soldiers were killed in all parts of the city.

Chap. CVII.—Having observed this, he ordered other legions to be brought to him from Asia, which he had made up out of Pompey's soldiers; for he was himself detained against his will, by the etesian[1] winds, which are totally unfavorable to persons on a voyage from Alexandria. In the mean time, considering that the disputes of the princes belonged to the jurisdiction of the Roman people, and of him as consul, and that it was a duty more incumbent on him, as in his former consulate a league had been made with Ptolemy the late king, under sanction both of a law and a decree of the senate, he signified that it was his pleasure that king Ptolemy, and his sister Cleopatra, should disband their armies, and decide their disputes in his presence by justice, rather than by the sword.

Chap. CVIII.—A eunuch named Pothinus, the boy's tutor, was regent of the kingdom on account of his youthfulness.[2] He at first began to complain among his friends, and to express his indignation, that the king should be summoned to plead his cause: but afterward, having prevailed on some of those whom he had made acquainted with his views to join him, he secretly called the army away from Pelusium to Alexandria, and appointed Achillas, already spoken of, commander-in-chief

[1] The etesian or periodical winds so called from ετος, a year. They blow in different directions in different countries.

[2] We learn from Appian that the young king was thirteen years old at this time.

of the forces. Him he encouraged and animated by promises both in his own and the king's name, and instructed him both by letters and messages how he should act. By the will of Ptolemy the father, the elder of his two sons and the more advanced in years of his two daughters were declared his heirs, and for the more effectual performance of his intention, in the same will he conjured the Roman people by all the gods, and by the league which he had entered into at Rome, to see his will executed. One of the copies of his will was conveyed to Rome by his embassadors to be deposited in the treasury, but the public troubles preventing it, it was lodged with Pompey: another was left sealed up, and kept at Alexandria.

CHAP. CIX.—While these things were debated before Cæsar, and he was very anxious to settle the royal disputes as a common friend and arbitrator; news was brought on a sudden that the king's army and all his cavalry, were on their march to Alexandria. Cæsar's forces were by no means so strong that he could trust to them, if he had occasion to hazard a battle without the town. His only resource was to keep within the town in the most convenient places, and get information of Achillas's designs. However he ordered his soldiers to repair to their arms; and advised the king to send some of his friends, who had the greatest influence, as deputies to Achillas, and to signify his royal pleasure. Dioscorides and Serapion, the persons sent by him, who had both been embassadors at Rome, and had been in great esteem with Ptolemy the father, went to Achillas. But as soon as they appeared in his presence, without hearing them, or learning the occasion of their coming, he ordered them to be seized and put to death. One of them, after receiving a wound, was taken up and carried off by his attendants as dead: the other was killed on the spot. Upon this, Cæsar took care to secure the king's person, both supposing that the king's name would have a great influence with his subjects, and to give the war the appearance of the scheme of a few desperate men, rather than of having been begun by the king's consent.

CHAP. CX.—The forces under Achillas did not seem despicable, either for number, spirit, or military experience; for he had twenty thousand men under arms. They consisted partly of Gabinius's soldiers, who were now become habituated to the licentious mode of living at Alexandria, and had forgotten the name and discipline of the Roman people, and had married wives there, by whom the greatest part of them had children. To these was added a collection of highwaymen, and freebooters, from Syria, and the province of Cilicia, and the adjacent countries. Besides several convicts and transports had been collected: for at Alexandria all our runaway slaves were sure of finding protection for their persons on the condition that they should give in their names, and enlist as soldiers: and if any of them was apprehended by his master, he was rescued by a crowd of his fellow soldiers, who being involved in the same guilt, repelled, at the hazard of their lives, every violence offered to any of their body. These by a prescriptive privilege of the Alexandrian army, used to demand the king's favorites to be put to death, pillage the properties of the rich to increase their pay, invest the king's palace, banish some from the kingdom, and recall others from exile. Besides these, there were two thousand horse, who had acquired the skill of veterans by being in several wars in Alexandria. These had restored Ptolemy the father to his kingdom, had killed Bibulus's two sons; and had been engaged in war with the Egyptians; such was their experience in military affairs.

Chap. CXI.—Full of confidence in his troops, and despising the small number of Cæsar's soldiers, Achillas seized Alexandria, except that part of the town which Cæsar occupied with his troops. At first he attempted to force the palace; but Cæsar had disposed his cohorts through the streets, and repelled his attack. At the same time there was an action at the port: where the contest was maintained with the greatest obstinacy.[1] For the forces were divided, and the fight maintained in several streets at once, and the enemy endeavored to seize with a strong party the ships of war; of which fifty had been sent to Pompey's assistance, but after the battle in Thessaly, had returned home. They were all of either three or five banks of oars, well equipped and appointed with every necessary for a voyage. Besides these, there were twenty-two vessels with decks, which were usually kept at Alexandria, to

[1] Otherwise thus, "and that action was productive of by far the greatest danger."

guard the port. If they made themselves masters of these, Cæsar being deprived of his fleet, they would have the command of the port and whole sea, and could prevent him from procuring provisions and auxiliaries. Accordingly that spirit was displayed, which ought to be displayed when the one party saw that a speedy victory depended on the issue, and the other their safety. But Cæsar gained the day, and set fire to all those ships, and to others which were in the docks, because he could not guard so many places with so small a force; and immediately he conveyed some troops to the Pharos by his ships.

CHAP. CXII.—The Pharos is a tower on an island, of prodigious height, built with amazing works, and takes its name from the island. This island lying over against Alexandria, forms a harbor; but on the upper side it is connected with the town by a narrow way eight hundred paces in length, made by piles sunk in the sea, and by a bridge. In this island some of the Egyptians have houses, and a village as large as a town; and whatever ships from any quarter, either through mistaking the channel, or by the storm, have been driven from their course upon the coast, they constantly plunder like pirates. And without the consent of those who are masters of the Pharos, no vessels can enter the harbor, on account of its narrowness. Cæsar being greatly alarmed on this account, while the enemy were engaged in battle, landed his soldiers, seized the Pharos, and placed a garrison in it. By this means he gained this point, that he could be supplied without danger with corn, and auxiliaries; for he sent to all the neighboring countries, to demand supplies. In other parts of the town, they fought so obstinately, that they quitted the field with equal advantage, and neither were beaten (in consequence of the narrowness of the passes); and a few being killed on both sides, Cæsar secured the most necessary posts, and fortified them in the night. In this quarter of the town was a wing of the king's palace, in which Cæsar was lodged on his first arrival, and a theater adjoining the house which served as for citadel, and commanded an avenue to the ports and other docks. These fortifications he increased during the succeeding days, that he might have them before him as a rampart, and not be obliged to fight against his will. In the mean time Ptolemy's younger daughter, hoping the throne would become vacant, made her escape from the palace to Achillas, and assisted him in prosecuting the war. But they soon quareled about the command, which circumstance enlarged the presents to the soldiers, for each endeavored by great sacrifices to secure their affection. While the enemy was thus employed, Pothinus, tutor to the young king, and regent of the kingdom, who was in Cæsar's part of the town, sent messengers to Achillas, and encouraged him not to desist from his enterprise, nor to despair of success; but his messengers being discovered and apprehended, he was put to death by Cæsar. Such was the commencement of the Alexandrian war.

THE

COMMENTARIES OF AULUS HIRTIUS

ON THE

ALEXANDRIAN WAR.

THE ARGUMENT

I. Cæsar begins to lay siege to Alexandria. II.-III. The inhabitants make a vigorous defense. IV.-VI. Cæsar gets possession of the person of King Ptolemy; Arsinoe seizes the sovereign power, and puts Achillas to death; Ganymedes prepares to cut off the supply of water from Cæsar's troops. VII.-IX. Cæsar relieves their anxiety by sinking wells, which furnish a copious supply. X.-XVIII. Is successful in a naval engagement, and makes himself master of the Pharos. XIX.-XXI. He suffers severely in an attack on the bridge and mole. XXII.-XXV. Restores the young king to the Alexandrians at their earnest request, who treacherously renews the war: Euphranor, the Rhodian, distinguished for his bravery and knowledge of naval tactics, falls in action. XXVI.-XXXI. Mithridates of Pergamus brings assistance to Cæsar, takes Pelusium by storm, and defeats the Egyptian troops; whose king is conquered by Cæsar in a bloody battle, and drowned in the Nile. XXXII., XXXIII. Cæsar, on gaining possession of Alexandria, confers the supreme authority on the younger Ptolemy and Cleopatra: he dethrones Arsinoe and proceeds to Syria. XXXI.-XLI. In the mean time, Deiotarus, king of Armenia, requests assistance from Domitius Calvinus against Pharnaces; the Roman army is defeated, and forced to retreat into Asia: Pharnaces takes possession of Pontus, and treats the Roman citizens with great cruelty. XLII.-XLVII. Galinius marches to support Cornificius, who commanded for Cæsar in Illyricum, and suffers severe loss: Vatinius, by defeating Octavius, Pompey's general, restores Cæsar's influence in that province. XLVIII.-LXIV. Cassius Longinus propraetor in Spain, makes himself generally detested by his avarice: a conspiracy is formed against him, from which he with difficulty escapes: a mutiny breaks out among a division of the soldiers on the march to Africa, and Cassius, being afraid to intrust his personal safety to Marcellus, Lepidus, and Trebonius, flees from Spain, and is drowned in the Ebro. LXV.-LXVIII. Cæsar arranges the affairs of Syria, Cilicia, Asia, and Cappadocia: he confers the guardianship of the temple of Bellona, in the latter country, on Lycomedes, the Bithynian; he pardons Deiotarus, the tetrarch of Gallogræcia, who had espoused Pompey's party. LXIX.-LXXVIII. He speedily conquers Pharnaces, who acted with great treachery, and recovers Pontus: he creates Mithridates of Pergamus, king of Pontus, and tetrarch of Gallogræcia: he suddenly embarks for Italy.

CHAP. I.—When the war broke out at Alexandria, Cæsar sent to Rhodes, Syria, and Cilicia, for all his fleet; and summoned archers from Crete, and cavalry from Malchus, king of the Nabatheans.[1] He likewise ordered military engines to be provided, corn to be brought, and forces dispatched to him. Meanwhile he daily strengthened his fortifications by new works; and such parts of the town as appeared less tenable were strengthened with testudos and mantelets Openings were made in the walls, through which the battering-rams might play; and the fortifications were extended over whatever space was covered with ruins, or taken by force. For Alexandria is in a manner secure from fire, because the houses are all built without joists or wood, and are all vaulted, and roofed with tile or pavement. Cæsar's principal aim was, to inclose with works the smallest part of the town, separated from the rest by a morass toward the south: with these views, first, that as the city was divided into two parts, the army should be commanded by one general and one council; in the second place, that he might be able to succor his troops when hard pressed, and carry aid from the other part of the city. Above all, he by this means made sure of water and forage, as he was but ill provided with the one, and wholly destitute of the other. The morass, on the contrary, served abundantly to supply him with both.

CHAP. II.—Nor were the Alexandrians remiss on their side, or less active in the conduct of their affairs. For they had sent deputies and commissioners into all parts, where the powers and territories of Egypt extend, to levy troops. They had carried vast quantities of darts and engines into the town, and drawn together an innumerable multitude of soldiers. Nevertheless workshops were established in every part of the

[1] Strabo and Pliny give the name of Nabathæa to Arabia Petræa. They are said to have derived their origin and name from Nabaioth, the eldest son of Ismael. Malchus, their king, subsequently sent auxiliaries to Pacorus, the king of the Parthians, for which act he was compelled by Ventidius, Mark Antony's lieutenant, to give a large sum of money.

city, for the making of arms. They enlisted all the slaves that were of age; and the richer citizens supplied them with food and pay. By a judicious disposition of this multitude, they guarded the fortifications in the remoter parts of the town; while they quartered the veteran cohorts, which were exempted from all other service, in the squares and open places; that on whatever side an attack should be made, they might be at hand to give relief, and march fresh to the charge. They shut up all the avenues and passes by a triple wall built of square stones, and carried to the height of forty feet. They defended the lower parts of the town by very high towers of ten stories: besides which, they had likewise contrived a kind of moving towers, which consisted of the same number of stories, and which being fitted with ropes and wheels, could, by means of horses, as the streets of Alexandria were quite even and level, be conveyed wherever their service was necessary.

CHAP. III.—The city abounding in every thing, and being very rich, furnished ample materials for these several works: and as the people were extremely ingenious, and quick of apprehension, they so well copied what they saw done by us that our men seemed rather to imitate their works. They even invented many things themselves, and attacked our works, at the same time that they defended their own. Their chiefs every where represented: "That the people of Rome were endeavoring by degrees to assume the possession of Egypt; that a few years before Gabinius[1] had come thither with an army; that Pompey had retreated to the same place in his flight; that Cæsar was now among them with a considerable body of troops, nor had they gained any thing by Pompey's death; that Cæsar should not prolong his stay; that if they did not find means to expel him, the kingdom would be reduced to a Roman province: and that they ought to do it at once, for he, blockaded by the storms on account of the season of the year, could receive no supplies from beyond the sea."

CHAP. IV.—Meanwhile, a division arising between Achillas, who commanded the veteran army, and Arsinoe, the youngest

[1] Ptolemy, king of Egypt, being driven from his throne by his subjects, requested the Romans to re-instate him. The latter, in compliance with his request, sent an army, and completely defeated Berenice and Archelaus, who had usurped the sovereign power, A.U.C. 699, about seven years before the present war.

daughter of king Ptolemy, as has been mentioned above, while they mutually endeavored to supplant one another, each striving to engross the supreme authority, Arsinoe, by the assistance of the eunuch Ganymed, her governor, at length prevailed, and slew Achillas. After his death, she possessed the whole power without a rival, and raised Ganymed to the command of the army; who, on his entrance upon that high office, augmented the largesses of the troops, and with equal diligence discharged all other parts of his duty.

CHAP. V.—Alexandria is almost quite hollow underneath, occasioned by the many aqueducts to the Nile,[1] that furnish the private houses with water; where being received in cisterns, it settles by degrees, and becomes perfectly clear. The master and his family are accustomed to use this: for the water of the Nile being extremely thick and muddy, is apt to breed many distempers. The common people, however, are forced to be contented with the latter, because there is not a single spring in the whole city. The river was in that part of the town which was in the possession of the Alexandrians. By which circumstance Ganymed was reminded that our men might be deprived of water; because being distributed into several streets, for the more easy defense of the works, they made use of that which was preserved in the aqueducts and the cisterns of private houses.

CHAP. VI.—With this view he began a great and difficult

[1] The river Nile was the largest river in the world known to the ancients. It derived its name from the Hebrew word Nachal, or Nahal, signifying merely "the river," and hence, in the book of Exodus it is mentioned only under this appellation. It was also called Siris by the Æthiopians; and we find it mentioned by the prophet Jeremiah, as the Sihor; it was surnamed Ægyptus, from its being the great fertilizer of the country. The most interesting phenomenon connected with the Nile, is its periodical inundation, upon which all the vaunted fertility of Egypt entirely depends; without it, the whole country, excepting such parts as are immediately on the banks of the river or on the innumerable canals, with which the natives have endeavored to supply the want of rain, would be no better than the rest of the Libyan desert. The ancients, who witnessed the inundation of this river, exhausted their imagination in conjectures as to its cause, and it is only of late years that it has been ascertained to arise from the periodical rains, which fall in the tropical regions from June to September, assisted by the etesian winds, which blow violently from the north-east, and thus hinder the waters from throwing themselves with their usual volume into the sea.—Arrowsmith's Ancient Geography.

work; for having stopped up all the canals by which his own cisterns were supplied, he drew vast quantities of water out of the sea, by the help of wheels and other engines, pouring it continually into the canals of Cæsar's quarter. The cisterns in the nearest houses soon began to taste salter than ordinary, and occasioned great wonder among the men, who could not think from what cause it proceeded. They were even ready to disbelieve their senses when those who were quartered a little lower in the town assured them that they found the water the same as before. This put them upon comparing the cisterns one with another, and by trial they easily perceived the difference. But in a little time the water in the nearest houses became quite unfit for use, and that lower down grew daily more tainted and brackish.

CHAP. VII.—All doubt being removed by this circumstance, such a terror ensued among the troops that they fancied themselves reduced to the last extremity. Some complained of Cæsar's delay, that he did not order them immediately to repair to their ships. Others dreaded a yet greater misfortune, as it would be impossible to conceal their design of retreating from the Alexandrians, who were so near them; and no less so to embark in the face of a vigorous and pursuing enemy. There were besides a great number of the townsmen in Cæsar's quarter, whom he had not thought proper to force from their houses, because they openly pretended to be in his interest, and to have quitted the party of their fellow-citizens. But to offer here a defense either of the sincerity or conduct of these Alexandrians, would be only labor in vain, since all who know the genius and temper of the people must be satisfied that they are the fittest instruments in the world for treason.

CHAP. VIII.—Cæsar labored to remove his soldiers' fears by encouraging and reasoning with them. For he affirmed "that they might easily find fresh water by digging wells, as all sea-coasts naturally abounded with fresh springs: that if Egypt was singular in this respect, and differed from every other soil, yet still, as the sea was open, and the enemy without a fleet, there was nothing to hinder their fetching it at pleasure in their ships, either from Parætonium[1] on the left, or from the

[1] A city and harbor of Egypt, situated on the Campic branch of the Nile, called at present *Porto Rassa.*

island[1] on the right; and as their two voyages were in different directions, they could not be prevented by adverse winds at the same time; that a retreat was on no account to be thought of, not only by those that had a concern for their honor, but even by such as regarded nothing but life; that it was with the utmost difficulty they could defend themselves behind their works; but if they once quitted that advantage, neither in number or situation would they be a match for the enemy: that to embark would require much time, and be attended with great danger, especially where it must be managed by little boats: that the Alexandrians, on the contrary, were nimble and active, and thoroughly acquainted with the streets and buildings; that, moreover, when flushed with victory, they would not fail to run before, seize all the advantageous posts, possess themselves of the tops of the houses, and by annoying them in their retreat, effectually prevent their getting on board; that they must therefore think no more of retreating, but place all their hopes of safety in victory."

Chap. IX.—Having by this speech re-assured his men, he ordered the centurions to lay aside all other works, and apply themselves day and night to the digging of wells. The work once begun, and the minds of all aroused to exertion, they exerted themselves so vigorously that in the very first night abundance of fresh water was found. Thus, with no great labor on our side, the mighty projects and painful attempts of the Alexandrians were entirely frustrated. Within these two days the thirty-seventh legion, composed of Pompey's veterans that had surrendered to Cæsar, embarking by order of Domitius Calvinus, with arms, darts, provisions, and military engines, arrived upon the coast of Africa, a little above Alexandria. These ships were hindered from gaining the port by an easterly wind, which continued to blow for several days; but all along that coast it is very safe to ride at anchor. Being detained, however, longer than they expected, and distressed by want of water, they gave notice of it to Cæsar, by a dispatch sloop.

Chap. X.—Cæsar, that he might himself be able to determine what was best to be done, went on board one of the

[1] This island is Pharos, of which Cæsar gave a description at the end of tho last book.

ships in the harbor, and ordered the whole fleet to follow. He took none of the land forces with him, because he was unwilling to leave the works unguarded during his absence. Being arrived at that part of the coast known by the name of Chersonesus,[1] he sent some mariners on shore to fetch water. Some of these venturing too far into the country for the sake of plunder, were intercepted by the enemy's horse. From them the Egyptians learned that Cæsar himself was on board, without any soldiers. Upon this information, they thought fortune had thrown in their way a good opportunity of attempting something with success. They therefore manned all the ships that they had ready for sea, and met Cæsar on his return. He declined fighting that day, for two reasons, first, because he had no soldiers on board, and secondly, because it was past four in the afternoon. The night, he was sensible, must be highly advantageous to his enemies, who depended on their knowledge of the coast, while he would be deprived of the benefit of encouraging his men, which could not be done with any effect in the dark, where courage and cowardice must remain equally unknown. Cæsar, therefore, drew all his ships toward the shore, where he imagined the enemy would not follow him.

CHAP. XI.—There was one Rhodian galley in Cæsar's right wing, considerably distant from the rest. The enemy observing this, could not restrain themselves, but came forward with four-decked ships, and several open barks, to attack her. Cæsar was obliged to advance to her relief, that he might not suffer the disgrace of seeing one of his galleys sunk before his eyes; though, had he left her to perish, he judged that she deserved it for her rashness. The attack was sustained with great courage by the Rhodians, who, though at all times distinguished by their valor and experience in engagements at sea, yet exerted themselves in a particular manner on this occasion, that they might not draw upon themselves the charge of having occasioned a misfortune to the fleet. Accordingly they obtained a complete victory, took one four-banked galley, sunk another, disabled a third, and slew all that were on board, besides a great number of the combatants belonging to the other ships. Nay, had not night interposed, Cæsar would have made

[1] This Chersonesus is placed by Ptolemy about seven leagues to the west of Alexandria.

himself master of their whole fleet. During the consternation that followed upon this defeat, Cæsar, finding the contrary winds to abate, took the transports in tow, and advanced with the victorious fleet to Alexandria.

CHAP. XII.—The Alexandrians, disheartened at this loss, since they found themselves now worsted, not by the superior valor of the soldiers, but by the skill and ability of the mariners, retired to the tops of their houses, and blocked up the entrances of their streets, as if they feared our fleet might attack them even by land. But soon after, Ganymed assuring them in council, that he would not only restore the vessels they had lost, but even increase their number, they began to repair their old ships with great expectation and confidence, and resolved to apply more than ever to the putting their fleet in a good condition. And although they had lost above a hundred and ten ships in the port and arsenal, yet they did not relinquish the idea of repairing their fleet; because, by making themselves masters of the sea, they saw they would have it in their power to hinder Cæsar's receiving any reinforcements or supplies. Besides, being mariners, born upon the sea-coast, and exercised from their infancy in naval affairs, they were desirous to return to that wherein their true and proper strength lay, remembering the advantages they had formerly gained, even with their little ships. They therefore applied themselves with all diligence to the equipping a fleet.

CHAP. XIII.—Vessels were stationed at all the mouths of the Nile, for receiving and gathering in the customs. Several old ships were likewise lodged in the king's private arsenals, which had not put to sea for many years. These last they refitted, and recalled the former to Alexandria. Oars were wanting; they uncovered the porticos, academies, and public buildings, and made use of the planks they furnished for oars. Their natural ingenuity, and the abundance of all things to be met with in the city, supplied every want. In fine, they had no long navigation to provide for, and were only solicitous about present exigences, foreseeing they would have no occasion to fight but in the port. In a few days, therefore, contrary to all expectation, they had fitted out twenty-two quadriremes, and five quinqueremes. To these they added a great number of small open barks; and after testing the efficiency of each in the harbor, put a sufficient number of soldiers on board, and prepared every thing necessary for an engagement. Cæsar had nine Rhodian galleys (for of the ten which were sent, one was shipwrecked on the coast of Egypt), eight from Pontus, five from Lycia, and twelve from Asia. Of these, ten were quadriremes, and five quinquerimes; the rest were smaller, and for the most part without decks. Yet, trusting to the valor of his soldiers, and being acquainted with the strength of the enemy, he prepared for an engagement.

CHAP. XIV.—When both sides were come to have sufficienr confidence in their own strength, Cæsar sailed round Pharos, and formed in line of battle opposite to the enemy. He placed the Rhodian galleys on his right wing, and those of Pontus on his left. Between these he left a space of four hundred paces, to allow for extending and working the vessels. This disposition being made, he drew up the rest of the fleet as a reserve, giving them the necessary orders, and distributing them in such a manner that every ship followed that to which she was appointed to give succor. The Alexandrians brought out their fleet with great confidence, and drew it up, placing their twenty-two quadriremes in front, and disposing the rest behind them in a second line, by way of reserve. They had besides a great number of boats and smaller vessels, which carried fire and combustibles, with the intention of intimidating us by their number, cries, and flaming darts. Between the two fleets were certain flats, separated by very narrow channels, and which are said to be on the African coast, as being in that division of Alexandria which belongs to Africa. Both sides waited which should first pass these shallows, because whoever entered the narrow channels between them, in case of any misfortune, would be impeded both in retreating and working their ships to advantage.

CHAP. XV.—Euphranor commanded the Rhodian fleet, who for valor and greatness of mind deserved to be ranked among our own men rather than the Grecians. The Rhodians had raised him to the post of admiral, on account of his known courage and experience. He, perceiving Cæsar's design, addressed him to this effect: "You seem afraid of passing the shallow first, lest you should be thereby forced to come to an engagement, before you can bring up the rest of the fleet. Leave the matter to us; we will sustain the fight (and we will not disappoint your expectations), until the whole fleet gets clear of the shallows. It is both dishonorable and afflicting that they should so long continue in our sight with an air of triumph." Cæsar, encouraging him in his design, and bestowing many praises upon him, gave the signal for engaging. Four Rhodian ships having passed the shallows, the Alexandrians gathered round and attacked them. They maintained the fight with great courage, disengaging themselves by their art and address, and working their ships with so much skill, that notwithstanding the inequality of number, none of the enemy were suffered to run alongside, or break their oars. Meantime the rest of the fleet came up; when, on account of the narrowness of the place, art became useless, and the contest depended entirely upon valor. Nor was there at Alexandria a single Roman or citizen who remained engaged in the attack or defense, but mounted the tops of the houses and all the eminences that would give a view of the fight, addressing the gods by vows and prayers for victory.

CHAP. XVI.—The event of the battle was by no means equal; a defeat would have deprived us of all resources either by land or sea; and even if we were victorious, the future would be uncertain. The Alexandrians, on the contrary, by a victory gained every thing; and if defeated, might yet again have recourse to fortune. It was likewise a matter of the highest concern to see the safety of all depend upon a few, of whom, if any were deficient in resolution and energy, they would expose their whole party to destruction. This Cæsar had often represented to his troops during the preceding days, that they might be thereby induced to fight with the more resolution, when they knew the common safety to depend upon their bravery. Every man said the same to his comrade, companion, and friend, beseeching him not to disappoint the expectation of those who had chosen him in preference to others for the defense of the common interest. Accordingly, they fought with so much resolution, that neither the art nor address of the Egyptians, a maritime and seafaring people, could avail them, nor the multitude of their ships be of service to them; nor the valor of those selected for this engagement be compared to the determined courage of the Romans. In this action a quinquereme was taken, and a bireme, with all the soldiers and mariners on board, besides three sunk, without any loss on our side. The rest fled toward the town, and protecting their ships under the mole and forts, prevented us from approaching.

CHAP. XVII.—To deprive the enemy of this resource for the future, Cæsar thought it by all means necessary to render himself master of the mole and island; for having already in a great measure completed his works within the town, he was in hopes of being able to defend himself both in the island and city. This resolution being taken, he put into boats and small vessels ten cohorts, a select body of light-armed infantry, and such of the Gallic cavalry as he thought fittest for his purpose, and sent them against the island; while, at the same time, to create a diversion, he attacked it on the other with his fleet, promising great rewards to those who should first render themselves masters of it. At first, the enemy firmly withstood the impetuosity of our men; for they both annoyed them from the tops of the houses, and gallantly maintained their ground along the shore; to which being steep and craggy, our men could find no way of approach; the more accessible avenues being skillfully defended by small boats, and five galleys, prudently stationed for that purpose. But when after examining the approaches, and sounding the shallows, a few of our men got a footing upon the shore, and were followed by others, who pushed the islanders, without intermission; the Pharians at last betook themselves to flight. On their defeat, the rest abandoning the defense of the port, quitted their ships, and retired into the town, to provide for the security of their houses

CHAP. XVIII.—But they could not long maintain their ground there: though, to compare small things with great, their buildings were not unlike those of Alexandria, and their towers were high, and joined together so as to form a kind of wall; and our men had not come prepared with ladders, fascines, or any weapons for assault. But fear often deprives men of intellect and counsel, and weakens their strength, as happened upon this occasion. Those who had ventured to oppose us on even ground, terrified by the loss of a few men, and the general rout, durst not face us from a height of thirty feet; but throwing themselves from the mole into the sea, endeavored to gain the town, though above eight hundred paces distant. Many however were slain, and about six hundred taken.

CHAP. XIX.—Cæsar, giving up the plunder to the soldiers, ordered the houses to be demolished, but fortified the castle at the end of the bridge next the island, and placed a garrison in it. This the Pharians had abandoned; but the other, toward the town, which was considerably stronger, was still held by the Alexandrians. Cæsar attacked it next day; because by getting possession of these two forts, he would be entirely master of the port, and prevent sudden excursions and piracies. Already he had, by means of his arrows and engines, forced the garrison to abandon the place, and retire toward the town. He had also landed three cohorts which was all the place would contain; the rest of his troops were stationed in their ships. This being done, he orders them to fortify the bridge against the enemy, and to fill with stones and block up the arch on which the bridge was built, through which there was egress for the ships. When one of these works was accomplished so effectually, that no boat could pass out at all, and when the other was commenced, the Alexandrians sallied, in crowds from the town, and drew up in an open place, over against the intrenchment we had cast up at the head of the bridge. At the same time they stationed at the mole the vessels which they had been wont to make pass under the bridge, to set fire to our ships of burden. Our men fought from the bridge and the mole; the enemy from the space, opposite to the bridge, and from their ships, by the side of the mole.

CHAP. XX.—While Cæsar was engaged in these things, and in exhorting his troops, a number of rowers and mariners, quitting their ships, threw themselves upon the mole, partly out of curiosity, partly to have a share in the action. At first, with stones and slings, they forced the enemy's ships from the mole; and seemed to do still greater execution with their darts. But when, some time after, a few Alexandrians found means to land, and attack them in flank, as they had left their ships without order or discipline, so they soon began to flee, with precipitation. The Alexandrians, encouraged by this success, landed in great numbers, and vigorously pressed upon our men, who were, by this time, in great confusion. Those that remained in the galleys perceiving this, drew up the ladders and put off from the shore, to prevent the enemy's boarding them. Our soldiers who belonged to the three cohorts, which were at the head of the mole to guard the bridge, astonished at this disorder, the cries they heard behind them, and the general rout of their party, unable besides to bear up against the great number of darts which came pouring upon them, and fearing to be surrounded, and have their retreat cut off, by the departure of their ships, abandoned the fortifications which they had commenced at the bridge, and ran, with all the speed they could, toward the galleys: some getting on board the nearest vessels, overloaded and sank them: part, resisting the enemy, and uncertain what course to take, were cut to pieces by the Alexandrians. Others, more fortunate, got to the ships that rode at anchor; and a few, supported by their bucklers, making a determined struggle, swam to the nearest vessels.

CHAP. XXI—Cæsar, endeavoring to re-animate his men, and lead them back to the defense of the works, was exposed to the same danger as the rest; when, finding them universally to give ground, he retreated to his own galley, whither such a multitude followed and crowded after him, that it was impossible either to work or put her off. Foreseeing what must happen, he flung himself into the sea, and swam to the ships that lay at some distance. Hence dispatching boats to succor his men, he, by that means, preserved a small number. His own ship, being sunk by the multitude that crowded into her, went down with all that were on board. About four hundred legionary soldiers, and somewhat above that number of sailors and rowers, were lost in this action. The Alexandrians secured the fort by strong works, and a great number of engines; and having cleared away the stones with which Cæsar had blocked up the port, enjoyed henceforward a free and open navigation.

CHAP. XXII.—Our men were so far from being disheartened at this loss, that they seemed rather roused and animated by it. They made continual sallies upon the enemy, to destroy or check the progress of their works; fell upon them as often as they had an opportunity; and never failed to intercept them, when they ventured to advance beyond their fortifications. In short, the legions were so bent upon fighting, that they even exceeded the orders and exhortations of Cæsar. They were inconsolable for their late disgrace, and impatient to come to blows with the enemy; insomuch, that he found it necessary rather to restrain and check their ardor, than incite them to action.

17*

CHAP. XXIII.—The Alexandrians, perceiving that success confirmed the Romans, and that adverse fortune only animated them the more, as they knew of no medium between these on which to ground any further hopes, resolved, as far as we can conjecture, either by the advice of the friends of their king who were in Cæsar's quarter, or of their own previous design, intimated to the king by secret emissaries, to send embassadors to Cæsar to request him, "To dismiss their king and suffer him to rejoin his subjects; that the people, weary of subjection to a woman, of living under a precarious government, and submitting to the cruel laws of the tyrant Ganymed, were ready to execute the orders of the king: and if by his sanction they should embrace the alliance and protection of Cæsar, the multitude would not be deterred from surrendering by the fear of danger."

CHAP. XXIV.—Though Cæsar knew the nation to be false and perfidious, seldom speaking as they really thought, yet he judged it best to comply with their desire. He even flattered himself, that his condescension in sending back their king at their request, would prevail on them to be faithful; or, as was more agreeable to their character, if they only wanted the king to head their army, at least it would be more for his honor[1] and credit to have to do with a monarch than with a band of slaves and fugitives. Accordingly, he exhorted the king, "To take the government into his own hands, and consult the welfare of so fair and illustrious a kingdom, defaced by hideous ruins and conflagrations. To make his subjects sensible of their duty, preserve them from the destruction that threatened them, and act with fidelity toward himself and the Romans, who put so much confidence in him, as

[1] Dion assigns a different motive for Cæsar's conduct on this occasion; his words are as follows: "Cæsar thought that the Ægyptians had really changed their minds (for he had heard that they were cowardly and fickle), and imagined that they were intimidated by their losses. Being unwilling to appear averse to peace, although they might have treacherous intentions, he said that he would comply with their wishes, and then sent Ptolemy to them, from whom he thought that he had nothing to fear on account of his youth and neglected education. He was in hopes also that the Ægyptians would agree to a peace on his own terms, or if they should not, that he could with more justice defeat and subject them, and it would also furnish him with a plausible pretext for conferring the sovereign power on Cleopatra. For he never suspected that he would be conquered by them, especially after the late increase to his army."

to send him among armed enemies." Then taking him by the hand, he dismissed the young prince who was fast approaching manhood. But his mind being thoroughly versed in the art of dissimulation, and no way degenerating from the character of his nation, he entreated Cæsar with tears not to send him back; for that his company was to him preferable to a kingdom. Cæsar, moved at his concern, dried up his tears; and telling him, if these were his real sentiments, they would soon meet again, dismissed him. The king, like a wild beast escaped out of confinement, carried on the war with such acrimony against Cæsar, that the tears he shed at parting seemed to have been tears of joy. Cæsar's lieutenants, friends, centurions, and soldiers, were delighted that this had happened; because his easiness of temper had been imposed upon by a child: as if in truth Cæsar's behavior on this occasion had been the effect of easiness of temper, and not of the most consummate prudence.

CHAP. XXV.—When the Alexandrians found that on the recovery of their king, neither had they become stronger, nor the Romans weaker; that the troops despised the youth and weakness of their king; and that their affairs were in no way bettered by his presence: they were greatly discouraged; and a report ran that a large body of troops was marching by land from Syria and Cilicia to Cæsar's assistance (of which he had not as yet himself received information); still they determined to intercept the convoys that came to him by sea. To this end, having equipped some ships, they ordered them to cruise before the Canopic branch of the Nile, by which they thought it most likely our supplies would arrive. Cæsar, who was informed of it, ordered his fleet to get ready, and gave the command of it to Tiberius Nero.[1] The Rhodian galleys made part of this squadron, headed by Euphranor their admiral, without whom there never was a successful engagement fought. But fortune, which often reserves the heaviest disasters for those who have been loaded with her highest favors, encountered Euphranor upon this occasion, with an aspect very

[1] The Tiberius Nero mentioned here, was the father of the emperor Tiberius, who succeeded Augustus. He served Cæsar most zealously throughout the whole of this war, and, on account of his meritorious conduct, was created Pontifex Maximus in room of Scipio, and commissioned to conduct several colonies to Gaul, among other places to Narbo and Arelate.

different from what she had hitherto worn. For when our ships were arrived at Canopus, and the fleets drawn up on each side had begun the engagement, Euphranor, according to custom, having made the first attack, and pierced and sunk one of the enemy's ships; as he pursued the next a considerable way, without being sufficiently supported by those that followed him, he was surrounded by the Alexandrians. None of the fleet advanced to his relief, either out of fear for their own safety, or because they imagined he would easily be able to extricate himself by his courage and good fortune. Accordingly he alone behaved well in this action, and perished with his victorious galley.

CHAP. XXVI.—About the same time Mithridates[1] of Pergamus, a man of illustrious descent, distinguished for his bravery and knowledge of the art of war, and who held a very high place in the friendship and confidence of Cæsar, having been sent in the beginning of the Alexandrian war, to raise succors in Syria[2] and Cilicia, arrived by land at the head of a great body of troops, which his diligence, and the affection of these two provinces, had enabled him to draw together in a very short time. He conducted them first to Pelusium, where Egypt joins Syria. Achillas, who was perfectly well acquainted with its importance, had seized and put a strong garrison into it. For Egypt is considered as defended on all sides by strong barriers; on the side of the sea by the Pharos, and on the side of Syria by Pelusium, which are accounted the two keys of that kingdom. He attacked it so briskly with a large body of troops, fresh men continually succeeding in the place of those that were fatigued, and urged the assault with so much firmness and perseverance, that he carried it the same day on which he

[1] We learn from Strabo that this Mithridates was born at Pergamus, and was descended from the tetrarchs of Galatia. When Mithridates the Great, king of Pontus, overran Asia, he took with him this man, who from this circumstance derived his name. He attached himself to Cæsar's party in the civil war, and received as the reward of his services, the tetrarchy of Galatia, and the sovereignty of the Cimmerian Bosphorus; the possession of the latter was disputed by Asander, who then held it. After the death of Cæsar, Mithridates of Pergamus endeavored to establish his claims by an appeal to arms, but was defeated and put to death.

[2] Josephus informs us that a large army was sent to the aid of Cæsar on this occasion, by Hyrcanus, the king of the Jews, under the command of Antipater, the father of king Herod. These forces contributed largely to the success of Cæsar.

attacked it, and placed a garrison in it. Thence he pursued his march to Alexandria, reducing all the provinces through which he passed, and conciliating them to Cæsar, by that authority which always accompanies the conqueror.

CHAP. XXVII.—Not far from Alexandria lies Delta, the most celebrated province of Egypt, which derives its name from the Greek letter so called. For the Nile, dividing into two channels, which gradually diverge as they approach the sea, into which they at last discharge themselves, at a considerable distance from one another, leaves an intermediate space in form of a triangle. The king understanding that Mithridates was approaching this place, and knowing he must pass the river, sent a large body of troops against him, sufficient, as he thought, if not to overwhelm and crush him, at least to stop his march, for though he earnestly desired to see him defeated, yet he thought it a great point gained, to hinder his junction with Cæsar. The troops that first passed the river, and came up with Mithridates, attacked him immediately, hastening to snatch the honor of victory from the troops that were marching to their aid. Mithridates at first confined himself to the defense of his camp, which he had with great prudence fortified according to the custom of the Romans: but observing that they advanced insolently and without caution, he sallied upon them from all parts, and put a great number of them to the sword;[1] insomuch that, but for their knowledge of the ground, and the neighborhood of the vessels in which they had passed the river, they must have been all destroyed. But recovering by degrees from their terror, and joining the troops that followed them, they again prepared to attack Mithridates.

CHAP. XXVIII.—A messenger was sent by Mithridates to Cæsar, to inform him of what had happened. The king learns from his followers that the action had taken place. Thus, much about the same time, Ptolemy set out to crush Mith-

[1] Josephus mentions this engagement in the sixteenth chapter of the fourteenth book of the Jewish War, and informs us that the Jews, under the command of Antipater, made the first impression on the Ægyptian ranks; and that the place where the action was fought, was called the "Expedition of the Jews," and that the Jews, who dwelt in that country, acted as guides to Mithridates and his army, on beholding the letters of king Hyrcanus.

ridates, and Cæsar to relieve him. The king made use of the more expeditious conveyance of the Nile, where he had a large fleet in readiness. Cæsar declined the navigation of the river, that he might not be obliged to engage the enemy's fleet; and coasting along the African shore, found means to join the victorious troops of Mithridates, before Ptolemy could attack him. The king had encamped in a place fortified by nature, being an eminence surrounded on all sides by a plain. Three of its sides were secured by various defenses. One was washed by the river Nile, the other was steep and inaccessible, and the third was defended by a morass.

CHAP. XXIX.—Between Ptolemy's camp and Cæsar's route lay a narrow river with very steep banks, which discharged itself into the Nile. This river was about seven miles from the king's camp; who, understanding that Cæsar was directing his march that way, sent all his cavalry, with a choice body of light-armed foot, to prevent Cæsar from crossing, and maintain an unequal fight from the banks, where courage had no opportunity to exert itself, and cowardice ran no hazard. Our men, both horse and foot, were extremely mortified, that the Alexandrians should so long maintain their ground against them. Wherefore, some of the German cavalry, dispersing in quest of a ford, found means to swim the river where the banks were lowest; and the legionaries at the same time cutting down several large trees, that reached from one bank to another, and constructing suddenly a mound, by their help got to the other side. The enemy were so much in dread of their attack, that they betook themselves to flight; but in vain: for very few returned to the king, almost all being cut to pieces in the pursuit.

CHAP. XXX.—Cæsar, upon this success, judging that his sudden approach must strike great terror into the Alexandrians, advanced toward their camp with his victorious army. But finding it well intrenched, strongly fortified by nature, and the ramparts covered with armed soldiers, he did not think proper that his troops, who were very much fatigued both by their march and the late battle, should attack it; and therefore encamped at a small distance from the enemy. Next day he attacked a fort, in a village not far off, which the king had fortified and joined to his camp by a line of communication, with a view to keep possession of the village. He attacked it with his whole army, and took it by storm; not because it would have been difficult to carry it with a few forces; but with the design of falling immediately upon the enemy's camp, during the alarm which the loss of this fort must give them. Accordingly, the Romans, in continuing the pursuit of those that fled from the fort, arrived at last before the Alexandrian camp, and commenced a most furious action at a distance. There were two approaches by which it might be attacked; one by the plain, of which we have spoken before, the other by a narrow pass, between their camp and the Nile. The first, which was much the easiest, was defended by a numerous body of their best troops; and the access on the side of the Nile gave the enemy great advantage in distressing and wounding our men; for they were exposed to a double shower of darts: in front from the rampart, behind from the river; where the enemy had stationed a great number of ships, furnished with archers and slingers, that kept up a continual discharge.

Chap. XXXI.—Cæsar, observing that his troops fought with the utmost ardor, and yet made no great progress, on account of the disadvantage of the ground; and perceiving they had left the highest part of their camp unguarded, because, it being sufficiently fortified by nature, they had all crowded to the other attacks, partly to have a share in the action, partly to be spectators of the issue; he ordered some cohorts to wheel round the camp, and gain that ascent: appointing Carfulenus[1] to command them, a man distinguished for bravery and acquaintance with the service. When they had reached the place, as there were but very few to defend it, our men attacked them so briskly that the Alexandrians, terrified by the cries they heard behind them, and seeing themselves attacked both in front and rear, fled in the utmost consternation on all sides. Our men, animated by the confusion of the enemy, entered the camp in several places at the same time, and running down from the higher ground, put a great number of them to the sword. The Alexandrians, endeavoring to escape, threw themselves in crowds over the rampart in the quarter next the river. The foremost tumbling into the ditch, where they were crushed to death, furnished an easy

[1] This Carfulenus, of whom Hirtius speaks so favorably, was subsequently killed in the battle of Mutina, while fighting against Mark Antony.

passage for those that followed. It is ascertained that the king escaped from the camp, and was received on board a ship; but by the crowd that followed him, the ship in which he fled was overloaded and sunk.

CHAP. XXXII.—After this speedy and successful action, Cæsar, in consequence of so great a victory, marched the nearest way by land to Alexandria with his cavalry, and entered triumphant into that part of the town which was possessed by the enemy's guards. He was not mistaken in thinking that the Alexandrians, upon hearing of the issue of the battle, would give over all thoughts of war. Accordingly, as soon as he arrived, he reaped the just fruit of his valor and magnanimity. For all the multitude of the inhabitants, throwing down their arms, abandoning their works, and assuming the habit of suppliants, preceded by all those sacred symbols of religion with which they were wont to mollify their offended kings, met Cæsar on his arrival and surrendered. Cæsar, accepting their submission, and encouraging them, advanced through the enemy's works into his own quarter of the town, where he was received with the universal congratulations of his party, who were no less overjoyed at his arrival and presence, than at the happy issue of the war.

CHAP. XXXIII.—Cæsar, having thus made himself master of Alexandria and Egypt, lodged the government in the hands of those to whom Ptolemy had bequeathed it by will, conjuring the Roman people not to permit any change. For the eldest of Ptolemy's two sons being dead, Cæsar settled the kingdom upon the youngest, in conjunction with Cleopatra, the elder of the two sisters, who had always continued under his protection and guardianship. The younger,[1] Arsinoe, in whose name Ganymed, as we have seen, tyrannically reigned for some time, he thought proper to banish the kingdom, that she might not raise any new disturbance, through the agency of seditious men, before the king's authority should be firmly established. Taking

[1] Cæsar subsequently brought Arsinoe to Rome to grace his triumph, but perceiving that the populace felt compassion for the youthful princess, he did not imprison her or put her to death (the usual dark scene that clouded the triumphs of the Roman generals), but restored her to freedom. She was afterward slain by Cleopatra, who, being desirous of having the sovereignty of Cyprus, which she held in common with Arsinoe, prevailed on Mark Antony to sacrifice her to her ambition.

the sixth veteran legion with him into Syria, he left the rest in Egypt to support the authority of the king and queen, neither of whom stood well in the affections of their subjects, on account of their attachment to Cæsar, nor could be supposed to have given any fixed foundation to their power, in an administration of only a few days' continuance. It was also for the honor and interest of the republic that if they continued faithful our forces should protect them; but if ungrateful that they should be restrained by the same power. Having thus settled the kingdom, he marched by land into Syria.

CHAP. XXXIV.—While these things passed in Egypt, king Deiotarus[1] applied to Domitius Calvinus, to whom Cæsar had intrusted the government of Asia and the neighboring provinces, beseeching him "not to suffer the Lesser Armenia which was his kingdom, or Cappadocia, which belonged to Ariobarzanes,[2] to be seized and laid waste by Pharnaces, because, unless they were delivered from these insults, it would be impossible for them to execute Cæsar's orders, or raise the money they stood engaged to pay." Domitius, who was not only sensible of the necessity of money to defray the expenses of the war, but likewise thought it dishonorable to the people of Rome and the victorious Cæsar, as well as infamous to himself, to suffer the dominions of allies and friends to be usurped by a foreign prince, sent embassadors to Pharnaces, to acquaint him, "That he must withdraw immediately from Armenia and Cappadocia, and no longer insult the majesty and right of the Roman people, while engaged in a civil war." But believing that his deputation would have greater weight, if he was ready to second it himself at the head of an army; he repaired to the legions which were then in Asia, ordering two of them into Egypt, at Cæsar's desire, and carrying the thirty-sixth along

1 Deiotarus had been made tetrarch of Galatia by the assistance of Pompey, and in return for this favor, aided him with all his forces in war against Cæsar. After the battle of Pharsalia, he was pardoned by Cæsar, who, however, deprived him of the tetrarchy of Galatia, and bestowed it on Mithridates Pergamenus. Deiotarus was subsequently accused of having planned the assassination of Cæsar, and defended by Cicero in a brilliant oration which is still extant. When a very old man, he sent auxiliaries to Brutus.

2 Ariobarzanes, king of Cappadocia, on the breaking out of the civil war between Pompey and Cæsar, espoused the party of the former. Cæsar appears to have pardoned him after inflicting a pecuniary fine upon him.

with him. To the thirty-sixth legion Deiotarus added two more, which he had trained up for several years, according to our discipline; and a hundred horse. The like number of horse were furnished by Ariobarzanes. At the same time, he sent P. Sextius to C. Plætorius the questor, for the legion which had been lately levied in Pontus; and Quinctius Partisius into Cilicia, to draw thence a body of auxiliary troops. All these forces speedily assembled at Comana,[1] by orders of Domitius.

Chap. XXXV.—Meanwhile his embassadors bring back the following answer from Pharnaces: "That he had quitted Cappadocia; but kept possession of the Lesser Armenia, as his own, by right of inheritance: that he was willing, however, to submit every thing to the decision of Cæsar, to whose commands he would pay immediate obedience." C. Domitius, sensible that he had quitted Cappadocia, not voluntarily, but out of necessity; because he could more easily defend Armenia, which lay contiguous to his own kingdom, than Cappadocia, which was more remote: and because believing, at first, that Domitius had brought all the three legions along with him, upon hearing that two were gone to Cæsar, he seemed more determined to keep possession; and insisted "upon his quitting Armenia likewise, as the same right existed in both cases; nor was it just to demand that the matter should be postponed till Cæsar's return, unless things were put in the condition in which they were at first." Having returned this answer, he advanced toward Armenia, with the forces above-mentioned, directing his march along the hills; for from Pontus, by way of Comana, runs a woody ridge of hills, that extends as far as Lesser Armenia, dividing it from Cappadocia. The advantages he had in view, by such a march, were, that he would thereby effectually prevent all surprises, and be plentifully supplied with provisions from Cappadocia.

Chap. XXXVI.—Meantime Pharnaces sends several embassies to Domitius to treat of peace, bearing royal gifts. All these he firmly rejected, telling the deputies: "That nothing was more sacred with him, than the majesty of the Roman people, and recovering the rights of their allies." After long and continued marches, he reached Nicopolis (which is a city

[1] Comana, a very celebrated city of Pontus, supposed to be the modern Tabachzè.

of Lesser Armenia, situated in a plain, having mountains, however, on its two sides, at a considerable distance), and encamped about seven miles from the town. Between his camp and Nicopolis,[1] lay a difficult and narrow pass, where Pharnaces placed a chosen body of foot, and all his horse, in ambuscade. He ordered a great number of cattle to be dispersed in the pass, and the townsmen and peasants to show themselves, that if Domitius entered the defile as a friend he might have no suspicion of an ambuscade, when he saw the men and flocks dispersed, without apprehension, in the fields; or if he should come as an enemy, that the soldiers, quitting their ranks to pillage, might be cut to pieces when dipersed.

CHAP. XXXVII.—While this design was going forward, he never ceased sending embassadors to Domitius, with proposals of peace and amity, fancying, by this means, the more easy to ensnare him. The expectation of peace kept Domitius in his camp; so that Pharnaces, having missed the opportunity, and fearing the ambuscade might be discovered, drew off his troops. Next day Domitius approached Nicopolis, and encamped near the town. While our men were working at the trenches, Pharnaces drew up his army in order of battle, forming his front into one line, according to the custom of the country, and securing his wings with a triple body of reserves. In the same manner, the center was formed in single files, and two intervals were left on the right and left. Domitius, ordering part of the troops to continue under arms before the rampart, completed the fortifications of his camp.

CHAP. XXXVIII.—Next night, Pharnaces, having intercepted the couriers who brought Domitius an account of the posture of affairs at Alexandria, understood that Cæsar was in great danger, and requested Domitius to send him succors speedily, and come himself to Alexandria by the way of Syria. Pharnaces, upon this intelligence, imagined that protracting the time would be equivalent to a victory, because Domitius, he supposed, must very soon depart. He therefore dug two ditches, four feet deep, at a moderate distance from each other, on that side where lay the easiest access to the town, and our forces might, most advantageously, attack him; re-

[1] We learn from Strabo, that this Nicopolis was built by Pompey. Ptolemy places it in Lesser Armenia.

solving not to advance beyond them. Between these, he constantly drew up his army, placing all his cavalry upon the wings without them, which greatly exceeded ours in number, and would otherwise have been useless.

CHAP. XXXIX.—Domitius, more concerned at Cæsar's danger than his own, and believing he could not retire with safety, should he now desire the conditions he had rejected, or march away without any apparent cause, drew his forces out of the camp, and ranged them in order of battle. He placed the thirty-sixth legion on the right, that of Pontus on the left, and those of Deiotarus in the main body; drawing them up with a very narrow front, and posting the rest of the cohorts to sustain the wings. The armies being thus drawn up on each side, they advanced to the battle.

CHAP. XL.—The signal being given at the same time by both parties, they engage. The conflict was sharp and various, for the thirty-sixth legion falling upon the king's cavaly, that was drawn up without the ditch, charged them so successfully, that they drove them to the very walls of the town, passed the ditch, and attacked their infantry in the rear. But on the other side, the legion of Pontus having given way, the second line, which advanced to sustain them, making a circuit round the ditch, in order to attack the enemy in flank, was overwhelmed and borne down by a shower of darts, in endeavoring to pass it. The legions of Deiotarus made scarcely any resistance; thus the victorious forces of the king turned their right wing and main body against the thirty-sixth legion, which yet made a brave stand; and though surrounded by the forces of the enemy, formed themselves into a circle, with wonderful presence of mind, and retired to the foot of a mountain, whither Pharnaces did not think fit to pursue them, on account of the disadvantage of the place. Thus the legion of Pontus being almost wholly cut off, with great part of those of Deiotarus, the thirty-sixth legion retreated to an eminence, with the loss of about two hundred and fifty men. Several Roman knights, of illustrious rank, fell in this battle. Domitius, after this defeat, rallied the remains of his broken army, and retreated, by safe ways, through Cappadocia, into Asia.[1]

[1] Asia seems here to refer to that part of Asia Minor, under the dominion of the Romans, which was subsequently called by them Asia Proconsularis.

CHAP. XLI.—Pharnaces, elated with this success, as he expected that Cæsar's difficulties would terminate as he [Pharnaces] wished, entered Pontus with all his forces. There, acting as conqueror and a most cruel king, and promising himself a happier destiny than his father, he stormed many towns, and seized the effects of the Roman and Pontic citizens, inflicted punishments, worse than death, upon such as were distinguished by their age or beauty, and having made himself master of all Pontus, as there was no one to oppose his progress, boasted that he had recovered his father's kingdom.

CHAP. XLII.—About the same time, we received a considerable check in Illyricum; which province, had been defended the preceding months, not only without insult, but even with honor. For Cæsar's quæstor, Q. Cornificius, had been sent there as proprætor, the summer before, with two legions; and though it was of itself little able to support an army, and at that time in particular was almost totally ruined by the war in the vicinity, and the civil dissensions; yet, by his prudence, and vigilance, being very careful not to undertake any rash expedition, he defended and kept possession of it. For he made himself master of several forts, built on eminences, whose advantageous situation tempted the inhabitants to make descents and inroads upon the country; and gave the plunder of them to his soldiers (and although this was but inconsiderable, yet as they were no strangers to the distress and ill condition of the province, they did not cease to be grateful; the rather as it was the fruit of their own valor). And when, after the battle of Pharsalia, Octavius had retreated to that coast with a large fleet; Cornificius, with some vessels of the inhabitants of Jadua,[1] who had always continued faithful to the commonwealth, made himself master of the greatest part of his ships, which, joined to those of his allies, rendered him capable of sustaining even a naval engagement. And while Cæsar, victorious, was pursuing Pompey to the remotest parts of the earth; when he [Cornificius] heard that the enemy had, for the most part, retired into Illyricum, on account of its neighborhood to Macedonia, and were there collecting such as survived the

[1] Jadua was a maritime city of Illyria, traces of the name are still preserved in the modern *Zara*.

defeat [at Pharsalia], he wrote to Gabinius, "To repair directly thither, with the new raised legions, and join Cornificius, that if any danger should assail the province, he might ward it off, but if less forces sufficed, to march into Macedonia, which he foresaw would never be free from commotions, so long as Pompey lived."

Chap. XLIII.—Gabinius, whether he imagined the province better provided than it really was, or depended much upon the auspicious fortune of Cæsar, or confided in his own valor and abilities, he having often terminated with success difficult and dangerous wars, marched into Illyricum, in the middle of winter, and the most difficult season of the year; where, not finding sufficient subsistence in the province, which was partly exhausted, partly disaffected, and having no supplies by sea, because the season of the year had put a stop to navigation, he found himself compelled to carry on the war, not according to his own inclination, but as necessity allowed. As he was therefore obliged to lay siege to forts and castles, in a very rude season, he received many checks, and fell under such contempt with the barbarians, that while retiring to Salona, a maritime city, inhabited by a set of brave and faithful Romans, he was compelled to come to an engagement on his march; and after the loss of two thousand soldiers, thirty-eight centurions, and four tribunes, got to Salona with the rest; where his wants continually increasing, he died a few days after. His misfortunes and sudden death gave Octavius great hopes of reducing the province. But fortune, whose influence is so great in matters of war, joined to the diligence of Cornificius, and the valor of Vatinius, soon put an end to his triumphs.

Chap. XLIV.—Vatinius, who was then at Brundusium, having intelligence of what passed in Illyricum, by letters from Cornificius, who pressed him to come to the assistance of the province, and informed him, that Octavius had leagued with the barbarians, and in several places attacked our garrisons, partly by sea with his fleet, partly by land with the troops of the barbarians; Vatinius, I say, upon notice of these things, though extremely weakened by sickness, insomuch that his strength of body no way answered his resolution and greatness of mind; yet, by his valor, surmounted all opposition, the force of his distemper, the rigor of the winter, and the difficulties of a sudden preparation. For having himself but a very few galleys, he wrote to Q. Kalenus, in Achaia, to furnish him with a squadron of ships. But these not coming with that dispatch which the danger our army was in required, because Octavius pressed hard upon them, he fastened beaks to all the barks and vessels that lay in the port, whose number was considerable enough, though they were not sufficiently large for an engagement. Joining these to what galleys he had, and putting on board the veteran soldiers, of whom he had a great number, belonging to all the legions, who had been left sick at Brundusium, when the army went over to Greece, he sailed for Illyricum; where, having subjected several maritime states that had declared for Octavius, and neglecting such as continued obstinate in their revolt, because he would suffer nothing to retard his design of meeting the enemy, he came up with Octavius before Epidaurus; and obliging him to raise the siege, which he was carrying on with vigor, by sea and land, joined the garrison to his own forces.

CHAP. XLV.—Octavius, understanding that Vatinius's fleet consisted mostly of small barks, and confiding in the strength of his own, stopped at the Isle of Tauris. Vatinius followed him thither, not imagining he would halt at that place, but being determined to pursue him wherever he went. Vatinius, who had no suspicion of an enemy, and whose ships were moreover dispersed by a tempest, perceived, as he approached the isle, a vessel filled with soldiers that advanced toward him, in full sail. Upon this he gave orders for furling the sails, lowering the sail-yards, and arming the soldiers; and hoisting a flag, as a signal for battle, intimated to the ships that followed to do the same. Vatinius's men prepared themselves in the best manner their sudden surprise would allow, while Octavius advanced in good order, from the port. The two fleets drew up Octavius had the advantage in arrangement, and Vatinius in the bravery of his troops.

CHAP. XLVI.—Vatinius, finding himself inferior to the enemy, both in the number and largeness of his ships, resolved to commit the affair to fortune, and therefore in his own quinquereme, attacked Octavius in his four-banked galley. This he did with such violence, and the shock was so great, that the beak of Octavius's galley was broken. The battle raged with great fury likewise in other places, but chiefly around the two admirals; for as the ships on each side advanced to sustain those that fought, a close and furious conflict ensued in a very narrow sea, where the nearer the vessels approached the more had Vatinius's soldiers the advantage. For, with admirable courage, they leaped into the enemy's ships, and forcing them by this means to an equal combat, soon mastered them by their superior valor. Octavius's galley was sunk, and many others were taken or suffered the same fate; the soldies were partly slain in the ships, partly thrown overboard into the sea. Octavius got into a boat, which sinking under the multitude that crowded after him, he himself, though wounded, swam to his brigantine; where, being taken up, and night having put an end to the battle, as the wind blew very strong, he spread all his sails and fled. A few of his ships, that had the good fortune to escape, followed him.

CHAP. XLVII.—But Vatinius, after his success, sounded a retreat, and entered victorious the port whence Octavius had sailed to fight him, without the loss of a single vessel. He took, in this battle, one quinquereme, two triremes, eight two-banked galleys, and a great number of rowers. The next day was employed in repairing his own fleet, and the ships he had taken from the enemy: after which, he sailed for the island of Issa, imagining Octavius had retired thither after his defeat. In this island was a flourishing city, well affected to Octavius, which however, surrendered to Vatinius, upon the first summons. Here he understood that Octavius, attended by a few small barks, had sailed, with a fair wind, for Greece, whence he intended to pass on to Sicily, and afterward to Africa. Vatinius, having in so short a space successfully terminated the affair, restored the province, in a peaceable condition, to Cornificius, and, driven the enemy's fleet out of those seas, returned victorious to Brundusium, with his army and fleet in good condition.

CHAP. XLVIII.—But during the time that Cæsar besieged Pompey at Dyrrachium, triumphed at Old Pharsalia,[1] and

[1] Strabo informs us that there were two cities of this name, the Old and New. We learn from the passage before us, that the battle which gave the empire of the world to Cæsar was fought at Old Pharsalus.

carried on the war, with so much danger, at Alexandria, Cassius Longinus,[1] who had been left in Spain as proprætor of the further province, either through his natural disposition, or out of a hatred he had contracted to the province, on account of a wound he had treacherously received there when quæstor, drew upon himself the general dislike of the people. He discerned this temper among them, partly from a consciousness that he deserved it, partly from the manifest indications they gave of their discontent. To secure himself against their disaffection, he endeavored to gain the love of the soldiers; and having, for this purpose, assembled them together, promised them a hundred sesterces each. Soon after, having made himself master of Medobriga, a town in Lusitania, and of Mount Herminius,[2] whither the Medobrigians had retired, and being upon that occasion saluted imperator by the army, he gave them another hundred sesterces each. These, accompanied by other considerable largesses, in great number, seemed, for the present, to increase the good-will of the army, but tended gradually and imperceptibly to the relaxation of military discipline.

CHAP. XLIX.—Cassius, having sent his army into winter quarters, fixed his residence at Corduba, for the administration of justice. Being greatly in debt, he resolved to pay it by laying heavy burdens upon the province: and, according to the custom of prodigals, made his liberalities a pretense to justify the most exorbitant demands. He taxed the rich at discretion, and compelled them to pay, without the least regard to their remonstrances; frequently making light and trifling offenses the handle for all manner of extortions. All methods of gain were pursued, whether great and reputable, or mean and sordid. None that had any thing to lose could escape accusation; insomuch, that the plunder of their private fortunes was aggravated by the dangers they were exposed to from pretended crimes.

CHAP. L.—For which reasons it happened that when Longinus as proconsul did those same things which he had

[1] This was the Cassius that, in conjunction with Mark Antony, served Cæsar so effectually at the commencement of the civil war. He was at that time tribune of the commons.

[2] Herminius, a mountain of Lusitania, whose modern name is *Arminia*.

done as quæstor, the provincials formed similar conspiracies against his life. Even his own dependents concurred in the general hatred; who, though the ministers of his rapine, yet hated the man by whose authority they committed those crimes. The odium still increased upon his raising a fifth legion, which added to the expense and burdens of the province. The cavalry was augmented to three thousand, with costly ornaments and equipage: nor was any respite given to the province.

CHAP. LI.—Meanwhile he received orders from Cæsar, to transport his army into Africa, and march through Mauritania, toward Numidia, because king Juba had sent considerable succors to Pompey, and was thought likely to send more. These letters filled him with an insolent joy, by the opportunity they offered him of pillaging new provinces, and a wealthy kingdom. He therefore hastened into Lusitania, to assemble his legions, and draw together a body of auxiliaries; appointing certain persons to provide corn, ships, and money, that nothing might retard him at his return; which was much sooner than expected: for when interest called, Cassius wanted neither industry nor vigilance.

CHAP. LII.—Having got his army together, and encamped near Corduba, he made a speech to the soldiers, wherein he acquainted them with the orders he had received from Cæsar, and promised them a hundred sesterces each, when they should arrive in Mauritania: the fifth legion, he told them, was to remain in Spain. Having ended his speech, he returned to Corduba. The same day, about noon, as he went to the hall of justice, one Minutius Silo, a client of L. Racilius, presented him with a paper, in a soldier's habit, as if he had some request to make. Then retiring behind Racilius (who walked beside Cassius), as if waiting for an answer, he gradually drew near, and a favorable opportunity offering, seized Cassius with his left hand, and wounded him twice with a dagger in his right. A shout was then raised and an attack made on him by the rest of the conspirators, who all rushed upon him in a body. Munatius Plancus killed the lictor, that was next Longinus; and wounded Q. Cassius his lieutenant. T. Vasius and L. Mergilio seconded their countryman Plancus; for they were all natives of Italica.[1] L. Licinius Squillus flew upon

[1] Italica, a town of Spain, situated on the banks of the Guadalquivir, supposed to be the modern *Sevilla la Vieja*. It was built by Publius

Longinus himself, and gave him several slight wounds as he lay upon the ground.

CHAP. LIII.—By this time, his guards came up to his assistance (for he always had several beronians[1] and veterans, armed with darts, to attend him), and surrounded the rest of the conspirators, who were advancing to complete the assassination. Of this number were Calphurnius Salvianus and Manilius Tusculus. Cassius was carried home; and Minutius Silo, stumbling upon a stone, as he endeavored to make his escape, was taken, and brought to him. Racilius retired to the neighboring house of a friend, till he should have certain information of the fate of Cassius. L. Laterensis, not doubting but he was dispatched, ran in a transport of joy to the camp, to congratulate the second and the new-raised legions upon it, who, he knew, bore a particular hatred to Cassius; and who, immediately upon this intelligence, placed him on the tribunal, and proclaimed him prætor. For there was not a native of the province, nor a soldier of the newly-raised legion, nor a person who by long residence was naturalized in the province, of which class the second legion consisted, who did not join in the general hatred of Cassius.

CHAP. LIV.—Meantime Laterensis was informed that Cassius was still alive; at which, being rather grieved than disconcerted, he immediately so far recovered himself, as to go and wait upon him. By this time, the thirtieth legion having notice of what had passed, had marched to Corduba, to the assistance of their general. The twenty-first and fifth followed their example. As only two legions remained in the camp, the second, fearing they should be left alone, and their sentiments should be consequently manifested, did the same. But the new-raised legion continued firm, nor could be induced by any motives of fear to stir from its place.

CHAP. LV.—Cassius ordered all the accomplices of the conspiracy to be seized, and sent back the fifth legion to the camp, retaining the other three. By the confession of Minutius, he learned, that L. Racilius, L. Laterensis and Annius Scapula, a man of great authority and credit in the province, and equally

Scipio, after his successes in Spain, and had the honor of giving birth to the emperors Trajan, Hadrian, and Theodosius.

[1] Some think that Vettones, or Bigerones (two tribes of Spain), is the true reading. Morus, however, thinks that the meaning of the word is lost.

in his confidence with Laterensis and Racilius, were concerned in the plot: nor did he long defer his revenge, but ordered them to be put to death. He delivered Minutius to be racked by his freed-men; likewise Calphurnius Salvianus; who, turning evidence, increased the number of the conspirators; justly, as some think; but others pretend that he was forced. L. Mergilio was likewise put to the torture. Squillus impeached many others, who were all condemned to die, except such as redeemed their lives by a fine; for he pardoned Calphurnius for ten, and Q. Sextius for fifty thousand sesterces, who, though deeply guilty, yet having, in this manner, escaped death, showed Cassius to be no less covetous than cruel.

Chap. LVI.—Some days after, he received letters from Cæsar, by which he learned that Pompey was defeated, and had fled with the loss of all his troops, which news equally affected him with joy and sorrow. Cæsar's success gave him pleasure; but the conclusion of the war would put an end to his rapines: insomuch, that he was uncertain which to wish for, victory or an unbounded licentiousness. When he was cured of his wounds, he sent to all who were indebted to him, in any sums, and insisted upon immediate payment. Such as were taxed too low, had orders to furnish larger sums. He likewise instituted a levy of Roman citizens, and as they were enrolled from all the corporations and colonies, and were terrified by service beyond the sea, he called upon them to redeem themselves from the military oath. This brought in a vast revenue, but greatly increased the general hatred. He afterward reviewed the army, sent the legions and auxiliaries, designed for Africa, toward the straits of Gibraltar, and went himself to Seville, to examine the condition of the fleet. He staid there some time, in consequence of an edict he had published, ordering all who had not paid the sums in which they were amerced, to repair to him thither; which created a universal murmuring and discontent.

Chap. LVII.—In the mean time, L. Titius, a military tribune of the native legion, sent him notice of a report that the thirteenth legion, which Q. Cassius his lieutenant was taking with him, when it was encamped at Ilurgis, had mutinied and killed some of the centurions that opposed them, and were gone over to the second legion, who marched another way toward the Straits. Upon this intelligence he set out by night with five cohorts of the twenty-first legion, and came up with them in the morning. He staid there that day to consult what was proper to be done, and then went to Carmona, where he found the thirtieth and twenty-first legions, with four cohorts of the fifth, and all the cavalry assembled. Here he learned that the new-raised legion had surprised four cohorts, near Obucula, and forced them along with them to the second legion, where all joining, they had chosen T. Thorius, a native of Italica, for their general. Having instantly called a council, he sent Marcellus to Corduba to secure that town, and Q. Cassius, his lieutenant, to Seville. A few days after, news was brought that the Roman citizens at Corduba had revolted, and that Marcellus, either voluntarily or through force (for the reports were various), had joined them; as likewise the two cohorts of the fifth legion that were in garrison there. Cassius, provoked at these mutinies, decamped, and the next day came to Segovia,[1] upon the river Xenil. There, summoning an assembly, to sound the disposition of the troops, he found that it was not out of any regard to him, but to Cæsar, though absent, that they continued faithful, and were ready to undergo any danger for the recovery of the province.

CHAP. LVIII.—Meantime Thorius marched the veteran legions to Corduba; and, that the revolt might not appear to spring from a seditious inclination in him or the soldiers, as likewise to oppose an equal authority to that of Q. Cassius, who was drawing together a great force in Cæsar's name; he publicly gave out that his design was to recover the province for Pompey; and perhaps he did this through hatred of Cæsar, and love of Pompey, whose name was very powerful among those legions which M. Varro had commanded. Be this as it will, Thorius at least made it his pretense; and the soldiers were so infatuated with the thought, that they had Pompey's name inscribed upon their bucklers. The citizens of Corduba, men, women, and children, came out to meet the legions, begging "they would not enter Corduba as enemies, seeing they joined with them in their aversion to Cassius, and only desired they might not be obliged to act against Cæsar."

[1] The Segovia mentioned here was a town of Bætica: Hirtius calls it Segovia upon the Xenil, to distinguish it from another town of that name, in Hispania Tarraconesis, situated on the river Areva, modern *Eresma.*

CHAP. LIX.—The soldiers, moved by the prayers and tears of so great a multitude, and seeing they stood in no need of Pompey's name and memory to spirit up a revolt against Cassius, and that he was as much hated by Cæsar's followers as Pompey's; neither being able to prevail with Marcellus or the people of Corduba to declare against Cæsar, they erased Pompey's name from their bucklers, chose Marcellus their commander, called him prætor, joined the citizens of Corduba, and encamped near the town. Two days after, Cassius encamped on an eminence, on this side the Guadalquivir, about four miles from Corduba, and within view of the town; whence he sent letters to Bogud, in Mauritania, and M. Lepidus, proconsul of Hither Spain, to come to his assistance as soon as possible, for Cæsar's sake. Meanwhile he ravaged the country, and set fire to the buildings around Corduba.

CHAP. LX.—The legions under Marcellus, provoked at this indignity, ran to him, and begged to be led against the enemy, that they might have an opportunity of engaging with them before they could have time to destroy with fire and sword, the rich and noble possessions of the inhabitants of Corduba. Marcellus, though averse to a battle, which, whoever was victorious, must turn to Cæsar's detriment, yet unable to restrain the legions, led them across the Guadalquivir, and drew them up. Cassius did the same upon a rising ground, but as he would not quit his advantageous post, Marcellus persuaded his men to return to their camp. He had already begun to retire, when Cassius, knowing himself to be stronger in cavalry, fell upon the legionaries with his horse, and made a considerable slaughter in their rear upon the banks of the river. When it was evident from this loss, that crossing the river was an error and attended with great loss, Marcellus removed his camp to the other side of the Guadalquivir, where both armies frequently drew up, but did not engage, on account of the inequality of the ground.

CHAP. LXI.—Marcellus was stronger in foot, for he commanded veteran soldiers of great experience in war. Cassius depended more on the fidelity than the courage of his troops. The two camps being very near each other, Marcellus seized a spot of ground, where he built a fort, very convenient for depriving the enemy of water. Longinus, apprehending he should be besieged in a country where all were against him, quitted his camp silently in the night, and, by a quick march, reached Ulia, a town on which he thought he could rely. There he encamped so near the walls, that both by the situation of the place (for Ulia stands on an eminence), and the defenses of the town, he was on all sides secure from an attack. Marcellus followed him and encamped as near the town as possible. Having taken a view of the place he found himself reduced, by necessity, to do what was most agreeable to his own inclination; namely, neither to engage Cassius, which the ardor of his soldiers would have forced him to, had it been possible, nor to suffer him, by his excursions, to infest the territories of other states, as he had done those of Corduba. He therefore raised redoubts in proper places, and continued his works quite round the town, inclosing both Ulia and Cassius within his lines. But before they were finished, Cassius sent out all his cavalry, who he imagined might do him great service by cutting off Marcellus's provisions and forage, and could only be a useless encumbrance to him, by consuming his provisions if he was shut up in his camp.

CHAP. LXII.—A few days after, king Bogud, having received Cassius's letters, came and joined him with all his forces, consisting of one legion, and several auxiliary cohorts. For as commonly happens in civil dissensions, some of the states of Spain at that time favored Cassius, but a yet greater number, Marcellus. Bogud came up to the advanced works of Marcellus, where many sharp skirmishes happened with various success: however, Marcellus still kept possession of his works.

CHAP. LXIII.—Meanwhile Lepidus[1] came to Ulia, from the hither province, with thirty-five legionary cohorts, and a great body of horse and auxiliaries, with the intention of adjusting the differences between Cassius and Marcellus. Marcellus submitted without hesitation: but Cassius kept within his works, either because he thought his cause the justest, or from an apprehension that his adversary's submission had prepossessed Lepidus in his favor. Lepidus encamped at Ulia, and forming a complete junction with Marcellus, prevented a battle, invited Cassius into his camp, and pledged his honor to act without prejudice. Cassius hesitated long, but at last desired that the

[1] We learn from Dion that Cæsar was so partial to Lepidus that he conferred a triumph on him for this slight service.

circumvallation should be leveled, and free egress given him. The truce was not only concluded, but the works demolished, and the guards drawn off; when king Bogud attacked one of Marcellus's forts, that lay nearest to his camp, unknown to any (except perhaps Longinus, who was not exempt from suspicion on this occasion), and slew a great number of his men. And had not Lepidus interposed, much mischief would have been done.

CHAP. LXIV.—A free passage being made for Cassius, Marcellus joined camps with Lepidus; and both together marched for Corduba, while Cassius retired with his followers to Carmona. At the same time, Trebonius,[1] the proconsul, came to take possession of the province. Cassius having notice of his arrival, sent his legions and cavalry into winter quarters, and hastened, with all his effects, to Melaca, where he embarked immediately, though it was the winter season, that he might not, as he pretended, intrust his safety to Marcellus, Lepidus, and Trebonius; as his friends gave out, to avoid passing through a province, great part of which had revolted from him; but as was more generally believed, to secure the money he had amassed by his numberless extortions. The wind favoring him as far as could be expected at that season of the year, he put into the Ebro, to avoid sailing in the night: and thence continuing his voyage, which he thought he might do with safety, though the wind blew considerably fresher, he was encountered by such a storm, at the mouth of the river, that being neither able to return on account of the stream, nor stem the fury of the waves, the ship sank, and he perished.

CHAP. LXV.—When Cæsar arrived in Syria, from Egypt, and understood from those who attended him there from Rome, and the letters he received at the same time, that the government at Rome was badly and injudiciously conducted, and all the affairs of the commonwealth managed indiscreetly;[2] that the contests

[1] The Spaniards had previously written to Cæsar, requesting him to send another person in the room of Cassius. Cæsar complied with their wishes, and sent Trebonius to succeed Cassius.

[2] We learn from the Epitome of 113th book of Livy, that a serious sedition was at this time excited at Rome in consequence of Publius Dolabella, tribune of the commons, bringing forward a bill for an abolition of debt. These disturbances were with great difficulty quelled by Mark

of the tribunes were producing perpetual seditions, and that, by the ambition and indulgence of the military tribunes, many things were done contrary to military usage, which tend to destroy all order and discipline, all which required his speedy presence to redress them; thought it was yet first incumbent upon him to settle the state of the provinces through which he passed; that, freeing them from domestic contentions, and the fear of a foreign enemy, they might become amenable to law and order. This he hoped soon to effect in Syria, Cilicia, and Asia, because these provinces were not involved in war. In Bithynia and Pontus indeed he expected more trouble, because he understood Pharnaces still continued in the latter, and was not likely to quit it easily, being flushed with the victory he had obtained over Domitius Calvinus. He made a short stay in most states of note, distributing rewards both publicly and privately to such as deserved them, settling old controversies, and receiving into his protection the kings, princes, and potentates, as well of the provinces as of the neighboring countries. And having settled the necessary regulations for the defense and protection of the country, he dismissed them, with most friendly feelings to himself and the republic.

CHAP. LXVI.—After a stay of some days in these parts, he named Sextus Cæsar, his friend and relation, to the command of Syria and the legions appointed to guard it; and sailed himself for Cilicia, with the fleet he had brought from Egypt. He summoned the states to assemble at Tarsus, the strongest and finest city of the province; where having settled everything that regarded either that province or the neighboring countries, through his eagerness to march to carry on the war he delayed no longer, but advancing through Cappadocia with the utmost expedition, where he stopped two days at Mazaca, he arrived at Comana, renowned for the ancient and sacred temple of Bellona,[1] where she is worshiped with so much veneration, that her priest is accounted next in power and

Anthony, the master of the horse, who filled the city with soldiers, and put eight hundred of the people to death.

[1] We have the authority of Strabo for asserting, that in his time there were 6000 slaves connected with this temple, subject to the authority of the chief priest. Cæsar took away the priesthood from Archelaus, who had embraced Pompey's interests, and gave it to Lycomedes.

dignity to the king. He conferred this dignity on Lycomedes of Bithynia, who was descended from the ancient kings of Cappadocia, and who demanded it in right of inheritance; his ancestors having lost it upon occasion of the scepter being transferred to another line. As for Ariobarzanes, and his brother Ariarates, who had both deserved well of the commonwealth, he confirmed the first in his kingdom, and put the other under his protection; after which, he pursued his march with the same dispatch.

CHAP. LXVII.—Upon his approaching Pontus, and the frontiers of Gallogræcia, Deiotarus, tetrarch of that province (whose title, however, was disputed by the neighboring tetrarchs) and king of Lesser Armenia, laying aside the regal ornaments, and assuming the habit not only of a private person, but even of a criminal, came in a suppliant manner to Cæsar, "to beg forgiveness for assisting Pompey with his army, and obeying his commands, at a time when Cæsar could afford him no protection: urging, that it was his business to obey the governors who were present, without pretending to judge of the disputes of the people of Rome.

CHAP. LXVIII.—Cæsar, after reminding him "of the many services he had done him, and the decrees he had procured in his favor when consul; that his defection could claim no excuse for want of information, because one of his industry and prudence could not but know who was master of Italy and Rome, where the senate, the people, and the majesty of the republic resided; who, in fine, was consul after Marcellus and Lentulus; told him, that he would notwithstanding forgive his present fault in consideration of his past services, the former friendship that had subsisted between them, the respect due to his age, and the solicitation of those connected with him by hospitality, and his friends who interceded in his behalf: adding, that he would defer the controversy relating to the tetrarchate to another time." He restored him the royal habit, and commanded him to join him with all his cavalry, and the legion he had trained up after the Roman manner.

CHAP. LXIX.—When he was arrived in Pontus, and had drawn all his forces together, which were not very considerable either for their number or discipline (for except the sixth legion, composed of veteran soldiers, which he had brought with him from Alexandria, and which, by its many labors and dangers, the length of its marches and voyages, and the frequent wars in which it had been engaged, was reduced to less than a thousand men, he had only the legion of Deiotarus, and two more that had been in the late battle between Domitius and Pharnaces) embassadors arrived from Pharnaces, "to entreat that Cæsar would not come as an enemy, for he would submit to all his commands." They represented particularly that "Pharnaces had granted no aid to Pompey, as Deiotarus had done, whom he had nevertheless pardoned."

CHAP. LXX.—Cæsar replied, "That Pharnaces should meet with the utmost justice, if he performed his promises: but at the same time he admonished the embassadors, in gentle terms, to forbear mentioning Deiotarus, and not to overrate the having refused aid to Pompey. He told them that he never did any thing with greater pleasure than pardon a suppliant, but that he would never look upon private services to himself as an atonement for public injuries done the province; that the refusal of Pharnaces to aid Pompey had turned chiefly to his own advantage, as he had thereby avoided all share in the disaster of Pharsalia; that he was however willing to forgive the injuries done to the Roman citizens in Pontus, because it was now too late to think of redressing them; as he could neither restore life to the dead, nor manhood to those he had deprived of it, by a punishment more intolerable to the Romans than death itself. But that he must quit Pontus immediately, send back the farmers of the revenues, and restore to the Romans and their allies what he unjustly detained from them. If he should do this, he might then send the presents which successful generals were wont to receive from their friends" (for Pharnaces had sent him a golden crown). With this answer he dismissed the embassadors.

CHAP. LXXI.—Pharnaces promised every thing: but hoping that Cæsar, who was in haste to be gone, would readily give credit to whatever he said, that he might the sooner set out upon more urgent affairs (for every body knew that his presence was much wanted at Rome), he performed but slowly, wanted to protract the day of his departure, demanded other conditions, and in fine endeavored to elude his engagements. Cæsar, perceiving his drift, did now, out of necessity, what he was usually wont to do through inclination, and resolved to decide the affair as soon as possible by a battle.

CHAP. LXXII.—Zela is a town of Pontus, well fortified, though situated in a plain; for a natural eminence, as if raised by art, sustains the walls on all sides. All around is a great number of large mountains, intersected by valleys. The highest of these, which is celebrated for the victory of Mithridates, the defeat of Triarius,[1] and the destruction of our army, is not above three miles from Zela, and has a ridge that almost extends to the town. Here Pharnaces encamped, with all his forces, repairing the fortifications of a position which had proved so fortunate to his father.

CHAP. LXXIII.—Cæsar having encamped about five miles from the enemy, and observing that the valleys which defended the king's camp would likewise defend his own, at the same distance, if the enemy, who were much nearer, did not seize them before him; ordered a great quantity of fascines to be brought within the intrenchments. This being quickly performed, next night, at the fourth watch, leaving the baggage in the camp, he set out with the legions; and arriving at daybreak unsuspected by the enemy, possessed himself of the same post where Mithridates had defeated Triarius. Hither he commanded all the fascines to be brought, employing the servants of the army for that purpose, that the soldiers might not be called off from the works; because the valley, which divided the eminence, where he was intrenching himself from the enemy, was not above a mile wide.

CHAP. LXXIV.—Pharnaces perceiving this, next morning ranged all his troops in order of battle before his camp. Cæsar, on account of the disadvantage of the ground, believed that he was reviewing them according to military discipline; or with a view to retard his works, by keeping a great number of his men under arms; or through the confidence of the king, that he might not seem to defend his position by his fortifications rather than by force. Therefore, keeping only his first line in order of battle, he commanded the rest of the army to go on with their works. But Pharnaces, either prompt-

[1] Triarius was one of Lucullus's lieutenants: he was desirous of having the honor of defeating Mithridates before the arrival of Lucullus, and coming to an engagement on most disadvantageous ground, was defeated with great loss. Seven thousand soldiers, one hundred and fifty centurions, and more than twenty-four military tribunes, are said to have fallen in this engagement.

ed by the place itself, which had been so fortunate to his father; or induced by favorable omens, as we were afterward told; or discovering the small number of cur men that were in arms (for he took all that were employed in carrying materials to the works to be soldiers); or confiding in his veteran army, who valued themselves upon having defeated the twenty-second legion; and at the same time, despising our troops, whom he knew he had worsted, under Domitius; was determined upon a battle, and to that end began to cross the valley. Cæsar, at first, laughed at his ostentation, in crowding his army into so narrow a place, where no enemy, in his right senses, would have ventured: while, in the mean time, Pharnaces continued his march, and began to ascend the steep hill on which Cæsar was posted.

Chap. LXXV.—Cæsar, astonished at his incredible rashness and confidence, and finding himself suddenly and unexpectedly attacked, called off his soldiers from the works, ordered them to arms, opposed the legions to the enemy, and ranged his troops in order of battle. The suddenness of the thing occasioned some terror at first; and our ranks not being yet formed, the scythed chariots[1] disordered and confused the soldiers: however, the multitude of darts discharged against them, soon put a stop to their career. The enemy's army followed them close, and began the battle with a shout. Our advantageous situation, but especially the assistance of the gods, who preside over all the events of war, and more particularly those where human conduct can be of no service, favored us greatly on this occasion.

Chap. LXXVI.—After a sharp and obstinate conflict, victory began to declare for us on the right wing, where the sixth legion was posted. The enemy there were totally overthrown, but, in the center and left, the battle was long and doubtful; however, with the assistance of the gods, we at last prevailed there also, and drove them with the utmost precipitation down the hill which they had so easily ascended before. Great numbers being slain, and many crushed by the flight of their own troops, such as had the good fortune to escape were nevertheless obliged to throw away their arms; so

[1] For an accurate and complete description of the scythed chariots used by the ancients, see my translation of Livy, book xxxvii. chap. xliii.

that having crossed, and got upon the opposite ascent, they could not, being unarmed, derive any benefit from the advantage of the ground. Our men flushed with victory, did not hesitate to advance up the disadvantageous ground, and attack their fortifications, which they soon forced, notwithstanding the resistance made by the cohorts left by Pharnaces to guard it. Almost the whole army was cut to pieces or made prisoners. Pharnaces himself escaped, with a few horse; and had not the attack on the camp given him an opportunity of fleeing without pursuit, he must certainly have fallen alive into Cæsar's hands.

CHAP. LXXVII.—Though Cæsar[1] was accustomed to victory, yet he felt incredible joy at the present success; because he had so speedily put an end to a very great war. The remembrance, too, of the danger to which he had been exposed, enhanced the pleasure, as he had obtained an easy victory in a very difficult conjuncture. Having thus recovered Pontus, and abandoned the plunder of the enemy's camp to the soldiers, he set out next day with some light horse. He ordered the sixth legion to return to Italy to receive the honors and rewards they had merited; and sent home the auxiliary troops of Deiotarus, and left two legions with Cælius Vincianus to protect the kingdom of Pontus.

CHAP. LXXVIII.—Through Gallogræcia and Bithynia he marched into Asia, and examined and decided all the controversies of the provinces as he passed, and established the limits and jurisdictions of the several kings, states, and tetrarchs. Mithridates of Pergamus, who had so actively and successfully served him in Egypt, as we have related above, a man of royal descent and education (for Mithridates, king of all Asia, out of regard to his birth, had carried him along with him when very young, and kept him in his camp several years), was appointed king of Bosphorus, which had been under the command of Pharnaces. And thus he guarded the provinces of the Roman people against the attempts of barbarous and hostile kings, by the interposition of a prince firmly attached to the interests of the republic. He bestowed on him likewise the tetrarchy of Gallogræcia, which was his by the law of nations and family

[1] It was on this occasion, that writing to the senate, he used the memorable words, "*Veni, vidi, vici.*"

claims, though it had been possessed for some years by Deiotarus. Thus Cæsar, staying nowhere longer than the necessity of the seditions in the city required, and having settled all things relating to the provinces with the utmost success and dispatch, returned to Italy much sooner than was generally expected.

HIRTIUS'S COMMENTARIES

ON THE

AFRICAN WAR.

THE ARGUMENT.

I. Cæsar sails for Africa, IV.-VI. And, after an unsuccessful effort to take Adrumetum, encamps at Ruspina. VII. Leptis surrenders to him, and is made the rallying point for his auxiliaries. IX.-XI. Cæsar endeavors to procure supplies of provisions, XII.-XIX. And skirmishes with Labienus. XXI. He increases his army while encamped before Ruspina, and procures arms and supplies. XXII., XXIII. Cato, who was in command of Utica, urges young Pompey to invade the territory of Bogud, king of Mauritania: Pompey complies with his wish, but is unsuccessful at Ascurum. XXIV. Scipio, Labienus, and Petreius, unite their forces; Cæsar suffers severely from want of corn. XXV. Sitius and King Bogud invade Juba's territories, and compel him to march to the assistance of his subjects. Cæsar assures the Africans of his arrival, and draws together auxiliaries. XXVII. Scipio trains his elephants. XXVIII. Two brothers of the name of Titius are taken prisoners by Virgilius, and put to death by the orders of Scipio. XXIX. Labienus besieges Leptis, but is repulsed. XXX.-XXXII. Cæsar is unwilling to come to an engagement with Scipio. A great number of Gætulians and Numidians desert to him. XXXIII. The state of Achilla surrenders to Messius, XXXIV. And the island of Cercina to Sallustius. XXXV. Some Gætulians are sent by Scipio as spies to discover the amount of Cæsar's forces: they desert to Cæsar. XXXVI. The inhabitants of Tisdra send embassadors to Cæsar, offering to surrender. Sitius takes by storm one of Juba's strongest fortresses. XXXVII.-XLII. The maneuvers of Cæsar and Scipio. XLIII. Considius abandons the blockade of Achillas; and retreats to Adrumetum. XLIV.-XLVI. Cæsar's ships are intercepted by the enemy. Some veterans are taken prisoners, and put to death by Scipio's orders, because they refused to desert. XLVII. Cæsar's troops are much harassed by a violent storm. XLVIII. Juba brings auxiliaries to Scipio. XLIX.-LII. Cæsar defeats the enemy near Uzita. LIII. The ninth and tenth legions arrive from Sicily. LIV. Cæsar breaks some of his officers, on account of their disgraceful conduct LV. A revolt of the Gætulians compels Juba to send back part of his army to defend his own kingdom. LVII. Cæsar's soldiers hold frequent conference with Scipio. Aquinius, when engaged in conversation with Saserna, is ordered by Juba to cease. LVIII.-LXIV. The hostile armies immediately come to an action between Uzita and Adrumetum; the victory is for a long time doubtful, but at length Cæsar gains the day. LXV.-LXXIII. Cæsar takes Zeta, and trains his soldiers in the method of opposing elephants. LXXIV. Vacca declares in favor of Cæsar: it is sacked and demolished by Juba. LXXV.-LXXVII. Cæsar marches against Sarsura, and takes it; Thabena shares the same fate. LXXVIII. The battle of Tegea. LXXIX.-LXXXVIII. Cæsar conquers the enemy at Thapsus and marches to Utica; Cato commits suicide, and Cæsar obtains possession of the city. LXXXIX., XC. Cæsar pardons Quintus Legarius, enters Utica, and fines many of the inhabitants. XCI.-XCII. The inhabitants of Zama shut their gates against Juba. XCIII. Considius flees from Tisdra; Virgilius surrenders. XCIV. The death of Juba and Petreius XCV P. Sitius conquers Sabura; the latter is slain in the action. Death of Faustus and Afranius, XCVI. And likewise of Scipio. XCVII. Cæsar sells the properties of his enemies at Zampa and Utica. He reduces Numidia to the state of being a province, and exacts heavy fines from the inhabitants of Thapsus, Adrumetum, Leptis, and Tisdra. XCVIII. He passes over to Carales in Sardinia, and subsequently repairs to Rome.

CHAP. I.—CÆSAR, advancing by moderate journeys, and continuing his march without intermission, arrived at Lilybæum,[1] on the 14th day before the calends of January. Designing to embark immediately, though he had only one legion of new levies, and not quite six hundred horse, he ordered his tent to be pitched so near the sea-side that the waves lashed the very foot of it. This he did with a view that none should think he had time to delay, and that his men might be kept in readiness at a day or an hour's warning. Though the wind at that time was contrary, he nevertheless detained the soldiers and mariners on board, that he might lose no opportunity of sailing; the rather, because the forces of the enemy were announced by the inhabitants of the province, to consist of innumberable cavalry not to be numbered; four legions headed by Juba, together with a great body of light-armed troops; ten legions under the command of Scipio; a hundred and twenty elephants, and fleets in abundance. Yet he was not alarmed, nor lost his confident hopes and spirits. Meantime the number of galleys and transports increased daily; the new-levied legions flocked in to him from all parts;

[1] A promontory and town in Sicily, opposite to Africa.

among the rest the fifth, a veteran legion, and about two thousand horse.

CHAP. II.—Having got together six legions and about two thousand horse, he embarked the legions as fast as they arrived, in the galleys, and the cavalry in the transports. Then sending the greatest part of the fleet before, with orders to sail for the island of Aponiana, not far from Lilybæum; he himself continued a little longer in Sicily, and exposed to public sale some confiscated estates. Leaving all other affairs to the care of Allienus[1] the prætor, who then commanded in the island; and strictly charging him to use the utmost expedition in embarking the remainder of the troops; he set sail the sixth day before the calends of January, and soon came up with the rest of the fleet. As the wind was favorable, and afforded a quick passage, he arrived the fourth day within sight of Africa, attended by a few galleys: for the transports, being mostly dispersed and scattered by the winds, with the exception of a few were driven different ways. Passing Clupea and Neapolis with the fleet, he continued for some time to coast along the shore, leaving many towns and castles behind him.

CHAP. III.—After he came before Adrumetum, where the enemy had a garrison, commanded by C. Considius, and where Cn. Piso[2] appeared upon the shore toward Clupea, with the cavalry of Adrumetum, and about three thousand Moors, he stopped awhile, facing the port, till the rest of the fleet should come up, and then landed his men,[3] though their number at that time did not exceed three thousand foot and a hundred and fifty horse. There, encamping before the town, he continued quiet, without offering any act of hostility, and restrained all from plunder. Meantime the inhabitants manned the walls, and assembled in great numbers before the gate, to defend themselves, their garrison within amounting to two legions. Cæsar, having ridden round the town, and

[1] This is the Allienus to whom Cicero addresses his Eighteenth Epistle. On the death of Cæsar, he espoused the party of Brutus and Cassius.

[2] This was the father of Piso, who was accused, in the reign of Tiberius, of having poisoned Germanicus.

[3] When Cæsar was leaving his ship, he accidentally fell; perceiving that the soldiers looked on it as an unfavorable omen, he dispelled their superstitious fears by saying, "Africa, I embrace thee."

thoroughly examined its situation, returned to his camp. Some blamed his conduct on this occasion, and charged him with a considerable oversight, in not appointing a place of meeting to the pilots and captains of the fleet, or delivering them sealed instructions, according to his usual custom; which being opened at a certain time, might have directed them to assemble at a specified place. But in this Cæsar acted not without design; for as he knew of no port in Africa that was clear of the enemy's forces, and where the fleet might rendezvous in security, he chose to rely entirely upon fortune, and land where occasion offered.

CHAP. IV.—In the mean time, L. Plancus, one of Cæsar's lieutenants, desired leave to treat with Considius, and try, if possible, to bring him to reason. Leave being granted accordingly, he wrote him a letter, and sent it into the town by a captive. When the captive arrived, and presented the letter, Considius, before he received it, demanded whence it came, and being told from Cæsar, the Roman general, answered, "That he knew no general of the Roman forces but Scipio." Then, commanding the messenger to be immediately slain in his presence, he delivered the letter, unread and unopened, to a trusty partisan, with orders to carry it directly to Scipio.

CHAP. V.—Cæsar had now continued a day and a night before the town, without receiving any answer from Considius; the rest of the forces were not yet arrived; his cavalry was not considerable; he had not sufficient troops with him to invest the place, and these were new levies: neither did he think it advisable, upon his first landing, to expose the army to wounds and fatigue; more especially, as the town was strongly fortified, and extremely difficult of access, and a great body of horse was said to be upon the point of arrival to succor the inhabitants; he therefore thought it advisable not to remain and besiege the town, lest while he pursued that design, the enemy's cavalry should come behind and surround him.

CHAP. VI.—But as he was drawing off his men, the garrison made a sudden sally; and the cavalry which had been sent by Juba to receive their pay, happening just then to come up, they took possession of the camp Cæsar had left, and began to harass his rear. This being perceived, the legionaries immediately halted; and the cavalry, though few in number, boldly charged the vast multitude of the enemy. An incredible event occurred, that less than thirty Gallic horse repulsed two thousand Moors, and drove them into the town. Having thus repulsed the enemy and compelled them to retire behind their walls, Cæsar resumed his intended march: but observing that they often repeated their sallies, renewing the pursuit from time to time, and again fleeing when attacked by the horse, he posted a few of the veteran cohorts which he had with him, with part of the cavalry, in the rear, and so proceeded slowly on his march. The further he advanced from the town, the less eager were the Numidians to pursue. Meantime, deputies arrived from the several towns and castles on the road, offering to furnish him with corn, and to perform whatever he might command. Toward the evening of that day, which was the calends of January, he fixed his camp at Ruspina.

CHAP. VII.—Thence he removed and came before Leptis, a free city and governed by its own laws. Here he was met by deputies from the town, who, in the name of the inhabitants, offered their free submission. Whereupon, placing centurions and a guard before the gates, to prevent the soldiers from entering, or offering violence to any of the inhabitants, he himself encamped toward the shore, not far distant from the town. Hither by accident arrived some of the galleys and transports; by whom he was informed that the rest of the fleet, uncertain what course to pursue, had been steering for Utica.[1] In the mean time Cæsar could not depart from the sea, nor seek the inland provinces, on account of the error committed by the fleet. He likewise sent the cavalry back to their ships, probably to hinder the country from being plundered, and ordered fresh water to be carried to them on board. Meanwhile the Moorish horse rose suddenly, Cæsar's party not expecting it, on the rowers who had been employed in carrying water, as they came out of the ships, and wounded many with their darts and killed some. For the manner of these barbarians is, to lie in ambush with their horses among the valleys, and suddenly launch upon an enemy; they seldom choosing to engage hand to hand in a plain.

CHAP. VIII.—In the mean time, Cæsar dispatched letters and messengers into Sardinia and the neighboring provinces, with orders, as soon as they read the letters, to send supplies

[1] A town of Africa, which, after the destruction of Carthage, became the principal city of that continent.

of men, corn, and warlike stores; and having unloaded part of the fleet, detached it, with Rabirius Posthumus,[1] into Sicily, to bring over the second embarkation. At the same time he ordered out ten galleys, to get intelligence of the transports that had missed their way, and to maintain the freedom of the sea. He also ordered C. Sallustius Prispus, the prætor,[2] at the head of a squadron, to sail to Percina, then in the hands of the enemy, because he heard there was great quantity of corn in that island: he gave these orders and instructions in such a manner as to leave no room for excuse or delay. Meanwhile, having informed himself, from the deserters and natives, of the condition of Scipio and his followers; and understanding that they were at the whole charge of maintaining Juba's cavalry; he could not but pity the infatuation of men, who thus chose to be tributaries to the king of Numidia, rather than securely enjoy their fortunes at home with their fellow-citizens.

CHAP. IX.—Cæsar moved his camp on the third day before the nones of January; and leaving six cohorts at Leptis, under the command of Saserna, returned with the rest of the forces to Ruspina, whence he had come the day before. Here he deposited the baggage of the army; and marching out with a light body of troops to forage, ordered the inhabitants to follow with their horses and carriages. Having by this means got together a great quantity of corn, he came back to Ruspina. I think that he acted with this intention, that by keeping possession of the maritime cities, and providing them with garrisons, he might secure a retreat for his fleet.

CHAP. X.—Leaving therefore P. Saserna, the brother of him who commanded at Leptis, to take charge of the town, with one legion, he orders all the wood that could be found to be carried into the place; and set out in person from Ruspina, with seven cohorts, part of the veteran legions who had behaved so well in the fleet under Sulpicius and Vatinius; and marching directly for the port, which lies at about two miles' distance, embarked with them in the evening, without imparting his intentions to the army, who were extremely inquisitive concern-

[1] This is the Rabirius Posthumus for whom Cicero pleaded in a speech which is still extant.

[2] The famous historian; he was expelled the senate by Appius Claudius, the Censor, upon which he embraced the cause of Cæsar, who subsequently restored him.

ing the general's design. His departure occasioned the utmost sadness and consternation among the troops; for being few in number, mostly new levies, and those not all suffered to land, they saw themselves exposed, upon a foreign coast, to the mighty forces of a crafty nation, supported by an innumerable cavalry. Nor had they any resource in their present circumstances, or expectation of safety in their own conduct; but derived all their hope from the alacrity, vigor, and wonderful cheerfulness that appeared in their general's countenance; for he was of an intrepid spirit, and behaved with undaunted resolution and confidence. On his conduct, therefore, they entirely relied, and hoped to a man, that by his skill and talents, all difficulties would vanish before them.

CHAP. XI.—Cæsar, having continued the whole night on board, prepared to set sail about day-break; when, all on a sudden, the part of the fleet that had caused so much anxiety, appeared unexpectedly in view. Wherefore, ordering his men to quit their ships immediately, and receive the rest of the troops in arms upon the shore, he made the new fleet enter the port with the utmost diligence; and landing all the forces, horse and foot, returned again to Ruspina. Here he established his camp; and taking with him thirty cohorts, without baggage, advanced into the country to forage. Thus was Cæsar's purpose at length discovered: that he meant, unknown to the enemy, to have sailed to the assistance of the transports that had missed their way, lest they should unexpectedly fall in with the African fleet. And he did not wish his own soldiers who were left behind in garrison to know this, lest they should be intimidated by the smallness of their numbers, and the multitude of the enemy.

CHAP. XII.—Cæsar had not marched above three miles from his camp, when he was informed by his scouts, and some advanced parties of horse, that the enemy's forces were in view. As soon as this announcement was made, a great cloud of dust began to appear. Upon this intelligence, Cæsar ordered all his horse, of which he had at that time but a very small number, to advance, as likewise his archers, only a few of whom had followed him from the camp; and the legions to march quietly after him in order of battle; while he went forward at the head of a small party. Soon after, having discovered the enemy at some distance, he commanded the soldiers to repair to their arms, and prepare for battle. Their number in all did not exceed thirty cohorts, with four hundred horse, and one hundred and fifty archers.

CHAP. XIII.—Meanwhile the enemy, under the command of Labienus, and the two Pacidii, drew up, with a very large front, consisting not so much of foot as of horse, whom they intermixed with light-armed Numidians and archers; forming themselves in such close order, that Cæsar's army, at a distance, mistook them all for infantry; and strengthening their right and left with many squadrons of horse. Cæsar drew up his army in a single line, being obliged to do so by the smallness of his numbers; covering his front with his archers, and placing his cavalry on the right and left wings, with particular instructions not to suffer themselves to be surrounded by the enemy's numerous horse; for he imagined that he would have to fight only with infantry.

CHAP. XIV.—As both sides stood in expectation of the signal, and Cæsar would not stir from his post, as he saw that with such few troops against so great a force he must depend more on stratagem than strength, on a sudden the enemy's horse began to extend themselves, and move in a lateral direction, so as to encompass the hills and weaken Cæsar's horse, and at the same time to surround them. The latter could scarcely keep their ground against their numbers. Meanwhile, both the main bodies advancing to engage, the enemy's cavalry, intermixed with some light-armed Numidians, suddenly sprang forward, from their crowded troops, and attacked the legions with a shower of darts. Our men, preparing to return the charge, their horse retreated a little, while the foot continued to maintain their ground, till the others, having rallied, came on again, with fresh vigor, to sustain them.

CHAP. XV—Cæsar perceived that his ranks were in danger of being broken by this new way of fighting, for our foot, in pursuing the enemy's horse, having advanced a considerable way beyond their colors, were wounded in the flank by the nearest Numidian darts, while the enemy's horse easily escaped our infantry's javelins by flight; he therefore gave express orders that no soldier should advance above four feet beyond the ensigns. Meanwhile, Labienus's cavalry, confiding in their numbers, endeavored to surround those of Cæsar:

who being few in number, and overpowered by the multitude of the enemy, were forced to give ground a little, their horses being much wounded. The enemy pressed on more and more; so that in an instant, the legions, being surrounded on all sides by the enemy's cavalry, were obliged to form themselves into a circle, and fight, as if inclosed with barriers.

CHAP. XVI.—Labienus, with his head uncovered, advanced on horseback to the front of the battle, sometimes encouraging his own men, sometimes addressing Cæsar's legions thus: "So ho! you raw soldiers there!" says he, "why so fierce? Has he infatuated you too with his words? Truly he has brought you into a fine condition! I pity you sincerely." Upon this, one of the soldiers said: "I am none of your raw warriors, Labienus, but a veteran of the tenth legion." "Where's your standard?" replied Labienus. "I'll soon make you sensible who I am," answered the soldier. Then pulling off his helmet, to discover himself, he threw a javelin, with all his strength at Labienus, which wounding his horse severely in the breast—"Know, Labienus," says he, "that this dart was thrown by a soldier of the tenth legion." However, the whole army was not a little daunted, especially the new levies; and began to cast their eyes upon Cæsar, minding nothing, for the present, but to defend themselves from the enemy's darts.

CHAP. XVII.—Cæsar meanwhile, perceiving the enemy's design, endeavored to extend his line of battle, as much as possible, directing the cohorts to face about alternately to the right and left. By this means, he broke the enemy's circle with his right and left wings; and attacking one part of them, thus separated from the other, with his horse and foot, at last put them to flight. He pursued them but a little way, fearing an ambuscade, and returned again to his own men. The same was done by the other division of Cæsar's horse and foot, so that the enemy being driven back, and severely wounded on all sides, he retreated toward his camp, in order of battle.

CHAP. XVIII.—Meantime M. Petreius, and Cn. Piso, with eleven hundred select Numidian horse, and a considerable body of foot, arrived to the assistance of the enemy; who, recovering from their terror, upon this reinforcement, and again resuming courage, fell upon the rear of the legions, as they retreated, and endeavored to hinder them from reaching their camp. Cæsar, perceiving this, ordered his men to wheel about, and renew the battle in the middle of the plain. As the enemy still pursued their former plan, and avoided a closing engagement, and the horses of Cæsar's cavalry had not yet recovered the fatigue of their late voyage, and were besides weakened with thirst, weariness, wounds, and of course unfit for a vigorous and long pursuit, which even the time of the day would not allow, he ordered both horse and foot to fall at once briskly upon the enemy, and not slacken the pursuit till they had driven them quite beyond the furthest hills, and taken possession of them themselves. Accordingly, upon a signal being given, when the enemy were throwing their javelins in a faint and careless manner, he suddenly charged them with his horse and foot; who in a moment driving them from the field, and over the adjoining hill, kept possession of that post for some time, and then retired slowly, in order of battle, to their camp. The enemy, who, in this last attack, had been vary roughly handled, then at length retreated to their fortifications.

CHAP. XIX.—Meanwhile the action being over, a great number of deserters, of all kinds, flocked to Cæsar's camp, besides multitudes of horse and foot that were made prisoners. From them we learned that it was the design of the enemy to have astonished our raw troops, with their new and uncommon manner of fighting; and after surrounding them with their cavalry, to have cut them to pieces, as they had done Curio; and that they had marched against us expressly with that intention. Labienus had even said, in the council of war, that he would lead such a numerous body of auxiliaries against his adversaries, as should fatigue us with the very slaughter, and defeat us even in the bosom of victory; for he relied more on the number than the valor of his troops. He had heard of the mutiny of the veteran legions at Rome, and their refusal to go into Africa; and was likewise well assured of the fidelity of his troops, who had served three years under him in Africa. He had a great number of Numidian cavalry and light-armed troops, besides the Gallic and German horse, whom he had drawn together out of the remains of Pompey's army, and carried over with him from Brundusium: he had likewise the freedmen raised in the country, and trained to use bridled horses; and also the immense number of Juba's forces, his hundred and twenty elephants, his innumerable cavalry and legionaries, amounting to above twelve thousand. Emboldened by the hope such mighty forces raised in him, on the day before the nones of January, three days after Cæsar's arrival, he came against him, with sixteen hundred Gallic and German horse, nine hundred under Petreius, eight thousand Numidians, four times that number of light-armed foot, with a multitude of archers and slingers. The battle lasted from the fifth hour till sun set, during which time Petreius, receiving a dangerous wound, was obliged to quit the field.

CHAP. XX.—Meantime Cæsar fortified his camp with much greater care, reinforced the guards, and threw up two intrenchments; one from Ruspina quite to the sea, the other from his camp to the sea likewise, to secure the communication, and receive supplies without danger. He landed a great number of darts and military engines, armed part of the mariners, Gauls, Rhodians, and others, that after the example of the enemy he might have a number of light-armed troops to intermix with his cavalry. He likewise strengthened his army with a great number of Syrian and Iturean archers whom he drew from the fleet into his camp: for he understood that within three days Scipio was expected to unite his forces to Labienus and Petreius, and his army was said to consist of eight legions and three thousand horse. At the same time he established workshops, made a great number of darts and arrows, provided himself with leaden bullets and palisades, wrote to Sicily for hurdles and wood to make rams, because he had none in Africa, and likewise gave orders for sending corn; for the harvest in that country was like to be inconsiderable, the enemy having taken all the laborers into their service the year before, and stored up the grain in a few fortified towns, after demolishing the rest, forcing the inhabitants into the garrisoned places, and exhausting the whole country.

CHAP. XXI.—In this necessity, by paying court to private individuals, he obtained a small supply, and husbanded it with care. In the mean time he went round the works in person daily, and kept about four cohorts constantly on duty, on account of the multitude of the enemy. Labienus sent his sick and wounded, of which the number was very considerable, in wagons to Adrumetum. Meanwhile Cæsar's transports, unacquainted with the coast, or where their general had landed wandered up and down in great uncertainty; and being, attacked, one after another, by the enemy's coasters, were, for the most part, either taken or burned. Cæsar, being informed of this, stationed his fleet along the coast and islands for the security of his convoys.

CHAP. XXII.—Meanwhile M. Cato,[1] who commanded in Utica, never ceased urging and exhorting young Pompey, in words to this effect: "Your father, when he was at your age, and observed the commonwealth oppressed by wicked and daring men, and the party of order either slain or driven into banishment from their country and relations, incited by the greatness of his mind and the love of glory, though then very young, and only a private man, had yet the courage to rally the remains of his father's army, and assert the freedom of Italy and Rome, which was almost crushed forever. He also recovered Sicily, Africa, Numidia, Mauritania, with amazing dispatch, and by that means gained an illustrious and extensive reputation among all nations, and triumphed while very young and only a Roman knight. Nor did he enter upon the administration of public affairs, distinguished by the shining exploits of his father, or the fame and reputation of his ancestors, or the honors and dignities of the state. Will you, on the contrary, possessed of these honors, and the reputation acquired by your father, sufficiently distinguished by your own industry and greatness of mind, not bestir yourself, join your father's friends, and give the earnestly required assistance to yourself, the republic, and every man of worth?"

CHAP. XXIII.—The youth, roused by the remonstrances of that grave and worthy senator, got together about thirty sail, of all sorts, of which some few were ships of war, and sailing from Utica to Mauritania, invaded the kingdom of Bogud. And leaving his baggage behind him, with an army of two

[1] After the battle of Pharsalia, Cato fled into Africa, where he still possessed great influence among Pompey's party. When the command of the army in Africa was offered him, he would not accept it, as he considered that it ought to be conferred on Scipio, who was then proconsul. The appointment of Scipio to the supreme command was a fatal measure for Pompey's partisans, and contributed in a great measure to their subsequent defeat. Cato employed all his time and talents in fortifying Utica, and earnestly advised Scipio and the other generals to avoid coming to an action with Cæsar. The neglect of his advice led to the ruin and total overthrow of his party.

thousand men, partly freedmen, partly slaves, some armed, some not, approached the town of Ascurum, in which the king had a garrison. On the arrival of Pompey, the inhabitants suffered him to advance to the very walls and gates; when, suddenly sallying out, they drove back his troops in confusion and dismay to the sea and their ships. This ill-success determined him to leave that coast, nor did he afterward land in any place, but steered directly for the Balearean Isles.

CHAP. XXIV.—Meantime Scipio, leaving a strong garrison at Utica, began his march, with the forces we have described above, and encamped first at Adrumetum; and then, after a stay of a few days, setting out in the night, he joined Petreius and Labienus, lodging all the forces in one camp, about three miles distant from Cæsar's. Their cavalry made continual excursions to our very works, and intercepted those who ventured too far in quest of wood or water, and obliged us to keep within our intrenchments. This soon occasioned a great scarcity of provision among Cæsar's men, because no supplies had yet arrived from Sicily and Sardinia. The season, too, was dangerous for navigation, and he did not possess above six miles in each direction, in Africa, and was moreover greatly distressed for want of forage. The veteran soldiers and cavalry, who had been engaged in many wars both by sea and land, and often struggled with wants and misfortunes of this kind, gathering sea-weed, and washing it in fresh water, by that means subsisted their horses and cattle.

CHAP. XXV.—While things were in this situation, king Juba, being informed of Cæsar's difficulties, and the few troops he had with him, resolved not to allow him time to remedy his wants or increase his forces. Accordingly he left his kingdom, at the head of a large body of horse and foot, and marched to join his allies. Meantime P. Sitius, and king Bogud, having intelligence of Juba's march, joined their forces, entered Numidia, and laying siege to Cirta, the most opulent city in the county, carried it in a few days, with two others belonging to the Getulians. They had offered the inhabitants leave to depart in safety, if they would peaceably deliver up the town; but these conditions being rejected, they were taken by storm, and the citizens all put to the sword. They continued to advance, and incessantly harassed the cities and country; of which Juba having intelligence, though he was upon the point of joining Scipio and the other chiefs, determined that it was better to march to the relief of his own kingdom, than run the hazard of being driven from it while he was assisting others, and, perhaps, after all, miscarry too in his designs against Cæsar. He therefore retired, with his troops, leaving only thirty elephants behind him, and marched to the relief of his own cities and territories.

Chap. XXVI.—Meanwhile Cæsar, as there was a doubt in the province concerning his arrival, and no one believed that he had come in person, but that some of his lieutenants had come over with the forces lately sent, dispatched letters to all the several states, to inform them of his presense. Upon this, many persons of rank fled to his camp, complaining of the barbarity and cruelty of the enemy. Cæsar deeply touched by their tears and complaints, although before he had remained inactive, resolved to take the field as soon as the weather would permit, and he could draw his troops together. He immediately dispatched letters into Sicily, to Allienus and Rabirius Postumus the prætors [to tell them] that without delay or excuse, either of the winter or the winds, they must send over the rest of the troops, to save Africa from utter ruin: because, without some speedy remedy, not a single house would be left standing, nor any thing escape the fury and ravages of the enemy. And he himself was so anxious and impatient, that from the day the letters were sent, he complained without ceasing of the delay of the fleet, and had his eyes night and day turned toward the sea. Nor was it wonderful; for he saw the villages burned, the country laid waste, the cattle destroyed, the towns plundered, the principal citizens either slain or put in chains, and their children dragged into servitude under the name of hostages; nor could he, amid all this scene of misery, afford any relief to those who implored his protection, on account of the small number of his forces. In the mean time he kept the soldiers incessantly at work upon the intrenchments, built forts and redoubts, and carried on his lines quite to the sea.

Chap. XXVII.—Meanwhile Scipio made use of the following contrivance for training and disciplining his elephants. He drew up two parties in order of battle; one of slingers, who were to act as enemies, and discharge small stones against the elephants: and fronting them, the elephants themselves, in one line, and his whole army behind him in battle-array;

that when the enemy, by their discharge of stones, had frightened the elephants, and forced them to turn upon their own men, they might again be made to face the enemy, by the volleys of stones from the army behind them. The work however, went on but slowly, because these animals, after many years' training, are dangerous to both parties when brought into the field.

CHAP. XXVIII.—While the two generals were thus employed near Ruspina, C. Virgilius, a man of prætorian rank, who commanded in Thapsus, a maritime city, observing some of Cæsar's transports that had missed their way, uncertain where Cæsar had landed or held his camp; and thinking that a fair opportunity offered of destroying them, manned a galley that was in the port with soldiers and archers, and joining with it a few armed barks, began to pursue Cæsar's ships. Though he was repulsed on several occasions he still pursued his design, and at last fell in with one, on board of which were two young Spaniards, of the name of Titius, who were tribunes of the fifth legion, and whose father had been made a senator by Cæsar. There was with them a centurion of the same legion, T. Salienus by name, who had invested the house of M. Messala, Cæsar's lieutenant, at Messana, and made use of very seditious language; nay, had even seized the money and ornaments destined for Cæsar's triumph, and for that reason dreaded his resentment. He, conscious of his demerits, persuaded the young men to surrender themselves to Virgilius, by whom they were sent under a strong guard to Scipio, and three days after put to death. It is said, that the elder Titius begged of the centurions who were charged with the execution, that he might be first put to death; which being easily granted, they both suffered according to their sentence.

CHAP. XXIX.—The cavalry that mounted guard in the two camps were continually skirmishing with one another. Sometimes too the German and Gallic cavalry of Labienus entered into discourse with those of Cæsar, after promising not to injure one another. Meantime Labienus, with a party of horse, endeavored to surprise the town of Leptis, which Saserna guarded with three cohorts; but was easily repulsed, because the town was strongly fortified, and well provided with warlike engines; he however renewed the attempt several times. One day, as a strong squadron of the enemy had posted themselves before the gate, their officer being slain by an arrow discharged from a cross-bow, and pinned to his own shield, the rest were terrified and took to flight; by which means the town was delivered from any further attempts.

CHAP. XXX.—At the same time Scipio daily drew up his troops in order of battle, about three hundred paces from his camp; and after continuing in arms the greatest part of the day, retreated again to his camp in the evening. This he did several times, no one mean while offering to stir out of Cæsar's camp, or approach his forces; which forbearance and tranquillity gave him such a contempt of Cæsar and his army, that drawing out all his forces, and his thirty elephants, with towers on their backs, and extending his horse and foot as wide as possible, he approached quite up to Cæsar's intrenchments.

CHAP. XXXI.—Upon perceiving this, Cæsar, quietly, and without noise or confusion, recalled to his camp all that were gone out either in quest of forage, wood, or to work upon the fortifications: he likewise ordered the cavalry that were upon guard not to quit their post until the enemy were within reach of dart; and if they then persisted in advancing, to retire in good order within the intrenchments. He ordered the rest of the cavalry to be ready and armed, each in his own place. These orders were not given by himself in person, or after viewing the disposition of the enemy from the rampart; but such was his consummate knowledge of the art of war, that he gave all the necessary directions by his officers, he himself sitting in his tent, and informing himself of the motions of the enemy by his scouts. He very well knew, that, whatever confidence the enemy might have in their numbers, they would yet never dare to attack the camp of a general who had so often repulsed, terrified, and put them to flight; who had frequently pardoned and granted them their lives; and whose very name had weight and authority enough to intimidate their army. He was besides well intrenched with a high rampart and deep ditch, the approaches to which were rendered so difficult by the sharp spikes which he had disposed in a very skillful manner, that they were even sufficient of themselves to keep off the enemy. He had also a large supply of cross-bows, engines, and all sorts of weapons necessary for a vigorous defense, which he had prepared on account of the fewness of his troops, and the inexperience of his new levies. It was not owing to being influenced by the fear of the enemy or their numerical strength, that he allowed himself to appear daunted in their estimation. And it was not owing to his having any doubts of gaining the victory that he did not lead his troops to action, although they were raw and few, but he thought that it was a matter of great importance, what sort the victory should be: for he thought that it would disgrace him, if after so many noble exploits, and defeating such powerful armies, and after gaining so many glorious victories, he should appear to have gained a bloody victory over the remnants who had rallied after their flight. He determined, in consequence of this, to endure the pride and exultation of his enemies, until some portion of his veteran legion should arrive in the second embarkation.

CHAP. XXXII.—Scipio, after a short stay before the intrenchments, as if in contempt of Cæsar, withdrew slowly to his camp: and having called the soldiers together, enlarged upon the terror and despair of the enemy, when encouraging his men, he assured them of a complete victory in a short time. Cæsar made his soldiers again return to the works. and under pretense of fortifying his camp, inured the new levies to labor and fatigue. Meantime the Numidians and Getulians deserted daily from Scipio's camp. Part returned home; part came over to Cæsar, because they understood he was related to C. Marius,[1] from whom their ancestors had received considerable favors. Of these he selected some of distinguished rank, and sent them home, with letters to their countrymen, exhorting them to levy troops for their own defense, and not to listen to the suggestions of his enemies.

CHAP. XXXIII.—While these things were passing near Ruspina, deputies from Acilla, a free town, and all the neighboring towns, arrived in Cæsar's camp, and promised "to be ready to execute Cæsar's commands, and to do so withal, and that they only begged and requested of him to give them garrisons, that they might do so in safety and without danger to themselves, that they would furnish them with corn and whatever supplies they had, to secure the common safety. Cæsar readily complied with their demands, and having assigned a garrison, sent C. Messius, who had been ædile, to command in Acilla. Upon intelligence of this, Considius Longus, who was at Adrumetum

[1] In the Jugurthan war.

with two legions and seven hundred horse, leaving a garrison in that city, hastened to Acilla at the head of eight cohorts: but Messius, having accomplished his march with great expedition, arrived there before him. When Considius, therefore, approached, and found Cæsar's garrison in possession of the town, not daring to make any attempt, he returned again to Adrumetum. But some days after, Labienus having sent him a reinforcement of horse, he began to besiege the town.

CHAP. XXXIV.—Much about the same time, C. Sallustius Crispus, who, as we have seen, had been sent a few days before to Cercina with a fleet, arrived in that island. Upon his arrival, C. Decimus the quæstor, who, with a strong party of his own domestics, had charge of the magazines erected there, went on board a small vessel and fled. Sallustius meanwhile was well received by the Cercinates, and finding great store of corn in the island, loaded all the ships then in the port, whose number was very considerable, and dispatched them to Cæsar's camp. At the same time Allienus, the proconsul, put on board of the transports at Lilybæum the thirteenth and fourteenth legions, with eight hundred Gallic horse and a thousand archers and slingers, and sent the second embarkation to Africa, to Cæsar. This fleet meeting with a favorable wind, arrived in four days at Ruspina, where Cæsar had his camp. Thus he experienced a double pleasure on this occasion, receiving at one and the same time, both a supply of provisions and a reinforcement of troops, which animated the soldiers, and delivered them from the apprehensions of want. Having landed the legions and cavalry, he allowed them some time to recover from the fatigue and sickness of their voyage, and then distributed them into the forts, and along the works.

CHAP. XXXV.—Scipio and the other generals were greatly surprised at this conduct, and could not conceive why Cæsar, who had always been forward and active in war, should all of a sudden change his measures; which they therefore suspected must proceed from some very powerful reasons. Uneasy and disturbed to see him so patient, they made choice of two Getulians, on whose fidelity they thought they could rely; and promising them great rewards, sent them, under the name of deserters, to get intelligence of Cæsar's designs. When they were brought before him, they begged they might have leave to speak without personal danger, which being granted, "It is now a long time, great general," said they, "since many of us Getulians, clients of C. Marius, and almost all Roman citizens of the fourth and sixth legions, have wished for an opportunity to come over to you; but have hitherto been prevented by the guards of Numidian horse, from doing it without great risk. Now we gladly embrace the occasion, being sent by Scipio under the name of deserters, to discover what ditches and traps you have prepared for his elephants, how you intended to oppose these animals, and what dispositions you are making for battle." They were praised by Cæsar, and liberally rewarded, and sent to the other deserters. We had soon a proof of the truth of what they had advanced; for the next day a great many soldiers of these legions, mentioned by the Getulians, deserted to Cæsar's camp.

CHAP. XXXVI.—While affairs were in this posture at Ruspina, M. Cato, who commanded in Utica, was daily enlisting freed-men, Africans, slaves, and all that were of age to bear arms, and sending them without intermission to Scipio's camp. Meanwhile deputies from the town of Tisdra came to Cæsar to inform him, that some Italian merchants had brought three hundred thousand bushels of corn into that city, and to demand a garrison as well for their own defense as to secure the corn. Cæsar thanked the deputies, promised to send the garrison they desired, and having encouraged them, sent them back to their fellow-citizens. Meantime P. Sitius entered Numidia with his troops, and took by storm a castle situated on a mountain, where Juba had laid up a great quantity of provisions, and other things necessary for carrying on the war.

CHAP. XXXVII.—Cæsar, having increased his forces with two veteran legions, and all the cavalry and light-armed troops that had arrived in the second embarkation, detached six transports to Lilybæum, to bring over the rest of the army. He himself on the sixth day before the calends of February, ordering the scouts and lictors to attend him at six in the evening, drew out all the legions at midnight, and directed his march toward Ruspina, where he had a garrison, and which had first declared in his favor, no one knowing or having the least suspicion of his design. Thence he continued his route, by the left of the camp, along the sea, and passed a little declivity, which opened into a fine plain, extending fifteen miles, and bordering upon a chain of mountains of moderate height, that formed a kind of theater. In this ridge were some hills that rose higher than the rest, on which forts and watch-towers had formerly been erected, and at the furthest of which, Scipio's guards and out-posts were stationed.

CHAP. XXXVIII.—After Cæsar gained the ridge, which I have just mentioned, and began to raise redoubts upon the several eminences (which he executed in less than half an hour[1]), and when he was not very far from the last, which bordered on the enemy's camp, and where, as we have said, Scipio had his out-guard of Numidians, he stopped a moment; and having taken a view of the ground, and posted his cavalry in the most commodious situation, he ordered the legions to throw up an intrenchment along the middle of the ridge, from the place at which he was arrived to that whence he set out. When Scipio and Labienus observed this, they drew all their cavalry out of the camp, formed them in order of battle, and advancing about a mile, posted their infantry by way of a second line, somewhat less than half a mile from their camp.

CHAP. XXXIX.—Cæsar was unmoved by the appearance of the enemy's forces, and encouraged his men to go on with the work. But when he perceived that they were within fifteen hundred paces of the intrenchment, and saw that the enemy were coming nearer to interrupt and disturb the soldiers and oblige him to draw off the legions from the work, he ordered a squadron of Spanish cavalry, supported by some light-armed infantry, to attack the Numidian guard upon the nearest eminence, and drive them from that post. They accordingly, advancing rapidly, attacked the Numidian cavalry: they took some of them alive, severely wounded several in their flight, and made themselves masters of the place. This being observed by Labienus, he wheeled off almost the whole right wing of the horse, that he might the more effectually succor the fugi-

[1] It is incredible that the work could have been executed in so short a space of time, not even though we should have recourse to the supposition that each redoubt was fortified in half an hour, or that the old redoubts were almost perfect. Guischard considers this passage spurious, because the time assigned would not be sufficient for the men to reach the hill, without considering the time requisite for fortifying.

tives. Cæsar waited till he was at a considerable distance from his own men, and then detached his left wing to intercept the enemy.

CHAP. XL.—In the plain where this happened was a large villa,[1] with four turrets, which prevented Labienus from seeing that he was intercepted by Cæsar's cavalry. He had therefore no apprehension of the approach of Cæsar's horse till he found himself charged in the rear; which struck such a sudden terror into the Numidian cavalry that they immediately betook themselves to flight. The Gauls and Germans who stood their ground, being surrounded on all sides, were entirely cut off. This being perceived by Scipio's legions, who were drawn up in order of battle before the camp, they fled in the utmost terror and confusion. Scipio and his forces being driven from the plain and the hills, Cæsar sounded a retreat, and ordered all the cavalry to retire behind the works. When the field was cleared, he could not forbear admiring the huge bodies of the Gauls and Germans, who had been partly induced by the authority of Labienus to follow him out of Gaul, and partly drawn over by promises and rewards. Some being made prisoners in the battle with Curio, and having their lives granted them, continued faithful out of gratitude. Their bodies, of surprising symmetry and size, lay scattered all over the plain.

CHAP. XLI.—Next day, Cæsar drew all his forces together, and formed them in order of battle upon the plain. Scipio, discouraged by so unexpected a check, and the number of his wounded and slain, kept within his lines. Cæsar, with his army in battle array, marched along the roots of the hills, and gradually approached his trenches. Cæsar's legions were, by this time, not more than a mile from Uzita, a town possessed by Scipio, when the latter, fearing lest he should lose the town, whence he procured water and other conveniences for his army, resolved therefore to preserve it, at all hazards, and brought forth his whole army, and drew them up in four lines, forming the first of cavalry, supported by elephants with castles on their backs. Cæsar believing that Scipio approached with the intention of giving battle, continued where he was posted, not far from the town. Scipio meanwhile, having the town in the center of

[1] A house of this description in which one or more turrets were built to command the view, was frequently called "turris."

his front, extended his two wings, where were his elephants, in full view of our army.

CHAP. XLII.—When Cæsar had waited till sunset, without finding that Scipio stirred from his post, who seemed rather disposed to defend himself by his advantageous situation, than hazard a battle in the open field, he did not think proper to advance further that day, because the enemy had a strong garrison of Numidians in the town, which besides covered the center of their front: and he foresaw great difficulty in forming, at the same time, an attack upon the town, and opposing their right and left, with the advantage of the ground; especially as the soldiers had continued under arms and fasted since morning. Having therefore led back his troops to their camp, he resolved next day to extend his lines nearer the town.

CHAP. XLIII.—Meantime Considius, who was besieging eight mercenary cohorts of Numidians and Getulians in Acilla, where P. Messius commanded, after continuing long before the place, and seeing all his works burned and destroyed by the enemy, upon the report of the late battle of the cavalry, set fire to his corn, destroyed his wine, oil, and other stores, which were necessary for the maintenance of his army; and abandoning the siege of Acilla, divided his forces with Scipio, and retired through the kingdom of Juba, to Adrumetum.

CHAP. XLIV.—Meanwhile one of the transports, belonging to the second embarkation, which Allienus had sent from Sicily, in which were Q. Cominius, and L. Ticida, a Roman knight, being separated from the rest of the fleet, in a storm, and driven to Thapsus, was taken by Virgilius, and all the persons on board sent to Scipio. A three-banked galley likewise, belonging to the same fleet, being forced by the winds to Ægimurum, was intercepted by the squadron under Varus and M. Octavius. In this vessel were some veteran soldiers, with a centurion, and a few new levies, whom Varus treated without insult, and sent under a guard to Scipio. When they came into his presence, and appeared before his tribunal: "I am satisfied," said he, "it is not by your own inclination, but at the instigation of your wicked general, that you impiously wage war on your fellow-citizens, and every man of worth. If, therefore, now that fortune has put you in our power, you will take this opportunity to unite with the good citizens, in the defense of the commonwealth, I am determined to give you life and money: therefore speak openly your sentiments."

Chap. XLV.—Scipio having ended his speech, and expecting a thankful return to so gracious an offer, pemitted them to reply; one of their number, a centurion of the fourteenth legion, thus addressed him: "Scipio," says he ("for I can not give you the appellation of general), I return you my hearty thanks for the good treatment you are willing to show to prisoners of war; and perhaps I might accept of your kindness were it not to be purchased at the expense of a horrible crime. What! shall I carry arms, and fight against Cæsar, my general, under whom I have served as centurion; and against his victorious army, to whose renown I have for more than thirty-six[1] years endeavored to contribute by my valor? It is what I will never do, and even advise you not to push the war any further. You know not what troops you have to deal with, nor the difference betwixt them and yours: of which, if you please, I will give you an indisputable instance. Do you pick out the best cohort you have in your army, and give me only ten of my comrades, who are now your prisoners, to engage them: you shall see by the success, what you are to expect from your soldiers."

Chap. XLVI.—When the centurion had courageously made this reply, Scipio, incensed at his boldness, and resenting the affront, made a sign to some of his officers to kill him on the spot, which was immediately put in execution At the same time, ordering the other veteran soldiers to be separated from the new levies, "Carry away," said he, "these men, contaminated by the pollution of crime, and pampered with the blood of their fellow-citizens." Accordingly they were conducted without the rampart, and cruelly massacred. The new-raised soldiers were distributed among his legions, and Cominius and Ticida forbade to appear in his presence. Cæsar, concerned for this misfortune, broke, with ignominy, the officers whose instructions were to secure the coast, and advance to a certain distance into the main sea, to protect and facilitate the ap-

[1] As Cæsar had been engaged in war sixteen, and not thirty-six years, we may naturally infer that this is one of the many corruptions of the text. Some commentators, who defend the text, refer the time to the duration of the services of the veteran army.

proach of the transports, but who had neglected their duty on that important station.

CHAP. XLVII.—About this time a most incredible accident befell Cæsar's army; for the Pleiades being set, about the second watch of the night, a terrible storm arose, attended by hail of an uncommon size. But what contributed to render this misfortune the greater was, that Cæsar had not, like other generals, put his troops into winter quarters, but was every three or four days changing his camp, to gain ground on the enemy; which keeping the soldiers continually employed they were utterly unprovided with any conveniences to protect them from the inclemency of the weather. Besides, he had brought over his army from Sicily with such strictness, that neither officer nor soldier had been permitted to take their equipages or utensils with them, nor so much as a vessel or a single slave; and so far had they been from acquiring or providing themselves with any thing in Africa, that, on account of the great scarcity of provisions, they had even consumed their former stores. Impoverished by these accidents, very few of them had tents; the rest had made themselves a kind of covering, either by spreading their clothes, or with mats and rushes. But these being soon penetrated by the storm and hail, the soldiers had no resource left, but wandered up and down the camp, covering their heads with their bucklers to shelter them from the violence of the weather. In a short time the whole camp was under water, the fires extinguished, and all their provisions washed away or spoiled. The same night the shafts of the javelins belonging to the fifth legion, of their own accord, took fire.

CHAP. XLVIII.—In the mean time, king Juba, having been informed of the cavalry actions with Scipio, and being earnestly solicited, by letters from that general, to come to his assistance, left Sabura at home with part of the army, to carry on the war against Sitius, and that he might add the weight of his authority to free Scipio's troops from the dread they had of Cæsar, began his march, with three legions, eight hundred regular horse, a body of Numidian cavalry, great numbers of light-armed infantry, and thirty elephants. When he arrived he lodged himself, with those forces which I have described, in a separate camp, at no great distance from that of Scipio. (Great alarm had prevailed for some time previously in Cæsar's camp, and the report of his approach had increased and produced a general suspense and expectation among the troops. But his arrival, and the appearance of his camp, soon dispelled all these apprehensions; and they despised the king of Mauritania, now that he was present, as much as they had feared him when at a distance.) After this junction, any one might easily perceive that Scipio's courage and confidence were increased by the arrival of the king. For next day, drawing out all his own and the royal forces, with sixty elephants, he ranged them, in order of battle, with great ostentation advancing a little beyond his intrenchments, and, after a short stay, retreated to his camp.

Chap. XLIX.—Cæsar, knowing that Scipio had received all the supplies he expected, and judging he would no longer decline coming to an engagement, began to advance along the ridge with his forces, extend his lines, secure them with redoubts, and possess himself of the eminences between him and Scipio. The enemy, confiding in their numbers, seized a neighboring hill, and thereby prevented the progress of our works. Labienus had formed the design of securing this post, and as it lay nearest his quarters, soon got thither.

Chap. L.—There was a broad and deep valley, of rugged descent, broken with caves, which Cæsar had to pass before he could come to the hill which he wished to occupy, and beyond which was a thick grove of old olives. Labienus, perceiving that Cæsar must march this way, and having a perfect knowledge of the country, placed himself in ambush, with the light-armed foot and part of the cavalry. At the same time he disposed some horse behind the hills, that when he should fall unexpectedly upon Cæsar's foot, they might suddenly advance from behind the mountain. And thus Cæsar and his army being attacked in front and rear, surrounded with danger on all sides, and unable either to retreat or advance, would, he imagined, fall an easy prey to his victorious troops. Cæsar, who had no suspicion of the ambuscade, sent his cavalry before; and arriving at the place, Labienus's men, either forgetting or neglecting the orders of their general, or fearing to be trampled to death in the ditch by our cavalry, began to issue in small parties from the rock, and ascend the hill. Cæsar's horse pursuing them, slew some, and took others prisoners; then making toward the hill, drove thence Labienus's detachment, and immediately took possession. Labienus, with a small party of horse, escaped with great difficulty by flight.

CHAP. LI.—The cavalry having thus cleared the mountain, Cæsar resolved to intrench himself there, and distributed the work to the legions. He then ordered two lines of communication to be drawn from the greater camp, across the plain on the side of Uzita, which stood between him and the enemy, and was garrisoned by a detachment of Scipio's army, and place them in such a manner as to meet at the right and left angles of the town. His design in this work was, that when he approached the town with his troops, and began to attack it, these lines might secure his flanks, and hinder the enemy's horse from surrounding him, and compelling him to abandon the siege. It likewise gave his men more frequent opportunities of conversing with the enemy, and facilitated the means of desertion to such as favored his cause; many of whom had already come over, though not without great danger to themselves. He wanted also, by drawing nearer the enemy, to see if they really intended to come to an action, and in addition to all these reasons, that the place itself being very low, he might there sink some wells; whereas before he had a long and troublesome way to send for water. While the legions were employed in these works, part of the army stood ready drawn up before the trenches, and had frequent skirmishes with the Numidian horse and light-armed foot.

CHAP. LII.—A little before evening, when Cæsar was drawing off his legions from the works, Juba, Scipio, and Labienus, at the head of all their horse and light-armed foot, fell furiously upon his cavalry; who, being overwhelmed by the sudden and general attack of so great a multitude, were forced to give ground a little. But the event was very different from what the enemy expected; for Cæsar, leading back his legions to the assistance of his cavalry, they immediately rallied, turned upon the Numidians, and charging them vigorously while they were dispersed and disordered with the pursuit, drove them with great loss to the king's camp, and slew several of them. And had not night intervened, and the dust raised by the wind obstructed the prospect, Juba and Labienus would both have fallen into Cæsar's hands, and their whole cavalry and light-armed infantry have been cut off. Meanwhile Scipio's men, of the fourth and sixth legions, left him in crowds, some deserting to

Cæsar's camp, others fleeing to such places as were most convenient for them. Curio's horse likewise, distrusting Scipio and his troops, followed the same counsel.

CHAP. LIII.—While these things were being carried on by Cæsar and his opponents around Uzita, two legions, the ninth and tenth, sailing in transports from Sicily, when they came before Ruspina, observing Cæsar's ships that lay at anchor about Thapsus, and fearing it might be the enemy's fleet stationed there to intercept them, imprudently stood out to sea; and after being long tossed by the winds, and harassed by thirst and famine, at last arrived at Cæsar's camp.

CHAP. LIV.—Soon after these legions were landed, Cæsar, calling to mind their former licentious behaviour in Italy, and the rapines of some of their officers, seized the slight pretext furnished by C. Avienus, a military tribune of the tenth legion, who, when he set out for Sicily, filled a ship entirely with his own slaves and horses, without taking on board one single soldier. Wherefore, summoning all the military tribunes and centurions to appear before his tribunal next day, he addressed them in these terms, "I could have wished that those, whose insolence and former licentious character have given me cause of complaint, had been capable of amendment, and of making a good use of my mildness, patience, and moderation. But since they know not how to confine themselves within due bounds, I intend to make an example of them, according to the law of arms, in order that others may be taught a better conduct. Because you, C. Avienus, when you were in Italy, instigated the soldiers of the Roman people to revolt from the republic, and have been guilty of rapines and plunders in the municipal towns; and because you have never been of any real service, either to the commonwealth or to your general, and in lieu of soldiers, have crowded the transports with your slaves and equipage; so that, through your fault, the republic is in want of soldiers, who at this time are not only useful, but necessary; for all these causes, I break you with ignominy, and order you to leave Africa this very day. In like manner I break you, A. Fonteius, because you have behaved yourself as a seditious officer, and as a bad citizen. You, T. Salienus, M. Tiro, C. Clusinus, have attained the rank of centurions through my indulgence, and not through your own merit; and since you have been invested with that rank, have neither shown bravery in war, nor good conduct in peace, and have been more zealous in raising seditions, and exciting the soldiers against your general than in observing forbearance and moderation. I therefore think you unworthy of continuing centurions in my army: I break you, and order you to quit Africa as soon as possible." Having concluded this speech, he delivered them over to some centurions, with orders to confine them separately on board a ship, allowing each of them a single slave to wait on him.

CHAP. LV.—Meantime the Getulian deserters, whom Cæsar had sent home with letters and instructions, as we related above, arrived among their countrymen: who, partly swayed by their authority, partly by the name and reputation of Cæsar, revolted from Juba; and speedily and unanimously taking up arms, scrupled not to act in opposition to their king. Juba, having thus three wars to sustain, was compelled to detach six cohorts from the army destined to act against Cæsar, and send them to defend the frontiers of his kingdom against the Getulians.

CHAP. LVI.—Cæsar, having finished his lines of communication, and pushed them so near the town, as to be just out of reach of dart, intrenched himself there. He caused warlike engines in great numbers to be placed in the front of his works, wherewith he played perpetually against the town; and to increase the enemy's apprehensions, drew five legions out of his other camp. When this opportunity was presented, several persons of eminence and distinction earnestly requested an interview with their friends, and held frequent conferences, which Cæsar foresaw would turn to his advantage. For the chief officers of the Getulian horse, with other illustrious men of that nation (whose fathers had served under C. Marius, and from his bounty obtained considerable estates in their country, but after Sylla's victory had been made tributaries to king Hiempsal), taking advantage of the night, when the fires were lighted, came over to Cæsar's camp near Uzita, with their horses and servants, to the number of about a thousand.

CHAP. LVII.—When Scipio and his party learned this, and were much annoyed at the disaster, they perceived, much about the same time, M. Aquinius in discourse with C. Saserna. Scipio sent him word that he did not do well to correspond with the enemy. Aquinius, however, paid no attention to this reprimand, but pursued his discourse. Soon after, one of Juba's guards came to him and told him, in the hearing of Saserna, "The king forbids you to continue this conversation." He, being terrified by this order, immediately retired, and obeyed the command of the king. One can not wonder enough at this step in a Roman citizen, who had already attained to considerable honors in the commonwealth; that though neither banished his country, nor stripped of his possessions, he should pay a more ready obedience to the orders of a foreign prince than those of Scipio; and choose rather to behold the destruction of his party than return into the bosom of his country. And still greater insolence was shown by Juba, not to M. Aquinius, a man of no family, and an inconsiderable senator, but even to Scipio[1] himself, a man of illustrious birth, distinguished honors, and high dignity in the state. For as Scipio, before the king's arrival, always wore a purple coat of mail, Juba is reported to have told him, that he ought not to wear the same habit as he did. Accordingly, Scipio changed his purple robe for a white one, submitting to Juba, a most haughty and insolent monarch.

CHAP. LVIII.—Next day they drew out all their forces from both camps; and forming them on an eminence not far from Cæsar's camp, continued thus in order of battle. Cæsar likewise drew out his men, and disposed them in battle array before his lines; not doubting but the enemy, who exceeded him in number of troops, and had been so considerably reinforced by the arrival of king Juba, would advance to attack him. Wherefore, having ridden through the ranks, encouraged his men, and gave them the signal of battle, he stayed, expecting the enemy's charge. For he did not think it advisable to remove far from his lines: because the enemy having a strong garrison in Uzita, which was opposite to his right wing, he could not advance beyond that place without exposing his flank to a sally from the town. He was also deterred by the following reason, because the ground before

[1] Plutarch, in his life of Cato, gives the following instance of the pride of Juba. On the occasion of a conference between Cato, Scipio, and Juba, the latter wished his chair to be placed in the middle (the seat of honor among the Numidians), Cato, however, would not concede the point, but insisted on conferring the honor on Scipio.

Scipio's army was very rough, and he thought it likely to disorder his men in the charge.

CHAP. LIX.—And I think that I ought not to omit to describe the order of battle of both armies. Scipio drew up his troops in the following manner: he posted his own legions and those of Juba in the front; behind them the Numidians, as a body of reserve: but in so very thin ranks, and so far extended in length, that to see them at a distance you would have taken the main body for a simple line of legionaries, which was doubled only upon the wings. He placed elephants at equal distances on the right and left, and supported them by the light-armed troops and auxiliary Numidians. All the regular cavalry were on the right; for the left was covered by the town of Uzita, nor had the cavalry room to extend themselves on that side. Accordingly, he stationed the Numidian horse, with an incredible multitude of light-armed foot, about a thousand paces from his right, toward the foot of a mountain, considerably removed from his own and the enemy's troops. He did so with this intention, that, when the two armies should engage, his cavalry at the commencement of the action should take a longer sweep, inclose Cæsar's army and throw them into confusion by their darts. Such was Scipio's disposition.

CHAP. LX.—Cæsar's order of battle, to describe it from left to right, was arranged in the following manner: the ninth and eighth legions formed the left wing: the thirteenth, fourteenth, twenty-eighth, and twenty-sixth, the main body; and the thirtieth and twenty-eighth the right. His second line on the right consisted partly of the cohorts of those legions we have already mentioned, partly of the new levies. His third line was posted to the left, extending as far as the middle legion of the main body, and so disposed, that the left wing formed a triple order of battle. The reason of this disposition was, because his right wing being defended by the works, it behooved him to make his left stronger, that they might be a match for the numerous cavalry of the enemy; for which reason he had placed all his horse there, intermixed with light-armed foot; and as he could not rely much upon them, had detached the fifth legion to sustain them. He placed archers up and down the field, but principally in the two wings.

CHAP. LXI.—The two armies thus facing one another in order of battle, with a space of no more than three hundred paces between, continued so posted from morning till night without fighting, of which perhaps there was never an instance before. But when Cæsar began to retreat within his lines, suddenly all the Numidian and Getulian horse without bridles, who were posted behind the enemy's army, made a motion to the right, and began to approach Cæsar's camp on the mountain; while the regular cavalry under Labienus continued in their post to keep our legions in check. Upon this, part of Cæsar's cavalry, with the light-armed foot, advancing hastily, and without orders, against the Getulians, and venturing to pass the morass, found themselves unable to deal with the superior multitude of the enemy; and being abandoned by the light-armed troops, were forced to retreat in great disorder, after the loss of one trooper, twenty-six light-armed foot, and many of their horses wounded. Scipio, overjoyed at this success, returned toward night to his camp. But fortune determined not to give such unalloyed joy to those engaged in war, for the day after, a party of horse sent by Cæsar to Leptis in quest of provisions, falling in unexpectedly with some Numidian and Getulian stragglers, killed or made prisoners about a hundred of them. Cæsar, meanwhile, omitted not every day to draw out his men and labor at the works; carrying a ditch and rampart quite across the plain, to prevent the incursions of the enemy. Scipio likewise drew lines opposite to Cæsar's, and used great exertions lest Cæsar should cut off his communication with the mountain. Thus both generals were busied about their intrenchments, yet a day seldom passed, without some skirmish between the cavalry.

Chap. LXII.—In the mean time, Varus, upon notice that the seventh and eighth legions had sailed from Sicily, speedily equipped the fleet he had brought to winter at Utica; and manning it with Getulian rowers and mariners, went out a cruising and came before Adrumetum with fifty-five ships. Cæsar, ignorant of his arrival, sent L. Cispius, with a squadron of twenty-seven sail toward Thapsus, to anchor there for the security of his convoys; and likewise dispatched Q. Aquila to Adrumetum, with thirteen galleys, upon the same errand. Cispius soon reached the station appointed to him: but Aquila being attacked by a storm could not double the cape, which obliged him to put into a creek at some distance, that afforded convenient shelter. The rest of the fleet which remained at sea before Leptis, where the mariners having landed and wandered here and there upon the shore, some having gone into the town for the purpose of purchasing provisions, was left quite defenseless. Varus, having notice of this from a deserter, and resolving to take advantage of the enemy's negligence, left Adrumetum in Cothon[1] at the commencement of the second watch, and arriving early next morning with his whole fleet before Leptis, burned all the transports that were out at sea, and took without opposition two five-benched galleys, in which were none to defend them.

CHAP. LXIII.—Cæsar had an account brought him of this unlucky accident, as he was inspecting the works of his camp. Whereupon he immediately took horse, and leaving every thing else, went full speed to Leptis, which was but two leagues distant, and going on board a brigantine ordered all the ships to follow him. He soon came up with Aquila, whom he found dismayed and terrified at the number of ships he had to oppose; and continuing his course, began to pursue the enemy's fleet. Meantime Varus, astonished at Cæsar's boldness and dispatch, tacked about with his whole fleet, and made the best of his way for Adrumetum. But Cæsar, after four miles' sail, recovered one of his galleys, with the crew and a hundred and thirty of the enemy's men left to guard her; and took a three-benched galley belonging to the enemy which had fallen astern during the engagement, with all the soldiers and mariners on board. The rest of the fleet doubled the cape, and made the port of Adrumetum in Cothon. Cæsar could not double the cape with the same wind, but keeping the sea at anchor all night, appeared early next morning before Adrumetum. He set fire to all the transports without Cothon, and took what galleys he found there, or forced them into the harbor; and having waited some time to offer the enemy battle, returned again to his camp.

CHAP. LXIV.—On board the ship he had taken was P. Vestrius, a Roman knight, and P. Ligarius, who had served in Spain under Afranius, the same who had prosecuted the war against him in Spain, and who, instead of acknowledging the conqueror's generosity, in granting him his libety, had joined Pompey in Greece; and after the battle of Pharsalia, had gone

[1] About nine at night.

into Africa, to Varus, there to continue in the service of the same cause. Cæsar, to punish his perfidy and breach of oath, gave immediate orders for his execution. But he pardoned P. Vestrius, because his brother had paid his ransom at Rome, and because he himself proved, that being taken in Nasidius's fleet and condemned to die, he had been saved by the kindness of Varus, since which no opportunity had offered of making his escape.

CHAP. LXV.—It is the custom of the people of Africa to deposit their corn privately in vaults, under ground, to secure it in time of war, and guard it from the sudden incursions of an enemy. Cæsar, having intelligence of this from a spy, drew out two legions, with a party of cavalry, at midnight, and sent them about ten miles off; whence they returned, loaded with corn to the camp. Labienus, being informed of it, marched about seven miles, through the mountains Cæsar had passed the day before, and there encamped with two legions; where expecting that Cæsar would often come the same way in quest of corn, he daily lay in ambush with a great body of horse and light-armed foot.

CHAP. LXVI.—Cæsar, being informed of the ambuscade of Labienus by deserters, delayed there a few days, till the enemy, by repeating the practice often, had abated a little of their circumspection. Then suddenly, one morning ordering eight veteran legions with part of the cavalry to follow him by the Decuman gate, he sent forward the rest of the cavalry; who, coming suddenly upon the enemy's light-armed foot, that lay in ambush among the valleys, slew about five hundred, and put the rest to flight. Meantime Labienus advanced, with all his cavalry, to support the fugitives, and was on the point of overpowering our small party with his numbers, when suddenly Cæsar appeared with the legions, in order of battle. This sight checked the ardor of Labienus, who thought proper to sound a retreat. The day after, Juba ordered all the Numidians who had deserted their post and fled to their camp to be crucified.

CHAP. LXVII.—Meanwhile Cæsar, being distressed by want of corn, recalled all his forces to the camp; and having left garrisons at Leptis, Ruspina, and Acilla, ordered Cispius and Aquila to blockade with their fleets, the one Adrumetum, the other Thapsus, and setting fire to his camp at Uzita, he set out, in order of battle, at the fourth watch,[1] disposed his baggage on the left, and came to Agar, which had been often vigorously attacked by the Getulians, and as valiantly defended by the inhabitants. There encamping in the plain before the town, he went with part of his army round the country in quest of provisions; and having found a large store of barley, oil, wine, and figs, with a small quantity of wheat, after allowing the troops some time to refresh themselves, he returned to his camp. Scipio meanwhile hearing of Cæsar's departure, followed him along the hills, with all his forces, and posted himself about six miles off, in three different camps.

CHAP. LXVIII.—The town of Zeta,[2] lying on Scipio's side of the country, was not above ten miles from his camp, but might be about eighteen from that of Cæsar. Scipio had sent two legions thither to forage; which Cæsar having intelligence of from a deserter, removed his camp from the plain to a hill, for the greater security; and leaving a garrison there, marched at three in the morning with the rest of his forces, passed the enemy's camp, and possessed himself of the town. He found that Scipio's legions were gone further into the country to forage: against whom, setting out immediately, he found that the whole army had come up to their assistance, which obliged him to give over the pursuit. He took, on this occasion, C. Mutius Reginus, a Roman knight, Scipio's intimate friend, and governor of the town; also P. Atrius, a Roman knight, of the province of Utica, with twenty-two camels, belonging to king Juba. Then leaving a garrison in the place, under the command of Oppius, his lieutenant, he returned to his own camp.

CHAP. LXIX.—As he drew near Scipio's camp, by which he was obliged to pass, Labienus and Afranius, who lay in ambuscade among the nearest hills with all their cavalry and light-armed infantry, started up and attacked his rear. When Cæsar perceived this, he detached his cavalry to receive their charge, ordered the legions to throw all their baggage into a heap, and face about upon the enemy. No sooner was this order executed than, upon the first charge of the legions, the enemy's horse and light-armed foot began to give way, and were with incredible ease driven from the higher ground. But when Cæsar, supposing them sufficiently deterred from

[1] About three in the morning.

[2] Zeta, a town of Africa, the name of which is derived from Zeith, an olive.

any further attempts, began to pursue his march, they again issued from the hills; and the Numidians, with the light-armed infantry, who are wonderfully nimble, and accustom themselves to fight intermixed with the horse, with whom they keep an equal pace, either in advancing or retiring, fell a second time upon our foot. As they repeated this often, pressing upon our troops when we marched, and retiring when we endeavored to engage, always keeping at a certain distance, and with singular care avoiding a close fight, and considering it enough to wound us with their darts, Cæsar plainly saw that their whole aim was to oblige him to encamp in that place, where no water was to be had; that his soldiers, who had tasted nothing from three in the morning till four in the afternoon, might perish with hunger, and the cattle with thirst.

CHAP. LXX.—When sun-set now approached, and Cæsar found he had not gained a hundred paces in four hours, and that by keeping his cavalry in the rear he lost many horse, he ordered the legions to fall behind, and close the march. Proceeding thus with a slow and gentle pace, he found the legions fitter to sustain the enemy's charge. Meantime the Numidian horse, wheeling round the hills, to the right and left, threatened to inclose Cæsar's forces with their numbers, while part continued to harass his rear: and if but three or four veteran soldiers faced about, and darted their javelins at the enemy, no less than two thousand of them would take to flight: but suddenly rallying, returned to the fight, and charged the legionaries with their darts. Thus Cæsar, at one time marching forward, at another halting, and going on but slowly, reached the camp safe, about seven that evening, having only ten men wounded. Labienus too retreated to his camp, after having thoroughly fatigued his troops with the pursuit: in which, besides a great number wounded, his loss amounted to about three hundred men. And Scipio withdrew his legions and elephants, whom, for the greater terror, he had ranged before his camp within view of Cæsar's army.

CHAP. LXXI.—Cæsar, to meet enemies of this sort, was necessitated to instruct his soldiers, not like a general of a veteran army which had been victorious in so many battles, but like a fencing master training up his gladiators, with what foot they must advance or retire; when they were to oppose and make good their ground; when to counterfeit an attack; at what place, and in what manner to launch their javelins. For the enemy's light-armed troops gave wonderful trouble and annoyance to our army; because they not only deterred the cavalry from the encounter, by killing their horses with their javelins, but likewise wearied out the legionary soldiers by their swiftness: for as often as these heavy-armed troops advanced to attack them, they evaded the danger by a quick retreat.

CHAP. LXXII.—Cæsar was rendered very anxious by these occurrences; because as often as he engaged with his cavalry, without being supported by the infantry, he found himself by no means a match for the enemy's horse, supported by their light-armed foot: and as he had no experience of the strength of their legions, he foresaw still greater difficulties when these should be united, as the shock must then be overwhelming. In addition to this, the number and size of the elephants greatly increased the terror of the soldiers; for which, however, he found a remedy, in causing some of those animals to be brought over from Italy, that his men might be accustomed to the sight of them, know their strength and courage, and in what part of the body they were most vulnerable. For as the elephants are covered with trappings and ornaments, it was necessary to inform them what parts of the body remained naked, that they might direct their darts thither. It was likewise needful to familiarize his horses to the cry, smell, and figure of these animals; in all of which he succeeded to a wonder; for the soldiers quickly came to touch them with their hands, and to be sensible of their tardiness; and the cavalry attacked them with blunted darts, and, by degrees, brought their horses to endure their presence.

CHAP. LXXIII.—For these reasons already mentioned, Cæsar was very anxious, and proceeded with more slowness and circumspection than usual, abating considerably in his wonted expedition and celerity. Nor ought we to wonder; for in Gaul he had under him troops accustomed to fight in a champaign country, against an open undesigning enemy, who despised artifice, and valued themselves only on their bravery. But now he was to habituate his soldiers to the arts and contrivances of a crafty enemy, and teach them what to pursue, and what to avoid. The sooner therefore to instruct them in these matters, he took care not to confine his legions to one place, but under pretense of foraging, engaged them in frequent marches, and counter-marches; because he thought that the enemy's troops would not lose his track. Three days after, he drew up his forces with great skill, and marching past Scipio's camp, waited for him in an open plain; but seeing that he still declined a battle, he retreated to his camp a little before evening.

CHAP. LXXIV.—Meantime embassadors arrived from the town of Vacca, bordering upon Zeta, of which we have observed Cæsar had possessed himself. They requested and entreated that he would send them a garrison, promising to furnish many of the necessaries of war. At the same time, by the will of the gods, and their kindness to Cæsar, a deserter informed him, that Juba had, by a quick march, before Cæsar's troops could arrive, reached the town and surrounded it, and after taking possession of it, massacred the inhabitants, and abandoned the place itself to the plunder of his soldiers.

CHAP. LXXV.—Cæsar, having reviewed his army the twelfth day before the calends of April, advanced next day, with all his forces, five miles beyond his camp, and remained a considerable time in order of battle, two miles from Scipio's. When he saw distinctly that the enemy, though frequently and for a long time challenged to a battle, declined it, he led back his troops. Next day he decamped, and directed his march toward Sarsura, where Scipio had a garrison of Numidians, and a magazine of corn. Labienus being informed of this motion, began to harass his rear with the cavalry and light-armed troops: and having made himself master of part of the baggage, was encouraged to attack the legions themselves, believing they would fall an easy prey, under the load and encumbrance of a march. However, this circumstance had not escaped Cæsar's attention, for he had ordered three hundred men out of each legion to hold themselves in readiness for action. These being sent against Labienus, he was so terrified at their approach, that he shamefully took to flight, great numbers of his men being killed or wounded. The legionaries returned to their standards, and pursued their march. Labienus continued to follow us at a distance along the summit of the mountains on our right.

CHAP. LXXVI.—Cæsar, arriving before Sarsura, took it in presence of the enemy, who durst not advance to its relief; and put to the sword the garrison which had been left there by Scipio, under the command of P. Cornelius, one of Scipio's veterans, who, after a vigorous defense, was surrounded and slain. Having given all the corn in the place to the army, he marched next day to Tisdra, where Considius was, with a strong garrison and his cohort of gladiators. Cæsar, having taken a view of the town, and being deterred from besieging it by want of corn, set out immediately, and after a march of four miles, encamped near a river. He marched from it on the fourth day, and then returned to his former camp at Agar. Scipio did the same, and retreated to his old quarters.

CHAP. LXXVII.—Meantime the inhabitants of Thabena, a nation situated on the extreme confines of Juba's kingdom, along the sea-cost, and who had been accustomed to live in subjection to that monarch, having massacred the garrison left there by the king, sent deputies to Cæsar to inform him of what they had done, and to beg he would take under his protection a city which deserved so well of the Roman people. Cæsar, approving their conduct, sent M. Crispus the tribune, with a cohort, a party of archers, and a great number of engines of war, to charge himself with the defense of Thabena. At the same time the legionary soldiers, who, either on account of sickness or for other reasons, had not been able to come over into Africa with the rest, to the number of four thousand foot, four hundred horse, and a thousand archers and slingers, reached Cæsar by one embarkation. With these and his former troops, he advanced into a plain eight miles distant from his own camp, and four from that of Scipio, where he awaited the enemy in order of battle.

CHAP. LXXVIII.—There was a town below Scipio's camp, of the name of Tegea, where he had a garrison of four hundred horse. These he drew up on the right and left of the town; and bringing forth his legions, formed them in order of battle upon a hill somewhat lower than his camp, and which was about a thousand paces distant from it. After he had continued a considerable time in one place, without offering to make any attempt, Cæsar sent some squadrons of horse, supported by his light-armed infantry, archers, and slingers, to charge the enemy's cavalry, who were on duty before the town. After

Cæsar's troops advanced and came to the charge with their horses at a gallop, Placidius began to extend his front, that he might at once surround us and give us a warm reception. Upon this Cæsar detached three hundred legionaries to our assistance, while at the same time Labienus was continually sending fresh reinforcements, to replace those that were wounded or fatigued. Our cavalry, who were only four hundred in number, not being able to sustain the charge of four thousand, and being besides greatly harassed by the light-armed Numidians, began at last to give ground: which Cæsar observing, detached the other wing to their assistance: who, joining those that were like to be overpowered, fell in a body upon the enemy, put them to flight, slew or wounded great numbers, pursued them three miles quite to the mountains, and then returned to their own men. Cæsar continued in order of battle till four in the afternoon, and then retreated to his camp without the loss of a man. In this action Placidius received a dangerous wound in the head, and had many of his best officers either killed or wounded.

CHAP. LXXIX.—After he found that he could not by any means induce the enemy to come down to the plain and make trial of the legions, and that he could not encamp nearer them for want of water, in consideration of which alone, and not from any confidence in their numbers, the Africans had dared to despise him; he decamped the day before the nones of April at midnight, marched sixteen miles beyond Agar to Thapsus, where Virgilius commanded with a strong garrison, and there fixed his camp, and began to surround the town the very day on which he arrived, and raised redoubts in proper places, as well for his own security, as to prevent any succors from entering the town. In the mean time, Scipio, on learning Cæsar's designs, was reduced to the necessity of fighting, to avoid the disgrace of abandoning Virgilius and the Thapsitani, who had all along remained firm to his party; and therefore, following Cæsar without delay, he posted himself in two camps eight miles from Thapsus.

CHAP. LXXX.—Now there were some salt-pits, between which and the sea was a narrow pass of about fifteen hundred paces, by which Scipio endeavored to penetrate and carry succors to the inhabitants of Thapsus. But Cæsar anticipating that this might happen, had the day before raised a very strong fort at the entrance of it, in which he left a triple garrison; and encamping with the rest of his troops in the form of a half moon, carried his works round the town. Scipio, disappointed in his design, passed the day and night following a little above the morass; but early next morning advanced within a small distance of the last mentioned camp and fort, where he began to intrench himself about fifteen hundred paces from the sea. Cæsar being informed of this, drew off his men from the works; and leaving Asprenas the proconsul, with two legions, at the camp, marched all the rest of his forces with the utmost expedition to that place. He left part of the fleet before Thapsus, and ordered the rest to make as near the shore as possible toward the enemy's rear, observing the signal he should give them, upon which they were to raise a sudden shout, that the enemy, alarmed and disturbed by the noise behind them, might be forced to face about.

CHAP. LXXXI.—When Cæsar came to the place, he found Scipio's army in order of battle before the intrenchments, the elephants posted on the right and left wings, and part of the soldiers busily employed in fortifying the camp. Upon sight of this disposition, he drew up his army in three lines, placed the tenth and second legions on the right wing, the eighth and ninth on the left, five legions in the center, covered his flanks with five cohorts, posted opposite the elephants, disposed the archers and slingers in the two wings, and intermingled the light-armed troops with his cavalry. He himself on foot went from rank to rank, to rouse the courage of the veterans, putting them in mind of their former victories, and animating them by his kind expressions. He exhorted the new levies who had never yet been in battle to emulate the bravery of the veterans, and endeavor by a victory to attain the same degree of fame, glory, and renown.

CHAP. LXXXII.—As he ran from rank to rank, he observed the enemy about the camp very uneasy, hurrying from place to place, at one time retiring behind the rampart, another coming out again in great tumult and confusion. As many others in the army began to observe this, his lieutenants and volunteers begged him to give the signal for battle, as the immortal gods promised him a decisive victory. While he hesitated and strove to repress their eagerness and desires, exclaiming that it was not his wish to commence the battle by a sudden sally, at the same time keeping back his army, on a sudden a trumpeter in the right wing, without Cæsar's leave, but compelled by the soldiers, sounded a charge. Upon this all the cohorts began to rush toward the enemy, in spite of the endeavors of the centurions, who strove to restrain them by force, lest they should charge withal the general's order, but to no purpose.

CHAP. LXXXIII.—Cæsar perceiving that the ardor of his soldiers would admit of no restraint, giving "good fortune" for the word, spurred on his horse, and charged the enemy's front. On the right wing the archers and slingers poured their eager javelins without intermission upon the elephants, and by the noise of their slings and stones, so terrified these animals, that turning upon their own men, they trod them down in heaps, and rushed through the half-finished gates of the camp. At the same time the Mauritanian horse, who were in the same wing with the elephants, seeing themselves deprived of their assistance, betook themselves to flight. Whereupon the legions wheeling round the elephants, soon possessed themselves of the enemy's intrenchments, and some few that made great resistance being slain, the rest fled with all expedition to the camp they had quitted the day before.

CHAP. LXXXIV.—And here we must not omit to notice the bravery of a veteran soldier of the fifth legion. For when an elephant which had been wounded in the left wing, and, roused to fury by the pain, ran against an unarmed sutler, threw him under his feet, and kneeling on him with his whole weight, and brandishing his uplifted trunk, with hideous cries, crushed him to death, the soldier could not refrain from attacking the animal. The elephant, seeing him advance with his javelin in his hand, quitted the dead body of the sutler, and seizing him with his trunk, wheeled him round in the air. But he, amid all the danger, preserving his presence of mind, ceased not with his sword to strike at the elephant's trunk, which enclasped him, and the animal, at last overcome with the pain, quitted the soldier, and fled to the rest with hideous cries.

CHAP. LXXXV.—Meanwhile the garrison of Thapsus, either designing to assist their friends, or abandoning the town to seek safety by flight, sallied out by the gate next the sea, and wading navel deep in the water, endeavored to reach the land. But the servants and attendants of the camp, attacking them with darts and stones, obliged them to return to the town. Scipio's forces meanwhile being beaten, and his men fleeing on all sides, the legions instantly began the pursuit, that they might have no time to rally. When they arrived at the camp to which they fled, and where, having repaired it, they hoped to defend themselves they began to think of choosing a commander,[1] to whose, authority and orders they might submit; but finding none on whom they could rely, they threw down their arms, and fled to the king's quarter. Finding this, on their arrival, occupied by Cæsar's forces, they retired to a hill, where, despairing of safety, they cast down their arms, and saluted them in a military manner. But this stood them in little stead, for the veterans, transported with rage and anger, not only could not be induced to spare the enemy, but even killed or wounded several citizens of distinction in their own army, whom they upbraided as authors of the war. Of this number was Tullius Rufus the quæstor, whom a soldier designedly ran through with a javelin; and Pompeius Rufus, who was wounded with a sword in the arm, and would doubtless have been slain, had he not speedily fled to Cæsar for protection. This made several Roman knights and senators retire from the battle, lest the soldiers, who after so signal a victory[2] assumed an unbounded license, should be induced by the hopes of impunity to wreck their fury on them likewise. In short all Scipio's soldiers, though they implored the protection of Cæsar, were in the very sight of that general, and in spite of his entreaties to his men to spare them, without exception put to the sword.

CHAP. LXXXVI.—Cæsar, having made himself master of the enemy's three camps, killed ten thousand, and putting

[1] For Afranius, Scipio, and the others had fled.

[2] Plutarch relates that several writers assert that Cæsar was not in the action at all, being at the time attacked by a fit of epilepsy.

the rest to flight, retreated to his own quarters with the loss of not more than fifty men and a few wounded. In his way he appeared before the town of Thapsus, and ranged all the elephants he had taken in the battle, amounting to sixty-four, with their ornaments, trappings, and castles, in full view of the place. This he did in hopes that possibly Virgilius and those that were besieged with him might give over the idea of resistance on learning the defeat of their friends. He even called and invited him to submit, reminding him of his clemency and mildness; but no answer being given, he retired from before the town. Next day, after returning thanks to the gods, he assembled his army before Thapsus, praised his soldiers in presence of the inhabitants, rewarded the victorious, and from his tribunal extended his bounty to every one, according to their merit and services. Setting out thence immediately he left the proconsul C. Rebellius, with three legions, to continue the siege, and sent Cn. Domitius with two to invest Tisdra, where Considius commanded. Then ordering M. Messala to go before with the cavalry, he began his march to Utica.[1]

CHAP. LXXXVII.—Scipio's cavalry, who had escaped out of the battle, taking the road to Utica, arrived at Parada; but being refused admittance by the inhabitants, who heard of Cæsar's victory, they forced the gates, lighted a great fire in the middle of the forum, and threw all the inhabitants into it, without distinction of age or sex, with their effects; avenging in this manner, by an unheard of cruelty, the affront they had received. Thence they marched directly to Utica. M. Cato, some time before, distrusting the inhabitants of that city, on account of the privileges granted them by the Julian[2] law, had disarmed and expelled the populace, obliging them to dwell without the Warlike gate, in a small camp surrounded by a slight intrenchment, around which he had planted guards, while at the same time he put the senators under arrest. The cavalry attacked their camp, knowing them to be favorers of Cæsar, and intending to wipe out by their destruction, the

[1] Cæsar was anxious to take Cato alive, and besides, several belonging to Scipio's army had fled to Utica.

[2] The object of the Julian law was the preservation of the freedom of such of the provincials as had been free previously. It was termed by Cicero, "*lex justissima atque optima.*"

disgrace of their own defeat. But the people, animated by Cæsar's victory, repulsed them with stones and clubs. They therefore threw themselves into the town, killed many of the inhabitants, and pillaged their houses. Cato, unable to prevail with them to abstain from rapine and slaughter, and undertake the defense of the town, as he was not ignorant of what they aimed at, gave each a hundred sesterces to make them quiet. Sylla Faustus did the same out of his own money; and marching with them from Utica, advanced into the kingdom.[1]

CHAP. LXXXVIII.—A great many others that had escaped out of the battle, fled to Utica. These Cato assembled, with three hundred[2] more who had furnished Scipio with money for carrying on the war, and exhorted them to set their slaves free, and in conjunction with them defend the town. But finding that though part assembled, the rest were terrified and determined to flee, he gave over the attempt, and furnished them with ships to facilitate their escape. He himself, having settled all his affairs with the utmost care, and commended his children to L. Cæsar his quæstor, without the least indication which might give cause of suspicion, or any change in his countenance and behavior, privately carried a sword into his chamber when he retired to rest, and stabbed himself with it. When the wound not proving mortal, he fell heavily to the ground, his physician and friends suspecting what was going on, burst into the room and began to stanch and bind up his wound, he himself most resolutely tore it open, and met death with the greatest determination. The Uticans, though they hated his party, yet in consideration of his singular integrity, his behavior so different from that of the other chiefs, and because he had strengthened their town with wonderful fortifications, and increased the towers, interred him honorably. L. Cæsar, that he might procure some advantage by his death, assembled the people, and after haranguing them, exhorted them to open their gates, and throw themselves upon Cæsar's clemency, from which they had the greatest reason to hope the best. This

[1] The kingdom is here put for the kingdom of Juba, as in the ninety-second and ninety-third chapters.

[2] These were Roman citizens who were employed as merchants in Africa, whom Cato had formed a senate of.

advice being followed, he came forth to meet Cæsar. Messala having reached Utica, according to his orders, placed guards at the gates.

CHAP. LXXXIX.—Meanwhile Cæsar, leaving Thapsus, came to Useeta, where Scipio had laid up a great store of corn, arms, darts, and other warlike provisions, under a small guard. He soon made himself master of the place, and marched directly to Adrumetum, which he entered without opposition. He took an account of the arms, provisions, and money in the town; pardoned Q. Ligarius, and C. Considius; and leaving Livineius Regulus there with one legion, set out the same day for Utica. L. Cæsar, meeting him by the way, threw himself at his feet, and only begged for his life. Cæsar, according to his wonted clemency, easily pardoned him, as he did likewise Cæcina, C. Ateius, P. Atrius, L. Cella, father and son, M. Eppius, M. Aquinius, Cato's son, and the children of Damasippus. He arrived at Utica in the evening by torch-light, and continued all that night without the town.

CHAP. XC.—Early on the morning of the following day he entered the place, summoned an assembly of the people, and thanked them for the affection they had shown to his cause. At the same time he censured severely, and enlarged upon the crime of the Roman citizens and merchants, and the rest of the three hundred, who had furnished Scipio and Varus with money; but concluded with telling them, that they might show themselves without fear, as he was resolved to grant them their lives, and content himself with exposing their effects to sale; but that he would give them notice when their goods were to be sold, and the liberty of redeeming them upon payment of a certain fine. The merchants, half dead with fear, and conscious that they merited death, hearing upon what terms life was offered them, greedily accepted the condition, and entreated Cæsar that he would impose a certain sum in gross upon all the three hundred. Accordingly, he amerced them in two hundred thousand sesterces, to be paid to the republic, at six equal payments, within the space of three years. They all accepted the condition, and considering that day as a second nativity, joyfully returned thanks to Cæsar.

CHAP. XCI.—Meanwhile, king Juba, who had escaped from the battle with Petreius, hiding himself all day in the villages, and traveling only by night, arrived at last in Numidia.

When he came to Zama, his ordinary place of residence, where were his wives and children, with all his treasures, and whatever he held most valuable, and which he had strongly fortified at the beginning of the war; the inhabitants, having heard of Cæsar's victory, refused him admission, because, upon declaring war against the Romans, he had raised a mighty pile of wood in the middle of the forum, designing, if unsuccessful, to massacre all the citizens, fling their bodies and effects upon the pile, then setting fire to the mass, and throwing himself upon it, destroy all without exception, wives, children, citizens, and treasures, in one general conflagration. After continuing a considerable time before the gates, finding that neither threats nor entreaties would avail, he at last desired them to deliver up his wives and children, that he might carry them along with him. But receiving no answer, and seeing them determined to grant him nothing, he quitted the place, and retired to one of his country-seats with Petreius and a few horse.

CHAP. XCII.—Meantime the Zamians sent embassadors to Cæsar at Utica, to inform him of what they had done, and to request "that he should send them aid before the king could collect an army and besiege them; that they were determined to defend the town for him as long as life remained." Cæsar commended the embassadors, and sent them back to acquaint their fellow-citizens that he was coming himself to their relief. Accordingly, setting out the next day from Utica with his cavalry, he directed his march toward the kingdom. Many of the king's generals met him on the way, and sued for pardon; to all of whom a favorable hearing was given, and they attended him to Zama. The report of his clemency and mildness spreading into all parts, the whole Numidian cavalry flocked to him at Zama, and were there relieved from their fears.

CHAP. XCIII.—During these transactions, Considius, who commanded at Tisdra, with his own retinue, a garrison of Getulians, and a company of gladiators, hearing of the defeat of his party, and terrified at the arrival of Domitius and his legions, abandoned the town; and privately withdrawing, with a few of the barbarians, and all his money, fled hastily toward the kingdom. The Getulians, to render themselves masters of his treasure, murdered him by the way, and fled every man where he could. Meantime, C. Virgilius, seeing himself shut up by sea and land, without the power of making a defense; his followers all slain or put to flight; M. Cato dead by his own hands at Utica; Juba despised and deserted by his own subjects; Sabura and his forces defeated by Sitius; Cæsar received without opposition at Utica; and that of so vast an army, nothing remained capable of screening him or his children; thought it his most prudent course, to surrender himself and the city to the proconsul Caninius, by whom he was besieged.

CHAP. XCIV.—At the same time king Juba, seeing himself excluded from all the cities of his kingdom, and that there remained no hopes of safety; having supped with Petreius, proposed an engagement, sword in hand, that they might die honorably. Juba, as being the stronger, easily got the better of his adversary, and laid him dead at his feet: but endeavoring afterward to run himself through the body, and wanting strength to accomplish it, he was obliged to have recourse to one of his slaves, and, by entreaties, prevailed upon him to put him to death.

CHAP. XCV.—In the mean time, P. Sitius, having defeated the army of Sabura, Juba's lieutenant, and slain the general, and marching with a few troops through Mauritania, to join Cæsar, chanced to fall in with Faustus and Afranius, who were at the head of the party that had plundered Utica, amounting in all to about fifteen hundred men, and designing to make the best of their way to Spain. Having expeditiously placed himself in ambuscade during the night, and attacking them by day-break, he either killed or made them all prisoners, except a few that escaped from the van. Afranius and Faustus were taken among the rest, with their wives and children: but some few days after, a mutiny arising among the soldiers, Faustus and Afranius were slain. Cæsar pardoned Pompeia,[1] the wife of Faustus, with her children, and permitted her the free enjoyment of all her effects.

CHAP. XCVI.—Meanwhile Scipio, with Damasippus and Torquatus, and Plætorius Rustianus, having embarked on board some galleys, with the intention of making for the coast of Spain; and being long and severely tossed by contrary winds,

[1] Pompeia was the daughter of Pompey the Great, married to Faustus, the son of Sulla the dictator.

were at last obliged to put into the port of Hippo, where the fleet commanded by P. Sitius chanced at that time to be. Scipio's vessels, which were but small, and few in number, were easily surrounded and sunk, by the larger and more numerous ships of Sitius; on which occasion Scipio, and all those whom we have mentioned above, as having embarked with him, perished.

CHAP. XCVII.—Meanwhile Cæsar, having exposed the king's effects to public sale at Zama, and confiscated the estates of those who, though Roman citizens, had borne arms against the republic; after conferring rewards upon such of the Zamians as had adopted the design of excluding the king, he abolished all the royal tribunes, converted the kingdom into a province; and appointing Crispus Sallustius to take charge of it, with the title of proconsul, returned to Utica. There he sold the estates of the officers who had served under Juba and Petreius, fined the people of Thapsus twenty thousand sesterces, and the company of Roman merchants there thirty thousand; he likewise fined the inhabitants of Adrumetum in thirty thousand, and their company fifty thousand; but preserved the cities and their territories from insult and plunder. Those of Leptis, whom Juba had pillaged some time before, and who, upon complaint made to the senate by their deputies, had obtained arbitrators and restitution, were enjoined to pay yearly three hundred thousand pounds of oil; because from the beginning of the war, in consequence of a dissension among their chiefs, they had made an alliance with the king of Numidia, and supplied him with arms, soldiers, and money. The people of Tisdra, on account of their extreme poverty, were only condemned to pay annually a certain quantity of corn.

CHAP. XCVIII.—These things being settled, he embarked at Utica on the ides of June, and three days after arrived at Carales in Sardinia. Here he condemned the Sulcitani in a fine of one hundred thousand sesterces, for receiving and aiding Nasidius's fleet; and instead of a tenth which was their former assessment, ordered them now to pay an eighth to the public treasury. He likewise confiscated the estates of some who had been more active than the rest, and weighing from Carales on the third day before the calends of July, coasted along the shore, and after a voyage of twenty-eight days, during which he was several times obliged by contrary winds to put into port, arrived safe at Rome.[1]

[1] On his arrival at Rome he celebrated four different triumphs, over the Gauls, Pharnaces, Egypt, and king Juba. It was a principle in the Roman constitution, that no triumph could be gained in civil wars. Hence Lucan:

"Bella geri placuit nullos habitura triumphos."

COMMENTARIES ON THE SPANISH WAR.

AUTHOR UNKNOWN.

FORMERLY ATTRIBUTED TO HIRTIUS.

THE ARGUMENT.

I. The commencement of the Spanish war. II. Cæsar marches to attack Corduba. III. At the same time throws succors into Ulia, besieged by Pompey. IV. The attempt upon Corduba obliges Pompey to raise the siege of Ulia. V. Pompey advancing to the relief of Corduba, Cæsar attacks Ategua, whither he is followed by Pompey. VII. Both intrench themselves in mountainous places, of difficult access. IX. Pompey, attacking a fort belonging to Cæsar, is repulsed. X. Cæsar continues the siege of Ategua, XI. And repulses a sally from the town. XII. Various skirmishes between the two armies. XV. Cruelty of the townsmen. XVI. Cæsar repulses them in a second sally. XVII. Tullius treats with Cæsar about a surrender. XVIII. Continuation of the siege. XIX. The town surrenders. XX. Pompey removes his camp toward Ucubis. XXII. Behavior of the Bursavolenses. XXIII. Cæsar and Pompey both encamp near Ucubis, where some skirmishes happen. XXV. Single combat between Turpio and Niger. XXVI. Great numbers of the enemy desert to Cæsar. Some of Pompey's letters intercepted. XXVII. Both parties encamp in the plain of Munda. XXVIII. A great battle ensues, XXXI. In which Pompey is totally defeated. XXXII. Cæsar besieges the fugitives in Munda. XXXIII. Attacks and makes himself master of Corduba, XXXV. Likewise of Hispalis; whence he is expelled, but again recovers it. The inhabitants of Munda, under pretense of a surrender, preparing to attack our men, are themselves put to the sword. XXXVII. Carteia surrenders to Cæsar. Pompey makes his escape, XXXIX. But is slain. XL. Some of Cæsar's ships burned. XLI. Cæsar's troops take possession of Munda and afterward invest Uraso. XLII. Cæsar's speech to the people of Hispalis.

CHAP. I.—On the defeat of Pharnaces and reduction of Africa,[1] those who escaped from those battles fled to young

[1] Africa had been lost on the death of Curio.

Cn. Pompey,[1] who had taken possession of Further Spain, while Cæsar was detained in Italy in exhibiting games.[2] Pompey began to throw himself on the protection of every state, in order the more readily to establish the means of defense against him. Accordingly, with a considerable force which had been collected, partly by entreaty, partly by force, he began to lay waste the province. Under these circumstances some states voluntarily sent him supplies, others shut the gates of their towns against him. If any of these chanced to fall into his hands by assault, although some citizen in it had deserved well of Cn. Pompey (his father), yet some cause was alleged against him on account of the greatness of his wealth,[3] so that, he being dispatched, his fortune might become the reward of the soldiers. Thus the enemy, being encouraged by a few advantages, their forces increased much, wherefore those states which were opposed to Pompey, by continual messages dispatched to Italy, sought protection for themselves.

CHAP. II.—When Cæsar, now a third time dictator, and elected a fourth time, having already proceeded many marches into Spain with prompt dispatch,[4] was coming to finish the war, he was met on the way by embassadors from Corduba, who had deserted Cn. Pompey; these informed him that it would be an easy matter to make himself master of the town by night, because the enemy as yet knew nothing of his

[1] He was scarcely twenty-four years of age. He left Africa in disgust at his ill success, and repaired to the Balearic isles, with the intention of going to Spain, in which he had many partisans, and in which active levies were going on against Cæsar. He was then attacked by a severe illness, which detained him there for some time. On his arrival in Spain he met with a most favorable reception, and was saluted imperator.

[2] *Munera* was the name given to the gladiatorial shows which the Roman nobility displayed to the people to gain their favor and support. The person who gave the exhibition was called editor, munerator, or dominus, and if a private person, was honored during the day of exhibition with the official signs of a magistrate. Suetonius says that Cæsar exhibited many of these spectacles to the people, and that they were on a very grand scale.

[3] This is the accusation that Cæsar urges with such vehemence against the Spaniards at the end of this book, namely, that they had received Pompey when a refugee, and by this act had renewed the war.

[4] Appian, Strabo, and Eutropius have recorded that Cæsar came from Rome to his camp which was pitched before Obulco, a town of Spain, in twenty-seven days. Dion says that he was seen by his friends and enemies before it was reported that he was in Spain at all.

arrival in the province, as the scouts sent out by Cn. Pompey to inform him of Cæsar's approach had been all made prisoners. They alleged besides many other very plausible reasons. He, therefore, immediately sent intelligence of his arrival to Q. Pedius, and Q. Fabius Maximus his lieutenants, to whom he had left the command of the troops in the province, ordering them to send him all the cavalry they had been able to raise. He came up with them much sooner than they expected, and had not the protection of the cavalry, according to his desire.

CHAP. III.—Sextus Pompey, the brother of Cneius, commanded at this time at Corduba, which was accounted the capital of the province. Young Cneius Pompey himself was employed in the siege of Ulia,[1] which had now lasted some months. Notice of Cæsar's arrival having been received, messengers having passed Pompey's guards came to him from that town and besought him to send them relief as soon as possible. Cæsar, knowing that this people had deserved very well oft he Romans, detached, about nine o'clock, at night eleven cohorts, with a like number of horse, under the command of L. Julius Paciecus, a man known in that province, and also well acquainted with it. When he arrived at Pompey's quarter, a dreadful tempest arising, attended with a violent wind, so great a darkness ensued that you could scarcely have distinguished even the person next you. This accident proved of great advantage to Paciecus: for being arrived at Pompey's camp, he ordered the cavalry to advance two by two, and march directly through the enemy's quarters to the town; one of their guards calling to know who passed, one of our troopers bade him be silent, for they were just then endeavoring by stealth to approach the wall, in order to get possession of the town; and partly by this answer, partly by favor of the tempest, the sentinels were prevented from examining things diligently. When they reached the gates, upon a signal being given, they were admitted; and both horse and foot raising a loud shout, after leaving some troops to guard the town, sallied in a body upon the enemy's camp. This came upon them so unexpectedly that the greater number of the men in the camps thought that they were captured.

[1] This was the only town of Bœtica that Pompey had failed to make himself master of.

Chap. IV.—Ulia being relieved, Cæsar, to draw Pompey from the siege, marched toward Corduba; sending the cavalry before, with a select body of heavy-armed foot; who, as soon as they came within sight of the place, got up behind the troopers. By this stratagem they could not possibly be perceived by those of Corduba. Upon their approach to the walls, the enemy sallied in great numbers to attack our cavalry; when the infantry, whom we have mentioned above, leaping down, fell upon them with such fury that out of an almost infinite multitude of men, very few returned to the town. This so alarmed Sextus Pompey that he immediately sent letters to his brother, requesting him to come speedily to his relief, lest Cæsar should make himself master of Corduba before his arrival. Thus Cn. Pompey, moved by his brother's letters, quitted the siege of Ulia, which was upon the point of surrendering, and set out toward Corduba.

Chap. V.—Cæsar, arriving at the river Guadalquivir, which he found too deep to be forded, sank several baskets of stones in it. Thus having formed a bridge, he transported his troops in three bodies to the camps. As I have just mentioned, the beams of the bridge stretched over against the tower in two rows. Pompey, arriving soon after with his troops, encamped directly over against him. Cæsar, to cut off his provisions and communication with the town, ran a line from his camp to the bridge. Pompey did the same; so that a struggle arose between the two generals, which should first get possession of the bridge; and this daily brought on skirmishes, in which sometimes the one, sometimes the other party had the better. When these merged into a serious engagement, both sides fought hand to hand; in the heat of the struggle for this position, owing to the narrowness of the bridge, they were pressed together, and in their efforts to extend themselves toward the river-side, many fell headlong. Thus the loss was pretty equal; for on either side lay heaps of slain, and Cæsar for many days used all possible endeavors to bring the enemy to an engagement on equal terms, that he might bring the war to a conclusion as soon as possible.

Chap. VI.—But finding that they carefully avoided a battle, with a view to which chiefly he had quitted the route of Ulia; he caused great fires to be lighted in the night, repassed the river with all his forces, and marched toward Ategua, one of their strongest garrisons. Pompey, being informed of this by the deserters, on the same day brought back many carriages and machines[1] by narrow paths, and betook himself to Corduba. Cæsar began his attack upon Ategua, and carried lines quite round the town. Pompey, having intelligence of this, set out upon his march the same day. In order to guard against his arrival, Cæsar possessed himself of many forts; partly to shelter his cavalry, partly to post guards of infantry for the defense of his camp. Pompey's arrival happened at a time when the mist was very thick, so that he found means, with some cohorts and troops of cavalry, to hem in a party of Cæsar's horse, and fell upon them in such manner that very few escaped slaughter.[2]

CHAP. VII.—The following night Pompey set fire to his camp, passed the river Rio Salado, and, marching through the valleys, encamped on a rising ground, between the two towns of Ategua and Ucubis. Cæsar cast up a mound and brought forward his machines, with other preparations which were necessary for storming the town. The country all around is mountainous, and seems formed for war, being separated from the plain by the river Rio Salado, ascending on the side toward Ategua, about two miles from the river. Pompey's camp was upon these mountains, within view of both towns; he could, however, send no relief to his friends. He had the emblems and standards of thirteen legions, but of those on whom he trusted for support two were natives[3] which had deserted from Trebonius; one was formed out of the Roman colonies in those parts; and a fourth, belonging to Afranius, he had brought with him from Africa; the rest were for the most part made up of fugitives and deserters; in light-armed foot and cavalry we far exceeded him in both courage and numbers.

CHAP. VIII.—Another reason why Pompey was enabled to protract the war was that the country was full of mountains

[1] Oberlin in this passage reads "lanistas," but the common reading seems preferable.

[2] We can not infer clearly from the construction whether Pompey's cavalry cut Cæsar's to pieces, or the reverse. However, as Dion says that Pompey succeeded in his attempt, I follow his authority in translating as in the text.

[3] These native legions served at first under Varro, Pompey's lieutenant. They then deserted to Cæsar, who gave the command of them to Longinus, and on his death to Trebonius, from whom they revolted, and declared in favor of young Pompey.

and extremely well adapted to encampments. For almost the whole province of Further Spain, though of an extremely fertile soil, and abounding in springs, is nevertheless very difficult of access. Here too, on account of the frequent incursions of the natives, all the places remote from great towns, are fortified with towers and castles, covered as in Africa, not with tiles but with earth, on these they place sentinels, and their high situation commands an extensive view of the country on all sides. Nay, the greatest part of the towns of this province are built on mountains, and places exceedingly strong by nature, the approaches to which are extremely difficult. Thus sieges are rare and hazardous in Spain, since it is not easy to reduce their towns by force; as happened in the present war. For Pompey having established his camp between Ategua and Ucubis, as related above, and within view of both towns, Cæsar possessed himself of an eminence very conveniently situated, and only about four miles from his own camp, on which he built a fortress.

CHAP. IX.—Pompey, who, from the nature of the ground, was covered by the same eminence, which was besides at a sufficient distance from Cæsar's quarters, became sensible of the importance of this post; and as Cæsar was separated from it by the river Rio Salado, he imagined that the difficulty of sending relief would prevent his attempting any thing of that kind in its defense. Influenced by this belief, he set out about midnight and attacked the fort, that he might bring assistance to the besieged. Our troops, upon their approach, setting up a shout, discharged their javelins in great numbers, and wounded multitudes of men. After this, when those in the camp began to resist, and when tidings of it was conveyed to the great camps to Cæsar, he set out with three legions, and when he approached them, many were killed, owing to their trepidation and flight, and a great number made prisoners. Among these two * * *; and many others, having thrown down their arms escaped, so that fourscore shields were found.

CHAP. X.—The next day Arguetius arrived from Italy with the cavalry, and five standards taken from the Saguntines;[1]

[1] The inhabitants of Saguntia or Sagunthus, a town of Hispania Bætica. We must not confound it with Saguntum, *Morviedro*, originally founded by colonists from Zacynthus, who were afterward joined by some Rutuli from Ardea. The inhabitants of the latter of these two towns are dis-

but was forced to quit his post by Asprenas, who likewise brought a reinforcement from Italy to Cæsar. The same night Pompey set fire to his camp, and drew toward Corduba. A king, named Indus, who was bringing some troops to Cæsar, with a party of cavalry, following the pursuit of the enemy too briskly, was made prisoner, and slain by the Spanish legionaries.

Chap. XI.—On the next day, our cavalry pursued those who were employed in carrying provisions from the town to Pompey's camp, almost to the very walls of Corduba, and took fifty prisoners besides horses. On the same day, Q. Marcius, a military tribune in Pompey's army, deserted to us. At midnight, a keen encounter took place in the town, and they hurled fire, and every means was resorted to by which fire could be cast. When the attack was ended, C. Fundanius, a Roman knight, quitted the enemy, and came over to us.

Chap. XII.—On the next day, two Spanish legionaries, who pretended to be slaves, were made prisoners by a party of our horse; but being brought to the camp, they were known by the soldiers, who had formerly served under Fabius and Pedeius, and deserted from Trebonius. No pardon was extended to them, and they were slaughtered by our troops. At the same time, some couriers, sent from Corduba to Pompey, entering our camp by mistake, were seized, had their hands cut off, and then were dismissed. About nine at night, the besieged, according to custom, spent a considerable time in casting fire and darts upon our soldiers, and wounded a great number of men. At day-break they sallied upon the sixth legion, while we were busy at the works, and began a sharp contest, in which, however, our men got the better, though the besieged had the advantage of the higher ground. Those who had begun the attack, being vigorously opposed on our side, notwithstanding all the inconveniences we fought under, were at length obliged to retire into the town, with many wounds.

Chap. XIII.—On the next day Pompey began a line from the camp to the river Rio Salado; and a small party of our horse,

tinguished for the memorable stand which they made against Hannibal, who besieged them, 219 B.C. The siege lasted for eight months till at length the Saguntines, who were pressed severely by famine, destroyed themselves and their property by fire. This was the immediate cause of the second Punic war.

being attacked by a much larger body of the enemy, were driven from their post, and three of their number slain. On the same day, A. Valgius, the son of a senator, whose brother was in Pompey's camp, mounted his horse and went over to the enemy, leaving all his baggage behind him. A spy, belonging to Pompey's second legion, was taken and slain. At the same time, a bullet was shot into the town, with this inscription: "That he[1] should set up a shield on whatever day they advanced to storm the town." This encouraging some to hope that they might scale the walls, and possess themselves of the town without danger, they fell the next day to sapping them, and threw down a considerable part of the outward wall. * * In this action, being captured and protected by the townsmen, as if they had been of their own party, they requested Cæsar to dismiss in armor even those who were appointed over the city by Pompey to guard it. To this Cæsar answered, "That it was his custom to give, not accept of conditions:" which being reported to the garrison, they set up a shout, and began to pour their darts upon our men from the whole circuit of the wall; which gave reason to believe that the garrison intended that day to make a vigorous sally. Wherefore, surrounding the town with our troops, the conflict was for some time maintained with great violence, and one of our engines threw down a tower belonging to the enemy, in which were five of their men, and a boy, whose office it was to observe the engine.

CHAP. XIV.—After this Pompey erected a fort on the other side of the Rio Salado, in which he met with no interruption from our men, and exulted not a little in the idea of having possessed himself of a post so near us. Also the following day, extending himself in like manner still further, he came up with our out-post of cavalry; and charging them briskly, obliged several squadrons and the light-armed foot to give ground: many of whom, owing to the smallness of their numbers and their light armor, were trodden down by the enemy's horse. This passed within view of both camps, and not a little animated the Pompeians, to see our men pushed so far: but the latter, being afterward reinforced by a party from our camp, faced about with the intention of renewing the fight.

CHAP. XV.—It invariably happens in encounters of cavalry

[1] Viz., he who wrote the inscription on the bullet.

that when the troopers dismount to charge the infantry, the match proves unequal, as happened on the present occasion. For a select body of the enemy's light-armed foot, coming unexpectedly upon our horse, they alighted to sustain the charge. Thus in a very little time, from a cavalry it became an infantry engagement, and again from an infantry changed to a cavalry engagement, in which our men were driven back to their very lines; but being there reinforced, about a hundred and twenty-three of the enemy were slain, several forced to throw down their arms, many wounded, and the rest pursued quite to their camp. On our side, three were slain, besides twelve foot-soldiers and five troopers wounded. Toward the evening of the same day, the fight, as usual, was renewed before the walls: and the enemy having thrown many darts, and a great quantity of fire from the battlements, proceeded afterward to an action of unexampled cruelty and barbarity: for in the very sight of our troops they fell to murdering the citizens, and tumbling them headlong from the walls, as is usual among barbarians: no parallel to this is to be found in the memory of man.

CHAP. XVI.—When night came on, Pompey sent a messenger unknown to us, to exhort the garrison to set fire to our towers and mound, and make a sally at midnight. Accordingly, having poured upon us a great quantity of darts and fire, and destroyed a considerable part of the rampart, they opened the gate which lay over against and within view of Pompey's camp, and sallied out with all their forces, carrying with them fascines to fill up the ditch; hooks and fire to destroy and reduce to ashes the barracks, which the soldiers had built mostly of reeds to defend them from the winter; and some silver and rich apparel to scatter among the tents, that while our men should be employed in securing the plunder, they might fight their way through and escape to Pompey; who, in expectation that they would be able to effect their design, had crossed the Rio Salado with his army, where he continued all night in order of battle, to favor their retreat. But though our men had no apprehension of this design, their valor enabled them to frustrate the attempt, and repulse the enemy with many wounds. They even made themselves masters of the spoil, their arms, and some prisoners, who were put to death next day. At the same time, a deserter from the town informed us that Junius, who was employed in the mine when the citizens were massacred, exclaimed that it was a cruel and barbarous action—"that they had never deserved such treatment at their hands—for that they had received them in their temples and their homes—that it was in violation of all hospitality." He added many things besides, which made such an impression upon the garrison that they desisted from the massacre.

CHAP. XVII.—The next day, Tullius, a lieutenant-general, accompanied by C. Antonius of Lusitania, came to Cæsar, and addressed him to this effect:—"Would to Heaven I had been one of your soldiers rather than a follower of C. Pompey, and given those proofs of valor and constancy in obtaining victories for you, rather than in suffering for him. The only advantage we reap from following his banners are wretched applauses; being reduced to the condition of indigent citizens, and by the melancholy fate of our country ranked among its enemies; we, who having never shared with Pompey his good fortune, yet find ourselves involved in his disgrace; and after sustaining the attack of so many armed legions, employing ourselves day and night in the works of defense, exposed to the darts and swords of our fellow-citizens; vanquished, deserted by Pompey, and compelled to give way to the superior valor of your troops, find ourselves at last obliged to have recourse to your clemency, and implore that you will not show yourselves less placable to fellow-citizens, than you have so often been to foreign nations."[1] "I shall," said Cæsar, "prove myself the same to fellow-citizens, as I have been to conquered nations."

CHAP. XVIII.—The embassadors being dismissed, when Tiberius Tullius arrived at the gate of the town, and C. Antony did not follow him, he returned to the gate and laid hold of him, upon which drawing a poniard from his breast, he wounded him in the hand, and in this condition they both fled to Cæsar. At the same time the standard-bearer of the first legion came over to our camp, and reported that the day when the skirmish happened between the horse, no less than thirty-five of his company fell; but it was not allowed to mention it in Pompey's camp, or so much as own the loss of one man. A slave, whose master was in Cæsar's camp, and who had left his wife and son in the city, cut his master's throat, and deceiving the guards, escaped privately to Pompey's camp; whence, by means

[1] Pontus, Egypt, and Gallogræcia.

of a bullet, on which he inscribed his intelligence, Cæsar was informed of the preparations made for the defense of the place. When we had read the inscription, those who were employed to throw the bullet returning to the city, two Lusitanian brothers deserted, and informed us that Pompey in a speech made to his soldiers, had said: "That as he found it impossible to relieve the town, he was resolved to withdraw in the night from the sight of the enemy, and retire toward the sea;" to which one answered "that it was better to hazard a battle than take refuge in flight," but he who said so was instantly put to death. At the same time some of his couriers were intercepted, who were endeavoring to get into the town. Cæsar sent the letters to the inhabitants, and ordered one of the messengers begging his life, to set fire to the townsmen's wooden turret, promising that if he did this he would grant him all. The enterprise was not without difficulty: he undertook it, however, but was slain in the attempt. The same night a deserter informed us that Pompey and Labienus were greatly offended at the massacre of the citizens.

Chap. XIX.—About nine at night, one of our wooden towers, which had been severely battered by the enemy's engines, gave way as far as the third story. A sharp encounter ensued under the walls, and the besieged, assisted by a favorable wind, burned the remaining part of that tower and another. Next morning a matron threw herself from the wall, and came over to the camp, reporting, "that the rest of her family had intended the same, but were apprehended and put to death;" likewise, a letter was thrown over, in which was written—"L. Minatius[1] to Cæsar; Pompey has abandoned me; if you will grant me my life, I promise to serve you with the same fidelity and attachment I have hitherto manifested toward him." At the same time deputies who had been sent before to Cæsar by the garrison, now waited on him a second time, offering to deliver up the town next day, upon a bare grant of their lives: to which he replied, "That he was Cæsar, and would perform his word." Thus, having made himself master of the place, on the nineteenth of February he was saluted imperator.

Chap. XX.—Pompey, being informed by some deserters

[1] Pompey had given him the command of the garrison of the city. Dion Cassius and Valerius Maximus accuse him of all the cruelty that was displayed at Ategua.

that the town had surrendered, removed his camp toward Ucubis, where he began to build redoubts, and secure himself with lines. Cæsar also decamped and drew near him. At the same time a Spanish legionary soldier deserting to our camp, informed us that Pompey had assembled the people of Ucubis, and given them instructions to inquire diligently who favored his party, who that of the enemy. Some time after in the town which was taken, the slave, who, as we have related above, had murdered his master, was apprehended in a mine and burned alive. About the same time eight Spanish centurions came over to Cæsar, and in a skirmish between our cavalry and that of the enemy, we were repulsed, and some of our light-armed foot wounded. The same night we took of the enemy's spies, three slaves and one Spanish soldier. The slaves were crucified,[1] and the soldier was beheaded.

Chap. XXI.—The day following, some of the enemy's cavalry and light-armed infantry deserted to us; and about eleven of their horse falling upon a party of our men that were sent to fetch water, killed some and took others prisoners; among which last were eight troopers. On the next day Pompey beheaded seventy-four persons supposed to be favorers of Cæsar's cause, ordering the rest who lay under the same suspicion to be carried back to the town, of whom a hundred and twenty escaped to Cæsar.

Chap. XXII.—Some time after, the deputies from Bursavola (whom Cæsar had taken prisoners at Ategua, and sent along with his own embassadors to their city, to inform them of the massacre of the Ateguans, and what they had to apprehend from Pompey, who suffered his soldiers to murder their hosts, and commit all manner of crimes with impunity), arriving in the town, none of our deputies, except such as were natives of the place, durst enter the city, though they were all Roman knights and senators. But after many messages backward and forward, when the deputies were upon their return, the garrison pursued and put them all to the sword, except two who escaped to Cæsar, and informed him of what had happened. Some time after, the inhabitants of Bursavola, sending spies to Ategua to know the truth of what had happened, and finding the report of our deputies confirmed, were for stoning to death him who had been the cause of the murder of the deputies, and were with

[1] The usual method, among the Romans, of putting slaves to death.

difficulty restrained from laying violent hands upon him, which in the end proved the occasion of their own destruction. For having obtained leave of the inhabitants to go in person to Cæsar and justify himself, he privately drew together some troops, and when he thought himself strong enough, returned in the night, and was treacherously admitted into the town, where he made a dreadful massacre of the inhabitants, slew all the leaders of the opposite party, and reduced the place to subjection. Soon after, some slaves who had deserted informed us that he had sold all the goods of the citizens, and that Pompey suffered none of his soldiers to quit the camp but unarmed, because, since the taking of Ategua, many despairing of success fled into Bæturia, having given over all expectation of victory; and that if any deserted from our camp, they were put among the light-armed infantry, whose pay was only sixteen *asses* a day.

CHAP. XXIII.—The day following Cæsar removed his camp nearer to Pompey's, and began to draw a line to the river Salado. While our men were employed in the work, some of the enemy fell upon us from the higher ground, and as we were in no condition to make resistance, wounded great numbers. Here, as Ennius says, "our men retreated a little." This occurrence, so contrary to our usual custom, being perceived, two centurions of the fifth legion passed the river, and restored the battle; when, pressing upon the enemy with astonishing bravery, one of them fell overwhelmed by the multitude of darts discharged from above. The other continued the combat for some time, but seeing himself in danger of being surrounded, endeavored to make good his retreat, but stumbled and fell. His death being known, the enemy crowded together in still greater numbers, upon which our cavalry passed the river, and drove them back to their intrenchments; so that, while they too eagerly desired to slay them within their lines, they were surrounded by the cavalry and light-armed troops. Many of these would have been captured alive, had not their valor been pre-eminent, for they were so confined by the space included in the fortress, that the cavalry could not well defend itself. Many of our men were wounded in these two encounters, and among the rest Clodius Aquitius, but, as the fight was carried on mostly from a distance, none of our men fell, except the two centurions who sacrificed themselves in the cause of glory.

Chap. XXIV.—Next day both parties withdrawing from Soricaria, we continued our works. But Pompey, observing that our fort had cut off his communication with Aspavia,[1] which is about five miles distant from Ucubis, judged it necessary to come to a battle. Yet he did not offer it upon equal terms, but chose to draw up his men upon a hill, that he might have the advantage of the higher ground. In this respect, when both parties were seeking the superior position, our men anticipating them, drove them into the plain, which gave us the advantage. The enemy yielded on all hands, and we made immense havoc among them. The mountain and not their valor protected them; of which advantage, and of all relief, our men, though few in number, would have deprived them had not night intervened. Three hundred and twenty-four light-armed foot, and about a hundred and thirty-eight legionary soldiers of their number fell, besides those whose armor and spoils we carried off. Thus the death of the two centurions, which happened the day before, was fully revenged.

Chap. XXV.—The day after, Pompey's cavalry advanced, according to their usual custom, to our lines; for they only dared venture to draw up on equal ground. They therefore began to skirmish with our men who were at work, the legionaries calling out to us at the same time to choose our field of battle, with a view to make us believe that they desired nothing so much as to come to blows; upon this our men quitted the eminence where they were encamped, and advanced a great way into the plain. But none of the enemy had the boldness to present themselves, excepting Antistius Turpio; who, presuming on his strength, and fancying no one on our side a match for him, offered us defiance. Upon this, as is recorded of Memnon and Achilles, Q. Pompeius Niger, a Roman knight, born in Italy, advanced from our ranks to the encounter. The fierce air of Antistius having engaged the attention of all, the two armies drew up to be spectators of the issue of this challenge, and expressed as much impatience as if the whole fortune of the war had depended upon it. The wishes on both sides for success were equal to the anxiety and concern each felt for his own combatant. They advanced into the plain with great courage, having each a resplendent buckler

[1] Aspavia, a town of Spain, situated on the Rio Salado, near Corduba. Some suppose it to be *Apea*, others *Cestro el Rio*.

of curious workmanship. And doubtless the combat would have been soon decided, had not some light-armed foot drawn up near the lines, to serve as a guard to the camp because of the approach of the enemy's horse, which we have before alluded to. * * * Our horse, in retreating to their camp, being warmly pursued by the enemy, suddenly faced about with great cries; which so terrified the Pompeians, that they immediately betook themselves to flight, and retreated to their camp with the loss of many of their men.

CHAP. XXVI.—Cæsar, to reward the valor of the Cassian troop, presented them with thirteen thousand sesterces, distributed ten thousand more among the light-armed foot, and gave to the commander of the cavalry five golden collars. The same day, A. Bebius, C. Flavius, and A. Trebellius, Roman knights of Asta,[1] with their horses richly caparisoned and adorned with silver, came over to Cæsar, and informed him, that all the rest of the Roman knights in Pompey's camp, had like them conspired to come and join him, that, on the information of a slave they had all been seized and cast into custody; that out of this number they only had escaped. The same day letters were intercepted, sent by Pompey to Ursao, with the usual greeting, and stating, "That hitherto he had all the success against the enemy he could desire, and would have ended the war much sooner than was expected, could he have brought them to engage him upon equal terms; that he did not think it advisable to venture new-levied troops on a plain; that the enemy, depending on our supplies, as yet protract the war, for they storm city after city, thence supplying themselves with provisions: that he would therefore endeavor to protect the towns of his party, and bring the war to as speedy an issue as possible: that he would send them a reinforcement of some cohorts, and that having deprived them of provisions he would necessitate the enemy to come to an engagement.

CHAP. XXVII.—Some time after, as our men were carelessly dispersed about the works, a few horse were killed, who had gone to a grove of olives to fetch wood. Several slaves deserted at this time, and informed us that ever since the action at Soritia on the 7th of March, the enemy had been under continual alarms, and appointed Attius Varus to guard

[1] Asta, which still retains its ancient name, was a town of Hispania Bætica. A Roman colony was founded there.

the lines. The same day Pompey decamped, and posted himself in an olive-wood over against Hispalis. Cæsar, before he removed, waited till midnight, when the moon began to appear. At his departure he ordered them to set fire to the fort of Ucubis, which Pompey had abandoned, and to assemble in the greater camp. He afterward laid siege to Ventisponte, which surrendered; and marching thence to Carruca, encamped over against Pompey, who had burned the city, because the garrison refused to open the gates to him. A soldier who had murdered his brother in the camp, being intercepted by our men, was scourged to death. Cæsar, still pursuing his march, arrived in the plains of Munda, and pitched his camp opposite to that of Pompey.

Chap. XXVIII.—Next day as Cæsar was preparing to set out with the army, notice was sent him by his spies, that Pompey had been in order of battle ever since midnight. Upon this intelligence he ordered the standard to be raised. Pompey had taken this resolution in consequence of his letter to the inhabitants of Ursao, who were his firm adherents, in which he told them that Cæsar refused to come down into the plain, because his army consisted mostly of new-levied troops. This had greatly confirmed the city in its allegiance. Thus relying on this opinion, he thought that he could effect the whole, for he was defended by the nature of his situation, and by the position for defense of the town, where he had his camp: for, as we observed before, this country is full of hills which run in a continued chain, without any plains intervening.

Chap. XXIX.—But we must by no means omit to mention an accident which happened about this time. The two camps were divided from one another by a plain about five miles in extent, so that Pompey, in consequence of the town's elevated position, and the nature of the country, enjoyed a double defense. Across this valley ran a rivulet, which rendered the approach to the mountain extremely difficult, because it formed a deep morass on the right. Cæsar had no doubt that the enemy would descend into the plain and come to a battle, when he saw them in array. This appeared evident to all; the rather because the plain would give their cavalry full room to act, and the day was so serene and clear that the gods seemed to have sent it on purpose to favor the engagement. Our men rejoiced at the favorable opportunity: some however were not altogether exempt from fear when they considered that their all was at stake, with the uncertainty of what might be their fate an hour after. He advanced however to the field of battle, fully persuaded that the enemy would do the same; but they durst not venture above a mile from the town, being determined to shelter themselves under its walls. Our men still continued before them in order of battle; but although the equality of the ground sometimes tempted them to come and dispute the victory, they nevertheless still kept their post on the mountain, in the neighborhood of the town. We doubled our speed to reach the rivulet, without their stirring from the place where they stood.

CHAP. XXX.—Their army consisted of thirteen legions; the cavalry was drawn up upon the wings, with six thousand light-armed infantry and about the same number of auxiliaries. We had only eighty heavy-armed cohorts, and eight thousand horse. When we reached the extremity of the plain, the real seat of disadvantage, the enemy were awaiting us above, so that it would have been exceedingly dangerous to proceed. When Cæsar perceived this, he pointed out the locality, lest any disagreeable occurrence should result from the temerity of his troops. The army murmured greatly, as if they had been kept back from a certain victory, when this was told them. The delay, however, served to enliven the enemy, thinking that Cæsar's troops shrank from an encounter through fear: they therefore had the boldness to advance a little way, yet without quitting the advantage of their post, the approach to which was extremely dangerous. The tenth legion, as usual, was on the right, the third and fifth on the left, with the auxiliary troops and cavalry. The battle began with a shout.

CHAP. XXXI.—But though our men were superior to the enemy in courage, the latter nevertheless defended themselves so well by the advantage of the higher ground, and the shouts were so loud, and the discharge of darts on both sides so great, that we almost began to despair of victory.[1] For the first onset

[1] Of Cæsar's danger in this battle, Plutarch speaks in the following manner: "The great battle which decided the war was fought under the walls of Munda. Cæsar at first saw his men so hard pressed, and making so feeble a resistance, that he ran through the ranks, amid the swords and spears, exclaiming, 'Are you not ashamed to deliver your general into the hands of boys?' The great and vigorous effort this reproach produced, at last made the enemy turn their backs, and there were more

and shout, by which an enemy is most apt to be dismayed, were pretty equal in the present encounter. All fought with equal valor; the place was covered with arrows and darts, and great numbers of the enemy fell. We have already observed that the tenth legion was on the right, which, though not considerable for the number of men, was nevertheless formidable for its courage; and so pressed the enemy on that side that they were obliged to draw a legion from the right wing to reinforce the left, lest we should come upon their flank; but they fought so bravely that the reinforcement could not find an opportunity of entering the ranks. Upon this motion, our cavalry on the left fell upon Pompey's right wing. Meanwhile the clashing of armor mingled with the shouts of combatants, and the groans of the dying and the wounded, terrified the new-raised soldiers. On this occasion, as Ennius says, "they fought hand to hand, foot to foot, and shield to shield;" but though the enemy fought with the utmost vigor, they were obliged to give ground, and retire toward the town. The battle was fought on the feast of Bacchus, and the Pompeians were entirely routed and put to flight; insomuch that not a man could have escaped, had they not sheltered themselves in the place whence they advanced to the charge. The enemy lost on this occasion upward of thirty thousand men, and among the rest Labienus and Attius Varus, whose funeral obsequies were performed upon the field of battle. They had likewise three thousand Roman knights killed, partly Italian, partly provincial. About a thousand were slain on our side, partly foot, partly horse; and five hundred wounded. We gained thirteen eagles, and several standards, and emblems of authority, and made seventeen officers prisoners. Such was the issue of this action.

CHAP. XXXII.—The remains of Pompey's army retreating to Munda, with the intention of defending themselves in that town, it became necessary to invest it. The dead bodies of the enemy, heaped together, served as a rampart, and their javelins and darts were fixed up by way of palisades. Upon

than thirty thousand of them slain, whereas Cæsar lost only a thousand, but those were some of the best men he had. As he retired after the battle, he told his friends, 'he had often fought for victory, but that was the first time he had fought for his life.'"

these we hung their bucklers to supply the place of a breastwork, and fixing the heads of the deceased upon swords and lances, planted them all around the works, to strike the greater terror into the besieged, and keep awake in them a sense of our prowess. Amid these mournful objects did they find themselves shut in, when our men began the attack, which was conducted chiefly by the Gauls. Young Valerius, who had escaped to Corduba with some horse, informed Sextus Pompey of what had happened; who, upon receipt of the mournful news, distributing what money he had about him to the troopers, left the town about nine at night, under pretense of going to find out Cæsar, to treat of an accommodation. On the other side, Cn. Pompey, attended by a few horse and foot, took the road to Carteia, where his fleet lay, and which was about a hundred and seventy miles distant from Corduba. When he was arrived within eight miles of the place, he sent P. Calvitius his camp-marshal before, to procure a litter to carry him to the town, as he found himself unwell. The litter came, and when he entered the town, those of his party waited on him privately, to receive his orders about the management of the war. As they assembled round the place in great crowds, Pompey quitting his litter put himself under their protection.

CHAP. XXXIII.—After the encounter, Cæsar seeing the circumvallation of Munda completed, marched to Corduba. Those of the enemy who had escaped the slaughter, possessing themselves of a bridge, upon the approach of our men, called out to them with an air of derision—"What! we who are no more than a handful of men escaped from the battle, shall we be allowed no place of retreat?" They immediately prepared to defend the bridge. Cæsar passed the river[1] and encamped. Scapula,[2] who had stirred up the freedmen to a revolt, escaping after the battle to Corduba, when he found himself besieged, assembled all his followers, ordered a funeral pile to be erected

[1] The Guadalquivir.

[2] Scapula, even before the arrival of Cneius Pompey in Spain, when the news of the total defeat of Scipio at Thapsus reached him, was elected general by the soldiers. Apollonius was declared his colleague. Scapula succeeded in debauching all Hispania Bætica from its allegiance to Cæsar, and then formed a junction with Pompey. His subsequent fate is related in the chapter before us.

and a magnificent supper served up; when, putting on his richest dress, he distributed his plate and money among his domestics, supped cheerfully, anointed himself several times, and, last of all, ordered one of his freedmen to dispatch him, and another to set fire to the pile.

CHAP. XXXIV.—Cæsar had no sooner encamped before the place than a division arose among the inhabitants, between the parties of Cæsar and Pompey, till the dispute almost reached to our camps. During the contest, some legions, composed partly of deserters, partly of slaves made free by Pompey, came and surrendered themselves to Cæsar. But the thirteenth legion prepared to defend the town, and with that view possessed themselves of the walls and some towers, in spite of all opposition, which obliged the other party to send deputies to Cæsar for aid. Upon this those who had escaped out of the battle set fire to the place, and our men entering at the same time, slew about twenty-two thousand of them, besides those who were slain without the walls; thus Cæsar obtained the town. While he was employed in this siege, those who, as we have said, were blockaded at Munda made a sally, but were driven back into the town with considerable loss.

CHAP. XXXV.—Thence Cæsar marched to Hispalis, which sent deputies to sue for pardon. Though the citizens assured him that they were able to defend the town, he sent Caninius his lieutenant thither with some troops, and encamped before the place. There was in the town a strong party of Pompeians, who, displeased to see Cæsar's troops received within the walls, secretly deputed one Philo, a zealous partisan of Pompey, and well known in Lusitania, to beg assistance of Cecilius Niger, one of the barbarians, who lay encamped near Lenius, with a strong army of Lusitanians. He is received into the town of Hispalis by night, surprises the sentinels and garrison, shuts the gates, and begins to defend the place.

CHAP. XXXVI.—During these transactions deputies arrived from Carteia, with accounts of their having secured Pompey; hoping by this service to atone for their former fault of shutting their gates against Cæsar. Meantime, the Lusitanians in Hispalis plundered the town, which, though known to Cæsar, did not yet determine him to press it too hard, lest they should in despair set fire to it, and destroy the walls. It was resolved in council to suffer the Lusitanians to escape in the night by a sally, yet so that the thing might not appear designed. In this sally, they set fire to the ships that were in the river Guadalquivir, and while our men were employed in extinguishing the flames, endeavored to get off; but being overtaken by the cavalry, were mostly cut to pieces. Thence Cæsar marched to Asta, which submitted. Munda having been now a long while besieged, many of those who had escaped out of the battle, despairing of safety, surrendered to us; and being formed into a legion, conspired among themselves, that upon a signal being given, the garrison should sally out in the night, while they at the same time should begin a massacre in the camp. But the plot being discovered, they were next night, at the changing of the third watch, all put to death outside the rampart.

CHAP. XXXVII.—The Carteians, while Cæsar was employed in reducing the other towns upon his route, began to disagree about young Pompey. One party had sent the deputies to Cæsar, and another was in the Pompeian interest. These last prevailing, seized the gates, and made a dreadful slaughter of their adversaries. Pompey himself was wounded in the fray, but escaping to his ships, fled with about twenty galleys. Didius, who was at Gades with Cæsar's fleet, hearing of what had happened, immediately sailed in pursuit of them; stationing at the same time some cavalry and infantry along the coast, to prevent his escaping by land. Pompey had left Carteia with so much precipitation, that he took no time to furnish himself with water, and this circumstance obliging him to stop by the way, Didius came up with him after four days' sailing, took some of his ships, and burned the rest.

CHAP. XXXVIII.—With a few friends, Pompey escaped to a place strongly fortified by nature; of which the troops sent in pursuit of him having certain intelligence by their scouts, followed day and night. He was wounded in the shoulder and left leg, and had besides sprained his ankle, all which greatly retarded his flight, and obliged him to make use of a litter. A Lusitanian having discovered the place of his retreat, he was quickly surrounded by our cavalry and cohorts. Seeing himself betrayed, he took refuge in a post fortified by nature, and which could easily be defended by a few men, the approach to it being extremely difficult. We attempted to storm it, but were repulsed, and pursued by the enemy; and meeting with no better success after several trials, we at length resolved to lay siege to the place, it seeming too hazardous to force it. Accordingly, a terrace was raised, and lines drawn round the place; which the enemy perceiving, thought it best to betake themselves to flight.

CHAP. XXXIX.—Pompey as we have observed above being lame and wounded,[1] was in no condition to make a speedy retreat; and the rather, because the place was such that he could use neither horse nor litter. Slaughter was dealt on all hands by our troops, his fortress having been stormed, and his resources cut off. In this extremity he fled to a cave, where he could not easily be discovered, unless by the information of the captives. Here he was slain, his head was brought to Hispalis on the day before the ides of April, and exhibited before the people when Cæsar was at Gades.

CHAP. XL.—After the death of young Pompey, Didius, proud of his success, retired to the nearest fortress and hauled some of his vessels on shore to be refitted. The Lusitanians, who had escaped from the battle, rallying in great bodies, advanced to Didius. Though the preservation of the fleet principally engaged his attention, he was obliged to leave his fort in order to restrain the frequent sallies of the enemy. These daily skirmishes gave them an opportunity of projecting an ambuscade; for which purpose they divided their troops into three bodies. Some were prepared to set fire to the fleet, and in the mean time others were to come to their relief. These were so arranged that they could advance to the battle without any one seeing them. Didius sallied out according to custom; when upon a signal being given, one of the parties advanced to set fire to the fleet; and another, counterfeiting a retreat, drew him insensibly into the ambuscade, where he was surrounded and slain with most of his followers, fighting valiantly. Some escaped in boats which they found upon the coast; others endeavored to reach the galleys by swimming; and, weighing anchor, stood out to sea. A great many saved themselves

[1] We learn from Appian, that when Pompey saw those who were carrying him despair of safety, he fled, lest they should give him up to the enemy. As he hastily entered the boat, his foot got entangled in a rope, and, in his haste to extricate himself and cut the rope, he wounded his foot.

in this manner, but the Lusitanians got all the baggage. Cæsar meanwhile returned from Gades to Hispalis.

CHAP. XLI.—Fabius Maximus, whom he had left to continue the siege of Munda, conducted it with great zeal; so that the enemy, seeing themselves shut up on all sides, sallied out, but were repulsed with great loss. Our men seized this opportunity to get possession of the town, and took the rest prisoners, in number about fourteen thousand. Thence they retreated toward Ursao, a town exceedingly strong both by nature and art, and capable of resisting an enemy. Besides, there is not, within eight miles of the place any spring but that which supplies the town, which was a decided advantage to the besieged. In addition to all this, the wood necessary for building towers and other machines had to be fetched from a distance of six miles. And Pompey, to render the siege more difficult, had cut down all the timber round the place, and collected it within the walls, which obliged our men to bring all the materials for carrying on the siege from Munda, the nearest town which they had subdued.

CHAP. XLII.—During these transactions at Munda and Ursao, Cæsar, who had returned from Gades to Hispalis, assembled the citizens, and made the following speech: "That when he was advanced to the quæstorship,[1] he had chosen their province in preference to all others, and during his continuance in that office, had done them every service in his power; that during his prætorship, he had obtained for them from the senate the abolition of the taxes imposed by Metellus,[2] declared himself their patron, procured their deputies a hearing at Rome, and

[1] Suetonius says that when Cæsar was quæstor, he obtained the province of Further Spain. Plutarch's account is that Cæsar went to Spain as quæstor with the prætor Tubero, and subsequently held the prætorship there.

[2] Q. Metellus Pius, the first Roman general who was successful against Jugurtha. He failed in his attempt to crush the rising ambition of the great Marius, through whose instrumentality he was subsequently banished. He was afterward recalled to Rome and on the downfall of the Marian faction, commanded against Sertorius in Spain. Metellus was unable to cope with his vigorous and talented opponent, and, in consequence, Pompey was sent to his aid. Sertorius, however, was equal to the crisis, and proved himself more than a match for both; and it was not until he was assassinated by Perpenna that Spain was reduced. As the Spaniards were much attached to Sertorius, we may suppose that the severe impost to which Cæsar here alludes was inflicted as a punishment for their fidelity.

made himself many enemies by undertaking the defense both of their private and public rights. In fine, that when he was consul, he had, though absent, rendered the province all the services in his power; that instead of making a suitable return for so many favors, they had always discovered the utmost ingratitude both toward him and the people of Rome; as well in this last war as the preceding. You," says he, "though no strangers to the law of nations and the rights of Roman citizens, have yet like barbarians often violated the sacred persons of Roman magistrates. You attempted in open day, in the public square, to assassinate Cassius. You have been always such enemies to peace that the senate could never suffer the province to be without legions. You take favors for offenses, and insults for benefits, are insolent and restless in peace, and cowardly and effeminate in war. Young Pompey, though only a private citizen, nay a fugitive, was yet received among you, and suffered to assume the ensigns of magistracy. After putting many citizens to death, you still furnished him with forces, and even urged him to lay waste the country and province. Against whom do you hope to be victorious? Can you be ignorant that even if I should be destroyed, the people of Rome have still ten legions, capable not only of opposing you, but even of pulling down heaven?[1] With whose praises and virtues" * * * *

[1] This boastful language is very foreign to Cæsar's natural disposition, and the passage is evidently spurious. In like manner in some of the old copies, we find the absurd addition to "with whose praises and virtues" —"the whole world exults." The end of this book is lost. We learn from Plutarch that this was the last war in which Cæsar was engaged, as he returned to Rome in the month of October, A.U.C. 709, and was assassinated on the following ides of March, A.U.C. 710.

A FRAGMENT

OF THE

HISTORY OF JULIUS CÆSAR.

FROM THE VATICAN COPY.

All that we can ascertain of this fragment is that it was found in the copy of Cujacius, without any name; but in the Paduan copy with the name of Petrarch; as it seems to have some connection with the last book, I translate it here.

For the length of the war called imperatively for peace, their toils sought repose, and their victories deserved a triumph; not their victories over their fellow-citizens, but their victories over the foreign enemy, of which we have previously spoken. But in what manner could he triumph, or on what principle could he rest, of whom it has been written that he believed nothing done if any thing remained to be done? Cneius and Sextus, the sons of the great Pompey, had seized the Spains, and were aided in doing so not by the heritage of their father's virtues, but by his popularity and name. Thus fortune had raised up two Pompeys instead of one. Cneius, the elder, who had more energy and intellect than his brother, had already effected the acquisition of great power, by throwing himself on the protection and support of all the states of Spain. The Spaniards could not resist his entreaties and earnest appeal to their mercy, and the memory of his father's kindnesses. In levying his army he resorted to violence when entreaties were ineffectual, and began to ravage the province in such a manner as gradually to alienate those who had been at first warmly in his favor. Cæsar thought that he ought by no means to neglect this, the last of his wars, and therefore set out at once for the scene of action. On this occasion, two almost incredible circumstances occurred. In the first place he traversed so rapidly the distance between Rome and Further Spain, that he arrived there in twenty-four days: a degree of speed seldom obtained by a traveler, much less an army. This was certainly a great feat, but the second was still greater. Although there were so many things to distract his attention, yet in this short time he wrote a poem, which he called the "Journey," because he composed it on this occasion. So completely had he learned the art of introducing refinement and unceasing mental activity into the camp. Cæsar's arrival in Spain created great excitement among the different states, and embassadors and deserters repaired to him from every quarter. Pompey's sons had already begun to excite the hatred or disgust of their followers, and this was a necessary result, even though there might have been no misconduct on their part, for it has been an ancient practice among states to be fond of new masters and change. Besides the reputation of Cæsar had very justly surpassed that of all others, and consequently the world was dazzled by the brilliancy of his exploits, and was desirous of seeing in person the hero whose acts had excited their admiration. At the very straits of Gibraltar, where the Atlantic dashes its waves against the Spanish coast, even the extremity of the Mediterranean becomes the scene of mutual embassies. Didius representing one party, Varus the other, while the storm proved the relentless foe of both. Nor had the contending parties less danger to dread from the winds and waves than from the cruelty of the foe. On one side was the merciless enemy, on the other the fury of the combatants was lulled into a passing repose by the violence of the storm: and during the time that the hostile fleets had to struggle against war and shipwreck, there were two distinct factions, two seas, and a mutual frenzy, the war of the elements and the rage of man partaking alike of this two-fold character. About this period two infantry soldiers were taken by Cæsar's troops, and alleged that they were slaves. Cæsar was not permitted to display his usual lenity toward them, for before they could be brought into his presence, they were recognized by the soldiers as deserters from Cæsar's army, and were immediately put to death. Some letter-carriers, who were on their way to Pompey at Corduba, were taken prisoners. Their hands were cut off, and then they were sent away. In like manner one of Pompey's spies was taken and slain. I am of opinion that the soldiers were irritated at the war, and, being aware of the character and mercy of their general, had invented this method of frustrating him, to prevent any of the prisoners from seeing his face, and thus insure their destruction. The Pompeys occupied Corduba, while Cæsar laid siege to it. In the absence of the generals many bloody battles took place before the walls: and when on one occasion the struggle was maintained, by fire and sword, with greater spirit than usual, the anger of the besieged changed into madness, and, in the sight of Cæsar's army, they cut the throats of some guests who were staying with them, confiding in the protection of the tie of hospitality—just as if victory was the prize of cruelty and not of courage—a wretched and horrid spectacle. One of the besieged who was stationed in a mine under ground to protect the wall, on learning this act from the groans of the dying, shouted aloud: "You have committed a dreadful and enormous crime, one that meets with the detestation of every nation, even the most barbarous, and justly too; for they deserved no evil who had done no evil, who with misplaced confidence threw themselves on you and on your altars and homes for protection. You alone have despised the rights of hospitality which are respected by all nations, and would that you had been contented with despising them only. You have violated them by an inhuman crime." When he uttered many words of a similar tendency, the besieged began to feel ashamed of their conduct, and left off the massacre of their guests. Thus the voice of a single good man occasionally prevails among many bad men, and even among enemies virtue meets its reward. This circumstance was first made known in Cæsar's camp by the narration of a deserter. On the next day, a certain Tullius with Cato, a Lusitanian, came as an embassador from the town to Cæsar. The first part of Tullius's speech was the expression of a wish that he had had the good fortune to espouse Cæsar's party, rather than be a suppliant for his mercy. The end of it was, that the besieged, being deserted by Pompey, and conquered by Cæsar, surrendered themselves and the town, and begged that he would not deny to his fellow-citizens the mercy which he had shown to conquered foreigners. He used many other arguments which have been so confused by the carelessness of transcribers that they can not be understood. One thing, however, is plain enough, that although many speeches were made on both sides, no progress was made to a surrender at the time. The blockade became more close every day, as is generally the case, and Pompey neither brought nor sent the promised succors. Furthermore he is reported to have said in an assembly, that as he could not assist them they ought to avail themselves of the kindness of night, and flee forth from the face of the enemy. When he made this remark, one of the bystanders answered that he ought to give the signal for fight rather than flight; and the person who used the expression was immediately put to death, as his language seemed to them a sarcasm on the cowardice of the general. We were informed of this circumstance also by deserters. . . . . In the mean time the calamities of the besieged increased hourly. A matron jumped over the wall, and said that she had concerted with her maid-servant to flee; that their intention happened to transpire, and the latter was slain: that herself had escaped by a precipitate flight. Letters also were found that had been cast from the wall, of which the following is a transcript to the very letter: "Lucius Munatius to Cæsar.—If you give me my life, since I am deserted by Pompey, I promise that I will serve you with as much zeal and energy as ever I served him." At the same time the embassadors who came first, returned to Cæsar. Their language was simple, frank, and brief: "That they would surrender the town the next day if he would grant them their lives;" to whom Cæsar made this brief reply: "I am Cæsar; I will not break my word." Thus it happened that Cæsar obtained possession of the town on the eleventh day before the calends of March. When Pompey was acquainted with this, relinquishing all hope and anxiety for the defense of Corduba and decamping, he departed and repaired to the town of Ucubis, and there assembling those whom he considered most attached to him, he ordered them to find out with the greatest diligence those who favored his party, and those who favored Cæsar's. When information was laid before him, he beheaded sixty-four of those who were said to have rejoiced at Cæsar's victory, just as if it were a great crime to be attached to Cæsar. He shut up the rest in the town

. . . they burst through their guards with one hundred and twenty horsemen, and fled to Cæsar. Besides, many cruel acts were performed by the Pompeians themselves at the same time, as if they foresaw that their doom was at hand, and were anxious (according to the custom of some barbarous nations) to send before them an offering to the infernal deities. Pompey at this time pretended that he was confident of the result, and that Cæsar was afraid. Letters of his were found asserting that Cæsar did not dare to lead his forces into the field of battle, distrusting his raw levies; and that, if Cæsar should at any time give him an opportunity of coming to action on level ground, he would finish the business sooner than any one could expect, and that he was waiting and even hoping for such an opportunity. Besides, he went round the different states of Spain to canvass them; or, as he himself said, to keep them in their allegiance; he therefore went to Hispalis and pitched his camp in an olive grove opposite to the city; and afterward went from one state to the other. At last he stopped at Munda, which fortune had selected for the closing of his career. Cæsar arrived there also, and pitched his camp opposite to Pompey. The latter had written to Faustus, who, as far as we can learn, was within the town: "That Cæsar was unwilling to descend into the midst of the valley, because a great part of his army was composed of raw soldiers." This letter exercised a strange influence in raising the hopes of the besieged. For all men eagerly grasp at hope, and even imagine those things which they feel neither are nor can be. So sweet it is, I will not say to hope, but even to think of a pleasing subject. I can not readily conceive how a person will hope for impossibilities; but we can think of any thing. While Pompey was thus encouraging himself and the others, but was, in reality, tortured by intense anxiety, as far as I can learn, he remained for a great portion of the night with his army in battle array: Cæsar came forth from his camp with the intention of marching in some direction, but, as soon as he was informed of the posture of the enemy, he halted and formed in line of battle. The hostile armies engaged with loud shouts and still greater fury, proceeding from inexpressible and undying hatred, and fought resolutely and obstinately, and (enough to make us blush for human frailty) never was Cæsar engaged in a more dubious struggle, either against foreign enemies or fellow-citizens, and never was he nearer defeat. To such a degree that (to borrow the eloquent words of Florus) fortune seemed to be undecided in her deliberations, which were, I suppose, whether she should attend on her favorite with a fidelity rarely met with and quite unprecedented, or whether she should desert him at the end of his career, and pass over to another. And so long did she remain undecided, that in the heat of the struggle, victory inclining to neither party, even the veteran soldiers, the conquerors in a hundred fields, gradually retreated (a sight that never met Cæsar's eyes before), and were prevented by shame rather than courage from an open flight. Cæsar began to doubt and distrust, a thing which he never did before, and even stood in front of his army with a grief expressed in his features that never was witnessed before. Still he showed in that perilous hour all the qualities of a consummate commander; he sprang from his horse, and, like a madman, rushed to the foremost ranks of the combatants, shouting, reproaching, beseeching, and exhorting. Using not only his voice and eyes, but also his hands and strength, to stop the flight, he began at last to bring back by force to the battle those that commenced to flee. Finally, so great was the alarm, and so undecided the issue of the combat, that several writers have recorded that Cæsar thought of putting an end to himself, and that his features bore the rigid impress of one who was meditating suicide; and yet there is no mention of this circumstance made by those who were on the field. It is truly difficult, not only for the absent, but even for the present, to divine a man's thoughts; but I have no hesitation in believing, that if Cæsar once doubted his success, he began to think of death at the same time. For at what time or with what feelings could Cæsar run away from a youth? Cæsar, who had so often compelled so distinguished an individual as the great Pompey, and so many kings and generals, states and nations, to flee before him. If, therefore, he was apprehensive of being conquered, he must have wished to die, for he was the child of victory, not of defeat. But who knows whether he was really afraid of being conquered? Some, however, say that he was, and others assert it as a positive fact. The battle remained in this undecided state for some time, until five cohorts of the enemy, which were sent by Labienus to assist his camp, which was attacked, hastening along the line, presented the appearance of flight. Oh, fortune, powerful in every thing, as is the general belief, but by far the most powerful in war! Cæsar, either imagining that they were fleeing, or pretending to think so, as he was a most skillful general, attacked them as if they were running away, and thereby gave courage to his own men who supposed that they were pursuing a fleeing enemy, and dispirited the enemy to such a degree that they fled under the impression that their fellow soldiers were running away. Thus Labienus, who betrayed Cæsar and deserted from him, and was the implacable enemy of his old general, was the means of procuring an unhoped-for victory for him whose destruction he sought, and death for himself: for he fell in that battle, and along with him Attius Varus, and thirty thousand men. A greater number would have perished, had not the city been so near to shelter them. About three thousand of the victors were slain, and a great number of the cavalry and infantry were wounded. Therefore Cæsar's troops marched to storm the town over a dreadful and ghastly heap of corpses, which were compacted by darts and swords, as if imbedded in lime, and over this mound they mounted to scale the city, the bodies of the slain serving as a wall. Go now, misguided men, engage in civil wars and while you envy others, destroy yourselves. Behold the survivors are attacked from your corpses. Do you seek any thing else, or is the climax of your madness still wanting? Or is Labienus with his burning insults still restless? Thousands have fallen the victims of your advice, Labienus; though you lie among the dead a single corpse, yet tombs were raised for you and Varus. And as I am of opinion that your own party had not time to do this while in such a wretched condition, I attribute them to the generosity of Cæsar, which you so little deserved: and I am convinced that had it rested with you, you were so obstinate that you would prefer to be left unburied. Cneius Pompey fled from the battle through the midst of the carnage, wounded in the shoulder and left leg. When he fled into the recesses of the woods, in an abject and lowly plight (carried on a litter because he could not use either a horse or vehicle, and concealed himself in the caves), Cæsonius, one of Cæsar's lieutenants, followed him to Lauso (that is the name of the place), still resisting, and still cherishing the expiring embers of hope. His head was brought to Cæsar who was accustomed to gifts of this nature, but by no means delighted with them. They say that fortune concealed his brother Sextus Pompey in Celtiberia, lest food for civil wars should ever be wanting. Munda was afterward taken by storm by Cæsar, but not without great bloodshed. At the same period Corduba was attacked a second time: I do not find it stated in what manner it revolted. There were then great commotions and great dissensions in the state, one part inclining to Cæsar, the other to the contrary faction; and when they had recourse to arms, the party which favored Cæsar conquered, and gave up the town to him. Twenty-two thousand of the opposite party fell, a remarkable havoc for the citizens of even the largest city. Cæsar left Hispalis on the ides of April and went to Gades. He went back again to Hispalis to finally arrange the affairs of Spain, as he did not intend to return again. Then having convened a public assembly, he recounted both his former and recent favors to that city. Finally, he accused them of returning evil for good in every case, and of being seditious in peace and cowardly in war. Because Cneius Pompey who was a mere youth, supported by their aid had slain his fellow-citizens, and laid waste their country and the vicinity, and had assumed the fasces and military authority there against him, or rather against the Roman people, of whom he had the control. What! could the inhabitants of Hispalis imagine that they could conquer the Romans, because they laid waste their province? Did they not know that even if Cæsar died, who was a mere mortal, still the Romans were immortal, and had at present ten legions, which were able not only to resist the inhabitants of Hispalis, but even to pull down heaven itself. In which expression there is not only the lofty diction evident to all, but also a latent meaning, because, in enumerating the forces of Rome, he recounts not all, but only his own legions, as if he considered the rest of no value, and not even worth being mentioned. Many other circumstances are related in this part of the history, but they are so confused by the carelessness of transcribers, that I pass them by, as I am anxious to conclude the subject. This was the termination of the civil wars.[1]

[1] Gerardus Johannes Vossius, in his treatise on Latin Historians, attributes this fragment of the Spanish war to Julius Celsus, because it is taken from his Commentaries on the life of Julius Cæsar.

THE FRAGMENTS

OF

CAIUS JULIUS CÆSAR.

THE FRAGMENTS CONTAINED IN HIS EPISTOLARY CORRESPONDENCE WITH M. T. CICERO.

CÆSAR[1] IMPERATOR TO CICERO IMPERATOR, GREETING.

Although I merely saw our mutual friend Furnius,[2] and he had not an opportunity of addressing me, or listening to my instructions, as I was in a hurry, and was advancing to meet my[3] legions whom I had sent on before me, yet I could not neglect the opportunity of writing and sending him to you and returning my thanks:[4] although I have often before executed the same duty, yet I think that I will do it oftener; you have laid me under so many obligations to you; I particularly request of you, that[5] as I trust that I shall soon arrive in the city,

[1] It is not at all strange that Cæsar, after his many great exploits in Gaul, should style himself Imperator, but few know the reason why Cicero, whose military achievements are but little celebrated, should receive that title from Cæsar. This, however, is explained in one of Cicero's epistles to Atticus, in which he writes that he was saluted Imperator on the occasion of his slaying a great number of Cilician robbers who were sheltered in the numerous fastnesses of Mount Amanus. Plutarch bears testimony to the same circumstance in his life of Cicero. Cæsar is not the only one that called Cicero Imperator, but also Pompey, in his letter to him.

[2] As far as we can infer from the epistles to Atticus, Furnius appears to have espoused Cæsar's party. After the assassination of Cæsar, he became the lieutenant-general of Plancus, and it was through him that Cicero endeavored to win over Plancus to the republic.

[3] In the direction of Brundusium, to which Pompey had retreated, as Cæsar was determined to pursue him wherever he went.

[4] Cicero remained in Italy, and this was the reason why Cæsar was so grateful to him.

[5] Cicero, by his prudence and care, crushed Catiline's conspiracy in his consulate, and thereby acquired vast influence, particularly among the aristocracy. Cæsar and Pompey made great efforts at the com-

I may see you there; that I may avail myself of your[1] advice, influence, dignity, and assistance in every thing. I must resume business: you will excuse my haste and the brevity of my letter: you will learn the rest from Furnius. Farewell.—*Cicero to Atticus*, 9, 6.

CÆSAR IMP. TO CICERO IMP.

You were right in the opinion you entertained of me (for you know my character well), that nothing is more foreign to my nature than cruelty,[2] and in addition to the pleasure that I derive from that very circumstance, I am also highly delighted that my conduct in this respect has earned your approbation: nor has it any influence on me that those who have been pardoned by me are reported to have departed, with a view to

mencement of the civil war, to attach him to their different parties. Cicero, in his seventh epistle to Atticus, tells us what his sentiments really were in the following passage: "Both of them [Cæsar and Pompey] consider me their own, unless, perhaps Cæsar is only pretending; for Pompey has no doubts (and he judges right) that his sentiments on the state of the republic are highly approved of by me. I received letters from both at the same time that I received yours, so that each of them seems to value no man's support more highly than mine." Cicero refers to the present letter.

1 No one can interpret this place better than Cæsar, who, in his eleventh epistle to Atticus, writes in the following manner: "The very base and mean individual who asserts that the elections for appointing a consul can be held by a prætor is the same as ever he was in matters connected with the commonwealth. Therefore, what Cæsar writes in the letter of which I have sent you a copy is surprising, viz., that he wished to avail himself of my advice. Well, suppose this to be a general expression;" *influence*—"this is rather absurd, but I suppose he refers to my getting him the support of some of the senators." *Dignity!*—"Perhaps my opinion as a man of consular rank. The last expression is, *assistance in any thing.* I began to suspect that this had the following meaning, or something very like it. It is a matter of great importance that the government should not come to an interregnum. Cæsar gains his object if consuls are appointed by prætors. But we have it stated in our books that prætors have not the right of appointing consuls, or even of appointing one another. They have not the right of appointing consuls because it is against the law that a higher magistrate should be appointed by a less. But the prætors, because they are elected in such a manner that they are considered colleagues of the consuls, whose magistracy is a greater one. He will be very likely to refer this to me, and not to rest satisfied with the opinion of Galba, Scævola, Cassius, and Antonius. Then may the wide earth open to swallow me."

2 Cæsar, on the capture of Corfinium, had shown great clemency to such of Pompey's party as fell into his hands, and had spared Domitius and Vibullius, as we read in the first book of the civil war.

make war against me again.[1] For I would wish nothing more than that I should be always like myself, and they like themselves. I should like your presence in Rome, that I might avail myself of your advice and assistance in every thing as usual. Be assured that nothing gives me greater delight than the society of your friend Dolabella, I take so much pleasure in it. Nor can he fail to be agreeable, so great is his natural politeness, and such his feelings and good-will toward me. Farewell.—*Cicero to Atticus*, 9, 16.

CÆSAR IMP. TO CICERO IMP. GREETING.

Although I was of opinion that you were not likely to do any thing rashly or imprudently, yet being influenced by the report[2] of these men, I thought that I ought to write to you and request that you would concede to our friendship,[3] that you would not go to any greater lengths in the declining state of Pompey's affairs than you would have thought it necessary to go to when his power was still unbroken.[4] For by doing so you will err most grievously against our friendship, and you will act with less judgment for your own interests, if you should appear to be influenced not by the course of events (for all things seem to have turned out most favorable to us,[5] and most adverse to our enemies), nor by attachment to the cause (for it was the same then when you came to the determination of absenting yourself from their councils),[6] but by condemnation of some act of mine: and no conduct on your part toward me could be more distressing; now I beseech you, by the claims of friendship, not to do so. Lastly, what conduct is more suitable to a good man, and a good and quiet citizen, than to keep aloof from all civil broils; although several approved of his conduct, yet they were prevented from adopting it by personal danger; you, after a careful examination of the testimony of my life, and the esteem of friendship, will find no

[1] Domitius did this at Massilia and in Thessaly, and Vibullius in Spain.

[2] A report spread at this time that Cicero was going over to Pompey.

[3] For they were mutual friends, and Quintus Cicero, the orator's brother, had been one of Cæsar's lieutenants in Gaul.

[4] Before the disastrous events of Corfinium and Brundusium.

[5] Cæsar, at this time, had driven Pompey from Italy, and was completely in possession of it.

[6] For it was not until Corfinium was lost that Pompey acquainted Cicero with his plans.

course more safe or honorable than to keep aloof from all strife. The 15th of the calends of May, on my journey. Farewell.—*Cicero to Atticus*, 10, 8.

I shall make your protégé M. Orsius, either king of Gaul, or lieutenant of Lepta: send another if you choose to me, and I will likwise do him honor.—*Cicero Epist. ad Fam.* 7, 5.

You ask what Cæsar has written to me. What he has frequently said; that he was much pleased with my remaining quiet, and he begs me to continue so.—*Cicero to Atticus*, 8, 11.

With regard to what you write about the tribunate, I requested it for Curtius, and mentioned his name, and Cæsar sent back to me that it was ready for Curtius.—*Cicero to his brother Quintus*, 3, 1, 3.

From Cæsar's letter it appears that I might almost do this with his consent; for he says that I can do nothing more honorable or more safe than to withdraw from all contention. —*Cicero to Atticus*, 10, 9.

Cæsar by letter excuses me for not going up, and says that he takes it in good part. I do not regard what he adds, that Tullius and Servius have complained of his not granting the same liberty to them as to me.—*Cicero to Atticus*, 10, 3.

I have had Sestius with me; and yesterday Theopompus arrived. He reported that letters had been received from Cæsar, who said that he had determined to remain at Rome, and added the same reason which was mentioned in my letter, namely, lest in his absence his laws[1] should be disregarded, as had been the case with the sumptuary law.—*Cicero to Atticus*, 13, 7.

On the sumptuary law see Suetonius, Julius Cæsar, ch. 43, and Cicero ad Fam. 9, 15.

But, my brother, I think that you are not aware what opinion Cæsar expressed about our verses. For he wrote to me that he had formerly read the first book, and his opinion of the first was, that he had never read better verses even in Greek. He says that the rest in some places were rather careless, for this is the word that he uses, etc.—*Cicero to Quintus his brother*, 2, 16.

From Britain Cæsar wrote to me on the calends of September, and I received his letter the fourth day before the calends

[1] The laws which Cæsar enacted a short time before he went to Spain to carry on war against the sons of Pompey.

of October, it contained satisfactory information concerning Britain; in which letter he informed me that you were not with him when he went down to the sea, to prevent my being surprised at receiving no letter from you, etc.—*Cicero to his brother Quintus*, 3, 1.

When I was folding up this letter, carriers came from you on the eleventh day before the calends of September, after being twenty days on their journey. Oh! my anxieties, how deeply I sympathized with Cæsar's misery on perusing his feeling letter, but the more feeling it was the more grief did his misfortune[1] cause.—*Cicero to his brother Quintus*, 3, 1, 5.

FROM THE LETTERS TO C. OPPIUS[2] AND BALBUS CORNELIUS.

CÆSAR TO OPPIUS AND CORNELIUS, GREETING.

I am truly delighted that you have declared to me by letter how highly you approve of the transactions that took place at Corfinium. I will gladly adopt your advice, and the more cheerfully because I myself had determined to be as merciful as possible, and to exert myself to reconcile Pompey. Let us endeavor, in this manner, to win the affections of all, and make our victory a lasting one; since others[3] could not escape the hatred that arises after a time, nor continue in the possession of victory, except Lucius Sulla[4] alone, whom I am very

[1] It is probable that the misfortune here alluded to is the death of Julia, Cæsar's daughter, of which he was informed on his return from Spain. Her death broke the ties between Pompey and Cæsar, and was followed by the civil war.

[2] This Oppius was an intimate friend of Cæsar's. Some attribute to him the eighth book of the Gallic War, and the others usually assigned to Hirtius. We find mention of Balbus in the nineteenth chapter of the third book of the Civil War. He was wounded at a conference.

[3] As, for instance, Marius and Cinna.

[4] The following extract from Plutarch will well explain the reason why Cæsar was so unlikely to imitate Sylla: "When Sylla had made himself master of Rome, he endeavored to bring Cæsar to repudiate Cornelia, daughter of Cinna, one of the late tyrants, and, finding he could not effect it either by hopes or fears, he confiscated her dowry. Indeed, Cæsar, as a relation of Marius, was naturally an enemy to Sylla. Old

unlikely to imitate. It would be a novel plan of conquest to secure ourselves by mercy and liberality; many suggestions present themselves to my mind as to the best way of carrying it into operation, and many plans can be devised. I ask you to consider these things; I took Cneius Magius, Pompey's prefect, prisoner; of course I acted on my previous resolution, and released him immediately. Already two officers of Pompey's engineers have fallen into my hands, and have been sent away by me. If they should wish to prove their gratitude, they ought to advise Pompey to prefer being my friend rather than the friend of those who have always been most hostile, both to him and me; to whose machinations it is owing that the commonwealth has come to such a state.—*Cicero to Atticus*, 9, 8.

CÆSAR TO OPPIUS AND CORNELIUS, GREETING.

I reached Brundusium on the seventh day before the ides of March, and encamped before the walls. Pompey is in Brundusium, and sent[1] to me Cneius Magius to negotiate. I made a fitting reply; I wished you to know it at once. Whenever I shall begin to entertain hopes that I have made some progress toward a reconciliation, I will immediately acquaint you.—*Cicero to Atticus*, 9, 13.

I had forgotten to write to you about Cæsar; for I see the letters which you expected. But he wrote to Balbus that the packet of letters which contained my letter and that of Balbus, was given to him completely soaked with water; to such

Marius had marred Julia, Cæsar's aunt, and, therefore, young Marius, the son he had by her, was Cæsar's cousin-german. At first Sylla, amid the vast number of proscriptions that engaged his attention, overlooked this enemy; but Cæsar, not contented with escaping so, presented himself to the people as a candidate for the priesthood, though he had not yet arrived to the age of manhood. Sylla, however, exerted his influence against him, and prevented his obtaining it. The dictator afterward thought of having him slain, and when some said there was no need to put such a boy to death, he answered, 'Their sagacity was small if they did not in that boy see many Mariuses.'"

[1] Yet Cæsar says, in the first book of the Civil War, that he was sent by him, and not sent back by Pompey. These statements can be reconciled in the following manner. Pompey first sent Cneius Magius to Cæsar. Cæsar made a fitting reply, and sent the same Magius to Pompey to bring back his answer, and thought he would return. But Pompey, being displeased with Cæsar's answer, did not allow him to do so.

a degree that he did not even know that there was a letter of mine there at all. But he understood a few words in Balbus's letter, to which he replied in the following language: "I see that you have written something concerning Cicero, which I did not understand; but as far as I could conjecture the meaning, the communication was of such a nature as I would consider the object of my wishes rather than my hopes." On that account I subsequently sent to Cæsar a copy of the same letter. But that you may not despise his jest about his own party, etc.—*Cicero to his brother Quintus*, 2, 12.

There are the books of the epistles of Caius Cæsar to Caius Oppius and Balbus Cornelius, who managed his affairs in his absence. In these epistles single letters are found in several places without any connection in syllables, and such as you would consider placed there without any arrangement; for no words can be formed from these letters. But there was a secret understanding between them about changing the position of the letters, so that one should occupy the name and import of another; but in reading the epistle, the proper arrangement and meaning should be restored. There is in existence rather an interesting treatise written by Probus the grammarian concerning the secret meaning of the letters in the epistles of Cæsar.[1]—*Gellius*, 17, 9.

FROM THE EPISTLE TO Q. PEDIUS.

CÆSAR TO QUINTUS PEDIUS, GREETING.

Pompey confines himself within the town; we are encamped at the gate; we are endeavoring to raise a difficult work, one that will require some time, on account of the depth of the water, but it is our grand object at present. We are building moles on both sides of the harbor, to compel him to transfer, as soon as possible, such forces as he has at Brundusium, or else prevent him from leaving it.—*Cicero to Atticus*, 9, 14.

[1] This is a specimen of stenography, very different from the stenography, or short-hand, which we see in the notes of Tyro and Seneca. We must not confound the work of Probus the grammarian, to which allusion is here made, with his treatise "On the Notes of the Romans," which is still extant.

FROM THE EPISTLE TO PISO.

I send you the little box sealed.

FROM THE BOOK OF THE EPISTLES TO ANTONIUS.

For Antonius has sent to me a copy of Cæsar's letter to him, in which was written that he had heard that Cato and L. Metellus had arrived in Italy, and appeared in public at Rome; that this did not please him, lest any disturbance should arise out of it; and that all should be excluded from Italy, except those whose case he had examined in person. He wrote warmly on this subject.—*From Cicero to Atticus*, 11, 7.

FROM THE BOOK OF THE EPISTLE TO SERVILIUS.

P. Servilius,[1] the father, on perusing the letter which he said was sent to him, intimated to me that you made him deeply your debtor, because you spoke of his kind feelings toward Cæsar, in a most polite and serious manner.—*From Cicero to his brother Quintus*, 3, 1, 6.

TESTIMONIES OF THE LETTERS OF CAIUS JULIUS CÆSAR.

His letters to the senate are still extant, and he appears to have been the first who reduced them to pages, and the form of a regular memoir; since, before his time, the consuls and generals did not send any letters that were not written across the whole length of the paper. His letters to Cicero are likewise extant, and likewise those to his intimate friends on private matters. In these letters, if it was requisite to convey some secret intelligence, he wrote it by signs; that is, in such an arrangement of the letters that no word could be formed out of them; but if any one should wish to investigate the subject and prosecute the inquiry, he must change the fourth letter of the alphabet; that is, put D for A, and likewise the others.—*Suetonius, Cæsar*, c. 56.

[1] This is the Servilius who is mentioned at the commencement of the third book of the Cival War, who was Cæsar's colleague in his second consulate, and had been his friend for a long time, as we infer from the passage before us; for this letter was written when Cæsar was in Britain.

We have heard that Cæsar was accustomed to read, write, dictate, and listen at the same time, and that he often dictated four letters at one time on the most important subjects to his secretaries, or even seven, if he had nothing else to do.—*Pliny*, 7, 25.

I have no doubts but that on the receipt of your letter, of which I have read a copy, that you gave to Blesamius at Tarraco to carry to Deiotarus, the latter was more encouraged and relieved from all anxiety; for you bade him "hope for the best and be of good spirits," which I know you do not usually write in vain.—*Cicero's Oration for Deiotarus*, c. 14.

Pompey ordered his infantry, etc. Appian, Civil War, 2, 72, mentions the tactics of Pompey on that occasion, which you will find in the Cæsar, Civil War, 3, 92. He writes that Cæsar expressed his disapprobation of them in his letters. When Cæsar, the founder of your family, first entered Britain, he wrote that he discovered a new world, thinking it so large, that instead of being surrounded by the ocean, it embraced the ocean in its bosom.—*From the Panegyric of Eumenius on Constantius, Cæsar*, c. 11.

In this expedition he also accustomed himself to dictate letters as he rode on horseback, and found sufficient employment for two secretaries at once, or, according to Oppius, for more. It is also said that Cæsar was the first who contrived to communicate his thoughts to his friends, by a peculiar arrangement of the letters.—*Plutarch, Cæsar*, c. 17.

BELONGING TO HIS ORATIONS PRONOUNCED AT THE OBSEQUIES OF JULIA AND CORNELIA.

When quæstor, he pronounced the funeral orations, according to the usual custom,[1] before the rostra, on his aunt, by the father's side, Julia, and his wife Cornelia. In the eulogium on his aunt, he speaks in the following manner of his own origin and that of his father: "The family of my aunt Julia sprang from the kings by the mother's side, on the father's it is united

[1] This custom, according to Livy, originated in the following circumstance: when there was not sufficient gold in the public treasury to pay the money which the Romans had stipulated to give the Gauls on the evacuation of the citadel, the matrons made up the sum by voluntary contributions. The right of having a funeral eulogium pronounced over them was granted to them as a reward for their patriotism.

to the immortal gods; for the Marcian kings[1] are descended from Ancus Martius, which name my mother bore; the Julians, to whom our family belongs from Venus. We have, therefore, in our family the sacred regard due to kings, who are the most powerful among men, and the religious worship of the gods, under whose power the kings themselves are."—*Suetonius, Julius Cæsar*, c. 6.

When the wife of Marius died, Cæsar, being her nephew, pronounced a splendid funeral eulogium in the forum, and at her obsequies had the daring to bring forth publicly the states of Marius.—*Plutarch, Cæsar*, c. 5, who adds: "It was a usual custom among the Romans to pronounce funeral orations over aged matrons, but it was not usual in the case of young women. Cæsar was the first to do so, and pronounced a eulogium over the corpse of his wife.

FROM THE ORATIONS IN BEHALF OF THE BYTHINIANS.

Caius Cæsar, when Pontifex Maximus, used the following exordium in the speech which he pronounced in behalf of the Bithynians: "Considering either my tie of hospitality with king Nicomedes,[2] or my intimate connection with the individuals whose interests are at stake, I could not, Marcus Vinicius, shrink from this duty; for on the death of a man, his memory is not altogether blotted out, but is preserved by his friends: nor can we desert our clients without the greatest disgrace to ourselves, since we are bound to protect them even against our relations."—*Gellius*, 5, 13.

What, then? They are not promissory notes, but the matter is foreign to our subject.—*Julius Rufinianus.*

FROM THE ORATION IN FAVOR OF THE PLAUTIAN LAW.[3]

However, I have found in the speech of Caius Cæsar, which he delivered in favor of the Plautian law, the word *necessitas*,

[1] To this family belonged Q. Marcius Rex, who was made consul the year before Cicero, with Lucius Metellus, and was sent by the senate into Etruria against Manlius, the leader of Catiline's army.

[2] When Cæsar was proscribed by Sylla he fled to Nicomedes, king of Bithynia, for protection.

[3] The Lex Plotia, or Plautia, was enacted against those who occupied public places and carried arms. The lex proposed by the consul, Q.

used instead of *necessitudo*, to express a tie of intimacy. He uses the following words: "Indeed, I think that considering our intimacy, I have not been deficient in labor, exertion, or industry."—*Gellius*, 13, 3, and *Nonius on the word Necessitas*, 4, 323.

FROM THE ORATION AGAINST CNEIUS DOLABELLA.[1]

Cæsar, in his third speech against Dolabella says, "Then the men whose statues were placed in the temples and shrines conferred both honor and dignity." In his books on Analogy he expresses his opinion that all words of the same kind as *ornatui*, the dative of *ornatus*, should be written without the letter *i*.—*From Gellius*, 4, 16.

L. Crassus, in his nineteenth year brought an action against C. Carbo; Cæsar, in his twenty-first year, against Dolabella; Asinius Pollio, in his twenty-third year, against Cato; and Calvus, when not much older, against Vatinius: their speeches are still extant, and we read them even now with admiration. —*From the Dialogue on Orators*, c. 34.

But after this civil commotion[2] was appeased, he impeached for extortion Cornelius Dolabella, a man of consular and triumphal rank, and when he was acquitted, he determined to retire to Rhodes.—*Suetonius, Julius Cæsar*, c. 4.

Also the deified Julius, a most perfect specimen as well of the divinity of heaven as of the human intellect, used peculiarly expressive language in speaking of Cneius Dolabella, whom he accused, viz., that the best of causes was wrested from him by the patronage of L. Cotta.—*Valerius Maximus*, 8, 2.

Lest perhaps you might fall into the mistake of supposing that this was the same Cneius Dolabella, against whom Cæsar delivered his oration, you must know that there were at that

Catulus, on this subject, and carried by the assistance of Plautius, the tribune, appears to be the Lex Plautia. There was a Lex Julia, of the dictator Cæsar, on this subject, which imposed the penalty of "aquæ et ignis interdictis."—See Smyth's Dictionary of Greek and Roman Antiquities.

[1] Suetonius and Plutarch inform us that he was a man of consular rank, and had enjoyed the honor of a triumph. He was accused of extortion by the judges, but was acquitted.

[2] The disturbances referred to were caused by Marcus Lepidus, who, when consul, endeavored to annul the laws of Sylla, but was unsuccessful in his attempt, and was driven from Italy by Quintus Catulus, his colleague.

time two Dolabellas: Cæsar brought an accusation against one of them, but did not succeed in having him condemned.—*Pedianus in the speech for Marcus Scaurus.*

He informs us that Cæsar, when a young man, accused Dolabella, who, however, was not condemned, owing to the influence of Hortensius.—*From Pedianus in Divin.*

Upon his return to Rome, he impeached Dolabella for misdemeanors in his government; and many cities of Greece supported the charge by their evidence. Dolabella however was acquitted.—*Plutarch, Cæsar*, c. 4.

FROM HIS SPEECH TO HIS SOLDIERS.

And when his soldiers were disheartened by reports of the arrival of the enemy, he encouraged them not by denying the truth of what was said and mincing the matter, but by enlarging and exaggerating it. And, accordingly, when his army were under terrible apprehensions about the arrival of king Juba, he called them together and said: "You are given to understand that the king will be here in a few days with ten legions, thirty thousand horse, a hundred thousand light-armed foot, and three hundred elephants: and therefore let none presume to trouble their heads with further inquiry, or declare their sentiments on the matter, but take my word for what I saw; which I have upon very good authority; otherwise I shall put them on board a crazy old vessel, and leave them exposed to the mercy of the winds."—*Suetonius, Julius Cæsar*, c. 66.

Caius Cæsar, when haranguing his troops about their sufferings, says: "I will not deceive you, soldiers."—*Diomedes.*

ON HIS SPEECH IN BEHALF OF DECIUS,[1] THE SAMNITE.

Neither the oration of Cæsar in behalf of Decius the Samnite, or that of Brutus in behalf of king Deiotarus, are generally read; nor others of the same nerveless cast.—*Dialogue on Orators*, c. 21.

ON THE ORATION FOR SEXTILIUS.

For with what stormy and violent language ought the impious head of Sextilius to be overwhelmed for his conduct to Cæsar, who defended him so ably and successfully when he was accused of a capital offense.—*Val. Max.*, 5, 3, 3.

[1] Who this Decius was has not been ascertained.

ON HIS SPEECH ABOUT THE ACCOMPLICES OF CATILINE'S CONSPIRACY.

He supposes that Cato was the first to propose the sentence of death on the members of Catiline's conspiracy, whereas every body had proposed it before except Cæsar; and because the sentence of Cæsar himself, then speaking in the place of prætor, was so severe.—*Cicero to Atticus*, 12, 21.

But Cæsar, when it came to his turn, being asked his opinion by the consul, delivered a speech to the following effect: "It becomes all men."—*Sallust*, *Cat.*, chap. 51.

Then Cæsar rose up and, in a studied speech, represented, "that it seemed neither agreeable to justice, nor to the customs of the country, to put men of their birth and dignity to death without public trial, except in a case of extreme necessity; but that they should rather be kept in prison, in any of the cities of Italy that Cicero might select on, till Catiline was subdued; and then the senate might take cognizance of the crimes of each conspirator at their leisure, when peace was restored." As there appeared something humane in this opinion, and as it was powerfully enforced by the orator, those who gave their voices afterward, and even many who had declared for the other side of the question, adopted it. But Cato and Catulus carried it for death.—*Plutarch*, *Cæsar*.

You may come to this conclusion, that since these miseries, that is from the time that they have begun to contend with arms concerning the rights of the republic, nothing has been done with dignity. For Cæsar himself, after blaming the harshness of Marcellus[1] (as he termed it), and after commending in terms of the highest praise, your justice[2] and prudence, suddenly, contrary to the expectations of all, said that he would not refuse the request of the senate concerning Marcellus.—*Cicero's Epistles ad Fam.*, 4, 4.

[1] Marcellus had been a most bitter opponent of Cæsar. He had proposed to the senate that Cæsar should be deprived of his consulship before the allotted period had expired, and that Cæsar should not be permitted to stand for the consulate in his absence, and that the rights of citizenship should be taken away from the colony which Cæsar had planted at Novocomum.

[2] For Servius Sulpicius, to whom this letter is written, one of the consuls that year, was in favor of Cæsar, and it was through him that Cæsar resisted Marcellus.

DIFFERENT TESTIMONIES CONCERNING THE ORATIONS OF CAIUS JULIUS CÆSAR.

Then Brutus says, Cæsar's speeches are highly admired by me; and I have read several of them.—*Cicero*, *Brutus*, c. 75.

He has left some speeches behind him; among which are inserted some that are not his, as that for Quintus Metellus,[1] which Augustus supposes, and with reason, to have been an incorrect copy, taken by short-hand writers, that were not able to keep pace with him in the delivery, rather than any thing published by himself: for I find in some copies the title is not for Metellus, but what he wrote for Metellus; whereas the speech runs in the name of Cæsar, vindicating Metellus and himself against the aspersions cast upon them by their common defamers. The speech to his soldiers in Spain, the same Augustus too looks upon to be not his. There are indeed two of them; one made, as is pretended, in the first battle; and the other in the second;[2] at which time, Asinius Pollio says, he had not time to speak to the soldiers, by reason of the sudden assault of the enemy.—*Suetonius*, *Julius Cæsar*, c. 55.

ON HIS TREATISES AGAINST CATO.

He has left behind him likewise two books of Analogy, and as many under the title of Anti-Cato.—*Suetonius*, c. 56.

Cæsar in his first book against Cato, says: "For with the exception of him whom nature has formed in a different manner from all others, each considers his own relations dear."—*Priscian.*

There are certain duties which bring passengers into the

[1] Metellus, tribune of the Commons, promulgated a law, in which he proposed "that it should be assigned to Pompey to see that the commonwealth received no injury from the danger which threatened it from Catiline, and that he should bring his army into Italy to defend Rome." But the real object was that the commonwealth should be handed over to Pompey, under the pretext of driving out Catiline. Cæsar, who was then prætor, most actively supported this law. Cato firmly resisted the multitude, who were urged on by the tribune, and prevented the law from being passed, on the ground that it was likely to excite sedition and civil war at Rome.

[2] Cæsar fought two battles in Spain against the sons of Pompey, one at Corduba, the other at Munda. Appian says that in the last battle he shouted to his soldiers, "Seize me, if you have no shame in you, and give me over to the hands of the boys."

streets at midnight, and which Cato himself could not discharge with propriety; though I must confess that Julius Cæsar, when he reproaches him with that circumstance, exalts the character he meant to expose; for he describes those persons who met this reeling patriot as blushing when they discovered who he was; and adds, you would have thought that Cato had detected them, and not they Cato. Could he place the dignity of Cato in a stronger light than represent him thus venerable, even in his cups? As for ourselves, nevertheless, let temperance not only spread our table, but regulate our hours; for we are not arrived at so exalted a reputation that our enemies can not censure our conduct without applauding it at the same time.—*Pliny*, *Epistles*, 3, 12.

Caius Cæsar, also an important authority in the Latin language, says in his treatise against Cato: "A man of unparalleled arrogance, pride and domineering temper."—*Gellius*, 4, 16.

TESTIMONIES CONCERNING C. JULIUS CÆSAR'S WRITINGS AGAINST CATC.

What will be the nature of Cæsar's censure in opposition to my commendation I see from the book which Hirtius has sent me, in which he collects together the faults of Cato, while he speaks very highly of me. I have therefore sent the book to Musca, that he might give it to your librarians; for I wish to have it made public.—*Cicero to Atticus*, 12, 40.

If you have read Hirtius's letter, which I consider a specimen of the censure that Cæsar has written upon Cato.—*Cicero to Atticus*, 12, 41.

Balbus lately told me in my farm at Lanuvium, that he and Oppius had written to Cæsar, and informed him of my having read and greatly commended his book against Cato.—*Cicero to Atticus*, 13, 50.

Cæsar used all these methods with too great effrontery against my friend Cato.—*Cicero*, *Topics*, c. 25.

When Cicero wrote a book in which he lauded Cato to the skies, what did Cæsar do but reply to it, as if pleading his cause before judges?—*Tacitus*, *Annals*, 4, 34.

Cicero has remarked that Caius Cæsar used them while abusing Cato.—*Quintilian*, 3, 7, 28.

Like Tullius, eulogizing Cato, and Cæsar accusing him in two volumes.—*Mart. Capell.*, lib. 5.

But hearing that he [Cato] had made away with himself, he was evidently chagrined, but the reason was not manifest: however, he said at last, "Cato, I envy thee thy death, since thou didst envy me the glory of giving thee thy life." Nevertheless, by the book which he wrote against Cato after his death, it does not seem as if he had any favorable intentions to him before; for how can it be thought that he could have spared the living enemy, when he poured so much venom afterward on his grave? Yet from his clemency to Cicero, to Brutus, and others without number, who had borne arms against him, it is conjectured that the book was not written with a spirit of rancor, but of political ambition; for it was composed on the following occasion. Cicero had written an encomium upon Cato, and to which he gave the name of Cato. It was highly esteemed by several of the Romans, as might be expected, as well from the superior eloquence of the author as the dignity of the subject. This annoyed Cæsar, as he considered that the praise conferred on the dead implied censure on his own conduct: he therefore wrote an answer to it, which he called Anti-Cato, and which contained a variety of charges against that great man. Both books have still their admirers, as a regard to the memory of Cæsar or Cato predominates.—*Plutarch*, *Cæsar*.

He himself afterward in his Anti-Cato, which he wrote in answer to a book of Cicero's, desired his readers "not to expect in the performance of a military man, the style of a complete orator, who had bestowed all his time on such studies."—*Plutarch*, *Cæsar*.

Cæsar continued to treat him with great kindness and respect, insomuch that when he [Cicero] had written an encomium on Cato, which bore that name, Cæsar in his answer, entitled Anti-Cato, praised both the eloquence and conduct of Cicero; and said that he greatly resembled Pericles and Theramenes. —*Plutarch*, *Cicero*.

And when Cicero wrote an encomium on him [Cato], and inscribed on it the name of Cato, Cæsar wrote an accusation in reply, and gave it the name of Anti-Cato.—*Appian*, book 2.

For he admired Cicero so much that when he subsequently wrote an encomium on Cato, he was not angry, although Cato had made war against him, but wrote a treatise which he called Anti-Cato.—*Dion Cassius*, book 43.

FROM HIS BOOKS ON ANALOGY DEDICATED TO MARCUS TULLIUS CICERO.

He left also two books on Analogy.—*Suetonius*, c. 56.

FROM BOOK I.

Nay, too, said Atticus, when Cæsar was employed in most important business,[1] and wrote to you, looking toward me [Cicero], concerning the method of speaking Latin with the utmost accuracy; and said in his first book, that the selection of words was the origin of eloquence, and bestowed the highest praise, my Brutus, on this friend of ours who nevertheless wishes that I [Atticus] should speak of him [Cæsar] rather than he himself (for he wrote in the following words when he addressed him by name: "And if some have labored by study and practice to attain to the faculty of clearly expressing their ideas, we ought to consider that you who are the inventor of this copious flow of language, in which you so much excel, have deserved well of the name and dignity of the Roman people)," that he disliked easy and common-place language, must be considered as certain. Then Brutus said, by Hercules, my friend, I consider that you have been nobly praised, since he styled you not only excelling in but also the inventor of this copious flow of language (and this was great merit in itself), and one who has deserved well of the name and dignity of the Roman people.—*Cicero in Brutus*, 72.

That Caius Cæsar the perpetual dictator, the father-in-law of Cneius Pompey, from whom the family and name of Cæsar was subsequently derived, a man of surpassing genius, whose style was the chastest of the men of that day, delivered it as his opinion in the book which he wrote to Marcus Cicero on Analogy, that it was improper to use *arena*, because *arena* can never be looked upon as a part of a multitude, and likewise neither *cœlum* nor *triticum*; and on the contrary, is of the opinion, that *quadrigæ*, even although a chariot drawn by four horses is a single object, must always be used in the plural; and likewise *arma*, *mœnia*, *comitia*, and *inimicitiæ*, *etc.* * * * * Then, when the work on analogy was published, I

[1] Cæsar wrote the books on Analogy to Cicero while crossing the Alps, after holding the provincial assizes in Hither Gaul, on his way to join his army in Further Gaul

committed a few words out of it to memory, for when he asserted that neither *cœlum*, or *triticum*, or *arena* included the idea of multitude; "Do you think," said he, "that it happened by the nature of these things, that we can say land in the singular, and lands in the plural; city and cities, empire and empires, and yet can not reduce *quadrigæ* to a singular noun, nor *arena* to a plural."—*Gellius*, 19, 8.

And always keep in mind and reflect on the advice given by Caius Cæsar, a man of surpassing talents and judgment, in the first book of his Treatise on Analogy, "that you should avoid as a rock an unusual or obsolete word."—*Gellius*, 1, 10; *Macrob. Saturn*, 1, 5.

BOOK II.

Caius Cæsar, in his second book on Analogy, thinks that we should use *die* and *specie* as the genitives of *dies* and *species*. —*Gellius*, 9, 14.

Cæsar, in his second book on Analogy, says that we ought to use *panium* as the genitive of *panis*, but Verrius, on the contrary, says that we should cancel the *i*, and use *panum*.—*Charisius*, book 1.

Cæsar, in his second book on Analogy, *fagos*, *populos*, *ulmos*.—*Idem*.

Cæsar, in his second book on Analogy, says that we should use *turbonem*, and not *turbinem*, as the accusative of *turbo*, a storm, following the analogy of *Cato Catonis*, not *homo hominis*.—*Idem*.

Lacer, or *laceris*, etc., Cæsar in his second book on Analogy. —*Idem*.

Is homo makes the compound *idem*, except that Cæsar, in his second book on Analogy, asserts that we should use *idem* in the singular, *iidem* in the plural. But this practice is not generally observed.—*Idem*.

From the same writers, without distinguishing the book, C. Cæsar, a weighty authority in the Latin language, says that we should write all words of this class (the datives of the fourth declensions) without the letter *i*.—*Gellius*, 4, 16.

Hic et hæc Samnis, hujus Samnitis.—*Priscian*, book 6.

Cæsar on Analogy, prefers *partum* to *partium*.—*Charisius*, book 1.

PROBABLY CONCERNING THE SAME, BUT WITHOUT MENTIONING THE WORK TO WHICH THEY REFER.

My opinion is, that we should follow the Latin declension, as far as euphony permits. I would not use *Calypsonem* as the accusative of *Calypso*, as we use *Junonem* as the accusative of *Juno*, although C. Cæsar, following the ancients, declines it in this manner.—*Quintilian*, 4, 5, 63.

Marcus Tullius and Caius Cæsar used *mordeo memordi*, *pungo pepugi*, and *spendeo spepondi*.—*Gellius*, 7, 9.

Caius Cæsar says that neuter nouns ending in *l*, in the nominative singular, assume the same form as nouns ending in the letter *e*: for instance, *animali* and *puteali*, in the dative and ablative.—*Charisius*, book 1.

Aplustre.—Pliny says that Cæsar decided that all nouns of the neuter gender which end in *e* are the same in the ablative as in the dative singular.—*Charisius*, book 1.

Cæsar says that neuter nouns in *ar* are the same in the dative and the ablative, as we learn from Pliny.—*Idem*.

Jubar.—Pliny says that Cæsar, among other precepts, gave the following one, that neuter nouns, ending in *ar* in the nominative, make the dative and ablative singular in *i*; but that *jubar* and *far* are exceptions so this rule; for we use *jubari* in the dative, *jubare* in the ablative, and *farri* in the dative, *farre* in the ablative.—*Charisius*, book 1.

The form has not been adopted which Cæsar lays down for the feminine; for instance, *puppis*, *restis*, *pelvis*, and in like manner *cani* and *cane* in the ablative.—*Idem*.

What sort of a syllable can be made out of three *iii* joined together? The last must not be considered a vowel, which was Cæsar's opinion, who was well acquainted with grammar; it is also supported by Victor.—*Priscian*, book 1.

V, placed as a consonant, has the same sound in all Latin words as the Aeolic digamma *F*, for which Cæsar wished to write this Ⅎ; although this appeared correct, yet the ancient custom prevailed.—*Priscian*, book 1.

Hæc pollis, pollinis; so, *Charisius*. But Probus and Cæsar declined it, *hoc pollen, pollinis*.—*Priscian*, book 6.

Besides, Cæsar declines *pubis, puberis*; Probus *pubes, puberis*; others, *puber, puberis*.—*Idem*.

Although Cæsar is favored by analogy in deriving *ens* from the verb *sum, es, est.*—*Idem*, book 18.

Remember that the termination in the singular is *lutum* and *macellum;* although Ennius says *macella*, and Cæsar *luta.*—From *Caper.*

It is a question whether we ought to write *lacrumæ* or *lacrimæ, maxumus* or *maximus*, and similar words. Terentius Varro has recorded that Cæsar was accustomed both to write and pronounce words of this sort with an *i*, and that it became a general custom on account of the authority of so distinguished a man.—*Cassiodorus*, from *Annæus Cornutus on Orthography.*

For *mancupium, aucupium*, and *manubiæ*, have been differently spelled, since C. Cæsar wrote these with the letter *i*, as appears from his inscriptions.—*Velius on Orthography.*

Was Marcus Tullius a less distinguished orator because he was also most strict in his grammar; and in the case of his son, as we learn from his letters, rigorously exacted from him that he should speak with propriety? Or did the books that Cæsar wrote on Analogy injure his power.—*Quintilian*, 1, 7, 34.

WITTY SAYINGS.

Cæsar himself has a very acute judgment; and as Servius your brother, whom I consider to have been very well versed in literature, could easily say, "This verse belongs to Plautus, or it does not," because his ears are familiarized to the different styles of the different poets, and the habit of reading: so I hear that Cæsar while compiling his volumes of witty sayings, if any thing was brought to him as mine, which really did not belong to me, used to reject it: and he does so now the more because some of his intimate friends almost live with me. But in a conversation on different subjects many expressions are used, which perhaps appeared to them with whom I was in conversation devoid neither of learning or wit. These are mentioned along with the rest of our proceedings. So he himself ordered. Thus it happens, that if he should hear any thing else of me, he thinks that he ought not to pay attention to it.—*Cicero ad Fam.* 9, 16.

A COLLECTION OF SAYINGS.

Some treatises likewise pass under his name said to have been written by him when he was a boy, or a very young man, as the Encomium of Hercules, a tragedy entitled Œdipus, and a collection of sayings; all of which Augustus forbade to be published.—*Suetonius*, c. 56.

THE JOURNALS.

When Julius Cæsar was carrying on one of his campaigns in Gaul, he was taken prisoner by the enemy and hurried along, when one of them recognizing him ran up and insultingly said, Cecos Cæsar,[1] which signifies in the Gallic language, let him go: and thus it occurred that he escaped. Cæsar himself says this in one of his journals where he records his good fortune.—*Servius*, *Virgil*, *Ae.* 11, 743.

We do not know the source from which Servius derived this story. There was a learned debate concerning the meaning of the expression, which is attributed to a Gaul. Le Brigant, in his Dissertation sur les Celtes gives it as his opinion that we should read Cetos Cæsar, for Chetò Cæsar, Chtò Cæsar, behold Cæsar. On the contrary, De la Tour d'Auvergne Corret, says that we ought to read skò Cæsar, that is, slay Cæsar. Le Brigant subsequently in a letter to a friend, came to the conclusion that we ought to return to the meaning that Servius gives, and conjecture that Cæsar did not hear him distinctly, for the enemy must have said, losk Cæsar, let Cæsar go.

THE BOOKS OF THE AUSPICES.

On the other hand, Julius Cæsar, in the 16th book of the Auspices, denies that an assembly can be convened on market-days; in other words, denies that business can be transacted with the people, and therefore that the elections can not be held on market-days.—*Macrobius*, *Sat.* 1, 16.

AUGURALIA.

Cæsar in the Auguralia: if the sheep was without blemish. —*Pris.* book 6.

[1] Some read Cetos Cæsar; others, Cæsar Cæsar.

ON DIVINATION.

Cæsar when he was young seems to have preferred Strabo as his model, out of whose oration for the Sardinians he has transcribed some things word for word into his Divination.—*Suetonius*, c. 55.

ASTRONOMICA.

For as Julius Cæsar borrowed from the Egyptian school the motions of the stars, on which he left some learned treatises; so he borrowed from the same system the plan of prolonging the time of the termination of the year according to the course of the sun.—*Macrobius*, *Saturn*. 1, 16.

Now there were of these astronomers three sects, namely, the Chalcidians, the Egyptians, and the Greeks. To which there may be added a fourth which, among us, Cæsar the dictator first instituted, who reduced each year to the course of the sun, which was previously in advance of it.—*Pliny*, 18, 25.

According to Cæsar, these are the notable stars which are significant, and do rule that quarter, which is between the winter *solstice*, and the rising of the western wind, *favonius*. Upon the third day before the calends of January, the dog-star sets in the morning. According to Cæsar's account, the Dolphin rises in the morning the day before the ides of January, and the next *Fidicula*, upon which day the star *Sagitta* sets in the evening in Egypt. Now with regard to the entrance of the new spring, which is from the rising of the said wind to the equinox in March, Cæsar sets down for it the time which, for three days together, is variable and inconstant weather, viz., fourteen days before the calends of March, also eight days before the said calends upon the sight of the first swallow, and the morrow after, upon which day the star *Arcturus* appears in the evening. In like manner Cæsar has observed, that the said wind begins to blow three days before the nones of March, just with the rising of *Cancer*. Cæsar has observed, that the star *Scorpio* rises upon the ides of March, so fatal to himself. The spring equinox seems to be always past the eighth day before the calends of April, from which day forward, according to Cæsar's calculation, the calends of April are significant, as in them the star *Vergiliæ* begins to rise and appear in the morning; however, in Attica, and the parts thereabouts, the said star seems to set or be hidden in the evening upon the third day before the nones of April; and similarly in Bœotia the day after; but, according to Cæsar and the Chaldeans, on the nones of April. According to Cæsar, the constellation *Libra* sets in Italy the sixth day before the ides of April, and portends heavy rain. The fourteenth day before the calends of May, the *Hyades* (a violent constellation causing tempests both by land and sea) set in the evening in Egypt, but in Attica two days before, and in Italy, according to Cæsar, the day before, and are significant for three days together. According to Cæsar, they rise in the morning the sixth day before the nones of May, and also the rainy *Capella*, the eighth day before the ides of May.—*Pliny*, 18, 26.

According to Cæsar, the day after the rising of *Vergiliæ*, the setting of the star *Arcturus*, in the morning, becomes significant; and the rising of *Fidicula* the third day before the ides of May, and the setting of *Capella* twelve days before the calends of June and the setting of the *Dog-star* in Attica; the day after *Orion's* Sword begins to set. The third day before the nones of June, according to Cæsar, *Aquila* begins to rise in Assyria, and appear in the evening; and on the eleventh day before the same calends, the Sword of *Orion* begins to set, according to Cæsar.—*Pliny*, 18, 27.

Among other stars which rule the season from the solstice to the setting of *Fidicula*, six days before the calends of June (according to Cæsar), *Orion* rises. On the thirteenth day before the calends of August, *Aquila* sets in Egypt in the morning, and then the forerunners of the *Etesian* winds begin, which Cæsar thought was felt in Italy the tenth day before the calends: on which day *Aquila* is known to rest and go out of sight in the region of Attica in the morning. The royal star seated in the breast of *Leo*, according to Cæsar, merges in the morning, the third day before the calends of August.—*Pliny*, 18, 28.

CONCERNING THE STARS.

He wrote a work in poetry.

Now none of the Latin writers wrote any book on this subject except Julius Cæsar: and even this he borrowed from the work of another, Julius Firmicus. Aratus,[1] a most accomplished poet, wrote a treatise in Greek on the number of the stars;[2] Cæsar did the same in Latin, as also Tullius, that glory of eloquence. These only gave their names and dates of their rising but did not give the authority of their influences: so that they appear to me to have shown merely their knowledge of language, being inspired, not by any knowledge of astrology, but rather by a poetic vein.—*Julius Firmicus.* 8, 5.

POEMS.

He has left behind him likewise two books of Analogy, and as many under the title of "Anti-Cato," and a poem, too, entitled "The Journey." Of which he compiled the first two in the passage of the Alps, as he was returning to his army from holding the Assizes in Hither Gaul; and the other about the time of the battle of Munda; and the last, during the four and twenty days he was upon the expedition from Rome to Further Spain, —*Suetonius*, c. 56.

The wild cabbage has also three leaves, and is celebrated in the verses of the deified Julius and the military jokes; as they told him in reproach, while finding fault with the parsimony of his rewards, that they lived on wild coleworts at Dyrrachium, But this is the *Cyma sylvestris.*—*Pliny*, 19, 18.

Donatus, in his Life of Terence, brings forward these verses under the name of Julius Cæsar.

Thou too, O Meander! divided into two, art placed in the first rank, and deservedly—thou lover of pure language. Would that the true spirit of a comic poet were added to the gentle flow of your writings; that your merit might be as transcendent,

[1] Aratus was a Greek poet, born at Sili, at Cilicia. At the request of Antigonus Gonatus, son of Demetrius Poliorcetes, he composed an astronomical poem, entitled, Phœnomena, treating of the heavenly bodies. He wrote also another poem, named Diosemata. It is to Aratus that St. Paul alludes in the twenty-eighth verse of the seventeenth chapter of the Acts. He flourished about 270 years B.C.

[2] The Delphin Commentator asserts that the allusion is not here to Julius Cæsar, or Germanicus, the renowned conqueror of Arminius, which is the generally received opinion, but to Domitian. In support of this he quotes Statius, to prove that Domitian was addressed by the title of Germanicus, and the following passage from Quintilian: "To them we have given the title of poets, because the care of governing the world has taken off Germanicus Augustus from the pursuit of his favorite studies, the gods having thought it but little to make him the greatest of poets."

and rank as high as that of the Greek poets; and that you did not fail in that. I am grieved, and I lament that this one thing is wanting to you, Terence.

Some attribute the following Epigram to Caius Julius Cæsar; others to Germanicus.

While a Thracian boy was sporting on the Hebrus, bound with ice, he by his weight broke the waters frozen with the cold. While the lower part of his body was swept away by the rapid river, the smooth ice cut off his tender head. When his bereaved mother found it, and lodged it in an urn she said, "I brought forth this for the flames, and the rest for the water."

And also this distich:—"Feltria condemned to the rigor of eternal snows, thou land in which I never again must dwell, Farewell," was falsely ascribed to Cæsar, although some say that it is preserved on parchment, others on stone. They say also that one of Cæsar's decrees was found at Viterbium, in Etruria, of which the following is a copy:—We, Caius Julius Cæsar, give orders, that Marcus Tullius Cicero, on account of his surpassing virtues and singular mental powers, shall be safe and uninjured throughout the whole world which has been subjected by our arms and prowess.—*C. Jabolenus.*

UNAUTHENTICATED.

Ointments are named from the place in which they are produced, as Telinum of which Julius Cæsar mentions, saying, "and we anoint our body with the sweet ointment of Telinum." This was made in the island of Telos, which is one of the Cyclades. —*Isidorus Orig.* 4, 12.

Strabo makes Telos an island of the Sporades, therefore we ought to read in Isidorus, either Delino, and Delo, or ex Sporadibus.

In Cæsar, and Calvus, and Catullus we read, "When now you shall be yellow ashes," (*cinis fueris*).—*Nonius in voce Cinis.*

Hail! thou that was first called Father of thy Country, that first won in the garb of peace a triumph and the laurel for language, then the parent of eloquence and Latin literature: and (as Cæsar, the Dictator, formerly your enemy described you) thou that hast gained a laurel greater than all triumphs, in proportion as it is a more noble achievement to advance so far the limits of the Roman genius, than those of the Roman empire.—*Pliny*, 7. 30.

Cicero says, "*re vendita iterum empta*," from which it is evident that we can not say "*venita*," but either "*venundata*," or "*vendita*," like Cicero, C. Cæsar: *possessiones redimi, eas postea pluris venditas.*—*Diomedes*, book 1.

The *esseda* was a sort of wagon or chariot, from which the Gauls were accustomed to fight. Cæsar in his third book to Cicero is our authority; "he has many thousand horse, and men that fight from the war-chariot."

From this circumstance, those gladiators who fight on horseback are called "*essedarii*."—*Junius Phylargyrius on the Georg. Virgil.*

Augustus also, in the letters which he wrote to Caius Cæsar, blames him for preferring the use of *calidum* to *caldum* (perhaps in his books on Analogy), not that the latter is bad Latin, but because it is affected, and as he himself signified by a Greek term "frivolous."—*Quintilian*, 1, 6, 19.

The inhabitants of Castile also, are called by Cæsar venales.—*Pliny, H. N.*, iii. 3.

Whatever new occurs (and I expect a great deal) I beg you will not fail to write. Among other things, whether this is true about Sextus;[1] but above all about our friend Brutus; of whom Cæsar used to say (as I heard from him with whom I have been), that "it is of great importance what he writes: for whatever he wishes he wishes ardently." He took notice of this when he spoke for Deiotarus at Nice, "that he seemed to speak with great vehemence and freedom." Likewise (for I like to write every thing as it occurs), very lately, when I was at his house by desire of Sextius, and sat down till I was called, he said, "Can I doubt of my being greatly hated when Marcus Cicero is obliged to wait, and can not get an audience at his own convenience? Yet, if any body is gracious it is he: nevertheless, I doubt not that he hates me bitterly."—*Cicero to Atticus*, 14, 1.

He said that Cæsar had observed to him, upon the occasion of my being kept waiting, when I went to him at Sextius's request: Can I now be so foolish as to suppose that this good-

[1] He alludes to Sextus, the surviving son of Pompey the Great, who was at that time preparing for war in Sicily.

natured man will be friendly to me, after he has been kept so long waiting for my convenience?"—*Cicero to Atticus.*

Upon which being transported with joy he could not forbear boasting in a full house a few days after, that he had, in spite of his enemies, and to their great mortification, got all he desired, and should for the future play upon them at pleasure, and some one insultingly replying "that that would not be very easy for a woman to do," he answered as if in jest, "that Semiramis had formerly reigned in Assyria, and the Amazons had formerly held a great part of Asia."—*Suetonius*, 22.

Asinius Pollio says, that Cæsar, upon viewing the vanquished and slaughtered enemy in the field of Pharsalia, used these very words:—"They would have it so; I, Caius Cæsar, after all my noble exploits should have been condemned, if I had not appealed to the army for assistance."—*Suetonius*, 30.

And coming up with his troops on the banks of the river Rubicon, which was the boundary of his province, he stood musing for some time on the greatness of his attempt; and then turning to those about him said:—"We may still retreat, but if we once pass this little bridge, we must make our way by force of arms."—*Suetonius*, 31.

While he was demurring upon the matter there happened something very strange. A person of surpassing size and beauty. * * Upon which Cæsar cried out "Let us march whither divine prodigies and the perverseness of our enemies call us. The die is now cast," says he.—*Suetonius*, 32.

He directed his march to Rome, and, after addressing the senate on the state of the republic, went to attack a very strong army of Pompey, which was in Spain, under the command of three lieutenants, M. Petreius, L. Afranius, and Marcus Varro, declaring among his friends, before he set out, "that he was going against an army without a general, and should return from it against a general without an army."—*Suetonius*, c. 34.

And chancing to fall upon his landing, he gave a lucky turn to the omen by crying out, "I hold thee fast, Africa."—*Suetonius*, c. 59.

Cæsar used to say, that he adopted the same system against an enemy that a majority of the physicians use against diseases of the body, namely, conquering them by famine rather than the sword.—From *Strat.* 4, 7, 1.

He was accustomed to boast "that his soldiers could fight

well even when perfumed;" and he was accustomed to call them in speeches, not by the name of soldiers, but the kinder name of fellow-soldiers.—*Suetonius*, c. 67.

They bore want and other hardships to such a degree that Pompey, when blockaded in the neighborhood of Dyrrachium, upon seeing a sort of bread made of a herb, upon which they lived, said he had to do with wild beasts.—*Suetonius*, chap. 68.

He advanced some of his friends, though of very mean extraction, to the highest post in the government. And when he was censured for it he openly declared, "That if he had availed himself of the services of robbers and assassins, in the defense of his honor, he would have made them the same requital.—*Suetonius*, c. 72.

And being asked why he had divorced his wife? "Because," says he, "I would have my family not only clear of all crime, but suspicion too."—*Suetonius*, c. 74.

On the field of Pharsalia he shouted out "to spare the citizens."—*Suetonius*, c. 75.

And to be convinced of the truth of the remark of Cæsar the Dictator, "that the recollection of cruelty was a miserable provision for old age."—*Amm. Marcel.*

He was guilty of the late extravagance in his public conversation, as Titus Ampius informs us. He said, "The commonwealth was nothing but a name, without substance, or so much as the appearance of any; that Sylla was an illiterate fellow to lay down the dictatorship."

That men ought to be more cautious in their conversation with him, and look upon what he said as law.

And he proceeded to such a degree of arrogance, that when a soothsayer brought him word that the entrails of a victim opened for sacrifice were without a heart, he said that the entrails would be more favorable when he pleased, and that it ought not to be looked upon as an ill omen if a beast did want a heart.—*Suetonius*, c. 77.

When Pontius Aquila, one of the tribunes of the commons, did not rise up to him, as in his triumph he passed by the place where he sat, he was so angry with him that he cried out, "Wilt thou, tribune Aquila, take the commonwealth out of my hands?" And for some days he never promised any thing unless with this proviso, "If Pontius Aquila will allow me to do it."—*Suetonius*, c. 78.

He replied to the people when saluting him by the title of king, "that he was Cæsar, not a king."—*Suetonius*, c. 79.

Of which class we have heard that C. Cæsar, while yet a young man, made the following witty remark:—"If you sing, you sing badly; if you read, you sing."—*Quintilian*, 1, 8.

There is a twofold method of depreciating, according as a person would diminish favor or boasting. As Caius Cæsar said to Pomponius, when showing a wound which he had received in the mouth in the Sulpician sedition, which he boasted he had suffered while fighting for Cæsar. You never will look back again in your flight. Or an accusation urged as Cicero.—*Quintilian*, 6, 3.

There is also the fiction from irony, which Caius Cæsar used. For when a witness said that the accused had endeavored to wound the inside of his thigh, and it was easy to refute him, from the circumstance of his attacking that part of the body in particular. "What could he do," said Cæsar, "when he had a helmet and coat of mail on?"—*Quintilian*, 91.

Dolabella, at my request, obtained the rights of citizenship from Julius Cæsar for Demetrius Mega, a Sicilian, in which affair I bore a part. Therefore he is now called Publius Cornelius. And when Cæsar, on account of some mean persons who sold his kindness, ordered the tablet to be torn down, on which the names of those whom he had presented with the rights of citizenship were engraved, Cæsar said to the same Dolabella, while I was listening, "That he had nothing to fear for Mega; that his kindness would be continued to him."—*Cicero ad Fam.* 13, 36.

And when the day of election was coming on, and Cæsar's mother attended him to the door with tears in her eyes, he embraced her and said, "To-day, mother, you will see your son either chief priest or an exile."

But he said to them seriously, "I would rather be the first among them, than the second among the Romans."

Do you not think that I have sufficient reason for grief, if Alexander, at such an age, ruled over so many, but nothing noble has been achieved by me.

It was enough, said Cæsar, not to use it if you disliked it; he that finds fault with rusticity, is himself a rustic.

Cæsar said, "Arms and laws do not flourish together; if you

are not pleased with my acts, now withdraw, for war does not require much freedom of language. Whenever I may lay down my arms, and a treaty may be made, then come forward and harangue."

Go forward, my noble fellow, have courage and fear nothing, for you have Cæsar and his fortunes in the same galley with you.

And when a horse was brought to Cæsar, he said, when I shall conquer I will use it for the pursuit; now let us march against the enemy; and rushing on he charged on foot.

To-day the victory would have been with the enemy, if they had had a general who knew how to conquer.

Cæsar is said to have observed "That Cassius urged the juster claim, but he could not pass by Brutus."

Brutus will wait for this skin.

What think you are the intentions of Cassius; for he does not please me very much, being very pale?

I do not fear at all those fat and luxurious men, but rather these pale and slender men; meaning Brutus and Cassius.

The ides of March are come; but he replied in a low voice, Yes, they are come, but they are not past yet.

When the subject was casually introduced what death was the best, Cæsar anticipated all and shouted out eagerly, "An unexpected one."—*Plutarch.*

They say that Cæsar answered the person making the announcement by striking the hilt of his sword, and saying, "This will give it to me."

He pardoned the Athenians at their request, and remarked: "How often will the glory of your ancestors save you perishing through your own conduct?"

This will be the end of my life and of your campaigns ——. They report that Cæsar said "that he had often fought for victory, but now for life."

Nothing is more wretched than constant apprehensions, for they are always the mark of a coward.—*Appian.*

CONCERNING CAIUS JULIUS CÆSAR.

But, however, said Atticus, addressing Brutus; I myself really entertain this opinion of Cæsar—an opinion, too, that I hear very often expressed of this connoisseur in this art, that he speaks the Latin language with the greatest purity and elegance of all the orators that have yet appeared, and that not merely for domestic habit, as we have lately heard it observed of the families of the Lælii and Mucii (though even here I believe this might partly have been the case), but he chiefly acquired it, and brought it to its present perfection, by a studious application to the most intricate and refined branches of literature, and by a careful and constant attention to the purity of his style.—*Cicero in Bruto*, c. 75.

But proceed, my Pomponius, with Cæsar, and give us the remainder of his character.

We see then, said he, from what has just been mentioned, that a pure and correct style is the ground-work and the very basis and foundation upon which an orator must build his other accomplishments, etc. But Cæsar, summoning to his aid the principles of the art, has corrected the imperfections of a vicious custom, by adopting the rules and improvements of a good one, as he found these occasionally displayed in the course of polite conversation. Therefore when he adds to the elegance of the Latin terms (which is necessary, although you may not be an actor but a well-bred Roman citizen), all the varied ornaments of elevation; then he seems to exhibit the finest paintings in the most advantageous light. As he has such extraordinary merit, even in the common run of his language, I must confess that there is no person I know of to whom he should yield the preference. Besides, his manner of speaking, both as to his voice and gesture, is imposing and splendid, without the least appearance of artifice or affectation; his presence, too, is dignified and noble. Indeed, said Brutus, his orations please me highly, for I have had the satisfaction of reading several of them. He has likewise some commentaries or short memoirs of his own transactions, and such as merit the highest approbation; for they are simple, correct, and elegant, and divested of all the ornaments of language, so as to appear (if I may be allowed the expression) in a kind of undress. For while he pretends to furnish only the loose materials for such as might be inclined to furnish a regular history he may perhaps have gratified the vanity of a few literary coxcombs, who wish to set off the incidents by a flourish of words but he has certainly prevented all sensible men from an improvement on his plan.—*Cicero in Bruto*, c. 74.

What? Which of the orators, who have made speaking the

sole business of their lives could you prefer to him (Cæsar)? Who is more pointed or brief in his sentences?—*Cicero ad Cor. Nep. Suetonius*, chap. 55.

Caius Julius Cæsar can not be considered a writer of Roman history. His commentaries on the Gallic war, the reputation of which has spread far and wide, are his only compositions extant: nor did he write any other historic composition as far as I can ascertain: for Hirtius his secretary undertook the task of completing the sequel to his commentaries, comprising his other achievements after Cæsar, but imposed on him the burden of deciding on the causes of almost the entire world.—*Lupi Abbatis Ferrariensis.*

But the reputation of the Catuli[1] for eloquence was not inferior; but in wit and humor Cæsar[2] surpassed them all.—*Cicero, de Officiis.*

He has likewise left memoirs of his own transactions both in the Gallic and Civil War with Pompey; for the author of the Alexandrian, African, and Spanish war has not been ascertained. Some think it was Oppius, others Hirtius, who also wrote a suppliment to the last book of the Gallic war which was left unfinished. Pollio Asinius thinks that they were not carefully compiled or with a due regard to truth; for Cæsar, as he will have it, is a little too hasty in believing what was done by others under him, and he has given no very just account of what he himself transacted in person, either through design, or a defect of memory, and he is of opinion that he intended a new and more correct draught of them.—*Suetonius*, c. 56.

If Cæsar had made the bar his principal object, no other of our orators could have better disputed the prize of eloquence with Cicero. So great is his energy, so sharp his wit, such his power of exciting emotions, that he appears to have spoken with the same power as he fought; he embellished all the talents of eloquence by a surprising elegance of language which he made his particular study.—*Quintilian*, 10, 1.

What should hinder our occasionally adopting the energy of

[1] There were two Catuli, father and son. The allusion here seems to be to the father, for the son was not considered a great orator.

[2] The reference here is not to Cæsar the Dictator, but to another of the same name, of whom Brutus says that he was deficient in fire, and that many of his speeches were quite tame.

Cæsar, the asperity of Cœlius,[1] the accuracy of Pollio, and the judgment of Calvus.—*Quintilian.*

Calvus was more concise, Asinius more copious, Cæsar more brilliant, Cœlius more bitter, Brutus more dignified, Cicero more vehement, rich and powerful.—*Dialogue on Oratory*, ch. 25.

Cæsar is said to have possessed great natural gifts for oratory, and he did not want ambition to cultivate them, so that he was, undoubtedly, the second orator at Rome.—*Plutarch, Cæsar.*

The eloquence Cæsar displayed at Rome in defending persons impeached, gained him considerable interest.—*Ibid.*

In answer to this he usually had recourse to authorities, and produces Lysias among the Grecians, together with Cato and the two Gracchi, among our own countrymen, as instances in favor of the concise style. In return I name Demosthenes, Æschines, Hyperides,[2] and many others, in opposition to Lysias, and I oppose Cato and the Gracchi, Pollio, Cæsar, Cælius, and above all Cicero, whose longest speech is generally esteemed the best.—*Pliny, Epistle* 1, 20.

Shall I fear that that would not become me which became Marcus Tullius, Caius Calvus, Asinius Pollio, Marcus Messala, etc., the deified Julius, the deified Augustus, the deified Nerva, T. Cæsar, etc.—*Pliny, Epistle* 5, 3.

Cæsar the Dictator was the rival of the most distinguished orators.—*Tacitus Annales.*

That most distinguished writer, the deified Julius.—*Tacitus, de Moribus Germanorum.*

Caius Cæsar the Dictator was engaged alternately in the

[1] None of the speeches of Cœlius, Pollio, and Calvus, have descended to us.

[2] Hyperides was a celebrated Athenian orator cotemporary with Demosthenes. He embraced the same political party, and was sent along with Ephialtes on a secret mission to the court of Persia, to procure aid against Philip, King of Macedon. After the disastrous defeat at Chæronea, Hyperides proposed that the Athenians should place their wives, children, and valuable property in the Piræus, recall their exiles, and give liberty to their slaves, to enable them to make a desperate struggle against Philip. By these measures Athens obtained an honorable peace. Hyperides was put to death by the orders of Antipater, B.C. 322. His body, which had been left without burial, was carried off by his relations and interred in Attica.

pursuits of war, dictation, and reading. And although he was the most distinguished man of the day, and was as celebrated for his speeches in the camp as in the forum, yet he thought that he had not a strong enough position in the citadel of either art until he was preferred to other men by the decision of the orator of Arpinum.—*Sidonius Apollonicus.*

INDEX.

N.B. The numerals refer to the book, the figures to the chapter. G. stands for the Gallic War, C. for the Civil, A. for the Alexandrian, Af. for the African, and H. for the Spanish War.

Celtillus, the father of Vercingetorix, assassinated by the Arverni, G. vii. 4.

Cenimagni, or Iceni, an ancient people of Britain, inhabiting the counties of *Suffolk, Norfolk, Cambridgeshire*, and *Huntingdonshire*.

Cenis Mons, that part of the Alps which separates Savoy from Piedmont.

Cenni, an ancient people of Celtic extraction.

Cenomāni, a people of Gallia Celtica, in the country now called *Le Manseau*, adjoining to that of the Insubres.

Centrŏnes, an ancient people of Flanders, about the city of *Courtray*, dependent on the Nervians.

Centrŏnes, an ancient people of Gaul, inhabiting the country of Tarantaise.

Ceranni Montes, Mountains of Epirus, *Monti di Chimera*.

Cercīna, an island on the coast of Africa, *Chercara, Cercare*.

Cevennes, mountains of, Cæsar passes them in the midst of winter, though covered with snow six feet deep, G. vii. 8.

Chara, a root which served to support Cæsar's army in extreme necessity, C. iii. 48; manner of preparing it, *ibid.*

Chariots, manner of fighting with them among the Britons, G. iv. 33; dexterity of the British charioteers, *ibid.*; chariots armed with scythes in Pharnaces' army, A. 75.

Cherronēsus, a peninsula of Africa, near Alexandria.

Chersonēsus Cimbrīca, a peninsula on the Baltic, now *Jutland*, part of *Holstein*, *Ditmarsh*, and *Sleswic*.

Cherusci, a great and warlike people of ancient Germany, between the Elbe and the Weser, about the country now called *Mansfield*, part of the duchy of *Brunswick*, and the dioceses of *Hildesheim* and *Halberstadt*. The Cherusci, under the command of Arminius (Hermann), lured the unfortunate Varus into the wilds of the Saltus Teutoburgiensis (Tutinger Wold), where they massacred him and his whole army. They were afterward defeated by Germanicus, who, on his march through the forest so fatal to his countrymen, found the bones of the legions where they had been left to blanch by their barbarian conqueror.—See Tacitus's account of the march of the Roman Legions through the German forests, Annals, b. i. c. 71.

Cicero, Quintus, attacked in his winter quarters by Ambiŏrix, G. v. 39; informs Cæsar of his distress, who marches to relieve him, 46; attacked unexpectedly by the Sigambri, who are nevertheless obliged to retire, vi. 36.

Cimbri, *the Jutlanders*, a very ancient northern people, who inhabited Chersonesus Cimbrica.

Cinga, a river of Spain, *Cinca*, or *Senga*.

Cingĕtŏrix, the leader of one of the factions among the Treviri, and firmly attached to Cæsar, G. v. 3; declared a public enemy, and his goods confiscated by Indutiomărus, 56.

Cingŭlum, a town of Picēnum, in Italy, *Cingoli*.

Cirta, a town in Africa, *Constantina*, or *Consantina*, al. *Tadel*.

Cleopatra, engaged in a war with her brother Ptolemy, C. iii. 103; she and her younger brother made king and queen of Egypt, A. 33.

Clodĭus, sent by Cæsar to Scipio, to treat about a peace, but without effect, C. iii. 90.

Clupĕa, a maritime city of Africa, *Quipia*.

Clusinas, a centurion, dismissed from Cæsar's army with ignominy, Af. 54.

Cocasātes, a people of Gaul, according to some the *Bazadois*.